# THE FIRST WARRIOR
## A LEGEND OF KHOTAN
## GABRIELLA CREIGHTON

GabriellaCreighton.com

**ISBN Information**

**eBook:** 979-8-9939808-6-7
**Print:** 979-8-9939808-7-4
**Hardcover:** 979-8-2445477-8-8

You can find more books by this author at:

GabriellaCreighton.com

# ABOUT THE AUTHOR

Gabriella Creighton is a life long lover of the Fantasy and Science Fiction Genres. She has been fascinated by Dragons and other mythical creatures from a young age and grew up dreaming of being a writer. Inspired by great authors like Jane Yolen, Anne McCaffrey, JRR Tolkien and Phillip Pullman, she loves to take an alternative view of myth and weave her own versions. After a long life of working, gaming and enjoying the works of others, she has finally decided to put her nigh on useless Masters Degree in English Literature to work to tell stories of her own.

Growing up in Rural New York, as well as having been thrown all over the United States, Gabriella has learned she has only three desires. To write until the nail her coffin shut, to never answer the phone and for a cool glass of Salted Caramel Crowne Royal mixed with Cream Soda and Dr Pepper, which she calls a magic elixir.

It helps get the writing done.

You can find more of her works at:
GabriellaCreighton.com

For Bryan "Drukas" Springer,

You were a comrade at the gaming tables.
We fought insurmountable odds.
However Mortality is that one we can't fight.

You will be missed.
You will be remembered.
Gone but never forgotten.

# Contents

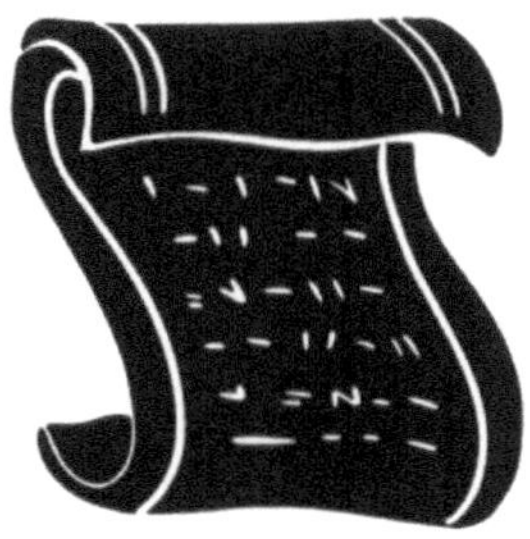

# The Place Where it All Began
## Prologue

Many years after, when I tried to tell this story the right way, I learned there are two kinds of people in the world.

There are the ones who want the truth to start at the beginning, with gods and fire and the first stone laid under the sky.

Then there are the ones who want the truth to start where it matters, with a door that sticks in winter, with a hungry stomach, with a girl tightening the strap on her sword belt, with a boy realizing his hands are shaking and deciding that is fine, so long as he does not drop the knife.

I have always been greedy. I wanted both.

So I will begin where the old songs begin, up where the world looks round and quiet and harmless, and then I will bring you down to where it was never quiet at all.

They say the world was made by dragons, not the kind you find in carved tavern signs, all snarls and treasure piles and bad manners. These were the Three, the ones people speak of like they are weather, like they are law, like they are the reason your hearth catches and your crops grow and your nightmares have teeth.

The Dragon Above, the Dragon Here, and the Dragon Below.

The first breath came from the Dragon Above. That is what the priests say, and the sky agrees with them most days. The Dragon Above shaped the high places, the airs that birds cut through, the peaks that catch sunlight first, and the cold clear spaces where prayers go when nobody is listening. Out of that breath came the Celestials and the Winged Ones, the Elves who walk like they are carrying old music in their bones, and the Birdfolk who never stop watching the horizon. Those peoples still tend to look upward when they speak of hope, as if hope has an address and it lives above the clouds.

The Dragon Here was different. The Dragon Here did not sing creation into being, or so the dwarves say. The Dragon Here worked. The Dragon Here pressed hands into clay, carved rivers through stubborn land, and built a world that could be walked on without falling forever. The Dragon Here made humans first, because humans are good at living in unfinished places. The Dragon Here made Beastfolk, because the world needed teeth and grace and wild sense. The Dragon Here made dwarves and gnomes, because the world needed builders who would argue with stone until stone surrendered. When dwarves speak of the Dragon Here, they do not bow, they nod, the way you nod at a craftsperson whose work you respect.

Then there was the Dragon Below.

Most people tell that part like a warning. They whisper it the way you whisper about wolves when the door latch feels loose. The Dragon Below was the dark sibling, the one who took what was made and learned how to twist it. Some say the Dragon Below was born angry. Some say it was born lonely. In the end it does not matter much. The world has enough stories about reasons. What the world remembers is the result.

From the Dragon Below came the drakes first, smaller dragons with hunger where wisdom should have been. Then goblins, then orcs, then trolls, and the Dark Elves, who share a name with the Elves of the high places but not the same heart. The Dragon Below made monsters that were not just dangerous, but useful, because usefulness is how evil spreads. A monster that only bites is a problem. A monster that obeys is an army.

That is how the world began, according to the three most common prayers and the four most common arguments, and if you have grown up anywhere with a hearth and a neighbor, you have heard some version of it. Children learn it as a bedtime tale. Adults learn it again when they need something to blame.

The peoples of the world rose the way grass rises through cracks. Slowly at first, then everywhere. Villages became towns. Towns became cities. Roads grew between them like veins. Markets and wars followed, because markets bring people close and wars bring people closer than they wanted to be.

The Winged Ones built monasteries on cliffs where the wind never slept. They wrote oaths in feathers and ink and believed, fiercely, that the Dragon Above was watching every promise. The Elves grew forests into living walls and called it peace. The Birdfolk carried messages across oceans that humans still stare at like miracles.

Humans did what humans always do. We spread. We made kingdoms and borders and laws and we broke them as soon as they got in the way. We made heroes and we built statues and then we argued about whether the statues looked enough like the heroes. Beastfolk became guides, hunters, and kings in places where human maps turned to lies. Dwarves dug deep and found stone that remembered older songs than any choir. Gnomes made tools that made other tools, and then acted surprised when the tools changed the world.

And beneath it all, where the Dragon Below's breath lingered, old caves filled with new voices. Goblins learned to count. Orcs learned to march. Trolls learned that bridges are powerful things. Drakes learned the scent of fear and began to crave it.

History, as I learned later, is not a straight line. It is a rope pulled between hands that do not agree. Some generations pull toward peace. Others pull toward conquest. The rope frays either way.

Empires rose in the east and fell into dust in the west. Great fleets crossed seas and discovered that other shores had their own gods and their own wars and their own bad weather. Old cities burned and new cities were built right on top of the ash, because people hate leaving good stone unused. Families moved. Cultures blended. Languages traded words like coins.

And always, always, the shadow of the Dragon Below pressed against the edges of things. Sometimes it did not need to attack. Sometimes it only needed to wait for people to do what people do when they are frightened and proud at the same time.

In the land of Galtreah, where my story lived, kingdoms fought like siblings who shared a house and could not agree who owned the table. The Kingdom of Lionel grew strong through stubbornness and good farmland and the kind of rulers who understood that a sword is useful, but a road is useful longer. Lionel had knights and squires and soldiers, the sort of people who wore their duty like armor and their opinions like weapons. Lionel had mages too, though in my village those were more rumor than neighbor.

There had been a great war, not so long before my childhood that the adults stopped flinching when they heard thunder. The war touched every border and every hearth. It took fathers and mothers and left children behind, and then it kept moving, because war is greedy and rarely satisfied. When it ended, the world did not become kinder. It became tired. Sometimes tired looks like peace. Sometimes tired is only a pause between storms.

Old King's Walk was one of the places the war had stepped on and then forgotten. It was not important on most maps. It was a village that lived on the edge of things, near the mountains and the forests and the old roads that had once carried armies. People there worked hard and laughed when they could and prayed when they remembered. They told stories about the Three Dragons the way you tell stories about winter, with respect and a little dread and a lot of hope that it would not be worse this year.

If you looked at the world from above, you would have seen Old King's Walk as a speck. You would have seen the mountains behind it like teeth on the horizon, and the forests like dark cloth spread over the land. You would have seen the rivers that carried trade to bigger towns, and you would have seen the roads that carried soldiers away and sometimes brought them back broken.

If you kept zooming in, you would have seen a cluster of homes with smoke curling from chimneys, the narrow path that passed for a main road, the small training yard where a man named Dratmar Blackenstone tried to teach a group of half-grown children how to keep their feet under them when life tried to sweep them away.

You would have seen a girl named Jaime Durandal, shoulders squared, eyes sharp, taking drills seriously because she had learned early that seriousness can keep you alive.

You would have seen me, Elric Shaddar, trying very hard to be the kind of person who made things easier for others, because I had seen what it did to people when life only got harder.

You might even have seen Maximus laughing too loud as he talked about knighthood, because dreaming big is a brave thing when you live somewhere small. You would have seen Anya running with that fearless kind of speed only young children have, and Bobo looking at the sky like it might answer him, and Ianteen carrying a piece of wood like it was already a finished tool.

And you would have seen, far out in the trees beyond the fields, a movement that did not belong there. A hush in the birds. A wrongness in the wind.

At the time, I did not notice any of that.

At the time, I woke up thinking it was going to be an ordinary day, which is the sort of mistake youth makes best.

Later, I learned that the world does not bother making ordinary days. It only makes days, and we decide how to remember them.

# Chapter 1

## A Good Morning for Trouble

THE FIRST THING I remember about that morning is the smell.

Woodsmoke, mostly, with a little bit of damp wool and bread that had been warmed too long on the hearthstone. Old King's Walk always smelled like that when the frost came, like the village was a single living thing and every chimney was a slow breath. Years later I have traveled through cities that burned sweeter incense and wore better perfume, but none of them ever felt as honest as smoke and bread.

Our house sat near the edge of the village, where the road narrowed into a path and the trees started acting like they owned the place. It was not a big house, and it had never been meant for as many bodies as we fit into it. It creaked when the wind leaned against it. It popped and sighed like it was thinking hard. It had a roof that tried its best and a door that stuck in winter, which meant someone had to shoulder it open like they were assaulting a fortress. We called it home anyway. Home is not a thing you buy, it is a thing you decide.

I had been up first, because I always was. Dratmar said it was because I was disciplined. Jaime said it was because I could not sit still. Both were probably true, and neither of them mentioned the third reason, which was that mornings were the easiest time to feel hopeful. When the day is new, you can pretend you are starting fresh, even if you are not. As a half-human, I had extra requirements in my morning routine, my mother's half was Cat Tribe, which left me with cat like furred ears that stuck out of my hair and a tail that required extra tailoring and effort in my clothing. Tufts of fur the same shade as my skin covered parts of my body even in my youth and it was always an annoyed exertion to clean.

The charm above the door caught the firelight as I moved around the room. It was a small carving, no bigger than my palm, made from dark wood polished by a hundred passing hands. Three dragons curled around each other in a circle, heads pointed in different directions. The Dragon Above had wings carved like sharp leaves. The Dragon

Here had thick legs and a broad back. The Dragon Below had a longer neck and a mouth cut with too many teeth. Some people in Old King's Walk touched that charm like it was a lock, and their fingers were the key. Some people spat when they passed under it, just in case the Dragon Below was listening.

I touched it out of habit. Not because I thought it made me safe, but because it made me feel like I belonged. There is a difference, and I did not learn that difference until later.

The kettle began to grumble on the hearth. I turned it down before it could start screaming, because if the kettle screamed, Anya would wake up, and if Anya woke up early, she would spend the rest of the morning finding new ways to be awake.

That was the plan, anyway.

Anya woke up like a bird shot out of a sling.

I heard her first, the quick little inhale she always took before she started talking, like she was drawing breath for a long race. Then her bare feet slapped the floorboards, and she burst into the room with her hair sticking up in the back and her shirt half twisted, grinning as if she had been invited to something fun.

"Elric," she said, and she said it the way people say the word "cake."

"Good morning," I told her. "Did you sleep well?"

"I slept," she said. "That is the same."

"It is not," I said, and I smiled because she was too young to understand the difference and too stubborn to admit it even if she did.

Anya scrambled up onto the bench and leaned across the table like she was crossing a ravine. She grabbed a piece of bread from the cloth and held it up in triumph, as if I might chase her for it. In those days she still believed food was a contest. She took a bite that was mostly air and then asked, "Are we training today?"

"We train every day," I said.

"I mean real training," she said, mouth full. "The kind where you hit things."

I pointed at the kettle. "If you want to hit something, hit that after it boils over."

She looked at the kettle with suspicion, as if it might fight back.

Behind her, Ianteen moved in the small corner by the window where the best light came in. She had a piece of wood on her knees and a knife in her hand, and she worked with the quiet focus of someone who liked making order out of mess. The shaving curls fell into her lap like pale ribbons.

"Do not hit the kettle," Ianteen said without looking up. "It will dent."

"I will not dent it," Anya said.

"You dent everything," Ianteen replied, calm as daylight.

"I do not," Anya said.

Ianteen lifted her eyes just enough to look at Anya over the top of her work. "You dent me."

Anya opened her mouth, prepared to argue the point, then stopped because she could not think of a clever lie fast enough. She made a face and went back to chewing.

Ianteen went back to carving. She was the kind of person who could take a broken chair leg and turn it into a tool handle, and if you praised her, she would pretend it did not matter, even though it did. Some people dream of knighthood, some people dream of magic, and some people dream of making something that lasts. Ianteen's dreams smelled like sawdust and oil. In a village like ours, that mattered.

Bobo was sitting on the floor near the hearth, watching the fire like it was speaking a language he almost understood. He held his hands out near the heat, palms up, fingers spread. Every now and then he moved them, slow and careful, like he was trying to catch something invisible between them.

"You are going to set your sleeves on fire," I told him.

Bobo blinked at me, then looked down at his sleeves as if they had surprised him by existing. "I was not touching it."

"You do not have to touch fire for fire to win," I said.

Anya leaned over and whispered loudly, "He thinks he is a mage."

Bobo's cheeks went pink. He did not deny it. He never denied it. That was one of the things I liked about him, even when it made him an easy target. He wanted something, and he was not ashamed of wanting it. In a world that teaches children to want smaller, that is a kind of bravery.

"He might be," I said, and I meant it.

Anya looked at me like I had announced that bread could fly. "He cannot even lift the bucket when it is full."

"Magic does not care about buckets," I said.

"It should," Anya insisted. "Buckets are important."

I let that one go. Some arguments are not meant to be won. They are meant to be remembered.

A thump came from the back room, followed by a low groan that sounded like someone wrestling with their own blankets. Then Maximus appeared in the doorway, hair flattened on one side, wearing his shirt inside out with complete confidence. He had a sword at his hip. It was not a real sword, not like the ones soldiers carried on the old road. It was a wooden training blade Dratmar had made, weighted just enough to teach you respect, not sharp enough to ruin your life. Maximus wore it like it was Exalted Steel.

"Morning," he announced, and then, because he could not help himself, he drew the wooden blade and made a slow sweeping salute at the room.

Anya clapped.

Bobo looked up from the fire and stared at the sword like it was the sun.

Ianteen did not look up at all. "Put that away," she said. "You will knock something over."

"I will not knock anything over," Maximus replied, the same way Anya had, which was proof that bad habits spread faster than colds.

"You knocked over the flour last week," I said.

"That was tactical," he said.

"Tactical flour," Ianteen murmured, and if you did not know her well you might have missed the humor hiding in her voice.

Maximus sheathed the wooden blade with extra care, like he wanted the moment to feel official. "We train today," he said, as if this was new information and not the same rhythm we lived by.

"Yes," I said. "We train today."

Maximus grinned and sat down at the table, then leaned forward and lowered his voice as if he was sharing a secret war council. "I dreamed I was knighted."

Anya immediately leaned in too, because anything whispered sounded exciting. "By who?"

"By the captain of the king's guard," Maximus said, and his eyes shone like he could see it. "He said, 'Maximus, you have defended the realm.' Then he tapped my shoulders with a sword and everyone cheered."

Bobo breathed, "Wow," like it was a holy word.

I smiled, because I knew what that dream meant. It meant Maximus wanted the world to see him as important. It meant he wanted to matter. In Old King's Walk, that kind of wanting was not foolish. It was survival.

"Did you bow?" Anya asked.

"Of course I bowed," Maximus said. "You always bow. It is proper."

Anya tried to bow and almost fell off the bench. I caught her by the back of her shirt before she could hit the floor.

"Careful," I told her.

"I am careful," she said, which was another lie she told with her whole heart.

The kettle started to hiss, and I poured water into chipped mugs, setting one aside with a little more than the others. Dratmar liked his tea strong, and he liked his portions fair, but he also tended to forget to eat when he was thinking. Someone had to remember for him.

"Is Dratmar coming?" Maximus asked.

"He will," I said. "He always does."

Maximus nodded like that was comforting, and it was. Dratmar Blackenstone was not our father by blood. He was something else, something made out of choice and stubbornness and the kind of loyalty that does not talk much because it does not need to. He had taken us in after the war left us scattered like loose nails, and he had turned a house that was too small into a place that felt safe. He trained us because he believed training was mercy. If you know how to stand, you fall less.

I had learned early that adults who survived wars carry their fear differently than children do. Children carry fear like a stone in their hands. Adults carry it like a scar under their shirt. They pretend it is not there until the day it aches.

While everyone ate, I listened to the house. I listened to the wind brushing the shutters. I listened to the pop of the fire. I listened to the distant sounds of the village waking up. A door opening. A cart wheel creaking. Someone laughing near the well.

It all sounded normal, and that should have comforted me.

Looking back, I can tell you that "normal" is not a promise. It is only the shape things take when danger is not currently biting you. In those days, I still thought normal was something you could keep if you worked hard enough. The front door rattled, and a gust of cold air shoved its way inside like it owned the place. Dratmar stepped in, stamping snow from his boots. He had his coat pulled tight and his hair tied back, and his eyes swept the room in one quick glance that counted heads without looking like it counted.

"All present," he said.

"That is because we live here," Ianteen replied.

Dratmar's mouth twitched, which for him was a grin. "Good. Eat. Then we drill."

Maximus sat up straighter. "Yes, sir."

Dratmar gave him a look. "Do not call me sir."

"Yes, sir," Maximus said, then winced as if he had bitten his tongue.

Dratmar set his gloves near the hearth and took the larger mug of tea I had saved. He did not thank me. Dratmar did not thank people for the things he believed were obvious acts of care. He treated them the same way he treated breathing. You did it because you were alive, and because someone needed you to do it.

His gaze flicked to the charm over the door. Just a glance, quick and thoughtful.

"You touch it?" he asked me.

"I always do," I said.

"Habit," he said, and he sounded neither approving nor disapproving.

"Is that bad?" Anya asked, immediately interested.

Dratmar looked down at her. His voice softened in a way that made the room feel warmer. "It is not bad to remember stories," he said. "It is only bad when stories replace thinking."

Anya frowned like that was unfair. "Stories are easier."

"Yes," Dratmar said. "That is why people use them."

I remember that line clearly. I did not understand it then, not fully. I only thought it was another one of Dratmar's lessons, like how to hold a stance and how to wrap a sprained wrist. Later, when the world started demanding choices, I learned what he meant. Stories can comfort you, but they can also give you someone to blame.

Outside, somewhere in the village, a dog barked once, sharp and loud, then went quiet. I noticed it because I always noticed things. I told myself it meant nothing. Dogs bark. That is what they do. With all that I know now, I still think that is true.

I also know that was the first sound of the day that did not belong.

WE ATE QUICKLY AFTER that, the way you do when you know the real part of your day is waiting outside and you do not want to meet it on an empty stomach. Anya kept sneaking bites from Maximus's plate, Maximus kept letting her because he loved being a hero even when the battle was a crust of bread, and Ianteen pretended not to see any of it while quietly sliding the basket a little closer to Anya's elbow. Bobo stayed near the hearth as if the fire might tell him a secret if he stared long enough, hands held out to the heat like he was praying to it, and Dratmar watched all of us with that steady look of his, the one that counted heads without making you feel like a number.

Jaime arrived just as I was rinsing mugs, stamping snow off her boots like she was annoyed at winter for daring to exist. Her hair was braided tight, her coat buckled properly, and her belt sat where it should, which told me she had been up and moving long before I thought I was being responsible. Jaime always woke like the day had an appointment with her, and the day had better not be late.

"You started without me," she said.

"You are late," I told her.

"I am early," she replied, and a grin flickered across her face for a moment before she smoothed it away. She ruffled Anya's hair with two careful fingers, just enough to make Anya beam without turning her braid into a nest, then her eyes swept the room in that fast way of hers, checking the door, the windows, the hearth, and Dratmar's posture. It was not fear, not exactly. It was the habit of someone who did not like surprises and did not want anyone else to be caught by them either.

Dratmar nodded once toward the door. "Ready?"

Jaime nodded back. "Ready."

Maximus sat up straighter like the word had been a trumpet. "Ready, sir."

Dratmar's eyes narrowed. "Do not call me sir."

Maximus opened his mouth, thought better of it, and shut it again. That was progress, and in our house we learned to celebrate progress wherever we found it.

We layered up, pulling on gloves and belts and thick scarves that always smelled faintly like smoke. I slipped my training knife into its sheath out of habit. It was not sharp enough to do anything dramatic, but it sat right on my hip, and I liked the weight. Jaime checked her wooden sword strap the way other girls checked their hair ribbons. She did not fuss, she confirmed, and when she caught me watching she lifted one brow like she was daring me to say something about it.

When we stepped outside, the cold slapped me awake, sharp enough to make my eyes water for a second before pride made me pretend it was nothing. Old King's Walk lay under a thin sheet of snow that made everything look cleaner than it was. Chimney smoke rose in lazy lines and flattened as the wind pushed it toward the forest, and the village road was packed down by boots and cart wheels into a pale ribbon that led to places most of us only talked about. Dratmar's training yard sat behind his workshop, fenced with split logs and stubborn hope, the ground inside swept clean and marked by scuffed lines where we drilled formations. There were striking posts, a few old shields hanging from pegs, and a rack of practice blades that had seen more bruises than glory. Dratmar believed that if you learned on poor ground with simple tools, you would not panic when the ground got worse and the tools got real.

He set us in a loose line and started us on footwork, because Dratmar always said that a sword is only as smart as the feet carrying it. We stepped forward and back, side to side, pivot and reset, the kind of drill that looks boring until you realize boring keeps you alive. Jaime moved like she had rhythm in her blood, each shift clean, each turn sharp, her weight always where it needed to be. Maximus tried to match her and overdid it, boots scuffing wider than necessary, and Dratmar stopped in front of him with the patience of a man who had seen ambition get people hurt.

"Your spacing is too wide," Dratmar said.

"It gives me reach," Maximus insisted.

"It gives you a hole," Dratmar replied. "Close it. Reach is useless if you cannot recover."

Maximus adjusted, cheeks pink, and tried again. Better. Dratmar moved down the line and tapped Bobo's elbow into place, then made that same correction he always made, the one that sounded harsh until you realized it was mercy.

"Do not apologize," he told Bobo. "Correct."

Bobo swallowed and nodded, face tight with concentration, trying to hold his guard up without thinking about his arms. Ianteen did her drills steady and quiet, not fast but right, and I saw Jaime notice and give her a small nod as they passed each other. It was nothing, and it was also everything, because in our house praise was not poured out like ale. You earned it, and when you got it you held onto it.

When Dratmar called for blades, Jaime and I paired off, Maximus sparred Ianteen, and Bobo worked the post like it was a stubborn enemy that refused to fall. Jaime held her wooden sword with the same seriousness she would have held steel, and she gave me a look that meant she expected me to try something clever.

"Slow first," she said.

"I am always slow," I lied.

Her eyes narrowed with amusement. "Try."

We circled, boots squeaking faintly on packed dirt. I tested her with a feint that would have fooled plenty of village boys. It did not fool Jaime. She tracked my shoulders instead of my blade, waited for me to commit, and when I pushed faster she parried clean and stepped into my space at the same time, forcing me back. Jaime's left hand hovered near her chest, ready to shove or grab, and I had learned the hard way that her left hand was just as dangerous as her sword.

"Your feet," she said. "You are dancing."

"I like dancing," I said, because I could not help myself.

"This is not a festival," she replied, and the way she said it meant she was trying not to smile.

Dratmar's voice cut across the yard. "Elric. Stop trying to be clever. Be clear."

"I am being clear," I protested.

"You are being cute," he corrected, and I felt my ears warm.

Jaime's blade tapped my shoulder. "Clear," she echoed, and yes, she was enjoying that a little.

So I dropped the flourish and stepped in honest. Wood met wood with a sharp click, the vibration running up my arm like a stern warning. Across the yard, Maximus overextended again and Ianteen stepped aside and tapped him in the ribs with her practice blade. He made a wounded sound as if the world had insulted him personally.

"That would have been lethal," Maximus complained.

"It would have been avoidable," Ianteen replied, calm as daylight.

Jaime's mouth twitched. She liked competence, and she liked when people learned.

After a few rounds Dratmar halted us and paced in front of the line, hands clasped behind his back, breath visible in the cold. There were moments when he looked like a man built for marching down roads toward wars nobody wanted, and that was not my imagination, not entirely.

"You are not soldiers," he told us.

Maximus frowned. "Why not?"

"Because you do not belong to an army," Dratmar replied. "Because you have not sworn to a banner. Because you have not been given orders by a commander who would spend you like a coin."

He let that sit for a moment, then kept going, because Dratmar did not just train bodies, he trained choices. He spoke of the names people fought under in Lionel, Soldiers, Squires, Knights, Mages, and how those words were systems and promises. If you ever left the village and claimed a title, people would expect you to act like it. Anya, watching from outside the fence, raised her hand like she was in a schoolhouse.

"What about Warriors?" she asked.

The air went a little still, not from magic, just from habit. "Warrior" was a story word in Old King's Walk, a word adults used with a smile when they wanted to entertain children, and a word they stopped using when the fire burned low and the wind made the shutters rattle.

Dratmar studied Anya a moment, then answered carefully. "Warrior is an old word. Some say it means a fighter blessed by the Dragon Here. Some say it means a person who takes on the strength of dragons. Some say it is only a tale people tell when they want to believe one person can fix what an army failed to fix. Legends as old as time say a Warrior is born to fight monsters beyond those that any mere mortal can face."

Maximus leaned forward, hungry for it. "Is it real?"

Dratmar's gaze flicked briefly toward the carved charm on his workshop door as if he was checking his own memory, then he looked back at us. "People use stories to explain things they do not understand," he said. "The names help them sleep. They help them blame. They help them hope."

Anya's brow furrowed. "So the Dragon Below is not real?"

Dratmar's voice hardened the smallest bit. "There are things in this world that want to hurt you," he said. "Call them monsters. Call them evil. Call them the Dragon Below if you must. The name does not matter. The fact matters. You stay alert. You stay together. You do not go looking for dark places because you think bravery is the same as wisdom."

Jaime had been quiet through that, but I saw her eyes flick once toward the tree line beyond the village, the way she always looked toward danger when someone named it. Jaime liked knowing where trouble lived. She thought knowledge was armor. I liked knowledge too, but I also liked believing people could be better. That was my armor, thinner than hers, and easier to dent.

Dratmar clapped once, brisk, and put us back into formation drills, advance and hold, flank cover and rally, retreat and reset, commands that sounded like a game until you understood they were meant for days when games ended. Jaime's voice cut in at points, correcting spacing without turning it into a scolding.

"Do not bunch," she said. "If one of you falls, the rest of you need room to move."

Maximus adjusted immediately, eager to do it right. Ianteen moved smooth and quiet. Bobo strained to keep up, face tight with effort, and Dratmar's shoulders settled as he watched us find the shape of a line and hold it.

For a little while the world felt simple again, snow and breath and wood and the clean certainty of movement. Then a shout carried from the village road, faint but urgent, and a dog barked fast and high, not the bored bark of a farm dog seeing a squirrel, but the sharp bark of warning. Dratmar's head snapped up, Jaime froze mid-step, and I froze too, because everyone freezes when the day stops behaving.

"Stay," Dratmar said, lowering his hand, palm down, the signal for stillness. He listened, eyes narrowed, and for one brief second I tried to convince myself it was nothing, a cart upset or a fox in the hens, because Old King's Walk had small troubles all the time and we handled them because that was what villages did. Years later I still believe most troubles start small, and I also know some troubles start small only so they can get close enough to bite.

DRATMAR HELD UP HIS hand, palm down, and the whole yard obeyed him like we were all tied to the same rope. Even Anya stopped bouncing at the fence and went still with her fingers clenched around the top rail. The shout came again, closer this time, and it was not a cheer or a greeting. It was a jagged sound, the kind a person makes when they are trying to get someone's attention before something gets worse.

Dratmar tilted his head, listening, the way he did when the wind shifted and he wanted to know if it meant snow or trouble. Then he glanced at Jaime and me, and I saw the decision settle into his eyes before he spoke it out loud.

"Elric. Jaime. Go see," he said. "Do not run blind. Look first. If it is nothing, come back. If it is something, you come back anyway."

"Yes," Jaime said immediately.

"Understood," I said, and I meant it, even though my feet were already eager.

Dratmar's voice sharpened. "Together."

"Together," Jaime echoed, and she took one step closer to me, not touching, just close enough that the space between us felt like an agreement.

We left the yard at a fast walk, not a sprint, because Dratmar hated wasted energy and he hated panic more. The village road curved past the workshop and toward the well, where most commotion in Old King's Walk gathered like ducks to grain. Snow squeaked under our boots, and the cold made my nose sting, but I could smell something new under the usual winter mix of smoke and wet wool. It was faint and easy to ignore, and that is the kind of detail the world loves to hide behind. It smelled like old ash, like a fire that had burned somewhere it was not supposed to.

At the well, a small crowd had formed, which in our village meant maybe twelve people, but twelve people could feel like a whole army when they were all talking at once. The mayor was there, Gregory Randmar, wrapped in a heavy cloak that made him look broader than he was. He had the posture of a man who had practiced authority in front of mirrors, chin lifted, shoulders square, hands folded as if he was always one breath away from declaring a meeting. In a bigger city, he might have been a clerk with a loud voice. In Old King's Walk, he was the closest thing we had to a king.

Beside him stood Mykel Randmar, his son, and even now as I look back my first thought when I picture Mykel is that he always looked like he had just won something, even when he had not done a single thing to earn it. Mykel had good boots, a clean scarf, and the kind of confidence that comes from knowing your mistakes will be forgiven before you make them. He was older than Anya but not old enough to be a man, which meant he lived in that dangerous space where he wanted power and did not yet understand the cost of it.

The source of the shouting was a farmer named Tovin, face red from cold and anger, pointing down the road that led toward the fields.

"I told you I saw tracks," Tovin insisted. "Not deer. Not wolves. Small feet, a lot of them, and they were not wandering. They were moving like they knew where they were going."

Mykel laughed, loud enough to make people turn. "You saw rabbits," he said. "Or you saw your own fear and put feet on it. It is winter, Tovin. Everything looks like a monster when the days get short."

Tovin's hands clenched. "I know what I saw."

Mayor Gregory lifted both palms as if he could press the crowd into calm. "We are not going to stir panic," he said. "We have patrols. We have hunters. We have men who can watch the tree line. This is not a time for shouting."

"That is rich," Tovin snapped. "Shouting is how you get someone to listen."

Mykel stepped forward, smiling as if he was enjoying the argument. "If you want someone to listen, you go to Dratmar and ask him to swing his little practice swords at the woods," he said, then his eyes found Jaime and me as if we had been placed there for his entertainment. "Or you ask the village heroes. Here they are now."

I felt Jaime's shoulders tighten beside me. She did not raise her chin. Jaime did not play those games. She just watched Mykel like she was measuring him for a uniform he would not fit.

"Morning," I said, because that is what I did in those days. I said hello to storms. I greeted snarling dogs. I tried to treat problems like they were people who might become polite if you gave them a chance.

Mykel's smile widened. "Elric," he said, drawing my name out like it was a joke he expected everyone to understand. "Training already? What is it today, learning to trip over your own feet in a new pattern? Perhaps how to use that furred appendage to hold a shield over your rear?"

"We were drilling," Jaime said, flat and calm. "What happened?"

Mykel made a show of looking around. "Tovin thinks goblins are coming," he announced. "Because he saw footprints. Footprints, Jaime. In winter. Can you imagine?"

Tovin looked like he wanted to throw something. He did not, because the mayor was there and because Mykel had that invisible shield of importance around him. In a small village, shields like that are made from other people's silence.

Mayor Gregory cleared his throat. "No one has said the word goblins," he corrected, even though Tovin had not needed to. The world has certain fears prepackaged, and you can call them up without saying their names. "Tovin believes he saw unusual tracks. We are discussing it calmly."

Mykel tilted his head toward Jaime. "Maybe Jaime can command the snow to stop falling. Or perhaps Elric can run very fast around the village and scare the monsters away." He looked back at me and his eyes narrowed, not with anger, but with the kind of casual cruelty that always surprised me, even though it should not have by then. "I hear you are good at running. Good at running away like a little kitten."

It was not clever. It was not even accurate. It was just meant to sting, and it did, mostly because it was said in front of people who might repeat it later. Shame spreads in villages faster than fire.

I smiled anyway, because I had learned that if you did not give Mykel the reaction he wanted, he got bored sooner. "Running is useful," I said. "If I see something dangerous, I can get help faster."

Mykel blinked as if he had not expected a sensible answer. Then he recovered, because bullies recover like cats, quick and graceful and always convinced they landed on purpose. "Help," he repeated. "From who? Dratmar? You mean your uncle-father? The man who plays soldier behind his shed?"

Jaime's eyes sharpened. "Do not talk about him like that," she said, still quiet, but the words had an edge.

Mykel lifted his hands in mock surrender. "I am only saying what people say," he replied, which was the easiest lie in the world, because it hid behind other voices. "Besides, if there was danger, the mayor would know. Wouldn't you, Father?"

Mayor Gregory's jaw tightened. For a moment he looked tired, and I almost felt sorry for him. Almost. Being responsible for a village is heavy, and being responsible for a son like Mykel is heavier. Still, the mayor did not correct him, not properly. He just smoothed his cloak and tried to steer the conversation back to where he felt safe, which was anything that did not require him to admit he had lost control of his own household.

"Elric," the mayor said, and his tone shifted into something official, as if that might keep the world orderly. "Jaime. You train with Dratmar. You are alert youths. Have you seen anything unusual this morning?"

Jaime answered honestly. "We heard shouting. We came."

I decided to be useful. "Tovin, where did you see the tracks?"

Tovin looked relieved that someone had asked him a real question. He pointed down the road toward the fields, past the last cluster of houses, where the land opened into white slopes and fence lines that looked like thin black scratches against snow. "Near the split oak," he said. "Right at the edge of the trees. A lot of feet. And drag marks, like they were hauling something."

Mykel made a sound of disbelief. "Hauling what," he asked, "your imagination?"

Jaime ignored him, which was its own kind of discipline. She looked at me. "We can check," she said.

Mayor Gregory hesitated. "I do not want you two wandering into the woods," he said, and that would have sounded protective if it had not come from the same mouth that had just allowed Mykel to spit on our names. "If there is trouble, it is a matter for adult men."

Jaime's expression did not change, but I could feel her anger like heat near a fire. "Then send adult men," she said. "Now."

Mykel laughed again, softer this time. "Listen to her," he said. "She talks like a captain. Maybe she thinks the king will hear her from all the way out here."

I kept my voice light, because light was my habit, even when I was carrying something heavier inside. "We are not asking to lead an army," I said. "We are asking to look at tracks in snow. If it is nothing, you lose nothing but a few minutes. If it is something, you gain time."

That, at least, Mayor Gregory understood. Time is a kind of currency even rulers respect. He nodded once, sharp. "Fine," he said. "You will not go alone. Mykel will accompany you. He is my son, and he needs to learn vigilance."

Jaime's eyes flicked to me, and I could read the entire argument she wanted to have in that single glance. The mayor had just turned our caution into Mykel's field trip, and he had done it without asking us if we wanted his son at our backs. Jaime's jaw set, but she did not refuse, because refusing in front of a crowd would only give Mykel another story to twist later.

Mykel's grin returned, bright and pleased. "Of course," he said. "I will keep them safe."

I wanted to say something clever. I wanted to say something sharp. What I did instead was nod, because I was still the boy who believed the world could be improved with patience. Even to this day, I still believe patience matters, but I also learned patience is not the same as surrender.

We walked out toward the fields, the three of us, with the village watching. Jaime moved at a steady pace, not rushed, not slow, and Mykel fell in behind us like he was already bored with the job he had been given. As we passed the last houses, I glanced back once and saw the mayor standing at the well, shoulders squared again, as if he could hold the village together by standing very still. For a heartbeat I felt sympathy, because I knew he was scared and did not want to admit it. Then Mykel kicked a clump of snow at my heel, hard enough to sting through my boot, and sympathy slipped away.

"You do not have to pretend you are brave," Mykel said, voice low so Jaime would not hear, though she did, of course. Jaime heard everything. "If there are goblins, you will run. That is what you do."

I gave him my easiest smile. "If there are goblins, I will do what keeps people alive," I said. "Sometimes that means running. Sometimes it means standing. You will learn that eventually."

Mykel scoffed, but he did not have a quick answer, which made his silence satisfying in a small way. Jaime did not comment. She just kept walking, eyes on the tree line ahead, the place where the world changed from open white field to dark branches. I watched her profile, the tight braid, the calm face, and I knew she was thinking about angles and distance and what Dratmar would want us to do. Jaime did not borrow courage from hope. She built it out of planning.

We reached the split oak, its trunk cracked and twisted like it had once been struck by lightning and had survived out of stubbornness. The snow around it looked undisturbed at first glance, smooth and innocent. Then Jaime crouched, brushed a gloved hand across the surface, and revealed the marks beneath, packed down and scarred.

They were not rabbit tracks. They were not deer. They were small, too close together, a mess of prints that churned the snow like a crowd had passed through. There were scuffs where something had been dragged, long lines cut into the white leading back toward the trees. Jaime traced them with her eyes, and I saw her mouth tighten.

Mykel stepped closer, and for the first time that morning his smile faltered. "That could be anything," he muttered.

"It is not anything," Jaime said. Her voice stayed level, but it had changed. It was the voice she used when she stopped pretending a problem might be polite. "It is a group. Moving with purpose."

I leaned in, and the faint ash smell hit me again, stronger here, mixed with something sour, like old sweat and damp fur. I did not know what goblins smelled like then. I only knew that this smell did not belong to our fields.

Jaime stood and looked toward the forest. I followed her gaze, and that is when I saw it. Not a monster, not a blade, not anything that would make a good story in a tavern. Just a thin thread of smoke rising behind the trees, too far to be any chimney in the village, too steady to be mist. It curled upward and flattened in the wind, the same way our hearth smoke did, but it was coming from the wrong place.

Mykel saw it too. He swallowed. "That could be a hunter's fire," he said, and he sounded like he wanted it to be true.

"Hunters do not build fires that big," Jaime replied.

I stared at that smoke for a long moment, trying to make it fit into something harmless, because that is what I did. I tried to excuse the world the way I excused people. After many hard lessons now, I can admit that the world does not always deserve it. I almost miss the times when I thought like this.

Jaime turned back toward the village, already moving. "We go," she said. "Now."

I nodded and fell into step beside her, and Mykel hurried after us, suddenly very interested in staying close. As we ran back across the field, the smoke behind the trees kept rising like a quiet warning, and the snow under our boots stopped feeling clean. It started feeling thin, like a sheet over something deep and hungry.

# Chapter 2

## THE MAYOR'S SON

THE BELL ABOVE THE mayor's door never did learn to ring for trouble. It jangled the same no matter who came through, tax man or tinker, gossiping auntie or panicked child. That afternoon it chimed in its thin, cheery way as Jaime shouldered the door open, and the sound struck me as wrong, like a laugh in the middle of a funeral.

The mayor's hall always smelled of beeswax and old paper. Dratmar said if you wanted to know what peacetime did to a village, you need only sniff its town hall. Ours was layered in comfort, the glowsmell of polished wood, the faint sweetness of ink, none of the sour metal tang that clung to places where hard decisions were made. We tracked mud across the clean board floor. Jaime didn't bother wiping his boots. Maximus did, out of habit, then realized halfway through that Ianteen was watching and trying not to smirk. He left the other boot dirty out of pride.

The reception room was empty. A shaft of pale sun cut through the front windows, catching the dust in lazy swirls. Somewhere deeper in the house someone coughed and a chair creaked.

"Hello?" I called.

Bobo slid in behind me, quiet as smoke. Anya's hand dropped to his shoulder by reflex. She was breathing hard, cheeks flushed from our run back from the northern woods. Goblin tracks. Smoke. The word had a taste in my mouth, bitter and metallic like over-steeped tea. Jaime stalked straight to the inner door and thumped twice without waiting.

"Hold," came a man's voice. Mayor Gregory Randmar, too well-fed to move quickly, too concerned with manners to not say something first.

We waited. The moment stretched. I studied a crack in the plaster near the ceiling, where damp had turned it the color of old bones. When you're seventeen and your heart is racing with what you've seen, silence like that feels like an insult. At last the door opened. The mayor stepped out, smoothing his vest.

Gregory Randmar was not a bad man. That might be the worst thing I can say about him. Evil men, at least, believe in something, greed, power, their own right to rule. The mayor believed in comfort, in order, in not making a fuss. It's a quiet sort of faith, but no less dangerous. He had thinning blond hair he tried to tame with oil, and a nose that reddened in the cold or when he drank. That day it was the color of soft apples. He smelled faintly of pipeleaf. His eyes flickered over us, Jaime's set jaw, my hands clenched at my sides, the dirt on Anya's dress, the smear of black soot on Bobo's cheek, and for a heartbeat, concern creased his brow. Then habit smoothed it away.

"What's this?" he asked. "You lot look like you've run from the Dragon Below himself."

"It's goblins," Jaime said. No preamble, no softening. "Tracks in the northwood. Smoke beyond the ridge. Not a campfire. A signal, maybe. Or a…"

"Jaime," I cut in, because he sounded like he was building to something and my mind was still full of shapes between trees. "We went up to Old Barrow Path for the morning drills. Near the stream crossing we found tracks." I nearly said "prints" like Dratmar, but I knew better than to use soldier words in this house. "Small, bare feet. Lots of them. Fresh. They weren't there yesterday."

The mayor's fingers tightened around the edge of the door, then loosened. "Bare feet? Could be children. Trappers' brats. Or those Riverfolk that came through last month, remember? Little one with the…"

"These weren't children," Jaime snapped. "Three toes. Claws. Deep in the mud. And we heard them last night, up past the far orchard." He jerked his chin toward me. "Elric heard them too."

I had. A thin, skittering call between the trees like someone rattling bones in a tin cup, too high and too fast to be any bird I knew. But telling a man who'd never camped outside his own fields what goblins sounded like wouldn't help.

"Tracks were small, but there were a lot," I said. "More than a dozen. Maybe two dozen. Heading south."

"Toward us," Anya added in a quiet voice. She had Bobo half behind her now. You could hardly see his round face over her shoulder.

"Toward the village." Jaime took a step closer. "Dratmar thinks"

"Dratmar," the mayor said, and there it was, the faint curl of his lip when that name entered any room. "I thought as much. He sent you, did he? Couldn't come himself?"

"He's keeping the little ones calm," Maximus said. His tone was respectful in that way of his that somehow made it sound like a rebuke. "He asked us to come. We're quick on our feet."

Gregory sighed and rubbed his forehead as if we were the headache and not what we'd brought. "Children," he said. "We've had peace on this stretch of road for near on twenty years. The Kingdom of Lionel is whole again, praise the Dragon Here. The last time a goblin raiding party came this close, some of you weren't even born." He smiled, the way someone smiles when they mean to reassure you that your fear is foolish. "I know you train very hard out there with old Dratmar. Play your war-games, swing your wooden swords. And that's good. Discipline is good. But the world does not jump every time a squirrel leaves a mark in the mud."

"It wasn't a squirrel," Jaime hissed.

I watched the mayor watching him. Jaime's hair was damp with sweat, curls sticking to his forehead; there was a tear in the sleeve of his tunic where a thorn had caught him in our rush back. His eyes were bright, too bright, the way they got before a fight. The mayor didn't see that. He saw an orphan boy trying to be important in the mayor's house.

"You must understand," Gregory went on, "what kind of trouble stories like this can cause. You run around shouting about goblins in the woods, and next thing you know every fool with a rusty pitchfork is out in the rain chasing shadows. That's how people get hurt."

"People get hurt when no one listens," Jaime said.

"Jaime," Dratmar's voice said from the doorway.

I hadn't heard the bell ring this time, but there he was, filling the frame in his patched gray coat. He'd put his uniform away years ago, but there was no hiding the way he carried himself: back straight, every line of him angled toward the exit, the window, the threat.

"Sir," I said without thinking.

The mayor's jaw flexed at that. He nodded at Dratmar, not quite managing a bow, not with the children watching.

"Gregory," Dratmar said. He used the mayor's name the way you use a knife on fruit, clean, efficient, with a faint twist at the end. "I sent them. They saw what they saw."

Gregory forced a chuckle. "You do keep them in training, Dratmar. I'll give you that. But goblins, this close? In Lionel's peace? It seems unlikely."

"War doesn't ask what seems likely," Dratmar said. "It asks where the soft places are." His eye flicked over the polished hall, the neat ledgers on the desk behind the mayor. "I've ridden with King Lionel's border scouts. Goblins don't range this far south on a whim. If they're here, they're hungry or desperate. Or someone's pushed them."

"Border scouts," Gregory repeated. "Yes, well, you're not on the border anymore. You're in Old King's Walk. We have fences, and good neighbors, and nothing worth a raiding party's trouble."

"Nothing worth their trouble," Ianteen muttered at my elbow. "Except a whole village of fat sheep."

Anya smothered a cough that might have been a laugh. Bobo's fingers worried the hem of her skirt until she gently pried them loose.

Dratmar took a slow breath. When he spoke again, his tone was different, lighter, almost casual. It fooled the mayor, but not me. "I'm not sounding an alarm. I'm asking for precautions. Go up to the tower at dusk. Put a man on watch. Send a runner to Greenglade, tell them we've seen goblin sign, ask if they have. That much, at least."

The mayor's eyes slid toward the window, where the sky was a clear washing-day blue, the kind that made laundry flap on lines and men think about crops instead of swords. "At dusk," he said, "I always go up to the tower. I like to watch the sun go down. It reminds me" He stopped, perhaps hearing himself. "If I see anything, I'll send word. As for runners and watches..." He spread his hands, calling upon the invisible weight of his office. "The people have their work. Harvest's not far. They don't need a scare over a few, what, toes in the mud and some smoke where some poacher lit an illegal fire."

Jaime's hands balled. I saw the muscles flex along his jaw.

"And if you're wrong?" Dratmar asked.

"If I'm wrong," the mayor said with a confidence I envied and hated, "we'll handle it. Old King's Walk has stood a century. She'll stand another night." He smiled. "I'll ask Alrin to keep his boys' dogs in, hm? That way, if there's anything out there, we'll hear them barking."

The conversation was over. You could feel it, the way you feel the air go still before a storm. Gregory turned back toward his office. "Do make sure your trainees don't spread panic, Dratmar. Stories have a way of growing. We've peace now. Best to enjoy it."

He left us in the beeswax quiet. The bell chimed again as the inner door shut. Dratmar watched the closed door for a count of three. His shoulders, which had been tight as drawn bowstrings, eased, not with relief, but with resignation.

"We did what we could," he said. He looked at each of us in turn. Jaime was all sharp edges; Maximus looked as if he'd swallowed a stone. Anya had that distant look she got when she was cataloguing everyone's hurt and figuring how to patch it. Bobo's eyes were on the far window, where the light fell in a perfect square on the floor. Ianteen's lip curled.

"He didn't even ask how many," I said. It bothered me more than I expected. A man who'd seen war would have asked that first. How many. How armed. How fast.

"He doesn't know which questions to ask," Dratmar said. "That's not his fault. It's mine, and men like me, for not teaching him when we had the chance." He turned toward the door. "Back home. Eat. Rest if you can. We'll go over the drills again before evening."

Jaime exploded. "We can't just—"

"We can," Dratmar said, and there was steel in it. "We will. We are six children and one retired soldier. We are not a garrison, and this is not a fortress. We prepare what we can prepare. No more speeches in the square. No more running from house to house. Panic will do more harm than goblins if they don't come."

"And if they do?" Ianteen asked.

Dratmar's good eye met hers. For all his scars and age, in that moment he looked young, the way a tree looks when lightning is close. "Then you'll be glad you spent the afternoon with a full belly and sharpened steel."

THE VILLAGE SQUARE OUTSIDE the mayor's hall might as well have been in another world. Sunlight lay thick over the cobblestones. A cooper's boy rolled a hoop past the well, laughing. Old Mara sat on her stool outside the bakers', knotting twine through loops of bread like she did every day till her fingers ached. Men leaned in front of the tavern, bare arms crossed, arguing the price of barley. Somewhere a lute clinked out a simple harvest tune.

Smoke from morning cookfires still hung low, sweet and greasy. Someone had spilled a basket of late apples by the fountain, and children scrambled after them, the skins flashing red and gold against gray stone. A pair of girls about our age walked arm in arm past us, their heads inclined toward each other, giggling. One had a fresh ribbon in her hair. Her eyes slid over us, our plain clothes, our sweat, Dratmar's shadow at our backs, and then slid away, as if we were a smell to be ignored. I'd been born elsewhere, but my memories started here. For me, Old King's Walk had never been a place at peace; it had been a place that happened to be between battles. Yet looking at it that afternoon, I understood why the mayor couldn't imagine flames licking those thatched roofs. There are days so ordinary they feel like armor.

We were halfway across the square when a voice like sour milk called out, "Well, if it isn't Dratmar's little soldiers."

The sound grated down my spine. Jaime's shoulders tensed under his shirt. Mykel Randmar, mayor's son, budding tyrant, lounged on the low stone lip of the fountain with his boot heels on the carved face of some old king. His hose were clean, his tunic a fine blue wool with a silver thread at the cuff, like a poor man's idea of nobility. A leather strap held back his blond hair; the style made boys think they looked older than they were. Half the merchant sons in town wore their hair that way, now that Mykel did. His smile was sweet and empty as bakery icing.

Two other village boys flanked him, elbows propped on the fountain: Jarron, whose father owned half the river fields, and Tolan, whose uncle had once worn a guard's cloak in the city and wouldn't let anyone forget it. Their clothes were a shade rougher than Mykel's, but still finer than ours. They could go home and change if they tore them. Most of us had one good set and one patched one.

A skinny girl with plaits sat a little apart, feet in the dust, chewing a reed and watching everything with hawk eyes. I'd seen her running household errands for the Randmars. Lysa, her name was. She never spoke to us, but she never joined in Mykel's games either.

"Out playing war again?" Mykel asked. His voice carried easily across the square. People's gazes flicked toward us, then away. No one moved to interfere. They knew the shape of this dance. They'd seen it before.

"We were reporting to your father," Jaime said. He kept his voice level. Polite, even. He was better at that than he wanted to be.

Mykel snorted. "Reporting. Listen to you. Like real scouts. What was it this time, wolves? Bandits? A tree stump you mistook for the Dragon Below?" The boys beside him laughed, not because it was funny but because it was theirs.

"Goblins," Bobo said softly.

Heads turned. Not just the local boys now. Mara's hands stilled on her bundles of bread. A man at the tavern shifted his weight, eyes narrowing.

"Bobo," Anya murmured.

Mykel's eyebrows shot up. "Goblins," he repeated, drawing the syllables out. "Did you go out the north road like Dratmar's supposed to? I hear he keeps you on a leash." More laughter. "What did you see, little Bobo? Monsters in the shadows? Maybe your own reflection in the stream?"

"Tracks," Bobo said. He wasn't looking at Mykel. He was looking at the trickle of water over the fountain's carved lip, the way it caught the sun. "Three-toed. Claws. Going south."

Mykel's smile thinned. He didn't like being ignored, especially by someone smaller. "Is that so?" He swung his legs off the stone. "A great discovery, then. I'm sure Father will have a feast held in your honor." His gaze flicked to me and Jaime. "Except, hm. You've already been to him, haven't you? To tell your big goblin tales."

Ianteen muttered at my elbow, too low for the others to hear. "I'll take tales from the field over tales from your father's wine cup." I couldn't help a flash of pride.

"What did he say?" Jarron called. "You going to save us from the Dragon Below, Elric?" He always used my name like it stung his tongue.

"He said what you'd expect," I answered. "That everything's fine as long as he says so."

It was careless, saying it like that. The words slipped out of the tight place between my ribs. I felt Jaime's sharp glance. A hush rippled out from us, subtle yet unmistakable. You didn't mock the mayor in public. Not if you had anything to lose, and we had less than most.

Mykel's eyes went cold. That was when you saw the part of him that would have done well in another sort of world, the one where cruelty is a coin you spend openly.

"What was that, gutter boy? Say it louder stray." he asked. His voice no longer carried a light singsong; it was flat as a slap.

"Leave it, Elric," Maximus said under his breath.

I could have swallowed it. I should have. Mykel's voice made my claws come out and my fur stand on end. Mykel had called us Dratmar's soldiers. Soldiers owe each other more than silence.

"I said," I began.

Jaime stepped in front of me. Smoothly. That was his gift, not just the steel, but the timing.

"We saw what we saw," Jaime said. "We told your father. He made a choice. That's his right." There was no mockery in what he said, only that same terrible precision he carried into everything. "If we're wrong, no harm done. If we're right, then it won't matter who believed us first."

Mykel studied him. Jaime was almost exactly his age, but if you'd stripped them both bare of clothes and pride, you would have thought Jaime the older. There's a way hunger carves years into a face.

"Always so noble," Mykel said. "You practice that in Dratmar's yard? 'Sir, yes, sir, we'll throw our useless little lives away for the good of the village, sir!'" He mimicked a salute. Jarron and Tolan guffawed like they'd never heard anything so clever.

Jaime's cheeks flushed, but he didn't rise. Mykel's gaze drifted over us. He was looking for a weak point. That's the thing bullies and generals have in common. They poke until someone yelps, and his eyes landed on Bobo.

Bobo had drifted a step closer to the fountain. His hand hovered over the sheet of water, not quite touching. Light played over his fingers, thin and pale.

"I hear you still wet the bed, Bobo," Mykel said. "That true? Heard Dratmar has to hang your sheets in the yard, next to the laundry from the pigsty. Makes the whole place smell." Some of the villagers around us shifted uncomfortably. A few laughed. It's easier to laugh than to choose a side.

Bobo's hand stilled. He looked down at his bare feet. I could see his ears reddening, the way they did when he was trying not to cry.

Anya stepped forward, but Mykel was faster. He hopped down from the fountain ledge and skimmed over to Bobo, all smiling charm again. He reached out as if to muss Bobo's hair, like they were friends. Then, in that soft, carrying voice of his, he said, "Maybe that's why the goblins are here. They smelled your piss from the northwood."

The words struck like a thrown stone. The square filled with a little burst of ugly laughter. Not everyone; not even most. But enough. Enough to lay a path brick by brick for the cruelty to walk on.

"Stop it," Anya said. Her voice shook. She put her arm around Bobo and tried to pull him back. "Don't talk to him like that."

Mykel's eyes flicked to her. There was a different kind of calculation there. He was old enough to know which sorts of hurt were sharper.

"Why?" he said. "You think they'll take you instead, Anya? Goblins like pretty girls, don't they?" He made a mock-terrified face. "Oh, the Dragon Below's brides. That's what they tell us in temple. Might be they'd trade one of their little ratlings for you, if we asked nice."

Anya went very still. Her fingers dug into Bobo's shoulder hard enough to leave marks. Tears shimmered in her eyes, but they didn't fall. Fierce, that girl, even when the floor dropped from under her.

Maximus moved. He didn't shout or snarl. He simply stepped into Mykel's space, planting his wide frame like a wall.

"Stop," he said.

It was a gentle word in his mouth, but there was nothing gentle in his stance.

Mykel recoiled half a pace, then caught himself, glancing swiftly around to see who'd seen that instinctive step back. Too many faces were turned our way. He had to reclaim the ground.

"What, big Ox?" he sneered. "Going to hit me? In the middle of the square? Hit the mayor's son?" His voice lifted on the last words, making sure they carried.

Maximus's hands curled. I could see the veins standing out under his skin, dark against his lighter forearms. He could have broken Mykel in two. The older boys from the river sometimes challenged Maximus to wrestling matches when they were half-drunk; he always won. He didn't move now.

"Leave him," Jaime said quietly. Not to Mykel. To Maximus. That was the cruelty of it. We were always talking each other down, never them. "We need to get back."

Mykel saw the retreat and pounced. "That's right," he said. "Run home, strays. Go hide under Dratmar's bed. Maybe he'll tell you another story about the big bad goblins that came and ruined his life. That's all they are now, you know. Stories. Old men's ghosts." He leaned around Maximus to look at me, because he knew I watched more than I spoke. "You know why my father's not afraid?" he asked. "Because no one ever comes here. There's nothing to come for. Not even you."

He turned his back on us then. That was the true dismissal, more than the words. One by one, the boys around him followed suit, like dogs when their master moves on.

"Careful in the woods, Bobo," he called over his shoulder. "Wouldn't want you to get lost like your parents."

That did it. Bobo's breath hitched loud in the stillness. Anya made a sound I'd only heard from her once before, when she cut her hand to the bone on a rusted plow share. Ianteen swore under her breath, a word Dratmar would have made her scrub her tongue for.

"Enough," Dratmar said.

He hadn't spoken through any of it. He'd stood by the edge of the square, watching not with indifference but with the kind of hard, tired patience you see in men who know exactly how much the world will allow. Now his voice cracked like a sapling under an axe. The sound made Mykel glance back. His face worked, a dozen expressions chasing each other: indignation at being rebuked, a flicker of fear, then the lofty disdain he'd seen his father use on petitioners. But he didn't push it, not with Dratmar. Not yet. There were some old habits left in the village, the instinct not to poke a man who'd worn a commander's cloak.

"Yes, Master Dratmar," he said, in a tone that made the honorific an insult. Then he strolled away, Jarron and Tolan loping after him, their voices rising in easy, unaffected chatter now that the show was over.

Lysa, the plaited girl, lingered a heartbeat longer. Her eyes met mine. There was something like apology there, or maybe just curiosity. Then she spat out her reed, tucked her hair behind one ear, and trotted off after the boys. The square exhaled. People went back to their errands, quicker than before, as if they could outrun what they'd seen. No one came over. No one asked if we were all right.

We gathered ourselves like scattered pieces. Bobo's face was blank now. That scared me more than tears would have. He'd gone inward, to that place he did when the world pressed too hard. Anya cupped his cheek, murmuring nothing words, the way you soothe a babe. He leaned into her touch, but his eyes had that too-bright shine.

"It doesn't matter what he says," she whispered.

"It does," Jaime said, too sharp. "That's the problem."

Dratmar's jaw was tight. "Back," he said again. "Now."

We went.

# Chapter 3

## SMOKE ON THE WIND

OUR HOUSE SAT ON the edge of the village, where the cottages thinned and the fields began, a squat, stone-shouldered building with a thatched roof and a low wall around the yard. Once it had been a barracks for King Lionel's levy men when the road was younger and more dangerous. You could still see the outline of the old training yard beneath our vegetable patch, the hard-packed earth where men had swung steel instead of hoes.

Inside, it smelled of stew and oil and the sharp tang of metal filings. The long room that served as both hall and dormitory was lined on one side with hammocks and straw pallets, on the other with weapon racks and a scarred oak table. Dratmar's old campaign banner, Lionel's rearing stag in faded crimson on black, hung over the hearth, moth-chewed and smoke-darkened.

The moment we crossed the threshold, the rest of the little ones swarmed us. Mira, all of eight and still missing half her front teeth, latched onto Anya's skirt. Thom and Vara popped up from behind the table, wooden swords clattering.

"Did you see them?" Thom demanded. "Did you see real goblins?"

"Did they have horns?" Vara asked. "Old Mara says they have horns and fangs down to their bellies and they eat bones whole."

Maximus chuckled despite himself. "If they had horns that big they'd get stuck in the trees, Tiny. Hard to sneak up on anyone with branches in your antlers."

"They don't have horns," Ianteen said. She threw herself onto a bench, stretching her legs out until her bare heels touched the opposite support. "They have ears. Big ugly ears. Like yours." She flicked Thom's.

"Ow!"

Dratmar closed the door behind us and slid the wooden bar across. It wasn't much against goblins. It was enough to shut out the village for a bit.

"Enough," he told the younger ones. "Let them breathe." He nodded toward the big iron pot hanging over the banked coals. "Stir the stew, Mira. If it sticks again, we'll be chewing charcoal for supper."

Mira scampered to obey. The others dispersed to their own small tasks, drawn as much by habit as by hunger. Chores were comfort. Chores made the world predictable: chop, stir, sweep, mend. Dratmar jerked his head at me and Jaime. We followed him to the corner by the hearth, where his old campaign chest squatted. The leather straps were cracked with age; the iron fittings had been polished so often by his hands they were almost silver.

He knelt, opened it, and eased the lid back. The smell that rose from within was like opening an old wound, oil, old leather, and something cold and sharp that wasn't quite metal. War has a scent that doesn't wash out. Inside lay the pieces of his past. A pair of greaves, dented and mended. A cloakpin in the shape of Lionel's lion icon. Three knives, each with a different sigil etched into the hilt from men who'd fallen beside him. And beneath a folded shirt of mail, seven short swords wrapped in oiled cloth.

He'd shown us the chest a year ago, on the day he'd decided our training was no longer a game. Before that, we'd swung sticks and practiced falling without breaking bones. After, we learned to sleep with the weight of steel within reach. He unwrapped two blades now and handed one to me, one to Jaime. We'd used them in drills, of course, out in the yard, under his supervision. They were ordinary soldier's swords, unadorned, double-edged, the grips bound in rough leather. Familiar weight settled into my palm. Today it felt different. He didn't say "practice." He didn't say "yard."

"Keep them close," he said quietly. "Not on your belts. Not where they'll draw eyes. Somewhere you can reach in the dark."

Jaime's back straightened. "You think they'll come."

"I think," Dratmar said, "that the Dragon Below's children don't often waste steps. If they're this close, they're moving toward something. And I think the mayor is wrong about how much we have that's worth taking."

He glanced around the room, at Thom trying to lift Vara into the hammock above his, at Mira's tongue peeking out the corner of her mouth as she stirred the pot, at Bobo sitting on the stone hearth, right hand held too close to the banked coals.

"Bobo," Dratmar said mildly. "Hands."

Bobo jerked like he'd woken from a dream and pulled his fingers back. The skin on his knuckles was already pink. Anya shot Dratmar a grateful look and went over to check Bobo's hand, blowing on it gently, murmuring, "You'll have no prints left if you keep kissing the fire."

"I like the way it moves," Bobo mumbled. "It's never the same. Like it's...thinking."

"Fire doesn't think," Ianteen said. "It just eats."

I knew better than to be comforted by that. Plenty of thinking things only know how to eat, too.

"Jaime," Dratmar said. "Elric. After you eat, take Maximus and Ianteen and walk the inside of the wall. Quietly. Make a note of every ladder, every stack of wood, every place a small body could slip through or over."

"This isn't a fortress," Jaime said bitterly. "You said it yourself."

"No," Dratmar agreed. "But we can pretend, for an afternoon. Anya, you and Bobo and the little ones stay close to the house. No wandering. If anyone asks why, say I have you on extra drills for the festival procession." He grimaced. "The mayor may not fear goblins, but he fears an untidy parade."

"What about you?" I asked.

He closed the chest and rested his hand on the lid. "I'll walk the fields. Talk to Weller and the other old boys who still remember which end of a spear is which. Quietly. We can't raise an alarm, but we can make sure a few of us don't sleep too deeply tonight."

"Do you think...could they pass us by?" Maximus asked. Hope clung to the question like lichen to stone.

"They could," Dratmar said. He didn't add the other half: they probably wouldn't. "People in this village have lived a long time without being frightened enough. That doesn't change in an afternoon. But fear's not the only thing that moves a body. Love will do it too." He nodded at us. "Eat. Then do as I said."

WE TOOK OUR BOWLS outside. The yard felt smaller than usual. The world beyond the low stone wall, the strip of weed-choked ditch, the dirt road, the sloping fields beyond, seemed brighter, louder, as if the sun had turned up its own voice.

Jaime ate standing, gaze flicking constantly toward the tree line. Maximus sat with his back to the house, spoon moving from bowl to mouth in automatic motions. Ianteen picked through her stew, fishing out the fattier bits for Mira, who sat at her feet like a tame dog. Anya sat on the step with Bobo, coaxing him to take more than two bites. He obeyed out of habit if not hunger.

The air had that late-summer heaviness that made shirts stick to skin. Flies buzzed. Somewhere a cow lowed, its voice lazy. Normal sounds, stretched thin over something I couldn't name yet.

"Dogs are loud today," Mira commented. She was right. Distant barking floated over from various parts of the village, sharper and more frequent than usual. I could pick out Old Harn's deep-voiced hound from down by the mill, and the yappy pair the Alrin boys kept by their woodpile. Those ones had a thing about trying to bite my tail, I knew them well.

"They smell us eating," Ianteen said. "Or a fox."

I listened closer. There was a particular tone to a dog's bark when they scented a fox or a rabbit, a high, excited yip. This wasn't that. This was throaty, insistent. Warning.

"You think the goblins can get past the wall?" Thom piped up. "Maybe they'll just run into it and bonk their heads."

"Goblins can climb," Jaime said quietly. He didn't raise his voice, but Thom heard the edge in it and subsided.

"Birds are quiet," Bobo murmured.

I frowned. He was right. Earlier, coming through the square, I'd heard swallows under the eaves and sparrows in the grain. Now, as I lifted my head, the only winged sound was the slow, heavy beat of a crow flapping off the tavern roof. The hedgerows along the road were still. No chitter of finches, no rustle of wings.

"Maybe they're napping," Mira suggested. Children always had an explanation that hurt less.

"Maybe," Bobo said, but his eyes had gone to the northern horizon, where the thin line of trees marked the start of the woods. He squinted, as if trying to see smoke where the sky was clear.

"What if Mykel's right?" Maximus said suddenly. "What if we're just...making trouble? Dratmar's seen war. Maybe it haunts him. Maybe we're seeing ghosts too."

Jaime's spoon clinked hard against his bowl. "You saw the tracks," he said. "You saw which way they pointed."

"I know," Maximus said quickly. "I'm just saying" He gestured helplessly. "Heir of the mayor, heir of the campaign chest. Two old stories pulling."

"Only one of them has blood on his hands," Ianteen said. "And it's not Mykel."

"That we know of," Anya added, surprising us all. There was bitterness in her voice; Mykel's words about brides hadn't been forgotten.

Mira looked between us, brow furrowed. "If the goblins are children of the Dragon Below," she asked, "and we're children of the Dragon Here, why don't we just...ask the Dragon Above to make them go away?"

"Because the Dragon Above doesn't care," Ianteen said, but Dratmar's bark from the doorway cut her off.

"The Dragons care in their own way," he called. "But none of them ever came down here to swing a sword for me. Eat," he said again. "Then work."

We worked.

Walking the wall with Maximus and Ianteen, I tried to see our village like a goblin might: the low stone barrier that marked its edge, knee-high in some places where the earth had sunk; the gaps where boys had kicked through rocks to make shortcuts; the places where woodpiles and rain barrels leaned invitingly, offering handholds and cover.

At one corner, near the old tannery, someone had stacked barrels of cured leather so high they made a neat little stair up to the top of the wall, then down the other side.

Convenient, if you wanted to run and jump. Or convenient if you were small and nimble and carried a knife.

"Here," I said, touching the rough stone. "We could push these barrels down. Block the gap."

"And stink up the whole lane," Ianteen said. "Might keep more than goblins away." She flicked a beetle off the wall with her thumb.

In the field beyond, a pair of boys our age were chasing one another with sticks, shrieking mock battle cries. One of them waved his makeshift sword and shouted, "For Lionel!" The other shrieked, "For the Dragon Below!" and tackled him into the stubble. They rolled, laughing. Neither of them saw us watching.

We moved on.

By the time we'd circled three-quarters of the village, the quality of the light had begun to change. Afternoon slid toward evening, the sun leaning west, casting longer shadows. The blue of the sky deepened. The warmth didn't fade, that would come later, but there was a tiredness in the air now, the way the land sighs after a long day of being trod upon.

Smoke curled from chimneys as women lit their supper fires. The smell of onions frying reached us from Old Mara's cottage. The dogs, which had been barking more or less steadily, were quieter now, as if their throats had gone hoarse. Occasionally one would let out a single sharp bark, then fall silent.

We passed the temple of the Three, its whitewashed walls turning golden in the low sun. The little dragon statues over the door, Above with her wings spread, Here with his claws dug into a stylized hill, Below coiled in shadow, watched us with their blank stone eyes. Someone had stuck a fresh sprig of rosemary in the crack by the Dragon Below's mouth. It hung there limp and unwatered.

The temple bell tolled once. Not for danger. For evening prayer.

"Do you think the Dragons ever talk to each other?" Mira had asked me once, lying on her pallet staring up at the smoke-stained rafters. "Do they fight over us?"

Back then, I'd said something flippant about them squabbling over who had to take responsibility for our mess. Now, staring at the indigo shadow pooling under the trees to the north, I wondered if the Dragons simply watched, the way the villagers had watched Mykel.

We finished the circuit and returned home. Dratmar was waiting by the door, arms folded. He listened as we reported what we'd found: the low points, the weak points, the barrel-stair.

"Arrin Weller still has his old pike," he said. "He'll stand by the gate tonight." He paused, then added, almost grudgingly, "The mayor did go up to the tower. I saw him there when I crossed the square. Leaning on the parapet like a painting. He waved."

"That'll scare them off," Ianteen said.

Dratmar looked past us, toward the northern line. His face was a map drawn in small, hard lines. "Maybe," he said. "Stranger things have happened."

The afternoon thinned.

We slipped back into routine because the body needs that. The little ones finished their chores. Jaime had us run footwork drills in the yard, small, precise movements, pivot and turn, step and strike without weapons. "If you can't move your feet right," he said, "you'll trip over them whether you hold a sword or a spoon." He made us do it twice as long as usual, as if he could burn the fear out through our soles.

Anya and Mira folded laundry, their fingers quick and sure. Thom and Vara argued over who got which hammock. Bobo sat on the step with a bit of charcoal, sketching in the dust. Circles and triangles, spirals that knotted back on themselves. Fire patterns.

The sun slid lower. The shadows of the village roofs reached long fingers across the road. A cart rattled past, heading in from the west fields, the driver humming tunelessly. Swallows began to dart and sweep in the sky, catching the evening gnats. Life, clinging stubbornly to its grooves.

For a while, I almost believed the mayor. Almost let myself think we'd laugh about this one day, tell the story of the time we'd thought we'd seen goblins and it had been nothing but stray farm dogs and smoke from some fool poacher's fire. We would complain about the extra drills. Mira would mimic Dratmar's gruff commands until we wheezed with helpless laughter.

Almost.

But then a wind came.

It wasn't much. A breath, really. It slipped over the wall and into our yard, carrying with it a faint smell that did not belong to Old King's Walk. Not woodsmoke. Not manure. Something sour and musky, like wet leather left too long in the dark. Under it, a tang of metal, old blood on iron.

Dratmar, who had been mending a strap by the door, lifted his head. His nostrils flared. He rose in one smooth motion that belied his years.

"What is it?" Maximus asked. His voice sounded thick in my ears.

"Inside," Dratmar said. Not a shout. A command. "All of you. Now."

We obeyed without thinking. The body knows when to stop arguing.

Jaime shepherded the younger ones through the door. Anya scooped Bobo's sketches away with her foot and tugged him in. Maximus held the doorframe a heartbeat longer, straining to see over the wall toward the north. Dratmar slapped his shoulder.

"Inside."

"But"

"Now."

They went. I went last. As I stepped over the threshold, my bare arm brushed the rough stone of the wall, and the hairs there rose. The air felt thick, charged, like right before lightning when the world holds its breath.

Dratmar dropped the bar into place. It thudded home with a dull, final sound.

"What's happening?" Vara whispered.

"Could be nothing," Dratmar said. He crossed to the weapons rack and took down a spear. It was old, the shaft worn smooth by years of hands, but the point had been kept sharp. "Could be a stray herd upwind. Could be a storm brewing." He glanced toward the shuttered window, where a sliver of dimming light leaked through the crack. "We'll wait."

We waited.

The minutes stretched like taffy. The only sounds inside were the crackle of the banked fire and the small, restless movements of bodies trying not to fidget. Outside, the world went oddly muffled. The usual evening noises, the clatter of pots from neighboring houses, the rise and fall of distant conversation, seemed to fade.

"Look," Bobo breathed.

He was peering through a knot-hole in the wall. Anya moved to block him, then hesitated when she saw his face.

"What do you see?" Jaime asked, moving up beside them.

"Light," Bobo said. "Where it shouldn't be."

I pressed my eye to the crack next to his.

At first, all I saw was the familiar: our yard, the low wall, the strip of road beyond. The sky above the northern trees had deepened to a dusky purple, banded with orange where the sun still lingered in the west. Shadows lay thick under the eaves of neighboring houses.

Then, at the far edge of my vision, where the road curved toward the north gate, a flare of color licked up suddenly. Orange and yellow and a furious white at the heart. Fire.

One fire wasn't so strange. People lit torches. Barns caught sparks. But torches didn't scream.

The sound reached us a breath later.

It wasn't words. It was raw, torn from lungs, high and human and full of something so primal it bypassed the mind. A child's scream, we thought for an instant. Then another voice joined it, deeper, then another, until the air itself seemed to vibrate with them.

"Stay," Dratmar said, already moving for the door. He lifted the bar with hands that didn't tremble and eased it open a crack.

Heat rushed in. Not the soft, familiar warmth of a hearth, but a greedy, grasping heat that smelled of pitch and hair. Over it came other sounds, shouts, the crash of something heavy falling, the ugly, wet noise of metal meeting flesh. Above it all, a new sound cut in, a shrill, ululating cry that made the pit of my stomach drop. I had heard it in the northwood the night before, faint and far. It was closer now, multiplied.

Goblins.

There is a way they scream when they charge, part battle cry, part laughter, part dare to the world. It is not like a wolf's howl or a man's roar. It skitters up and down the spine, all sharp edges.

"Dratmar," Anya began.

"They're here," I whispered, as if saying it softly would make it less true.

More light flickered past the crack. Another flare, closer this time. The air thickened with smoke. It clawed its way in under the door, under the shutters, snaking along the floor.

Someone in the village was shouting orders now, or maybe just shouting. Dogs barked, then cut off with yelps. Glass shattered. A roof beam groaned.

"Jaime," Dratmar said, not looking away from the door. "Elric. Swords. Exactly what we practiced."

My hand was already reaching for the hilt tucked under my pallet. The leather felt slick under my fingers, whether from oil or sweat I didn't know. Jaime's face had gone very calm, the way it did when he was doing numbers in his head. Maximus swallowed hard and grabbed a heavy oak staff from the rack.

"What do we do?" Mira whimpered.

"Stay low," Anya told her. Her voice shook, but her hands were steady as she pulled the younger girl toward the hearth. "Stay away from the windows. Don't scream unless I tell you."

Bobo's eyes reflected the flickering light from outside. "Fire," he said softly, almost in wonder. "It's everywhere."

Another explosion of sound, this time a roar of flame as something big caught, followed by a crash like a wall giving way. Sparks danced in the smoky air that had crept under our door. Somewhere very close, a woman shrieked a name over and over, until her voice broke.

Dratmar opened the door another hand's breadth. Through the gap, I caught a brief, staggering glimpse: the thatched roof of Harl's barn at the bend of the road, engulfed in a curtain of fire; dark shapes darting before it, low to the ground, fast, their silhouettes all angles and ears and blades; a man I recognized, Old Harn himself, stumbling backward with an arrow jutting from his shoulder, eyes wide and uncomprehending.

Then something small and fast flashed past the door, so close I could have reached out and touched the matted hair on its arm. A goblin. Its skin was the color of old bruises, its eyes too large, catching the firelight with a sickly yellow gleam. It held a crooked knife in one hand and a burning brand in the other. Its mouth was open wide, teeth bared not in fear but in exultation.

Our eyes met for a heartbeat.

There was nothing mythical about it. No horns, no fangs down to its belly. Just a body, small and hard-used, wrapped in scraps of leather and bone. Just a child of the Dragon Below, come up to feed.

It screeched, a sound like tearing metal, and turned toward our house.

Dratmar slammed the door.

"Positions!" he barked.

Outside, Old King's Walk screamed, and burned, and broke. Inside, with the bar dropping back into place and the sword's weight solid in my hand, my childhood ended. The goblin raid had begun.

# Chapter 4

## Hold the Line

The first blow rattled the hinges.

"Jaime. Left of the door. Elric, right."

Dratmar's voice cut clean through the roar building in my ears. "Maximus—brace it."

The second blow came, low and mean, right at the part of the wood that had split last winter in the frost. We'd always meant to fix it. We'd joked about it, even. Dratmar swore the door had another season in it.

We found out who was right.

Maximus lunged forward, shoulders slamming into the crossbar, boots skidding on the packed-earth floor. The bar groaned against the leather hinges, but held, for the moment.

The house was all breath and shadows, lamplight turned smoky, the air thick with the bitter tang of fear-sweat and sheep tallow. We had dragged in the feed chest, the cedar trunk with Dratmar's old things, the low bench, everything heavy shoved against the door while smoke was still a suggestion above the thatch and the screaming outside hadn't grown teeth.

Now the screaming had teeth.

"Max, down," Jaime snapped.

Maximus ducked without arguing, big body folding like he'd been training under her his whole life and not just four years. A spearhead, no, not spear, iron scrap lashed to a stick, punched through the bottom panel between the hinges. It came in fast, furious, a snapped piece of plow blade bound in greasy leather. It tore a ragged, splintered mouth into our door.

A gray-green hand, bristling with wiry black hair, shot through the gap, fingers hooked like claws.

Jaime moved first. Her sword came down in a single clean stroke, more like she was cutting cloth than flesh. The wrist parted. The hand dropped, still flexing, to the dirt by Maximus's knee.

Thick, tar-dark blood spattered his cheek. He flinched, more in surprise than pain.

Mira whimpered by the hearth. Anya's hand covered her mouth before the sound fully formed. The little ones and Anya huddled in the corner where the chimney stones met the back wall, a nest of blankets and wide eyes. Thom's knuckles were white around the little wooden horse he always refused to put down. Vara trembled so hard her braids shook.

"Quiet," Anya whispered. "Like when we play hiding from Dratmar, remember? Whoever makes a sound first has to scrub the privy."

Vara clamped both hands over her own mouth. Tears streaked the ash on her cheeks.

"Eyes on the door," Dratmar said.

His ruined eye stared straight ahead, vacant and pale. The good one flicked like a hawk's, taking in the splintering wood, the shadows under the sill, the faintest flicker at the window where something moved outside.

Another blow. The bar jumped in its brackets. The wall heaved with it. Outside, shapes scuttled against the logs, fast and erratic. Nails or blades scraped along the beams where the roof met the wall.

"Roof," Ianteen hissed from the foot of the ladder.

She had planted herself there without being told, short staff in both hands, jaw folded tight as a trap. Smoke from the thatch gave the air above her a gray halo.

"Let them try," Dratmar said. "They come down half-cooked, you finish 'em."

Something heavy thudded on the roof. The thatch rustled, dry and betraying, like hands running through it. Then another thud, the creeping sound of weight testing old beams. They sounded like children in the loft, playing a game, running from rafter to rafter. The goblins laughed, high and harsh, the sound knifing down through the smoke.

"We should—" I started.

"No shoulds," Dratmar cut in. "Not now. Count."

"What?"

"You can still count, boy?"

Another blow against the door, then another, quick and excited, like fists when a joke gets good.

"One," I muttered.

"Out loud."

"One."

"Again."

The rind of fear around my ribs loosened, just enough. "Two."

"Tighter," he told Maximus. "Feel the force before it hits. You're not a post, you're a spring. Jaime—blade high. Don't stab unless you're sure. They're low and slippery. Use the edge. Elric, watch the gaps."

Outside, something shrieked, human, high and raw, then cut off too fast.

Thom's eyes found mine in the half-dark. He had Anya's worst blanket around his shoulders, the one with the frayed corner she always meant to mend. He pressed his lips together so hard they turned white. The wooden horse shook in his hand.

"Three," I said.

The next impact was heavier, more controlled. They'd brought something, log, beam, whatever they'd found, ramming in rhythm. The nails Dratmar had driven years ago into the jambs shrieked in protest.

"Four. Five—"

The world flashed orange through the cracks around the door as if someone had opened an oven. Heat pushed in with the light. The goblins howled, close, vicious, the sound crawling under my skin.

"Fire," Bobo said softly from the hearth.

We'd set him there with a pail of water and the hooked ladle, as if that would matter when the roof went. His eyes gleamed in the firelight, calm and far away, like a boy watching storm clouds roll in over the river.

"It's all right," Anya murmured to the little ones. "Our house is stout. Master Dratmar built it himself. Remember how he says he hates shoddy work?"

Vara nodded too hard. Mira buried her face against Anya's shoulder. Anya's arms tightened around them. She sounded almost convincing.

"Maximus," Dratmar said, "say it."

"S-say what?"

"What you're doing."

"Bracing the door," Maximus ground out through his teeth.

"Against what?"

"Against..." His breath came rough. "Against goblins. Against... against their ram."

"Against the world," Dratmar said. "Hold the line."

Another impact. The cracks around the lintel bloomed a brighter orange. Smoke, bitter and oily, wormed through, rolling along the ceiling.

"Jaime?"

"High line," she answered, voice as steady as his. "Left."

"Elric?"

"Right." My hands were slick on the sword hilt. I didn't remember drawing it. "Middle if they duck."

"Ianteen."

"Ladder, roof rats."

"Bobo."

"Fire," Bobo said again, but this time his hand was already dipping the ladle into the pail, instinctive, like a priest making a sign.

"Anya."

She hesitated. I heard it. She wasn't on a line; she was behind it. "Keep them quiet. Keep them safe."

"Good." Dratmar rolled his shoulders, loosened his neck. Sword in one hand, shield in the other, he moved like old leather re-oiled, creaking for only a breath before it turned supple. "They're testing. When they come, they'll come crawling and climbing and screaming. They want you scared. Don't hurry. Don't chase. Let them break themselves on you."

"Dratmar," I said, because saying his name anchored me, "what if they set the roof..."

The next blow turned the top of the door into a mouth.

The upper hinge tore free with a crack like snapping ice. The bar tilted, wood shrieking, one end still seated, the other jolting up with the sudden slack. Maximus staggered as the door twisted inward, one top corner bowing into the room.

Cold night air knifed in, smoke-sharp and hot at the same time. I had a flashing image of the street beyond, the well, the Mayor's big house looming like a smug rock, the thatch of the other cottages, and then that was all gone.

All I could see was an eye.

Yellow and too large for the face around it, with a pupil a thin black slit like a snake's or a cat's. It bulged through the crack between the warped planks, searching. The skin around it was stretched thin and gray-green, like nasty scraped meat.

It laughed. Not the goblin. The sound that came with it. It was as if the eye itself laughed, a liquid, pleased little sound.

My chest tightened, ribs locking around nothing. I had never, none of us had ever, seen a goblin this close. Sacks from hunting trips, sure. Dead ones from the patrols, laid out stiff and gray in the square when larger towns sent back message. But dead was different. Dead was small, pitiful, wrong-colored meat.

Alive was fast. Alive was watching.

The eye rolled, then fixed on me.

I moved without thinking. I drove the point of my sword through the crack, aiming for the center of that yellow.

The wood shifted as the creature jerked back. My blade hit something harder than flesh, bone, doorframe, I couldn't tell. The shock ran up my arm. The goblin shrieked, a sound like a piglet under the knife. Another shriek answered, and another.

Then they all came at once.

The door exploded inward in a spray of splinters and smoke. The bar ripped free of its bracket, one end smashing into Maximus's shoulder. He roared and staggered aside. For a heartbeat the doorway was all jagged wood and swirling black, nothing to hit, nowhere to stand.

Then they poured through.

They moved like rats but with the minds of men. Small, all elbows and jutting knees, hunched low to the ground. They slid under the half-hanging door, vaulted over it, sprang from it. Blades caught the lamplight, scraps of iron hammered into wicked edges, bone sharpened to points, hooks meant for meat.

The first one hit Dratmar's shield so hard its teeth snapped.

He took the impact with a tiny step back, but his boots never left the ground. His sword was already moving, sliding along the shield's rim. The goblin's neck found it. Its head did not so much fall as come loose, as if the spine had decided to take a different path than the skull.

Blood sprayed in a hot, surprising arc. The smell hit me: copper and filth, rank and thick. Not like the clean, sweet blood of a pig in slaughtering season. This was swamp-rot and iron, wrong and heavy.

I gagged.

"Feet!" Jaime shouted.

Another goblin dove low, trying to scuttle past Dratmar's legs. Jaime stepped in, cut down. Her blade caught it just where shoulder met neck. The creature screamed, high and furious, then went rag-doll limp. She shook it off her sword with a sharp twist, mouth set in a bloodless line.

She looked... empty. Focused in a way that didn't have room for fear. It scared me worse than the goblins.

A flicker of motion to my right. Another goblin, this one smaller, teeth bared, eyes wild, came straight for me, skittering sideways like a crab. Its knife caught the lamplight, a wavering line too close, too fast.

I froze as everything went muffled, like thick wool shoved into my ears. The goblin's mouth moved, shrieking, but the sound was distant. My heart lurched behind my ribs, tripping and stumbling as if it had forgotten how to pump. My training rose in my mind, all wrong. Dratmar's voice, weeks ago, in the yard, sun on my neck, birds gossiping in the hedges as if the world would always be gentle.

Drop your weight. Angle the blade. Don't stare at the steel. Stare at the shoulder. The steel follows. The goblin's shoulder rolled. Something in my spine unlocked. My feet moved, one sliding back, one planting. The world rushed back in, screams, smoke, steel on bone and at that moment, I cut.

The sword felt too light and too heavy all at once, an awkward extension of my arm that somehow landed exactly where it needed to. Edge to bone, halfway up the creature's collar. There was a moment, a sliver of eternity, when the resistance was almost gentle. Then it gave.

The goblin crashed into me, dead weight slamming my chest, breath coughing out of me in a startled, ugly sound. The knife it held skittered along the floor, carving a white line in the packed earth. We went down together.

Its skin was hot and clammy against my hands. Its breath, no, not breath anymore. Just the stink of it, sour and sharp. Its head lolled at a wrong angle, almost looking back over its own shoulder. The cut I'd made gaped, mouth-like, showing flashes of pink and white and glistening black that would haunt me for years.

I had to get it off. I shoved at the small, muscular chest, fingers slipping in the blood slicking its jerkin. For a heartbeat, the goblin's limp hand slid along my forearm, fingers closing by sheer dead weight.

I screamed then, a noise that didn't sound like me at all.

"Up!" Dratmar's voice snapped like a whip over my panic. "Elric, on your feet!"

A blade flashed where my head had been a moment before. I rolled, my shoulder grinding in the dirt, something hard digging into my back. Pain flared under my ribs. Another goblin had come in under the dead one, using its comrade's body as cover. It grinned at me. Goblins shouldn't grin. Their mouths are too wide, teeth too many and too small, like broken shells washing up on the riverbank. Its eyes were huge and delighted, as if this were a game and I'd played my part well. It lunged, arm whipping forward.

There was no time to get my sword up. Instead of cut, there was a dull crack, a sound like someone hitting meat with a floured rolling pin. The goblin's head jerked sideways, jaw snapping shut with a click. It slumped, then toppled away from me.

Ianteen stood over it, both hands on her staff, knuckles white. The end of the staff was wet and dark. Her breath came in quick, shallow pulls.

"Off your backside," she snapped. Her voice shook only a little. "You're blocking my way."

I scrambled to my feet, snatching my sword up from where it had fallen. "Thanks."

"Don't mention it," she muttered. "Ever."

Another goblin scrambled for the ladder, heedless of us as it clawed for the roof. Its back was to her. She swung again, hard and precise. The staff cracked into its spine. It gave a choked yelp and dropped, half-twisting in the air to land on its shoulder with a crunch.

She jabbed the end of the staff into its throat before it could pull itself up. I had thought, once, that Ianteen's weapon looked like a toy next to our swords. Now, with her small frame braced, her arms taut, the staff an extension of her entire body, I saw how wrong I'd been.

"Roof!" she shouted again. "They're up there, I can hear..."

The ceiling above us bloomed orange. Fire licked between the thatch bundles, greedy tongues tasting dry straw. Smoke turned from gray suggestion to thick, black river, rolling down from the rafters. The heat hit in waves, heavy as wet wool. Sweat popped along my brow, stung my eyes, mixed with the sting of woodsmoke until tears blurred everything.

"Bobo," Dratmar called without looking back, "mind the sparks."

"Yes, Master," Bobo whispered.

His small hand moved in smooth, careful arcs, slopping water along the driest edges of the hearth, dousing the embers that jumped free. His eyes barely left the fire above, following it, measuring it, as if he could hold it with his gaze alone.

By the door, Jaime moved like the blade she held. She slid in and out of the line, not wasting a step, cutting where she could, withdrawing where she couldn't. Her hair was plastered to her forehead, cheeks streaked with soot and blood she hadn't noticed. There was no triumph in her face when a goblin fell. No fear either. Just a cold, clear intent that made my throat tighten.

Maximus had taken Dratmar's place at the door's edge, his big body in the space where goblins crowded. He wasn't quick like Jaime, but he was relentless. Every swing of his sword was a promise. Every time metal met bone or leather or wood, you could hear exactly what he was saying, even if there were no words in it:

*You are not getting past me.*

He bellowed as he fought, raw and wordless. The sound was part battle cry, part plea. His eyes darted past the goblins, again and again, to where Anya crouched with the little ones.

Her face was turned away from the door, wholly for them. Mira's arms were locked around her neck. Thom had wedged himself under her other shoulder, the wooden horse forgotten on the floor. Vara sat practically in Anya's lap, head buried against her chest, small shoulders shaking. Anya's hands stroked Vara's braids with slow, steady motions that had nothing to do with the speed of her heartbeat. She hummed under her breath, some nonsense lullaby she made up on the spot, tuneless but soft.

"Can they see us?" Vara whispered into her dress.

"No," Anya breathed. "They're busy with Dratmar and the big idiots." She forced a tiny, choked laugh. "They'd rather break their teeth on them first."

The goblin Maximus had been facing dodged under his swing, quick as thought. It darted sideways, reaching with its free hand, fingers stretching for Thom's ankle.

Thom froze. His mouth opened, but no sound came out.

Anya suddenly and quickly moved. Her hand shot down, slapping Thom's leg aside. She kicked out, heel catching the goblin's hand with a crack. It hissed, jerking back, just as Maximus's return swing kissed its neck. The head went one way, the body another.

Blood sprayed over the hearthstones. Some of it caught Anya's cheek, a red line across pale skin.

"Eyes on me," she told Thom quietly. "Not on them. On me."

He nodded, but his gaze slid, unsteady, back to the door anyway.

"Elric!" Dratmar barked.

A goblin was on the table, scrambling for the far side to get behind Maximus. It had climbed in through the shattered window above the bench, glass glittering in its hair like ice. Its blade was longer than the others, a broken sword, maybe, scavenged from some caravan.

I didn't think. I didn't plan. I ran.

The table's edge caught my thigh as I charged, sending a bolt of pain up my leg. My sword swung up, clumsy and too wide. The goblin laughed, rolling under the arc. It slashed up at my side as it came, its knife catching the edge of my tunic. Cloth parted with a ripping sound. Skin burned a heartbeat later.

I stumbled, heat blooming along my ribs.

The goblin coiled to spring, knife coming for my belly where the leather was thinner. Its eyes flicked, just for a second, to the spot on my side where the blood welled. Like it wanted to see what it had done.

Dratmar had told us, over and over, that every fighter gives you a gift.

A tell. A habit. A moment when they want to admire themselves.

I took it.

I dropped my weight, like he taught. The sword in my hand suddenly felt heavier, anchored. I didn't slash this time. I didn't swing. I pushed. The point went in low, under the goblin's ribs, the way Dratmar demonstrated on sacks of grain. This was no sack. It was hot and struggling and screaming, breath in my face, spit and bile flecking my cheeks. Its hands scrabbled at the blade, too late. I felt everything.

The give of skin. The catch at cartilage. The moment of terrible softness when the tip slid into something vital. The way its body bowed around the steel as if trying to reject what I had done, to spit it back out. I wanted to let go. To drop the sword, to be anywhere but there, with this creature's life pouring down my hands. The wrongness of it screamed through me.

Yet still, out of sheer instinct and primal fear, I kept pushing.

Dratmar had said, the first time he put a real blade in our hands, that there's no such thing as a gentle kill. Only a clean one. I don't know if that one was clean. I know it ended. The goblin shuddered, then sagged against me. Its breath stuttered once, twice. Then nothing. Only weight. I wrenched the blade free. It came with a wet, sliding sound. The goblin slumped off the table, hitting the floor with a thump and a jingle of bone ornaments.

The room seemed to tilt.

"Elric." Dratmar's voice again, quieter now but no less anchoring. "Leave it. Eyes up."

I left it.

The doorway was a churn of bodies, smoke, and steel. Dratmar in the middle, Maximus to his right, Jaime to his left. Goblins clawing and shrieking and dying in front of them. The fire on the roof ate through another beam with a crack. Flaming thatch tumbled in clumps, bursting on the packed-earth floor. Sparks flew like angry bees.

Bobo darted, pail in hand, sloshing water where he could, stamping others with bare feet. His face had gone distant, somewhere deep. Not magic, not exactly, just a boy and his element. He understood fire the way Anya understood tears. It listened to him, a little.

"Too many," Jaime grunted, parrying a blow that would have taken Maximus in the neck. Her arm shook. She swallowed it down.

"Then kill faster," Dratmar said.

The goblin he'd just smashed skidded limp into my boots. I stepped over it, taking my place at his side without thinking. My back was to the hearth now. Heat kissed the nape of my neck, the fur there feeling singed. Smoke scratched at my throat, thick and bitter. We made a jagged half-circle inside the doorway. Dratmar at the peak, Maximus and Jaime flanking, I just behind Dratmar's right shoulder, close enough to smell the old leather and sweat of his coat. Ianteen darted in the gaps, staff cracking knees, wrists, skulls that slipped through.

"Hold the line," Dratmar murmured, low enough that the goblins couldn't hear. "They come, they break. We don't."

"Easy for you to say," Ianteen panted.

"We've got this," Maximus gasped. "We've got this, we've..."

The wall behind us cracked.

Not from fire. From force.

The logs shuddered under an impact from the rear. Dry clay dust rained down on Anya's bowed head. Thom flinched. Mira squeaked, a small, animal sound.

"They're at the back," Jaime snapped. "How..."

"The alley," I said, throat dry. The narrow run between our house and the old grain shed, where the pallets leaned, never mended properly because no one ever thought anyone would come crawling through muck for us. "They can climb the stones."

Another blow. The back wall yawned, a plank giving way where rot had eaten at it under the eaves. A gap the size of a boy's head opened. In it, smoke and night and yellow eyes. Dratmar's jaw clenched. He didn't look back.

"They'll get in," I said.

"Aye."

"What do we do?"

The wall groaned again. More wood cracked, then snapped. The gap widened. A long, sinewy gray arm wormed through, fingers groping.

"Jaime," Dratmar said calmly, as if asking her to pass the salt. "Take Elric. Guard the breach."

She didn't argue. She didn't say she was better at the door. She just moved.

"Elric."

"Right." My legs felt like rotten twine, but they carried me. I skidded on blood, caught my balance on the table's edge, then surged for the back of the house.

The gap in the wall was now large enough for a goblin's shoulders. A long nose pushed through, sniffing. Then teeth. It smiled, an awful stretch of lips.

We hit it together.

Jaime's blade flashed down, chopping at the wrist as the goblin tried to brace itself. I shoved with my shoulder, slamming the plank inward. The goblin, halfway through, shrieked as the wood bit into its ribs, pinning it for a heartbeat.

"Now," Jaime grunted.

We both drove our swords in, a messy, two-handed shove. The blades punched through skin and muscle, sliding between ribs. Hot blood sprayed the inside of the wall, streaking the clay. The goblin sagged, more pressure on the planks. They creaked ominously.

"Again," Jaime said, breathless.

We yanked our swords free. Wood caved with a splintering crack. The goblin's dead weight tore more of the wall away as it collapsed inward, dumping a tangle of limbs and a rain of cold night air into the room.

Beyond the new gap, I saw the alley: a narrow strip of churned mud and old straw. More shapes lurked there, hunched and eager.

"Back," Jaime ordered. "We make a choke."

We fell into another half-circle, small, tight. Jaime in front, me at her right hip, the broken wall just at our shoulders. We didn't have Dratmar's steadiness, his terrifying surety. But we had been taught how to stand where he told us, how to fill gaps.

The first goblin shouldered through the opening, ducking low. Jaime's sword took it in the eye. It never got to scream. She yanked the blade free, already turning.

"Count," she said between panting breaths.

"What?"

"Like he told you. One."

"One," I echoed.

The next goblin darted in to the left. I stepped in, swords crossing, catching its knife on mine while Jaime swept in from above, her edge kissing its ear. The top half of its head went with it.

"Two," she said.

"Two."

My voice steadied.

We killed three, four, five. At six, I lost count because one of them made it past us, a small, fast shape that slipped through our blades and darted for the hearth.

"Vara!" Mira shrieked.

The goblin's hand fastened in Vara's hair. She screamed, high and shattering. Anya moved faster than thought. She surged to her feet, dragging Vara with her, twisting out of the goblin's grip. Half of Vara's braid tore free in the creature's fingers. It stared at the tangled hair, offended, then lunged again.

Anya put herself between it and the little ones.

She didn't have a sword. She had a kitchen knife, long and narrow, the one she used to cut bread and apples and Maximus's stitching when he wouldn't sit still. Her hands shook as she brought it up, but she brought it up.

The goblin laughed and came at her, and yet she stabbed without a hint of intimidation.

Not like Dratmar. Not like Jaime. There was no training in it, no angled weight or measured breath. It was sheer, frantic will. The blade went into the goblin's neck, just under the jaw. She shoved it in to the hilt. Its laughter cut off in a strangled gargle. Black blood spat over her hand, the knife, Vara's dress, Thom's wooden horse. Anya tried to yank the knife out yet it stuck fast.

Another goblin, larger, clambered half through the broken wall by the hearth, where the clay had crumbled with that last impact. Its eyes fixed on Anya, blood-slick and off-balance.

"Anya!" Maximus roared from the front. I heard the panic rip the word from him, torn from somewhere deep.

He shoved backward, throwing his shoulder into a goblin, knocking it into Dratmar. The older man snarled something wordless as his shield skewed, opening a gap. Blades darted for it.

"I've got her," I shouted, lunging.

Jaime's hand clamped on my collar, jerking me back. "Line!" she snapped. "You break, we all die."

I hated her for a heartbeat. Utterly. My vision went red with it.

She was right.

The big goblin shoved into the room. It moved differently than the others, with a predatory confidence. Its knives were longer, curved, catching the firelight in wicked hooks. A leather harness across its chest jingled with teeth and small bones. Its gaze flicked between Anya and the smaller children, weighing. Choosing.

It chose wrong, as far as Maximus was concerned.

"Come on, then," Anya whispered, voice shaking. "Come on, look at me, don't look at them, just me…"

The goblin lunged.

Raw sound tore my throat. I couldn't even shape her name.

Something inside Maximus broke. He roared, a sound more animal than man, and threw his entire weight sideways, slamming his back against Dratmar's shoulder. The sudden shift sent both of them skidding, their line bowing inward. Goblins poured at the gap like water finding a crack in a dam.

"Maximus!" Dratmar bellowed, furious. "Hold…"

Maximus was already running. He left a wake of goblins behind him, some slashed, some merely knocked aside by the sheer force of his passage. His sword whistled in one hand. With the other, he flung a stool, hitting a goblin that had almost reached Anya from behind.

"Anya!" he shouted. "Get down!"

She did, ducking under the big goblin's sweeping blade, dragging Vara and Thom with her. The curved knife skimmed her hair, slicing off a lock. Maximus's sword crashed into the goblin's shoulder a heartbeat later, the edge biting deep. The creature screamed, stumbling. It recovered faster than I liked, jamming its knee into Maximus's thigh. He grunted, staggered. Another goblin, small and clever, slipped past his swinging sword and went for Anya's flank.

She yanked Thom and Vara behind her, shoving them into the space between the cupboard and the wall. "Stay," she cried. "Don't move, stay…"

Too late. The little goblin twisted his way in after them, fingers like hooks. Thom fought, kicked, bit. Vara screamed and clung to his shirt. The goblin's hand closed on Vara's ankle.

"Dratmar!" I screamed. "The back…"

The roof answered for him. A beam, burnt through at one end, surrendered all at once. It cracked with a sound like the world breaking. Flaming thatch dropped in a curtain. Smoke whooshed in a fresh, choking wave as the air above the hearth turned to fire.

For a moment, I couldn't see. Heat slammed into my face, scorching my eyebrows. Sparks peppered my exposed skin. Bobo screamed, not in fear but anger, as his carefully contained fire betrayed him.

"Get them out!" Dratmar roared. "Move the little ones! Now!"

Suddenly there was no line. There was no front or back. There was just chaos. The house became a spinning wheel of needs and threats. Goblins pouring from the broken wall. Fire from above. Smoke from all sides. Little bodies that needed lifting. Anya in the middle of it, blood on her hands, hair in her eyes. Jaime yanked at my sleeve. "We drag them to the door," she shouted into my ear. "We make the fight out there. The house is killing us faster than they are."

"Vara..." I choked.

Anya had one arm locked around Vara's middle, the little girl's legs kicking uselessly as the goblin clamped onto her ankle and hauled with gleeful cruelty. Another had Thom by the back of his shirt, dragging him toward the widening gap by the hearth where clay and wood had finally surrendered under goblin hands and falling fire. Thom's fingers raked trenches into the dirt floor, dirt that was already turning to ash. His wooden horse lay a few feet away, tipped on its side, smoldering where a coal had kissed it and decided to stay.

"Maximus!" Anya sobbed. "Max..."

As though summoned, he was there. He drove his sword clean through the goblin's back, the point punching out through its ribs. The creature shrieked and went rigid, lifted off the ground by the force of the thrust as Maximus slammed it into the wall like he was pinning a board. Its feet bicycled in the air, flailing at nothing. Maximus didn't waste a breath. He dropped his grip, seized Thom under the arms, and yanked him free so hard the boy's boots skidded. Thom sucked in a ragged breath that sounded like he'd been underwater too long.

"I've got you," Maximus panted, voice shredded. "I've got you, I've..."

Something hit him from behind. A roof goblin dropped out of the smoke like a burning spider, landing square across Maximus's shoulders. Clawed fingers hooked into his collar and hair. Its weight drove him forward. He crashed onto hands and knees, and Thom tumbled out of his grasp, rolling in the dirt, coughing.

Anya gave a raw, broken cry and lunged instinctively, but the goblin on Vara's ankle yanked hard, heels digging into the floor as it tried to pull the child through the breach. Vara slid a hand's breadth, screaming, fingernails carving furrows that filled instantly with ash and soot.

"Jaime, Elric!" Dratmar roared. "Door..."

"I know!" Jaime snapped back, and the fact that she had breath to snap at all felt like a miracle.

Then she shoved me toward the hearth instead, hard enough that I stumbled.

"Get them!" she barked. "We'll hold the bloody door."

For a heartbeat our eyes met. Her pupils were blown wide, almost swallowing the blue. Sweat and soot made streaks down her cheeks like someone had tried to draw lines and given up. She looked terrified, not the controlled kind that still breathes steady, the real kind that lives in the throat and the wrists. She moved anyway, turned, and was swallowed back into the crush at the front, disappearing behind Dratmar's solid form as the doorway howled with bodies and steel.

I lurched toward the hearth with my lungs already on fire. Every breath tore like sandpaper. Heat crawled across my skin like hands, reaching for my hair, sucking the moisture from my mouth until my tongue felt too big.

Bobo jumped into my path, flinging the last of the pail's water at a clump of falling thatch. It hissed and boiled up steam, buying us a few heartbeats and nothing more.

"Go," he coughed, eyes streaming. "I'll... I'll keep it from eating the floor."

"Don't you burn," I rasped.

He bared his teeth in something that might have been a grin if the smoke hadn't been choking him. "I won't. Fire likes me."

Vara slid again, another awful hand's breadth. Anya's grip slipped on the child's calf, slick now with sweat and soot and panic. On the far side of the broken wall a goblin cackled, bracing its feet in the alley mud and hauling like a fisherman with a strong line.

"I've got you," Anya choked, voice cracking. "Vara, hold, hold onto me..."

Vara obeyed with the desperation of a drowning girl. Her hands locked in Anya's dress like claws. Then another goblin arm shot through the gap and snapped around Anya's wrist, without waiting for anything it yanked. Her shoulder wrenched with a sound I felt in my own bones. Anya screamed, a sharp, white sound that cut through everything else. Her body buckled, but she did not let go of Vara.

I charged, swinging my sword at the reaching arms, hacking without finesse because there was no time for finesse. Steel bit flesh. A goblin howled and jerked back, leaving part of itself behind on my blade. Another hand replaced it immediately, then another. There were always more hands, more fingers, more hunger.

Thom, dazed and coughing, tried to crawl back toward Anya. Maximus, still pinned under the roof goblin, strained with muscles cording in his neck as he fought to push up.

"Move!" I shouted at him, voice breaking on the word. "Max, get up, you have to get up, they're..."

"I know!" he roared back.

He had no sword in his hands now. He grabbed the goblin's arm, rolled, and slammed it into the edge of the table. Bone cracked like dry kindling. The creature shrieked and loosened. Maximus flung it off and staggered upright, limping, one knee refusing him for half a step.

He looked at Anya.

Everything else vanished from his face. The fight, the fire, the goblins at the door, the screams from outside, all of it fell away until there was only her and the child being dragged out of her arms.

He moved.

He had never run so fast in his life, not even the day Dratmar chased us out of the orchard with a switch for stealing apples. He barreled past me and shouldered me aside as if I were smoke. I almost went down, catching myself on the hearthstone, fingers blistering as my palm slapped the hot rock.

"Max..." Anya gasped, and her voice held his name like a prayer and a warning at once.

He reached her and Vara in the same breath the wall gave way completely.

The goblins had overreached. The clay, baked and cracked, finally surrendered. The half-burned logs behind it splintered. Suddenly there was nothing between the inside of our home and the alley but smoke and the cold bite of night air.

Hands poured through. They weren't careful anymore. They didn't have to be. They grabbed whatever they could find, cloth, hair, limbs, anything that could be dragged away. Maximus seized Anya around the waist with both arms and pulled as Goblins seized her too. For a moment she was just a scrap of cloth in a tug-of-war, her feet sliding, her eyes blown wide with white showing all around the blue. Her mouth opened around a sound that would not end.

"Max!" she screamed. "Maximus!"

"Let go," he sobbed, voice splintering. "Let go, Anya, let..."

"Not you!" she cried, frantic and furious. "Them. Let..."

A goblin swung the butt of a hooked spear into Maximus's temple. His head snapped to the side. His arms spasmed. He did not fall, not fully, but something in him buckled for a heartbeat. He lost strength. Just enough. Anya slid in his grasp, their hands locking as if instinct could hold the world together. Fingers twined desperately, nails digging into skin. For one heartbeat everything narrowed to that single point, their joined fists, the last clean thing in a room of smoke.

Her face, streaked with blood and ash, turned toward him. There was terror in it, yes, but there was also fury, and something older than either of them had any right to carry.

"Don't you come after me," she gasped.

"You know I will," he choked, and the promise sounded like a curse.

"Idiot." Her fingers slipped another fraction. "Don't let them take Vara..."

A goblin clawed up Anya's back and latched into her hair. It yanked. Her head snapped back with a cry. Another wrapped its arms around her waist from behind, planted its heels in the mud, and hauled.

Maximus roared and pulled until the veins stood out in his neck, until his shoulders shook.

For a heartbeat, he won. The goblins slid in the muck, boots scrabbling, bodies tipping. Anya jerked forward, a hand's breadth closer to the room, to him, to us, to the world she belonged in. Then more joined the tug. Hands on hands, bodies on bodies, lean muscle and vicious intent stacking into a chain. The weight on the other side doubled, then tripled. The pull became a certainty.

Maximus's feet slipped.

Dratmar appeared beside him like iron given a body, one massive hand planting on Maximus's back, adding his weight to the pull as if he could anchor the boy by force alone. His sword arced and severed a reaching goblin arm, blood snapping through the smoke. It was not enough.

"Jaime!" Dratmar shouted. "Get the little ones out! Elric, Maximus, let her go."

Neither of us moved. My hands were white around my hilt, useless, because the thing I wanted to cut was the whole moment and you can't cut a moment.

"I said..."

"Don't you dare," Maximus snarled through gritted teeth. Blood ran down the side of his face, black in the firelight. "Don't you make me..."

"Max." Anya's voice dropped, somehow, through the screaming, through the fire. She locked her eyes on his and the world narrowed again, as far as it could narrow. Even the chaos seemed to dim for a second. "You have to."

He shook his head once, a broken, helpless motion.

"They'll kill you," she panted. "They'll kill Vara. You have to…"

He made a sound low in his throat, animal and useless against physics and numbers.

"Maximus," Dratmar said quietly, over his shoulder, and it was the only time all night his voice sounded almost gentle. "Son. Let go."

Maximus made a sound like something tearing. It might have been his heart. His fingers opened. Anya's hand tore free from his. She slid back into the smoke and the press of gray bodies. Vara shrieked, "No!" as an arm wrapped around her middle and yanked her away. Thom lunged and caught Vara's wrist for a heartbeat, then a goblin seized his hair and ripped him backward, his cry turning sharp with pain.

"Anya!" Maximus screamed, and the sound lodged itself in my skull like a nail.

She reached for us, for him, for the house, for any anchor at all.

"Max!" she cried. "Don't…"

The goblins surged, hauling. Her arm vanished into the press. Her face disappeared behind smoke, behind bodies, behind crude blades that caught firelight in jagged flashes. The last glimpse of her was not her face or her hair or her hands. It was the edge of the kitchen knife still buried in the neck of the first goblin she'd killed. It tore free as they dragged her, clattered onto the hearthstone, and spun once. Blood flicked across the floor. The knife came to rest point-down in a crack in the clay like it had chosen a grave.

Maximus stared at it as if it had betrayed him. Then something in him went quiet. Not calm. Not peace. Just silence, the kind you get after something inside you breaks and stops making sound. The world around us did not quiet. Goblins screamed and whooped, triumphant, dragging their prizes back into the alley and the smoke. Vara's wails faded into the night. Other cries rose from outside, from other homes, other stolen children, a chorus of grief that made the village feel suddenly too small for the sky above it.

I could not move. My legs had turned to stone. My lungs were empty bellows. All I could see was the space where Anya had been, the shape of her absence burning brighter than the fire.

"Elric!"

Jaime's hand cracked across my cheek.

My head snapped to the side. Pain bloomed hot and electric. For a heartbeat I saw nothing but white, then smoke again, and her face inches from mine, wild and furious and terrified.

"Move!" she shrieked. "We're burning. Get Thom!"

Her calm was gone now, shattered. What she held together was held together by habit and sheer refusal. Behind her the front of the house had become a wall of fire and smoke. The door was gone, swallowed by heat and bodies. Goblins were already scattering back into the street, shadows against the flames. Some limped. Some crawled. Others leaped away laughing, flinging torches onto neighboring roofs like children flinging stones.

Dratmar stood in the doorway's ruin, shoulders heaving, sword dripping. His coat smoked. His hair was singed. He looked like something carved from burn-scarred oak.

"Out!" he roared. "Everyone out!"

Jaime grabbed the torn scrap of Vara's braid with one hand and Thom's arm with the other and hauled him bodily away from the crumbling wall. He screamed Anya's name until his voice cracked, but his feet moved because Jaime made them move.

Bobo shoved at me with both hands. "Elric, Elric, you have to get Mira," he coughed, eyes streaming. "I've got the fire here. Go."

Mira was frozen against the chimney, small fingers dug into cracks in the stone. Her lips moved in silent prayer, one Anya had taught her. A god of hearths and safe homes, a god that was either deaf tonight or dead. I staggered toward her, lungs sawing. The smoke tasted of burning wool and meat and a sharp, sick tang I refused to name.

"Mira," I rasped. "We have to go."

She shook her head hard, eyes squeezed shut. "Can't. Can't. If I move, they'll see me."

"They already saw us," I said, because lying was suddenly beyond me. My voice broke anyway. "She's... she's gone, Mira. We have to go or we burn too."

Her eyes snapped open. Understanding flashed in them, horrible and clear. Children learn quickly when the world makes it necessary. I scooped her up. She was lighter than she should have been. Too many dinners stretched thin. Anya had fretted about it all summer. I clutched Mira to my chest now and felt the hard flutter of her heart against my own. The roof groaned. Timbers shifted. A beam crashed down where she'd been standing, throwing a geyser of sparks and flaming thatch into the room. Bobo ducked and threw his empty pail over his head like a shield.

"Go!" Dratmar bellowed again, voice hoarse. "Out the back. The front's a slaughter-house. Jaime, lead them. Maximus, move!"

Maximus stood where Anya had been torn away, staring into empty air as if he could fill it by will. Smoke blurred him. Ash dusted his hair. Dratmar crossed the room in two strides, grabbed him by the collar, and shook once, hard enough that Maximus's teeth clicked.

"Son. Out."

Maximus's eyes found his. For a heartbeat there was nothing there, no focus, no light, just shocked emptiness. Then something sparked. Not at Dratmar. Not at us.

At the world.

He nodded once, jerkily, and turned. We spilled out through the broken back wall into the alley, coughing, half-blind. Smoke and shadow tangled there too. Bodies slumped against the grain shed. The air reeked of spilled offal and scorched wood. Goblins skittered along fence tops and rooflines, some fleeing, some still hunting for stragglers like wolves who had tasted blood and wanted more.

The village that had been Old King's Walk when the sun rose was gone.

What remained was a ring of fires, some big, some small, houses burning like torches as thatch roared and collapsed inward. The Mayor's house on the hill smoldered at the edges, stone walls refusing to catch as if pride could stop flame. The well in the square glowed faintly with embers fallen in, steam rising like ghost-breath. Screams still rose from some houses. From others there was only silence, heavy and unnatural.

We stumbled toward the square because there was nowhere else to go.

The air felt colder out here despite the fires, the shock of night against burned skin. The cold had teeth. It found every raw patch on my arms, every place my shirt had torn, and it bit with the same steady patience the goblins had shown. Above us the stars looked wrong, too still, too indifferent, like someone had nailed them to the sky and forgotten they were supposed to flicker. Smoke smeared them into pale scars, white streaks across black, like the heavens had been scraped by claw marks.

People stumbled out of alleys and doorways in staggered waves, as if the village itself was vomiting up survivors. Some were bleeding. Some were blackened. Some dragged others by wrists and collars, pulling bodies that did not always help. A woman I knew only as Marta lurched past with half her hair burned off, clutching a bundle tight to her chest. For a terrible moment my mind insisted it was a child, charred and limp.

Then she shifted, and cloth unfurled in the firelight. Linens; her best ones, white once, now gray with soot and spattered with mud. She tripped and dropped them, the whole precious stack sliding into the muck. She stared at them as if she'd forgotten what they were, as if the idea of "best" had stopped making sense. Then she left them where they fell and walked on with her hands empty.

"Here," Dratmar rasped, and his grip on my shoulder was the first solid thing I'd felt in minutes. He hauled us into the lee of the well. The stone was rough and cool against my back, so cold it felt like a kindness. Mira clung to my neck still, her breath sobbing hot into my ear, little hitches that made her whole body tremble.

Jaime sank down beside me with her head in her bloody hands. Her shoulders shook once, convulsively, then stilled. She drew in a long, shuddery breath and forced herself upright again, spine straightening like she'd tied it to an invisible post and dared the world to cut the string.

"We... we all here?" I croaked. My throat felt skinned. My tongue was too thick in my mouth.

"Vara?" Jaime asked, voice raw, eyes darting as if the dark might still steal someone while she looked away.

"Here," Vara whispered from somewhere near Jaime's knees. Soot streaked her cheeks. Her eyes were enormous, pupils swallowing nearly all the green. She held the torn half of her braid in both hands, gripping it like a rope she could climb out of this night with.

"Thom?" I said.

He didn't answer. He couldn't. His voice was gone. He huddled against the well, staring at nothing, hands clenched on air as if he was still gripping someone's wrist, as if his fingers had not gotten the message that they were empty. His wooden horse had not made it out.

"Bobo?" Jaime tried again.

"Present," Bobo coughed. His face was black with soot except for two pale tracks where tears had carved channels. His hair smoked faintly, a thin ghost of steam rising whenever a breeze caught it. He smelled of boiled leather and singe. "Master, the house is…"

"I know," Dratmar said, and he didn't need to look because his voice already carried the weight of seeing.

We turned anyway. In spite of ourselves, we turned.

Our house was an orange beast at the end of the lane, roaring and spitting sparks. The roof had gone entirely now. Flames clawed at the night sky where our loft used to be, where we'd played cards and whispered secrets and complained about chores and pretended tomorrow was guaranteed. The front wall bowed inward, then collapsed in a fountain of sparks that arced up and drifted down like vicious snow.

Everything we owned turned to ash in that moment, but that wasn't the part that hurt. Maximus stood swaying, watching it burn.

"Anya," he said. The name came out like he'd swallowed glass. "She's…"

"Gone," Dratmar said.

Maximus turned on him. His fist bunched in Dratmar's burned coat and hauled him forward, dragging the older man nearly to his knees. Maximus's face was streaked with soot and blood, his eyes fever-bright, too bright, as if the fire had moved into him and decided to live there.

"We go after her," he snarled. Spittle flew from his lips. "Now. We go now."

"Max," Jaime said softly, and she sounded like she was trying to hold a collapsing roof up with her voice.

"No." He didn't even glance at her. "No, you don't get to soft-voice me now. We go after her. She's still screaming. You heard her. You heard…"

His voice shattered. The sound that came out of him then was not words. It was something broken trying to become a weapon.

Dratmar didn't hit him. He could have. Maximus's grip, for all its fury, was clumsy. The old soldier could have put him on his back in a heartbeat and made him stay there. He let the boy shake him. When Maximus's arms finally failed, when the rage burned down to ash and left only shudders and shaking breath, Dratmar set his big scarred hands on Maximus's shoulders and held him upright like a man holds a post that's about to fall.

"We will," he said.

"You're lying," Maximus spat, though even the spit was half blood. "You always say wait, and watch, and count. You'll make plans and make me sit while they, while they…"

"We. Will." Dratmar's good eye bored into his. "We're not a company on campaign. We're not a garrison. We're a handful of children and one half-burnt old fool. We run into the dark now, we join them on spits or chains before dawn. We wait an hour, we watch where they go. We count who's missing. Then we hunt. You hear me?"

"An hour," Maximus whispered, and the words sounded poisonous in his mouth.

"Less, if we can. I swear it. On my good eye, if that means anything to you."

Maximus stared at him, chest heaving, and for a moment I thought he might hit him anyway just to make the pain go somewhere else.

"Swear it on her," he whispered. "On Anya."

Dratmar's jaw worked. I watched him swallow whatever it cost.

"I swear," he said finally. "On Anya. We don't leave her in their hands if I can put my blade in the bastard that took her."

Maximus let go. His hands fell to his sides as if cut away.

"You can't…" someone nearby said weakly. "You can't go after them. They're goblins. They'll be halfway to the… to the… mountains by morning…"

It was the Mayor, of all people. He sat slumped against the far side of the well, his fine shirt blackened at the sleeves, his velvet vest smudged, his hair hanging lank around his face where it used to be oiled and curled. A shallow cut marked his cheek, already swelling. His eyes skittered everywhere but at us, like he thought looking straight at our grief would make it contagious.

"You," Ianteen hissed.

She would have gone for him then, I think, if she'd had any strength left. As it was, she just glared, thin shoulders trembling, hands curled into fists she didn't use.

"You said they wouldn't come," she spat. "You said it was stories."

"They never come this far north," he protested, voice pinched and brittle. "Not in years. My father…"

"Your father is dead," Dratmar cut in, flat as a blade laid on a table. "And his father before him. Goblins don't care whose son you are."

The Mayor's mouth opened and closed. No sound came out. For once, his talent for speeches deserted him. Around us the square slowly filled. Survivors gathered in sluggish knots, drawn to the well as if by old habit, as if water and stone were the last rules the world still followed. Mothers counted children with shaking fingers. Fathers stared at ruined homes as if they were trying to remember what the walls had looked like before they became fire. Old men from the far cottages leaned on sticks, faces gray, eyes too tired to widen anymore.

Names began, quiet at first. They wound through the square like smoke.

"Have you seen Lina?"

"Where's Joros? He was just…"

"Bram? Bram!"

"Anya," Maximus whispered, over and over, a prayer with no god to answer. "Anya. Anya…"

Dratmar's mouth was a hard line. He rose slowly, surveying the wreckage, the people, the glowing arcs of fire around us with the grim calm of a man reading a battlefield.

"Elric," he said.

I jerked as if he'd struck me, my ears flicked up high to listen better, the left one knicked in the fight stung as the cut hit the cold air. "Yes."

"Jaime. Ianteen. Bobo." He waited until each of us dragged our gaze up to him. "Go. Listen. Count. I want the names of every child not standing in this square by sunrise. You understand me?"

Jaime blinked like he'd slapped her. "Master, Anya…"

"Is one name," he said sharply. "There will be more. We go blundering after only her, we trip over the bones of the others. We bring them all back, or none. Move."

There was iron in him that would not bend. We'd trained against it, bruised our knuckles on it, cursed it under our breath when he made us do the same drill again and again. It held now when everything else had burned. We obeyed. We scattered into smoke and alleys and half-collapsed doorways, moving through clusters of stunned villagers, asking questions with voices that barely worked. We gathered names like you gather splinters from a wound, each one small, each one sharp.

Marta's youngest son, gone from his bed with the window smashed.

Old Greer's twin granddaughters, missing from the loft where they'd hidden.

The baker's boy, last seen throwing stones at goblins from his doorway before the roof came down.

Teo, who used to sneak apples to Maximus to bring to Anya when she'd skip meals tending us, insisting she wasn't hungry when her stomach growled loud enough for everyone to hear.

On and on.

Anya's name threaded through all the others like a blade through beads. Every time someone said it, my chest tightened. Every time I said it, it felt like I was doing violence with my own tongue.

By the time the first pale gray seeped into the sky above the eastern ridge, my throat was raw from smoke and questions. My hands shook too much to hold a cup of water steady. My legs felt like they'd been swapped for someone else's, old and stiff and uncooperative, like they were offended I still expected them to carry me. We reconvened by the well. Jaime had ten names. Ianteen had four. Bobo had three, his quiet voice even more distant than usual as he recited them. I had five. Nineteen children in a village that had held maybe seventy. Maximus listened with his jaw clenched so hard I could see the muscles jump. He flinched each time another name joined the list, as if each one were a blow. When I said, "Anya," he closed his eyes. His lips moved, but no sound came. As if saying her name again would shatter him.

"Write them," Dratmar said.

"With what?" Jaime demanded, ragged. "On what? The houses are..."

Dratmar walked to the nearest intact wall, what was left of the smithy's underpinning, soot-streaked but standing. He picked up a charred beam from the ground, its end still smoking faintly, and pressed it to the stone. Charcoal marked black against gray. He wrote each name as we spoke it, letters blocky but clear, the way he taught us to carve practice runes on wood. No flourishes, no wasted motion. Just a roll call of absence.

Anya. Teo. Lina. Bram.

Vara... no. Vara was clinging to Ianteen's leg, her small fingers locked tight like she was afraid the ground might open. I struck her name from my tongue before it could slip out by habit, and the fact that my mind even tried made me feel sick. When he finished, Dratmar stepped back.

"Look at them," he said quietly to us, not to the weeping parents, not to the blank-eyed Mayor. "Go on. Look."

We did. Nineteen names. Nineteen reasons. Dratmar turned to the Mayor.

"You'll send to Northwatch," he said. His voice was polite enough, and that was the dangerous part. "Tell them what happened. Tell them goblins hit Old King's Walk proper, not just a caravan or a shepherd in the woods. Tell them how many took. Tell them where they went."

"How am I to know that?" the Mayor snapped, desperation making him bold. "You expect me to follow them? I'm no soldier. I'm the Mayor of a respectable..."

"They went north," Bobo said softly.

Heads turned.

He stood a little apart from us, gaze fixed beyond the burning rooftops, beyond the tree line, to the jagged line of mountains that loomed like teeth along the edge of the world.

"How do you know?" Ianteen asked, sharper than she meant. Grief makes knives out of voices.

Smoke had cleared enough that the night wind had a way again. It carried faint, fading echoes of something else. Drums, maybe, or just many small feet moving fast. The sound was so thin I couldn't trust my own ears.

"Fire tells me," Bobo said simply. "They took torches. It leans that way."

Dratmar nodded once. "North, then. Into the foothills. Likely to their dens in the low caves before sunup. They'll rest there. We don't catch them by then, we never will."

The Mayor made a strangled noise. "You're not suggesting... surely you're not mad enough to... you can't go after them. You're few. You're..." He gestured helplessly at us, soot-streaked and blood-spattered. "They'll eat you alive. Better to mourn and rebuild than throw more lives after..."

Dratmar's gaze pinned him to the stone as cleanly as a nail.

"You rebuild," he said. "You mourn. You send for help that will come too late. You do your duty, in your way."

He turned back to us.

"We do ours."

Jaime straightened, as if he'd pulled a string inside her spine. I felt something settle heavy and cold in my gut. Not dread, that had already had its way with me. This was weight. Responsibility. The sense that the world had handed us a burden and would not accept it back.

"Pack what you can carry that won't slow you," Dratmar went on, voice hoarser than I'd ever heard it, but steady. "Food. Water. Rope. Bandages. Flint, if Bobo doesn't burn the mountains down for us. We go light and fast."

"When?" Maximus whispered.

Dratmar looked east.

The first smear of dawn painted the mountain tips in thin, sickly gold. It did nothing to warm the square. The village fires still burned brighter, hungry and loud.

"As soon as the sun shows her face," he said. "Goblins'll make for their holes then. They like dark. We don't have that luxury."

Jaime nodded once. Ianteen wiped her eyes with the back of her hand and nodded too. Bobo just stared north, as if he could already see the distant campfires, as if the fire had whispered more than direction into his ear.

Maximus looked at the wall again. At Anya's name, dark and sharp among the others.

"We're going to get her," he said.

It wasn't a question.

For a moment I wished, brief and fierce, that I could tell him yes as surely as he needed. That the world worked that way. That wanting something hard enough, bleeding for it, would guarantee its return.

"We're going after her," I said instead, because it was the only promise I could afford to make.

He gripped the hilt of his sword until his knuckles shone pale under the grime. He nodded once to himself, a motion so tight it looked like it hurt.

"Then I'm coming," he said.

Of course he was. Of course we all were. There was nowhere else to go. The house was ash. The village was broken. The little ones clung to us because we were what was left. Dratmar turned away from the ruined square and the names on the wall and the Mayor's sputtering protests. His one good eye locked on the black line of the northern hills.

"Eat what you can," he said. "Drink. Piss. Say whatever prayers you think might help."

He rolled his shoulders, the motion weary and resolute, like he was settling armor onto bones that ached.

"Then we go into the mountains."

# Chapter 5

## THE CHASE

Dratmar's words should have landed like a bell, clean and unquestionable, something that cut through smoke and grief and left a single clear note behind it. Instead they settled on my ribs like another weight, the kind you carry because there's no place to set it down.

Then we go into the mountains.

The square around the well did not answer him with anything so neat as courage. It answered with the slow noises of people trying to become real again. Coughs that turned wet. A woman sobbing until her throat ran out of sound. A baby crying somewhere, thin and stubborn, as if it had not received the message that the world had ended. Firelight made faces copper and soot, eyes too bright, pupils blown wide by terror and heat. When the wind shifted, sparks lifted and drifted like tiny malignant stars, landing on roofs that had not yet caught.

Dratmar pointed, not with speeches, not with theatrics, just the same way he did in the yard when we drilled.

"Jaime. Take food that doesn't cook in your pocket. Bobo, waterskins. Maximus, bandage your head. You bleed out, you don't help anyone."

Jaime nodded once and moved. There was blood drying on her knuckles and soot caked in the crease beside her nose, but she moved like a blade being drawn, smooth and inevitable. Bobo went too, silent and tight-faced, the way he got when the world became an inventory of elements and problems: fire, smoke, wind, breath. People were harder. Maximus did not look at anyone. His gaze stayed on the northern hills as if his stare could drill through stone and find Anya's hands in the dark.

Dratmar's fingers closed on Maximus's shoulder. Not a shake this time, not a slap. A grip that anchored.

"Son."

Maximus blinked, and his eyes finally moved, not to Dratmar, but past him to the soot-streaked wall where the names had been written in charcoal. The list made the village feel too small, as if it had been hollowed out and left standing by habit alone.

Anya. Teo. Lina. Bram. Joros. Old Greer's twin girls. Marta's youngest.

Mykel.

The Mayor stood on the far side of the well, posture broken, fine clothes turned to scorched rags. His hands shook, not from cold, but from imagining. When Dratmar had first ordered the count, the Mayor had argued. When Mykel's name had been spoken, something inside him had snapped and rewired into desperation.

"You cannot wait," he said, stumbling toward us as if he might physically push us north. "An hour? You said an hour. They'll be gone. They'll be..."

He could not finish. His mouth worked like he was chewing sand.

"We go when we're ready," Dratmar said, calm enough to be dangerous.

"You are ready now!" the Mayor snapped, and it was not authority that made him loud. It was panic, naked and ugly. "Do you understand me? That is my son. Mykel is my son."

Ianteen made a sound that might have been laughter if it had not been full of knives. She stepped forward, shoulders trembling with exhaustion and fury.

"And Teo was Marta's," she said. "And Lina is the tanner's. And Bram is nobody's boy but his own, and still he is gone. They are all our children, you coward."

The Mayor flinched as if the word had a blade in it. He tried to stand taller, tried to remember he was used to being obeyed, but the firelight did not make him imposing. It made him look small and singed and afraid.

"I am not a coward," he protested, and even that sounded like begging. "I am trying to keep this village alive."

"You kept it alive by telling yourself stories," Ianteen spat. "Now the story has teeth and it is chewing on your house too, so suddenly you believe."

The Mayor's gaze latched onto Dratmar as if he was the only solid thing left in the world.

"Take men," he said, desperate. "I will send men with you. Coin, weapons, anything. I have a chest, I have..."

His eyes darted around as if his riches might rise out of the ashes and prove he still had power.

"You'll send to Northwatch," Dratmar said, ignoring the offer like it was smoke. "You'll send now, while the road is still passable. You'll tell them goblins took nineteen children from Old King's Walk. You'll tell them we're going after them. You'll tell them if they want the trail, they go north."

"I can come," the Mayor said, voice thinning with hope. "I can ride with you."

"You'll stay," Dratmar replied.

The Mayor's face tightened, and for a moment I saw the truth under his indignation. Staying meant helplessness. Waiting. Listening to mothers cry and fires crack and not being able to fix it with a signature or a speech.

"You cannot order me," he whispered.

"I can," Dratmar said, stepping closer, winter-calm. "Not because I am your Mayor, and not because I have coin. Because I have a sword, and you have a village full of people who will tear you apart if you try to make this about your blood instead of theirs."

The Mayor's mouth opened and closed. He looked around, finally seeing the way heads had turned, the way grief was beginning to harden into blame, searching for somewhere to land. His shoulders sagged like a man whose bones had become water.

"Please," he said, and the word sounded foreign in his mouth. "Bring him back."

Dratmar did not nod. He did not promise. He only said, "Do your duty."

Jaime returned with a sack slung over her shoulder, something that had once been flour. Now it held whatever she could rip from the bakery stall that had not burned: hard rolls, dried apples, a wedge of cheese wrapped in cloth. She shoved a roll into my hand.

"Eat," she said.

My fingers did not want to close around it. They wanted to keep shaking. I forced them anyway. The bread was stale and tasted like ash, because everything tasted like ash now, but the act of chewing did something simple and brutal to my body. It reminded it that we were still alive.

Bobo came with waterskins and a small bundle of flint, though he looked at the stones like they were a child's toy. He carried a clay jar too, stoppered tight.

"What's that?" I asked.

He did not look up as he answered. "Pitch. For sealing. For making fire behave, if you talk to it right."

Maximus sat on the well's edge and let Jaime wrap cloth around his temple. Dried blood cut a dark line down his cheek. His eyes stayed open the entire time, unblinking, as if closing them would show him Anya being dragged away again. When Jaime tied the knot, she touched his shoulder, gentle, and he flinched like tenderness hurt worse than blows.

"You come with us," Maximus said to Dratmar. It was not a question.

Dratmar nodded once.

"I'm going to kill every one of them," Maximus whispered, and his voice sounded scraped raw from the inside.

Dratmar did not scold him. He did not tell him not to speak such things. "Keep your head," he said. "Rage is a torch. It shows you the way, and it burns your hand if you hold it wrong."

Maximus swallowed hard and forced a nod, as if obedience was something he had to wrench out of himself with both hands.

Near my side, Mira stood wrapped in a blanket that smelled of wet wool and smoke. Her eyes were enormous, tracking every movement like she thought the world might collapse again if she looked away.

"You're coming too?" she asked, voice small.

"No," I said too quickly, and the word cut her. I saw it in the way her mouth tightened, in the way she tried not to cry like Anya had taught her, prideful and stubborn even now.

"Who watches us, then?" she whispered.

Dratmar crouched in front of her, slow and deliberate, so she would not think he was rushing away from her. "The old folk and the wounded," he said. "And the ones who can still stand without falling over. They'll gather in the Mayor's stone house. Stone doesn't burn like thatch. You watch each other, you stay where you can be found, and you do not wander. If goblins come back, you scream and you run to stone."

Mira's lip trembled. "Promise you'll come back."

Dratmar held her gaze and did not lie. "I promise we'll try."

She nodded like that was enough because children will tie whatever rope you offer around their hearts and call it certainty. The sky had begun to pale above the ridge, thin gray seeping into smoke. The fires still burned brighter than dawn. Dratmar rose and rolled his shoulders, coat scorched, seams smoking faintly. He looked older than yesterday, not frail, but sharpened, as if the night had scraped softness out of him and left only bone and iron.

"Listen," he said, and he did not have to shout. We turned toward him because his voice had always been the thing we trained against, the thing that held us upright when our knees wanted to fold.

"We go north. We follow the trail, not the anger. Jaime, you take point with me. Elric, two steps behind. You watch the ground and the trees. You do not lift your eyes into the sky looking for miracles. Miracles don't track goblins."

Heat rose in my cheeks, shame sharp and hot, because he had seen my eyes drifting, searching for some sign that this was a story where heroes arrive in time.

He looked at Bobo next. "No fires," he said. "Even if you can make it small. Even if you think you can hide it. Fire is a beacon, and it is a tongue. You use it only if you must, and if you do, you bury it."

Bobo's jaw tightened, but he nodded once, stiff.

Dratmar's gaze landed on Maximus. "You do not run ahead," he said. "You do not break formation. If you see her, you tell me. If you hear her, you tell me. You do not throw yourself into the dark alone, because the dark will swallow you and then we have two names on that wall, not one."

For a heartbeat Maximus looked like he might argue, like the rage in him was a living thing with teeth, but he swallowed and forced his head to dip. "I hear you," he said, voice rough, and it sounded less like agreement and more like something he was doing with both hands to keep from splitting apart.

Then Dratmar turned to me. "Elric," he said, and my spine straightened by instinct.

"You've killed now," he said quietly.

My stomach lurched. The table. The wet sound of the blade coming free. The weight of a body sagging like a sack of grain that had once been alive.

"Yes," I managed, and the word came out thin.

"There are moments ahead where you will want to freeze," Dratmar continued. "Where the world tilts and you think you cannot move because moving means choosing. You move anyway. You understand me?"

I swallowed ash and smoke and nodded, then forced my voice to work. "Yes."

Dratmar held my gaze for another heartbeat, then nodded once, satisfied. "Good. Because if we catch them, we catch them while they're tired, while they're loaded down with stolen children, while they think we are weeping in a square."

His eyes flicked to the wall where the names waited in charcoal. "We prove them wrong."

We left the well behind. I did not look back at Mira because I could not, but I felt her gaze on my shoulder like a hand. The village narrowed into lanes, then into the track that led north, past blackened fence posts and fields trampled into mud. The sun finally showed the edge of her face over the eastern ridge, and it did not feel like hope. It felt like exposure.

We found the trail sooner than I expected, not because it was subtle, but because goblins did not care about subtle when they believed no one would follow. Boot prints bit sharp into mud. Drag marks scored the ground. Broken branches showed where they had shoved through hedges. A scrap of cloth snagged on a thorn bush, pale and small enough that my throat closed around it.

I reached for it before I could stop myself and tore it free, the fabric soft and ordinary between my fingers. Maximus saw it and his breath caught. Dratmar's voice cut in at once, steady and hard. "Keep moving. That cloth is bait. They leave pieces to make you stop."

I still shoved it into my pocket, because I needed something real to hold onto, proof that this was not a nightmare that would dissolve if I woke. Then we moved into the trees, and the forest swallowed sound. The crackle of burning village faded behind us until there was only the hush of needles and damp earth under our boots, and the cold line of the foothills rising ahead like teeth at the edge of the world.

Now it felt like walking into a mouth.

The foothills had been bad enough, all those scrubby slopes and loose shale that shifted underfoot and threatened to announce every step, but the cut in the rock ahead of us was worse. The ravine narrowed as we went, the walls rising on either side like black teeth. Pine roots clawed from the stone, twisted and exposed, as if the mountain had tried to swallow the trees and failed. Smoke still clung to my hair from the night before, and every time I breathed too deep, my throat reminded me what fire had taken.

We moved in a rough line, close enough that I could reach out and touch the back of Jaime's shoulder if I had to. Maximus kept drifting forward like a hound on a scent, then catching himself and glancing back with that raw, hunted look, as if the act of slowing down was a sin. Bobo padded beside me, quiet as ever, his eyes flicking to the ground and then up to the branches, taking the world in as if it might speak to him again.

It did not feel like our village anymore. It felt like something older, something that did not care about names on a wall or a girl with a kitchen knife. The stones did not mourn. The wind did not apologize. The mountains simply existed, and in their existence they made everything smaller, including my anger.

The path bent, and the ravine tightened until we had to turn sideways in places to squeeze through. The air changed. It grew colder, yes, but not in the honest way dawn cold usually was. This cold sat on the skin like damp cloth. It brought a faint sourness with it too, a smell that was not pine or wet rock. Goblins. Rot. Old grease. The aftertaste of a cooking fire that had burned something it should not have.

Jaime lifted a fist and we stopped without needing to be told. That was one of the things Dratmar had carved into us with repetition. Stop before you need to stop. Stop before your enemy tells you to.

Maximus's breathing was loud in the narrow space, a rasp he could not seem to control. His knuckles stayed white on his sword hilt even in the dim light, and I could see a tremor running through his forearm every time his grip tightened. I thought of Anya's hand tearing free, her fingers slipping like wet rope, and my stomach turned hard enough I had to swallow twice.

Bobo paused. It was not the sharp, startled pause of fear, but the careful one, the kind that made the rest of the world lean in. His head tilted, and his brow furrowed. The frown looked wrong on him, too old, as if he was wearing someone else's face for a moment.

"What now?" I whispered, because the silence was worse than any answer.

He raised a hand, palm outward, not to stop us, but to ask the world to hush. The gesture was gentle, almost polite, like he was addressing an animal that might bolt if startled. Jaime held her position, eyes narrowed, listening too, but it was Bobo who seemed to be hearing something the rest of us were not yet brave enough to admit was real.

At first I heard only myself, the scrape of my own breath, the faint wet click of saliva in a mouth that had been too dry for too long. Somewhere above us a pine bough shifted and shed a dusting of needles. The ravine carried the sound and made it seem closer than it was, as if the mountain wanted to play tricks. Then it came, faintly, underneath everything, like something tapping on the far side of a wall. A rhythm.

It was not a song. It was not a drum I could name with certainty. It was a cadence that repeated with the stubbornness of marching, many feet moving together over stone. Between those beats there was another sound, irregular and ugly, as if something heavy was being dragged and occasionally caught on a rock, bumped, then lifted and dragged again. The rhythm never broke for long. Whatever was coming had numbers, and it had purpose.

Maximus's head snapped toward the sound, and for a moment he looked like he might bolt straight into it, sword first, sense last. Jaime's hand shot out and caught his sleeve in a hard grip. She did not yank him, not yet, but her fingers locked like a clamp, and he froze as if she'd driven a nail through his wrist.

"Don't," she mouthed at him, no sound, all command.

His jaw worked. A vein stood out in his temple beneath the soot. His eyes were bright in the dim, feverish, and I hated the part of me that understood him. Every beat of that rhythm felt like a countdown. Every scrape felt like someone's heel catching on Anya's ribs. The cadence drew closer by inches, not by leaps, because the ravine swallowed distance and fed it back slowly. Alongside it, a murmur threaded through the stone, low and shifting. It might have been goblin speech, all those clipped syllables and wet laughs, or it might have been wind in the cracks making nonsense that sounded like words if you were desperate enough to hear meaning. I was desperate enough. I heard meaning anyway.

Bobo's eyes went half-lidded, focusing inward. His lips moved once, almost a whisper, as if he was tasting the air. "They've got torches," he murmured, so softly I barely caught it.

"You can smell that?" I whispered. The scent was clear enough to me but the fact that Bobo picked up on it was surprising.

He shook his head once, small. "Not smell. It leans."

That was how he talked about fire when he did not want to call it magic. The fire likes me. Fire tells me. It leans. As if flame had opinions and directions, as if it could point like a finger. I did not know if any of that was true, but I knew Bobo had been right last night when the roof came down. He had bought us breaths with steam and stubbornness, and I did not have the right to doubt him now just because the world had turned cruel.

Jaime shifted her weight, careful to keep her boots from scraping. She glanced back at me, then at Bobo, then toward the narrowing dark ahead. In that look there was a whole plan, half-formed but functional. We were not Dratmar. We did not have his iron patience. But we had what he'd left us with, and we had the one thing goblins did not like to account for.

We had stubborn people who loved someone enough to become dangerous. Maximus swallowed hard. His gaze flicked toward the ravine's mouth ahead, where the path widened into a small bowl of stone and stunted trees. If the goblins came through there, we would see them. They would see us and it would be a collision few walked away from. His shoulders rose, fell. He was a forge about to spark, and I could feel Jaime reading him like a page.

"Max," she whispered, finally giving him the smallest amount of voice, the smallest amount of permission. "Look at me."

He did not, not at first. His eyes stayed fixed on the dark.

Jaime's grip tightened on his sleeve, and she leaned close enough that her breath brushed his ear. Her voice came out low and sharp, the kind of truth you could not argue with. "Your stress won't save Anya."

Maximus flinched as if she'd struck him. His eyes snapped to her then, furious, wounded, a boy being told his feelings were useless.

"They're dragging something," he hissed, and the words were ragged with helplessness. "You heard that. They're dragging... gods, Jaime, it's them. It's them."

"I heard it," Jaime said. She did not soften, but she did not pull away either. "And you rushing will get you killed before you see her. Then she has no one coming. Elric has no one coming. Those other children have no one coming. You want to help her, you stay breathing."

Maximus's gaze dipped, not in surrender, but in the act of forcing himself to swallow rage. His nostrils flared. He looked past Jaime at me as if he needed someone else to contradict her so he could keep being furious, however we both knew I could not. I tasted smoke in my mouth again, remembered the crack of Anya's shoulder popping when a goblin yanked her wrist, and the memory made my hands shake on my sword hilt. "She's right," I whispered. It came out like broken glass. "If we crash into them here, we're dead. We have to see them first."

Maximus's throat bobbed. For a heartbeat I thought he might refuse anyway, might rip free of Jaime's grip and sprint into that sound simply because standing still felt like betrayal. Then he did something I did not expect.

He nodded.

It was a small motion, stiff and ugly, like his neck was resisting. But it was a nod, and it held.

Bobo pointed with two fingers toward a narrow slit in the ravine wall, half-hidden by a curtain of roots and hanging moss. It was not a proper path, more like a wound in the stone, a place where water had been cutting for years. "Up," he whispered. "We go above. We look down."

Jaime's eyes narrowed. She assessed the climb in a single glance. "We can make that," she murmured. Then, quieter, to Maximus, "We can make that without them hearing you breathe like a dying bull."

Maximus's lips twitched, the ghost of offense, the ghost of a laugh that did not have permission to live yet. It died quickly, but something in his shoulders loosened. Purpose, finally, had somewhere to go.

We moved.

The climb tore at my palms immediately. Stone scraped skin, roots snagged sleeves, and the damp cold in the crack bit into my fingertips until they felt numb. I forced my hands to keep working anyway. Below us, the cadence grew louder. I could hear the little stutters of it now, the way feet adjusted on uneven ground, the occasional sharp yip of command, the clack of bone ornaments, the low, nasty laughter that traveled like oil on water.

Halfway up, I paused and pressed my forehead briefly against the stone, not in prayer, but in the act of not vomiting. My stomach was trying to climb out of my throat. The idea of looking down and seeing what they were dragging made my vision blur. Jaime climbed past me with grim efficiency, the way she did everything. She did not look down.

She looked up. She did not allow herself to imagine. She saved imagination for later, for when it could kill her quietly. Right now she needed it dead.

Bobo followed, light-footed, somehow steady even with smoke in his lungs. He did not look afraid. He looked attentive, like a boy in a lesson. I wondered, briefly, what it did to him to feel fire as if it were a thing with moods. I wondered what it would do to him when he started feeling other things the same way.

Maximus came last, climbing like he wanted to punch the mountain into a ladder. Jaime hissed at him once, a warning, and he forced himself to slow, breath shaking but quieter.

At the top, the crack widened into a ledge just big enough for four bodies to crouch without falling. Brush grew thick here, stunted pines and thorny scrub that grabbed at hair and clothing. We sank into it, keeping low, and the world below opened. The bowl of stone was lit by torchlight now, flickering orange on gray rock. Shadows jumped and stretched, made every moving goblin look bigger than it was. There were more of them than I wanted to count, a pack that moved with practiced confidence, some carrying sacks, some carrying spears, some dragging bundles that bumped and snagged on the stones.

My throat went tight. Among those bundles were small shapes. Limbs. Cloth. The pale flash of a child's bare foot. I did not know which one was Anya from this angle, from this distance. The torches turned everything into broken color, and fear made my eyes unreliable. But I knew, with a certainty that made my teeth ache, that she was down there somewhere, because the world did not feel empty enough yet to have taken her entirely.

Maximus's breath hitched beside me. Jaime's hand moved fast, clamping over his mouth before the sound could escape. Her other hand dug into his shoulder, anchoring him. He did not fight her, he simply stared down into that torchlit river of monsters and stolen children, and the hatred in his face was so pure it looked clean.

Jaime leaned to my ear, her voice barely more than air. "We follow," she whispered. "We don't strike yet. We find where they're going. We find where they stop."

"And if they stop to hurt them?" Maximus rasped, the words muffled against Jaime's palm.

Jaime's eyes did not leave the moving line below. "Then we choose the moment," she said, and there was something in her tone that made my skin prickle. Not mercy. Not patience. Calculation, sharpened by grief. "But we choose it smart. For Anya. For all of them."

Bobo's gaze tracked the torches like they were stars that had fallen too low. "North," he whispered again, as if confirming a compass. "Fire leans north."

Below, the goblin line shifted, turning toward a narrower cut between boulders, a place where the mountain broke open again and swallowed them one by one. For a moment the cadence sped up, as if something had barked an order. One of the bundles dragged too hard, and a small voice cried out, thin and sharp.

Maximus went rigid under Jaime's hand. My heart slammed once, furious and helpless. Jaime tightened her grip on him until his jaw clenched, and she hissed, so quietly it was almost nothing, "Breathe. Stay breathing."

We watched the last torches vanish into the stone throat ahead, the orange flicker dwindling until it was just a faint stain on the rock, then nothing. The ravine swallowed the sound too, and the rhythm faded into distance, leaving only the wind and our own breathing and the horrible knowledge of what was still moving in the dark. Jaime released Maximus's mouth slowly, as if she was afraid he might bite. He did not. He stayed silent, eyes fixed on the place the torches had gone.

"We move," Jaime whispered at last.

We rose, careful, and began to pick our way along the ledge to find a safer descent, following the path of the goblins from above, from the shadows, like we had become something thin and hungry ourselves. Behind us, far away now, Old King's Walk burned without us, and the smoke climbed into a sky that did not care.

WE FOUND IT WHERE the mountain folded in on itself, as if the world had once bitten down and never fully opened its jaw again.

The pines thinned, the ground turned to broken shale, and the air changed. It went damp and sharp, carrying a cold mineral taste that did not belong to morning. Even Bobo stopped talking to the fire under his breath. Jaime lifted a fist, and we all went still behind her, crouched among scrub and rock.

Below us, the cave mouth yawned wide enough to swallow a wagon. Old soot smeared the stone around it in fan-shaped streaks, like the cave had been breathing smoke for a long time. A trickle of water ran out from the darkness, thin as a thread, and vanished into the stones.

At first I saw only goblins. They moved in and out of the mouth in a rough rhythm, two in, one out, one in again, as if they were passing messages or tools. Their torches were not bright, more like bruised orange lumps of light, and it made their bodies look half-real, like bad thoughts.

Then I saw the huddle.

Close to twenty shapes, pressed together in a cluster on the flat rock just inside the mouth, where the torchlight licked them enough to show pale faces and dark hair and small shoulders. Some were sitting. Some were on their knees. Some lay curled like they had fallen and not managed to rise again. Rope looped their wrists. Cloth gags cut lines into cheeks. A few heads lolled with the slow sway of exhaustion.

My throat tightened so hard it felt like someone had grabbed me by the collar from the inside. I tried to find her.

I tried to find Anya the way you look for a candle in a storm, desperate for the shape of it, for the promise of warmth. I counted heads. I looked for her hair, for the angle of her shoulders, for the way she always held herself like she was between the little ones and the world. A girl lifted her face toward the cave ceiling, eyes glassy in the torchlight. For half a heartbeat I thought it was her, and my heart jumped, and my hands started to shake.

Then she turned, and the nose was wrong, the brow was wrong, and the hope that had surged up in me fell back down like a stone into a well.

Maximus made a noise beside me, barely more than breath. His fingers were white around his sword hilt, knuckles scraped raw from the night. I could feel the heat of him, coiled and ready to explode.

Jaime's voice came soft, rough as worn rope. "We watch."

"I'm watching," Maximus whispered, and it came out like he hated the words.

Below us, a goblin with a harness of teeth and small bones stepped into the torchlight. It was larger than the others, not tall like a man, but thick with muscle and confidence. It stalked toward the huddle and kicked at the nearest child, not hard enough to break something, just hard enough to prove it could. The child flinched. A second child tried to curl closer to them, as if the body could become a shield.

The goblin barked something, and the others moved. Not in a scramble, not in the sloppy frenzy they'd shown in our house, but in a practiced pattern. Two grabbed the rope line. Two took torches. One moved to the side of the cave mouth and crouched, doing something with its hands against the stone. I saw the faint glint of wire or cord.

*A trap.*

And the goblin did it with the casual speed of someone locking a door they had locked a thousand times.

Bobo's head tilted, eyes narrowed. He looked like a boy listening to a bedtime story that had turned into a warning. "They've been here before," he breathed.

"They live here," Jaime murmured, and I heard the grim satisfaction in her voice. A den meant a place to fight. A den meant they could not run forever.

The goblins hauled the rope line, and the children stumbled to their feet in a wave of weakness. One child fell, knees slamming stone. A goblin jerked the rope, dragging them a hand's breadth before the child managed to crawl up and stagger again. Then they started moving deeper, away from the mouth, away from the flat rock, into the black.

The torches went first, and the darkness swallowed them in bites, one step at a time. A goblin paused at a certain point and stepped sideways, placing its foot on a stone that looked no different to me than any other. Another goblin hopped over a narrow crack in the floor that was too dark to read. Another ducked under a low shelf of rock without slowing, as if it had memorized the shape of the cave with its bones.

They moved faster as they went.

They did not hesitate at the dark holes. They did not glance down. They did not test the ground. They slid through the cave like water through a channel they had carved themselves, and the children were just debris caught in the current.

Maximus shifted, a muscle twitching in his shoulder.

Jaime's hand closed around his forearm, hard. "No."

He glared at her, eyes bright with fever. "If we wait, she's gone."

Jaime did not flinch. She held his stare like she was pinning him to the rock. "Your stress won't save Anya," she said, low enough that only we could hear. "It won't save any of them. You charge in there blind, and you will die in a hole, and the only thing you'll have protected is your pride."

Maximus's jaw flexed. The anger in him looked for somewhere to land.

Jaime leaned closer. "You want to do something useful, then breathe. Look. Learn. Give me the shape of what we're walking into."

His nostrils flared. For a heartbeat, I thought he might tear free anyway. Then his shoulders dropped a fraction. Not surrender, not peace, just the smallest click of something being forced into place. He swallowed, and I saw the wet shine in his eyes that he refused to let fall.

"Fine," he rasped. "Fine. Tell me what you see."

Jaime nodded once, satisfied, cruelly gentle. She turned her gaze back to the cave. Below, the last torch dipped and vanished. The cave mouth sat open and empty again, as if nothing had ever happened, as if the mountain itself was innocent. But the air held the echo of footsteps. The faint murmur of goblin speech. The soft, thin sound of rope sliding against stone.

Dratmar, crouched behind us, shifted his weight. His one good eye stayed on the darkness like it was a living enemy. "They're taking them deeper," he said. "They know we're near, or they're assuming we will be. Either way, they've planned for it."

"How deep?" I whispered.

Dratmar's mouth tightened. "Deep enough that daylight won't matter."

Bobo's voice came quiet, almost reverent, as if he hated the truth but respected it. "They move like they've got a path," he said. "Like the dark is their road."

"It is," Jaime replied.

Maximus exhaled through his teeth, and the sound shook. "Then we take it away."

Dratmar looked at each of us in turn. Me, Jaime, Maximus, Bobo. Four people against a mountain full of teeth. "You go in," he said. "Not running. Not shouting. You go in like thieves and locate the kids. If they come to danger, you act."

He gestured to the stone under our feet. "Rope. Chalk, if you've got it. Knots. Mark every turn, every shelf, every drop. Do not lose the way back out, not for gold, not for pride, not even for love."

Maximus made a sound that was almost a laugh and not at all one. "Love's the only reason I'm here."

Dratmar did not argue. He only rose, slow and careful, and motioned for us to continue. "There's a station of the North Guard not far from here. If I go there, they'll come. You need to control yourselves and act as my scouts for now. Mark the path so I can bring em' in fast."

Jaime was the first to rise and move forward, I followed, because there was nowhere else in the world that made sense anymore to go.

# Chapter 6

## THE MOUTH OF THE MOUNTAIN

THE MOUNTAINS DID NOT look like a destination up close. They looked like an argument the world had tried to make with itself and never finished, all jagged edges and stubborn mass. Behind us, Old King's Walk still burned in pockets, not one grand blaze anymore but a dozen separate wrong lights, roofs collapsing with dull, distant sighs. Smoke hung low over the valley, dragged along the ground like a mourner's cloak, and every time the wind shifted it brought the taste of our house back into my mouth. Ash, wet thatch, and something I tried not to name.

Ahead of us, the mouth to the caves awaited, our mission from Dratmar clear as day. Somehow the cold coming from it bit into my fur more than the snow and the wind outside could.

Jaime set the pace. She did not look back to see if we were following, and somehow that made it easier to follow her, because it meant she was not asking permission to lead. She was just leading. Her sword hung low at her side, close enough to scrape stone if she let her wrist slack. She kept it steady.

Maximus walked like a man already halfway dead, shoulders locked, hands opening and closing as if he could practice the exact grip he would need to pull Anya back out of the dark. Bobo moved quieter than the rest of us, a small bundle hugged to his ribs, flint and cloth and whatever food he had managed to grab before the roof finally surrendered. I kept my eyes on the ground because every time I looked up, I saw the wall where Dratmar had written the names, black charcoal on gray stone. Nineteen absences. Nineteen holes carved clean through the village's future.

Anya was one of them. Mykel was another, and that one had turned the Mayor into something frantic and sharp edged, as if other children were tragedy but his child was the end of the world. No doubt he was already doing what Dratmar set out to do himself, so my doubts about backup coming were close to none. My dread was that they would be too late either way.

The entrance to the caves was low and narrow, half hidden behind a slant of rock, its opening choked with bramble and dead branches that did not belong there. Someone had dragged them into place to make the dark look harmless.

My stomach tightened. The world behind us had been open, even burning, even ruined. This looked like the world narrowing down to teeth.

We approached slowly. The ground shifted from soil to stone, and our boots sounded different, less forgiving. Every scrape felt too loud. Dampness rolled out of the cave mouth in cold breaths, carrying the smell of old earth, stale water, and something faintly greasy under it. Rot. Animal. Life lived too long without sunlight.

Jaime crouched and studied the threshold like it was a battlefield map. "Look."

At first it was just darkness. Then my eyes adjusted enough to catch shapes where roots should have been. A shallow arc of stones laid too deliberately to be natural, and smeared with something dark that caught no light.

"Marker stones," Jaime murmured.

Trap stones, Dratmar's voice corrected in my head, as if he were standing behind my shoulder the way he always did when he wanted us to feel watched. The memory of his lessons came back sharp and unwelcome. Goblins were not clever like men, he used to say. They were clever like rats. They learned what hurt and what fed, and they built their world around that.

Bobo picked up a pebble and rolled it between his fingers, then tossed it lightly inside.

The pebble clicked against one of the stones. Nothing happened for a heartbeat, long enough that my skin crawled with anticipation. Then the ground just inside the entrance shifted. A fitted slab of rock tilted under its own weight, revealing a narrow hole beneath. The pebble vanished with a sharp clatter, followed a second later by a deeper sound, wet and final, then a slow drip.

Maximus stared at the hole like he wanted to jump into it just to prove it could not stop him.

"How do they pass?" I asked, throat dry.

Jaime pointed at the wall rock. "There."

A narrow ledge ran along the side, no wider than my hand. The kind of thing you would never notice unless you already knew you needed it.

"Single file," I said.

"Aye," Jaime replied, and the word sounded strange in her mouth because it was not hers. It was something she had learned from Dratmar and kept because it worked.

Maximus made a sound that was half growl, half prayer. "We do not have time for careful."

"We do not have time for stupid," Jaime said, and this time there was no softness left in her at all. "If you fall, you bleed. If you bleed, they hear. Then we save no one."

The truth sat heavy and cold in my gut. This was not a chase anymore. This was a place with teeth and patience, and we were stepping into it on purpose.

Jaime tested the ledge with her boot, then shifted her weight onto it, shoulder close to the wall. "I go first."

I went after her, because my legs moved when she told them to and because Dratmar had built that obedience into me long before I understood why. The pit yawned at my left, waiting. I put my palm to the wall, grit and damp under my skin, and forced myself to breathe slow through my nose, the way he taught us when panic wanted to own our lungs.

One step. Then another. Halfway across, my boot slipped on wet stone. My stomach lurched. My fingers clawed at the rock, nails biting, and I froze with every muscle clenched, convinced the next breath would tip me into the hole.

"Bend your knees," Jaime said softly ahead of me. "Weight over your feet."

I did it, tiny and careful, and my balance found itself again. I took another step. Then another. When I reached solid ground on the far side, my legs trembled like they belonged to someone else, but they held.

Maximus crossed next, heavier, angrier, clumsier. Twice he nearly stepped into the pit, and twice he caught himself with a harsh intake of breath that sounded like pain. Bobo came after him, moving like a cat, quiet as smoke. Putting me to shame. When we were all through, Jaime nudged the stone slab back into place with her boot until the trap disappeared again beneath dust and shadow, as if the mountain had swallowed its own grin.

"Good," she murmured. "Now we are in."

The cave narrowed immediately, ceiling lowering until the stone felt close enough to press against my skull. The air changed, colder and heavier, carrying a faint vibration like the mountain was holding its breath. We moved in single file now, Jaime in front, then me, then Maximus, then Bobo. The mouth of the cave vanished behind the first bend. Light thinned, then died.

Somewhere deeper in the dark came the faintest echo of movement, a soft cadence that did not belong to wind or water. Many feet. Quick feet. Goblin feet, moving with the confidence of creatures walking through their own traps.

I tightened my grip on my sword and kept my eyes on Jaime's back, because that was what I had been taught. Follow the steady thing. Do not look at the pit. Do not look at the dark. Do not look at fear like it can bargain with you.

We went on, careful as thieves, quiet as a promise we had not earned yet, stepping deeper into the mountain where nineteen names waited to become either rescue or elegy.

THE TUNNEL TIGHTENED THE way a fist tightens, not all at once but with patient insistence. Stone pressed closer to our shoulders, the air turned wetter, and the smell changed from old earth to something lived-in. Goblins. Smoke. Unwashed bodies and animal fat rubbed into leather. Under it all ran a faint metallic tang that made my mouth water and my stomach roll, blood dried and re-wet by cave damp.

Jaime kept one hand on the wall as she walked, fingers brushing ridges and seams like she was reading a script only she could see. Her sword stayed low, point forward, ready to lift without scraping. Every few steps she paused just long enough to listen, not dramatic, not announcing it. Just a small stillness that made the rest of us still too.

I tried to do what Dratmar always demanded. I tried to breathe like a person who had time.

It did not work.

The darkness was not a blanket. It was a mouth. The deeper we went, the more it felt like we were walking into something that could close behind us and leave our bones there without comment.

Maximus walked behind me like a storm trapped in a boy's ribs. I could hear him, not by footsteps but by the way his breath kept catching, the way his throat made small, angry sounds when he swallowed. Every few minutes he would mutter Anya's name under his breath, so quiet it almost became the sound of water dripping somewhere far off. He did it like a charm, as if saying it enough would keep her tethered to him.

Bobo moved last, silent in a way that made me think of coals buried under ash. He was not calm. He was focused. His eyes kept lifting to the ceiling, to the bends in the tunnel, to places where shadows thickened. He watched the cave the way he watched fire, like it had moods and intentions you could learn if you paid the right kind of attention.

We followed the tunnel down through a long slope of stone that slicked our boots and made the air grow colder with every step. Then it flattened, and the sound came back, clearer now. Not just movement. Not just many feet.

*Voices.*

Gutters of goblin speech, clipped and ugly, with laughter threaded through it. The sound of something dragged, bumped, then lifted again. The cadence of a group that knew where it was going.

Jaime raised her fist, and we stopped with our bodies bunched close enough that I could feel Maximus's heat at my back. She leaned forward, careful as a thief, and crept to the edge of the next bend. I watched her shoulders tense. She did not speak right away. She listened, head tilted, eyes narrowed, breathing shallow and controlled. Then she eased back toward us, slow.

"There's a chamber ahead," she murmured. "Not big. Low ceiling. They're using it to rest. Or count. I can hear something being tied."

My stomach clenched. Rope. Chains. Knots around wrists small enough to bruise.

Maximus shifted, a blade in human form. "Then we take them now."

Jaime's eyes snapped to him. In the dark, her gaze felt like a hand on my throat. "No. Remember our mission."

"They're right there," he hissed, and I heard his nails scrape against his sword hilt. "Anya is right there."

"You don't know that," Jaime said. She kept her voice low, but the steel in it had teeth. "You run in, you make noise, you start a fight where the cave decides who lives. That is not a plan. That is a tantrum with a sword."

Maximus made a sound like he might spit, but he didn't. The cave air was too dry for waste.

I swallowed, throat burning, and forced myself to speak. "How many?"

Jaime closed her eyes for a heartbeat, listening again. "Close to twenty shapes," she said. "Hard to tell in sound alone, but it's crowded in there."

My heart knocked hard against my ribs. Nineteen taken. Close to twenty in the chamber. It should have felt like certainty.

It didn't.

Because a number was not a name. A shape was not Anya's face. A breath was not Mykel's voice. All I had was the ache of maybe.

Bobo shifted his weight, head tilted. "They're not just sitting," he whispered. "Hear that? That's not rest."

We listened. Under the goblin talk, under the scrape of dragged feet, there was another sound, softer and worse. A small, stifled sob, cut off too fast. A child trying not to be heard. Maximus surged forward a half-step before he could stop himself. Jaime caught his forearm, fingers biting in through cloth.

"You stress in silence," she whispered into his face, fierce and close. "You do not spend it out loud. Your stress won't save Anya. Your patience might."

Maximus's eyes flashed in the dark. For a heartbeat he looked like he might hit her. Then his shoulders shook once, a tiny, violent tremor, and he went still. Not calm. Contained.

Jaime released him and looked at me. "Elric. You see the ground?"

I dropped my gaze. She knew my eyes were better. The stone under our feet was not smooth. It was scored. Scratched lines, shallow grooves, places where something sharp had scraped again and again. At first I thought it was just wear. Then I saw the pattern. Marks that ran in parallel, they were too straight and too intentional. These were no natural formations.

"Drag lines," I whispered.

"Aye." Jaime pointed with the tip of her sword, not touching. "They've hauled things through here. Bodies. Sacks. Children. That means there's a route. A path they've used enough that it's carved itself into the stone."

Maximus's breath hitched again, and this time it sounded like pain.

Bobo crouched, palm hovering over one of the grooves as if he could feel the story in it. "They're moving deeper," he said quietly.

Jaime nodded once, like she had already decided before Bobo spoke. "They're not staying in that chamber. That's a huddle point. A check. Then they push on."

"Why?" I asked, though I hated that my voice sounded like a child.

Jaime's mouth tightened. "Because they know a village can chase for a while. They know we'll come. If they keep the children close to the entrance, they invite rescue. If they take them deeper, they force us to bleed for every step."

Maximus's fingers flexed. "Then we follow."

"We follow," Jaime agreed, "but we do it the right way."

She slid her pack off her shoulder and opened it with careful hands, as if noise itself was an enemy. Inside were scraps of cloth torn from bedding, a short length of rope, and a stub of chalk she must have grabbed from somewhere in the ruin. She held the chalk up, then looked at Bobo.

"Light?" she asked.

Bobo shook his head. "Not yet. Light is a shout in a cave."

Jaime nodded, accepting it, and pressed the chalk to the wall anyway, drawing a small mark low where it wouldn't catch the eye unless you were looking for it. A short line. Then another. A simple sign.

"Marking," I breathed.

"So we can get back out," she said. "So we don't become part of the mountain."

Maximus made a quiet, bitter laugh. "We're already part of it."

"Not yet," Jaime said, and the way she said it made me believe her for a second.

We crept forward again, closer to the bend. Goblin voices grew clearer. I caught bits of the harsh language, the way they snapped and clicked, and the occasional burst of laughter that made my skin crawl. The air carried a sour warmth now, a press of bodies in an enclosed space. Jaime eased her head around the corner again, slow enough that it felt like watching someone step onto thin ice. She stayed there longer this time. When she finally pulled back, her face had gone pale under soot, and her eyes were wide in a way that made them look younger than she ever let them be.

"They're there," she whispered. "Children. Huddled. Rope on wrists. Some sitting, some slumped. I can't see faces. Too dark, too many bodies between. But there are about twenty, and the goblins are pushing them, not feeding them, not bedding down. They're getting ready to move."

Maximus exhaled through his teeth, a sound like a blade sliding from a sheath. "Anya."

Jaime shook her head once. "I couldn't confirm her. I couldn't confirm Mykel either."

The Mayor's son. The name landed like a stone in my gut because it made the whole thing bigger than us again, bigger than Anya and Maximus, bigger than my own selfish terror. Nineteen children did not belong to one family. They belonged to the village, and the goblins had taken the village's future in their teeth.

"We wait until they move?" I asked.

Jaime nodded. "We do not attack in that chamber. Too tight. Too many. We attack when the cave forces them into a line. When they have to pass their own traps and shortcuts."

Maximus's jaw bunched. "They know their own traps."

"They know how to avoid them," Jaime corrected. "That's different. They will move fast. They will take paths we will not be able to take without breaking our necks. They will drop into holes we cannot drop into. That's the point."

Bobo's gaze stayed fixed on the bend, unblinking. "They'll go through places that hate us."

Jaime's mouth twitched, not a smile. "Aye. Which means we go through places that hate them too, if we can find them. We watch. We learn their route. We let the cave show us where it wants to kill."

My palms were slick on my sword hilt. I wiped them on my tunic, then hated myself for caring about cleanliness when children were tied up in the dark. From the chamber came a sudden barked order, sharp enough that even I could hear the difference. Goblin voices rose in reply. Then, underneath it, the soft scrape of movement, a shuffle of many small bodies being herded.

A child whimpered.

Maximus's shoulders jerked, and for a heartbeat he looked like he might burst. Jaime stepped closer, put her mouth near his ear, and spoke so quietly I almost didn't catch it. "If you break now, we lose them. If you hold now, you get a chance to die for them later, if that's what you're craving. Hold."

His eyes snapped to hers, furious, grief-struck, alive. Then he nodded once, a stiff, ugly motion, like a man swallowing nails.

We pressed ourselves back into the shadows, deeper into the side of the tunnel, making room as the sounds approached. The goblins began to move, and they moved with a confidence that made my blood run cold. Their feet did not hesitate where the grooves in the stone ran. They stepped around certain stones without looking. They ducked under a low point without slowing. They knew exactly where the cave would punish the uninvited.

The children came after, and the sound of them was worse because it was restrained. Shuffling feet. A chain clink. A soft sob swallowed down. The brittle silence of fear. We did not move. We let them pass, the way you let a predator pass when you do not yet have a spear in the right place. I held my breath until my lungs screamed. I listened until my ears felt full of the scrape of rope and the drag of small boots.

As the last of the group moved by, one of the goblins laughed, and in that laugh I heard triumph, and hunger, and the comfort of home. Then the sound began to fade deeper into the mountain, faster now, the goblins picking up speed as soon as the chamber was behind them. Their footsteps quickened, sure and light. The children's shuffles stumbled to match, forced forward by shouted words and sharp prods.

Jaime waited until the echoes thinned. Then she lifted her hand, two fingers, and pointed down the tunnel.

"Now," she whispered.

We followed, but not at their pace. Not with their certainty. We followed with care, with marking, with the slow understanding that the goblins were about to bypass their own defenses in ways we could not. They would take shortcuts into darkness, drop through holes that were not meant for us, vanish into passages the mountain had hidden and we would have to find another way.

The chalk mark on the wall sat behind us like a quiet promise: if we lived, we could return. If help was coming, they would know where to go.

If we did not make it, the mountain would keep our names too.

WE MOVED LIKE THIEVES in our own nightmare, slow enough that every sound had time to become a threat. The goblins' trail still clung to the air, rancid sweat and torch-smoke, the faint bite of pitch. It would have been easier if the cave had been honest, if it were just stone and dark, but it wasn't. It had been used. It had been taught. The mountain had grooves worn into it by goblin feet, and scars where they'd trained it to kill.

Jaime led, not because she was the strongest, but because she was the steadiest. She marked the walls with chalk when she could, small symbols low to the ground, and when the stone grew damp enough that chalk smeared, she tore strips from a ruined cloth bundle and knotted them around roots or jutting rock. Little pale flags that meant nothing to anyone who did not know to look. Maximus kept his eyes forward, jaw clenched hard, breathing too loud and too raw, his hand fused to his sword hilt like staring could punch a hole through stone and grief. Bobo brought up the rear, quiet as ash, a small stubborn heat we refused to let go out. I kept glancing back at him, needing the proof he was still there, still moving, and when he caught me looking once, he lifted his chin in a silent promise.

The tunnel narrowed and then stretched into a low run where we had to hunch, the floor rough and gritty, pebbles shifting underfoot. Jaime slowed even more, and I understood why when my boot nudged something that wasn't rock. A thin cord lay across the ground, nearly invisible in the dark, stretched from wall to wall. My stomach clenched and I froze with my foot hovering. Jaime turned her head just enough to see it, crouched, and brushed the cord with the back of her fingers, careful not to pull.

"It's a trigger," she whispered.

Maximus leaned forward, impatient, and Jaime snapped her hand up without looking, palm out. He bristled, but he stopped. That alone told me how close he was to breaking. I mouthed, "What does it do?" and Jaime's gaze tracked along the cord to where it vanished into a crack in the wall, then up, scanning the ceiling. Loose stone sat in shallow hollows, and thin wooden supports made no sense unless they were meant to fail.

"Drop rock," she breathed. "Enough to crush, or block the passage and steal time."

Bobo crept closer, eyes narrowing. "They'll reset it behind them," he murmured. "They don't just want to hurt us. They want us lost."

"Of course they do," Jaime said. She slid a small knife from her belt, lifted the cord a finger's breadth off the stone, and held it there. "Step over where I lift. One at a time."

Jaime went first, then Maximus, because she wanted him close where she could control him. I went next, palms pressed to the wall because my hands shook too hard to trust my balance. The stone was cold and wet. I lifted my foot, cleared the cord, set it down as softly as I could, like the mountain could feel weight through leather soles. Bobo stepped last, moving with a careful grace that did not fit a boy who'd grown up hauling water, and he didn't touch the cord at all. When we were past it, Jaime eased the line back down like she was tucking a child into bed. She did not cut it. If we had to run back, we'd need to know it was there.

The cave began to branch, side tunnels splitting off like cracks in old wood, each with its own smell: wet rot, stale air, a sharp animal sourness. Jaime paused at each fork, listened, and chose. Sound slid down here, curling and lying, and half the time I heard only my own blood, rushing in my ears. At one fork, where the air felt like it split into two kinds of cold, Bobo lifted his hand and tilted his head as if tasting the darkness.

"Left," he whispered.

Jaime glanced at him. "Why?"

He hesitated, suddenly just a boy again, then forced the words out anyway. "Smoke that way," he said. "Old torch smoke. The other way is dead air."

Jaime nodded once, accepting it as simply as reading tracks in mud. "Left, then." Maximus shot Bobo a look, and for a flicker his face held something that wasn't rage. It vanished fast, but I saw it.

The tunnel sloped down. Damp gathered on my lashes, made my eyebrows itch, and water dripped somewhere with the steady patience of a heartbeat. We passed a tight squeeze where Jaime signaled single file, and when it was my turn the stone scraped my ribs through my tunic and panic hit so fast I nearly gagged. For a second I could not breathe. For a second it felt like the mountain was closing around my chest. I shoved through anyway, teeth gritted, because if Anya could be dragged into the dark, I could walk into it.

On the other side, the tunnel opened into a low chamber with a ceiling rough enough to snag hair. Bones littered the floor, some old and clean, some newer and darkened, with scraps of dried flesh still clinging. My stomach lurched. Maximus saw them too, and his grip tightened until I thought the leather might tear. Jaime crouched, lifted a rock with the tip of her sword, and revealed a shallow hole beneath it, dug and lined with sharpened stakes fashioned from bone and splintered wood.

"They trap their own tunnels," I whispered.

"They trap what they don't use," Jaime murmured. "Or they trap it to slow anything that follows. They know where to step."

Bobo's gaze swept the floor. "There." He pointed to a line of stones arranged in a loose curve, subtle but deliberate. A path. Once you saw it, it was a seam in cloth. Jaime nodded. "We step where they stepped. Elric, you watch my boots. Maximus, you watch mine. Bobo, you watch both of ours."

We crossed the chamber following Jaime's steps exactly. Halfway across, the ceiling gave a soft creak. Jaime stiffened instantly. "Freeze," she breathed, and we froze. The creak came again, followed by a gritty shift. Jaime's eyes lifted and found it: a crude wedge of wood jammed between rocks, too straight, too intentional.

A deadfall.

Jaime raised her sword, not touching the wedge, just hovering near it, then glanced at Bobo. "Can you...?"

Bobo swallowed. He looked painfully young in that moment, then closed his eyes for a heartbeat and lifted his palm, not summoning flame, not lighting anything, just pushing at the air itself. A tiny warm draft kissed the wedge. It trembled. Jaime held perfectly still. The wedge slid free, silent as a falling leaf.

For a heartbeat, nothing happened. Then the rock shelf gave way.

Stone dropped in a sudden brutal rush, a cascade aimed at the spot we would have occupied if we'd taken one more step. It slammed down with a muffled roar, dust exploding up into our faces, pebbles skittering, one larger rock cracking in two with a sharp snap. The sound thundered down the tunnels behind us, echoing until the cave felt like it was beating a drum for our enemies.

Maximus's eyes went wide, not with fear of dying, but fear of being heard. Jaime's face went pale. She stared at the pile of stone, then at Bobo, and whatever gratitude she felt she swallowed with the rest of her panic. She leaned close, breath tight. "We can't do that again. That was loud. If they hear it, they'll move faster."

"They're already moving fast," Maximus rasped.

"Then we don't give them a reason to sprint," Jaime shot back.

Bobo's shoulders shook once, the effort costing more than he wanted to admit. He wiped his palm on his trousers, smearing damp grit. "It would have fallen on us," he said quietly, as if he needed to say it out loud to believe it.

"I know," I whispered. "You did good."

He didn't look at me. He only nodded and stared down the tunnel where the goblins had gone, as if he could hold the darkness open by will alone.

We moved again, faster now but still careful, edging around the fresh rockfall. Beyond it the air changed, warmer by a degree, and the smell of smoke strengthened. Torchlight flickered ahead in a way I could not see yet, but could feel against my skin like distant heat. Jaime crouched at a steeper slope and touched the wall with her fingertips, then lifted them and sniffed, face tightening.

"Pitch," she whispered. "Smeared in places. Fire trap."

"They want us to light a torch," Bobo murmured.

"They want us to panic," Jaime corrected. "They want us to think light is safety."

Maximus swallowed, throat working. "So what do we do?"

"We keep going blind," Jaime said, voice hard enough to be a blade. "We keep going quiet. We follow their trail until we can't, and when we can't, we make our own way. We don't start a fight until we see the children again and we can choose where the cave won't choose for us."

She pointed down the steep slope. "Step where I step."

We started down. The air warmed. The torch-smoke thickened. Somewhere far ahead, faint as a heartbeat under stone, I heard it again, the rhythm of many feet moving together, faster now, and beneath it a smaller sound that made my gut twist, the scrape of chains and the soft broken noise of children being forced to keep up. I tightened my grip on my sword and followed Jaime into the dark that waited like a throat, knowing that the deeper we went, the harder it would be to turn around.

THE SLOPE SPILLED US into a wider throat of stone where the air turned damp and warm at the same time, like breath held too long. My boots slid on slick grit. Jaime caught my sleeve before I went down hard, and her fingers were iron, even though her hand trembled once before she forced it still.

"Slow," she mouthed, not bothering to whisper now. Down here, sound carried like gossip.

We eased along the wall, shoulders brushing cold rock, following the faint pulse of torchlight that bled around a bend ahead. The smell of pitch was stronger here, and under it, something worse, unwashed bodies, old meat, the sharp copper tang of blood dried into cloth.

Bobo's eyes narrowed. He kept his hands close to himself, fingers flexing as if he were counting something invisible. I watched him do it and felt my own stomach tighten, because if Bobo was listening to fire, then there was fire ahead, and goblins did not light torches to be kind.

Jaime lowered herself into a crouch when the tunnel split into a shallow ledge above, a natural shelf that overlooked the bend. She crawled forward on her forearms, careful as a spider, and pressed her face to the stone lip. Maximus hovered behind her, breathing too loud, anger keeping his lungs working when shock wanted him to stop.

Jaime glanced back at us, then made a small, sharp motion with two fingers.

Come. Quiet.

I crawled up beside her, stomach scraping the stone, and lifted my head by an inch.

Below, the cave opened into a corridor made by hands, not just time. The walls were scored with tool marks, crude but deliberate, and shallow niches held torches that sputtered and popped. The light made everything look sickly, yellow and greasy. It threw long shadows that seemed to move on their own.

The goblins moved through it in a pack, two and three abreast, their feet sure on stone where ours had slipped. They did not glance at the walls, did not pause at the cracks and holes. They flowed, fast, like they knew every tooth in the mouth.

And in the middle of them, hunched and shivering, were the children.

Not walking in a line like a caravan, not led like guests. Herded. Pushed. Tugged by hair and wrists. Some stumbled and were yanked upright with a jerk that made their shoulders bow wrong. One boy fell to his knees and a goblin struck him with the butt of a spear, not hard enough to kill, just hard enough to remind him what he was.

I sucked in air and tasted smoke and bile.

There were more than I wanted to count. Small shapes in too-big nightshirts. Bare feet on stone. Hands bound in rough rope. Faces streaked with soot and tears, eyes huge and glassy in the torchlight.

My throat tightened so hard it felt like the cave was squeezing it for me.

"Do you see her?" Maximus whispered, voice so thin it barely existed.

I stared until my eyes burned, until the torchlight blurred and made ghosts of them. I looked for the shape of Anya the way you look for a star you know by heart. Her braid. Her shoulders. The way she would stand between someone else and danger even when she was terrified.

But goblins had torn braids and dignity away. In this light, every child looked like every other child. Every hunched figure was just a bundle of fear.

"I can't," I breathed. The words felt like betrayal.

Maximus's jaw worked. His hands were clenched so hard I could see the tendons in his wrists. Jaime's gaze flicked to him, measuring, and she shifted closer, like she meant to be a wall he could crash into without breaking the whole ledge.

A goblin shoved the group forward and a boy turned his head, just for a moment, as if he'd heard something above. The torchlight caught his face, and my stomach dropped.

Mykel.

He looked older than he had the day before, as if a night could carve years into a child's cheekbones. His hair was plastered to his forehead with sweat and soot. One side of his mouth was swollen, and he held his bound hands close to his chest like he was trying to keep his heart from shaking loose.

His eyes were open, though. Not empty. Not gone. He was watching. He was counting too, in his own way.

I felt Maximus shift, sensed the lunge that wanted to happen, the stupid heroic urge to leap down and start cutting.

Jaime's hand snapped out and clamped over his wrist. Her grip was not gentle. It was a command.

"Not here," she hissed, low and vicious. "Your strength won't save Anya. Not like this."

Maximus's eyes flashed. For a heartbeat I thought he would rip free, that he would rather die than be held back one more second. Then his gaze flicked down again, caught on the children, on how many goblins surrounded them, on the hooked spears and the curved knives and the way the goblins moved like this corridor belonged to them.

His chest heaved once. Twice.

He did not pull away.

The goblins drove the group onward, deeper into the carved corridor. As they moved, I began to see what Jaime had warned us about. Holes in the floor that looked like natural cracks until a goblin stepped over them without looking. Thin lines of cord stretched across side passages, not for goblins, for anyone foolish enough to chase with their eyes on prey instead of the ground. Little stacks of stone that would fall if brushed, loud enough to call half the den down on you.

The goblins did not slow. They knew every danger and every shortcut. One of them cut through a side notch that looked, to my eyes, like a dead end. The goblin pressed a palm to a wall and a slab of stone shifted, just enough to let them pass single file. It closed behind them with a soft grind like teeth.

Jaime's face tightened. "A gate," she breathed. "They've built gates."

Bobo's eyes tracked the torches. "And they've got air," he whispered. "These burn clean. This goes deep."

The children were pushed through after the goblins, swallowed by the moving walls of stone and firelight. Their feet scuffed. Someone sobbed. Someone else made a sound that might have been a prayer or might have been a name. Then the last goblin stepped through, the slab slid back into place, and the corridor below looked empty again, as if it had never held anything living. For a moment, the only sound was the pop of torches and the drip of water.

Maximus stared at the sealed stone as if he could glare a hole through it. His face was pale under the soot, and something in him was shaking, not his hands, not his knees, something deeper and worse.

Jaime let go of his wrist, but she stayed close, her shoulder nearly touching his. When she spoke again, her voice was quieter, not soft, just controlled.

"We go after them," she said. "We do it smart. We do it where the cave can't help them."

Maximus swallowed. "That was them going smart."

"Aye," Jaime said. "So we have to do smarter."

I forced myself to breathe, to take in the details instead of drowning in them. The sealed slab was not perfect. There was a seam along one edge, a hairline gap where smoke leaked, thin as thread. The floor near it was scuffed with goblin feet, and there were marks in the stone wall beside it, shallow scratches that looked like a warning to anyone who knew their own signs.

Jaime shifted her weight and pointed with two fingers, not at the slab, but at the wall above and behind it.

"There," she murmured.

A narrow fissure ran up into darkness, half hidden by a curtain of hanging roots. It looked like nothing. It looked like a crack that went nowhere. But cold air breathed out of it, steady and faint, and the roots had been disturbed, pushed aside and then tugged back into place.

A way around. A way the goblins used. A way that was probably worse than the corridor, because if they could move fast through it, it meant it was either safe to them or deadly to everyone else.

Maximus leaned toward it, impatient again, and Jaime caught his eye, held it.

"You go first," she told him, and there was a reason in the cruelty. "You're strong enough to haul us if it pinches tight. You keep your sword sheathed unless I say otherwise. Steel rings louder than you think down here."

His mouth twisted. "I'm not leaving my blade away."

"You're not leaving it," she snapped. "You're keeping it quiet."

He nodded once, jerky.

Bobo cleared his throat, small and tight. "If there's pitch," he whispered, "and if there's old torches, there will be smoke pockets. Bad air. I can feel it sometimes. Like a candle that doesn't want to stay lit."

Jaime looked at him, really looked at him, and something in her expression softened by a fraction. "Then you tell us," she said. "Before we breathe it."

Bobo nodded, eyes wide, taking the responsibility like a stone he did not have the right to carry.

I stared at the fissure and felt the cave staring back. The mountain was not just dark. It was full of edges, full of holes that wanted you, full of ways to die without ever seeing a blade. The goblins had turned it into a place that punished haste, punished grief, punished love.

I thought of Anya, somewhere ahead, somewhere deeper, and the thought hurt so sharply it almost made me fold.

Jaime's hand brushed my elbow, not comforting, just present. An anchor.

"You with me?" she whispered.

I swallowed smoke and nodded. "I'm with you."

Maximus slid into the fissure first, shoulders turning, breath held. The roots trembled as he pushed through. Jaime followed, then me, then Bobo, who paused with his palm on the stone for a heartbeat as if he were asking permission from the mountain, or warning it.

The crack swallowed us.

Behind us, the torches in the corridor below hissed and popped, indifferent as stars, while somewhere ahead the goblins moved fast through their own dark, carrying our village's children deeper into the teeth of the earth.

# Chapter 7

# THE GOBLIN KING'S COURT

THE CAVE MOUTH DID not look like a mouth from the outside. It looked like what it was, a split in the hillside where water had worried at stone for longer than anyone in Old King's Walk had been alive. We had found it the hard way, following scuffed mud, snapped fern stems, and a faint trail of soot where goblin torches had kissed the low branches. The hills had swallowed the last of the village's smoke hours ago, but I still tasted it every time I breathed. My tongue felt like old cloth, my throat raw enough that swallowing hurt.

Inside, the world turned into damp and dark and the constant press of rock. The air changed first, thickening, cooling, taking on the copper tang of minerals and the sour stink of too many bodies kept close. It was not just goblin. It was fear, sharp as vinegar. It was piss and old blood. It was the animal smell of children who had been crying until they had nothing left and then crying anyway.

Jaime moved ahead of us with her sword low and ready, the point angled down so it would not snag the ceiling. She did not walk like she was afraid. She walked like she was listening to the cave itself, weighing each drip and echo, deciding which ones belonged and which ones lied.

Maximus followed her, shoulders hunched to fit the tunnel, his blade held close to his chest. Ever since we'd seen Mykel farther up the trail, ever since Maximus had tried twice to bull straight at him and Jaime had shoved him back with a snarl and a fist in his shirt, something in Max had been vibrating under his skin. Not energy. Not courage. A kind of frantic, useless electricity that wanted to turn into motion, any motion, because standing still meant thinking, and thinking meant seeing Anya's hand slipping away again.

Bobo came behind him, one hand on the wall as if he could read it by touch. He carried a torch, but he kept it mean and narrow, a thin flame wrapped tight around the stick, more coal than light. The fire obeyed him. It did not flare. It did not spit. It breathed when he breathed, as if they shared lungs.

I brought up the rear because Jaime told me to. "Watch our back," she had said, like that was as simple as keeping your eyes open. Like there were not ten shadows behind every shadow, and a dozen holes in the rock that could vomit goblins into our spine. I tried anyway, jaw clenched, eyes stinging, sword sweating in my grip.

The tunnel dipped, then widened, then dipped again, as if the cave could not make up its mind whether it wanted to swallow us whole or just chew. Water dripped from the ceiling in slow, patient ticks. Somewhere deeper, something scraped along stone, a dragging sound that came and went. Once, faintly, I heard a child cough, then the rough hush of a goblin voice shoving it quiet.

We reached a narrow bend where the ceiling dropped low enough that Jaime had to crouch. She paused, held up two fingers, then closed her fist. Stop. Listen. We did.

At first there was only the cave, the drip, the hush of our breathing, the far-off wind that did not belong down here. Then, beneath it, a rhythm so faint it almost felt imagined. Not a drum, not quite. More like many feet moving in practiced cadence, small steps keeping time with each other. Every so often there was a heavier bump, something being dragged, then lifted, then dragged again.

Bobo's brows drew together. He leaned his head slightly, as if the sound had a direction you could taste.

"What is it?" Maximus whispered, and the words came out ragged, scraped raw.

"Children," Jaime murmured, eyes on the floor. There was a thin smear of mud where the cave's damp had kissed it, and in it were prints, narrow and sharp, and among them scuffs that looked like something had been pulled heel-first. "They're moving them."

Maximus's jaw jumped. The name Anya did not come out this time, but I saw it behind his teeth anyway, pressing at the back of his mouth until it hurt.

Jaime turned her head just enough to look at me. In the torch's thin light her face looked cut from stone, but her eyes gave her away, too bright, too alive. Fear and focus braided together so tight it might have been the only thing holding her upright.

"Same rules," she whispered. "No hero running. No shouting names."

Maximus made a harsh noise, half breath, half protest.

Jaime did not soften. "Your stress won't save Anya," she said, low and sharp. "Your arms will. Your feet will. Your head will. So keep it."

For a heartbeat I thought he would snap at her. He had the look of someone who wanted to bite the world back. Then he nodded once, jerky, and tightened his grip on his sword until the leather creaked. Bobo lifted his torch slightly. The flame bent forward, as if it was eager.

I wanted to tell them I understood. That I could be calm. That I could be steady like Dratmar. The thought nearly made me laugh, and the laugh nearly turned into a sob, so I swallowed it and tasted smoke.

Jaime shifted forward again, and we followed.

The bend opened into a wider passage, then into something that made my stomach drop. The tunnel spilled into a chamber. It was not a grand cavern like the stories, not a glittering cathedral of stone. It was a rough-bellied hollow, low-ceilinged and cramped, the walls sweating moisture. Torches were wedged into cracks around the perimeter, their flames stuttering in the stale air. Smoke clung under the ceiling in a greasy layer, turning the torchlight into a sick haze that flattened faces and made every movement look wrong.

On a raised shelf of rock at the far side, huddled close together like kindling, were the children.

*Too many.*

They were packed shoulder to shoulder, knees to chests, arms locked around themselves. Some had cloth over their mouths. Some had rope on their wrists, tied in pairs. A few sat very still, heads bowed, as if moving might remind the world they existed. My mind snagged on numbers anyway, because it always did when it needed something to hold onto. Close to twenty shapes, and I could not tell if it was all nineteen. I could not tell, from this distance and this smoke, where Anya might be inside that knot.

Maximus saw them and went rigid, whole body tightening as if someone had hooked a chain around his spine.

"Mykel," Jaime breathed, not because she had just noticed him, but because she was using him the way she had told us to, as a marker. A beacon.

And there he was, where we had expected him to be, shoved near the front edge of the huddle, a knot of rope across his wrists, his fine shirt torn and dark with dirt. His face was streaked with soot and tears that had dried into pale tracks. He was smaller than he should have been. He kept his head up anyway, eyes flicking again and again toward the chamber's entrance, searching. Waiting.

When he saw us, he did not shout. He did not even gasp. He just stared, and something in his expression loosened for half a breath, a desperate, fragile relief that made my throat tighten.

Maximus took a step.

Jaime's hand shot out and caught his sleeve, hard, a reminder rather than a rescue. Maximus's shoulders bunched like a bull about to charge, and for a terrifying heartbeat I thought he would rip free and run straight into whatever the cave had laid for us.

Jaime leaned close enough that only he would hear. "Not yet," she hissed. "Use him. Find the path. Then move."

Maximus shook once, like he was trying to fling the urge off his body. He swallowed, eyes fixed on Mykel as if staring hard enough could keep him alive.

Goblins moved around the pen. They were not the frantic, screaming things from the village firelight. These moved like they belonged. Like the cave was their skin. They wore harnesses of leather and bone, teeth strung across their chests, little trophies that clicked softly as they walked. Some had crude helmets made from old pots or hammered plates. A few carried longer blades, scavenged swords with nicks along the edge.

There were traps too, and I only saw them because Jaime's stillness forced me to look properly. Dark holes in the floor, round and hungry. Thin cords stretched low across the ground, almost invisible in the torch haze. A patch of mud that gleamed wrong, slick as oil. The goblins walked through it all without hesitation, stepping in the one safe line that zigzagged between holes and cords as easily as a farmer walking a path he had worn for years.

My mouth went dry.

Jaime's gaze swept the chamber once, twice. Her eyes caught the pen, the safe line, the holes, the goblins' positions. Then, at the near edge of the chamber where the passage widened, she lowered her sword and breathed out through her nose, slow and controlled, like she could force her heartbeat to behave.

"Bobo," she whispered. "Mark it."

Bobo nodded and crouched, pressing his palm near the ground. The flame on his torch shivered, then flowed, not away from him but along the floor like a living ribbon. It did not roar. It did not flare. It crawled forward in a thin, careful line of ember-light, licking stone, slipping into cracks, tracing the contour of the safest route he could guess. Where it hit slick mud it hissed, turning it into steam that curled up in pale strands. The steam clung low, a drifting veil that made the ground easier to read.

Bobo's face tightened with concentration. Sweat beaded at his hairline despite the cold.

"There," he whispered. "It leans that way. Like the fire knows the safe steps."

Jaime nodded, and for a heartbeat I saw Dratmar in her. Not in her shape, not in her youth, but in the way she made decisions like she was cutting rope. Clean. No wasted motion.

"Maximus," she murmured. "With me. We go for the pen. Elric, you cover our flank. You catch anything that slips around. You do not chase."

I nodded because words felt like they would fall apart in my mouth. I set my feet, tried to memorize the ember-line, tried to trust that if I stayed near it, the cave would not open under me.

We moved.

We stepped into the chamber the way you step into cold water, not all at once, not if you want to keep breathing. Bobo's ember-mark guided us, and I placed my boots exactly where Jaime placed hers, exactly where Maximus's weight landed. For a few heartbeats it worked, and the only sounds were our breathing and the damp click of goblin teeth ornaments in the distance.

Then a goblin at the far edge turned its head.

Its ears twitched. Its nose lifted. It sniffed.

It saw us, and its mouth opened on a sharp, rising yip, like a dog calling to its pack.

The chamber woke up. Goblins snapped to attention, heads turning, bodies shifting. A few rose from crouches I had not noticed, tucked behind rocks, hidden in shadow. The children on the shelf flinched as if the air itself had struck them. Mykel's eyes widened, and he leaned forward as far as his ropes allowed, trying to see past the goblins between him and us. Our scouting mission was at an end, combat was our only option.

Jaime did not stop. She surged forward, and Maximus surged with her, and the careful approach became a run whether we wanted it or not.

The first goblin that reached us came low, knife out, aiming for Jaime's thigh. Maximus met it without hesitation. He stepped into it and drove his shoulder into its chest hard enough that I heard breath explode out of it, then chopped down with his sword in a brutal, efficient arc. The blade cracked into collarbone. The goblin went down in a tangle, its knife skittering across stone.

Two more darted in from the left, trying to slip around Maximus's bulk. I caught the first on my sword, steel ringing, my arm jolting with the impact. The second tried to snake in for my ribs, fast and clever, aiming where my leather was thinner. Jaime's blade flashed across my vision and ended it, clean and immediate, before it could turn that cleverness into blood.

"Keep moving," Jaime snapped, and it was not just an order, it was the whole shape of our chance. "Do not stop."

We did not stop. We followed the ember-line through the goblins' net, and Bobo kept his torch tight, flaring heat in short, controlled bursts when a goblin tried to close too near. The air filled with the smell of singed hair and damp stone, with the metallic bite of blood and the harsh, animal yelps goblins made when they were hurt.

I felt the cave amplify everything, turning each scream and clang into an echo that came back at us sharper than it left. It made the fight feel endless, like we were trapped inside a bell.

Through the haze I saw Jaime reach the pen shelf. Maximus stayed on her shoulder, cutting at any goblin that tried to close the gap. Bobo angled his torch to keep the nearest cluster of goblins wary, and Jaime hacked at the crude bindings and ropes, hands moving fast. The children stared at her like she was a story they did not trust. Mykel stared like he was trying to survive on the sight of us alone.

Maximus's gaze kept darting across the huddle, searching for one face, one set of eyes. Every time his attention wavered, Jaime shoved him back into the work with a word or a shoulder, because the cave did not care what we wanted. It only cared what we did.

Then the fight changed shape. A presence stepped into the torchlight from deeper in the chamber, and the goblins reacted to it in a way they had not reacted to us. They pulled back, not in fear but in deference, like dogs making room for the one that bites last. A few slapped hands to their chests, teeth ornaments rattling. One lowered its head. The figure was taller than the others, thick through the shoulders, its skin a darker gray that looked almost blue in the torch haze. It wore a harness of leather and iron plates patched together from a dozen stolen pieces. Around its neck hung a circle of small bones threaded on cord, each one polished smooth by fingers.

It held a sword.

Not a proper one, not forged clean and balanced, but a scavenged blade that had been sharpened and reshaped, its tip wicked, its edge serrated by crude filing. The hilt was wrapped in cloth stained dark.

The Goblin King, or whatever title the thing used in its own mind, stopped near the center of the chamber and turned its head slowly until it found me.

Not Jaime, not Maximus.

**Me.**

Its lips peeled back in something like a grin. Its eyes were bright and clever, and the look it gave me was not surprise. It was appraisal, as if it had chosen the shape of this moment before we ever stepped inside. It pointed its sword toward the tunnel behind me, and two goblins darted into position, moving with practiced ease to block the approach. Then it pointed toward Jaime and the pen, and a different cluster shifted, forming a living line across the chamber. A wall of bodies and knives that tried to cut Jaime, Maximus, Bobo, and the children off from the only clean route back.

Jaime looked up from the ropes, saw the wall forming, and her eyes snapped to mine.

"Elric!" she shouted over the noise. "Hold him!"

My stomach dropped, but I understood at once. If the King kept me busy and the goblins sealed the path, Jaime would be trapped on the far side with a bundle of terrified children and no way to move them. The goblins would not need to kill us quickly. They could simply drag the children deeper while we bled out in the wrong place.

The Goblin King stepped forward, slow and confident. The goblins around it did not swarm. They shifted like a net tightening, each one taking a position that made it harder for me to step sideways, harder to retreat, harder to push through. They even left a narrow strip of clearer ground in front of the King, a pocket where the footing looked better, like the ground itself had been prepared.

A pre-cleared dueling space.

It wanted me there, and it wanted me alone.

Its voice rasped out a few words in broken Common, thick and ugly enough to make my skin crawl. "Little sword," it said, almost amused. "Little holder. Dirty Cat."

I did not answer. I could barely breathe. I lifted my sword anyway, sweat slicking my palm, and set my feet where Bobo's ember-mark was warmest under the stone, because the cave's traps did not care about bravery.

The Goblin King lunged.

Steel met steel with a shriek that made my teeth ring. The impact jarred up my arms to my shoulders. It was stronger than it looked, and fast, and it pressed in immediately, trying to drive me back toward darker patches of floor where the footing looked wrong. I pivoted, remembering Dratmar's barked lessons in the yard, and forced myself to give ground only on my terms. Give it when you choose, not when fear shoves you.

The King's blade flicked up in a clever slash for my wrist. I caught it, barely, the force numbing my fingers. It grinned wider, pleased, and drove again, knee forward, shoulder in, turning the fight into a crush. I took a glancing hit to my thigh that bloomed hot, and I swallowed the sound it tried to pull from me. A goblin darted in at my side, trying to take advantage of the King's pressure. I kicked it back and kept my eyes on the King, because the moment I looked away would be the moment its serrated edge found my throat. The cave amplified every breath and scrape, making the world feel too loud and too close.

Across the chamber, Jaime was cutting ropes and shoving children forward along the ember-line. Bobo's fire flared in short bursts to keep goblins from closing on small bodies. Maximus moved like a storm beside them, violent and focused, except for the way his eyes kept searching the huddle, hunting for Anya with a desperation that made my stomach twist.

The Goblin King pressed again, and our blades locked for a heartbeat, serrated teeth grinding against steel. Its face was close enough that I could smell its breath, rotten and damp. Its eyes flicked past me toward the tunnel mouth, toward escape, toward the path it was trying to cork.

Not for it.

For the children.

It thought it could hold me here long enough for the rescue to fail. It thought it could make me the hinge the whole plan broke on.

My muscles trembled. My arms burned. My breath came in ragged pulls that tasted of smoke and blood. Somewhere behind the wall of goblins, a child screamed. Somewhere else Maximus roared Anya's name like it could drag her into existence by force alone, and the sound clawed at my focus, tried to pull my eyes away. The King felt that flicker and took it like a gift. Dratmar had told us that the enemy always gives a gift, the problem is sometimes we accidentally do the same to our enemies.

It slammed its forehead into mine.

Pain burst white behind my eyes. My skull rang, and my feet slipped a half-step, heel skidding onto stone that felt slick. My stomach dropped as I realized my mistake and jerked my weight back just in time, boot scraping the edge of a dark hole that yawned without sound. The pebble I dislodged clicked once and vanished into black. The Goblin King chuckled, satisfied, because it knew the ground and I did not. It knew every lie in this chamber, every place stone gave way, every thread that would trip a foot and turn a body into meat.

I tightened my grip until my fingers screamed. I forced my feet back onto Bobo's ember-mark, onto safer stone, and lifted my sword again. There was no room for panic here. Panic was a gift. Panic was an opening.

The Goblin King lifted its sword. It stepped forward as if we were alone in the world. In that crush of smoke and bone and torchlight, I understood what it was making me. A single combatant pinned in place by responsibility, a line-holder in a cave that wanted to swallow us whole.

I swallowed blood and smoke and fear, and met its charge.

STEEL MET STEEL AGAIN, and the sound did not just ring, it scraped the inside of my skull like a file.

The Goblin King kept its feet in the clean strip of stone it had claimed, the little pre-cleared pocket where the ground felt almost honest. Almost. I could see the lies anyway now that I knew to look, the faint sheen where dampness pooled too slick, the hairline cracks that were not cracks so much as seams. The King's eyes kept flicking down to my boots as if it could steer me by watching where my weight landed, and every time I shifted wrong by even a thumb's breadth its grin widened, pleased the way Dratmar looked when I fell into a lesson the first time and had to learn it the hard way.

I held my sword up between us and tried to breathe through my nose. The air down here tasted like wet pennies and old piss. My throat kept catching on smoke that should not have been able to follow us this deep, but it lived in my lungs now, the village stitched into me with ash.

The King came at me with a short, brutal sequence, not pretty, not proud, just efficient. A low cut meant to hamstring, a quick lift to catch my ribs when I flinched, then a shove with its shoulder to crowd my space and make my sword feel too long. It wanted me close, where its serrated edge could chew at joints and tendons. I caught the first strike and let the second slide off my blade with a jolt that numbed my forearm. The third hit me in the chest like a battering ram. My heel skidded, and I felt, more than saw, the edge of something wrong underfoot.

The cave's mouth opened in my imagination, black and patient. A hole waiting. A trap that did not care about courage.

I forced my weight forward again, back onto the warmer line of stone where Bobo's ember-mark had kissed the ground. Heat rose faintly through my boot sole, not enough to burn, just enough to remind me where the safer steps lived. The King's eyes narrowed when it saw the correction, and it adjusted immediately, circling to my left, trying to angle me off the line and into a patch of stone that looked slightly darker, slightly slicker.

I did not let it.

I moved with it instead, matching its circle, keeping the ember warmth under me like a tether. It was work in the ugliest way, not the kind of work that made you feel brave, the kind that made you feel like you were hauling a cart out of mud with your teeth.

Across the chamber the fight had become a roar of smaller sounds. Goblins yipped and shrieked, blades clacking against Jaime's and Maximus's. The children made noises too, but quieter, the little trapped sounds of people trying not to be noticed by the world that wanted them.

I could not look away for long. Every time my eyes flicked toward the shelf, the King felt it. It pressed harder, tried to turn my attention into an opening, and if I gave it more than a blink it would take my throat like a prize.

So I stole glimpses the way you steal bread.

Jaime was on the shelf now, half-climbed up, one knee braced against the rock, her hands working fast at knots and rope. She did not waste motion. She cut, pulled, whispered, shoved. The children stared at her with the same wide-eyed disbelief they'd had when the roof goblins fell on us back in the village, like the world had become too strange to trust. Mykel was still where he had been, near the front of the huddle, shoulders trembling with the effort of holding himself upright. His hands were tied, but he leaned forward anyway, eyes fixed on Jaime's blade like he could learn safety by watching.

Bobo stood just off the shelf, torch angled down, flame tight and controlled. He did not swing it wildly. He let it breathe in short, mean flares that made goblins hesitate at the edge of their rush. When one got too close, Bobo would snap his wrist and the flame would lengthen and lick toward the goblin's face, not enough to start a blaze, just enough to remind it that fire bites. The goblin would recoil, and Bobo would pull the flame back in again, contained, obedient, like a dog on a short leash.

Maximus was a storm beside them, but a storm trying to stay inside a bottle. His sword moved with the ugly competence of someone who had trained under Dratmar until his arms shook. He hit goblins hard, he hit them fast, and he kept his body between the shelf and the largest cluster of attackers. Still, even as he fought, his eyes kept darting across the huddle, searching for one face among too many smeared with soot.

I felt the tug in him from here, even without looking. It was the same pull that had dragged him toward Mykel in the tunnel, that had made him try twice to rush and be stopped. It was worse now because the children were right there, close enough that hope could punch him in the ribs.

The Goblin King noticed it too.

It feinted left, then snapped its blade up for my wrist again. I caught it late, steel shrieking, and the force of the impact shoved me a half step. My boot slid on damp stone and my stomach dropped, because the ember warmth was suddenly not under me anymore.

The King's grin widened. It pressed, shoulder first, trying to ride the momentum into a shove. It wanted me on the darker patch. It wanted my heel on the cord I could not see. It wanted my next step to be into a hole.

I dug my toes in and shoved back. My muscles screamed. My thigh wound from earlier cracked open in hot protest. The King's blade rasped along mine, serrations chewing at steel, and sparks flicked in the torch haze. For a heartbeat we were locked, our faces close, and I saw a kind of sick delight in its eyes. It was not just fighting, it was playing with the idea of control.

Then it twisted its hilt sharply, trying to wrench my sword out of line, and at the same time it stomped its foot at the edge of that slick patch. The stomp was not random. It was a signal.

Two goblins that had been hanging back in the shadows lunged toward the ember-line behind me, trying to cork it, trying to cut me off from the safest route. They moved like they knew exactly where to place their feet, which told me the King had taught them, or the cave had, or both.

Bobo flared his torch in a narrow whip of heat. The nearest goblin shrieked as the flame kissed its cheek. It staggered back, hands up, and the second goblin hesitated long enough for Maximus to pivot and drive his shoulder into it, knocking it away from the line.

Maximus could have chased it. I saw the way his body wanted to, the way his weight pitched forward, the way he would have followed that goblin if he was thinking with anything but his blood. Jaime shouted something sharp, a word I could not make out through the echo, and Maximus snapped back into place like a dog called to heel. His jaw was clenched so hard I thought his teeth would crack.

Good. Stay there. Stay with them.

I tried to hold onto that thought as the King pushed again, and my mind kept pulling at the shelf like a wound you cannot stop touching.

The children were moving now, not all at once, not in a stampede, but in a slow, frightened trickle as Jaime freed wrists and cut ropes. Mykel was the first to stand when his bindings came loose, legs shaking. Jaime shoved him forward with her palm on his back, guiding him toward the ember-marked line on the floor, and Mykel did something strange and brave. He did not bolt. He did not scream. He looked down at the ember warmth, then looked back at the other children, and he nodded once, as if he understood his role.

A beacon.

He stepped where Jaime stepped. He pointed with his chin, tiny, sharp movements, showing the next child where to put their feet. It was clumsy, but it worked. One girl followed him, then another. A boy with blood crusted on his nose stumbled, and Mykel caught his elbow and steadied him with a gentleness that did not belong in the Mayor's son, not the one who had strutted around the square like the world owed him applause.

Maybe the cave made everyone honest.

The Goblin King's eyes flicked to Mykel, then to Jaime, then to Maximus. It tracked the movement the way a farmer tracks livestock, calm and calculating. It did not rush to stop them itself. It did not need to. It made a small motion with two fingers, and a cluster of goblins shifted, bodies forming a living line to slow the lane's progress.

Jaime's head snapped up. She saw the line forming, saw the way the goblins were trying to funnel the children off the safe route and into the traps like sheep into a ditch. She shouted something, and Bobo's torch flame tightened again, flaring low across the ground in a thin sheet that forced goblins back from the ember-mark. The heat did not fill the chamber. It did not set the cave on fire. It simply made a boundary line that goblins did not want to cross because they still feared what fire could do to skin.

It bought heartbeats.

That was all we ever had down here, heartbeats. Little coins of time we had to spend perfectly.

The King shoved into me again, harder, and my heel slipped. The slick patch kissed my boot sole like oil. I felt panic claw at my throat, quick and sharp, and I swallowed it and forced my weight forward onto the ember warmth again.

"Not today," I rasped, and I did not know if I was talking to the King or the cave or myself.

The King chuckled, a sound like stones grinding, and answered in broken Common, voice thick with old phlegm. "Little holder learns."

It snapped its sword down in a brutal chop meant to break my guard. I caught it, arms jolting, and my blade dipped dangerously low. The King used the opening to hook its serrated edge up and toward my face. I twisted my head aside and felt the teeth of the blade scrape across my cheek, shallow but enough to sting, enough to leave warmth trickling down toward my jaw.

Pain sharpened the world for a second. It made the torches flare brighter in my vision. It made the echoes cut cleaner. It made me remember Dratmar's voice, his flat bark, his insistence that a fight is not a story, it is math. Position. Breath. Footing.

I tightened my grip until the leather creaked. I shifted my stance to keep my front foot on the ember warmth and my back foot braced against a slight ridge in the stone. I used the ridge like a peg. When the King shoved, I did not slide. My bones held.

The King's grin faltered for the first time. Not fear. Irritation.

It snapped another quick series at me, trying to pry me off balance again. I met it, block for block, the way Dratmar had beaten into us. I was not elegant. I was not strong like Maximus. I was not precise like Jaime. I was stubborn, and stubbornness could be a weapon if you used it right.

A goblin darted in at the edge of my vision, trying to take my leg while the King kept me busy. I kicked out with my heel and felt my boot connect with ribs. The goblin wheezed and stumbled back. I did not look at it again. I could not afford to.

The King pressed me, and in the press I heard Maximus shout something, a word torn out of him raw.

"Anya!"

It hit me like a thrown stone. I could not see her. The huddle was still too tight, too many bodies, too many heads bowed and hair hanging. But Maximus's voice was not guessing. It was not the desperate calling he had been doing since the village burned. That was recognition. That was his eyes finally finding the shape of her in the smoke.

His attention snapped to one point on the shelf, and everything in him leaned toward it.

Jaime swore, a harsh sound that echoed off stone. "Maximus!" she barked, not kindly, not gently, as if she could yank his mind back by force. "Stay!"

He did, barely. His feet stayed. His sword stayed moving. But his eyes did not. His eyes were on Anya now, and I knew, with a sick certainty, that the Goblin King knew too.

The King's gaze flicked past my shoulder. It did not have to turn its head fully. It did not have to lose focus on me. It simply tasted the chamber the way a predator tastes air, and its lips peeled back wider.

There it was.

*The lever.*

It shoved its sword hard into mine again, forcing our blades to lock. The serrations ground against steel, and sparks spat. In the lock it leaned closer, eyes bright with malice, and hissed, almost conversationally, "Girl. Your big dog loves girl. Cat watch big dog die."

My stomach clenched. My ears folded backwards, my tail went straight.

I tried to wrench my sword free, but the King held the bind with practiced cruelty, twisting just enough to keep the teeth engaged. It wanted me stuck. It wanted my attention forced onto it while it played the rest of the chamber like a puppet show.

Behind me, goblins surged toward the shelf, not all of them, just enough, a disciplined wave. They did not charge Bobo's flame. They skirted it, stepping precisely where the ember warmth did not run, using their own safe line that zigzagged close to the traps. Their feet moved without hesitation because the cave was theirs. The line was theirs. The rules were theirs.

Jaime saw the surge. She moved faster, blade flashing as she cut the last knot on Anya's wrists. I caught a glimpse of her, just a glimpse, hair stuck to her face with sweat and soot, eyes hard as flint. She grabbed Anya by the upper arm and yanked her forward, shoving her into the line behind Mykel.

For a heartbeat Anya's face turned toward Maximus, and even through distance and smoke I saw the way her eyes widened. She looked thinner than she had in the village. Her cheek was bruised. Her mouth was split. There was dirt ground into the cut like someone had pressed her face into the cave floor to make her obey. She did not cry out. She did not call his name. She just looked at him, and something passed between them that made my throat tighten. Recognition. Fear. Relief sharp enough to hurt. And beneath it, a warning, because Anya was not stupid and she could see the same thing Jaime and I could.

The goblins were moving to cut her off.

Maximus made a sound that was half growl, half prayer. His sword chopped a goblin down at his feet, but his body was leaning toward Anya now, tugged by a force bigger than discipline.

Jaime's voice snapped again, low and vicious. "Your stress won't save her," she shouted, as if the cave had not already heard it once. "Move your feet where I tell you, or you will kill her yourself."

Maximus's head jerked, as if she had slapped him. He forced his weight back into position, forced his sword to keep moving, forced his breath into his chest. I watched him swallow the urge to run like it was poison.

Good. *Hold.* **Hold.**

The Goblin King felt the tension in him like blood in the water.

It released the bind suddenly and lunged low, not to kill me, not yet, but to drive me. The serrated edge whipped toward my thigh. I tried to pivot, but the slick patch caught my boot again. My foot skidded, and my heart lurched, and the King's blade kissed my leg with a shallow slice that burned like hot wire.

I hissed and stumbled, and the King used the stumble to shove me sideways, off the ember warmth, toward the darker stone.

*No. No, not there.*

I forced myself back, dragging my boot across stone, scraping, feeling the edge of a cord underfoot before I stepped fully on it. I froze for a fraction of a breath, weight balanced, then lifted my foot carefully and set it back on the ember line. The cord quivered. It did not snap. It did not pull. I had not given it enough pressure to trigger whatever it was tied to.

The King's eyes narrowed in irritation again, as if I had stolen a joke it wanted to make at my expense. It snapped at my sword, trying to break the pattern, but I held now, teeth gritted, mind locked on the ember warmth.

Across the chamber, Mykel was guiding children down the line one by one. The lane was moving. It was working.

But it was slow.

Too slow.

Each child took time to convince. Each child had to be shoved, coaxed, carried. Some were too stunned to move. Some were too afraid, bodies locked into place like the cave had turned them to stone. Jaime's hands were on them constantly, pushing, pulling, dragging them into motion, her voice a low stream of command and promise and threat. Bobo kept the goblins wary with small flares, but his sweat was heavier now, dripping off his nose, his jaw clenched with concentration. Fire obeyed him, but it cost him.

Maximus was still fighting beside the lane, and every time Anya took another step, his eyes tracked her. Every time a goblin got too close to her, he twitched, ready to break formation and become the hero Jaime had forbidden him from being.

The Goblin King watched all of it while it fought me, as if it had enough mind to spare for the whole chamber. It made a soft clicking noise in its throat, then barked something in goblin speech. The goblins near the lane shifted in response, not random, not panicked. They moved like a net tightening. A pair stepped onto the safe path the goblins used, not the ember line, and angled toward Anya's position in the procession.

They were not aiming for Jaime. They were not aiming for Mykel. They were aiming for the girl that made Maximus's breath hitch.

A planned cruelty.

Jaime saw them too. Her head snapped up, eyes blazing, and she shoved another child forward hard enough that the boy stumbled and nearly fell. Mykel caught him, steadied him, kept the line moving.

Jaime's hand closed on Anya's shoulder, and she pulled her closer to the inner edge of the ember line, trying to keep her away from the goblins' safe route. "Feet," Jaime hissed at her. "Feet, Anya. Look at the ground. Not at him. Feet."

Anya's gaze flicked toward Maximus again anyway, like a reflex she could not control. Her mouth moved, and I could not hear what she said over the clang of swords, but I saw her shape the word.

*Max.*

Maximus's face changed. Something in him softened and then broke. The Goblin King saw that too. It lunged at me again with a sudden viciousness, not because it had found an opening, but because it wanted me pinned. It wanted my attention trapped in the duel while it set the other pieces on the board. It drove me back a step, then another. My calf brushed stone that felt wrong, and my skin prickled with the certainty of a hole nearby. I twisted, blade up, and caught the King's strike with a jarring impact that made my arm go numb. The King leaned in, shoulder and hip, trying to crowd me and force me into the wrong placement.

I pushed back, teeth clenched, and for a heartbeat our blades locked again. The King's breath washed over me, rotten and damp, and it hissed in broken Common like it was telling a secret.

"Big dog runs," it rasped. "Girl dies. Cat will follow."

My stomach clenched so hard it hurt. Then the King's eyes flicked past me, toward Anya's place in the line, and its grin sharpened into something uglier.

It did not need to say it out loud for me to understand.

It had chosen.

It was going to use Anya to crack Maximus open, and it was going to do it while keeping me occupied, while the goblins moved like trained hands, while the lane stayed narrow and fragile and one wrong footstep could turn rescue into slaughter. I shifted my stance, forcing myself back onto the ember warmth again, anchoring my boots as if the stone could hold my will.

Across the chamber Anya took another step along the line, guided by Jaime's hand, eyes wide, chest heaving, trying to keep her feet where the ember heat ran. Mykel was ahead of her now, looking back over his shoulder, mouthing words without sound, trying to coax the next child forward. The goblins angled closer as Maximus's shoulders bunched.

Bobo's torch flame tightened, ready to flare, but he could not cover every angle at once.

Jaime's face hardened, and she shouted something sharp, a command to move faster, to keep the line going, to not stop for fear.

The Goblin King pressed in on me again, stronger, sharper, as if it could smell the moment it wanted, and my arms trembled under the strain. My breath came in ragged pulls that tasted like blood and wet stone. I realized, with cold clarity, that this was not just a duel. It was a leash. The King was holding me here so the chamber could become its trap. I raised my sword again, met its next strike, and held my ground with everything I had.

Because if I broke, if I slipped, if I let it push me off the ember warmth and into the cave's mouth, then Jaime and the children would be alone with a net tightening around them.

And Anya, the lever the King had chosen, would pay for it first.

# Chapter 8

## ONE FOR ALL

THE GOBLIN KING'S BLADE snapped at mine again, quick as a striking snake, and I caught it with a jarring block that sent a shock up my arms and into my teeth. The serrations on its edge worried at my steel like a saw, scraping and biting, trying to chew my guard apart by inches until my wrists gave out and my hands forgot how to hold. It did not fight like an animal. It fought like a cruel mind with patience, like it knew time was a weapon and fatigue was a certainty.

I refused to give it either.

The ember-warmth under my boots had become a border I would not cross, not because I was brave, but because I had already learned what the cave did to careless feet. The drip-drip-drip of water from the ceiling kept time above us, steady and indifferent, a small clock that made every heartbeat feel measured. Torch smoke clung to my tongue, and my breath came in ragged pulls that scraped my throat raw, but I kept my stance tight and my blade up, forcing the King to meet me on the ground Bobo had marked instead of the darker patches it wanted.

Across the chamber the rescue line was moving, and that was the only reason I could keep breathing.

Mykel was near the front, bound wrists held close to his chest as if he could keep them from shaking by force. He was not leading so much as enduring, but he made himself useful anyway, leaning and gesturing in quick, frantic little motions to help the smaller ones find the safe strip of stone. Jaime's hands were everywhere at once, cutting knots, yanking shoulders, dragging hesitant feet into motion. Bobo kept his torch tight and low, fire breathing small and controlled, flaring just enough to make goblins flinch back without lighting children on fire in the same breath. Maximus guarded the moving knot like it was the last living thing in the world, and every time he shifted his weight to block a goblin's angle, it looked like he was holding his body together by stubbornness alone.

Anya was in the line now.

I saw her between goblin shoulders and smoke haze, and the sight hit me like a fist in the ribs. Rope had chafed her wrists raw. A bruise had gone dark along her cheekbone. Ash clung to her hair, and there was a stubborn set to her jaw that did not belong on anyone her age. She moved like someone who had learned the hard way that stopping meant pain, so she kept going even when her legs trembled, even when her breath came in shallow, panicked pulls that looked like they were tearing at her chest from the inside.

Maximus saw her with the same terrible clarity, and his attention kept snapping toward her like a magnet. Every time he forced himself to look away, it looked like he was tearing muscle off bone. His sword stayed up, his feet stayed where Jaime had told them to stay, but his whole body vibrated with that frantic electricity, the desperate need to be closer, to put himself between her and everything sharp in the world.

The Goblin King noticed. Of course it did.

Its eyes flicked past my shoulder toward the rescue lane, then back to me, and the grin it showed was not joy. It was satisfaction, like it had just found the weakness it wanted most. It leaned into our bind again, shoulder driving forward, trying to turn the duel into a crush. Steel ground on steel. The serrations scraped and whined. My forearms burned as I held it, and I tasted blood where I had bitten my tongue without realizing.

"Big dog," it rasped in broken Common, breath rancid and damp, words wet as if it enjoyed the sound of them. "Big dog bleeds for girl."

I did not answer. I could not spare the breath. I shoved back and forced the blades apart, refusing to let it pin me in place, refusing to let it dictate the rhythm. The King's blade darted up for my wrist and I caught it just in time, the impact numbing my fingers. Its grin widened as if it had been hoping for that, as if it had been collecting small proofs that I could be made to fail.

Then it stamped its foot, once, sharp and deliberate, a rhythm against stone that did not belong to our fight.

A signal.

The goblins around the chamber shifted in response, not chaotic, not panicked. They moved like they had rehearsed this in the dark, like the cave itself had taught them where to step and when. Two of them broke from the pack near the shelf and angled toward the children's lane, taking their own safe route instead of the ember-mark. They stepped around holes and cords without looking down, as casual as men walking a familiar road. One carried a hooked spear with old stains dark on its head. The other had a short blade that looked less like a knife and more like a sharpened shard of stolen metal.

Jaime saw them and barked something sharp, an order that vanished under the echoing clang of steel. Bobo flared his torch in a narrow sheet across the floor to cut off their angle, but the goblins did not rush through heat like fools. They skirted it instead, patient and practiced, choosing the one line where fire could not easily reach. They were not trying to win a fight. They were trying to break the lane, to snag a child, to turn the rescue into a scramble.

Maximus turned half a step, ready to intercept, and the Goblin King used that half step like it was a gift handed to it clean.

It surged into me again, not aiming to kill, aiming to move me, aiming to tilt my balance just enough that I had to spend attention on my own footing. Its serrated edge scraped along my blade and snapped toward my throat in a flicker of silver. I jerked back and felt the cold kiss of air where steel should have been. My heel slid a fraction on damp stone and a cord twitched under the edge of my boot, a thin line that might as well have been a noose.

For the smallest possible heartbeat I froze. I held my weight like a suspended breath, then set my foot down again on warmer stone without tripping the line. My stomach lurched hard enough to make nausea rise, not from fear alone but from the awful understanding of how close I had come to giving the King exactly what it wanted. One wrong step, one snapped ankle, one body on the floor, and the cave would do the rest.

The King chuckled as if it had heard the exact shape of my fear.

It released the bind and sprang back in a way that was almost graceful, then lunged again. I met it and shoved us back into close range because I could not let it have room. If it had room, it could see everything, coordinate everything, steer everything. Up close it at least had to share its attention with my blade, had to respect the fact that I could still bite.

Even so, I felt the moment sliding.

The children were moving, but fear makes bodies hesitate, and a cave full of knives makes legs forget how to work. They bunched because someone stumbled. They bunched because someone turned their head to look back. They bunched because the dark around the torches felt alive, and the ceiling pressed low, and goblin voices hissed like threats in a language that did not need translation.

Anya was caught behind that tightening knot.

The spear goblin took advantage of the bottleneck and darted in, hooking low at ankles, not trying to pierce, trying to snag. A boy went down with a scream that ripped out of him raw and high. Two more children stumbled over him. The lane collapsed into a small pile of limbs and panic, and the goblin with the shard knife slid into the soft chaos behind the spear, moving like a shadow with intent.

Jaime pivoted and drove her sword at the spear goblin's hands. The goblin yanked back in time, but the damage was already done. The line was broken. The children were tangled and crying, and goblins loved tangles because tangles made grabbing easy.

Anya's eyes snapped toward the spear as it lifted again, and the expression on her face changed from fear into something sharper, something that made my throat tighten. She tried to move, but the bodies in front of her and behind her made her pinned. She was trapped in the lane's narrowness, in the simple geometry of too many people in too little space.

The spear rose higher.

This time it was not aimed for ankles.

I saw it and my breath seized so hard it hurt. I tried to surge forward, tried to break the duel, but the Goblin King drove into me and locked our blades again, forcing my attention back onto steel because it knew, it knew, it knew. It was holding me here on purpose. It was making me watch through gaps and smoke while it arranged another loss.

Maximus made a sound that was not a word. It was a raw animal noise, the kind a body makes when thought is too slow for love.

He launched.

Jaime shouted at him, fury and terror tangled together, but he did not listen. He could not. He moved off the ember-mark, off the safe line, off everything we had planned, and for a terrifying heartbeat I thought the cave would eat him before any goblin got the chance. He slammed into the edge of the children's knot like a wave, shoving bodies aside with his shoulder and dragging Anya toward him with one arm while his sword came up in the other.

"Feet, you idiot," Jaime snapped, voice cracking. "Your feet!"

Maximus did not even turn his head. His eyes were only on Anya and the spear.

The spear thrust.

Maximus moved faster than I thought a person could move in a cramped cave with bad footing and worse luck. He shoved Anya behind him and took the spear's point into his side, just under the ribs where his leather was worn thin from training and work. The impact hit him hard enough that his whole body jerked. The sound that came out of him was a choking grunt, shock turning instantly to pain.

Anya screamed his name, and the sound tore through the chamber like ripped cloth.

Maximus did not fall. Not yet. He grabbed the spear shaft with both hands, blood slicking his fingers almost immediately, and hauled the goblin toward him. He drove his forehead into its face with savage force. Bone cracked. The goblin reeled. Maximus wrenched the spear sideways as if he could break it by anger alone and bought himself half a breath of space.

The shard-knife goblin took that half breath and lunged for Anya, slipping around Maximus's wounded side to reach the softer target. It moved quick and low, like it had done this before, like children were easy prey and panic made them slower.

Maximus turned anyway, even as the spear still pinned him, and swung his sword in a brutal sideways cut that opened the goblin's throat. Black blood sprayed in a hot arc and pattered on stone. The creature collapsed, twitching, fingers still reaching for a prize it did not get to keep.

Maximus stayed upright for one more breath, one more stubborn heartbeat, because he refused to fall while Anya was standing.

He shoved her toward Jaime with his free hand. "Go," he rasped, voice wet. "Go with them."

Anya grabbed at him, frantic, fingers shaking so badly she could barely find purchase on his tunic. "Maximus, no. Max, please, please—"

Jaime caught her by the shoulders, hard enough to bruise. Her eyes were blazing, wet with tears she refused to let fall. "Move," she snapped, and it was not cruelty, it was the desperation of someone trying to keep the world from swallowing itself. "You want his blood to mean something, you put your feet on the line and you move."

Anya's face twisted, grief and terror and fury mashed together, but she obeyed because she had already learned tonight that obedience was sometimes the only way to survive. She stumbled back onto the ember-mark. Jaime physically pushed her forward, shoving her into the lane behind Mykel, and Mykel reached back with bound hands as if he could hold her up by touch alone.

The Goblin King watched all of it through the gaps in our duel. I felt it in the way its pressure changed, not heavier, not lighter, but angled. It was no longer trying to simply wear me down. It was positioning, measuring, preparing to break away at the exact moment it would hurt most.

It happened fast.

The King feinted high and smashed the flat of its blade into my forearm hard enough to numb my fingers. My sword dipped and my grip threatened to fail. It followed with a kick to my shin that forced me to step wrong. I caught myself before I tripped a cord, but the stumble was enough. It bought the King what it wanted, the smallest opening that might as well have been a door.

Space.

It slipped past me in a blur, not toward escape, not toward the tunnel, but straight toward the children's lane where Anya had just been forced back into motion. It shoved its own goblins aside as it moved, cutting through its pack like it owned their bones. Its serrated sword rose in the torch haze, and for a heartbeat the edge looked like the teeth of a saw, hungry and eager.

My mind lagged behind the sight. It felt like watching a door slam while my hand was still on the handle.

Then I moved.

I chased, but the cave would not let me run like a sane person. Traps yawned and cords waited and slick patches gleamed wrong, so I had to pick my steps even as my body screamed to sprint. Each choice of foot placement felt like an insult, like the cave was asking me to solve a puzzle while a blade came down toward the one person Maximus could not lose.

Anya turned at the sound, because some part of her sensed danger the way a deer senses wolves. Her eyes widened. She tried to move faster, but there were children in front of her and children behind her, and the lane was narrow and fragile. The Goblin King was almost on her, and the goblins around it surged in reflex, excited by the scent of a clean kill.

Maximus saw it too.

He was swaying where he stood, one hand pressed hard to the wound in his side. Blood pumped between his fingers in thick, dark pulses. His face had gone pale beneath soot, lips tinged blue at the edges, like the cold had found him even in all this heat. He should not have been able to move. He should have been down. He should have been done.

He did not hesitate.

He threw himself forward, wounded body and all, because there was nothing else left in him except that single decision. He hit the Goblin King from the side, slamming into its shoulder and ruining its angle. The King's blade came down anyway, because it was faster than mercy and uglier than fate, but not into Anya's chest.

It bit into Maximus instead.

The serrated edge sank near his collarbone, deep enough that the sound was dull and final, like chopping wet wood. Maximus made a strangled noise that was more breath than voice. His knees buckled. He still did not let go. He clung to the King's sword arm with both hands like he could keep that blade from lifting again by will alone.

Anya screamed, and the lane surged forward in a messy rush as fear finally did what discipline could not. Jaime dragged her, Bobo flared his flame to force goblins back from small bodies, and Mykel hauled the next child by the wrist with shaking arms. The children stumbled and ran and sobbed, feet slapping wet stone as they fled along the ember-mark, away from the shelf, away from the pen, away from the moment turning into a slaughter.

Maximus's fingers slipped.

The Goblin King wrenched its arm free with a savage jerk, and Maximus fell hard onto the stone. His body hit with a wet thud. He tried to rise, he tried, but his arms did not obey. His eyes stayed open anyway, fixed on Anya's back as she was dragged forward by the flow, as if some part of him refused to stop guarding her even when his body had already started to betray him.

The Goblin King turned, not satisfied, not finished.

It stepped toward Maximus with cruel patience, lifting its serrated blade over him as if it were taking its time on purpose, as if it wanted us all to understand exactly what it was about to do. Jaime's scream cut through the chamber, Bobo's fire flared, goblins shrieked and surged, but the King moved like none of it mattered. It had its prey on the ground and it meant to make a point out of the kill.

I reached them too late to stop the lift.

I reached them in time to see the blade poised.

Something inside me went cold and tight, like a cord drawn until it was ready to snap. My lungs forgot how to breathe for a heartbeat. My hands tightened on my sword until the leather bit into my palms. The cave, the traps, the goblins, the dripping water, the smoke, the screams, all of it narrowed until there was only the Goblin King standing over Maximus and the bright, ugly edge of what it meant to do next.

For a moment everything felt lost, as if the mountain had decided to keep its trophies and we had been foolish enough to offer ourselves as extra payment.

Then the Goblin King began to bring its blade down.

THE GOBLIN KING'S BLADE started down.

It was not a fast strike, not at first. It was a measured descent, deliberate enough to feel like mockery, as if the thing wanted us all to understand that it had time, that it owned the chamber and the air inside it, that it could choose when the killing happened and still have room left over to enjoy it. The serrated edge caught the torchlight and turned it into a jagged grin.

Maximus lay on the stone beneath it, blood spreading dark and warm under his ribs. His hand was still half-raised, not enough to stop anything, not even enough to plead. His eyes were open and glassy with pain, but they were fixed, not on the blade above him, not on the Goblin King's grin, but past it, toward the lane where Arya had been dragged forward. It looked like he was trying to memorize her back as if that could be an anchor, as if he could keep her safe simply by watching her leave.

Something inside me went silent.

It was not thought. It was not choice. It was a snapping, a cord pulled too tight for too long, and when it broke, everything that had been holding me together broke with it.

I was there.

I did not remember crossing the trapped stone. I did not remember the cords and the holes and the slick patches that had forced me to count my steps like a coward. I only remember the sound of my boots hitting the warmer line of stone, the sensation of air tearing past my face, and the moment my sword rose on its own, not careful, not practiced, but sure.

Steel met steel.

The Goblin King's blade hit mine with a hard, ringing crack that jolted all the way up my arms and into my skull. The serrations skated along my edge, spitting sparks. The force of the blow shoved me half a step sideways and drove my boots into the stone, but it did not drive me back. It did not drive me off the line. I locked my shoulders, braced, and held.

For an instant I was close enough to the King's face to smell its breath again, that damp rot, that cave-stink, and I saw its eyes widen, not in fear, but in sharp irritation. It had expected a clean end. It had expected a boy too slow to matter. It had not expected me to be there at all.

I shoved.

Not a neat push, not a measured parry, but a full-bodied heave, shoulder and hips and anger all at once. The King staggered a half step away from Maximus, its balance thrown off just enough to break the killing angle. I drove forward again, pressing it back, putting my body between it and the boy on the stone, and I felt something inside me flare so hot and so sudden that the world's edges blurred.

Maximus sucked in a breath behind me, wet and ragged.

Not a cry. Not a word. A breath that sounded like the last coin in a poor man's pocket.

I glanced down without meaning to, just a flicker, just enough to see his lips move and no sound come out. His eyes found mine for a heartbeat, and in them there was no panic anymore. There was only a strange, exhausted calm, like he had already stepped one foot out of the world and was trying to leave something behind with the other.

I did not have time to understand it.

I only understood that he was dying, and that the Goblin King had been trying to make a spectacle of it, and that the cave had already taken too much from us. The thought hit like a hammer, and my vision flushed with a red that did not come from torchlight. It came from something inside me that had been waiting for a reason.

The Goblin King hissed, quick and ugly, and snapped its blade back into guard. It circled, trying to reclaim the center, trying to herd me off the safe stone the way it had tried earlier. It moved like it always had, clever and practiced, but now, for the first time, it looked slightly wrong to me. Its steps were still precise, but they seemed slower, as if the cave itself had thickened around its ankles. Its timing, which had felt like a trap closing, felt like something I could see coming a heartbeat before it arrived.

It feinted high at my face and cut low for my thigh.

I caught it.

I did not even think about it. My blade was there, already in the right place, and the clash did not sting the way it had before. It was just contact. A fact. A door slamming in the King's face.

It tried again, a series of quick cuts meant to draw my guard apart, meant to force my arms to choose wrong. I answered each one, not elegant, not perfect, but relentless, turning its cleverness into noise. Each time it stepped to angle me toward darkness, I stepped with it, refusing to give it the ground it wanted. Each time it tried to bind my blade and chew it apart with those serrated teeth, I yanked free and struck back, forcing it to respect the simple truth that I could hurt it too.

The fight felt different now.

It felt easy, and that should have terrified me, because nothing about a Goblin King should ever feel easy. But my body moved as if a new rhythm had been laid down under my bones, as if something had decided it was finished with hesitation. My breath came hard, but it was not ragged with fear anymore. It was hard with effort, with drive, with the kind of purpose that does not ask permission.

The King swung again, a brutal overhead chop meant to break my guard by force alone.

I stepped inside it.

The blade whooshed past my shoulder close enough that I felt the cold of it. Before it could recover, I drove my pommel into its jaw with savage intent and heard teeth click together. It staggered, head snapping to the side. I did not let it reset. I struck again, a cut across its forearm that made dark blood bead and then spill. It snarled, more animal now, less amused, and it swiped at me with its free hand, claws aiming for my eyes.

I ducked and shoved my shoulder into its chest.

It went back another step, boots scraping, trying to find its safer strip of stone, trying to reclaim the pocket it had prepared. I did not give it space to breathe. I stayed close, tight as a collar, turning the duel into a collision. It had wanted to make me a hinge. It had wanted to pin the whole rescue on my weakness. Now I made it carry my weight instead.

Somewhere behind me, the chamber was chaos. Children sobbed and stumbled. Jaime shouted until her voice cracked, forcing bodies forward along the ember-mark. Bobo's fire flared in hard, controlled bursts that shoved goblins back without turning the lane into a pyre. Goblins shrieked and surged in broken waves, some trying to fight, some trying to grab, but the shape of them had changed. The discipline had started to fray. Their movements had more panic in them now, more hunger than plan, as if the King's certainty had been a thread holding the whole nest together.

I did not look. I could not.

The Goblin King was in front of me, and Maximus was behind me, and I could feel the thinness of time, the way it stretched and threatened to snap.

The King tried to retreat again, and I chased it with violence in my feet. It slipped on the slick patch near the edge of the chamber, the same place it had tried to force me earlier, and its balance faltered, only for a fraction, but fractions mattered now. I took that fraction and made it mine. I drove my sword into its shoulder, not a clean thrust but a hard punch of steel that sank deep enough to stop it in place.

It screamed.

The sound was high and ugly, echoing off stone, and it clawed at my blade, trying to wrench it free. Its blood ran hot down the metal and onto my hands. I could feel it slicking my grip, trying to make my fingers fail, trying to turn the weapon itself into a hazard.

I leaned in, face close enough to see the strain in its eyes.

It looked smaller in that moment. Not physically, but in a way I could not explain. Its cleverness was still there, its cruelty still sharp, but it suddenly felt like something I could break, like a door that had been locked all my life and had finally been kicked hard enough to splinter.

I ripped the sword free and struck again.

The cut was not pretty. It was not heroic. It was honest. It bit into the side of its neck, and the King's scream turned into a wet gargle. It swung at me wildly, the careful duelist gone, the planner reduced to flailing survival. I stepped aside and brought my blade around again, a second chop, harder than the first.

The Goblin King dropped to one knee.

It tried to rise. It tried to lift its serrated sword again, but its arm shook, and its fingers did not obey the way they had. I could see its gaze flick toward the tunnels, toward the dark places it could vanish into. I could see the decision forming, flight replacing dominance.

I did not let it choose.

I drove forward and ended it.

My sword went in with a dull, final resistance, and when I pulled back, the King toppled onto the stone like a puppet whose strings had been cut. Its blade clattered beside it, ringing once, and that single ring seemed to change the air. Goblins nearby froze, heads snapping toward the fallen body. Their eyes flashed white in the torch haze. The ones who had been pressing toward the children hesitated, and in that hesitation their courage broke.

They ran.

Not all at once, not orderly, but in sudden skittering bursts, diving toward side tunnels, scrambling over each other, tripping over their own safe lines because panic made them forget the cave's rules. Some vanished into holes with shrieks that cut off abruptly. Others threw themselves down passages without looking back, desperate to be anywhere that was not this chamber with a dead King and humans still standing.

Jaime seized the change like a weapon. Her voice cut through the noise, raw and furious. "Out. Keep moving. Do not stop."

The children surged along the ember-mark in a messy rush, fear turning into speed now that the net had loosened. Mykel hauled the next child by the wrist with shaking arms. Anya was among them, moving, stumbling, catching herself, looking back even as Jaime shoved her forward. Her face was wet and filthy, and her eyes were fixed on the place where Maximus had fallen, a grief so raw it looked like it might become hate if it did not have somewhere to go.

Bobo was already down beside Maximus, torch angled awkwardly away so it would not spill flame onto flesh. His hands were slick with blood. He pressed them hard against the wound as if he could physically hold the life in, as if force of will could stitch torn flesh. His mouth moved, words I could not hear over the ringing in my ears.

Maximus's chest rose, then fell, shallow as a tide that had run out too far. His eyes were still open, unfocused now. When Anya looked back, his gaze seemed to catch her for a heartbeat anyway, like some last part of him refused to stop guarding her.

Then the sound came, distant at first, rolling through the tunnels like thunder trapped in stone.

Human voices.

Boots scraping and slamming against rock, heavy and urgent, coming fast.

Torches bobbed in the far passage like a line of angry stars. Steel flashed in their hands. The fleeing goblins heard it too, and this time the fear that seized them was not the twitchy fear of prey. It was real, full-bodied terror, the kind that turns legs into frantic messes.

Dratmar's voice hit the chamber like a thrown hammer. "Push in. Hold your ground. Push in."

The villagers flooded the passage behind him, faces smeared with soot, eyes wild with grief and exhaustion. They carried whatever they had been able to grab in the dark, axes and pitchforks and woodcutting blades, a hammer blackened from a forge that was probably ash now. They did not look like an army. They looked like people who had been broken and decided, together, that they were done being broken quietly.

Dratmar led them like he led us in the yard, sword up, one good eye burning. He took in the scene in a single sweep, the children moving out, goblins scattering, the dead King on the stone, Bobo kneeling over Maximus.

His face tightened once, a small hard movement like a fist closing.

Then he moved.

He carved into the remaining goblins with the same brutal efficiency I had always feared in him, and the villagers followed his momentum, turning the chamber into a press of human fury. Goblins shrieked and died. Some slipped away into side tunnels only to slam into villagers at the mouth and get dragged down. The cave swallowed screams. The torches smoked. The air tasted like iron and soot and victory that did not feel clean.

Jaime kept the children moving toward the tunnel mouth, her hand on shoulders, her voice on a razor's edge, refusing to let anyone stop long enough to get grabbed again. Anya twisted once, tried to pull back toward Maximus, and Jaime caught her by the arm hard enough to bruise.

"Not now," Jaime hissed, eyes bright with tears she refused to spend. "You live first. You mourn after."

Anya's face crumpled, and she obeyed, because her legs were still working and that meant she still had something to obey with.

I stood over the Goblin King's corpse, chest heaving, sword dripping. My hands felt distant, like they belonged to someone else, and my breath was loud in my ears which burned from multiple knicks to the soft thin cartilage, drowning out everything I should have been hearing. The rage that had carried me here did not leave all at once. It lingered, hot and sharp, looking for another target, looking for another reason. The blood soaking into my fur was hot and burning, but also seemed to calm me. My enemy bled.

Dratmar reached me, boots splashing in dark blood. He looked at the fallen King, then at me, then past me to Maximus on the stone.

"Elric," he said, voice rough as gravel.

I tried to answer and found my throat too tight for words. My head nodded once, small and useless.

Dratmar's gaze stayed on Maximus. "Get the children out," he ordered, not to me alone, but to the room, to everyone who could still move. "Now. We do not lose anyone else to this damned hole."

His one good eye flicked back to me for a heartbeat, and there was something steady in it, something like a hand bracing the back of my neck. "Stay upright," he said quietly. "Stay upright until they're clear."

I did, because standing was the only thing holding me together.

Behind us, the goblins fled into the villagers' blades, and the cave swallowed their last frantic shrieks. Ahead of us, the children moved toward the mouth of the tunnels, guided by ember warmth and bruised hands and the hard refusal in Jaime's voice.

Bobo's hands would not stop shaking as he pressed them to Maximus's side. Maximus's breathing was a thin, broken thing, and every rise of his chest looked like a question the world might refuse to answer.

The people were being saved.

Someone had died for it, or was dying still, and the cost sat in the chamber heavier than smoke.

# Chapter 9

## FUNERAL WEIGHT, TRAVELING FEET

DAWN TOOK ITS TIME finding us in that valley. The light had to climb over the black shoulders of the mountains and filter past the low mist that clung to the stones. When it finally reached my eyes it did not feel like morning. It felt like someone had pulled a thin sheet over a body and called it enough.

I woke to the smell of blood already drying and the sour stink of goblin flesh. My cheek rested against cold rock. Every part of me remembered pain that was no longer there. My hands came up on their own and ran along my ribs, my stomach, my throat. The skin was smooth, only smeared with dirt and ash. No torn meat. No broken bone. Just the ache of having been used too hard.

Voices moved around me, low and steady. Metal scraped stone. A horse snorted and stamped. I turned my head and the cave mouth swam in and out of shape, bright with thin daylight. Dark shapes crossed it, men in North Guard colors, armor dulled by travel dust. They moved among bodies, goblin and human both, lifting and sorting them like firewood. The dead made a soft thudding sound when they were set aside. I knew that sound. It sat deep in the ear and did not go.

My tongue felt thick. When I tried to speak, only a grunt came out. Someone turned. A weight knelt beside me. A hand, rough with old scars, slid in under my shoulders and lifted me very gently.

"Elric," Dratmar said. "Easy, lad. Easy now."

His face hung over mine, lined and tired. New lines, it seemed. His beard was darker with blood near the chin, not his own by the way he moved. I blinked up at him and tried again.

"What... happened?"

He studied me a moment, his eyes moving as if counting things only he could see. The air around us came into clearer shape. We were just inside the main cavern, near the wall, away from the worst of the bodies. Our packs were stacked in a weary pile. A lantern guttered on a rock. The Goblin King's stone chair lay toppled, its back broken.

"We won," Dratmar said. There was no pride in his voice, only fact. "Goblins scattered or dead. Children safe. North Guard came just in time to make a show of it." He nodded past my shoulder. "How much do you remember?"

I closed my eyes. There was the rush down the passage, Anya's scream somewhere ahead, the Goblin King's stink like rotten bark. Maximus stepping in front of her. The sound of metal going into him, thick and wet. His weight hitting the stone. Anya's hands on him. My own breath, ragged, hot. After that, things broke apart. A flash of green torchlight. A roar that rattled my teeth. Or was that the mountain? My own fingers digging into rock that felt soft, then shattering under them. Fire, but not on my skin. In it.

I opened my eyes again. They stung.

"I remember him," I said. "Maximus. Then nothing. Did he..."

My voice did not want that last word. It came out in a dry whisper.

Dratmar did not answer at once. His hand stayed on my shoulder. It was a soldier's grip, meant to hold a line.

"Aye," he said. "He's gone, lad."

The words were simple. They did not crash over me. They stepped up and sat down in my chest. I turned my head slowly, as if sharp motion might cut something worse inside, and saw the stretcher.

It was just an old North Guard shield with spear shafts lashed along the sides. Maximus lay on it, wrapped in two cloaks. A lock of his hair showed where Anya had not tucked it in right. It was still the same dull brown. His big hands were folded, but not the way priests did it in stories. One thumb stuck out crooked. His boots were gone, set at the end of the stretcher, soles worn thin from his love of pacing when he talked. In that moment I hated the sight of those boots more than I had ever hated a goblin's face.

Anya knelt beside him, her head bowed, her hair hanging like a curtain. Her hand lay on his chest where the wound would be beneath the cloth. Jaime sat near her, back against the cave wall. She had her arms drawn around her knees, her shoulders tight. Her eyes were open and clear, but they saw something far away.

North Guard men moved around them, careful in that way hard men get when they enter an honest grief. They knew when to speak and when to hold their tongues. These had seen battle and worse. Their captain, a square-faced woman with a broken nose, spoke quietly with one of the villagers who had come with the patrol. I saw Old Harn, the miller, standing with them and staring at the dead goblins with a mixture of fear and some sour satisfaction.

I pushed myself up on one elbow. My arms trembled but held.

"How long was I out?" I asked.

Dratmar watched my movement and did not try to force me back down. He had never been one to coddle us.

"Some hours," he said. "You dropped like a stone when the last of them fell. We thought you were gone at first."

He hesitated. That alone told me whatever came next was not easy for him.

"Elric," he went on, voice low. "Do you feel... anything strange? Any pain? Heat?"

"Only tired," I said. I swallowed. My throat tasted of smoke and old bile. "And wrong. Like I'm walking around with my skin on the wrong way."

He snorted once, not a laugh, more a breath trying to find a softer shape.

"Fits what we saw," he said. "Look at your arms."

I glanced down. My sleeves were torn. Under the grime my forearms showed pale and unmarked, except for the thin white scars I already knew. No burns. No cuts. Yet I remembered blades. Claws. I had felt steel bite me, sure as rain on my face.

"It all closed," he said. "Right in front of us. Like watching wet clay dry and crack. And you... lad, you shone. Light came out of you. Not like a lantern. More like furnace coals when you open the iron door." He shifted, finding words that a village boy would understand. He knew his audience even then. "All your veins lit up, under the skin. The goblins ran from you. The big one tried to, but you caught him."

The Goblin King lay where he had fallen, near the broken chair. His thick neck was twisted at a bad angle. His jawbone hung on only one side. The stone around his body was crushed as if something heavy had dropped from a great height.

"I did that?" I asked.

"Aye."

I touched the stone with my fingertips. It was pitted and scored. There were prints there, faint but clear, the shapes of fingers sunk in as if the rock were fresh bread. They matched my own hand if I spread it just so. I drew my hand back as the North Warch Captain walked over. Her armor plates clicked softly. She glanced at me, then at Dratmar.

"This the one?" she asked.

Dratmar nodded once.

"Name?" she said.

"Elric," I said. My voice sounded small in my ears. I had spoken to soldiers before when they passed through Old King's Walk on patrol. I had always felt younger in front of them. Just then I felt like a boy caught stealing from the village storehouse.

She grunted.

"You gave us a light to steer by in the dark," she said. "Some of the lads thought they were seeing one of the old spirits come down out of the mountain."

Her eyes ran over me. They were not kind or unkind. Just measuring, as if weighing a sack of grain.

"You hurt anywhere?" she asked.

"No," I said.

"You keep it that way," she said. "Whatever trick you did, save it for when you must." She looked at Dratmar again. "We'll have words at the village, old dog. Lot in this that smells off."

Dratmar's jaw tightened. "That it does," he said.

She nodded once and turned away, already calling to her men to start loading the dead. Dratmar waited until she was out of earshot. Then he leaned closer.

"You heard her," he said. "Not one word of this light or healing to anyone not in this cave. Not to the villagers. Not to the priest when he starts sniffing. Not to any of those neat-sleeved merchants who ask too many questions. You understand me, Elric?"

"Why?" I said. It came out sharper than I meant. My head felt fogged, but a spark of anger pushed through. "You think I did it on purpose? Think I knew I could?"

His eyes flashed.

"Mind your tone," he said. Then the heat went out of his voice and left it flat. "I don't know what you did. I don't know what you are. I know this. Men fear what they don't understand. And fearful men do cruel things they call necessary. I've seen it with witches and hedge-healers and any soul who was born different. You keep your head down. You stay alive. That comes first."

He spoke like he was telling me how to hold a shield or swing a blade. That was how survival sounded in his mouth. Instruction, not comfort. I thought of the way the goblins had looked when I walked toward them, if that was not something I imagined. The way the air had thickened, the heat in my chest. I was not sure I wanted any part of that to be real. But the crushed stone under my fingers did not care what I wanted.

"Will it happen again?" I asked.

Dratmar looked at me, and something in his eyes had gone far behind the cave for a moment.

"I don't know," he said. "Best pray it doesn't. And if it does, pray we're the only ones close enough to see."

He squeezed my shoulder once and rose with a soft groan of old joints.

"Can you stand?" he asked.

I nodded. My legs swung under me like someone else's for a breath, then found themselves. The world tilted, steadied. I took in the cavern as one picture instead of broken pieces.

The North Guard were efficient. Goblin bodies were dragged toward the back where a deep pit yawned, maybe a natural sink, maybe dug. Two men and a woman heaved them in without ceremony. No one wanted to heap stones for goblins. The smell was getting worse as the day warmed.

The freed village children huddled near the wall, wrapped in spare cloaks. They were as quiet now as they had been loud in the village square. Their eyes were too big in their small faces. One or two were biting their knuckles to keep from making sounds. A Guard woman knelt with them, passing out water from a skin and broken bits of hardbread. They took each piece like it might vanish.

Jaime's face tilted toward me as I stepped closer. Her eyes were rimmed red, though I had not seen her cry. Her sword lay across her knees, its tip resting on the ground.

"You look like boiled leather," she said. Her voice aimed for wry but came up short.

"You don't look much better," I said. My throat hurt putting that much air to use. It still felt good to try. Words were how we kept things normal.

Her gaze flicked to Dratmar.

"He tell you?" she asked.

"Some," I said.

She looked back down at her sword.

"It was like something out of those old fireside tales," she said, softer. "Light pouring from you. Flesh knitting while blades bounced off. I thought you were going to fly or crack the world open."

Anya turned at that. Her face was streaked with grime and salt. Even with her eyes swollen, she had that sharp little-sister look, as if hunting for someone else's foolishness to point out.

"He saved us," she said. "Saved me. That's what he did."

Her hand still lay on Maximus's wrapped chest. She had not moved it since I woke. Her fingers were pale where she gripped the cloth.

"He also terrified a pack of goblins and half a patrol," Jaime said. There was no meanness in it, just plain speech. "Fright like that tastes a lot like awe."

"I don't remember doing anything," I said.

"That doesn't make it less real," she replied. "And it doesn't matter much how it felt to you. It matters how others saw it. Word like that spreads, Elric. Folk love a marvel, right up until they don't."

Dratmar nodded once, a sharp little dip of his chin to show she had hit the mark.

"Talk later," he said. "For now we put this place to use."

He turned from me and walked to the Goblin King's toppled throne. The stone had been roughly carved, the back high and narrow, like the broken tooth of some great beast. At its base, tucked almost out of sight, was a low opening.

"We found this when we dragged him off it," Dratmar said over his shoulder. "Hole goes back to a little chamber. Hoard of some sort. Goblins like to keep shiny things near where they sleep. Jaime, you and Elric take a look. Anya stays with Maximus."

Anya shook her head once in a small, hard gesture.

"I'm not leaving him," she said.

"No one asked you to," Dratmar replied. He did not soften the words. That was his kindness sometimes. "Jaime. Elric. Go."

We crouched and ducked into the hole. The air inside was cooler, stale with old sweat and metal. Someone had set a lamp in the passage. Its light shivered on the walls, catching on veins of dark ore. The space opened into a small hollow no larger than Harn's grain shed. Piles of scrap metal and bone lay off to one side, the chewed remains of meals. The other side was given over to treasure, if one had goblin tastes.

There were coins, of course. Copper mostly, a few silvers, scattered like spilled grain. A dented helm. A cracked shield with a faded crest I did not know. Broken bits of armor, none of it goblin sized, tangled like fish in a net. More interesting were the crates.

Three of them stood stacked neat as any merchant's, good pine planks reinforced with iron bands. Another had already been pried open. I stepped over to it and looked inside. Rows of short swords lay nestled in straw, their blades oiled and wrapped in cloth. We were used to village smithing, Dratmar's old work hammering farm tools and simple blades from scrap. These swords were another thing. Balanced. Clean. They looked like the ones the North Guard carried, though without the royal stamp.

Jaime ran her hand over one of the closed crates. Her fingers traced the inked mark on the side. A circle with three wavy lines running through it like water. I had seen it on casks that came up from the river trade.

"Merchant's seal," she said. "From the south-coast routes. My father used to make us memorize the common ones. Said it was the same as learning faces."

Her hand stilled. Her shoulders went tense in a way I knew well. It was how she stood when she had found something that fit a shape she had been holding in her mind.

"Elric," she said. "There."

She pointed at a leather satchel half-buried under a heap of chainmail. The bag was scuffed but well-made, the buckles of good brass. A scrap of blue cloth still clung to one strap. I had seen that exact shade once before, in a faded cloak folded at the bottom of Jaime's chest back home. It had belonged to her father. She did not rush to it. She walked slow, as if afraid a quick move might scare it away. Her hands lifted pieces from the pile. A broken helm. A bent spearhead. A leather belt, stained dark a third of the way up. Each item came away and was set aside with careful, automatic movements, the body knowing what to do while the mind lagged.

She reached the satchel at last and lifted it free. The strap tore where it had been trapped. She turned it over. There, on the flap, stamped into the worn leather, was the same merchant's mark as on the crates. Circle and three lines. Her breath left her in a short sound. Not quite a sob. More like the noise someone makes when they sit down hard without meaning to.

"Jaime," I said.

She swallowed and worked the buckle. Her fingers, that could tie bowstrings and catch knives in the air, fumbled once. Then the flap came open. Inside were papers, folded and refolded many times. A small leather-bound book. A ring on a thong of cord. The ring caught the lantern light. It was plain iron, but inlaid around the band in brass were three small knots joined together. I had seen it carved on the beam above Jaime's bunk. She had done that herself, with a paring knife she had borrowed and not returned. Her hand shook as she picked it up. She held it near her face. For a moment the hard set of her jaw broke. Her lips trembled. She did not cry, not like Anya could, all at once and loud. She just made her face very still, the way a person does when they will not let themselves fall apart in front of witnesses.

"It's his," she said. Her voice sounded like it belonged to someone else. "He never took it off, except to spar."

She slid the ring onto her little finger. It hung loose, but she curled that hand into a fist and it stayed.

I picked up the folded papers. The top one had writing on it in a neat, compact hand. My letters were decent, thanks to the priest who came twice a year and tried to beat scripture into us, but I was slow. Jaime, on the other hand, could strip words like bark off a stick.

"Here," I said, holding them out.

She wiped her face with the heel of her hand, took the sheets, and held them to the lamp. Her eyes moved left to right, then back again, faster as she found the rhythm of the writer.

"It's from him," she said after a moment. "Addressed to me. Never sent."

She cleared her throat once. When she read aloud, her voice firmed.

"'Jaime. If this finds you, it means I have finally learned to write and walk at the same time, and a courier has not run off with my coin to see the world on my purse. I imagine you taller now. Angrier, if that is possible. Still stealing knives from decent folk. Know first that I did not leave because of you.'"

She paused. Her eyes skipped ahead, but she backed up and read the line again, softer.

"'Know first that I did not leave because of you.'"

Her mouth pressed together. She went on.

"'Work took me north. Better work than caravan guard, I thought. Someone has been arming goblin tribes near the old passes. Well-made steel in filthy hands. Small bands at first. Test raids. I took coin to track the source and send word back south. I told myself it would be one season. Two at most. I told myself there would be time later to fix what I broke with you and your mother. I was wrong about many things in my life. I pray I am wrong about this danger at least, and that by the time you read this it will be done and you will have no need to forgive me for my absence.'"

The cave felt smaller while she read. Even the distant sounds of the Guard men moving seemed to quiet. Jaime turned the page slowly.

"'Their blades bear merchant marks I have seen before in honest trade. Someone in the river cities sells to both sides of the mountain, and they do not care where blood spills so long as the coin runs.'"

She glanced at the crate beside her, then back to the letter.

"'If I do not return, go to Old King's Walk. There is a man there named Dratmar, once of the North Guard, who owes me more than one favor and more than one beating. He will not say it gladly, but he has a good heart. Greener than he thinks. He will see you fed and fed firm. Trust him. Trust the boy he keeps close who looks at the horizon as if it has insulted him. There is iron in that one. I would like to have put a sword in his hand myself.'"

She stopped. The lamp flame jumped a little. I realized I had been holding my breath.

"He wrote about me?" The question came before I could weigh it. My skin felt too tight for my bones.

Jaime gave a small huff that might have been a laugh in an easier world.

"He writes about everyone," she said. Her thumb rubbed the edge of the paper. "Draws them in like he did marks on a map." She looked back at the sheet and kept reading, quieter so that some of the words blurred.

"'If the worst comes and you find this among my things, know again that I did not stop loving you, stubborn girl. I only stopped knowing how to carry that love and the work both. One of them was always going to fall. I chose wrong. This is a poor inheritance. Papers and old steel. But there is a better world for someone if we stop these raids before they turn into something larger. Perhaps that can polish the shame a little.'"

The last lines were scribbled faster, like he had been writing on horseback.

"'If by grace we are in the same room again when you read this, you have my permission to strike me once across the jaw before you speak. It is no less than I deserve. After that, I will ask if you are eating enough and if you still steal knives. I hope the answer to both is yes. All my failed best to you. Your father, Derrin.'"

The words hung in the lamplight. Jaime folded the letter smaller than it had been, edges worn from all the times he must have read it over and not sent it. Her fingers lingered on the crease.

"He didn't abandon us," she said. She did not look at me. She looked at the leather of the satchel, as if it might hold his answer. "He chose something else. Chose wrong, but not to forget."

"Feels different?" I asked.

"Yes," she said. The word carried a weight that pulled something down through her, setting it more solidly in the world. "Yes, it does."

She slid the folded note into her own jerkin, tucked behind the leather over her heart. Then she reached into the satchel again and pulled out the small book. She flipped through it, pages covered in cramped writing and draw lines, some smudged by damp.

"Journal," she said. "Routes, names, places, buyer marks. Look."

She turned it so I could see. One page had a careful list of symbols. The river-merchant seal. A jagged star. A crowned hammer. Beside each were notes. The circle and three lines had a single, harder underline.

"This is the same mark," she said, tapping the crate. "He traced the crates back to someone south, then followed the trail up here. He was close. If his things are here, he probably..." She stopped. Her throat worked. She did not finish the thought.

"Jaime," I said. "We don't know that he died here. He could have lost the bag. Been captured, then escaped."

She gave me a look that said not to waste her time with soft straw.

"There's dried blood on the strap," she said, flipping it over. The underside was dark and stiff. "Older than yesterday. The goblins would have taken a live man with them to their meals. This was left where they piled things to keep." She sighed through her nose.

"It's all right. I've been waiting to hear he was dead for years. Having a place to pin it to is almost a kindness."

She slipped the journal into her belt.

"It explains the goblins," I said, nodding at the crates. "They didn't forge those blades. Someone gave them steel and food and a sense of direction."

Jaime moved to the next crate and pried at the lid with a short sword. The nails squealed in the wood. Inside were more weapons. Axes with double heads for cleaving shields. Bundles of crossbow bolts, all tipped with well-shaped iron.

"Enough to arm a small company," Jaime said. "And black powder kegs, see? For blasting walls or mines." She pointed to two clay jars packed in straw at the bottom. "This isn't some goblin raiding party gone lucky. Someone spent real coin to give them teeth."

We opened the third crate. It held sacks of grain, salt meat, dried peas. Supplies meant to last men, not beasts, through a mountain winter. Each sack had the same mark.

She ran her hand along the edge of the wood again.

"I told you," she said. "My father always said the trouble that kills you rarely walks on two legs alone. There's always coin behind it. Always someone in a chair far away, fat and comfortable, counting how much blood they bought."

"And he followed that trouble up here," I said. "Then vanished."

She nodded once, jaw tight.

We gathered what needed gathering. Jaime took the journal and a few loose papers that looked like maps of passes and trails. I scooped coins into a spare pouch, leaving the scattered copper. It felt strange to take money from a pile beside packs that had belonged to other dead men, but Dratmar always said coin was the only thing that held its shape after trouble.

We crawled back into the larger cavern. The light from outside seemed harsher after the lamp glow. Dratmar stood conferring with the Guard captain about how many bodies to burn and how many to bury, given the rocky ground and the time before night. His hand chopped the air once. Barely. The captain nodded.

Anya had not moved much. She looked up when we approached. Her eyes clung to Jaime's face, then to the ring now resting on her little finger.

"You found something," she said. It was not a question.

Jaime eased herself down beside Maximus's shield-stretcher. She placed one hand gently on the cloaked form, just above Anya's.

"My father's ring," she said. "And his work. He was tracking who sent these." She jerked her chin at the crates behind us. "He got as far as here."

"And then?" Anya asked.

"And then goblins won a throw," Jaime said. She did not say more. Anya inhaled, shaky.

"At least you know," Anya whispered. "I don't even know if my real parents died in their sleep or on a road like this." Her hand tightened on the cloth. "All I know is Dratmar found me in a crate half-rotten with other children."

"Knowing doesn't feel like much just now," Jaime answered, just as quiet. "But it's something that isn't a hole."

WE BUILT LITTERS FOR the human dead. There were four beside Maximus. Two were North Guard. One was a trapper we recognized by his heavy coat, though his face had been taken by claws. The last was a youngster from the next village over, no more than twelve, who had followed the searchers without permission and paid for it. His name was Berit. He had tried to show off in front of Anya once by juggling apples and dropped all three. That was how my mind marked him, not with the way his limbs now lay too loose.

The captain assigned two men to each litter, rotating them as we walked. Dratmar, of course, insisted on taking one end of Maximus's himself. I moved to the other without asking. Jaime took charge of the crates from the hoard, selecting one to bring and marking the others with charcoal so the Guard could send for them later.

The freed children walked in the middle of the line, ringed by North Guard on all sides. Anya walked beside Maximus, one hand always resting on some part of the cloth as if anchoring him to the world for as long as she could.

We stepped out of the cave. The day was bright now, though the sun was thin so high in the mountains. The sky had that clear, cold look that cuts more than it warms. Smoke still drifted from the mouth where the Guard had burned piles of goblin debris.

The path down was narrow, cut by centuries of water and feet. We moved slow. Every now and then a loose stone would skitter down ahead of us, bouncing and pinging off the rock. Each sound was sharp, too bright. I felt like I was walking through a painting, my body doing what it knew to do while my mind watched from a few steps back.

We did not talk much. Breath went to walking and bearing. Once, when we had to pause to let a mule pick its way around a switchback, Anya spoke without looking up.

"I should have died," she said. Her voice was calm. That was worse than if she had wailed.

Dratmar, balancing the stretcher on one broad shoulder, grunted. "That's foolishness," he said.

"It was me he went in front of," she said. "Not you. Not Jaime. Me. He jumped in front of that blade because I was there. If I hadn't run, if I'd stayed like you told us, he'd still be alive." Her words came out flat and even. That evenness scared me more than any storm of anger would have.

Jaime, walking behind, shifted the crate she carried and stepped up close.

"He wouldn't have stayed," she said. "You know him. If you'd been safe in the village and he'd heard children taken, he'd have run anyway. Blade had his name on it, Anya. Some things do."

"That's a priest's talk," Anya snapped. A flicker of heat showed through the calm, then doused itself. "They say 'His time had come' when they don't want to say 'We failed him'."

"You did not fail him," Dratmar said, each word landing like a hammer on an anvil. "He made a choice. You had a choice too. You chose not to freeze and die in a corner. You fought. You are still fighting by putting one foot after another on this cursed path. Don't insult him by saying his death was a waste."

Anya bit her lip until blood beaded. Her eyes stayed on the path.

"He joked," she said, almost to herself. "He made that stupid joke about dying for something grand one day. Said he'd rather go down in a ballad than in a ditch." A harsh little laugh broke from her. "This wasn't a ballad. It was a hole full of goblin stink and no one singing."

I thought of the way his body had jerked when the sword went in. The noise he had made that was too small for a man his size. I said nothing. Some things were too big to touch with words.

We reached the lower slopes by afternoon. The air grew thicker, though my chest still felt hollow. Trees appeared, first in clumps, then as a proper wood. The village smoke came into view, a smudge against the sky where the valley opened. Old King's Walk looked almost the same as we had left it. Roofs. Fields. The crooked line of the stone wall. But one thing missing can make a whole picture strange. Knowing Maximus would not be popping his head up over one of those roofs to wave at us made the houses look like a row of teeth with a gap.

The first villager to see us was Sela, the weaver, standing outside her cottage with a basket of raw wool at her hip. She shaded her eyes, saw the stretchers, and dropped the basket. Wool rolled and tumbled into the dust. She did not even glance at it as she ran to meet us, skirts gathered in her hands.

Others followed. Faces we knew, some streaked with soot from putting out fires after the raid. In our small place news flew like sparks in a dry barn. By the time we reached the square, half the village walked beside us, slowing their pace out of respect without needing to be told.

The children we had freed were taken quickly from the Guard's ring into waiting arms. There were cries of joy, wails of recognition, names called again and again as if saying them could paste back the torn parts of the day. Not all were claimed. Two little ones stood alone, turning this way and that with that stunned look a kicked dog has. The priest's wife shepherded them away gently, promising to find them a warm corner and a meal.

We carried Maximus to the middle of the square. Dratmar lowered his end with great care. His broad hands trembled just once. I saw it because I was looking for it. Others might have missed it.

Anya knelt straightaway, both hands on the cloak now.

"Not here," she said, voice rough. "Not under all these eyes."

Dratmar rested his hand on her head like he often did when she had nightmares as a child.

"We'll take him home," he said. "Just for a time." He looked at the men around him. "We'll hold the funeral at dusk. Old way. No priest speech unless the family asks it."

There were nods. The priest himself, a narrow man with a watery gaze, opened his mouth as if to object. One look from Dratmar and he closed it again. The village knew who had kept its walls up when raiders came years before. Respect for the gods did not always outweigh respect for old soldiers.

We bore Maximus to Dratmar's house. It had been our house too, all of us crammed into its two rooms and loft, but in that moment it felt like it belonged mainly to the dead and to the man who had raised him.

Inside, the air was close and familiar. The big table sat where it always had, scarred by years of elbows and knife nicks. The tinderbox on the shelf sat just so. The spare boots by the door included Maximus's second pair, the ones he wore on feast days. These details stuck me like thorns.

We cleared the table and laid him there, cloaks and all. Anya fetched clean cloths from the trunk at the foot of her pallet. Her hands shook only once when she touched the stack. Jaime brought the good soap, the one Dratmar had traded for with a passing caravan three summers back and hoarded for special times. Births. Funerals.

Dratmar undid the cloaks. I turned my head aside, then forced myself to look. If Maximus had walked with me into that cave, I owed him the respect of not flinching from him now.

The wound in his chest was clean. The Goblin King had known his work. A single thrust, straight between ribs. Blood had dried dark around it. His face looked almost calm, lines of worry smoothed out. Only the slack jaw and the color of his lips set him apart from sleep.

We washed him in silence. The water in the basin went pink, then red, then finally a dull rusty shade as we wrung cloth after cloth. Anya's hair fell forward as she scrubbed his arms. A strand stuck to the corner of his mouth. She wiped it away with a tenderness that meant she had not yet fully believed he could not feel.

Jaime worked at his hands, cleaning under the nails, scraping out the dirt that always lived there from his habit of grabbing hold of everything. She pressed her thumb along each finger, as if checking the strength that had once been there. I washed his face. My own reflection flickered in the water, distorted. It looked like a stranger's.

When we were done, Dratmar brought out the good shirt. It was one he had had us stitch for Maximus last winter, muttering all the while that the boy would only grow out of it anyway. White, with blue thread at the cuffs. We had teased Maximus when he tried it on, said he looked like some lord's son trying to act like a farmer. Now we eased it onto him with more care than we would give a newborn.

Anya smoothed the cloth over his chest. Her hands hung there a long moment, then dropped.

"I'm sorry," she whispered. "I'm so sorry."

Dratmar closed his eyes. The cords stood out along his neck. His big shoulders, which had carried more than most, sagged for one small space of time. Then he squared them again.

"We'll dig his resting place on the hilltop," he said. "Like we did for your brother and sister when the fever came." He looked at me. "Elric. There's a spade by the shed. Take whoever offers a hand."

I welcomed the work. Swinging iron into dirt was simple. It did not ask what had lit my bones in the cave or why Maximus's heart had stopped while mine had not. It only demanded sweat and the feel of soil giving way. On the hill above the village, where the wind always tasted a little sharper, we had a small ring of stones. Two sat there already, marking where Dratmar's blood-children lay. We chose a spot beside them. It felt right. In death, he would stand watch over them the way he had tried to in life.

Berit's father and Harn came with me. No one spoke much. The sound of steel biting into earth said enough. The ground was half-frozen. Each cut of the blade jarred my arms up to the shoulder. I drove it in again and again until my back burned and breath dragged. It was good to feel something simple like muscle ache. By the time we finished, the sun had slid low. The light along the western ridge was that rich, dying gold that fools and poets talk about. We climbed down to the house, our boots heavy with mud.

The whole village gathered at the hill just before dusk. Fires were lit in town and along the path, a line of glowing eyes that led up to the stone ring. Children were shushed. Old women leaned on sticks. The Guard captain stood a respectful distance away with three of her people, hands clasped in front of them. We carried Maximus up together, four men at the corners of the door we used as a bier. Anya walked at his head. Jaime and I took the rear corners. Dratmar walked beside, his hand never leaving the wood. At the ring, we set him down. The grave gaped dark beside him. The earth around it smelled rich, turned over. Ravens watched from a bare tree a little way off, heads cocked.

Dratmar stepped forward. He did not wear any special clothes. He had on the same old tunic stained with the day's work. That felt fitting. Maximus had never fussed about appearances.

"In some places," Dratmar said, his voice carrying without needing to be raised, "they've got chants for this. Long pretty words about roads to other worlds and the mercy of gods with too many names. I have never been much for pretty words."

There was a murmur of wry agreement from a few of the older men. Even in grief, it was there. It helped.

"I have buried men," he went on. "Too many. On battlefields and in ditches. On ships. On hills like this. Most of them fought because someone with coin and a shiny bit of metal told them to. They died far from home, and the ground did not remember their names. Today is not that."

He looked down at Maximus.

"This boy was mine as much as any born from my blood," Dratmar said. "I did not sire him. I scolded him, fed him, beat sense into his thick skull, and watched him defend this village with more heart than men twice his years. He died in a dark place so that children would not be dragged there in chains. That is enough. More than enough."

His voice roughened, just a little. "If there is a hall beyond this one where men who did right sit with full cups, I expect to see him there. And if there isn't, then the world is smaller than I took it for."

He stepped back. It was not much of a speech, but it came from his boots up, and that was all we needed. The priest cleared his throat, looked about to say something, then thought better of it. He murmured a short blessing under his breath instead. The words floated off into the cold without clinging. Anya moved to the side of the bier. Her face was drawn. Her cheeks were raw from earlier tears, dried in salt tracks. She held something in her hand. It was a small wooden horse, the kind a child plays with. Maximus had carved it for one of the village little ones last year and then kept it on his own shelf because he liked the shape.

"He never finished the tail," Anya said, looking down at it. "Said he would get to it when there was a quieter day." Her fingers closed around it. "He always said that. 'When things quiet down.'"

She laughed on the word, bitter and soft.

"I'm sorry," she whispered again, this time to the whole hill, to the air, to the bones under the earth. "I should have listened. I should have..." Her voice broke. Her knees gave. She went down beside the bier, catching herself on her hands.

We all saw the moment when the dam she had been holding back cracked. It was not pretty. It was not noble. It was just a girl who had watched her brother die, keening into the clay.

"I'm sorry, Max," she sobbed. "I'm so sorry. I made you go. I made you. You said stay, and I said no. I said I could help. I said..." The words dissolved into broken sounds.

No one moved for a heartbeat. Grief like that makes people shy. They look away, afraid it might catch. Jaime stepped first. She knelt on Anya's other side and laid a hand on her back between the shoulder blades, firm and warm. I followed and took her hand. Her fingers crushed mine like a grip on a ledge.

"You didn't make him," I said, keeping my voice low so it barely carried past us. "You asked. He chose. He would have punched me flat if I tried to put this on you."

"He should be here yelling at me himself," she choked.

Jaime let out a breath that shook.

"I wish he were," she said. "He'd tell you you're being dramatic and then steal your bread. And you'd hit him with a spoon."

A strangled little laugh fought its way through Anya's sobs at that. It was a thin, wounded thing, but it was there. I felt her breathe, jerkily, against my side.

"You hear me, Anya?" I said. "You walking out of that cave wasn't some mistake. It wasn't stealing life that wasn't yours. Maximus wanted that. He did everything in that hole so you could be here yelling at the world. Don't you spit on that by wishing you were under this dirt with him."

She lifted her face. Her eyes were swollen almost shut.

"It hurts," she said, as if surprised.

"Aye," I said. "Means you're still here."

She sagged against us. We stayed kneeling until her sobs eased from ripping to ragged. The cold ground seeped through my trousers. My knees went numb. I did not stand until she did.

One by one, people stepped up to the bier. Each laid something small on his chest. Harn placed a barley stalk from his mill. Sela set a twist of dyed thread. Berit's father put down a little stone from their field. Even the Guard captain came and rested a North Guard badge beside his hands, a spare one she had on a thong.

"Would have taken you, if you'd come to us young," she said under her breath. "World needed you either way."

When it was my turn, I found my pockets empty of token-worthy things. In the end I slipped off the bit of leather I had always worn around my wrist. It was nothing more than an old strap with a hole punched through one end and a knot in the other. Maximus had tied it there for me seasons back when I complained about my hair getting in my eyes while I worked.

"Use it to tie your own hair back up there," I muttered as I looped it around one of his fingers. "Keep it out of your porridge."

When all had given what they would, Dratmar nodded at Berit's father. He and I took up the ropes. We lowered Maximus gently into the earth. The door-turned-bier became a bridge for just a moment, then tilted. The sound of the body settling at the bottom of the grave was soft, final. We each took up handfuls of dirt. There is an old saying in our valley that you do not truly lay someone to rest until your own hands have felt the weight of their return to the ground. One after another, soil fell on the white shirt. It darkened, disappeared. The thud of each clump was steady, like a slow drumbeat.

Anya stepped up last. Her hand shook so much some of the earth spilled from between her fingers before she could throw it. The bit that made it in hit almost without sound. She swayed. I was close enough to catch her elbow. We filled the grave by lamplight. Shovels scraped. Someone began a low humming tune, one of the old mountain songs without words. People picked it up. It was not pretty. Many of the voices were rough. But it sat in the gut. When the hole was level with the ground again, we placed a flat stone over it. Dratmar knelt and dragged his knife across the surface, carving Maximus's name in rough grooves. It did not need to be fine. It just needed to be there.

The villagers drifted away in twos and threes, speaking in low tones. The Guard took their leave, promising to send word north about the crates and to station a patrol nearer the valley for a time. The captain caught Dratmar's arm at the edge of the circle.

"Come with us," she said. "We could use an old bastard who remembers what a war smells like."

He shook his head.

"These are my hills," he said. "And my brats." His eyes flicked to us. "If something worse walks down from the north, I'll know soon enough without going to meet it."

She held his gaze a moment, then gripped his forearm.

"You always were too rooted," she said. "Keep them safe. And if more steel with merchant marks turns up, send a runner. This smells wrong."

"I know," he said.

When only we three remained at the stones with Dratmar, the sky had deepened to a blue so dark it was nearly black. The first stars pricked through. The air nipped at any bit of skin left exposed. Dratmar stood with his hands on his hips, looking down at the fresh mound.

"Maximus wasn't the only one who walked out of that cave changed," he said. His eyes shifted to me. "That light in you. The way wounds closed like they were never there. I have seen many things, Elric. Men on fire running three steps before they drop. Arrows in eyes. Horses split open. I have not seen that."

"I didn't ask for it," I said, speaking before I could bite the words back. "If you'd like to take it back with a shovel, be my guest."

Somewhere in the back of my mind, a part of me was still that boy who just wanted Dratmar's steady regard. The thought that I might have become something else, something other, weighed heavier than any crate. He studied me. The wind tugged at his grey-streaked hair.

"If I thought you had done it on purpose," he said, "I would have knocked you down myself and asked you who taught you. This is something in your bones. In your blood. Stories talk of folk like that. Fire-touched. Dragon-blooded. Some say there were lords once who could crack walls with a shout. I never put much store in those tales. Now I have to."

He stepped closer.

"Whatever this is, it can be a tool or a curse," he said. "Or both. I can't teach you how to carry it. All I can say is men will want it. Kings. Priests. Merchants. They'll dress it up as duty. As service. They'll tell you you're special and born for it. Remember this day when they do. Remember Maximus on that table. Remember that light did not save him. You did, as much as anyone, by standing where you did with the body you had. Not by shining."

I nodded. My throat had closed around any words worth saying.

Jaime, who had been standing a little apart, spoke up.

"Dratmar," she said. "I'm going after whoever filled those crates."

He looked at her, one brow lifting.

"The Guard will take it from here," he said. "They'll send word up the chain. There'll be letters and inquiries. Men whose only callous is from holding quills will sit on chairs and decide what to do about this."

"While more crates walk through passes we don't know, to goblins we haven't met," she said. "My father followed this trail until it killed him. His notes show he was close. I can't sit here and hope some captain's captain reads that journal and cares more about mountain folk than their own pocket."

Dratmar snorted softly.

"Can't say I blame you," he said. "You're his in more ways than your face." He turned his gaze north, where the mountains loomed. "Where will you go first?"

"River cities," she said. "Follow the mark on those crates back to the merchant house that stamped it. My father's notes mention a name or two. I'll see which doors he knocked on, and if any of those hands are still bloody."

She looked at me then. It was not the first time she had asked me to follow her somewhere. Since we were small, she had been picking paths and daring me to keep up. Up trees. Into old ruins. Along riverbanks. Never this far. Never beyond the valley.

"Elric," she said. "Come with me."

The words settled between us. The hilltop went very quiet in my ears. Wind hissed in the grass, but that was old talk, not ours.

"I can't leave them," I said. I jerked my head toward Anya, who stood with her arms wrapped around herself, staring at Maximus's stone. Toward Dratmar. "Not now."

"Now?" Jaime echoed. "No. Tomorrow morning. Or the morning after, if your feet need one more day in this dirt. But you can't pretend you belong here anymore. Not truly. Not with that fire in your chest and that look in your eye when you see the ridge line."

She stepped closer, lowering her voice.

"You think you can hide what happened in that cave? You might keep the light quiet a while. Word still spreads. They'll say you pulled down the Goblin King with your bare hands. That you walked out with no cuts while others bled. Priests will want to lay hands on you. Merchants will want to hire you. Boys will want to follow you into foolish fights." She shook her head. "You need to know what you are, Elric. Hiding in Old King's Walk will not teach you that. It will only make you stranger."

She had a point and she knew it. She pressed on.

"My father thought this worth his life," she said. "Stopping these raids before they turned into war. Finishing what he started is the only way I know to lay him down proper. I don't ask you to do it for him. I ask you because we walked into that cave once and saw a small piece of the ruin these weapons can bring. You've felt how small you are under a mountain. Imagine what happens when steel like that moves in ranks across fields."

Dratmar looked from her to me. He did not speak at once. He let the question hang. In my mind I saw the village as it would be if I stayed. The same fields. The same chores. The same coals in the forge, flaring under my hammer. Anya at the table. Dratmar in his chair. A gap in the noise where Maximus's laughter should be. And inside me, that light like a coal I dared not touch and dared not ignore.

I also saw Jaime walking north alone with only a journal and an old ring for company. I saw her walking into towns where people lied for a living, facing men who sold death by the crate. Her clever hands, quick with a knife, did not scare me as much as the thought of her back with no one to watch it. I looked at Anya. She met my gaze for the first time since Maximus went into the ground.

"You're going," she said. No question in it. She had ridden on my shoulders when she was little. She knew how I shifted before I moved.

I opened my mouth to give her the kind lie. She shook her head before I could form it.

"You've never looked right without a road in your eyes," she said. "Even when you were staring at a plow. It's worse now." She swallowed. "If you stay, every time you look at the mountains you'll break a little more. I'd rather have you whole and somewhere I can't see than cracked and sitting at our table."

"You'll be alone," I said. "Just you and Dratmar."

She gave a snort that was almost a laugh.

"Alone? With that old goat?" She glanced at Dratmar, and something like a smile tugged at the corner of her mouth. "He'll make me split every log in the valley just to keep me busy. Besides, someone has to stay and tell people the truth about Maximus. If you go, his story goes with you. Here, I can keep lighting it like a candle. Besides I've got Bobo and Ianteen. And the littler brats."

Dratmar stepped closer. He put one big hand on my shoulder and the other on Jaime's. His fingers dug in, grounding.

"I won't hold you," he said to me. "Never was my way to cage a thing that wanted the sky. You've given this village more than most your age ever will. You earned the right to choose your next path." He turned to Jaime. "You'll lead him into trouble. I reckon you know that."

Her mouth twitched.

"Of course," she said. "I do it all the time."

"You keep him from doing the kind of stupid that gets him on a pyre," Dratmar said. "And you, boy, you keep her from lighting fires she can't put out."

He reached into his belt and pulled out a small leather pouch. It clinked softly when he tossed it to me. My reflexes caught it without thinking.

"That's the bit I've set aside over the years," he said. "For mending roofs and buying extra grain when the harvest went bad. We had a few good years. Roof's sound. You'll need it more. Don't argue. Makes my jaw ache."

I held the pouch. It felt heavier than it should have.

"I can't take this," I said.

"You're not taking," he said. "You're carrying it for us. You go north with empty hands, they'll eat you alive before you get within spitting distance of anything important. Coin talks. You'll need to talk loud."

He turned and walked over to the house. For a moment I thought he was done. Then he came back with something wrapped in cloth. He unrolled it. Maximus's sword lay there, clean and dull in the evening light. It was no great weapon by a noble's measure. The handle was plain wood. The pommel was a simple iron ball. There were nicks along the blade where it had struck rock and bone. I knew each mark. I had watched him sharpen it by firelight, running the whetstone along with a patient rhythm.

"He'd want you to have it," Dratmar said, holding it out. "Jaime's got her own. Anya swings a staff better than a blade, and that's no shame. You fought beside this steel. Feels fitting you keep it singing. It's a blade that defended the innocent, let it do the same in your hands."

I hesitated. Taking that sword felt like admitting Maximus was not coming back for it. But he was already under a stone. The world had already admitted it. I reached out and gripped the hilt. It lay in my palm steady, almost familiar. Its weight pulled my arm down, anchoring me.

"Don't let it make you think you're invincible," Dratmar said. "The brightest steel breaks easy if the hand behind it is foolish."

"I know," I said.

He put his hand on the back of my neck and pulled my forehead briefly against his. It was a rough, half-hearted bump, as if he were afraid any softer touch might crack him.

"You come back when you can," he said into my hair. "If you can. If you don't, I'll assume you died for something worth the trouble, and I'll curse you at my table for leaving your boots lying around."

Anya came then. She threw her arms around both Jaime and me at once, burying her face between our shoulders. Her breath was warm through my shirt.

"You write," she mumbled. "Both of you. Even if it's just to say you're not dead yet. And if you see anything like those crates again, kick it over."

"We will," Jaime said.

We did not sleep much that night. Jaime spent the dark hours at Dratmar's table with her father's journal spread open, copying certain names and marks onto fresh scraps so she could carry them separate. I sat with Maximus's sword across my knees, running a cloth along the blade out of habit more than need. Anya dozed in the chair by the hearth, jerking awake every so often as if afraid her brother would have moved while her eyes were closed.

Near dawn, I stepped outside. The air bit my lungs. Frost silvered the thatch. The sky over the eastern ridge was just turning grey. I walked up to the hill one more time. The new stone over Maximus's grave looked slightly lighter than the older pair beside it, as if the weather had not quite claimed it yet.

I stood there a while. I did not talk to the stone. Words seemed small. I just let my boots press into the earth above him and hoped that counted for something. The wind tugged at my cloak and my hair. Somewhere a rooster crowed, shrill and foolish. When I went back down, Jaime already had her pack on. She had traveled light even before. Now her shoulders looked strangely bare without all the odds and ends she used to collect. Only the journal, wrapped in oiled cloth, bulged against her back.

"You ready?" she asked.

"As I'll ever be," I said.

Dratmar and Anya stood at the door. Anya's eyes were clear, though rimmed red. She had braided her hair back tight, in the way she did when she meant to get through something hard without it whipping in her face.

We walked together to the edge of the village. The sun had just pushed its rim above the mountains, blinding in that first break. Our road north was no more than a track of pounded earth between scrub and stone. Beyond the first rise, the land dropped and rose again and again, each hill hiding the next. I had walked parts of it before on hunts. It had never seemed so long.

The village turned out to see us off. Not with banners or cheering. They came with folded arms and quiet faces, the way folk go to watch a storm rolling in at the far end of the valley. Children peered from behind skirts. Old men squinted.

Harn stepped forward and shoved a wrapped bundle into my hands.

"Bread," he said. "From the last of yesterday's loaf. You can say it's Old King's Walk you're chewing on when the road gets rough."

Sela tied a length of blue thread around Jaime's wrist.

"For luck," she said. "Or for mending. Whichever you need more."

The Guard captain inclined her head to us.

"If you live long enough to find who's behind those crates," she said, "and you find you can't handle it alone, send word to the nearest post. Some of us still remember what oaths were meant for."

Jaime nodded.

"We'll try," she said. "If our tongues haven't been cut out."

The captain smiled, thin and brief.

"Fair," she said.

Dratmar stood solid beside Anya. He did not speak at first. His eyes took us both in, as if fixing our shapes in his mind.

"You walk out that gate as my brats," he said finally. "You walk back in the same way, no matter what bad habits you pick up out there. Don't let anyone convince you otherwise. Blood's what you make with your own two hands."

Anya took my hand and squeezed once, hard enough to hurt.

"Come back," she said. "Even if it's just to bring more trouble to our doorstep. I'll complain. Then I'll make you tea."

I leaned down and pressed my forehead to hers. It was an old gesture between us, from when she was small and frightened of thunder. Her breath hitched once.

"Take care of him," I said, tilting my head toward Dratmar.

She gave a watery snort.

"Someone has to," she said.

Jaime adjusted the strap of her pack. The ring on her finger caught the light and flashed once, like a small, stubborn star.

"Time," she said.

We stepped through the gap in the low stone wall that marked the village edge. My boots found the ruts I had walked since I was a boy, but each step away felt different, as if the ground's memory of me was already fading.

I did not look back at first. I focused on the feel of Maximus's sword at my hip, unfamiliar weight pulling on my belt. The pouch of Dratmar's coin thumped against my thigh. The air smelled of cold earth and smoke and something else, thin and sharp, that belonged to higher places. After a dozen paces I did glance over my shoulder. The village lay in its bowl of land, smoke rising from chimneys, tiny figures at the gate watching.

Dratmar's broad frame. Anya's slight one. The three stones on the hill just visible above the roofs.

The sight sat in my chest like another stone. Not crushing. Just there, solid, heavy, not to be ignored. I knew, even then, that whatever roads we took would carve something out of us that could not be put back. That is the weight of a first leaving. The door does not slam. It closes slow, inch by inch, until one day you turn and realize the hinge has rusted. Jaime walked beside me, eyes forward, jaw set. Her fingers brushed the ring now and then, as if checking it had not gone. Her father's words rode in her pack. Maximus's laughter rode somewhere between us, an echo waiting for a place to land.

The mountains ahead did not care who we were. Their peaks cut the sky the same as they always had, indifferent and cold. But as we walked toward them, with funeral dirt still under my nails and a strange warmth coiled deep where no one could see, I felt the ground shift a little under my feet. The path was the same. I was not.

# Chapter 10

## STONE WALLS AND TALL RULES

By the third day out of Old King's Walk the mountains stopped feeling like walls and started feeling like a memory.

The stone shoulders of home sloped away behind us, white-tipped and blue with distance. Ahead, the land unrolled itself into long ridges and shallow valleys, as if someone had pressed a giant hand over clay and smoothed it flat. The air grew thicker and warmer, the wind less sharp. Our breath did not steam so much in the mornings.

We walked.

For a while, that was all there was. Boot leather on dirt. The creak of our packs. The dull jangle of Maximus's sword at my hip, heavier than the old iron I had trained with back in the village. Crows haunted the bare trees, black commas against a gray sky. The path widened from a goat track to something rutted and sure, with wagon grooves baked hard from years of use instead of the faint scratch of the old road up to Old King's Walk.

We did not speak much the first day. There was too much lying behind us, crowding close. Every time I looked sideways and caught the edge of Jaime's profile, I saw her on her knees in that smoky cave, her face streaked with soot and tears and Goblin King blood, fingers closed around her father's ring. I heard Maximus's last breath more clearly than the birds.

I do not break easily, but my chest felt like someone had wedged a stone under my ribs and left it there.

We stopped at midday beside a stream, the sort that braided over rocks instead of cutting deep, water clear as melted glass. I filled our flasks while Jaime rummaged in the pack for bread and dried apples. My reflection rippled up at me from the current, long and blurrier than the boy I knew. Same brown hair hanging too near my eyes, same thin nose, but there was a drawn look about the mouth that did not belong to the blacksmith's apprentice from Old King's Walk.

I pushed a wet hand through my hair and the memory came quick and hot: my skin glowing in that green light, the Goblin King's claws in my shoulder, bone knitting together beneath my fingers like it was no more than snapped kindling.

I gripped the flask so hard the leather squealed.

When I turned, Jaime was standing with a piece of flatbread in each hand, eyes on me. The ring she wore on a thong at her neck caught a pale flash of sun as she shifted.

"You all right?" she asked.

"Yes," I said, too fast.

Her gaze stayed on me a moment longer, steady as a nail hammered true, then she passed me the bread without argument. We ate on a fallen log. The stream talked enough for both of us.

On the second day, the path joined a proper road. It came shouldering out of a stand of pines, laid with crushed stone that crunched underfoot. Weathered posts lined the edges, each painted with a faded white stripe. Wagon tracks grooved the surface into two long scars.

Jaime stopped short where the goat path kissed the new road. She frowned at the posts, then looked up and down the line of it, like a hunter studying a trail.

"So this is it," she said.

"What is?"

"The river road. The notes say the smugglers are using 'the lower river routes, by way of the South Gate.' That has to mean this." She slung the pack higher on her shoulders with a sharp hitch. "Stay to the road, head toward the river, we'll hit the city."

Her father's journal was tucked into the pack under her spare shirt and Maximus's neatly folded cloak. Every time she mentioned it her voice hardened. It was like watching metal go from red to white-hot.

"You sure?" I asked.

"Roads this wide don't lead nowhere." She gave me a thin smile that did not touch her eyes. "Trust me."

I did not trust roads. In the village, the only real road ran from the square to the mines and half of it changed every spring when the mountain shrugged and tumbled rocks over it. A road this certain felt wrong, like a river that refused to bend.

But I nodded and followed.

Traffic thickened as the hours wore on. At first it was only a cart or two, farmers with winter vegetables rattling by, carrots and parsnips bundled in damp-smelling heaps, cabbages tied in nets that knocked against the wheels. A man on a sway-backed mare passed us without a glance, cloak's hem crusted with old mud, a string of rabbit carcasses bumping his saddle.

By afternoon, more people moved alongside us. A pair of women walked together, each with a child strapped to her back, their skirts muddy to the knee. Two men pushed a wheelbarrow between them loaded with sacks that clinked like bottles. A group of lads about our age, all in matching brown jerkins, tramped behind a wagon with a black-and-gold sigil painted on its side, laughing loud enough to scare birds from the hedges.

Jaime watched everyone. Her eyes flicked over harness buckles, the color of wagon covers, the brands on sacks. It made my own gaze restless. I found myself checking faces, hands, the way people walked. Looking for what, I did not know. Goblins did not roam these roads in daylight, not so near a city. Still, I had trouble believing anything so large and alive as our fear could be contained by a line on a map.

We camped that night in a shallow hollow just off the road, ringed by low scrub. The sky pushed down close, thick with cloud. The fire we coaxed from damp twigs struggled, orange light flickering weakly over Jaime's face as she read by it.

She had the journal open on her knees. The leather was cracked, the spine bent the way it gets when a book has seen more hands than shelves. Her father's hand was tight and slanting, written with a man's haste. Names, dates, small notes. A sketch of a sigil shaped like a twisted river, ink bled at the edges where a drop of rain must have kissed it.

"Listen to this," Jaime said.

I lay on my back, staring at the nothing of the sky, but turned my head toward her voice.

"'Three crates of steel heads, marked as milling tools. Paid in full by Kaben & Sons. Shipment to be transferred at Riverside Warehouse, South Gate, upon arrival from northern forges.'" She squinted at the next line. "'Suspect Kaben shielding actual buyer. Frequent visits to warehouse at night. Tall man, red hair, heavy rings.'"

The fire snapped. Somewhere in the brush a small animal scurried.

"Kaben & Sons," I repeated. The name meant as much to me as a new kind of tree, but it sat heavy on her tongue.

"They're in the city, Elric. He was close." The pages rustled as she turned them. "He wrote this two months ago. If we can find this warehouse, or this Kaben, we can figure out who's paying for goblin steel. Then we take it to the guard. Or the Watch, or whatever they have. Someone will have to listen."

I thought of the guards in Old King's Walk, the way they shrugged when Maximus spoke of raiding parties and stolen ore. I thought of the Goblin King's hoard: coins from half the known world, tangles of silver wire, facedown medallions stamped with foreign crests, and on top of it all a hammer whose metal burned my skin.

"Will they?" I asked.

She snapped the journal closed. The sudden silence of it made the hairs on my arms rise.

"They will," she said. "Or we make them."

There was a new hard edge in her voice that had not been there back when we spent afternoons stealing apples and skipping stones into the quarry pond. Grief had taken the softness of her and filed it down. Part of me missed that girl, the one who laughed too loud and climbed too high and ripped her dresses. Part of me knew she had walked into the cave with us and never walked out.

Rain came sometime in the night, fine and steady, a sleepless patter on the canvas of our tent. By morning it had settled into a low mist that clung to the ground and turned the road into a gray tunnel. Our cloaks soaked through by midday, water tracking down my spine in cold little rivers.

More trade moved along the road now. Wider wagons, some with covers painted bright colors. One passed with its horses stepping high, flanks gleaming even through the mud, harness brass polished like gold. A dark-coated driver sat up front, hat pulled low. Behind him, two guards rode, cloaks plain but their swords clean.

I watched them go with a tight itch between my shoulders. Steel used as show felt stranger than steel used as tool.

The third day the air warmed again, the mist lifting into ragged shreds. Around noon, I smelled the river.

It reached us before the water itself did. A deep, living scent, part mud, part cold stone, part something green and far. It swallowed the smell of our damp wool and road dust, curled into my nose like woodsmoke. In the mountains, rivers cut narrow and wild, white water smashing itself to pieces against rocks. This smelled wider.

The road dropped, then leveled. The trees thinned. Far ahead, between two low hills, something flat and pale gleamed.

Jaime walked a little faster. Her hand brushed the journal's shape through the pack, an unconscious pat like you give a dog to let it know you are still there.

"There," she said.

At first I did not see what she meant. The horizon seemed cluttered with nothing more than haze and a long line of that pale gleam. Then the haze shifted, and I made it out.

Walls.

They rose from the flat land like someone had taken a slice of cliff and planted it upright. Not the stacked stone that held up frost-cracked fields, not the squat guard walls around the Old Walk. These were smooth and tall and long, made of big-cut blocks that caught the light in dull sheets. Towers broke their line at intervals, square-edged and massive, each topped with a little crown of merlons like teeth.

The first thought that came was that a mountain had lain down and grown edges.

I had never seen a city wall. I had heard traders describe them, of course, in the shade of Old Bram's alehouse, always with a certain swagger. They used words like "unbreachable" and "fortress" and "hundred men high." They talked about gates choked with carts and guards in bright colors and a maze of streets that could swallow a boy whole.

Words had not been enough.

Jaime stopped when I did, both of us standing in the wagon ruts like children watching a storm roll in. The walls looked close, but the way their size cheated the eye, I knew they were still a good walk off.

"Elric," she said, half astonished, half something else. I realized her hand had found mine without either of us thinking about it. Her fingers were cold and damp and strong.

"I see it," I said.

The road bent a little as it ran down toward the river, angling us so the wall's curve became obvious. It did not run straight like a fence but arced gently, the river a wide silver band pressing against it. Where road and water met the stone, there was a gap. The South Gate.

Even from a distance, the gate did not look inviting. Two squat towers flanked it, heavier than the rest, their sides bristling with arrow slits. The opening itself was tall enough that three of our old watchtowers could have been stacked and still not scraped its arch. Heavy wooden doors stood open, iron bands like scars across them. Above the arch, a carved crest peered down, rain-black and stern.

As we drew nearer, the trickle of traffic thickened into a steady current. People converged from side paths and roads, all drawn toward that dark mouth in the stone.

Carts creaked on swollen wheels. A herd of goats trotted past us driven by a boy even younger than Jory back home, his feet bare and quick in the mud. A woman balanced a bundle on her head so large it made me dizzy to look at it. Two men in faded blue jerkins argued briskly over a set of rolled-up carpets, words snapping as quick as twigs.

Noise grew. Not the clean echo of a shout off the quarry walls, but a layered murmur full of coughs, clucks, curses, laughter. A baby cried, sharp and thin. A hawker somewhere ahead called out what sounded like "hot pies," the last word drawn out into a rising song.

The smell changed too. River damp. Sweat. Cooked meat, sweet and greasy. Smoke that did not smell of pine or spruce but of something softer, like burning straw. Under it all, a sour note of too many people in one place for too long.

We were swallowed.

It happened so gradually I did not notice until I realized I could not stretch my arms out without touching someone. I had known crowds, of a sort. Harvest festival in the village square, the market days when all the miners were off-shift and everyone came out for roasted nuts and barley beer. But those had been crowds of faces you knew, shoulders you'd bumped before. Here, everyone was a stranger. Clothes cut in ways I had only seen on coins turned in the tavern. Headscarves woven with bright threads. Boots stitched from soft-looking leather that would not have lasted an hour in the scree above Old King's Walk.

A trader in a cloak of green so fine it shone brushed past. The edge of it tickled my wrist, and for a heartbeat I wanted to apologize for the smear of road dirt my sleeve might leave. His eyes flicked over me and Jaime, quick and dismissive, and slid on.

We moved with the tide until we could move no faster. Ahead, the press tightened as people funneled toward the gate. Cries rose and fell. I heard commands, laughter, a sharp shout of pain.

A line had formed without anyone saying the word. Wagons and carts in one slow-moving snake, people on foot in another. At the head of each, under the shadow of the gate, guards checked papers, peered into carts, took coins.

The guards looked nothing like the old men who patrolled Old King's Walk, leather jerkins cracked and patched, spearpoints dull but good enough to prod drunks home.

These wore cloth that fit well, in dark red and brown, sleeves outlined with thin gold stitching. Chain gleamed at their throats. Their spears were straight, iron points clean. At their belts hung short swords with metal pommels, polished from constant touch.

Jaime's grip on my arm tightened.

"We should get in line," I said quietly.

"To do what?" she asked, mouth close to my ear so she did not have to raise her voice.

"To get in."

It sounded stupid when I said it. As if there were another option, like walking around the wall. I imagined trying to circle that enormity, pounding palms against stone, looking for a crack big enough to slip through.

"All right," she said. "Stay with me."

We joined the line of people on foot. A woman with a basket of chickens eyed us, lips pursed. Behind us, a pair of men carrying a long pole between them, from which hung strings of dried fish, stopped so close I could smell the salt on their hands.

The line inched forward. Rainwater dripped from the edge of the gate onto the cobbles in a slow, steady rhythm. Every few heartbeats, a guard's voice would cut through the general murmur.

"Name."

"Business in Aramor."

"Coin for entry."

The first time I heard that last one clearly, I frowned. No one paid to walk into Old King's Walk, unless you counted the way Bram glared if you took up a stool and did not order a drink.

"Coin?" I murmured.

"Gate tax," the chicken woman said without looking at me. "You from the hills?"

Jaime answered before I could step on my own tongue. "First time to the city."

"Hnh." The woman adjusted her basket as one of the chickens made a bid for freedom. "They squeeze you when you come in and squeeze you when you go out. Like pressing cider. Guards have to be fed. Roads have to be kept. Walls don't mend themselves."

"How much?" Jaime asked.

"For you two?" The woman finally gave us a proper look, eyes flicking from our mud-stained boots to the sword at my hip to the pack on Jaime's shoulders. "Standard is a copper each, more if you look like trouble. Or like money. You don't look like money."

I did some quick counting inside my head, picturing Dratmar's coin bag as we had last opened it in the tent, its mouth yawning, a neat clink of comfort. We had paid for bread, for a new waterskin when Jaime's old one split, for a fresh leather strap for my pack. There was still a fair weight of copper and a few small silvers in the bag. Enough for a tax. Enough for a few nights at an inn, if we chose poorly. Not enough to waste.

"We'll manage," Jaime said.

Her jaw set, the same look she had worn trudging up to Goblin's Crown when the cold bit and her feet bled in her boots, but she refused to say she was tired.

When we reached the front of the line at last, the stone of the gate loomed over us, roughness of its individual blocks lost in the sheer idea of it. All the breath of the crowd seemed to wash toward that arch, like air itself needed to be checked and counted.

A guard stood in our path, a board on a stand beside him. On it, someone had written rows of names in chalk, each name with a mark beside it. A tally of who had come through? His eyes were dark and bored, his beard trimmed short. Rain speckled his felt cap.

"Names," he said, not unkindly, just in the flat tone of someone who had said the same word five hundred times already and would have to say it five hundred times more.

""Elric Shaddar," I answered, before my tongue could tangle. "From Old King's Walk."

He glanced at me, then at Jaime.

"Jaime Durandal," she said. I heard the slight hitch before the family name. Her father should have been the one to speak it here first. "Also from Old King's Walk."

"Business in Aramor?" He dipped the end of a bit of chalk in his mouth, ready to make his next mark.

"We're here to find my father," Jaime said.

Something in her voice made him pause. His gaze sharpened, climbed from the wet fringe of her hair to the ring that showed at the neck of her tunic, then to the sword I wore like a child playing at soldier.

"Missing?" he asked.

"Yes," she said. No tremor.

The guard looked at us a moment longer. Whatever he saw did not move him enough to break the script.

"Talk to the Watch if you want missing persons," he said. "Gate tax is a copper each." His eyes slid to the sword again. "Any weapons to declare?"

"Two swords," I said, resting my hand on Maximus's hilt and nodding toward Jaime's blade.

"You'll keep them sheathed inside the walls," the guard said. "Draw them in the city without cause and you'll answer for them."

Trouble goes before the magistrates. Understand?"

"Yes," I said.

His attention returned to the important part: coin. Jaime's hand found the purse at her belt and drew out two coppers. They were ordinary little circles, stamped with a pattern of wheat. They looked smaller between her fingers than they had in Dratmar's palm. She put them in the guard's outstretched hand. His fingers closed with an absent familiarity.

He marked two lines on the board, one beside each of our names, then moved without ceremony to the next in line. We were already dismissed.

Somewhere in the tangle of my chest, something bristled. Back home, if you told a man you were looking for someone, he asked who and why and who you had already spoken to. Old Rhena would have pressed a slice of bread into your hand and told you what the gossip said of where he'd gone. Here, the man just took his coin and pointed vaguely at "the Watch," which might as well have been a thundercloud for all I knew how to reach it.

"Come on," Jaime said. She started forward without looking back.

We stepped under the arch.

For a heartbeat, sound dampened. The air cooled. The stone gathered all the noise and smell against itself. The ceiling soared above us, beams running like ribs. Arrow slits pierced the thickness of the walls at intervals, narrow and mean, each one a dark eye. It felt like walking into a throat.

Then we were through.

THE CITY OPENED AROUND us, and all at once home shrank behind my eyes.

Streets stretched in three directions from the gate, all paved in close-fit stone. Buildings crowded them, three and even four stories tall, their upper stories leaning a little over the street as if trying to listen in on passersby. Roofs stacked at odd angles, tiles in varying shades of red and brown. Chimneys stabbed at the gray sky. Balconies jutted here and there, from which laundry flapped like flags.

People moved everywhere. Not just on the main street that ran inland from the gate, but in thin alleys cutting between houses, in doorways, hanging from windows. Children darted underfoot, their laughter breaking against the dull roar like little splashes against river rock. Dogs nosed at gutters, tails held high. A man drove a handcart nearly into my shins, muttering a curse I did not quite catch.

Scents hit like blows. Yeast from a bakery to our left, warm and thick, rolls piled behind a glass pane. Hot tallow from a candle seller. The sharp bite of vinegar, the comforting depth of roasting meat. Under and around it all, the sour, honest smell of refuse, human and animal both, and of water that had nowhere else to go.

Jaime had gone still beside me. Her eyes were so wide the brown of them looked almost black.

"It's..." I said, then realized I had no word.

"Big," she finished.

It was more than that. It was like standing too near a full wheel of a mill, feeling the size of it in your bones more than in your eyes. Everything was turning faster than seemed safe.

We stood there too long. A guard near the gate barked a brisk "Move along," and that broke the spell. Jaime flinched as if pricked, then set her shoulders and picked a direction.

"Riverside first," she said. "The notes say Riverside Warehouse. That would be by the river, right?"

"Seems likely," I said.

"We follow the downhill," she said, and started in the direction where the street sloped and the smell of wet stone strengthened.

I stuck at her shoulder, one hand on the strap of my pack, the other hovering near Maximus's hilt mostly for my own comfort. My eyes kept snagging on details. A man in a robe of some smooth cloth that caught the light soft as water. A woman perched on a stool outside a shop, painting tiny flowers on cups with a brush not much bigger than a pin. A boy balancing on a stacked pile of barrels, shouting song lyrics down at friends below.

Street vendors lined the wider road as we walked, their stalls jammed shoulder to shoulder. Bolts of cloth hung like frozen waterfalls, blues and greens more vivid than any dye we had at home. Pyramids of oranges glowed, bright as coals, their scent sharp. A woman held out a small wooden skewer threaded with cubes of something steaming and spiced.

"Best lamb in South Quarter," she called. "Hot, hot, fill your belly!"

My stomach woke with a painful twist. We had eaten our last hard heel of bread just before the gate. The meat on that skewer glistened with fat.

"Dratmar's coin," I started.

Jaime shook her head without even looking. "Find a room first. Then we see how much we have left." Her voice had the sharp, clipped quality it took on when she was forcing herself to be practical.

She was right. Hunger was an ache we knew how to bear. A roof in a city like this felt more urgent. I tore my eyes away from the food stall and tried to think.

"How do we find an inn?" I asked. "In Old King's Walk you just... know."

"Look for a sign with a bed?" Jaime suggested.

We both turned in a slow, awkward circle, scanning the buildings near the gate. Images swung above some doorways: a painted fish, a pair of scales, a hammer and anvil, a book. But no beds. My gaze snagged on a wooden sign carved into the shape of a foaming tankard, swinging in the damp air. Laughter and the clink of pottery spilled from the open door beneath it.

"Beer means beds, usually," I said. "Bram said that once when he was complaining about strangers taking tables."

Jaime followed my gaze. "The Foaming Tankard," she read, sounding each letter out from the faded paint. "Do we dare?"

"We can at least ask," I said.

Inside, the air was a punch of warmth and smell: spilled ale, sweat, a hint of stew. The room was larger than Bram's tavern but packed tighter. Men and women sat on benches at long tables, shoulders pressed together, voices a constant buzz. A low fire smoldered in a stone hearth, orange light glancing off a rack of cheap-looking tin cups. A serving girl wove through the crowd with a tray held high, posture of someone who had done the dance so often her feet knew it without asking her head.

Behind a scarred counter, a big man with a balding crown and a tangled beard wiped at a mug with a cloth that did not look much cleaner than the mug. His arms were thick as hams. A tattoo peeked from under one sleeve, some knotwork pattern.

We stood just inside the door, boots dripping on the threshold. A few faces turned our way, then turned back, our dampness nothing special in a room full of worn edges.

Jaime took a breath and stepped toward the counter. I went with her.

"Rooms?" she asked the bearded man.

He glanced up from his mug, took us in with a sweep that started at our boots and ended at our hair. His eyes were a gray that looked like they had seen a lot of mornings that came too early.

"Coin first," he said. His voice was low but carried.

Jaime tugged at the purse at her belt. "How much?"

"For what?" He set the mug down. "Common room pallet? Corner of the floor? Stable loft? Or you looking for a little better?"

Jaime's mouth worked as she calculated words she had not expected. "Just... a small room. Two beds. Or one bed and a bit of floor. For... how long, Elric?"

"Tonight," I said. "We'll see about the rest."

The man scratched his cheek, beard rasping against thick fingers.

"Two beds is a silver a night," he said. "One bed is eight coppers. Floor space in the common room is three." His gaze flicked to Maximus's sword again, the way the guard's had. "Meals are extra. I don't do charity. You and your lad can share, or you can sleep with the snorers. Don't care which."

Jaime stiffened. "He's not my lad."

The man shrugged, bored. "Your brother, then. Cousin. Pet wolf that learned to stand. It's all the same to me as long as the money is right."

"A silver," Jaime murmured, mostly to herself. She slid the purse's mouth open with her thumb and peered in, shading it from the eyes nearby. I could see the weight of the decision balancing on her face.

"Floor," I said quietly. "We can manage on the floor for one night. Gives us more for food and... finding things."

Her jaw clenched. Part of her did not want to give us less than beds, I could see it. Part of her had grown up in the same house I had, knowing how far a coin could be stretched if you pinched it tight enough.

"Floor," she told the innkeeper. "For both of us."

He nodded as if that had been the only sensible answer all along. "Pay now, or you lose your place if you go wandering and come back late smelling like the river." He held out his hand.

Jaime spilled three coppers into his palm, flesh and metal both dull in the candlelight. He made them disappear faster than any goblin.

"Name's Hadren," he said. "That pallet in the corner by the hearth, near the barrels, that's empty. You curl there after I rake the coals and you won't freeze. Your packs stay on you or under your heads. I'm not responsible for light fingers." He jerked his chin toward the far end of the room, where I saw two men in hats pulled low and expressions even lower pretending not to watch us. "You got business in the city, best get it done by dark. Watchmen don't love folks who look like they got lost from the mountain."

"We'll keep out of trouble," I said.

"Everyone says that," Hadren replied, and turned away to bellow at someone about spilled ale.

We found the indicated pallet later, but first we needed to breathe air that did not taste of other people's words. We backed out of the Tankard and into the damp street again, agreeing without saying it that we would find food elsewhere, somewhere cheaper, maybe from a cart.

The weight of what we had spent sat in my mind as tangible as the pack on my shoulders. Three coppers for a square of floor and a share of someone else's warmth. Two coppers for crossing a line on the ground. It made me think of what Old Bram always muttered when a tax collector came through Old King's Walk: "In the city they charge you for the air."

We followed the street that ran downhill. It narrowed in places, pinched by buildings that leaned toward one another, then spit us out into little squares where vendors clustered. At one such place a woman sold strips of fried dough dipped in honey, each bite a burn and a blessing. Jaime gritted her teeth and handed over a copper for two. The first bite filled my whole mouth with heat and sweetness, honey running down my wrist.

We licked the last of it from our fingers as the sound of the river grew.

The city's edge gave way with less drama than the wall had. One moment there were houses, the next their backs to us, doors turned away, and then the world opened.

The river here was indeed wider than any I had known. It rolled slow and deep, a gray-green muscle flexing under the dull sky. On the near bank, a forest of wooden piers thrust into it, ropes thick as my wrist looping from posts to cleats. Boats crowded them: flat-bellied cargo barges, their hulls scuffed from scraping against countless docks; smaller fishing boats with nets coiled neat; a few sleek, long-bodied craft that sat arrogant and still.

Warehouses loomed behind the docks, two and three stories of brick and timber, big double doors yawning, smaller doors set above with hoists and pulleys. Crates and barrels were stacked in the mud and on the boards, branded with symbols and numbers, unreadable to me. Men and women moved among them, shouting, checking ledgers, directing the loading and unloading with a sort of rough music of command.

Somewhere in that tangle was a place called Riverside Warehouse. Somewhere in that tangle, if the ink in Jaime's journal spoke truth, merchants handed off steel heads and spearpoints to goblin runners under cover of night.

Jaime stood staring, the river wind pushing the wet hair back from her face. Her hand had found the journal again, thumb working at the cracked leather.

"Tomorrow," she said.

I nodded. Today we had eaten, found a place to put our heads down that did not involve stealing a niche under a cart. That was enough for the first day.

The sky had sunk itself toward evening without my noticing. Lamps blinked to life one by one along the docks, yellow eyes sparking against the coming dark. Voices changed as the day's business slipped its shoulders into night's.

"Come on," I said. "Before the Watch decides we look especially lost."

We climbed back up the hill, legs heavier now. The streets felt different in the half-light. Shadows pooled thicker under archways. The same vendor who had cheerfully sung about lamb earlier now packed up, movements brisk and tight. A man bumped my shoulder hard enough to spin me half a step, then did not even bother with a curse, just moved on.

Inside The Foaming Tankard the air had thickened with evening business. More bodies, more noise, more of that faint metallic taste of too many people in one room for too long. Our pallet in the corner by the hearth looked smaller than it had in daylight. A thin straw mattress, two grayish blankets folded on top. It was no worse than the floor at home when the roof leaked and we all crowded by the stove, but it felt different because there were strangers' boots a yard away.

Jaime slid her pack from her shoulders and sat on the pallet with a sigh that seemed to escape her whole spine. She untied the thong around her neck and took off the ring there, holding it between thumb and forefinger. The stone caught the firelight and threw it back in a small, sullen glimmer.

"Give me the journal," I said gently, sitting cross-legged opposite.

She hesitated, then lifted it out and passed it to me. The leather was warm from where it had rested against her.

We spread it between us on the pallet, hunching together to keep it off the floor and out of sight. The script wavered a bit in the low light, but I had grown used to the shape of her father's letters. We turned to the page with "Riverside Warehouse" and the note about Kaben & Sons. The ink there looked no different from the ink on any other line, but it felt like something important pressed into the paper.

"We need to find where this is," Jaime said. Her voice had taken on that focused tone again, the rest of the room falling away for her. "There are probably a dozen warehouses by the river. More. But if we ask about Kaben & Sons, someone will know."

"If we ask the wrong someone, they might warn them," I said. The Goblin King's grin flickered behind my eyes, too-wide mouth full of old metal and meat. "Or worse."

"We can start with the honest people, then," she said tightly.

"Honest merchants," I said. "That's like asking for a snowstorm in midsummer."

She snorted despite herself, and for a heartbeat the old Jaime peeked out, the one who laughed in the middle of church when the priest's voice squeaked.

"The guilds," she said after a moment. "Father wrote about them. 'River Guild,' 'Mercers' Guild,' 'Dockworkers' Guild.' They take dues, settle disputes... keep order, in their way. If Kaben & Sons is a respectable merchant, he'll be on some list. The guild will know."

"And if he's not respectable?"

"Then the Watch should know," she said. "Missing shipments, strange crates. Father was talking to someone. It's in here." She flipped to a different page, finger running down cramped lines. "'Spoke with Captain Lerin of the Watch. Sympathetic, but hands tied. Suggested going higher. Note to self: next council session in three weeks.'" Her lips pressed thin. "He wrote that and then... nothing. No more entries. Just the ring in that filthy hoard."

We both sat with that a moment. The idea of Jaime's father in these streets, walking these docks, speaking to guards and guilds and councils, then vanishing so completely no one even thought to tell his daughter, made the city feel less like a marvel and more like a beast with too many teeth.

"Tied hands," I said quietly. "By what?"

"By who," she corrected. Her eyes burned with a small, contained fire. "Mayor. Magistrates. Guildmasters. Someone in this city took their coin and looked away while weapons went upriver. Someone knew he was asking questions. And someone decided to make sure he stopped."

The words hung between us, heavier than the damp blankets or the heat from the hearth.

The edge of the page brushed my fingers. My hand looked much the same as it had before the cave. Same scars from the forge, same thickened knuckles from years of hammering and hauling. Yet in my mind I could still see it blazing with that unnatural light, skin stretched over something more than bone.

"Jaime," I said slowly. "If the Watch could not help him, what makes you think they will help us? Two mountain kids with borrowed coin and a dead man's notebook?"

She looked at me very directly.

"Because we have something he didn't," she said.

"What?"

"Proof the weapons reached the goblins." Her hand went unconsciously to the pouch at her belt where the goblin-forged knife lay, wrapped in cloth, its metal wrong as a broken bone. "Proof of what they're paying for. And you."

I felt my shoulders go rigid. "Me?"

"You ripped those chains out of the rock," she said, keeping her voice low. The din of the tavern around us made sure no one could hear us clearly, but still she kept it to a murmur. "You bled and then you didn't. The Goblin King clawed you open, and then you stood up like you'd only taken a glancing blow. I saw your skin glow, Elric. I wasn't dreaming. Whatever that is, whatever you are, it is more than some boy from Old King's Walk. Whoever armed the goblins wanted that hammer. You touched it, and it burned you. There is something... connected there."

The words made my skin remember the taste of that heat. I could smell again the sharp, sour tang of my own flesh scalding. I had never felt so small and so huge at once.

"I don't want to be 'something,'" I said. It came out harsher than I intended. A nearby drinker glanced over, then away.

"I know," she said, softer. "I don't want my father to be a man whose story ends in a goblin cave. We don't always get what we want."

We let the murmur of the room swell to fill the space between us. Someone near the hearth started a quiet song about the river's moods. A man laughed too loud at a joke he did not find funny. A dog snored under a table, feet twitching.

Eventually, bones heavy, eyes burning with grit, we arranged ourselves to sleep. Jaime kept her pack between her and the wall, one arm slung over it. I lay on the outer edge of the pallet, body curled a little, one hand on Maximus's hilt, more comfort than threat. The fire in the hearth had sunk to a red sigh. Shadows played on the low rafters.

"Tomorrow," Jaime whispered into the dim. "We start with the River Guild. Or the Watch. Or both."

"In that order," I murmured back. City words. Guild. Watch. Council. Magistrate. Each one another stone in the wall between us and understanding.

"My father walked these streets," she said, voice drifting. "He saw these walls. He touched these doors. Somewhere in this city, someone knows what happened to him. I'm going to make them tell me."

"You won't have to do it alone," I said.

That, at least, was simple. Whatever strange fire had woken in me, whatever tall rules and stone walls the city held, my place was still the same as it had been since we were children racing across the frozen pond: at her shoulder, ready to pull her up if she fell through the ice.

Outside, the city creaked and muttered in its sleep. Carts rattled by long after midnight. Somewhere, water roared where it went over a sluice. Feet thudded overhead on the floor above.

I lay there, staring at the underside of the table a few feet from my nose, watching lamplight flicker through the gaps in the planks. Every groan of wood, every snore, every muffled shout sharpened the sense of how big the place was and how little we were inside it. Old King's Walk felt small as a thumbprint compared to this, a single knot in the grain of a huge board.

Sleep came not all at once but in stages, like walking into a dark room and waiting for your eyes to give up on finding shapes. My last conscious thought before I slipped under was not of Maximus's last stand, nor of the goblin caverns, nor even of the burning hammer.

It was of the city gate and the guard's hand closing around our coins without interest, our names turning to chalk on his board. The way the walls had loomed, indifferent, stone teeth biting into the sky.

In Old King's Walk, the mountains were our guardians, old and slow and sometimes cruel, but familiar. Here, stone had been stacked by human hands to make new mountains, and the rules written inside them seemed just as high and cold.

We had come down chasing a dead man's journal and questions about goblin steel. We had found stone walls and tall rules that took coin just to step through. Somewhere beyond them, wrapped in the city's endless coils, lay merchants and guilds and captains and councils.

We knew none of their games. But we had Dratmar's coin, Maximus's sword, her father's words, and whatever slept coiled in my bones.

For now, that would have to be enough.

# Chapter 11

## A Badge with Rotten Edges

Morning came slow and sticky.

For a moment I did not know where I was. The ceiling above me was too low, the beams too dark, the smell wrong. Back home it should have been smoke and iron and Anya's over-sweet porridge if I'd overslept. Here it was spilled ale, stale onions, and the thick breath of strangers seeping through the floorboards.

Then the ache in my shoulders reminded me of the road, and the weight at my side reminded me of Maximus's sword. Old King's Walk was three days behind us. Maximus was further than that.

The bed at The Foaming Tankard complained when I sat up. Straw shifted inside the mattress with the tired whisper of something that had already given all it had to give. Jaime was a bundle of gray blanket on the other bed, dark hair loose for once, the pointed tip of one ear just visible. She slept curled tight, knees to chest, like she was holding something in.

A thin band of light pushed around the edges of the shutters. Someone below shouted for more water. Someone else laughed in a way that sounded like they'd been laughing all night.

My mouth tasted of old smoke and city dust. I swung my feet to the floor and winced at the chill of the boards. Somewhere under my boots the kitchen was already awake; the air carried the hollow clang of pots and the sharp scent of onions frying, trying their best to hide the sour-bitter reek of yesterday's beer.

"Jaime," I said, and cleared my throat when it came out more gravel than word. "Sun's up."

She did not move at first. Then the blanket shifted, and a green eye blinked at me through a curtain of hair. Without her braids she looked younger, which was strange, since Jaime often carried herself like someone older than my father had ever managed.

"I was hoping that was a dream," she said, voice muffled.

"Which part?" I asked. "The goblins or the lumpy bed?"

"Both." She pushed herself up on her elbows and grimaced as her back cracked. "But I suppose the bed is proof the goblins were real."

I did not answer. Saying it made it heavier, like naming a thing forged it in iron.

She swung her legs over the side, toes searching for her boots. Her usual neatness was gone; clothing was in a rough pile at the foot of the bed, pack half-open, Derrin Durandal's journal peeking out like a secret that had rolled too near the light. The silver ring she wore on its cord glinted once when she reached for her shirt.

"We should eat while we can," she said. "Find the docks before they're crowded."

"They're docks," I said. "Aren't they always crowded?"

She gave me a look that said I was being particularly dense this morning. It was an old, familiar feeling; Maximus had used it often.

"Crowded is different from thick with eyes," she said. "Early is better. Fewer people watching."

She put her back to me while she dressed. It was not something she'd done on the road. The city had tightened something in her. Or maybe it had just reminded her that people watched different here.

I pulled on my own clothes, the same shirt I'd worn yesterday and the day before. The fabric had the stretched feel of something that wanted a rest and would not get it. My hands found the familiar weight of Maximus's sword-belt even before my eyes did. The leather was worn smooth, scuffed white in places where his hand had always settled. I buckled it on and felt both lighter and heavier.

Jaime braided her hair quickly, several small plaits drawn back from her face instead of the single thick one she'd worn at home. It made her look sharper, like she'd fitted herself for trouble.

"Ready?" I asked.

"As I'll be." She picked up her father's journal and slid it into her pack with careful fingers before buckling the flap shut. "We ask about Riverside Warehouse, and Kaben & Sons. And Captain Lerin, if we find anyone with a brain."

"You're sure he's in the city?" I asked, as we stepped into the narrow hall. The wood smelled of damp clothes and boiled cabbage.

"He was, when Father wrote the journal." Her mouth flattened. "If he's posted somewhere else now, Watch records will say. But first the river."

The main room of The Foaming Tankard was half full, which, judging by the sticky floor and the man snoring under a table, probably meant it had been full not long ago. The hearth held the ghosts of last night's fire. The light that did creep in through the glazed windows was the sort that made dust stubbornly visible: thick motes drifting like lazy snow.

The innkeeper's wife—broad shoulders, narrow eyes, apron losing its battle with grease—gave us one appraising look as we came down, decided we were not the sort of trouble she needed to worry about, and shoved two chipped bowls along the bar without a word.

Porridge. Thick enough to stand a spoon in, gray as sawdust, sweetened with something pretending to be honey. A heel of bread each that had seen better days, and maybe better mouths.

Jaime pushed hers around with her spoon like she was trying to divine answers from the lumps.

"Do you think they'll know him?" she asked suddenly.

"Your father?" I shoveled in a mouthful. It tasted like someone had boiled regret with oats. "Here? This is just... an inn."

"Not here," she said. "I meant at the docks. He worked with river merchants before, he said so. It's in the journal. Names of shipmasters, places upriver. Someone must have seen him."

"If he wanted to be seen," I said. "If he was sniffing after smugglers, maybe he kept his head low."

"Even smugglers love someone." Her jaw set. "Someone would remember if he vanished."

She spoke like remembering was a duty. Maybe for her it was.

We ate in quick, steady silence after that. Traveling had taught me that complaints did not fill bellies any faster, and city food cost coin we did not have enough of to waste.

I caught the innkeeper's wife watching the sword at my hip once, her eyes lingering on the pommel, but she said nothing. Folk in cities were like that, I was learning. They saw more than they said, saved their words like coin.

Outside, the air had the chill, sour tang of a place that had been washed recently but not well. Rain had come in the night and not stayed long. The cobbles glistened in the narrow street, wet but already spotted with new horse droppings, new mud. Aramor's buildings leaned over us like they were trying to gossip about the people walking underneath. Laundry hung limp between second stories, gray shirts and underthings sharing the same tired sway.

We turned downhill, following the smell.

You didn't need to know a city to find its river. You just needed a nose and a willingness to keep walking toward the sharp mix of tar and rot and fish guts. Back home our river was clear and cold, thinking only of the glacier it had descended from. Here, the river had learned other languages. It spoke of oil and old wood, of rope and rust and waste.

The streets widened as we went. Carts rattled by piled with crates stamped with symbols I did not know, children darted between wheels like they'd never been told that wood and iron did not care which bones they broke. Men in rough shirts and women with scarves over their hair moved with their shoulders set as if they expected to be jostled and did not intend to yield.

The first glimpse of the river itself came over the shoulder of a warehouse: a wide brown sheet, flat only from a distance, crowded with boats of all sizes. Barges low and heavy in the water, little skiffs flicking between them, fat-bellied river-ships riding higher with painted names on their sides. Masts and spars made a forest of their own, ropes and rigging crisscrossing like spiderwebs.

The noise rolled at us in waves. Men shouting, gulls screaming, the deep, wordless groan of wood under strain.

Jaime stopped for a heartbeat on the corner, eyes narrowed as she took it in. To someone like her, whose father had written about all the places a river could carry a person, this must have looked half like hope, half like betrayal.

"Which way?" I asked.

She pointed toward a stretch where the warehouses were particularly tight-packed, tall brick and timber with only narrow alleys between. "Riverside Warehouse will be along there somewhere. Father said it sat close to the old quay."

"That narrows it down," I said dryly, looking at the endless line of stone and wood.

"Ask, Elric," she said. "You know how to do that, at least."

I KNEW HOW TO ask. I just had not expected it to feel like walking with a bell tied to my neck.

We moved along the dock-edge, and I stopped the first man who did not look like he'd bite my hand off. He was leaning on a pile of coiled rope, a scar down one cheek like someone had once tried to cut his face in half.

"Excuse me," I said. "Do you know where I can find Riverside Warehouse?"

He looked me up and down, then let his gaze slide to the sword at my side. Something calculating passed through his eyes, though I could not read the sum.

"Lots of riverside round here, boy," he said. "Plenty of warehouses, too."

"This one's called Riverside," Jaime cut in. "By name. It's a... company, or a guild holding." She sounded like she was quoting.

His jaw worked a moment. He spat to the side, narrowly missing a rat that had been investigating an old fish head.

"Never heard of it," he said. "Move along. You're in the way."

He turned his shoulder to us. That was that.

The next dockworker, a woman with arms like wrought iron and a kerchief tied around her hair, actually laughed when I asked.

"Riverside? No such place," she said. "Not here. Try up-river, boy. Or better yet, go home."

Jaime stepped closer to her. "A man named Derrin Durandal worked there," she said, voice steady. "He came from upriver. From Harrowmere, from the lake-villages. He had a silver ring with—"

The woman's mouth, which had been amused, lost its curve. Not flattened in ignorance. Flattened in the way of someone who had just heard a word she did not want attached to her day.

"Don't know him," she said quickly. "Don't know a Riverside. Don't know you. Clear off."

She walked away before we could press, hauling a handcart as if it suddenly needed moving very urgently.

Jaime watched her go with a narrowed gaze. "She knew something," she murmured.

"Or just didn't like strangers poking questions," I said.

"Both can be true."

We kept on. The river wind threaded fingers under my collar, carrying damp and a fine grit of something that clung to my tongue. I asked a man patching a net, two boys carrying a crate between them, an old fellow with skin like dried river leather sitting mending a rope. Some claimed ignorance. Others said they'd heard of a warehouse by that name once, long ago, but it had burned, or closed, or become something else. They all had answers, but none of them lined up straight.

When I shifted the question to Kaben & Sons, the air changed.

"Oh, Kaben," said the net-mender too quickly. "Sure. Grain importers, them. Good folk. Never cheated me." His fingers sped up on the net, tangling more than fixing.

"Solid traders," another man said, without waiting for us to ask more. "Nothing strange there. Everybody does business with Kaben."

"Everybody?" I asked.

"Everybody that matters," he said, then seemed to realize what he'd implied. His eyes darted away, to the watchtower further down the quay where a flag hung limp in the still parts of the breeze. "You two don't look like you matter. Go find a tavern. Leave the docks to workin' folk."

By the time we'd gone a quarter-mile along the waterfront my throat hurt from talking, and my head hurt from all the sudden silences that followed our questions. It felt like trying to pound a bent bar straight when the iron had already cooled. You could hit it all you liked; it would only crack.

"We're not getting anywhere," I muttered.

Jaime had her arms folded, nails biting into her sleeves. She looked less like she was going to cry and more like she was going to bite someone.

"We're getting something," she said. "No one pretends not to know a big merchant, or a whole warehouse, unless they have a reason."

"Fear's a reason," I said. "Or coin."

"Yes." She scanned the line of warehouses. "Which means we're close."

"Close to what? The part where someone decides we're not worth the trouble and tosses us in the river?"

"Maybe." Her lips thinned into something that was not quite a smile. "Then we'll know we were asking the right questions."

In hindsight, that might have been the moment to stop. But I was seventeen, and angry, and I believed, still, that if something was wrong and you pointed it out loudly enough, the right person would fix it. That was the world I knew: you showed Master Harrod the crack in the wagon axle, and he sighed and fetched fresh iron. You told the elder about the wolf tracks near the sheep-pasture, and men with spears went out. Problems were things you could put your hands on.

Cities, I was learning, had problems like mold. Under the paint.

We turned down a narrow side passage between two warehouses, thinking to cut toward the street behind. The alley smelled of stale urine and damp stone. My boots slipped a little on something green trying to grow where the light did not.

"Maybe we should look for Captain Lerin instead," I said. "If he's Watch, he might keep his records near the tower."

Jaime opened her mouth to answer.

That was when a voice behind us said, "You two look lost."

I TURNED. THREE MEN filled the mouth of the alley.

They wore the city's colors, blue and dull iron gray, with breastplates over padded jerkins and short cloaks thrown back. Not the gold-trimmed surcoats I had seen on the Watch at the city gates, but the cheaper variant I'd spotted on the patrol that had driven drunkards from the inn district last night. City Guard, not Watch. I was only just starting to learn the difference.

Their leader was thick through the chest but not soft. He had the kind of muscles that came from using them, not showing them. His eyes were a flat, muddy brown, but there was nothing dull in them. They moved over us the way a butcher's eye moves over a pig: weighing cuts.

To his left stood a younger man with a narrow face and a nose that had been broken badly and left crooked. To his right, a broad-shouldered fellow with a blotchy beard and small, pale eyes that did not seem to agree on where to look.

"Not lost," I said. "We were just heading back—"

"To the river?" The leader's mouth pulled sideways, not quite a smile. "I've been watching you. All morning. Asking questions that don't belong to you."

Jaime took half a step forward. "Questions belong to whoever's got breath to ask them," she said. Her tone was light, but I could see the stiffness in her shoulders.

"We got ourselves a philosopher," the crooked-nose guard muttered. He sounded like he thought most ideas larger than an ale mug were a waste of air.

The leader ignored him. His gaze had settled on Jaime now, lingering on the slight point to her ears. His lip curled almost imperceptibly.

"What brings country brats like you down to the guild docks?" he asked. "Looking for a ship? Don't look like you've the coin for it."

Jaime's chin lifted. "We're looking for a man named Derrin Durandal," she said. "He's my father. He was investigating smuggling through these warehouses. Riverside. Kaben & Sons. We're following his trail."

If she'd thrown a lit coal into a dry haystack, the effect would have been much the same.

The blotchy-bearded guard's eyes, which had been half-lidded and bored, snapped sharp. His jaw worked; the tendons in his neck stood up. The crooked-nose one glanced at the leader, a question in that look: *Did you hear what I heard?*

The leader's face did not change. Not much. But I saw the small tightening at the corners of his mouth. I'd seen Master Harrod wear that expression when inspecting a flaw in iron he hoped no one else had noticed.

He stepped closer. The alley suddenly felt smaller.

"Smuggling?" he said mild as milk. "Those are big words. Dangerous, in the wrong mouths."

"I have a right," Jaime began.

"You have what we say you have," he said, and the softness dropped away like rotten plaster. Underneath was stone. "You're not Watch. You're not Guild. You're not even proper citizens, by the look of you. Yet here you are, poking around dock-business. Asking after respectable merchants. Interfering in city matters."

"Respectable?" The word scraped my throat. "Kaben & Sons were doing business with goblins. We saw Kaben crates in the Goblin King's hoard. In Old King's Walk, three days upriver. People died because of those weapons."

The crooked-nose snorted. "Goblins raid, folk die. That's country life. Don't see how that's Aramor's problem."

"Funny," I said, "since the crates had your city seal on them."

That was a guess. But I'd seen the way marks on those crates had matched the marks on some I'd glimpsed being unloaded earlier this morning. The leader's eyes flickered. Just a twitch, but enough.

"Careful, boy," he said softly.

Jaime took a tight breath. "Captain Lerin is sympathetic," she said. "That's in Father's journal. If you take issue with our questions, we can bring them to him. Or to the Watch commander instead."

At the mention of Lerin, the blotchy-bearded guard made a sound in his throat, half choke, half curse.

"You hear that, Cragen?" he said to the leader. "They know names."

So, Cragen. It suited him: short, hard, nothing wasted.

Cragen's gaze went from Jaime to me and back again, measuring something new now. "You've been reading things you shouldn't," he said. "Talking to people you shouldn't. That makes you suspicious. Could be you're the ones meant to be handing off crates to goblins. Might be this is all a game, throwing dirt on respectable folk to cover your own muck."

"That's a lie." My fists had balled without my noticing. "We're trying to stop—"

He lifted one hand, and the other two guards shifted, hands falling to sword-hilts.

"You're trying to get yourselves in deeper than you understand," Cragen said. "But I'm a fair man. I'll give you a chance to mend your ways."

His eyes went to my sword. Maximus's sword.

"First," he said, "you'll show us what you're carrying. Coin. Blades. Papers. For inspection."

"For theft, you mean," Jaime said quietly.

He smiled without humor. "For evidence," he said. "Of your suspicious activity. Interfering with city business. Investigating without authority."

I felt something hot flare in my chest. "Investigating without—? We're the ones who were attacked. My brother died because your 'respectable merchants' are arming monsters, and you're worried we're asking the wrong questions?"

His eyes cooled. "Your brother," he said, "died because he was where steel was swinging. That's all. Now give me the sword, boy. Before this has to get unpleasant."

The alley seemed to narrow further. My hand went to the hilt, thumb rubbing automatically at the nick just under the pommel Maximus had always meant to file out and never had. His handprint was worn into that leather. Giving it up felt like sawing off the last piece of him I had.

I did not move.

Cragen took one step closer. The other two shifted, the soft hiss of steel half-leaving scabbards like snakes tasting the air.

"Don't," Jaime said low, not to them, to me. "Elric."

Her voice snagged itself in me. I swallowed.

"If this were proper," I said, forcing the words between my teeth, "you'd take us to your commander. To Captain Lerin. Let him decide if we're—"

"Captain Lerin's Watch, not Guard," Cragen said. "Different banners. Different walls. You're on my stones now. And under my say." His hand came up, palm open. "Sword. Coin. Knife, girl. I can see the hilt. Slow."

He had seen more than I'd thought. Jaime's cloak barely showed the shape of the knife she wore at the small of her back, but his eyes had been counting edges since we met.

For half a heartbeat she looked like she would run. Or fight. Then she unhooked the knife, reversing the grip so she held the blade. She offered him the hilt.

It might have been her calm that undid me. That I could stand there and watch her hand over the last steel that had been hers, and do nothing, and call that wisdom.

When Cragen took the knife, his fingers brushed hers. He did not need to smirk; the satisfaction showed anyway.

He turned to me again. "Your turn."

My fingers tightened on the hilt until the leather creaked.

"Maximus carried this since he was fifteen," I heard myself say, like someone else had taken my mouth. "He—he took a goblin spear in the chest for my sister. He died holding this sword. And you—"

"And now you're going to hand it to me," Cragen cut in. "Because your dead brother won't miss it, and you'll still have your hands. Mostly."

Something cracked in me then. Not the big crack; that came later, when power had to run through it. This was smaller, but it let heat flood in.

The alley blurred at the edges. All I could see clearly was his smirking face and his hand on Maximus's hilt in my mind's eye, dragging it through mud, using it to lean on while he idled at a post. I saw him leaving it to rust in a rack, or selling it for a few extra coins in some backroom deal. Maximus's care, all those nights spent oiling the blade by lamplight, turned into nothing.

My thumb slid over the guard to my own blade. I could draw faster than he expected; I knew that. Smith's arms and long hours had given me a certain speed. I could see the line of it: steel out, across, that smug expression opening from ear to ear.

"Elric." Jaime's hand closed on my arm. Her grip found the muscle and pinched hard. Her voice was low and very clear. "Not here. Not like this."

I could hear my heart pounding in my ears. The world had become very small: my hand, the sword, his throat.

Cragen watched all of that pass through my face. He was not stupid. His stance shifted subtly, weight settling, hand ready.

"Try it," he said softly. "Give me the excuse."

Jaime's fingers dug in harder. "You swing," she hissed, "and they gut you, and I sit in a cell alone. Maximus doesn't get his sword back either way. Do you want your mother to lose both her sons?"

The words hit harder than any blow. The thought of my mother, standing in the smithy doorway with no more sons to send home, knocked some of the breath back into sense.

I dragged air into my lungs. It tasted of mildew and piss and the copper of my own bitten tongue.

Slowly, like I was forcing rusted hinges, I uncurled my hand from the hilt. It shook, just a little. I took the belt by the buckle instead, unfastened it, and let the sword hang between my fingers.

Cragen watched my face the whole time. When I held it out, he took it without looking at the blade, only at me. There was a satisfaction there that made me want to find that crack in myself again and widen it.

"See?" he said quietly. "You can follow orders."

He passed Maximus's sword back to the blotchy-bearded guard. "Logan," he said, "tag this for evidence. Interfering with city business. Illegal investigation. Suspected conspiracy with foreign raiders."

"Evidence?" I heard my voice tilt. "You can't just—"

He ignored me. "Coin," he said. "All of it."

Jaime's jaw clenched. She pulled the small leather pouch from inside her tunic and dropped it into his waiting hand. That was most of what the village had scraped together to help us, plus the few coppers we'd earned on the road mending pots. He weighed it quickly, nodded, and slid it out of sight under his cloak. My own purse followed, lighter to begin with, and looked almost small in his fist.

"Consider this a lesson," he said. "In Aramor, you don't go poking your nose where it doesn't belong. The Watch keeps the law. The Guard keeps the peace. And both answer to folk with more gold than you'll see if you live to be as gray as the river."

"You mean you answer to Kaben," Jaime said. Her voice was tight but did not shake. "Or whoever's paying them. You're thieves with uniforms."

The crooked-nose took a step forward, hand raised. "Watch your pretty mouth, half-blood—"

Cragen threw out an arm, blocking him without taking his eyes off her.

"Enough," he said. "You're done talking for today." He crooked a finger. "Hands. In front."

"Are you arresting us or robbing us?" I demanded.

"Both," he said. "You're under detainment for suspicion of interfering in city business and slander against reputable merchants. You'll sit a while and think about whether you want to keep sharing your tales. Maybe by the time we're done, you'll see it's better to forget what you think you know."

Cold, heavy bands closed around my wrists when Logan snapped the manacles on. They were iron, and they did not care who I was or why I was there, only that they could hold.

"Captain Lerin will hear about this," Jaime said. It sounded more like a promise than a hope.

Cragen's mouth twitched in something that might have been amusement, if amusement could be cruel.

"Oh, I don't doubt it," he said. "Walk."

THEY DID NOT PARADE us through the main streets. The Guard knew a thing or two about humiliation, and they were careful with it; show too much and people start to ask the wrong questions. We went by back ways instead, through narrow lanes that smelled of the things the city hid: rotting scraps, chamber pots emptied carelessly, the sour-sweet stink of someone having been sick too close to a wall.

My wrists burned where the metal rubbed. The chain between the cuffs was short enough that if I stumbled, I would pull Jaime with me.

"Keep your head down," she murmured once, when we crossed a wider lane and a wagon rattled past. "No point letting half the city remember our faces."

"I thought we wanted people to know," I said, keeping my voice low.

"Not like this." She kept her gaze on the cobbles. "Not as fools in chains."

The Guardhouse they brought us to sat squatting at the edge of one of the older squares, stones darkened by years of smoke and rain. It had the look of a building that had been repurposed more than once. What might have been arrow slits in older days had been widened into windows with iron bars. The door was thick oak bound with bands of black metal, edges polished by generations of hands pushing it open.

Inside, the air was heavy with sweat, ink, and old anger. A desk stood just beyond the door, manned by a clerk whose hairline had lost its own battles. He looked up, took in our manacles and country clothes, and barely bothered to conceal his boredom.

"Two more," Cragen said. He tossed a folded scrap of parchment onto the desk. "Interfering dockside. Asking questions they've no right to ask. Alleged ties to goblin raiders."

"Alleged?" Jaime snapped. "You made that up on the spot."

The clerk glanced at her. His eyebrows lifted the smallest bit, as if her nerve intrigued him for half a second before habit buried it.

"Name?" he asked, quill hovering.

"Elric son of Harrod," I said, before Cragen could put something else in my mouth.

"Jaime Durandal," she said. There was a tiny pause before she gave the surname, and when she did, it landed like a thrown stone.

The clerk's hand jerked. The quill left a blot of ink on the parchment. His eyes flicked to Cragen, then away so fast it might have been a trick of the light.

"Durandal, is it?" he said slowly.

Cragen's hand came down flat on the parchment, smearing the ink. "Just write," he said, voice gone very quiet.

The clerk swallowed. He wrote.

No one mentioned my brother's name. Maximus might as well have been nothing more than the weight hanging now at Logan's hip.

They took us down a short corridor that smelled of damp and the end of things, then down a set of stone steps into the belly of the Guardhouse. The temperature dropped with each stair, the air thickening and cooling until my breath ghosted faintly in front of my face.

The cells were small stone mouths, barred with iron, doors opening inward on hinges that groaned in complaint. Most were empty this time of morning. One held a drunk snoring so loudly it sounded like each breath fought with the next for passage. Another housed a bald man sitting with his back to the wall, staring at nothing with the patient eyes of someone who had learned that time moved whether he watched it or not.

They put us in the third.

The door squealed when Logan swung it open. The inside stank of mildew and old piss. The floor was stone, uneven, with a dark patch in one corner that might have been spilled ale once, or something worse. A single narrow slit meant to pass for a window let in a thin gray light high up on the wall, too small to fit even Jaime's shoulders through.

"Welcome to Aramor hospitality," Logan said, his smile showing crooked, yellowed teeth.

Cragen unhooked the manacles with quick, practiced movements. For half a heartbeat as the weight fell from my wrists, the temptation to move, to shove, to throw a punch and damn the consequences flared again. I could feel my muscles coil.

Jaime's hand brushed mine, a light touch this time, no pressure needed. It was enough.

"Enjoy the peace and quiet," Cragen said. "Might be a while before anyone has time to hear your little tales. We're very busy, you understand. Keeping the city safe."

"From who?" Jaime asked. "From smugglers working with monsters, or from anyone who might make that known?"

He met her gaze through the bars as Logan swung the door shut.

"From trouble," he said. "And you brought trouble with you." His eyes flicked once, almost involuntarily, to the ring's faint outline under her collar. "Some folk can't help it. It sticks to them."

The key turned in the lock with a heavy clunk, the sound of something settling into place.

Footsteps faded up the corridor. The drunk snored on. Water dripped somewhere out of sight at irregular intervals, a slow, maddening beat.

I stood in the center of the cell for a moment, not quite trusting my legs to move. The space was too small to pace properly, too big to pretend walls did not exist. Jaime crossed to the back wall and slid down it until she sat with her knees drawn up, arms draped over them.

"They took his sword," I said. It came out dull.

"I know," she said.

"They took your knife. Our coin. What little we had."

"I know," she said again. "They were going to, whether we fought or not."

"It shouldn't be like this," I said, and heard how childlike it sounded, even to my own ears. "If there's law, it should—should help. My father always said—"

"He said that in Old King's Walk," Jaime said, not unkindly. "Where law was the faces you knew and elders you'd watched sit at the same table since before you were born."

I looked around our stone box. The walls sweated slowly. Rust bled from the bolts that held the bars.

"When he came to Aramor," she went on, voice low, "my father wrote that law here wears armor. It answers to coin more than to conscience. He thought he could work with that. Bend it. Find the bits that still remembered what they were meant to be."

"Captain Lerin," I muttered.

"Yes." She rested her forehead briefly on her knees. When she lifted it again, her eyes were bright, but dry. "If he was 'sympathetic but with hands tied' when Father wrote that, how tight are those knots now?"

Something in my chest felt like an ember buried under ash: not enough air, not enough fuel, but still hot. It refused to go out.

"We can't do anything in here," I said. My wrists still tingled from the manacles. Without Maximus's sword at my side, I felt lopsided, like someone had taken one of my arms and left the sleeve hanging.

"For now," Jaime said. "We wait. Listen. Watch." She let out a breath that shivered on the way out. "If they mean to keep us, they'll have to bring us before someone who can sign a paper. And if they don't mean to keep us, then they'll let us go with words meant to scare us quiet. Either way, we'll know more than we do now."

"You said on the road you didn't want to see your father's city like this." I slid down the wall opposite her, the damp seeping into my trousers. "Rotten."

"I wanted to believe he fought the rot and won," she said. "Or at least held it back. Instead, it swallowed him." Her jaw tightened. "I don't know if I'm more afraid that he's dead, or that he's alive somewhere inside it."

We fell quiet after that.

The drip continued its uneven count. Somewhere above us, boots thudded, voices rose and fell. The stone at my back leached warmth from me steadily. Damp crept into the cut on my palm I'd forgotten about, making it sting anew.

In the village, wrong things had at least had shapes I recognized: wolves, storms, goblins. You could swing at those. You could drive them off or die trying. Here, the wrongness was in the walls, in the weight of keys on a man's belt, in a ledger's ink. It was a thing that did not care if I was angry, except perhaps to enjoy it.

I rested my head against the cold, gritty stone and shut my eyes for a moment.

I had thought, when we reached Aramor, that the city would be an answer. Instead, we were two country fools in a box, our weapons gone, our coin stolen under the name of law, with only a muffled ring of iron between us and everything we did not yet know.

The stone under my ribs had not gone anywhere. It had just got heavier.

# Chapter 12

## THE HOLDING BLOCK

THE HOLDING BLOCK STANK of old piss and wet stone.

They marched us down a narrow corridor, boots and shackles echoing off the walls. Torches spat and crackled in iron brackets, throwing sour light over everything. The air was thick and damp, like a cellar no one had bothered to empty of potatoes and ghosts.

"Nothing but the best for you two," Cragen said, walking just behind my shoulder. "Don't say the Watch never did anything."

My wrists itched where the manacles rubbed my fur bare. Every step, the chain between my ankles clinked. Jaime's chin was high, but I could see the tightness in her jaw. A pair of guards trailed us with hands a little too eager on their cudgels.

The corridor ended in a heavy oak door bristling with iron bands. Cragen rapped twice, then shouldered it open. It complained on tired hinges.

The holding room beyond was low-ceilinged and cramped, more storage cellar than justice. The air cooled another notch. A single slit window near the ceiling let in a slice of afternoon the width of my thumb. Below it, three barred doors opened into cells. Someone had scratched tally marks into the stone by the nearest.

"Rotated the stock, did we," Cragen said to no one in particular. "Good. Hate mixing the fresh trouble with the old."

He produced a ring of keys that jingled like bad news and walked to the middle cell. The two other guards dragged us along.

"Inside," Cragen said, unlocking it. "Mind the step. Hate to have you break your neck before you hang."

The cell was not much wider than a cart, and deeper than it was tall. Straw clumped damply in the corners. A bench of rough planks sat bolted to the back wall. That was all.

All, and two people.

They sat at opposite ends of the bench, as far apart as the bench allowed. The nearer was a woman a few years older than me, human at first glance but wrong around the edges. Her dark hair fell in chopped, uneven layers to her jaw, framing a pale face smudged with soot or dirt or both. Her eyes were the deep kind of brown that looks black in low light. She had the sort of stillness I'd only ever seen in ambush cats: loose and ready and considering.

The other was a dwarf. White-shot brown beard cropped short by dwarf standards, coppery skin, a nose that had been broken more than once and set without much fuss. His clothes might have been decent once—sleeves embroidered with tiny bronze sigils, good wool trousers—but they'd been slept in and sweated through. Even sitting hunched, there was a weight about him, like a boulder that had chosen that spot and would not be budged.

They both looked up as we filled the doorway. Not alarmed; just...adjusting their sums to account for two more.

The woman's gaze flicked, quick as a sparrow: manacles, ears, tail, then my face. Assessing. Jaime got the same treatment. The dwarf squinted as if we were an ink blot he had to make a picture out of and wasn't impressed with any of the options.

Cragen grinned, showing the gap where a left canine should be. "Make room for our honored guests."

The dwarf snorted. "You planning to stack us like firewood then, Sergeant?"

Cragen's smile didn't move, but his eyes did, a lazy drift to the dwarf and back. "Careful, Wrothburt. 'Honored' can mean 'hung first.'"

He waved the two guards forward. One shoved me between the shoulder blades. I stepped up into the cell, ducking instinctively under the low lintel. Jaime followed, brushing my arm. The woman slid her boots back, making space without making it look like she'd given ground.

"Nice and cozy," Cragen said, swinging the door shut. The key turned with a solid, final click. "You four behave. Or don't. Makes paperwork easier, either way."

The manacles came off our wrists through the bars, but they left the shackles at our ankles. Iron bit my skin, heavier now that there was nowhere to go.

Cragen pocketed the keys, then paused, head tilted. From the far cell—dark and empty, bars rusting at the bottom—a rustle and a wet cough came, then silence.

"Forgot we had a fifth," he muttered, not sounding like someone who'd truly forgotten anything. "Ah, he's quiet enough."

Jaime licked her lips. "Our belongings. Our swords. The coin you took."

"That so?" Cragen said, all innocence. "I remember contraband seized during arrest. Dangerous weapons. Evidence logged proper. Can't have it in here." He rapped the bars with a knuckle. "You'll hurt yourselves. Or, worse, someone who matters."

"They're not contraband," I said, before Jaime's temper got out ahead of her. "Maximus's blade—"

"Maximus," he repeated, as if testing the name on his tongue. Nothing in his face changed. "You're lucky we're generous souls. Belongings will be inventoried. Whatever the court doesn't take as fine, you might see again. If you live long enough."

He gave us a little bow, all mock flourish, then nodded to his men. They filed out. The door thudded shut. The heavy lock snicked on the other side.

For a moment, the only sound was the crackle of torches in the corridor and the faint, seeping drip of water somewhere above.

I BREATHED IN THE cell: old straw, dried sweat, stone dampness, and under it all, the sour tang of fear that clung to this place like lichen. The walls closed in, more felt than seen. I could stretch my arms almost to both sides.

The dwarf watched us, hands resting on his knees, fingers drumming absently. The woman had leaned back a little, slouching against the cold wall in a way that made it look like she owned it.

Jaime took two steps into the cell and turned so her back was not to anyone. I did the same, the old habit from tavern brawls, from alleys where you couldn't trust the dark not to have teeth. I shifted so my tail had space to curl, not be stepped on.

The woman eyed the shackles on our ankles. "They treat all the kittens like this," she said, voice low and dry, "or are you special?"

It took me a heartbeat to realize she meant me. My ears twitched before I could stop them. Heat pricked my neck.

"Maybe they're just scared of a Durandal," Jaime said before I could bark something deflecting. There was an edge to her voice I'd heard in her father's when a witness lied. "Since they know my family has friends who court."

The dwarf's brows rose a fraction. "Durandal," he repeated. "Interesting surname to be rotting in a city cell."

The woman's gaze sharpened. "You're Derrin's girl," she said. Not asked—stated. "The nose is the same. Less broken."

Jaime's eyes snapped to her. "You knew my father?"

"Knew of him," the woman said. "You listen enough in the right alleys, you learn which names not to touch and which ones get you paid double." Her eyes flicked to me again. "Shadow-Touched Elisah Nialath, since we're making friends."

The way she said "Shadow-Touched" wasn't apologetic. It was almost proud, like she was leaning into a rumor to see who flinched.

The dwarf snorted at that. "Nobody with sense calls themselves Shadow-Touched."

"Nobody with sense wears that beard in this damp, but here we are," she said calmly. "What are you, their grandfather?"

He folded his arms. "Rygial Wrothburt. And I've been grandfather to more promising fools than the three of you put together."

"Four," I said, before I could decide whether interrupting was smart. All their eyes went to me. I swallowed. "Maximus would tell you to count properly."

Jaime's shoulders eased just a hair at the name.

Elisah watched that, then tipped her head. "And you? Besides kitten. Got a name?"

"Elric," I said. "Shaddar." Saying the family name in this underground stone felt strange, like planting a seed in rock.

Her mouth quirked. "Sounds foreign. Smells like farm." She sniffed the air theatrically. "Hay, goats, poor choices."

"Village," I said, because there was no hiding it. The country clung. "Half a day's walk east. You?"

"Elisah's enough," she said, gaze sliding away, into the darker corner of the cell as if something there interested her more.

Rygial grunted. "If you lot are finished preening, maybe you'll tell me why the Watch is sweeping up teenagers with noble names, cursed girls, and dwarves who were minding their own business."

"You weren't minding your own business," Elisah said. "You were meddling in everyone else's."

"So you admit it," he said, satisfied.

"I admit you're loud," she muttered.

"Rygial," Jaime said, seizing on the familiar syllables, fighting the walls closing in. "Wrothburt. I've seen that name in my father's notes. You were consulting on...on time anomalies in the lower wards, three years ago."

His eyes narrowed. "Your father asked questions. That's what he did. Didn't mean he liked the answers."

"Better than sleepwalking," she shot back. "They've arrested us on false charges. They took our swords, Dratmar's coin. All part of something bigger tied to Kaben & Sons and the weapons shipments on the river. I don't intend to sit here and wait to be 'processed' while they clean their tracks."

Elisah's eyes glinted at the word "coin." "Dratmar's coin," she repeated, like she was tasting a story. "Pretty trinket to wave around in this city. Kind that gets things opened or gets throats cut."

"Where is it?" I asked before I could stop myself, heart kicking. My hand went to where the chain had ridden under my shirt. Empty. Dumb thing to say; I knew where it was. In a ledger somewhere. Or a pocket.

"Under lock and key," Rygial said. "With the rest of our things, most like. Unless a guard with more appetite than discipline has gone shopping early."

He shifted, the bench creaking. "They took my focus crystal. My satchel. Two decades of notes. Their souls should itch for a century."

"You're a wizard," I said. Obvious, maybe, but the word in a place like this still wanted saying.

"Among other indignities," he said. "What did they claim you did, then? Or did you blink at them wrong?"

"Assaulting an officer," Jaime said. Each word was clipped, like she was turning a knife over. "Disturbing the peace. Interfering with an investigation. Take your pick."

"All of them unearned," I added.

Elisah's smile was small and feline. "If I had a copper for every honest soul in here..." She held up empty hands. "See? Still poor."

"What about you?" Jaime asked her. "Your charges?"

"Existing," Elisah said. "Breathing in the wrong direction. The usual."

Rygial sighed. "The posted reason was 'suspected accomplice to theft and unlawful sorcery.'"

"Ah, you read the fancy script," Elisah said. "I just heard 'witch' and 'Dragon Below' and figured I'd be bored in a cage again. Shadow-Touched girls are useful when you need a culprit." Her eyes slid to me. "Or a monster, hm?"

My tail twitched. The fur on my arms prickled. I met her gaze. "They didn't say 'monster' to my face," I said. "They just grabbed my ears in the street and told jokes."

"That's restraint," she said. "Most days, they skip the jokes."

Jaime's hands had curled into fists. "They wanted a reason to get us off the street," she said. "I was following a lead. Kaben & Sons' ledger numbers don't line up with what's coming off the barges. Father flagged it months ago. Then he vanished." Her throat bobbed. "Now every time I get close to a shipment or a name, someone tries to shut me up. Badly, this time."

Rygial's eyes sharpened. "Kaben & Sons, you say. The weapons factors by the west docks."

"Yes," Jaime said.

He scratched his beard slowly. "They came to the Collegium four months back with a request. Wanted to hire temporal security. 'Ensure punctual cargo,' they said. Wanted me to help them...stretch certain nights. Shorten certain days. So some barges might, say, arrive before they left."

Elisah let out a low whistle. "That's one way to dodge tariffs."

"I told them to put that level of idiocy in writing so I could throw it at the magistrates," Rygial said. "They declined."

"And now they have a friend in the Watch," Jaime murmured. Her gaze went to the door. "Cragen works for them. Or with them."

"Or with whoever owns them behind the signboard," Elisah said. "Names on ledgers are like masks. The real face is in the shadows behind."

I tried to picture it: Cragen with his easy cruelty, men hauling crates off ships under cover of fog, coins passing from hand to hand. Somewhere in there, my brother Max dying on a road for reasons we still didn't fully understand. These people, this city, tugged on threads that ran straight back to my village field and the blood in the dust.

"Either way," Jaime said, "we need out. We need our equipment back. I need that coin. And my father's sword."

"Elric's brothers' sword," I corrected quietly.

She glanced at me and nodded. "And Maximus's sword."

Elisah stretched her boots out, ankles crossing. The iron around mine felt heavier. "You can list your needs all day," she said. "Out there, they sound very noble. In here, they sound like air in a jar."

"You've escaped from these cells before," Rygial said, not a question.

She smiled with only one corner of her mouth. "From worse. This place is just damp and lazy. The mortar's old. The guards are bored. Shadows are thick. If I had my tools, we would already be gone."

"Tools they took," I said.

"Yes," she agreed lightly. "Which is rude. And inconvenient. For them, mostly."

"If you had my focus crystal," Rygial said, "I could show you inconvenient. I had a very neat little temporal dilation field mapped out. Enough to slow this corridor to half-speed for a minute and a half. Walk right past them while they finish blinking. Would have been...elegant."

"Elves and their flourishes," she said. "No offense to your half."

"Dwarf," he grunted.

"Elves, dwarves. Pointed ears, blunt ears. You all want the same thing." She tipped her head back against the stone, studied the cracks in the ceiling. "You want time to behave. Stones to stay where you put them. Shadows to fall in straight lines. You like order."

"And you don't?" I asked.

She let her gaze drop to me. "I like knowing where the cracks are," she said. "And how deep they go."

For a while, we sat in restless silence. A shout drifted faint through the door, then the muffled thud of something dropped. Somewhere nearby, a man laughed, the sound ugly and short.

Jaime paced the width of the cell: three steps, turn, three steps, turn. Her boots scuffed the stone. Every time she turned, her eyes cut to the door, to the barred window, to the lock.

Rygial watched her once, then shut his eyes and leaned his head back, lips moving soundless. Counting, maybe. Or reciting spells he couldn't cast.

I sat on the floor with my back to the wall opposite the bench, knees up, tail around my ankles. I let my eyes half-close and listened like I would in the forest: for pattern, for break in pattern. Footsteps in the hallway came and went. Keys jangled far off. The drip kept its slow beat.

"Elric," Jaime said quietly, not pausing her pacing. "You all right?"

"Fine," I lied automatically.

"Your ears are flattened," she observed.

I forced them up. They drooped back of their own accord. "Just thinking."

"Think us out of here, then," Elisah murmured.

"You're the one who knows the cracks," I said. "What would you do, if you had a pick, a strip of metal, anything?"

She exhaled through her nose, considering. "Locks are like stubborn old men," she said. "They have their pattern. You learn where to push, where to pry. This one—" she nodded at the door "—looks like the sort they use everywhere in this city because they bought them cheap in bulk. Easy enough to tickle if I could get fingers inside. But your manacles are built to keep even a hairpin from slipping free. Someone's been robbed by a nimble girl before." Her smile was sharp.

"Could you pick with...without tools?" Jaime pressed.

"Could you write with no ink?" Elisah countered. "I can feel a lock. I can understand it. I cannot magic the pins into falling over for me. That's your wizard's territory."

Rygial didn't open his eyes. "I bend time, not metal. Very different disciplines."

"You bend time into knots," she said. "Maybe time could tie up a guard for us. Strangle him a little."

"If I had my focus," he said evenly, "I could do enough mischief to give us a chance. As I do not, I'm reduced to schoolyard tricks and old bones. They might get us out of the cell, if we don't mind loosing half the mortar and bringing the ceiling down."

"There's a thought," Elisah said. "We'd definitely be out."

Jaime stopped pacing. "There has to be some angle," she said, more to herself than to any of us. "They're arrogant. Cragen especially. He thinks he's untouchable. Men like that...they talk. They gloat. They slip."

"Maybe he'll come back and monologue his whole scheme," Elisah said. "Villains do that in old plays. Gives the heroes time to wriggle free."

"He'll come back," I said. The certainty surprised me, but it came on strong. "Men like him like to see what they've done. Like a boy who pulls wings off flies waits to see if they can still crawl."

Jaime looked at me, then gave one short nod. "Then when he does," she said, "we listen. We make him feel clever. And we make sure he tells us where our things are."

Elisah smiled that small smile again. "Now you're talking like you grew up in a city, Durandal."

"I grew up in my father's house," Jaime said. "Same thing."

Rygial cracked one eye. "If you're all through counting on the tender mercies of a corrupt sergeant," he said dryly, "save a sliver of thought for what comes after. Say we know where the evidence is. We still have to get to it. Odds are, it's in the property room behind two locked doors, a bored clerk, and an inventory ledger from here to the river."

"Do you have a better plan?" Jaime asked.

"Yes," he said. "But it involves not letting them catch me in the first place. A bit late for that one."

I huffed a laugh despite myself. It came out thin.

Elisah's head turned, just slightly. Her posture changed. A cat smelling a shift in the wind. A heartbeat later, I heard it too: the steady clomp of footsteps, heavier than the other guards', not hurrying.

Cragen.

He didn't rush. He didn't need to. The keys on his belt chimed a lazy accompaniment.

"Show's back on," Elisah murmured. Her eyes went flat and unreadable.

Jaime's mouth set. She moved to standing in the middle of the cell, feet braced, shoulders loose, as if about to argue a case before a magistrate instead of iron bars.

Rygial rolled his shoulders once, making some of the stiffness crack free, then settled his face into something bland and unimpressed.

Me? I shifted until I was half-crouched near the door, not close enough to grab at, but close enough to watch his eyes.

The outer door opened with its familiar complaint. Cragen stepped in alone this time. No need for backup, not with the iron between us. He sauntered to our cell, sucking something from between his teeth with a click of his tongue.

"Comfortable?" he asked.

"Just like home," Jaime said. She was good; the shake in her voice barely there. "Cold, cramped, and crawling with rats."

He laughed, genuinely amused. "Durandal wit. Your da had that. Less pretty when it got him in trouble, mind you."

Jaime's fingers tensed, but she kept her chin up. "You knew my father."

"Oh, everyone knew your father," Cragen said. "Man couldn't sneeze without three scribes writing it down. And you, playing at little magistrate, digging into things beyond your reach. Should have stuck to harp lessons and soft shoes."

"He was investigating Kaben & Sons when he disappeared," she said. "You know that."

Cragen tilted his head, considering. "Now that's an interesting word. 'Disappeared.' Makes it sound like he tripped and fell down a hole. Maybe wandered off. Old watchman's trick, that. You don't see a problem, you don't have to fix it."

"You arrested us because I was following the same trail," Jaime pressed. Her eyes didn't leave his. "Because Kaben & Sons don't like Durandals sniffing around their ledgers."

His smile thinned. "I arrested you because you started a fight in my streets."

"You know that's a lie."

"Truth is what ends up on the scrap of paper, girl," he said, voice gone flat. "Not whatever story you spin yourself to sleep with."

Elisah chuckled softly. "He has a point, you know."

He flicked a glance at her. "And you. Every back alley's favorite curse. I've hauled you in twice before. You keep slipping the noose. Someone up there—" he gestured vaguely toward the ceiling "—likes you. Or doesn't want to touch you."

"Dragon Below's children never hang," she said, her tone taking on a faint, ritual lilt. "Rope rots. Wood splits. Necks don't break. That's what they whisper in the gutters."

Cragen snorted. "I've seen plenty hang. Dragon Below or Above doesn't pay my wage. Men with full purses do." His gaze slid back to Jaime. "Men who move steel quietly, so the city can keep playing at peace. Men who don't like little girls with daddy's name poking their noses in."

"Men like Kaben," Jaime said.

"Kaben is a sign on a warehouse," he said. "A piece of painted wood. You think wood gives orders?" He shook his head in mock sorrow. "This is why your father got in so deep. Always thought the writing on the door meant something."

"Then who does give orders?" I asked, the words out before I could clamp my teeth on them. My voice came out rougher than I meant.

Cragen's eyes flicked to me, taking in the fur, the ears, the shackles. "You," he said, amusement curling his lip. "Another country stray who doesn't know when to keep his mouth shut."

His gaze slid off me like I wasn't worth the spit, turning instead to Jaime—the real problem in the room.

My skin crawled. "You knew Maximus."

"He was one of mine for a while," Cragen said. "Before he decided he liked the open road better than a proper wage. Good sword-arm. Better instincts than most. Shame, what happened on that pass."

My breath hitched. "What happened?"

"Bandits," Cragen said. "Or so the report said. You know how it goes: merchant caravan, wrong valley, right time for someone else. You want more, ask your betters. I just read what's handed to me and keep my streets clean."

Jaime stepped forward, as close to the bars as she could without touching them. "And the men with the full purses," she said. "They hand you the reports. They tell you what the truth is, don't they."

He leaned a shoulder against the bars, bringing his face level with hers. "Here's a truth," he said softly. "Kaben & Sons, and men like them, keep this city fed. Armed. Working. They buy swords from outlands that cost more than your father made in a year. They move them where they're needed. Quietly. Off the books. Because if every clerk and priest saw the numbers, they'd start to worry who all that steel is for."

"For war," Jaime said.

"For balance," Cragen countered. "When one baron arms up, his neighbors get nervous. They buy too. Steel flows. Coin flows. Men like me get enough to line our boots." He tapped his chest. "And the streets stay—more or less—in one piece. Your father wanted to drag all that into daylight. Put names on it. Limits. Laws. Thought the world cared for justice more than it did for not being on fire."

"He was right," she whispered.

"Maybe," Cragen said. "Maybe not. Either way, he made enemies higher than my pay grade. I take orders; I don't write them. But when a directive comes down from above, wrapped in a nice fat purse—'keep the Durandal girl busy, keep prying eyes off the west docks shipments'—I don't ask whose ink it's written in."

He paused, realized what he'd just stitched together aloud. His jaw flexed once.

Silence thudded between us. Elisah's eyes had gone very sharp. Rygial's fingers drummed a rapid rhythm on his knee, then stilled.

Cragen pushed off the bars, straightening. "Anyway," he said briskly, trying to toss the words away like scraps. "I've got three street brawlers, one suspected witch, and one doddering wizard to process. By tomorrow, you'll be in front of a magistrate who owes me favors, and by next week you'll be on a work gang mending the Kingsroad. Or worse, if anyone up top decides they'd rather you disappear quiet." His gaze lingered on Jaime at that last.

"You're not subtle," Jaime said. There was a sharp, brittle calm in her now. "For someone who likes to think he's clever."

He smiled slow. "I don't need to be subtle. I have bars." He tapped them with his knuckles again, an unconscious, possessive gesture. "And you have nothing. No swords. No coin. No friends who'll stick their necks out this far. Your father spent all that goodwill long ago."

"You talk a lot for a man who 'just takes orders,'" Rygial observed.

Cragen's eyes went flinty. "I talk because I can. Because down here, my word's the only one that counts." He turned to go, then paused, half-turned back. "Oh. And don't waste your time planning any tricks with that pretty little Dragon coin." He smirked at Jaime. "It's in the lockbox in the property room now. Along with your swords and the dwarf's toys. Three keys to that box: one on me, one on the captain, one in the clerk's desk. None of which you'll ever see."

He let that hang in the air like a dare, then walked away, boots thudding in that unhurried rhythm. The outer door shut behind him, the lock bar dropping with a heavy, satisfied clunk.

We listened to his footsteps fade, the echoes smearing out along the corridor, until the drip and torch crackle swallowed them.

Elisah blew out a slow breath. "Well," she said. "If you were hoping he'd monologue, Durandal, I'd say you've been blessed."

Jaime stood where she was for three heartbeats more, shoulders tight, then stepped back from the bars like they'd burned her. She turned to look at us, something clear and hard in her eyes. "Property room," she said. "Lockbox with three keys. One on Cragen. One on the captain. One with the clerk."

"Men with full purses giving orders from above," Rygial added. "This is bigger than a crooked sergeant. Which I suspected. But it's...convenient to have it confirmed by the man himself."

"And he thinks his bars make him safe," I said. I could still see Maximus as I'd last seen him, laughing as he swung into the saddle, promising to bring back something better than stories. Bandits, Cragen had said. Or so the report claimed.

"Bars help," Elisah said. "For a while."

Jaime moved to the bench, sat down abruptly beside Rygial, elbows on her knees, hands clasped under her chin. "He won't make the same mistake twice," she said. "He knows he said too much."

"Men like Cragen," Elisah said, "believe they can say anything in places like this. Words don't count in the dark. Only in ink." She flexed her fingers. "But we heard. And I don't forget what I hear."

Rygial gave her a sidelong look. "Nor do I," he said. "And I have the advantage of having spent two centuries training my memory. Every rune he traced in the air while he bragged is carved up here now." He tapped his temple.

Jaime nodded. "Then we're agreed. Whatever our reasons for being here, we're all pinched by the same hand. Kaben & Sons. The men behind them. Cragen, their hound. We all need what's in that property room, and we all have cause to make them pay."

Elisah's smile this time was wide enough to show teeth. "You talk like a magistrate and a gutter rat had a baby," she said. "I like it."

She leaned forward, shadows from the torchlight pooling under her eyes, making them look deeper. "So. Keys. Lockbox. Property room. A very arrogant sergeant who believes we are caged and declawed." Her gaze went from Jaime to Rygial to me. "We going to sit here and let him be right?"

"No," I said. The word settled in my chest like a stone in water, sinking to something solid. "Maximus didn't die so I could sit in a cell and wait to be told what truth is."

Rygial grunted, which could have meant agreement or heartburn. "I am not," he said, "ending my days patching potholes for a city that barely remembers my name. If there's a crack to be found in this little system of theirs, I'll find it. With or without a focus crystal."

Jaime met each of our eyes in turn. "Then we work together," she said. "Elisah, you know locks. The layout. The rumors of how things run behind these walls. Rygial, you know the Watch's procedures, from your time consulting. The way they think, where they cut corners. Elric..." Her gaze softened fractionally. "You see things. Hear things. You grew up fitting yourself into spaces that didn't want you. That's...useful."

Useful. Not monster. It warmed something cold in me.

Elisah's voice cut through. "We don't have tools, or spells, or allies on the outside we can count on," she said. "We have time, such as it is. Ears. Hands. Shadows."

She tilted her head back, studying the slice of light high in the wall. "First thing's first. We learn the rhythm. Guard shifts. Which ones drag their feet. Which ones talk too much. Who brings food, who carries keys. Everything else grows from that."

Rygial nodded slowly. "And we think carefully about timing. Cragen wants us before a magistrate tomorrow. That's both a threat and a deadline. They'll be busiest preparing, less watchful about the small things. Small things are where escapes live."

Jaime exhaled, some of the tremor leaving with the breath. "Then we watch," she said. "We listen. We plan."

"And when we get out," Elisah said lightly, "we have a sergeant, a factor, and their quiet wars to visit."

She held out her hand, palm up, in the space between us. The gesture wasn't grand. Just there.

One by one, we put our hands in. Mine, furred and callused from practice with a blade that wasn't mine. Jaime's, ink-stained at the edges, knuckles rubbed raw from cuffs. Rygial's, square and strong, faintly warm as if from some heat banked under stone.

Elisah's fingers curled around ours, surprisingly strong. Shadows clung in the lines of her wrist like bracelets. "To cracks," she said.

"To truth," Jaime added.

"To repayment," Rygial said.

I thought of Maximus's laugh, of my mother's hands in the earth, of Derrin Durandal's empty study. "To getting our things back," I said, not trusting myself with bigger words.

We let go. The walls didn't move; the air didn't sweeten. The shackles were still cold around our ankles.

But something else shifted in that small, sour cell. Not much. Just enough.

We were no longer four strangers waiting for whatever the Watch chose to do with us.

We were, for the first time since the manacles clicked shut, facing the same crack in the same wall, looking for the same way out.

# Chapter 13

## KEYS, CLOCKS, AND QUIET STEPS

WE WAITED A LONG time after Cragen left.

You can tell the hour by the way a cell sounds. Early on there's shouting, boots, a door somewhere slamming every few breaths. Later, the night settles into the stone. The quiet gets a weight to it, like wet wool on your shoulders. Voices turn low or stop altogether. You hear small things instead: rats chewing, someone coughing two cells away, the drip where the mortar never quite set right.

We lay on our pallets and listened to all that, not saying much. There's only so many times you can rehearse the moment when a guard might come back and hit you just because he can. After a while, your mind gives up and drifts to other dangers.

The lantern down the corridor had burned low, its light thinning out before it reached us. Our bars took what was left and turned it into ladders of shadow that climbed the wall. When I looked at them too long my eyes started to stitch them into shapes. Faces, mostly, and that always came back around to my own.

My ears had stopped ringing from the last scuffle, but my ribs still complained when I breathed too hard. I lay flat on my back, tail curled stiff along my leg to keep it from twitching, and watched the ceiling. It had a crack that ran corner to corner, like someone had tried to cut the sky out with a dull knife.

Jaime sat with her knees drawn up, back to the wall, wrists resting on the tops of her shins. In the dim I could make out the pale line of her jaw, the fall of her hair. She'd braided it again with quick fingers after they'd tossed us in here. I'd watched her do it in silence. We all held on to the small routines we could.

Rygial was a squat shadow by the bars, beard wisped against the iron. He'd been studying the lock for the last hour with the same annoyance as a man faced with a stubborn ledger. Every now and then he'd mutter under his breath, the kind of Dwarvish that sounded like someone clearing gravel from their throat.

Elisah had taken what they gave her—one threadbare blanket and a strip of floor—and made a nest in the corner opposite Jaime. She'd rolled the blanket double and leaned against the cold wall, boots still on. Mostly I knew she was awake because her eyes kept catching the lantern light whenever she glanced up. They reflected quick, like a cat's, except hers were human-dark in daylight.

The bruises along her jaw had gone from red to purple to that yellow edge that means healing. She touched them sometimes, absent-minded, like a person checking a loose tooth with her tongue.

No one talked for so long that when her voice finally came, it startled me.

"You seeing spirits up there, Elric, or just counting stones?"

Her tone was light, but quiet. It didn't bounce. It just lay between us.

"Cracks," I said. "Looks like a river on a bad map."

She snorted. "Hope this one leads out of here."

"Rivers don't help you much if you're downstream of the mill," Rygial said without looking back. "All they do is carry other people's waste to you."

"Spoken like a man who's never swum in summer," Jaime murmured.

"I have swum," the dwarf said, affront prickling his words. "We have underground lakes that'd put your surface ponds to shame. Crystal-clear. Freezing. Full of things with more teeth than sense."

"So... family reunions," Elisah said.

That earned a faint, surprised bark of laughter from Jaime. Even Rygial's shoulders eased a touch.

I found I was smiling, which felt strange, given the iron and stone. I rolled onto my side, facing them. "Seems we're stuck downstream of someone's mill tonight."

"Kaben's," Rygial said. He spat the name like a gristle. "Kaben & Sons. Sons and bastards and bought men."

"And Cragen," Jaime added. "Don't forget Cragen. He looked proud of himself, marching us in."

Elisah tipped her head back against the wall. "He's proud because he thinks he's on the winning side. Men like that always are."

"You sound like you've known a few," I said.

Her gaze slid over to me. In the half-light it was hard to read her expression. She'd been with us only days, and there was a habit about her shoulders still, a readiness to slip away the first time no one was watching. Not that it had done her much good against twenty guards and a locked gate.

"More than a few," she said. "Less than I might have, if I'd lived more careful."

Rygial sniffed. "You're nineteen."

"Which is more years of being kicked around than some of us have had," she shot back. "You want to trade, I'll take your two hundred and fifty and see how far I get."

"Two hundred and sixty-two," he corrected automatically. Habit again. "And you wouldn't make it ten years. Deep roads would eat you in a week."

Elisah's mouth twitched. "Might be worth it, just to see them."

Jaime rubbed at the inside of her wrist where the shackles had been earlier. "What did Cragen call you, Elisah? Shadow witch?"

"Shadow-cursed," I supplied. The word had stuck in my fur. The extra weight on it. "Dragon Below marked."

"Ah." Rygial made a level, assessing sound in his throat. "That."

"That," Elisah echoed. She pushed a breath out through her nose. "He's not the first to use it. Or the most creative."

I hesitated, then asked, "What does it mean, really? Where you're from. I know the stories we were told in the village but..." I shrugged. "Stories say a lot of things."

She watched me for another beat, like she was weighing something. The lantern down the hall guttered, steadied. A passing footstep scuffed, then faded.

"You ever see the underside of a bridge in flood season?" she asked.

I nodded. "River goes brown. Thick. Whole trees come down it, roots and all."

"Right. Imagine it from the river's point of view. Normally you go along, placid as an old nag, carrying leaves and frogs and the occasional drunk. Then one day the sky rips open and drops half the forest, three barns, and a dead cow on your head. You don't have time to sort what's what, you just have to shove it all under the bridge and hope none of it sticks."

"Charming," Jaime murmured.

"Point is," Elisah went on, "when the ones up top see what's come through after? The splinters, the bones, the mess? They don't think about how it got there. They curse the river."

She lifted a hand and flexed her fingers into the shadows pooled by her boots. The air there seemed to... bend, faintly, like heat above a forge.

"Magic's like that," she said. "Or whatever you want to call what's under things. Dark, deep, the bits the priests mutter about in bad weather. Sometimes it pushes something through, and if that something looks bad enough, scares enough people, they give it a name. Dragon Below. Demon-touched. Shadow-cursed. Easier to spit a word than to admit there's parts of the world that don't answer to your temple bell."

Rygial's bushy brows climbed. "You're saying you're innocent, then? That the shadows just... fell on you by accident?"

She gave him a thin smile. "I'm saying if the Dragon Below wants me, it should write me a letter instead of sending every fool with a blade and a sermon."

Jaime shifted, the chains of her ankles giving a small clink before she stilled them. "When did it start?"

"According to my mother?" Elisah said. "Before I was born. According to the women who helped push me into the world? Around the time the candles went out and the midwife's helper swore something cold touched her ankle under the bed."

The words hung between us, shaped by the hush.

"My first memory," she went on, voice level, "is this sound." She tapped her fingernails softly on the stone. Clack. Clack. "Nails on my nursery floor. Everyone else was downstairs. It was afternoon. Sun was coming in the window, catching dust. I remember watching the dust. And I remember the shadow under the crib not being where it should be."

Jaime's lips parted slightly. I felt the fur along my spine lift, though the air didn't change.

"Shadows normally fall away from the light," Elisah said. "This one... curled toward it. Like a slug under salt. And it reached. Not far. Just the length of a man's hand. Just enough to touch my fingers when I leaned down."

"And you... touched back?" Rygial asked.

"What can I say, master dwarf. I was an affectionate child." Her hand had gone still on her knee. "The wood went cold. Not the way metal gets cold. That's just heat leaving. This was... the opposite. The feeling of a room right before someone walks in who makes you nervous. Air holding its breath."

I thought of winter mornings, going out before dawn to check the hens, knowing there might be a fox in the coop. That sharp, careful feeling in my whiskers.

"This... thing under the crib?" I asked. "It was... you?"

"It was mine," she said. "As much as your claws are yours. Or your ears. I didn't ask for them, but I learned what to do with them."

"And what did everyone else do, when they saw?" Jaime asked softly.

Elisah laughed once, short. "What do you think? My mother screamed. Knocked over a candle. Nearly burned the house down trying to beat the 'curse' out of me with the wet end of a broom. My father looked at me like I'd grown a second head with teeth."

Rygial made a quiet, disapproving sound, which surprised me more than her story. Dwarves have their own tales about what lives under rock.

"The village priest got involved," she said. "He was the one who said the phrase. Dragon Below marked. Said he'd seen the signs once before, in a boy who'd made the grain in his father's barn rot just by standing near it."

"What happened to the boy?" Jaime asked.

"The priest said he 'took care' of the problem. Then he looked at me like he was bent on doing the same." Elisah's jaw flexed. "My mother begged. Cried. Said I was a good girl. They argued over me like I was a heifer at market. [We keep her—no, we slaughter her now before she brings trouble to the herd.]"

She said the words flat. My stomach tightened remembering the fair green where we'd done much the same over cows and pigs, voices loud and practical. Never about a child.

"What changed their minds?" I asked.

"The Baron's steward walked in," she said. "He'd come to see why the village bells had been ringing all morning. Found a crowd outside our door, my mother on her knees, the priest with his hands on my head like he was weighing a melon for bruises."

"Ours took coins," Rygial said dryly. "To let someone live."

"Ours took interest," Elisah replied. "The steward's wife was expecting. They'd lost three before. He thought..." She shrugged, a small, vicious motion. "Who wouldn't want a child who could make miracles? Or terrors. Sometimes the two are the same thing, viewed from one step to the left."

"So you went to the Baron's house," Jaime guessed.

"For a while. Learned to walk on polished floors. Learned which spoons you were allowed to use and which rugs you mustn't bleed on. Learned that when people look at you like you're a knife, you might as well learn where their soft parts are."

Her eyes were very still as she said it.

"Then?" I asked.

"Then I learned the most important lesson." She leaned her head back again, looking up at the same cracked ceiling I had. "That what scares people doesn't have to control you. You can... nudge it. Bend it. Use it."

"The shadows," Rygial said.

"The way light falls," she corrected. "Shadows are just the shape of the world where light can't reach. You learn what makes light, you learn what casts it, and you learn what happens in the places in between. It's not... evil. Any more than a wolf is evil for killing a sheep. It's just... another way the world is."

"And the Dragon Below?" Jaime asked.

"Maybe it's just the name we give to everything we don't like in ourselves," Elisah said. "Or maybe there's truly something under us all, watching. I've never heard it speak. If it is there, it's less talkative than priests would have you believe."

Her tone had gone softer toward the end. I heard the tiredness under it then. Not just from the scuffle, but from years of saying the same explanations to people determined not to hear.

"What about the streets?" I asked. "You said you learned where people's soft parts were."

She gave me a sideways glance. "You're quick for a farm boy."

"Village," I said automatically. "We had three whole streets."

"Luxury." She blew air through her lips. "Baron's wife had her miracle in the end. Healthy boy, all his fingers and toes, no shadows crawling out of the cradle. Turned out I'd been a hedge against fear more than anything. No need for a second monster in the house when the heir arrived."

"And so..." Jaime prompted.

"And so the priest came back into favor," Elisah said. "He convinced her that my presence offended the heavens. That I had to be sent away for some... purification." Her fingers traced an idle pattern on the stone, following some memory path. "They called it exile, but it felt more like being dropped out the back door during a thunderstorm."

"How old?" I asked, trying to picture her then. Thinner, smaller, eyes too large already.

"Eleven," she said. "Old enough to know when someone is lying to you for your own good. Young enough to believe maybe they're right."

She shifted, stretching her legs out. The chain of ink around her wrist—her only visible mark of any temple I didn't know—caught faint light.

"The city wasn't so bad," she went on. "You learn quick that the worst people you meet in some Baron's hall are just... practice. Out there you don't have polished floors. You have mud and cobbles and alleys that smell like piss and rotting cabbage. You have men like Cragen who think bruises on a girl's face are proof of something wrong with the girl."

"What did you have?" I asked.

She closed her eyes for a moment, as though searching for the correct tally.

"A bunk in a flophouse when I could pay. A corner under the eaves of a tannery when I couldn't. A baker who'd slide me yesterday's bread if I swept his step. A woman who'd teach me how to listen at doors without being seen. Others like me, more or less. Orphans. Runaways. People whose families had decided they looked a little too much like trouble."

"And the shadows," Jaime said.

"And the shadows," Elisah agreed. "You can hide in them, or you can make other people think you can be anywhere they are. Once you learn that, you learn fear cuts both ways."

She opened her eyes again, and now they were on me. "You grew up in a place where everyone knew your name," she said. "If they didn't like you, they still had to look you in the eye in the market, maybe trade eggs with your mother. In the city, no one knows your name unless you make it worth knowing. 'Shadow-touched' is a name, of a sort. So I made it mine."

"How?" Rygial asked, ever the scholar. "Beyond... melting into corners."

She considered. "I watched people. What made them flinch, what made them greedy. What they whispered about at night. You exaggerate a rumor here, you spread a story there. You let someone see less of you than is really there. Soon enough, 'Elisah' is less a person and more a... shape people see when they're already afraid. Means some doors open to you. Others slam shut. Some men toss you coins to go away; others to come closer."

"And the knives?" I asked quietly.

She smiled then. Not kindly, but not cruelly either. Just acknowledging a fact.

"You don't grow up on those streets without learning to put steel between yourself and their worst offerings," she said. "Little blades at first, then better ones when I could afford them. A chain, when I realized people never look up until it's too late. And the picks..." She shrugged one shoulder, rueful. "Locks are just doors with worse manners. I got tired of waiting for anyone else to open them for me."

Her gaze slid to the iron bars in front of Rygial.

"They took all that," Jaime said. "When they searched you."

Elisah's hand twitched briefly, as if remembering the weight of metal that wasn't there.

"They did," she said. "I feel naked without them. It's... disorienting. Like losing a limb, or your shadow at noon."

"Better than losing your head at dawn," Rygial muttered. "Which is still on the table, if Kaben has his way."

Silence wrapped around us for a stretch after that. The kind that comes when you've all told more than you meant to and are waiting to see if anyone will use it against you.

"Why didn't you run?" Jaime asked eventually. "When the guards came for us. You could have slipped away in that alley. We were the ones Cragen wanted."

Elisah huffed out a breath that could almost have been a laugh. "I told you. People already think I'm cursed. Doesn't pay to make them right too often. Besides, you'd just have bumbled your way into someone else's net. This way I get to see exactly which hole in the wall Kaben thinks is safe enough to stash his problems in."

"And then?" I asked.

"And then maybe I find where he keeps his ledger," she said. "And his purse. And his secrets. Men like that hate it when his secrets go walking."

Rygial gave a snort of reluctant approval. "You've an eye for long odds, girl."

"Says the dwarf who insulted Kaben & Sons to their faces," she shot back.

"I refused to commit a crime against time itself," he said, affronted again. "That's rather different than poking a smugglers' nest with a stolen knife."

"Is it?" She tilted her head. "Tell us that story, then. Since we're all baring our sad little tales for the stone."

RYGIAL PUFFED HIS CHEEKS out, beard bristling. For a moment I thought he'd refuse. Then he shifted his weight, settling his back more firmly against the bars, and his voice took on that measured cadence I already associated with his lectures.

"In my halls," he began, "we measure our lives in stone layers and sediment, in heat and cooling and the curling of roots that seek water where none should be. We do not... play with it. Time, I mean. Not beyond very strict diagrams."

"You're a chronomancer," Jaime said. "You told us."

"I am a practitioner of measured temporal invocation," he corrected. "Chronomancer is a surface word. Like calling a master vintner a man who 'makes grape juice go old.'"

"Both true," Elisah murmured.

He ignored her, though the corner of his mouth twitched.

"I grew up in the lower quarters of Baraz-Thuldor," he went on. "My mother polished crystal lenses for the great clock-windows. My father maintained the weights and coun-terweights of the Deep Pendulum. I learned my letters marking gear teeth and tallying swings. We Dwarves count ourselves lucky when we are allowed to be small parts of big mechanisms."

"How romantic," Elisah said dryly.

"It is," he insisted. "Or was, to me. To walk below the vast brass rings, to hear the slow, steady tick that has measured our city's heartbeats for ten thousand years... That is a kind of music you soft folk never hear."

I tried to imagine it. The inn clock back home was all I had to go on: the slow clack of the pendulum, the regular chime that told you when to start dinner or drive the cows home. Scale that up, down in the dark, until each swing was as heavy as a wagon. I could see why a dwarf might grow up thinking of time as something you could touch.

"I apprenticed under Master Tholgar of the Fourth Dial," Rygial continued. "A stern old rock with lichen for eyebrows. He taught me the basics of adjustment—tiny corrections. Speed a thing up a hair here, slow a thing down there. Enough that the great clocks all agree when festival comes and the miners are owed their rest. We bend time like you bend wood in a steam kettle. Gently. Patiently. No cracks."

"And then you came up to the Collegium," Jaime said.

"Eventually." He shifted, old joints complaining in small pops. "I showed some talent, they said. A knack for seeing the shape of a moment. They sent me to the Surface Collegium as an exchange. Imagine: a greybeard of ninety-eight, barely finished shedding his youthstone, sent up among humans who think someone my age must have all the answers."

"How old did they think you were?" Elisah asked.

"They never asked," he said, amused. "One of them once called me 'ancient.' I laughed until my ribs hurt. I was barely more than a beardling."

He fell quiet a moment, the memory softening his voice.

"I did good work," he said at last. "Taught a few, terrified more. Most surface mages treat time like it's fire: handy in a lantern, deadly in a forest. I tried to show them it's more like a river—"

"Ah," I said. "We're back to rivers."

"A slow river," he amended. "With banks that you can shore up if you know where to put the stones. You can't turn it around, but you can divert an eddy, strengthen a current. Small, careful things. That's what I insisted on."

"And Kaben wanted... something else," Jaime said.

Rygial's lips pressed together. The muscles in his jaw bunched above his beard.

"Kaben wants shipments to arrive before they leave," he said. "He wants to move contraband along roads no one else can walk yet. He wants debts to come due early and contracts to expire late. Men like him look at a river and think, 'If only it flowed uphill for me alone.'"

"You say that like it's not possible," Elisah said.

"It's not," he snapped. "Not without cost. Not without tearing banks and drowning villages and waking things in the depths we'd all be better off leaving to their silt."

He rubbed at his forehead with his thumb, suddenly looking every one of his years.

"He approached me months ago," Rygial said. "Smiling, of course. Always smiling. Offered me a private patronage. Materials. Rare ores for my lenses. Access to old texts locked in the Collegium's forbidden stacks."

"You said no," I said.

"Of course I said no." He glowered at the memory. "I explained, slowly and with diagrams, why what he wanted could not be done safely. He listened. He even asked clever questions. Then he thanked me and left half a purse on my desk 'for the trouble.'"

He spat again, dry, onto the stone.

"Next tenday he returned," Rygial said. "With his 'sons' and a man named Cragen in a uniform that fit too well. This time he had a warrant, signed by a magistrate who owed him something, I'm sure. Accused me of... What was the phrasing? 'Disturbing the civic calendar.' Using temporal magics without proper licensure. I tried to argue, but when a human with a pen decides a dwarf with a beard must be guilty, he does not listen to clocks."

"So they arrested you," Jaime said, frowning. "Brought you here. To a holding cell with us."

"Seems a waste of an education," Elisah remarked.

"Kaben doesn't waste anything," Rygial said grimly. "He repurposes. A man like me who won't work for him freely may be... persuaded. With the right leverage. Or he may serve as an example to others. 'See what happens when you refuse our generous offer.'"

He glanced down the corridor where Cragen had gone earlier, mouth tight.

"Or," he added, more quietly, "he may be locked away until someone weaker in the Collegium decides to take the offer I didn't. After all, an empty office is a temptation."

The thought of the city's timekeepers in Kaben's pocket made the fur along my arms bristle. Smugglers with ships that arrived a day before the watchmen expected. Contracts that never quite matched up with when they'd been signed. It would be like giving a fox not just the key to the henhouse, but the ability to make the farmer sleep in every morning.

"And you can't do what he wants?" I asked. "Even if you tried?"

Rygial hesitated. For the first time since we'd met him, his certainty wavered.

"There are... theories," he admitted. "Dwarven. Human. Elven. Ways you might... anchor a working to a moving frame. Walk with a bubble of slowed or hastened time around you. I have read about them. I have, in my foolish youth, scribbled margins about them. But they are half-glimpsed, like reflections in warped metal. To make them real would take years. Teams. Deep study. And even then..."

He shook his head hard, as though dislodging a bad thought.

"These are not things to hand to a man who smuggles powders in children's flour," he said.

Jaime's eyes hardened at that. "He does that?"

"I've seen the ledgers," Rygial replied. "Not that they were meant for me to see. Drugs, cursed objects, bound spirits. All things that move better in the dark. Time is just another kind of dark, to him."

"So he'll keep pressing," Elisah said. "On you. On the Collegium. On whoever sits near the levers he wants pulled."

"Unless someone breaks his fingers," Jaime said.

We all looked at her. Her tone had gone very even.

"Metaphorically," she amended after a beat. "Or not."

The quiet that followed had a different texture now. Less like waiting, more like choosing.

"I can get us out," Elisah said.

Her voice was matter-of-fact, like she was offering to fetch more firewood.

Rygial snorted. "With what? Your charm?"

"With these." She lifted her hands and wiggled her fingers. "And a little of what everyone's so afraid of."

I pushed myself up on my elbows. The cell felt smaller suddenly. The air seemed to thicken around her, like bread dough rising.

"You said the shadows were... yours," I said. "That you could... nudge them."

"I did." She rolled her shoulders, as if limbering them. "I also said I hate waiting for other people to open doors for me."

Her gaze tracked the line of darkness pooling along the bottom of our cell door. The lantern down the hall threw the bars' silhouettes long and thin, bars of shadow crisscrossing our floor.

"How solid would you say that door is, Master Rygial?" she asked.

He frowned at it. "Oak. Old. Iron bands. Surface work, which is to say adequate and no more. Why?"

"Because wood and iron are for people who live in one world at a time," she said. "I've never been very good at that."

"Elisah—" Jaime started. "You tried something in the alley, when they grabbed us. You staggered after. It took a lot out of you."

"And this will take more," she said calmly. "But unless you have a better plan..."

She looked at each of us in turn. No one spoke.

"I can go through," she said. "Slip into the armory shadows. Take back our things. Rygial, you can do something to the hinges, yes? I've seen you sour milk in a bottle from across a room."

He sniffed. "That wasn't souring, it was... never mind. Yes. I believe I can accelerate the rust along the hinge pins. The lock, too, perhaps. Make them brittle."

"Then it's simple," she said.

"Simple," I repeated. "Like walking on a pond in spring."

"Better than drowning in it come summer," she shot back. "Listen. I pull myself thin, here." She tapped the shadow by the door. "Slip along the cracks, like a draft. It's not... comfortable. It burns. Or freezes. Hard to explain. But I've done it before. Walls. Floorboards. Never something so thick as this, but shadows are cast on both sides. As long as there's some light in the armory, I'll have somewhere to come out."

"And what happens if there isn't?" Jaime asked.

Elisah held her gaze. "Then I bounce. Hit the skin of the world and slide along until I find a seam thin enough to push through. Probably come out in a coal chute or a chimney. Messy, but survivable."

"Probably," I said.

She bared her teeth, not quite a smile. "You're welcome to stay and take your chances with Cragen in the morning, kitten."

Rygial scratched at his beard, thinking. "Even if you get through, the armory will be locked. Your tools are in there with everything else."

She looked almost insulted. "Do you think I wouldn't memorize the pattern of their keys hanging on that board when they dragged us past? Locks are habits you can listen for. Once you know the song, you can hum it from either side."

"Assuming no one's in there," Jaime said. "If a guard is—"

"Then I scare him," Elisah said. "Or I don't, and I cut something that makes him quiet. I've done worse."

The way she said it left no room for doubt. Jaime's mouth tightened, but she didn't argue.

"What about timing?" I asked. "If we break the door while the wrong man's walking by..." I jerked my chin toward the corridor.

"Guard shifts," Rygial murmured. "There was a bell about half an hour ago. Change of watch for the outer walls, by my reckoning. Inner keeps usually stagger theirs a little after. Less chance of everyone in the hold yawning at once."

"So we wait for another bell," I said.

"And count the footsteps," Jaime added. "See if there's a pattern. How often they pass. If there's a gap."

We fell silent again, this time listening on purpose. The cell block breathed around us: snores, coughs, a mutter here or there, the faint clink of someone shifting chains. Farther off, a door creaked, closed. Boots thudded in pairs, then in fours. A man laughed, cut off quickly.

The seconds passed in the slow, viscous way they do when you're waiting for pain or relief. Eventually a bell tolled, distant but clear. One, two, three... Seven strokes.

"Half-watch," Rygial said. "About midnight."

Right on its heels came the shuffle of movement above. Men trading places. Voices low. The feel of the hold adjusting its weight.

We waited. In the ten breaths after the bell, boots clanged down the main corridor, passed our junction, faded. Then, for a little while, only the drip.

"That's our window," Jaime whispered. "Now, before the new rhythm settles."

Elisah pushed herself to her feet with a small grunt. I saw the lines of tension in her legs, the way she shook out her hands twice, as though slinging water from her fingers.

Up close, the shadows seemed... thicker somehow. Maybe it was just my imagination, primed by her story. The strip of darkness under the door looked no different than any I'd seen in a hundred barns at dawn. But as she stepped into it, the hair along my arms rose.

"You sure you're up for this?" I asked, low.

She glanced back at me over her shoulder. For all the bravado in her words earlier, there was something younger in her face now. Raw.

"I don't like cages," she said simply. "Never have. Never will."

Before I could answer, she knelt and laid both hands flat to the stone, fingers spread into the seam where floor met door.

The change was almost too subtle to see at first. The edges of her hands blurred, like looking at them through heat shimmer. The skin along her wrists darkened—not in color, exactly, but in depth, as though it were being soaked in ink from the inside out.

I felt it in the temperature before anything else. A sudden sinking, like stepping into a cellar in high summer. The air around her grew cold, but not the sharp, clean cold of snow. This was an absence, a pulling away of warmth that left gooseflesh in its wake.

The lantern down the hallway sputtered. Its flame dipped, then flared, thin and strained. The shadows on our floor thickened, lines going from soft gray to a hard, velvety black that seemed to eat what little light was left.

Elisah drew a breath through her teeth. Her shoulders hunched as though against a physical blow. For a heartbeat I smelled something like wet slate and old dust—air that hadn't been moved in a very long time.

Her fingers sank.

Not all at once. Not like putting your hand in water. More like pushing into packed earth that resisted at first, then grudgingly gave. The stone around her knuckles rippled, faint, like dough under a kneading palm. The darkness clung to her skin, climbed.

She bit down on a sound. Her jaw clenched so hard I could see the tendons stand out in the side of her neck. Sweat broke on her forehead, cold and shining.

"Elisah," Jaime whispered, half rising. "If it's—"

"Don't," Elisah hissed. Her voice sounded odd, blurred at the edges, as if coming from a greater distance than the length of our small cell. "If you pull me back now I'll get... stuck."

I didn't know what that meant, and I didn't ask. My claws had slid out of habit, pricking my palms.

Her hands had gone to the wrist now, submerged in nothing. The stone didn't part or crack. It held all its angles, as stubborn as ever. But her arms... thinned. The flesh paling, then darkening, then... flattening, somehow. Depth folding in on itself. It made my eyes ache to look at.

The cold deepened. My breath smoked in front of my face, though there was no draught. Jaime's fingers, resting on her knees, went pale.

"Almost," Elisah grated. Her eyes were tightly shut now. A tremor ran through her shoulders down into her spine. The ink-dark along her forearms spread, swallowing up color, swallowing up solidness. Her elbows met the stone and didn't stop.

There was a moment then—a single heartbeat—when she was wrong. Not in any way I could put to words. Just... wrong. The shape of her against the dim. Too thin. Too long in some dimensions, too short in others. My instincts screamed the same way they had when I'd once stepped into a patch of bog I'd thought was solid ground and felt the earth give way.

Then she... slid.

That's the only word that fits. One instant her shoulders were here with us, hunched, shaking; the next they weren't. The dark under the door flexed, gulped, and for a breath there was no sign that a person had ever knelt there. Just empty floor, old wood, iron, and a strip of black that looked like any other.

I realized I had my hands clenched so tight my claws had nicked my palms. I forced them to unclench, the small sting reminding me I was still, emphatically, on this side of the door.

Jaime let out the breath she'd been holding in a shudder. "I hate that," she said under her breath.

"I heard nothing," Rygial murmured. "No displacement. No echo. Remarkable."

"You and I have different ideas of 'remarkable,'" I said.

We waited. The quiet pressed harder than before. I strained my ears, but the thick stone swallowed most sound. Every creak could be her or a guard or nothing. My tail had coiled so tight around my calf it almost hurt.

Time stretched. Rygial's lips moved silently, counting, measuring. At what I guessed was a hundred heartbeats, a doubt crawled into my chest. At two hundred, it had built a house and started arranging furniture.

"What if she can't get back?" Jaime whispered.

"She's gotten out of worse," I said, more firmly than I felt.

I thought of Elisah at eleven, shoved into the city streets. Of her voice when she'd said she didn't like cages. That stubborn line of her jaw. If anyone could bully the skin between worlds into letting her through, it was her.

Another thirty heartbeats. Forty. Then—

A sound. Faint, muffled through wood and distance, but distinct: the soft, familiar snick of a lock yielding to persuasion.

Rygial's eyes lit. "She's in," he breathed.

Metal scraped. A hinge squealed protest, as if in complaint at being hurried. Then footsteps, light and quick, moving across what I pictured as a weapon room lined with racks.

I found myself gripping the bars beside Rygial, as if I might somehow see better through sheer will. All that stared back at me was the opposite wall, pitted and worn.

something slid along the floor outside. Soft, like leather on stone. Then a whisper came through the door, close and low.

"Miss me?"

I let out a breath that was almost a laugh. "Thought you'd decided to take a holiday in the coal chute," I replied just as quietly.

"You wish." Her voice was a little strained, like someone who'd run up too many stairs. "Move back. Whatever the dwarf's going to do, I don't want his magic licking my boots."

Jaime and I scrambled away from the door, pressing ourselves to the rear wall. Rygial stood, rolling his shoulders as though settling a cloak.

"This will not be pleasant," he warned. "For me. For you it should be mostly... unsightly."

"Unsightly?" Jaime repeated.

"You're about to watch a century of rust grow in a handful of heartbeats," he said crisply. "Steel is not meant to age that quickly. Nor are dwarves meant to push it so."

He raised his right hand, fingers curling inward until his nails—clipped short but thick as horn—pressed into his palm. With the other, he touched lightly to the hinge plate nearest him.

I'd seen Rygial work small magics before. The twist of time on a fruit, the souring of milk he'd mentioned. They'd been neat, almost invisible. This was... not.

The air around his fingers wavered, not with heat but with something like it. The metal under his touch darkened, the clean gray-brown of old iron deepening to near black. A smell hit me: sharp, metallic, biting the back of my throat. Like the inside of a forge left damp too long. Rust, but far thicker than anything I'd ever caught in the barn.

Tiny flakes began to curl up along the edge of the hinge, peeling away like bark from a diseased tree. They fell in a slow rain, dusting the stone at our feet.

Rygial muttered under his breath, words that weren't any language I knew. His voice had a rhythm, though, like a man marking time with a hammer on anvil. His forehead beaded with sweat. The tendons in his neck stood out as he poured... something... through his fingers into the stubborn metal.

I watched, transfixed, as the hinge seemed to... age. Fine hairline cracks spidered out from the pins into the surrounding plate. They bloomed, widening, deepening, the way cracks do in a dry riverbed. In the span of ten breaths, the solid, healthy iron looked like something that had been left in the rain for generations.

He moved his touch down to the lock itself, slower this time, more deliberate. The keyhole's lip flowered with rust. The interior gears—what I could see of them through that narrow slot—fuzzed, clotted, seized. The smell intensified, making my eyes water.

Rygial swayed. Jaime stepped forward, then halted when he snapped, "Stay back."

"Your nose is bleeding," I said. A thin red line had indeed begun to trickle from his left nostril, threading into his beard.

He sniffed irritably, which only smeared it. "Temporal inversion is thirsty work," he said between clenched teeth. "Do you want the door open or not?"

I shut my mouth.

He held the contact five more heartbeats, then tore his hand away as though from a hot stove. He staggered. Jaime caught his elbow, bearing more of his weight than her size suggested she could.

"Enough," he panted. "Any more and we risk collapsing the pin entirely, which would be... unpredictable."

"Unpredictable how?" I asked.

"Explosive," he said shortly.

Noted.

He put a shaky hand on Jaime's shoulder, steadying himself. His skin had gone pale beneath the ruddy tones. The lines around his eyes seemed deeper.

"Now you," he said, turning his gaze on me. "You're the one with the farmer's kicks. Make them count."

I approached the door, eyeing the hinge and lock. Close up, the metal looked... rotten. That was the only word for it. Soft in the way a mushroom is soft compared to wood. The iron bands had pitted too, spots of orange-brown blooming along their lengths where rust had jumped like a fungus.

I planted my feet where the wall and floor met, braced my tail, and set my shoulder just below the lock. The cell smelled of rust and old sweat and the faint mineral tang of Rygial's blood.

"On three," I said, more for myself than the others. "One. Two."

On two I drove my heel into the door, putting every bit of weight and anger and fear into the motion. Years of kicking at stubborn stall doors and frozen troughs paid off.

Something gave with a harvesting crack. The sound was half splintering wood, half crumbling stone, undercut by a dry, ragged snap as one of the rusted hinge pins sheared clean through.

The impact jolted up my leg and into my hip. Pain lit along an old bruise. The door, however, jumped in its frame, iron bands screeching in protest as they ripped rusty nails from ancient anchors.

Again. Before the metal had time to remember how to hold together.

I stepped back, sucked a breath, and kicked once more, foot slamming into the spot just below where Rygial had blackened the lock.

This time there was no half-measure. The weakened wood split along its grain, shooting a jagged crack from the keyhole down to the bottom edge. The lower hinge pin, brittle as a stale biscuit, snapped. The whole door sagged sharply inward and then, with a drawn-out tearing sound, fell forward into the cell.

It hit the stone floor with a thunder that seemed much too loud in the sleeping block. Dust billowed up, carrying with it a choking wave of rust flakes. I coughed, waving my hand in front of my face.

For a heartbeat, no one moved. Down the corridor, a voice muttered in its sleep, then subsided. No boots pounded. No shout went up.

We stared at the gape where the door had been. On the other side, the corridor stretched away, lit by the guttering lantern. For the first time since we'd been marched in, nothing stood between us and that thin, threadbare light.

"Elric," Jaime whispered. "You did it."

"Rygial did it," I corrected hoarsely. "I just kicked like a mule."

"Team effort," Elisah's voice said from the right.

I turned. She stood just beyond the threshold, pressed into the shadow of the wall. For a second she looked less like a person and more like a cut-out where the darkness had decided to take a woman's shape.

Then she stepped forward, and the illusion broke. She was very real. Very solid. And very pale.

Sweat plastered strands of her dark hair to her forehead. Her lips had a bluish tinge, and the skin under her eyes looked bruised. She moved stiffly, as if each motion hurt.

But her hands...

Her hands were full.

"Miss me?" she repeated, a little breathless.

She held out a familiar shape. My sword. Maximus's sword, truth be told, but Dratmar put it in my hands and told me to carry it, and that made it mine as much as his. The leather of the grip, worn just so by his fingers over the years, fit into my palm like a handshake from an old friend.

Behind it dangled a small leather pouch on its thong—Dratmar's coin, the weight of it unmistakable even at a glance. My throat tightened at the sight.

"Thought you'd left these with the quartermaster," Elisah said. "He has terrible taste in storage."

I took them gently, almost reverently. The sword's weight settled against my hip, as right as a well-balanced bucket in hand. I slid the coin's thong over my head, tucking the pouch under my shirt where it lay, a small, solid reassurance against my chest.

"Thank you," I said. The words felt thin compared to what it meant.

"Don't get sentimental on me, farm boy," she said, but there was no heat in it. Her hand shook as she reached into the shadow behind her and drew out another bundle.

She tossed a sheathed blade to Jaime, who caught it with a motion that spoke of long practice.

Jaime's fingers tightened on the hilt. Her father's sword. The simple, well-made grip was as familiar in her hand as any plow handle had ever been in mine. She ran her thumb along the worn leather, lips pressed together. Then she slid the blade just enough from its sheath to see the faint pattern of the steel, the small nick on the guard from that time she'd parried too close.

"Feels like coming home," she murmured.

Elisah followed it with a small ring on a strip of cloth. Jaime caught it almost clumsily, suddenly less soldier and more daughter. The ring was plain silver, nicked and dulled by years, with a shallow dent on one side where it had once been stepped on in a stable. She cradled it in her palm like something much more fragile than metal.

"He kept this on him?" Jaime asked, voice gone thin.

"Every watchman has a pocket," Elisah said. "Cragen thought hiding it in his made him clever. The man underestimates fingers thinner than his conscience."

Jaime slid the ring onto a chain around her neck, next to the small charm she always wore. Her eyes were bright in the low light, but she blinked whatever threatened to fall away and looked up, jaw set.

"You have my thanks," she told Elisah.

"Add it to my tab," Elisah said. She was swaying minutely where she stood. Her hands had gone to her own belt, buckling on twin sheaths at her hips with the familiarity of ritual. She slid daggers into them—slim, dark-bladed, the edges catching the lantern light with a hungry whisper.

She slung a coiled length of chain over one shoulder. It was finely made, each link precise, weighted at one end with a small, dense sphere of metal and at the other with a wicked hook. It looked as out of place in her delicate grip as a scythe in a child's, but she handled it like a part of herself.

Last came a narrow leather roll, tied with a thong. She tucked it into an inside pocket of her vest, patting it once. The lockpicks, I knew, even before she said, with quiet satisfaction, "Tools of the trade."

Rygial watched her, then cleared his throat pointedly.

She rolled her eyes but reached back into the gloom and drew out a cloth-wrapped bundle. "For you, rock-man."

He took it almost reverently. The cloth fell away to reveal a crystal, the size of a clenched fist, cut in many facets that seemed to catch light from angles that shouldn't exist in this dim corridor. It glowed faintly from within, not with any color I could pin down, shifting between pale blue and soft amber like a sky at different hours.

"My focus," he breathed. His fingers trembled as they closed around it. "By all the ticks and tocks..."

He cradled it against his chest a moment, eyes closed, as though greeting an old friend. Then he carefully slipped it into a padded pocket inside his robe. The slight straightening of his spine afterward had nothing to do with magic yet; it was simply the comfort of having something familiar, something that made sense in his hands.

Elisah then produced a leather satchel, bulging with odd shapes. "And this," she said. "Before you ask, yes, I put back everything else I saw before I touched it. Your notes are the driest thing in that room."

"Good," he said. "I'd hate for some half-wit to learn anything from them."

He slung the satchel across his body, wincing as the strap settled on a shoulder that had to be aching from his earlier working.

"Anyone else?" Elisah asked, looking between us. "Hidden keepsakes, smuggled sweets, a favorite sock?"

"That's all of us," I said, tightening my sword belt. "Four blades, one chain, one crystal, one bag of words, and a coin that's caused more trouble than it's worth."

"Don't you dare say that," Jaime said quietly.

She was right. The coin had brought us here, in a sense, but it had also carried promises, debts, and paths out of fields I'd once thought I'd never leave. Worth is a complicated thing.

Elisah took a step, stumbled, and caught herself with a hand on the wall. The move was small, but my eyes tracked it.

"You all right?" I asked.

"Shadow-walking isn't a stroll to market," she said, cheeks pale but set. "Feels like scraping the meat off your own bones and then stuffing it back in, wrong way round. I'll manage."

"You sure you can move quietly?" Jaime's hand hovered near Elisah's elbow, not quite touching.

Elisah gave her a look. "I could outrun you with my legs tied together and a bucket on my head."

Jaime's mouth twitched. "Prove it after we're not three steps from a gallows."

"Deal," Elisah said.

Rygial straightened with a small groan. "We have perhaps half an hour before the next patrol walks by," he said, eyes flicking down the corridor. "Less, if Cragen is nervous."

"Then we move." I stepped into the threshold, peering left, then right.

The cell block corridor stretched out, lined with iron doors like the one we'd just toppled. Some had eyes peering out, wide in the gloom. A hand reached through one set of bars, fingers clutching.

"Take me with you," a hoarse voice whispered. "Please. I can—"

Elisah touched my arm. "We can't," she said low. "We don't have keys for all, and we'd bring the whole guard down on us trying. Choose four free or fifty dead."

The calculus sat like a stone in my stomach. Back home, when a storm hit and the river swelled, you couldn't save every chick, every lamb. You did what you could reach and lived with the rest. It never felt clean.

"I'm sorry," I said to the reaching hand, meaning it. The fingers scrabbled, then withdrew, cursing under their breath.

Jaime's jaw worked. Rygial looked straight ahead.

We stepped over the shattered door and into the hallway together. The air out here tasted different. Stale, but less closed-in. The lantern's weak flame painted everything in thin yellows and deep, invasive shadows.

We moved.

Elisah took the lead, despite her obvious exhaustion. Her steps were ghosts on the stone. She kept to the edges where the wall met floor, sliding from shadow to shadow as though slipping into familiar coats. Jaime followed a pace behind her, sword at hand but not bared, her body angled to shield us if something came around the bend.

Rygial stumped along beside me, a little slower than before. He had one hand on the wall, fingers trailing, counting doors, distances. I could hear, very faintly, the almost inaudible tick from the crystal under his robe, matching his heartbeat.

I brought up the rear, ears straining, tail low to keep from brushing metal. The weight of the sword on my hip and the coin against my chest felt like anchors, but also like promises: of things yet owed, of debts yet to be paid.

As we reached the junction where the cell block met the main corridor, Elisah lifted a hand, signaling halt. We froze, listening.

Far down to the left, a cough. A bored voice saying something about dice. The faint clatter of bone on wood.

"Two at least," she mouthed. "Maybe three. If we go right..."

Rygial nodded. "Stair down to the lower store and then up to the yard. Less guarded at this hour. They don't expect traffic from the dead cells."

"Dead cells?" I whispered.

"Where they keep those scheduled for the noose," he said. "We were not meant to leave this corridor alive, Elric. Best to remember that when you next see Kaben's smile."

I swallowed. The stone under my pads felt suddenly thinner, like glass over deep water.

Elisah glanced back at us. Jaime met her eyes. Something unspoken passed there—agreements, regrets, the sharp knowledge that their paths, once separate, had tangled for good now.

"Ready?" Elisah whispered.

"No," Rygial said. "But go."

We slipped right, into the thicker dark, feet making barely more sound than the settling of dust. Behind us, the holding cells waited, full of men and women and one old ledger of a dwarf who had refused to bend time for a smuggler.

Ahead, the corridor bent toward a set of stairs and whatever waited beyond: Cragen, Kaben, the city, the Dragon Below or Above, I didn't know.

We went anyway.

Quiet steps. Borrowed time. Keys where they shouldn't be, clocks that had been nudged out of true. Four of us, moving together for the first time not just as prisoners shoved into the same cage, but as something like a unit.

An alliance, I might call it now. A fellowship, if I'm feeling grand. That night, with my heart in my throat and my fur prickling at every sound, it felt like something simpler and more necessary:

If we didn't hold to each other, we'd fall alone.

# Chapter 14

## Heroes Nobody Asked For

They never build prisons for quiet escapes. Every floorboard complains. Every lantern wants to draw eyes. Every corridor feels twice as long once you are not allowed to walk it.

We moved anyway. The corridor outside the armory lay empty, washed in the tired yellow of guttering lamps. The air smelled of grease, sweat and stale soup. Night air pushed faintly under the outer doors, cooler than the breath of the stone. The guardhouse slept in that way busy places do, one ear open.

Jaime slid ahead, the point of her sword low and ready, her shoulders loose. Once she had her blade in hand her whole body changed, like a plowhorse in spring pressed back into the traces. Familiar weight, familiar work. Elisah went opposite her, opposite in every way. Jaime was clean lines and disciplined steps. Elisah was a smear along the wall, coat brushing stone, the lamplight seeming to trip and slide off her. The shadows liked her. Or she liked them. Hard to say.

Rygial padded behind me, beard braided tight, that odd smell of charged air and old books hanging about him. His boots did not make a sound they ought to have made. Either he walked soft or the air had agreed not to tell on him. "Stairs first," Jaime whispered. "We need the ground door, not the tower. Elric, ears?"

I let my eyes close for a heartbeat and tilted my head, letting the world fill my skull. The creak of a distant door. A snore that shook someone's jowls. Two voices low and bored ahead and left. A wheeze to the right that might have been a man or an old pipeshaft. Above all that, the slow thunk of the tower clock. The dwarf's work had not disturbed that. "Two ahead. Left side, not moving," I murmured. "No boots on stone close. We move."

We went single file, no talking. The corridor ran straight, then jogged around a corner. Here the lamps failed, one out entirely, one guttering. Elisah smiled. She lifted a hand and the remaining light dimmed as if embarrassed at shining so bright. Shadow thickened, soft as wool between us and the sleeping guardhouse. She did something with her fingers, sketching a circle in the air. A rag of darkness peeled itself from the corner and crawled toward the ceiling. Watching her work, you could forget that shadows are just a lack of light. Hers had opinions.

We reached the corner. Jaime froze, raised two fingers. I let my weight down through my calves, claws just brushing the stone. The air smelled stronger here: boiled onions, lamp oil and sour wine. Voices swung into focus.

"Card's wrong," one man muttered. "You misdealt."

"I misdealt your face," another said. A muffled chuckle. "Turn it over."

"No. You're cheating." The scrape of a chair. A slosh of liquid. Cards on wood. A quiet night that had not yet realized it was about to end.

Jaime leaned close enough that her breath warmed my ear. "If we can pass, we pass," she exhaled. "No killing if we can help it."

"Passing four people through two bored men in a lit doorway," Elisah breathed from the other side, "sounds like not-helping."

"Then we put them to sleep," Rygial whispered. "Differently than they would prefer." He stepped forward before any of us could object, robes whispering. I saw the way his hands shaped the air, fingers walking some old practiced path. His voice buzzed under his breath like a hive.

The card players did not look up until the last word settled. Sound dragged. The chair's creak turned slow and deep. The mutter of complaint stretched like hot tar. I watched a droplet of spilled wine hang, swell, separate from the cup and fall as if it had all the time in the world to consider its choices. Rygial's jaw clenched. Sweat shone on his brow. "Now," he said through his teeth.

We moved. Jaime crossed the distance in three strides, the third a sliding stop that left her behind the first guard. Her sword flicked, quick and sure, not to kill but to bite deep into the muscle of his thigh. He grunted, or started to, but the sound lagged behind his pain. I rapped the second man's wrist with the flat of my blade. Where Rygial's time-trick held, even that simple motion felt like stirring porridge left to cool. Then the world snapped forward.

The wounded guard howled. The other's mug shattered, wine spattering his shirt all at once. Elisah's chain whispered. The loose end wrapped the second man's neck, shadow-dark metal against flesh. She yanked him backward, knocking the breath out of him. His shout turned to a choke. Jaime's boot drove the other man's knee sideways. He went down hard, cursing, hand reaching for the spear propped by his chair. I put my blade across his wrist just enough to sting and let my ears flare open.

No alarm. No pounding boots yet. "Quiet," I hissed. "Or you'll wake the honest ones and the crooked both."

The man on the floor spat at me. "You're all crooked."

"Then we're among our own," Elisah said in his ear. She twisted her chain a notch tighter. The man gagged.

"Hands," Jaime ordered. I used strips from a curtain to bind wrists. We dragged them behind their table, out of sight of the corridor. Rygial touched each, lips moving. Their blinks turned sticky. Their curses blurred. In a few heartbeats they were snoring into their own cards.

"I tilted their clock a bit," Rygial muttered, wiping at his brow. "They will wake in an hour. Or yesterday. I am never quite sure with wine in the gears."

"Yesterday would be nice," Elisah said. "They could warn themselves to stay out of our way."

Jaime's mouth twitched. She did not smile often in those days. War had taken that from her early. Prison had not helped. But the corners of her lips acknowledged the attempt. "Stairs," she said. "Elric?"

"Still clear," I said, ears sweeping the corridor. "Ground door is ahead, then right. Kitchen to the left. Night watch in the hall. Three men. One asleep. Two playing stones."

"We cannot dance through three," Jaime said. "Not with this lot." She meant me and Elisah without saying it. We did not have the look of saints.

"I can dim the hall," Elisah said. "Enough to slip behind."

"Or we walk into the kitchen," I said, picturing the fire, the pots, the smell of burning porridge. "Smoke route. Kitchens always have back doors. And sleeping cooks are easier than armed men with nothing to do."

"Cooks carry knives," Rygial pointed out.

"So do I," Elisah said. "Ask which of us sleeps deeper."

Jaime thought for a moment. She had a farmer's way of considering, like weighing grain in her palm. Not just counting what she wanted, but what it would cost. "Kitchen," she decided. "If there's trouble, we draw it there, not in the main hall. Fewer eyes."

We skirted the lit hall, slipping under the crackle of lanterns. Elisah pulled shadow behind us like a cloak, thinning our shapes. We reached the kitchen door without a shout raised. I eased it open.

Warmth hit first. Then the rich smell of bone broth and frying fat, onions cooked down to sweetness days ago and reawakened. My stomach cramped. Prison food did not count as food. The kitchen held two long tables, a soot-black stove and a bank of ovens that gave the only light. A single apprentice cook sagged on a bench, head back, mouth open, snoring with slow dedication. A panshelf stood between us and him.

"Rygial," Jaime whispered.

He looked offended. "What, I am the designated sleeper-maker now?"

"You are the one with the clock. Slow him if he stirs," she said, and stepped past him into the room. We moved around the tables, using the benches as cover. Elisah's fingers twitched. The oven flames guttered, low enough that we were shapes more than faces.

I could hear it then: a soft hiss from the far corner, air funneling narrow. "Smoke tunnel," I breathed. "There."

Guardhouses keep their fires hungry but controlled. No one wants to burn with the prisoners. A brick shaft punched through the wall rose above the main hearth, a blackened tunnel into the night. Jaime squinted. "Too small," she said. "For normal people."

"Luckily we brought a cat," Elisah murmured.

I eyed the opening. Soot ringed the stone like an old black halo. Two, maybe three body-widths at the narrowest, if those bodies were small and willing to come away smeared. Above, cool night drew the smoke, a draft that whispered against my whiskers. "I can go first," I said. "Make sure it's not bricked or barred at the top. Then Jaime, Elisah. Rygial last."

The dwarf sniffed. "Old bones squeezed through a chimney. My father would laugh himself right back to life just to see it."

"Tell him to wait until we're clear," I said.

Jaime nodded. "Go."

I slung my sword over my back, wrapped it in a rag from a butcher's hook to muffle the scrape, then put both hands on the smoke-black stone. Heat licked my palms. I pulled myself up, feet braced on the wall, shoulders compressing. The first breath filled my throat with the taste of ash and meat and long-burned wood. It was like climbing the throat of the guardhouse.

My claws found little purchase in the slick, baked soot, but elbows and knees and back all learned to press, twist, hunch. I wriggled, shoved, climbed. Once, halfway up, my shoulder stuck where a mason had not smoothed the join. Panic jabbed under my ribs. Above me, hungry dark. Below, dim orange. The smoke burrowed around my head like hot, damp fur. I exhaled until my chest was empty. Then I let my collarbones narrow and slid past.

The top flared wider. Cool air kissed my whiskers, blessed and sharp. I pushed my head out onto the roof and drew three deep breaths of night. The guardhouse roof spread flat and tarred, still warm from the day. Chimneys rose like blunt fingers. The prison wall beyond cut a heavier shape against the stars. Lamps burned in a few arrow slits.

I listened. No alarm yet. The city hummed in the distance. Somewhere a cart rattled past on late business. Somewhere a cat yowled for a lover or a fight. The world had not yet learned we were free again. "Clear," I whispered down the tunnel.

Jaime's boots scraped. A hand, then a shoulder. She wriggled up, face smeared like a chimney sweep's, hair coming loose from her prison tie. She hauled herself out with a grunt and lay flat for a moment, ribs rising and falling. "You all right?" I asked.

"Had to leave my pride stuck halfway," she said. "It will find its own way."

Elisah appeared next, all elbows and laughter. She came up like smoke, quicker than either of us, as if the dark wanted her out where it could see her properly. When she crouched beside me her teeth flashed white in her soot-blackened face.

Rygial took the longest. There were grunts. Old dwarven curses. At one point his beard wedged and there was a panicked mutter about strangling on his own magnificence. Then his bald head emerged, as offended as any chick dragged wet from an egg. "You are all too tall," he complained as I pulled him onto the tar. "This tower was not designed for honest dwarven shoulders."

"Next time we will ask them to build according to your measurements," Jaime said. "For now, we move."

WE CROSSED THE ROOF crouched low, shadows among shadows. At the edge, a lower outbuilding clung to the main block like a barn lean-to. Its roof sat ten feet down. Beyond that, the stable yard. Beyond that, a narrow lane and the city. "Easy," I said. "We jump, then the wall by the manure pile. Soft landing if we miss."

"No one wants that soft," Elisah muttered.

Jaime swung down first, hanging from the edge and dropping to the lower roof with a muted thump. Elisah followed, landing lighter than looked possible for her height. I went after, tail lashing for balance. Rygial eyed the drop.

"You lived two and a half centuries to die of a bruise?" I asked.

He sniffed. "I have fallen farther. Into worse." He sat on the edge, legs dangling, then let go. I braced for the impact. He hit, and the sound of it bent, came late. His descent had looked normal, but the landing took twice as long as it should. He straightened, joints creaking. "Slowed myself," he said. "Old trick. The ground is grateful."

We crept to the far edge. The stable yard lay below, a dark rectangle that smelled of hay, dung and horse sweat. One lantern burned near the door, left for whoever drew night-stable duty. A single gelding rustled in its stall. "Any ears?" Jaime asked.

I listened. The soft huff of that one horse. A man snoring somewhere above the stable, a thin wisp of sound from a loft. No boots. No mutter of guarding. "Clear," I said. "Drop by the muck pile. It is forgiving."

Rygial grimaced. "Forgiveness has a smell."

We dropped. The manure heap squished under our boots, warm and soft as overcooked porridge. My nose wrinkled instinctively. "Some of us are not meant for grace," I said.

"We were in a cell this morning," Elisah said. "I will bathe in worse if it means not going back."

We scaled the low wall, hands finding the chips in the mortar, and slid down into the lane outside. The air of the city wrapped us: wood smoke from a hundred hearths, nightsoil from the gutter, fish and rot and the faint sweet tang of spilled ale. It had never smelled so clean. I drew my first truly free breath and felt the space in my chest expand.

For a moment, there was a warmth there. Not the full flare I had felt in the swamp with the drakes, but a small coal. A reminder.

"Do we run?" Elisah asked. "If we keep to the alleys we can be in the outer wards before they sound the bell."

"We run," Jaime said, "but not away." She turned toward the river quarter, shoulders squaring again. Toward Kaben & Sons.

Elisah frowned. "You just climbed out of a cell. Most people head the other direction from the men who put them there."

"We are not most people," Jaime said. "Cragen framed us to protect Kaben. If we leave now, the drakes keep hitting the villages and Kaben keeps getting fat. If we go to ground, they find us again with the same lies. We need proof. We need to cut the rot."

I thought of home. Of the fields flattened by panicked feet. The smell of churned mud and drake blood. The look on my father's face when he saw the broken fence, the half-eaten goats. How small our village felt when something from the swamp took an interest. Swatting drakes had been like pulling weeds one at a time while something fed them from beneath the soil.

"Kaben's warehouse records will have something," I said. "No one moves creatures that big without paper trails. Feeding. Handling fees. Coin somewhere it should not go."

Rygial stroked his soot-clotted beard. "Ledgers are clocks of a sort. They show where time and money have gone. Men like Kaben never imagine their own numbers will turn against them."

Elisah shifted her weight, her shadows hugging closer. "So we walk back into the bear's den instead of away from it. To pick its pockets. In front of its snout."

"To break its snout," Jaime said quietly. "But yes."

Elisah looked at each of us in turn, eyes narrowing. She had been hired to open a lock and ended up with a jailbreak. Now we offered her a conspiracy. "You are all mad," she said.

"Yes," Rygial agreed. "But the other madmen own the guardhouse. Choose."

She snorted. "I have been running my whole life. Maybe I see what happens if I stop, just once. Fine. I am in. But if a drake eats me, I will haunt your clocks, dwarf."

He bowed. "I would be honored."

We slipped through the back lanes, keeping to the narrow places where the city forgot itself. Laundry lines brushed our faces. A sleeping dog lifted its head and did not bark. Lamps burned low, the hour between drinking and morning bread when most honest folk close one eye and dishonest ones open the other. Kaben's warehouse sat by the river like a satisfied tick. Big enough to impress a clerk. Not big enough to attract a noble's eye. The sign over the shuttered front boasted Kaben & Sons: Importers, Storage, Honest Brokerage. We went around the back.

THE RIVER STANK OF algae and old fish. Barges creaked in their moorings, black shapes against dull water. The warehouse's rear wall faced a narrow strip of cobble and a drop to the river, all weeds and broken crates. "No patrol," Elisah murmured, eyes scanning. "Too quiet."

"Men who trust their bribes sleep deep," Rygial said.

"Door?" Jaime asked.

Elisah approached the back door, a stout thing banded with iron. She ran fingertips along the lock, humming to herself. Her shadow stretched thin, sliding under the door crack like a probing tongue. "New bolts," she said. "He paid for better iron when he started making more coin. Good for us. This kind sings when you touch it."

She slipped two picks from her sleeve. They flashed, then were dark again as she worked them into the lock. The only sounds were the river's gurgle and the soft click, click of her tools. I listened hard. To our right, a drunk tried to find his way home, humming tunelessly. Farther away, a watch bell chimed twice. No alarm. The guardhouse had not yet realized we were not where we belonged. "Come on," she whispered to the lock. "You want to open. It is what you are made for."

The bolt slid back with a soft, pleased sigh. "Good girl," Elisah murmured.

Jaime eased the door open just enough to peer inside. She looked, listened, then nodded. "Empty," she said. "For now."

We went in. The warehouse was a dark sea of crates and barrels, their labels and chalk marks ghost-pale in the dim. Rafters loomed high above. The air was cold and dry, thick with the smell of burlap, salt and old wood. Kaben's business slept around us, neat and numbered.

"Office will be up," Rygial said quietly. "Men like their desks to look down on their labor."

We threaded the aisles. Jaime moved like she was counting steps, storing the pattern in case we had to run this path blind. Elisah's gaze flicked from shadow to shadow, measuring where she could disappear if someone came through the front. I padded ahead, ears spreading every whisper over my skin. At the western wall a staircase climbed to a platform and a door with a small glazed window. Faint lamplight bled around the frame.

"Occupied?" Jaime asked.

I listened. Quill scratching. Paper rustle. A cough, light and impatient. "He works late," I said.

Elisah smiled without humor. "Perfect. Men are so charming when surprised at their desks."

Jaime considered. We could have backed off, caught him later. But later did not exist. The guardhouse clock was chasing us. "We go loud only if we must," she said. "Elric and

I first. If he calls out, Elisah blinds the lamp. Rygial, you... do something unpleasant to his sense of speed."

"That I can do," the dwarf said.

We climbed. The office door was not locked. Kaben trusted the lock on the back door and the distance between his paperwork and the street. Jaime signaled three, two, one with her fingers. On one, she pushed the door in.

The man behind the desk looked up, quill pausing mid-stroke. I had seen Kaben once before, on the docks. He looked softer now. The prison air had not touched him. His tunic was fine linen, his belt heavy with coin and knife. His hair was thinning, combed carefully. His eyes were shrewd and small, used to weighing men like he weighed cargo.

"Who in the blessed name of coin are you," he began, then his eyes widened. He recognized Jaime. Then me. The quill dropped. Elisah flicked her hand. The lamp on his desk sputtered down, throwing most of the room into murk.

"Kaben," Jaime said, stepping into the half-light. "We need your books."

He recovered faster than I liked. "You are supposed to be in chains," he said.

"We were," I said. "The hospitality was lacking."

His hand went for the desk drawer. "Don't," Jaime warned. He pulled anyway. Rygial lifted his hand.

The drawer came out. The knife inside began to rise, point toward Jaime's gut. Then the motion froze thickened. The knife edged upward with the languor of a drowning man's last bubble. Kaben's arm trembled. His jaw worked faster than his fingers. "What is this," he snarled.

"Time enough for you to reconsider," Rygial said.

Jaime stepped forward and plucked the knife from the air. The moment her hand closed, it moved at normal speed. She dropped it into a box of quills. "We are not here to kill you," she said. "We are here for evidence that you bought those guards and set those drakes."

His eyes slid from face to face, calculating. "You have no idea what you are playing with."

"Probably not," I said. "I grew up counting goats. But I can read a ledger."

Elisah had already slipped past him, her shadow brushing his boots. She went to the shelves behind the desk, eyes scanning titles. Some were decoys, I knew. Generic shipping accounts, old tax records. "Real ones will be ugly," she murmured. "Bad handwriting. Coffee stains. Men hide their sin in the mess they understand."

Her fingers closed on a stack of worn, leather-bound books at the very bottom shelf. They had that saggy look of being opened and shut a hundred times. She tossed the stack onto the desk. "Those," she said.

Kaben lunged. Rygial's hand twitched. Time hiccuped. Kaben's forward motion turned syrup-thick again. Jaime caught his collar and slammed him back into his chair. The impact came slow, then fast at the last second, rattling his teeth.

"If you scream," she said, "I will not be gentle. Neither will the villagers when they learn what you did."

His lips pressed into a line. Sweat stood on his forehead. Elisah opened the first ledger.

The columns marched down the page in tidy ink. Receipts. Expenditures. Once you have seen a few, your eyes go heavy. But little anomalies shine like worms. "Here," I said, leaning over. "Payment to 'S.D. Handler' three months running. Same name that was on the crate we saw at the swamp crossing."

Jaime's jaw tightened. "The one the drakes followed."

"Here." Elisah flipped three pages. "Excess feed purchased. Not accounted for in known livestock. And a side note." She squinted. "'Special feed for big pets.' Charming."

Rygial peered closer. "Look at the dates. Coin leaves his hand every time a drake hits a village. Out, then in." He tapped the column of incoming. "And this... 'consulting fee, Captain C.' Twice a month. Same amount as the fines for 'unauthorized disruption of trade operations.' A tidy little wheel."

"Cragen," I said. "He fined us for interfering. Then Kaben paid him for the trouble."

"Bribes, not fines," Jaime said. "Different line in the book, same coin in the pocket."

Kaben's face had gone pale. "You do not understand," he said again, voice thin now. "I made a deal. Those beasts were supposed to stay in the marsh. Just scare caravans off the old road. Force trade onto the river where I could protect it. Then some idiot cut their feed and they started looking for food elsewhere. I tried to control it."

"By blaming villagers and wandering swords," Jaime said.

"By paying guards to create easy culprits," I said.

His eyes flashed. "By keeping trade running. You think your villages survive without this city's coin flowing? You think your fathers' plows do not depend on men like me?"

"Where I am from," I said, "plows depend on rain and calloused hands. Not on you feeding swamp monsters."

"You cannot pin this on me," he snapped suddenly, desperation bleeding through. "You are criminals. Escaped prisoners. No one will believe you."

"They will believe your handwriting," Elisah said. She flipped another ledger. There were coded notations in the margins now. S D H. C.C. F.D.

"What is F.D.?" Jaime asked.

"Further development," Rygial murmured. "Or future disaster."

It did not matter. We had enough. More than enough. "Take as many as we can carry," Jaime said. "We will run out of time before we run out of pages."

Elisah selected three ledgers, three letter bundles tied in blue string, and one thin book bound in expensive brown leather, no title on the spine. She opened it, scanned, and smiled. "Private correspondence," she said. "Dear Captain Cragen, enclosed please find your usual gratitude. Dear Mister Dorun at the city council, a small encouragement to overlook certain shipping incidents. My shelves are a better witness than any of us."

The warmth in my chest flared, small but insistent. We had our teeth in something that had only ever chewed on others. Kaben surged up again, this time going for the window. Time was thinning. Rygial swore, snapped a word. The air around Kaben thickened. His hand stretched toward the glass, fingers straining. He hung there, caught between one moment and the next, sweat rolling down his temple in slow beads.

"Ark," Rygial grunted. "Slowing a whole man is work. Take what you need. Decide if you want him to shout before or after we leave."

"After," Jaime said. "We want the honest guards here too."

"Elric," Elisah said. "You are quick. Go ahead. Find the nearest patrol that does not smell of Kaben's coin. Bring them running."

I hesitated. Leaving them felt wrong. But the longer we lingered, the more chance Cragen's men would arrive first. "Jaime?" I asked.

Her eyes met mine. "We need witnesses," she said. "We need someone in a clean coat to see these with us still holding them. You can hear them before they hear you. Go."

So I went.

THE CITY AT NIGHT is a living thing. It breathes in soft snores and muttered dreams. Its veins are alleys and its heart beats in taverns that never close. Boots beating on stone are its pulse. I slipped down the stairs, into the aisle maze, and back through the rear door. The river air hit my face. The lane was empty.

I ran. Not fast enough to draw eyes, not slow enough to lose the edge. Just that steady, long-stride pace my people use in the fields, crossing furrows at dawn when there is more to do than the day will hold. My ears cast wide, collecting the city's little sounds.

On Fishmonger's Cut, I caught a patrol. Two men and a woman, lantern swinging at the end of its pole, bored talk drifting in their wake. Their steps were even, professional. Their gear was serviceable, not new from bribes nor ragged from neglect. Their conversation was about a sick child and a wife's temper, not coin.

"Guards," I called softly from the shadow of a doorway.

Their hands went to hilts. The woman swung the lantern my way, light stabbing into the alley's black. "Show yourself," she barked.

I stepped into the fringe of light, hands open, not close to my sword. She took me in at a glance: the prison grime, the stolen guard cloak, the ears.

"Stop," she said. "Turn around. Hands on the wall."

"We do not have time for that," I said.

"Those are interesting words from a man in stolen uniform," she replied.

"You know Captain Cragen?" I asked.

Her jaw tightened. "He is my superior."

"You trust him?"

A muscle jumped in her cheek. "You are a breath from irons, cat. Choose next words carefully."

"Your Captain has been taking coin from Kaben & Sons to cover swamp attacks. Kaben has books that prove it. We have those books in our hands. In about three minutes, Cragen's personal men will arrive at Kaben's warehouse to kill us and burn the proof. If you want to know which side of that you were walking on tonight, you can keep pointing that lantern at me. Or you can come and see for yourself."

She stared at me, eyes searching my face for the idiot or the liar. She found neither, I think, only the ragged edges of someone already tired of running. "What is your name?" she asked.

"Elric," I said. "From Old King's Walk."

"Mine is Captain Mirel," she said quietly. "You are very unlucky that I am on duty tonight. Move." She gestured to her patrol. "Jarek. Pint. With me. Lantern low. If this is a trap, we kill him first."

"That seems fair," I said.

We ran back along the river.

Kaben's back door stood where I had left it, closed but not bolted. The lane still held only the river's whisper and the far-off murmur of the city. No sound of battle yet. "In there," I said.

Mirel signaled. Her men fanned, the lantern's light hooded now. They followed me into the shadowed canyon of crates. We almost made it to the office stairs.

"Elric," Jaime's voice rang out, somewhere above. "Company."

Boots thundered from the front main doors, many of them, no care for stealth. Men in city guard colors poured in, but their formation was sloppy, confidence born of habit and private orders, not training. Cragen strode in at their head, armor bright, jaw dark with stubble, eyes already hard. He did not expect to see Captain Mirel's lantern glow on the far side.

He hesitated one heartbeat. Sometimes that is all fate needs. "Mirel?" he snapped. "What are you doing here?"

"Responding to unlawful activity," she said, voice even. "Same as you. Apparently."

Cragen's gaze flicked from me to her to the stairs. Calculation flickered. "These four escaped my custody," he said. "They are armed, dangerous and in league with a known smuggler. Stand aside."

"Known smuggler that you happen to mention with convenient timing," Mirel said. "At his own warehouse. At night. Where you rushed ahead of the bell."

He bristled. "Do you question my deployment?"

"I question why your patrol moved without notifying central," she said. "And why this catfolk in stolen cloak knows more about Kaben's books than half my men do."

"You are being manipulated," Cragen snarled. "Stand down, Captain. That is an order."

Above us, Jaime's voice cut through. "If anyone is manipulated, it is the villagers Kaben fed to his beasts. We have his ledgers. We are coming down."

She emerged at the head of the stairs, Elisah at her shoulder with a stack of books clutched to her chest. Rygial followed, one hand flat on Kaben's back, urging him along at a painfully slow pace. Behind them, Kaben struggled, words tumbling from his mouth half as fast as his limbs moved.

"Captain Cragen," Kaben gasped. "They forced me. They are criminals." His protest came out stuttered, too late, mismatched with his mouth. It made him sound drunk or lying. Or both.

"That is enough," Cragen barked. "Men, seize them. Kill anyone who resists."

Mirel stepped forward, sword leaving scabbard with a clean rasp. "Anyone who draws blood in my presence tonight answers to me," she said.

Some of Cragen's men wavered. Some sneered. Two took a step back. One spat on the floor. "We serve the Captain," he said. "Not some bleeding-heart river patrol."

It did not matter whose order sparked it. Once steel comes out in a room full of fear and pride, the rest follows like rain from a dark cloud. Cragen drew. "Take them," he roared.

Chaos unrolled.

THEY CAME IN TWO waves. The first rushed the base of the stairs, trying to cut Jaime and Elisah off. The second spread to flank, to keep Mirel's patrol from closing ranks with us. Jaime moved first. She met the first guard three steps up from the bottom. Her sword caught his overhand swing, turning it aside with a sparking kiss. She slid, used his momentum to spin him into the man behind. They tumbled, knocking others off their stride.

"Elric, left," she snapped.

I went low. Claws, knees, the flat of my blade. I did not want to kill them. Some might have been like Mirel's men, just taking orders from the wrong mouth. But you cannot coddle a man swinging steel at your head. The first guard came in with a cautious jab. I batted it aside, then stepped in and drove my pommel into his gut. He oofed and folded. I kicked his knee, hard enough to make it buckle but not break. He went down, steel clattering.

Another came from my left, slashing high. I ducked, felt the wind of his blade over my ears. My second sword whispered from its sheath and my world narrowed. In tight quarters, speed is not about how fast you swing but how little you waste. I let the warmth in my chest feed my legs. I slipped between crates, each movement measured, no more and no less than needed. A parry here, a cut across a knuckle there, a shove that sent a man stumbling into Mirel's waiting blade.

Mirel fought like a woman who knew the cost of every inch. No wasted flourish. She kept her men back-to-back, forming a small circle that shifted to keep their exposed sides toward crates, not enemies. When a guard rushed in, she turned his sword aside and drove her hilt into his jaw. She did not kill unless she had to. It made me like her.

Elisah loosed her chain. It hissed out like a tongue of night, wrapping around an ankle, yanking a man off his feet. She stepped in, shadow-knives flickering. One cut the strap of a shield, dropping it. Another sliced a hand's tendons, sending a sword to the ground. "Eyes up," she called. "They like to circle."

A thrown dagger whistled toward her head. She tilted, barely, and it passed through her hair. For a moment her outline blurred, as if the lamp could not decide where she truly stood. "Missed," she said.

On the stairs, Rygial held one palm out, fingers crooked like claws. His lips moved constantly now, sweat dripping from his nose. The men who tried to reach Jaime found their legs strangely heavy on the last three steps. They swung, and their cuts came late. One man's thrust slowed long enough for Jaime to step aside, almost bored, and rap his helmet with the flat. He toppled backward.

Rygial's beard shook with the strain. "I cannot hold them all," he grunted. "My clock has only so many hands."

Cragen did not care. He pushed through his men like a bull, shouldering aside the ones too slow. His sword was broader than Jaime's, nicked from use. He fought with that ugly efficiency I had seen in career soldiers, no thought for grace, only for winning. He locked blades with Jaime halfway down the stairs.

"You should have stayed in your cell," he snarled.

"You should have stayed honest," she replied, teeth bared.

He drove forward, using his weight. She gave ground, step by step, jaw clenched. Sparks spat where their steel ground. Her footing skidded on a fallen man's spilled blood. "Elric," she hissed.

I wanted to go to her, but two more of Cragen's men barred my path, paired up now, learning. They came at me like they had practiced together, one high, one low. I had no room for cleverness. Just hard choices. I dropped my off-hand sword, took the high man's cut on my main blade, feeling the shock through shoulder and spine. I kicked sideways into a crate, forcing my weight the opposite direction. The low man's thrust missed my thigh by a whisker.

"Faster," that warmth inside whispered. "Faster."

For a moment, the world slowed. Not like Rygial's magic, not thick and sticky, but clear as winter air. I could see the next three moves if I wanted them. I could watch their shoulders, their breath. I did not let it eat me. Not this time. Just a sip. I twisted, slid my blade along the high man's, deflecting his point out and down. Then I stepped into his guard and drove my forehead into his nose.

Bone crunched. He staggered, dropping his sword. I grabbed his collar and yanked him into his friend's line. The second man's thrust sank into his own comrade's side instead of my ribs. He cried out. The second man stared, horrified. "You did that," I said, and slammed my hilt into his temple. He went limp.

On the stairs, Jaime and Cragen traded a flurry. She slipped his guard twice, cutting shallow lines across his arm and side. He grunted, but did not slow. "Captain," Mirel called. "Stand down. Look at him. Look at Kaben. You are on the wrong side of this."

Cragen's answer was a roar. He shoved Jaime back with a shoulder-check, swinging hard at her neck. She ducked by instinct. The sword whistled over. He overcommitted. She stabbed. Her point slid along his cuirass, looking for a gap. Found one at the edge of his hip plate. Skated in.

He gasped and spun, ripping himself off her blade, blood following. His sword came around wild. It would have taken her head if she had not dropped, literally, sitting down hard on the stair. The cut passed inches above her braids. His momentum took him forward two steps, onto the slick of his own blood.

He slipped. Rygial reached for him, perhaps on reflex, to slow his fall. His left hand twitched, but whatever spell he held on Kaben and the others faltered. He had nothing left to give. Cragen crashed sideways into the crate stack.

Wood splintered. The top crate tipped and fell, smashing open on the floor in a burst of straw and iron-bound bottles. Liquid spread, sharp with the smell of spirits. A lantern, knocked from a hook in the chaos, tumbled down.

Time has its own humor. The lantern's fall bent as it passed through the bubble of slowed air around Kaben. It drifted, turning lazily, flame licking at the oil. Rygial swore in a language older than the stones.

He flung his hand out, wrenching that little chunk of time aside. The lantern's trajectory shifted by a handspan. It missed the spirits, hit the wet straw instead. Fire leapt.

"Out!" Jaime shouted.

"We cannot leave the books," Elisah snapped.

"We do not," Jaime said. "Elric, get what you can. Mirel, pull your people. Rygial, if you can slow that fire, now would be blessed."

"Time is tinder," he grunted. "I can... pinch it."

He clenched his fist. The flames shivered, slowed, crawling instead of leaping. Smoke still poured up, thick and bitter. We moved fast.

Elisah shoved ledgers into a burlap sack, hands a blur. Jaime grabbed the correspondence bundle and stuffed it into her tunic, wincing. I scooped up the fallen thin brown book off the floor, clutching it to my chest. Cragen, groaning, pushed himself to hands and knees. Blood darkened his leg. He reached for his sword.

Mirel stepped between him and it. "Captain," she said low. "Stop. It is over."

His eyes burned. "You will regret this."

"Maybe," she said. "But not as much as them." She nodded at us.

Smoke climbed the rafters. Men coughed, stumbling back. "Kaben," Rygial said. "Choose."

The merchant stood panting in Rygial's grip, half-free of the temporal net. He could have bolted, but where? Through Cragen's men, who would hang him to save themselves? Into the river? Jump through the window into the street? He slumped. "You think they will thank you," he rasped. "You will be tools and then cast off. That is how it works."

"Better a used tool than rotten lumber," I said.

We half-dragged, half-hustled him and the sacks of ledgers toward the front door. Mirel's patrol formed a wedge around us, shields up to deflect any last foolish swing. Cragen's loyalists glared but did not attack again, not with fire licking at their ankles and their Captain on one knee. Outside, the night air tasted like freedom and smoke.

WE DID NOT STAND in the street arguing long. Kaben's warehouse was not the only building in the row. Flames and neighbors encourage haste. Mirel snapped orders.

"Jarek, Pint, bucket chain. Rouse anyone still sleeping. You, you and you," she pointed at three of Cragen's men, "drop your swords and help or so help me I will arrest you for arson as well as corruption."

They hesitated, then obeyed, more afraid of burning than discipline. She turned to us. "All of you," she said. "With me. Now."

She marched us two streets over, to a small square with a dry fountain. No one else was there at this hour. Smoke curled above rooftops behind us, but here the air held only damp and stone. We stood in a loose circle: Jaime, Elisah, Rygial and me on one side, Kaben groaning on the ground between us and Cragen, propped against the rim of the fountain, blood soaking his hip, on the others. Mirel held the middle.

"Put the ledgers on the stone," she ordered. We did. The brown correspondence book. The three fat trade ledgers. The bundle of letters.

She looked at me. "You said they prove corruption."

"They show coin moving when and where drakes attacked," I said. "They show bribes to Cragen, to a councilor, to handlers who moved beasts instead of cargo. Kaben can tell you the rest."

Kaben laughed, a dry, cracked sound. "Why should I say anything?"

"Because if those ledgers burn or disappear," Mirel said, "you hang alone. If you speak and they match your story, you might live long enough to see old age in a cell. Up to you."

He weighed it. Men like Kaben always weigh. Rygial leaned on his staff, breathing hard. His usual humor had burned away with the straw. "Time will tell with or without your tongue," he said. "Speak, and you at least get to hear it."

Kaben sagged. "Fine. Yes. I paid Cragen to steer blame. I paid handlers to lure drakes. I paid a councilor to look away. I never meant for villagers to die. It was supposed to be about trade routes. But when the beasts tasted easy flesh…" He shuddered. "You cannot reason with hunger."

Mirel's jaw tightened. She had grown up here, I guessed. She knew the villages better than she let on. She turned to Cragen.

"Captain," she said. "Response?"

He spat on the cobbles. "Convenient confession from a cornered man and the word of criminals. These... books could be forged."

"By who?" Elisah asked lightly. "I have fast fingers, Captain, but not that fast. And my handwriting is prettier."

Mirel flipped a ledger open. Her eyes moved down the columns. Her finger traced dates, then jumped to the correspondence. "Here," she said quietly. "Council docket eighteen. There was a complaint from the marsh villages about increased drake activity. I remember. It was delayed hearing for two months." She held up a letter. "And here is Kaben thanking Councilor Dorun for 'handling that little scheduling matter' and enclosing additional payment."

Her gaze shifted to Cragen. "Here is Kaben thanking you for 'neutralizing disruptive elements interfering with the natural flow of commerce' and enclosing your 'usual gratitude.'"

Cragen's lips peeled back. "You want to burn me," he hissed. "For what? For playing the same game every man with a title plays? Dorun will skate. Kaben will buy his way into a nicer cell. And you will go back to chasing drunks in the river quarter while the true rot moves up where your sword does not reach."

"Maybe," Mirel said. "But tonight I reach you. That is enough."

He lunged, faster than he should have been able with that wound. For Rygial, for Kaben, for anyone he could drag down. Jaime moved. Her sword slid between them, aimed not at heart or throat but at Cragen's reaching hand. It pierced his palm, pinning it to the fountain's stone lip.

He screamed. Blood sheeted. His fingers spasmed around the steel. She held his eyes. "No more killing tonight," she said. "Hurt if you must. But no more dying over your pride."

Mirel stepped in, cuffed Cragen on the back of the head hard enough to make him sag. When he slumped, she twisted his arm and slapped irons on his wrists. "I am placing you under arrest for corruption, conspiracy, and endangering citizens," she said. "By authority of the city guard and my own common sense."

He laughed once, bitter. "They will not let this stand."

"Then they can come say it to my face in the morning," she replied.

She turned to us at last. "You four broke out of a lawful holding cells, assaulted guards, stole property and set half a warehouse on fire," she said. "You also exposed a conspiracy that has been bleeding my people for months."

"The fire was an accident," Rygial muttered. "Mostly."

Her mouth twitched. "I cannot ignore the first part," she went on. "If I haul you in, the council will make a spectacle of you to cover their shame. If I let you walk free in my jurisdiction, every petty thief will claim they are exposing grand conspiracies when I catch them."

"So what then?" I asked. My bones felt hollow. The fight was catching up with me. The warmth in my chest was ashes again.

She looked at Jaime. "You said you were following the trail of those drakes," she said. "Out into the marsh, beyond the city's grip."

"Yes," Jaime said. "Whatever Kaben started, someone in the swamp finished. Those creatures did not just wander into villages by chance."

Mirel nodded slowly. "Then here is what will happen. At dawn, I will file paperwork stating that four dangerous prisoners escaped during a riot caused by Captain Cragen's negligence. I will attach evidence of his crimes and Kaben's, plus these ledgers." She rested a hand on the stack.

""I will also file an order of exile," she said. "For Elric of Old King's Walk, Jaime Durandal, Elisah...?"

Elisah's eyes flicked. "Just Elisah."

"Elisah Justelisah," Mirel said dryly, "and Rygial...?"

"Son of Rygial, of Rygial's Line," he said. "We are not inventive with names."

"Exile," Mirel repeated. "From this city and its holdings, effective immediately. You will not be welcome inside the walls again without my explicit writ. If you are found here after dawn, any guard will have the right to run you in on sight."

"Punishment fits the gossip," Elisah said. "Criminals run off. City cleanses itself."

"And in the same order," Mirel said, "I will note that as part of your sentence, you are to follow the trail of swamp activity beyond our borders and report to the nearest authority what you find. As far as my superiors are concerned, I will be sending problems away from my streets. What you do with your feet after that is up to you."

"You are formally ordering us," Jaime said slowly, "to keep doing what we were doing before you arrested us."

"Yes," Mirel said.

"That is... a strange mercy," Rygial said.

"It is not mercy," she replied. "It is the only way I can write the truth into the lies they will make me tell." She looked at me. Her eyes were tired, but clear.

"Your villages need someone willing to stand between them and whatever grew hungry in those reeds," she said. "It will not be me. I belong here, in these alleys, dealing with drunks and petty thieves and, occasionally, captains who forget what the badge is for."

"You send us out to be heroes," I said. "Heroes no one will thank. No one asked for."

"No one ever asks," she said. "They just cry when no one comes."

Jaime exhaled slowly. There was a set to her shoulders I had come to recognize, like a woman putting on a harness before dawn. "We were going that way anyway," she said. "With or without your exile."

Mirel nodded. "This way, I can tell myself I did not just turn loose four dangerous individuals. I set them to a task."

Elisah smirked. "Makes you sleep better?"

"Barely," Mirel said. "But in my line of work, you take what sleep you can."

She gathered the ledgers and letters under one arm, grunting at the weight. "Dawn is not far," she said. "If you have any love for this city, do not be in it when the bells ring. The council will wake angry. They will want someone to hurt. Let it be me, not you."

"You will not hang for this?" I asked.

She shrugged. "I am too useful. They will shout, they will threaten to cut my pay, they will move me to a less pleasant ward. Life will go on. Corruption does not vanish in a night. But tonight at least, we cut one rotten branch." She looked at each of us in turn. "Try not to die in the swamp," she said. "It reflects badly on my paperwork."

Rygial bowed, as much as his aching back would allow. "We will do our best to inconvenience your clerks with long reports."

Elisah flourished a half-salute. "If I come back, it will be to rob someone nicer."

Jaime extended her hand. Mirel took it, soldier to soldier. "Thank you," Jaime said simply.

"Do not thank me," Mirel replied. "Go."

We went.

WE LEFT BY THE river road, skirting the guardhouse lights and the waking grumble as word of fire spread through the ward. We stayed to back alleys until the walls loomed ahead, black and high. The east gate would not open until dawn for caravans. The sally postern, though, opened for no one but rats and men with keys.

"We are outlaws now," Elisah said. "We do not need gates."

She found us a forgotten culvert where runoff from the walls trickled into a ditch. Once it might have been properly barred. Rust had eaten half the iron away. Stone had cracked. There was just enough gap for a stubborn young man of mixed blood to wedge himself through. I went first, scraping shoulders, feeling moss and slime cold against my fur. Jaime followed, then Elisah, then Rygial, muttering about dignified dwarven ends. When we stood on the far side, in the wild weeds beyond the city's stone skin, the sky over the marsh glowed faintly with the promise of dawn.

Behind us, bells started to toll. First the fire-call, then the heavy, steady beat of the watch-change. The city was waking to its new cracks. Ahead of us, the swamp waited, black and silent. Mist crawled over the reeds like something alive. Somewhere within, a drake bellowed, low and hungry.

We were tired. My muscles shook with each step. Jaime's bandaged arm bled through in one thin line. Rygial's face was gray with spell-exhaustion. Elisah's usual quicksilver motions had slowed to something almost normal. None of us suggested stopping.

"Exiles," Elisah said quietly. "For doing the right thing."

"In my village," I said, "when a dog kills a fox in the henhouse, you still beat it for running through the cabbages to get there."

Jaime glanced at me. "And the dog?"

"Still gets fed," I said. "If the hens live."

The road ahead was nothing more than two ruts cutting into the marsh. The world beyond the city's walls did not know our names and did not care. The drakes would not weigh our good deeds before they bit. We walked toward that indifference with soot on our faces and someone else's coin in our pockets. Heroes nobody had asked for, with an order of exile in all but name and a swamp full of trouble waiting to see if we would sink or swim.

The sun's first edge broke over the reeds. "Forward," Jaime said. We went.

# Chapter 15

## THE SWAMP TAKES NAMES

THE MARSH BEGAN WHERE the last stone ended.

We stepped off the mossed slab of the culvert and the ground gave way. Not much. Just enough that my boots sank over the tops and cold, brown water poured in. The shock bit to the bone. I hissed and lurched forward. The mud let go with a sound like someone tearing raw meat.

Behind us, the city bells were still ringing. They carried thin over the marsh, stretched by distance until they sounded almost small. Jaime paused on the last bit of stone and looked back through the dripping arch.

"That's it, then," she said.

Her voice was flat. Not grief. Not yet. Just the statement of a thing done.

Rygial swung down beside me with far more grace than someone his age had any right to. The mud swallowed him halfway to the knee and held on. He did not bother to curse. He only sighed, like he had been expecting this particular indignity all morning.

"Old King's Walk," he said. "Mud's worse this side. Always was."

Jaime's mouth twitched. She knew he was lying. I did too. He had never been here with us before. But he said it in the tone of a man who had seen enough swamps that they had blurred together into one long stretch of rot.

Elisah came last, light as a stray shadow. She landed on a tuft of grass, not the mud, and did not sink at all. Of course she didn't.

"Try the green bits," she said over her shoulder, as if we hadn't already noticed the obvious. "They want you dead less."

The wind shifted. Marsh smell rolled over us. Rot and stagnant water. A sweetness that had gone wrong. Things drowned long ago, still softening. The mist was not thick yet, just a low veil over the water, clinging to the roots. It blurred shapes at the edge of vision.

The city bells went on. Then stopped.

No going back after that.

Jaime was the first to turn away from the culvert. She squared her shoulders the way I'd seen her do when her father sent her out into the fields in late frost to save what barley she could. Jaw set. Eyes lower, looking for rocks, not horizons.

"East," she said. "The ledger marked drake sign all along the Hagwater fork. Mirel said the main nest has to be past the split."

Rygial lifted his head, as if sniffing for something else. "Mirel says many things."

"Got any better ideas?" Jaime asked.

"Yes. Several. All worse."

He set off anyway, stumping through the mud with slow, short steps, feeling each one before he gave it his weight. His beard already held flecks of wet leaf. I followed in his prints, longer stride matching two of his. The mud still grabbed. Something slick slid over my boot and away.

Elisah ranged ahead and to the side. One moment she was on a root, the next on a leaning stone, the next balancing along a tangled mass of exposed roots as if she had lived her whole life on things that moved.

Maybe she had.

I did not know then how much of her childhood had been spent looking for places to stand that no one else could reach.

Jaime fell in behind me, the tip of her sword scabbard tracing a slow furrow. Her breath came hard already. We had not slept. The warmth I carried inside, that deep ember that always flared under my ribs in real danger, lay dull and sullen. It had spent itself in the prison yard when the sun was barely up. Now my limbs felt full of wet sand.

We left the culvert and with it the last glimpse of stone and straight lines. The ground rolled out in broken humps of peat and pools of brown water coated in green skin. Dead trees thrust up like fingers. The living ones leaned over, roots showing, drinking rot.

Flies found us within a dozen paces. They weren't the house flies of Old King's Walk. These were thick, dark things that bit through cloth. They came in clouds. They went for eyes, ears, the damp crease of the neck. Jaime cursed and tied a rag around her face. It muffled her voice.

"You could've let us keep our armor, at least," she said, speaking to nobody in particular. Captain Mirel was already far away. "If we get eaten in the swamp, I'm haunting his office."

"Paperwork is curse enough," Rygial said. "Leave the man some hope of rest."

The mud changed underfoot without warning. One moment it was thick and resistant, the next my leg plunged down to the thigh. I yelped and grabbed at nothing. My weight dragged me sideways. The swamp did not roar or hiss. It just held fast and tried to pull me apart.

A hand caught my collar. Cloth bit my throat. Jaime grunted and leaned back, boots sliding.

"Elric, stop flailing," she said through clenched teeth. "You're supposed to be the cat."

I froze. The mud tugged harder now that I had stopped fighting it. A slow, steady weight. I could feel it working past my boot top, creeping under, sucking at the bare fur of my leg. Cold. Grainy.

"Elisah," Jaime snapped. "Rope."

"On it."

Elisah uncoiled from a low limb. I hadn't seen her climb it. That was becoming a pattern. She had a coil of thin line in her hands. Not prison issue. Something she had not surrendered. She must have hidden it in the shadows when they stripped the cells. Or hidden herself from their eyes.

She looped the rope around my chest in two quick passes, both under my arms, knot biting down under my shoulder blades. There was a smell on the rope. Oil and metal and something faintly floral. Not hers.

"Rygial, brace," she said. "Jaime, pull with me. On three. Don't jerk. You'll tear him. One, two—"

I felt the line go taut. My ribs compressed. My trapped leg burned.

"—three."

They did not haul, exactly. It was more of a lean. Slow. Relentless. Jaime's boots slid, found a root, slid again. Rygial wedged himself behind a stone and made a low, unhappy sound. Elisah's shoulders bunched. Her eyes stayed on my face. Watching for something. Panic, maybe. Or that moment when people break and stop helping themselves.

I gritted my teeth and pushed down with my free leg, trying to give the pull something to work with. The swamp sucked at me, thick and obscene. For a heartbeat the rope seemed to stretch rather than move me. Then, with a wet, tearing groan, the mud let go.

I came up with an explosion of brown water and muck. It splashed over all of us. There was something in it. Grit. Bits of shell. I did not think too hard about what else.

I lay on my back, half across the tuft of ground, gasping. My trapped leg burned from hip to toes. My boot stayed behind. The marsh had claimed it. Brown water filled the hole with a slow burp.

"Lost a shoe?" Rygial peered down. "Only fair. You stole that from one of Kaben's men."

"I did not steal it," I said between breaths. "I borrowed. Long-term."

"Call it interest," he said.

Jaime was still braced, fists white on the rope. When she saw I was clear, she let go and sat down heavily in the muck beside me.

"New rule," she said. "We follow Elisah's feet. Not Rygial's memory. No offense, Rygial."

"All offense taken," he said. "I approve of competence where I find it."

Elisah slipped the rope off my shoulders. Her fingers were quick and impersonal. Her eyes flicked down my soaked leg, then away.

"You're lucky," she said. "Another few breaths and you'd have gone past knee. Past knee, you don't come back with all the joint working right. Or at all."

"You've seen that?" I asked.

She shrugged. "Seen worse. Marshes are cheap ways to hide things. Sometimes the things walk in by themselves."

She coiled the rope with three practiced turns and hooked it back on her belt.

I pushed myself upright. The mud tried to claim my bare foot at once. I yanked it up and swore.

"Take my left boot," Jaime said, already tugging at the laces. "I'll go barefoot."

"Your feet will rot," Rygial said.

"Yours won't?" Jaime shot back. "You're what, fifty? Sixty?"

Rygial snorted. "In dwarf years? I am the creak in the first snow-worn door you ever opened. I am the dust between stones your great-grandfather never noticed. Fifty, she asks."

He shook his head and trudged on. But a ghost of a smile pulled at one corner of his mouth.

Jaime handed me her boot. It was still warm from her foot. I tried not to think about that too much as I shoved my muddy leg into it. It was a little tight, but leather forgives. I tied it in a double knot and stood, testing my weight.

"Now we're uneven," Jaime said. "You're taller on one side."

"So are you," I pointed out.

She looked down at her bare foot, now deep in brown slime. "Fair."

We walked more carefully after that. Elisah chose the way. She did not do it loudly. She just happened to be where the ground held, and if we stayed in her wake, we took fewer bad steps.

Sometimes she tested with a stick first. Sometimes she just looked. I watched her eyes then. They moved too fast for comfort, always ahead, always searching for the slight sheen that meant open water, the drag in a branch that meant weight had broken it recently.

There was more to her than locks and quiet steps. She treated the swamp like a street with bad alleys and worse corners. You stayed where you could see. You did not walk where the color looked wrong.

Rygial marked our passage in his own way. Every so often he would stop, sigh, and pinch something in the air. The space between his fingers wavered, as if heat rose there. A ghost image of our group, smaller and paler, took three steps ahead and then blurred away.

Jaime watched that the first time and flinched. "What are you doing to us?"

"Nothing," Rygial said. "Trying to do something to what was. Hold still."

He closed his eyes. The tiny phantom of us sharpened, then reversed. It walked backward along our trail. Rygial's hand trembled.

"There," he said softly. "They're following us."

I turned, ears pricking, half expecting guards wading through mud with swords raised. There was only the grey of morning and the slow drip of water from branches.

"Who?" Jaime asked.

Rygial opened his eyes. They were a little bloodshot. He let the image go. It vanished with a pop.

"Nothing with legs yet," he said. "But the water's moving wrong behind us. Tides in a place that does not have them. Something big is stirring when we pass. It goes still when we stop."

"You can see that?" I asked.

"I paid a high price to see what should be left alone," he said. "Try not to make me use it more than I have to."

"How high?" Elisah asked without looking back.

"High enough I started stealing," he said.

The words hung there between us. It was the first time he had spoken of it plain. Why a dwarf with that much age in his eyes had ended up in a petty human prison.

Jaime made a low noise. "Stealing time?"

"Stealing hours," he said. "Mine. Others'. Time is a debtors' game. Borrow from your future, pay back in days you wish you hadn't spent in a cell. Borrow from someone else's... well. You end up here, with you three. No offense."

"All offense taken," Jaime said.

We walked.

The marsh did not change quickly. It was all the same things in different orders. Pools, hummocks, half-submerged logs. Trees growing out of the water with their roots bare like black lace. But the weight of it grew. The air got thicker. The mist began to cling in folds around our legs, then up to our waists.

Sound went strange. Sometimes a bird called close by and it seemed very far. Sometimes a branch snapped under my boot and the noise cracked out like a tree falling.

There were things in the water.

I heard the first one before I saw it. A soft slicking sound off to the right, too regular to be wind. Then a wet slap, as if something had rolled in mud and flopped back.

"Elisah," I said quietly. "Stop."

She did. One hand went out, palm back toward us. Wait. Her other hand found the hilt of her little knife.

We all froze.

The sound came again. Slither. Slap. Slow, patient movement. Not coming straight at us. Circling, almost. Judging distance.

The surface of the pool to our right bulged. Not breaking. Just rising. The green scum stretched, then split. A wedge of dark pushed through. Water poured off scaled hide. Two pale, lidless eyes rose above the surface, then a snout peeled open to show a long row of teeth meant for gripping and not letting go.

The thing was all jaw and tail. A marsh-croc, I realized, though I had only ever seen them dead and skinned in the market, their meat going cheap.

This one was not cheap. It was longer than a cart and half again. Its back was hooped with moss, as if the swamp had tried to claim it and failed.

It turned its head toward us, very slow. It had been moving for some time, I guessed, riding the current of our wake. Waiting to see which one of us would stumble.

My skin prickled. The warmth at my core stirred, not waking fully, just shifting like a sleeper hearing a noise. There was danger here, and it knew its work.

Jaime's hand found my sleeve. "Don't move," she breathed.

Rygial snorted very softly. "I was going to dance a jig."

The croc's eyes slid over us. Past us. It sank, soundless. Its bulk moved under the scum toward a different pool, away from the little rise we had found.

"If we hadn't stopped?" I whispered.

"It would have taken whoever was last," Elisah said. "Dragged them sideways. Rolled. That's how they drown you. No chance to yell. Just water and teeth. My old crew used to use them near the piers. Lure them with offal. Toss in a body you don't want found."

She spoke lightly. Too lightly. I pictured a young girl on a rotting pier with men who thought throwing bodies to reptiles was a joke.

"Your old crew sounds charming," Jaime muttered.

"They were warm in winter and you could trust them not to stab you facing away from you," Elisah said. "Most of the time. You take what you get."

She started down off the hump of ground.

"Wait," Rygial said. "You're walking us straight toward its wake."

"That's where the bottom's solid," she said without turning. "Something that heavy doesn't swim. It walks. Same as us. Step where it did, you don't sink. Just don't fall in."

"Oh, good," Jaime said under her breath. "We're following a man-eater's footsteps. Sense at last."

But she followed.

The day dragged. The light never got bright. It was a grey that seemed to come from everywhere and nowhere. My tail was a dull ache from keeping it lifted out of the water. Every muscle in my legs trembled from balancing on roots and narrow ridges of peat. My borrowed boot squelched. Jaime's bare foot bled from a cut she refused to look at.

We took a rest when the tremble reached our arms from gripping branches. Jaime found a patch of ground higher than the rest, crowned with a cluster of reeds and one stunted tree. It was only dry in comparison, but our feet did not vanish when we stood on it. That was enough.

"We sit ten breaths," she said. "No more. Mirel gave us a head start, not a holiday."

Rygial lowered himself against the tree with a wheeze. "You sound like a captain already."

"I sound like a farmer who knows if you stop when you're tired, you never reach the end of the row," she said, lowering herself with a wince. Mud had caked around her bare ankle. I could not see the cut, but I could smell the copper.

I sat near her without thinking, back to the reeds, knees drawn up. The ground was soft, molding to me. There was a faint vibration in it, like a big beast walking somewhere far off.

Elisah did not sit. She paced the perimeter of our little rise, eyes scanning. Every so often she would crouch and touch two fingers to the mud, then bring them to her nose and breathe in.

"You smell something?" I asked.

"Lots of somethings," she said. "Old water. Rot. Scale oil. Men. Not fresh men. A day, maybe two. Heavy. Like armor. Like Mirel's."

"Guards came this way?" Jaime straightened. The word men did that to her. To all of us, then.

"Came, yes," Elisah said. "Went..." She sniffed again, this time turning slowly, face wrinkling. "Harder to say. Two went back. One... doesn't go back."

Rygial's eyes flicked open. "Doesn't?"

She pointed with her chin toward a smear of churned mud leading off into thicker trees. "Body drag. Not human hands. Claw marks along with it. Mirel said three didn't make it back after their last chase. He was right about that, at least."

Jaime's jaw worked. "Drake?"

"Too small," Elisah said. "Or too careless. Drakes lift. They don't drag. Learned that from a man who caught one once."

"You keep interesting company," Rygial murmured.

"Kept," she said. "Past tense."

Rygial shifted, wincing. Sweat stood out on his forehead despite the cool air.

"You all right?" I asked.

He gave me a thin look. "Fine. Everything's fine. I just reached too far and my joints are reminding me I'm a collection of borrowed hours held together with spite."

"What did you reach for?" Jaime asked.

He hesitated. Then, with a little shrug, held up his hand.

In his palm, cupped carefully, lay a small silver disk. It was no larger than Jaime's thumb nail. It spun slowly, not on any surface, just above his skin. The air around it was warped, like the shimmer above a forge.

"What is that?" I breathed.

"Secondhand," he said. "Literally. I shaved it off the moment we left the culvert. Took a sliver of our near past and made it hold still. When I poke it, it shows me where we were in that instant. Who was near. How the water moved."

His fingers closed around it. When he opened his hand again, it was gone. Or maybe it had never been.

Jaime frowned. "And doing that makes you... what? Old?"

"Older," he said. "Every cut adds up. You lot count in years. I've started counting in spells."

"That why you were in that cell?" Elisah asked from the perimeter. Her tone was casual, but she had stopped pacing.

"That, and poor taste in patrons," he said. "A prince wanted more hours than he had. Thought he could hoard youth the way he hoarded land. I made it work. For a while. The bill always comes due. He went to the noose before his fortieth name day with a young man's face and an old man's eyes. I got a cell. Fair trade."

"Why didn't you leave?" Jaime asked. "Before us. You could have. You were doing tricks like that in the cell."

Rygial's gaze went distant for a heartbeat. "I walked out of that prison a dozen times," he said quietly. "Back, forward, sideways. It always ended the same. Rope. Bolt. Falling stones. Time I'd cut away came back looking for me. The first path that went anywhere different was the one where the idiot cat and the farm girl picked a fight in the yard."

"Elisah and I did most of the work," Jaime said automatically. Then blinked. "Wait. So you stayed because—"

"Because every future I stepped into without you three ended in a wall," Rygial said. He closed his eyes again. "Don't make me regret betting on the noisy option."

The swamp hummed. Flies buzzed in a slow halo around us. Somewhere out at the edge of hearing, something big moved through water and reeds with the indifference of a barge.

Jaime chewed that over, scowling. I did too. I had not asked to be anyone's changing point. I just wanted to keep my friends alive and prove I was more than Kaben's frightened stray.

"What about you?" I asked Elisah, because my tongue always moved faster than my wisdom. "You had ropes and tricks. Why'd you stay?"

She had gone still near the edge of the rise, half-crouched. For a moment I thought she had not heard me. Then she turned her head. Her eyes were very dark in that light.

"In the cell, you mean?" she asked.

"In the prison at all," I said. "You move like someone who doesn't get caught unless she wants to."

She snorted very softly. "Flatterer."

"I'm serious."

"So's he," Rygial murmured without opening his eyes.

Elisah straightened. She walked over, slow, and dropped cross-legged opposite me, careful to keep her boots out of the worst of the slime. Her fingers played with the hem of her sleeve, rolling it back, rolling it down again.

"Sometimes you get tired of running," she said finally. "Sometimes you want to see what happens if you stop."

"You wanted to be caught?" Jaime asked, incredulous.

"I wanted to be somewhere the men I owed weren't," she said. "City gaol's as good a place as any for that. Cheaper than paying off the Brotherhood. Safer than skipping town and hoping their knives are slower than your feet."

"Who'd you cross?" Rygial asked quietly.

She smiled without humor. "Everyone."

Her hand flipped, and for a moment, in the hollow of her palm, shadow pooled deeper than it had any right to. It had weight. Edges. Then it was gone as she closed her fingers.

"I took something that wasn't mine," she said. "Same as you, dwarf. Only what I took wasn't hours. It was a door. To places men in gilded masks weren't meant to walk."

"The Brotherhood of Veils," Rygial said under his breath. "Idiots. Dangerous idiots."

"Idiots who don't like being robbed," Elisah said. "So I went somewhere they wouldn't bother to look. A place with honest records and dull guards and a man like Kaben who thought shadows were something you beat out of people, not something that can bite back."

"You're working for them," Jaime said slowly. "Or you were."

"I was working for me," Elisah said. "Then they noticed I was good at opening things. So they started pointing at locks and saying please. Men who are used to being obeyed don't like it when you walk away. The prison was my way of walking. With walls between us."

"And now?" I asked.

She tilted her head, studying me. "Now you three are between me and them," she said. "Isn't that nice?"

"Comforting," Rygial said.

"You could still go," Jaime said. "We're exile, not chain gang. You could fade back to the city, to some other alley."

Elisah shook her head once. Tiny movement. "Can't go back," she said. "Word's out. They'll be watching the streets and docks and every fence I ever used. Out here? They're blind. If something's hunting us in this mess, it's not them. I'll take scales over silk for now."

It was as close to saying she chose us as I ever heard her, then or later.

Our ten breaths had turned into more. Jaime pushed up with a groan.

"Rest's over," she said. "Elisah, pick us a path where the ground hates us slightly less."

We moved on.

The day sagged toward a color that was not quite evening, just a dimming. The mist thickened. It hung in long, low curtains between the trees, moving slow as breath. Our clothes never dried. Sweat did not so much form as blend with the damp.

We found our first clear sign of drakes an hour after we left the rise.

They had not bothered to hide their passing.

A stretch of reeds lay flattened in a rough, wide band crossing our path. Mud was gouged out in great clawed scoops. In one place, a fallen log had been torn open as if by a blunt, furious hand. The air smelled of sulfur and iron and something else—an oily sharpness that cut through the rot.

Jaime knelt beside one of the grooves. Her fingers hovered just above it, not quite touching.

"Front claws," she said. "Deep. Back feet lighter. It's using its wings to carry some of the weight."

"Adult," Rygial said. "But not the big one."

"How can you tell?" I asked.

He pointed with his staff at the spread of the tracks relative to the log. "If it were the one Mirel whispers about—the hunter of hunters—that log would have been kicked aside by its chest alone. This one still has to climb."

"Still big enough to eat us," Jaime said.

"Everything out here is big enough to eat us," Rygial said. "Some just take more bites."

Elisah moved past them both, following the smashed reeds with her eyes.

"Two," she said. "Maybe three. One heavy. One lighter. They're not dragging meat. See? No parallel grooves. They were moving fast."

"Chasing?" I asked.

"Or being chased," she said.

I glanced around at the trees. They leaned in, their branches hung with ragged moss. Something black and glossy hung in strips from one limb that I first took for bark. Then I saw the claw marks on it. Scale, torn free in a fight.

Jaime saw it too. She stood slowly.

"If there are little ones," she said, "there's a nest. If there's a nest, there's a mother."

"And if there's a mother," Rygial said, "she will not like us near her children."

"We're supposed to find the nest," I reminded them, though my fur prickled at the thought. "Mirel, the ledger… the attacks start near here and spiral out. There's a center."

Jaime nodded once. "We follow," she said. "Carefully."

"Carefully," Rygial echoed. "Into a place where flying lizards teach their young to hunt. Lovely."

We trailed the marks deeper. The swamp shifted almost without us noticing. The ground lifted by slow degrees until our boots—boot—made more noise than the water. Patches of dry, cracked mud appeared between pools. The trees grew closer together, their roots a tangled lattice above ground. The smell changed, too. Less rot, more astringent sharpness. Like stone when rain first hits it.

Bones appeared.

They were not in tidy piles. They were scattered. A rib caught in a fork of branches. A jawbone half-buried in sludge. Horns tangled in roots. Some old and moss-grown. Some yellow-white.

"Deer," Jaime said quietly, toeing a hoof. "And boar. See the tusk stump?"

"Human," Rygial added, prodding a femur with his staff. "Or something close."

"Close enough," Elisah said. She stepped around a skull canted to one side. Its jaw was missing. Its teeth were ground flat.

I forced my ears to stay upright. They wanted to flatten back against my head. My inner warmth stirred again, this time with a nervous, eager flicker. Danger ahead. A place where it could sing.

We heard the first drake before we saw it.

A long, low hiss, like a bellows drawing in. Then a bellow that started in lungs and ended in throat, ragged. It came from the left, echoing weirdly through trees. Another answered from ahead, shorter, sharper. There was a splash. The sound of something heavy colliding, scales scraping.

"Listen," Rygial murmured. "Children fighting over scraps."

"Or practice," Jaime said. She had her sword in hand now, angled low. Not to charge. To guard.

Elisah vanished.

I knew, rationally, that she was still near. But one moment she was at my shoulder, the next the shadows between two trunks had swallowed her. It was not magic like Rygial's. No shimmer in the air. Just knowing where the darkness lay thickest and stepping into it.

"Stay where I can see you," Jaime hissed.

"Can't see anything in this mist anyway," Elisah's voice came back, disembodied. "Better one of us does. I'll circle. You four stomp forward and make friends."

"Four?" Rygial asked, glancing around. "Who else is joining us?"

She didn't answer.

We edged closer to the sounds. The trees thinned abruptly, opening on a broad, shallow basin. Water sheeted across cracked earth in a wide, glassy mirror. In the center, a black rock jutted up, slick and scored with claw marks. On it lay the carcass of a boar, half-eaten. Two drakes fought over it.

They were smaller than the one we'd seen outside the city walls. Leaner. Less scarred. Their wings were still slightly too big for their bodies, the way pups are all paws. But their teeth were real, and their tails lashed with enough force to crack bone.

They were not alone.

On the far side of the basin, half-hidden in the shadow of uprooted trees, lay a mound of peat and woven reeds and branches. It was huge. Its side steamed faintly where it rose from the water. The smell of sulfur was stronger here, threaded through with the copper of blood.

The mound moved.

No. Something within it moved.

A great, scaled head eased out of a gap near the top, like a snake from its burrow. Eyes the color of old gold slitted against the grey light. They watched the young ones brawl. The pupils were narrow, not round. Focused.

This drake was bigger than the prison-yard monster by half again. Maybe more. Her horns swept back in a crown of bone. Scars crossed her muzzle in pale lines. She did not bare her teeth. She did not need to. There was a stillness to her, a coiled weight, that made every instinct I had want to run.

My inner warmth flared, then flattened. This was not a fight. This was death.

"Mother," Jaime breathed.

The big drake's head turned, very slightly. Not toward the youngsters, but toward us. The distance between us and the basin edge was thick with trunks and shadow. We had crept well. Elisah was nowhere to be seen. But the mother's nostrils flared. Her pupils widened a fraction.

"She smells us," Rygial whispered.

"Back," I said. It came out as more of a croak.

Jaime did not argue. She had more sense than courage by half, which is the correct proportion for surviving.

We eased away, careful not to break twigs, careful not to splash. My tail felt like a flag someone was about to spot. Every breath sounded like thunder in my own ears. The young drakes kept brawling, oblivious, their shrieks echoing. The mother watched the trees where we were, not them.

We did not run until the sounds of their fight were wrapped again in distance and the trees hid the basin. Even then, it was not a full run. More a stumbling, hunched trot. Roots snagged our feet. Branches slapped faces. The swamp tried to pull us down and we did not have time to negotiate.

We didn't stop until my chest burned and spots danced at the edges of my sight. Jaime leaned against a tree, sword hand shaking. Rygial bent over, palms on his knees, breath coming in ragged pulls.

Elisah stepped out of a pool of darkness at my elbow, unsweaty, unruffled. Her eyes were too bright.

"Seen enough?" she asked.

Rygial laughed, a wheezing thing. "More than enough. We found our center. We can go home."

"We can't go home," Jaime said hoarsely. "We're exiles."

"Details," he said.

"We've seen a nest," I said. My heart was still hammering, but somewhere under the fear there was a thin thread of excitement. "Not the whole story. Mirel said something—someone—is using the drakes. That mother... she wasn't hunting the farms. She was teaching. The ledgers showed attacks patterned. Regular. That's not a beast's idea."

"So we go around," Elisah said. "Find who's tugging her tail from a distance."

"Can you smell it?" I asked her. "Like you smelled the men, the claw drag."

She made a face and sniffed the air. "Smell a lot of things, Elric. You'll have to be more specific. Wet rock. Drake oil. Burnt... something..."

She stopped.

"What?" Jaime asked sharply.

"Burnt magic," she said slowly. "Like a candle snuffed. Rygial?"

He looked up fast for a tired man. "Where?"

She pointed. "That way. Faint, but old. Not marsh-old. Days-old."

He straightened. "You're sure?"

"I know what it smells like when someone tears a hole in the dark," she said quietly. "This is that. But wrong. Sloppy."

We followed her nose.

The light was definitely failing now. Not full dark, but the color of boiled bone. The mist thickened into proper fog, clinging higher, wrapping trunks, swallowing mid-distance. The ground underfoot rose another hesitant handspan, enough that our steps squelched less and crunched more.

We came upon the place almost by accident. One moment the swamp was its usual chaos. The next, we stepped into a circle of black.

Not absence of light. Absence of life.

Everything within a space the size of Mirel's office lay dead. Reeds stood grey and limp, their tips crumbling to dust when my sleeve brushed them. A tree leaned over the circle, its branches reaching in, but the moment they crossed the invisible boundary, bark peeled and dropped in strips. The trunk ended in a jagged break, as if something had bitten it off.

The mud was cracked and dry. That alone was wrong enough. No water pooled here. No flies hovered. The silence was heavy.

In the center of the circle lay a stone. It had not been there long. It sat on top of the dead things, not under them. It was black, glossy, with veins of dull red. It hurt to look at. My eyes wanted to slide away.

Jaime swore softly.

"What is that?" she whispered.

"A mistake," Rygial said. There was no dry humor now. Only fatigue and something that might have been anger. "Someone opened a door and didn't close it properly."

"Like you?" Elisah asked.

"I carve windows in time, not doors in the dark between things," he said. He stepped up to the edge of the dead circle and stopped, toes just shy of crossing. "This is old craft. Badly copied. They bled something through and used it to bind. Predatory magic."

"Used it on the drakes?" I asked.

He nodded slowly. "You saw the mother. Alert. Patient. Too patient. Beasts hunt, they do not lay sieges. Not like that. Someone's mind is riding her. Or someone's will is knotted to hers. This is where they tied the knot."

"Can you untie it?" Jaime asked.

He barked a laugh that had no humor. "With what? My hands? You think I brought the proper knife for unmaking ancient wards to prison?"

"You brought that pebble thing," she said. "You could—"

"I could die," he snapped. Then seemed to catch himself. His shoulders dropped. "And take you with me. These are not games to play when your bones already owe too many hours to fate."

Elisah crouched just outside the dead zone. Her shadow angled wrong as it fell across the line. Instead of stretching naturally, it bent away from the stone, as if even absence didn't want to touch it.

"You said someone did this badly," she said. "Sloppy. Does that help us?"

"It means they likely burned out," Rygial said. "Or went mad. Or both. You've seen men who tried to juggle too many knives, thief?"

"I've seen the stains they left," she said.

"Imagine doing it with lightning," he said.

Elisah's mouth thinned.

Jaime squinted at the stone. "If we can't untie it, we can at least tell Mirel where to send someone smarter."

"We're exiles," Rygial reminded her. "We do not get to give orders anymore. Or requests."

"We can still bring word," she said. "Words move. Even when we don't."

I stepped closer, sniffing. The smell of burnt magic was strong here. Under it lurked something copper-black, like dried blood left too long on steel.

I did not realize I had crossed the line until my boot came down on dead mud.

The world tilted.

Sound dropped away. The fog around us froze in place. Jaime's hand, half-lifted, hung in the air. Rygial's eyes were widened, his mouth half-open on a word. Elisah's head was turned toward me, panic just starting to register.

I stood in a bubble of stillness.

The inner warmth in my chest didn't stir. It went flat and thin, like embers starved of air.

"Ah," a voice said.

It did not come from outside. It came from everywhere at once. From the stone. From the air. From the heat of my own blood.

"Another thread," the voice mused. It was not loud. It did not need to be. "Another little creature walking where it was not meant to walk."

My heart thudded once, twice. The only moving thing. My breath would not come faster. My hands would not lift.

"You carry a spark," the voice said. "How quaint. How... early."

A shape stirred within the black stone, not with light, but with lack of it. A deeper darkness moved. Stretched. I could not see it clearly. My eyes watered when I tried.

"I did not know then," I will say now, from years away, "just how close I stood to a hand that had been reaching into our world for a very long time."

In that moment, all I knew was fear, raw and simple.

"Walk away, little spark," the voice said. "Not because I am kind. Because you are not ready. Not yet. And I am patient."

The last word crawled along my spine like something with too many legs.

Time rushed back.

Sound slammed in. The wet buzz of flies, the slow drip of water, Jaime's shout.

"Elric! Get back!"

Her hand closed on my arm and yanked. My boot tore free of the dead mud as if from thick glue. I stumbled backward over the line and fell hard on my tail in the living muck. The air hit my lungs like a fist. I gasped. Coughed. My heart hammered wild and fast now.

Rygial was at my side in an instant, his hands on my shoulders, his face inches from mine. His eyes searched mine the way a doctor searches for fever.

"What did you see?" he demanded.

"Nothing," I lied, because I did not have words yet for that voice, that sense of a presence too large to fit in the shape the stone offered it.

Rygial's grip tightened. "Don't play patient games with me, boy. Did it speak to you?"

Jaime went still. Elisah's hand found her knife.

I swallowed. My mouth tasted of ash.

"It... noticed," I said finally. "Said I had a... spark. Told me to walk away. Said it was patient."

Rygial closed his eyes. When he opened them again, some of the color had gone from his face.

"Wonderful," he muttered. "It's watching. Through the link. Feels for minds that brush it. That explains the pattern. That explains the mother drake's new habits. Someone called of this, and it stuck a piece of itself in the call."

"We break the stone," Jaime said at once.

"No," Rygial snapped. "You break that anchor, and whatever is pressed against the other side comes through the hole all at once. The stone is a plug as much as a nail. We step away. We mark the place in our heads. We tell nobody who might be fool enough to meddle without years and books and an army."

"So we just... leave it?" Jaime's voice pitched up. "After all this? We see the nest, the trap, the thing in the middle, and we just walk?"

"Yes," he said. "If you want to see anything beyond tomorrow."

Elisah was not looking at the stone. She was looking into the trees beyond us, her head cocked slightly.

"You all can argue about fate and plugs later," she said quietly. "We need to go. Now."

"Why?" Jaime asked. "We've already angered—"

"Because we're being hunted," Elisah said.

The hairs along my arms rose. Not from her tone. From something else.

At first, all I heard was the normal swamp: water, flies, the occasional drip of something heavier. Then I caught it. A faint, deliberate sound. Not far. Not close.

A footfall on soft ground, placed with care.

Another. A shift of weight on a root, wood creaking in complaint. Then silence. Then the soft, high hiss of something exhaling through teeth held almost together.

My ears swiveled, trying to fix it. It was like chasing smoke. Every time I thought I had it, it slipped.

Jaime tightened her grip on her sword. "More drakes?"

"Not walking like that," Elisah said. "Drakes don't care if the ground hears them. This... does."

Rygial's eyes half-lidded. His fingers twitched, as if pulling threads.

"Don't," Elisah said sharply. "If it's watching for that kind of move, you'll light us up like a bonfire."

He ground his teeth. "I am not fond of flying blind."

"Then get used to it," she said. "Welcome to my life."

The feeling of eyes on us grew. Not from one direction. Several. Like we had stepped into the center of a ring we had not seen drawn.

"Back away from the circle," Jaime murmured. "Slow. Keep together. No sudden moves. Elric, ears up. Rygial, if you fall, I'm leaving you."

"Understood," he said dryly.

We edged away from the dead patch, each step measured. The sense of being watched did not lessen. If anything, it sharpened. I could feel it on my fur, on the back of my neck, between my shoulders. A predator's gaze. Not yet pouncing. Learning the measure of our steps.

Something moved in the fog ahead. Not big. Low. A ripple, like a dog passing behind a curtain.

Another faint creak of bark off to the right, too high up for men.

A gust of wind—or what I told myself was wind—carried a new scent. Drake. Smoke. And under it, something cold and metallic. Not iron. Not steel. Older. Like the smell that had clung to the stone, but thinner, spread out.

"The drake that hunts the hunted," Rygial said, very softly. "Mirel did not lie about everything."

"We're outside its nest," Jaime said. "Why would it be... the kids—"

"It's not protecting the young," Elisah said. "It's protecting the stone. Or whatever it thinks the stone protects. We stepped on its leash. It felt the tug."

I could not see it. That was the worst part. My eyes, good in dusk, showed me only trunks and fog and the pale smear of dead grass. But everything in me screamed that something waited just beyond where I could see. Pacing. Matching our retreat.

Waiting for us to stumble. Or to run.

I did not know then how long it stalked us through that next stretch of marsh. How many times it could have struck and didn't. How much of its restraint was its own mind, and how much was the will knotted through its head from that black stone.

All I knew was that every step away from that clearing felt like walking a razor. Every root was an ankle turned waiting to happen. Every shallow pool a mouth that might grab.

We did not speak. Even Rygial had nothing to say. Elisah's eyes never stayed on one place longer than a heartbeat. Jaime's bare foot bled more with every careful step. My inner warmth hovered between sleep and panic, wanting to flare, knowing if it did I would run, and running would mean teeth at my back.

The swamp closed in. The fog swallowed the dead circle, then the memory of it. The smell of burnt magic thinned, replaced again by rot and water and life.

The sense of being watched did not leave.

When we finally stopped—when even Jaime conceded that if we did not rest our legs would simply stop obeying—we chose a hummock with our backs to a half-fallen tree. It gave us the illusion of a wall. That was all. The fog pressed close on three sides.

We did not dare a fire. The damp would have made it hard anyway. We huddled together in the dripping dark, sharing heat, listening.

There were normal sounds here. Frogs. The occasional distant splash. The whirr of wings. But under it all, there was a waiting.

I sat awake long after the others' breathing had settled into something like sleep. Jaime's shoulder was a warm weight against mine. Elisah had curled herself small at our feet, back to the log, knife in hand even in rest. Rygial snored in little huffs, staff clutched tight.

I stared into the fog.

Somewhere out there, beyond the reach of my sight but not beyond the reach of my fear, something stared back.

I heard it once, in the deep of that half-sleep where thoughts blur. A scrape of scale on bark. The slow inhale of a vast chest, pulling in our scent, our sweat, our fear. Not closing in. Not yet.

Patient.

Out in the swamp's black heart, under a sky we could no longer see, the thing that hunted hunters settled itself, and waited for us to move.

# Chapter 16

# LANTERN LIGHT, LONG KNIVES

MORNING NEVER TRULY CAME in that swamp.

The sky only went from black to the color of old bruises, and the fog turned thin enough that you could see ten paces instead of five. Birds did not sing. Frogs did not croak. The insects hissed, and the water whispered, and somewhere a tree let go of another limb with the cracking sigh of wet bone.

We woke anyway.

Jaime shook me first. She always did. Said I was hardest to rouse, which was a lie. She just liked getting her hand clear before my claws twitched.

"Elric." Her voice came from a long way off. Then closer. "Elric. Up."

I surfaced from whatever thin, bitter sleep I'd managed. The world snapped back—stiff shoulders, damp fur, the stale taste of swamp rot in my mouth. The cold that came from the ground itself. Every joint felt packed with mud.

"Still alive?" I rasped. My voice came out wrong. Rougher.

"Unfortunately," Elisah muttered somewhere behind her. Fabric rustled. Metal clicked. A soft hiss as she tightened the straps on her bracers.

Rygial was already sitting up, back against the trunk of the drowned tree that had sheltered us. He rolled his neck until it popped, then set his hands on his knees and breathed slow, as if counting time. His beard was a sodden gray braid down his chest, clotted with bits of moss and grit he hadn't bothered to clean.

"Don't say it," I told him.

He raised an eyebrow. "Say what?"

"Whatever proverb you've got about bad sleep and worse days."

Rygial made a quiet sound. Might have been a laugh. "Boy, if the day cares what I say, we're all in trouble."

The lantern between us had burned down to a stub of wax and soot. Jaime snuffed it with her gloved fingers and clipped it back to her belt. The sudden absence of that weak warmth bit at the skin. The air felt larger and more dangerous without its small, defined circle of light.

The sense of being watched never left. It had settled around us sometime in the worst part of the night, when my eyes had been too tired to focus and every rustle sounded like leather scales sliding over bark. It stayed now—thin, like spider silk across the back of the neck. Not constant. It brushed. It withdrew. It brushed again.

The drake that hunts the hunted.

We had put a name to it, the way people do when something is too big to grasp otherwise. Naming did not make it smaller.

Jaime rose, squinting through the half-light. Her hair was a tangle, her armor dark with swamp stains. The lines at the corners of her eyes were deeper than any seventeen-year-old had a right to.

"Food first," she said. "Then we move. We don't want to be in its ground when the light goes again."

"There is no light," Elisah said. But she took the dried meat Jaime offered her. Ate without comment. She moved like someone counting each motion, measuring it against the strength she had left.

I chewed. The meat might as well have been leather. My jaw ached by the time I swallowed. I wanted something hot so badly it made my ribs hurt. A stew. A crust of bread that wasn't damp around the edges. I looked at the swamp water lapping against twisted roots and felt my stomach turn.

"The stone," I said. "We're still going toward it?"

Rygial's eyes flicked to me. "The anchor. Aye. We don't have a choice now."

We had found it the night before. Black stone sunk in the muck under the mother drake's corpse. A thing with no business in a living world—etched with lines that hurt to look at, pulsing with a slow, patient malignance that clung to the air. Bound not to the dead mother, but through her. Something older and deeper. Something that called.

Jaime slid her pack over one shoulder. "Rygial, you still feel it?"

The dwarf closed his eyes. His face slackened in that way it did when he listened for things that weren't sound. A stillness came over him. Even the insects seemed to fade a little, as if the swamp itself leaned closer to hear his answer.

After a moment, Rygial's eyelids twitched. "A pull. Like a tide. Not quite east, not quite south." He lifted his hand, fingers spreading, then turned it a hair. "There. Stronger than last night."

"In the mother's territory," I said. "And beyond."

"Below it," he murmured. "Deeper."

Jaime nodded once. Decision settled over her features like a mask she had worn often. "Then that's where we're going."

"No argument," Elisah said. "The sooner we find the big lizard, the sooner we can stop smelling like its toilet."

We checked our gear with the simple, automatic care of people who had lived too close to their mistakes. Fletching smoothed. Bowstrings waxed. Knife edges tested with a thumb. The lantern refilled from Rygial's dwindling flask of clear oil.

Light and blades. That was what we had to put between us and what waited ahead.

WE LEFT THE DROWNED tree behind. The fog rolled around our calves as we waded through brown water shot with veins of slick green. Shapes shifted just below the surface—fish, or eels, or things that were only teeth and hunger. The roots rose and fell in strange, looping tangles like the backs of half-buried beasts.

I took point. My ears twitched with every soft splash our steps made, every distant ripple. My pupils were wide, pulling in the dim. The swamp gave us sounds and took them away at random, as if having second thoughts. Some things echoed that should not have. Other noises died as soon as they were born.

The feeling of being watched scraped against my spine again. I stopped. The others went still behind me. For a heartbeat all I could hear was the drip of water from my own coat and the faint rasp of my breathing in my ears.

"Elric?" Jaime said quietly.

"Nothing," I lied.

Because I could not say: It's close.

Because I could not say: It's above us. Or below us. Or both.

At seventeen, pride still had teeth. I did not want them to see me afraid in ways that did not point to anything they could fight.

We went on.

Hours blurred. The swamp did not mark distance well. You could walk straight and end up somewhere you had already seen. You could turn around and find that what had been behind you was gone. The only constant was the sense of pressure building ahead, like the air tightening before a storm.

Twice we circled places we recognized—a broken cypress like a crooked finger, a patch of water lilies floating in a stagnant mirror. Each time, Rygial stopped earlier and corrected our heading with more force. Sweat gathered on his brow despite the chill. Time magic does not enjoy being contradicted by land that refuses to hold still.

"It doesn't want us forward," he said under his breath, the second time.

"What?" I asked.

He shook his head, beard dripping. "Keep moving, boy."

We moved.

NEAR WHAT MUST HAVE been midday—judging only by the faint paling of fog above—we entered a part of the swamp where the trees thinned. The ground dipped, and the water grew sullen and oily, coated with a sheen that caught the low light in bruised colors. The smell changed: deeper rot, sharp threads of sulfur like bitten match heads.

Jaime raised a hand, slowing us. "Drake sign?"

"Not fresh," I said. My nose wrinkled. "But close enough."

Elisah's gaze flicked from shadow to shadow. "Anything that smells like this often has teeth."

We should have turned back there. We didn't. That is how these stories go.

We reached a stretch where the mud rose into a low, wide bar, thick with dead reeds and the husks of long-rotted stumps. It looked almost like firm ground, in the way a bruise almost looks like color.

"Stay light," Jaime said. "Single file. Watch your footing."

She went first this time, testing each step with the butt of her walking stick. The mud accepted her. Elisah flowed after, feet barely seeming to sink at all. I followed, tail held high to keep it clear. Rygial came last, cursing softly every time the muck tried to steal his boots.

We were halfway across when the bar moved.

That is the only way to put it. Not a tremor from below. Not a subtle shift. The whole length of the thing shuddered, sagged, then heaved upward like a living thing shrugging off a blanket.

"Elric—" Jaime snapped.

"Back!" I barked, but there was nowhere that wasn't it. The mud bucked underfoot. My leg plunged up to the knee. Cold sludge closed over fur and skin, clutching tight. The reed husks around us rose on pillars of glistening black earth like skeletal fingers.

The bar split down its center with a wet sound. Dark water frothed up, boiling with trapped gas. Shape coalesced out of it. Limbs. Shoulders. A vague torso, wider than a wagon. A head like a half-melted statue, featureless but for deep hollows where eyes might have been. The smell hit us—ancient rot and slow ferment, peat cut open after centuries.

A bog elemental. I had heard stories. Back then, I thought they were for scaring children away from dangerous ground.

"Don't cut it!" Rygial shouted, voice cracking. "Steel wakes it!"

Too late. Jaime's sword had already come up out of reflex. The tip slashed across the rising arm of muck. The elemental shuddered. The cut closed in an instant, sucking the metal's brightness in with a liquid gulp. The thing's hollow gaze turned toward us.

The sense of being watched narrowed to a point and pressed down.

"We go around it?" Elisah asked, breath tight, weight already shifting on her toes as if to dance away.

"We're standing on it," I said.

The elemental's arms rose higher, each one tapering into vast, dripping fists. Ropes of weed and bone dangled from them—old victims knotted into its mass. Its chest swelled, and the bar under our feet dipped sharply, threatening to roll us into the surrounding deep.

"Rygial!" Jaime's voice clawed at the air. "Tell me you have a trick for this."

The dwarf's eyes were wide. There are few things that unsettle a chronomancer more than something that has lain in one place, undisturbed, for longer than kingdoms last. "It's old," he said. "Older than the city that fed it. Than the fields that rotted into it." He swallowed, throat working. "I can't break that much time."

The first fist came down.

I lunged to the side as mud the weight of a house slammed into the place where I'd been. The impact sent a spray of black filth in all directions. A clod struck Jaime in the shoulder, spinning her. Another hit me across the ribs with a sound like a fist into wet cloth. Pain flared. My breath vanished.

"Elisah!" I gasped, more instinct than thought.

She had already moved, of course. She was above the blow, having used that initial buck of the mud as a launch. Her body turned in the air, coat flaring. She landed on what passed for the thing's shoulder, daggers in her hands like stings of moonlight.

"Don't—" Rygial started.

She drove both blades down into its mass.

The reaction was instant. The elemental convulsed, its entire body rippling upward as if something had shocked it from the core. Elisah's blades vanished up to the hilt, then deeper as the mud tried to swallow them. She ripped one free, but the other stuck fast.

"Let go!" I yelled.

She didn't. Not at first. Good steel is hard to come by in the exile markets. Her jaw locked. Her arm strained. The elemental's surface bubbled, bulged.

It flung her.

The motion was grotesquely slow and fast at the same time. The shoulder reared, and for a heartbeat she hung there, fighting gravity, defiant. Then the mud flexed and snapped, and she arced outward, trailing clumps of black slop, toward the deeper water at the bar's edge.

Time did a small, mean thing then. It stretched the moment where she hung above the drop, arms flailing, eyes wide. Enough that I could see the exact instant realization sank in. Enough that I could almost hear the beat of her heart over the swamp's whisper.

"Elisah!" Jaime dove.

She hit the ground belly-first, sliding across the slick surface. One arm shot out. Her fingers closed on Elisah's wrist just as Elisah's lower body hit the water with a splash that swallowed sound.

For a second they hung like that—Jaime sprawled flat, boots digging into the mud, Elisah half-submerged and dragging her toward the edge. The elemental shifted under us, annoyed by their scrambling. The bar tilted another few degrees. Rygial cursed in a language older than the swamp.

I flung myself toward them, claws digging for purchase. The muck tried to hold me, to suck at my ankles. I pulled free with a pain like skin coming off. Jaime's face was contorted with effort, tendons standing out in her neck. Elisah's free hand thrashed in the water as something unseen brushed against her legs.

"Got you," I panted, seizing the back of Jaime's cuirass. The leather was slick, but I had claws. I sank them in. "On three. One—"

The elemental's second fist came down behind us. The shockwave traveled through the bar like a wave through flesh. It threw us all forward. For an instant, we were all weightless. Then the mud leapt up to meet us with bruising enthusiasm.

I lost my grip on Jaime. She lost hers on Elisah. Elisah vanished with a choking cry, pulled under in a whirl of bubbles and dark.

"Elisah!" Jaime choked, scrambling on all fours toward the edge.

Rygial appeared at her side, one hand locking around her arm. "Stop. You go in, you don't come back."

"Let go of me!" Jaime snarled. I had never heard that sound from her. It was feral, unshaped.

"Elric!" Rygial snapped. "Help me."

Duty over shock. That is what training gives you. Even when it is someone you care about vanishing into water thick as soup. Even when every instinct in you screams to dive after them. Even when every part of you wants to be braver than you are.

I moved. Between one heartbeat and the next I was beside them, adding my weight to Rygial's hold on Jaime. Together we dragged her back from the edge as the surface frothed and closed over where Elisah had been.

The bog elemental loomed above us, rearing higher, drawing itself taller out of its own substance. The reeds and bone fragments knitted tighter into its hide. The hollows of its eyes burned with a dull, earthy hate—not for us, exactly, but for the disturbance we represented. For the steel we had driven into its timeless decay.

"We're dead," Jaime said. Her voice had gone flat. Empty.

"No," Rygial grated. "We're not. She's not."

"You didn't see—"

"Shut up and listen." The old dwarf's eyes flashed. "You think that thing wants to chase three insects around? It wants to sink. To sleep. Give it what it wants."

"How?" I asked. My chest still ached where the mud had hit. My legs shook under me. "It's already awake."

Rygial's gaze flicked from the elemental's massive fists to the bar beneath our feet, then to the surrounding water. I saw something click into place behind his eyes. A line drawn between points in time and weight and erosion.

"It's holding more than us," he said. "It's holding the ground."

The elemental's arm began to fall again.

Rygial reached into his coat, fingers fumbling for something small and metallic. Not a weapon. A focus. Part of the strange toolkit of a man who argued with clocks. He found it—a thin ring of brass etched with tiny marks. He slid it over his thumb and bit down on a curse as if it tasted bad.

"I can't undo what made it," he muttered. "But I can make it old where it wants to be young. Just for a moment."

"Rygial—" Jaime started.

"Stay on your feet." The dwarf planted his staff, pressed his brass-ringed thumb to the soaked wood, and whispered a word that tore the air.

You don't see time magic when it happens. You feel its absence. The bog elemental shuddered. Its raised arm slowed as if pushing through honey. Lines formed in its mass—cracks where there should have been flow. The reeds woven through it went brittle in an instant, snapping with tiny pops.

The bar under us changed. What had been wet, clinging muck dried between one breath and the next, then crumbled. The whole structure sagged inward, its cohesion rotting at high speed.

The elemental tried to pull itself together, but its own body betrayed it. New cracks yawned. Segments sloughed off and hit the water not as animated limbs but as dead clods that sank with dull plunks.

"Run," Rygial hissed through his teeth. Sweat streamed down his face, his hand white on his staff. "Now. While it remembers how to fall apart."

We ran.

The bar disintegrated under our boots, collapsing into a slurry that tried to suck us down even as it lost the strength to hold us. I leapt from patch to patch, trusting my eyes, my balance, the twitch of my tail. Jaime stumbled once, and I caught her arm, hauling her over a gap where the bar had given way entirely to sucking, black water.

Behind us, the elemental howled. The sound was like wind through a graveyard. It was the groan of buried trunks giving way, the sigh of a collapsed peat bog exhaling a century of trapped gases. Its form caved in on itself, shoulders folding, head sinking. The hollow eyes flared once with muddy light, then dimmed as its essence slumped back into unconscious sludge.

Rygial staggered. I looked back once and saw him lurching after us, each step a small war. The brass ring on his thumb had gone black, hairline fractures spidering through it. He stumbled.

I doubled back without thinking. Got my shoulder under his arm. Nearly went to my knees with the weight of him and whatever strain he'd just pulled through his bones.

"Don't you dare fall here," I said, jaw clenched.

"I'm not... that considerate," he panted.

We made the far side of what had been the bar as it finally gave up the pretence of being anything but mud. It collapsed with a slow, sucking roar, pulling chunks of reed and bone down into a new, ugly hollow. The elemental vanished into it, its last coherent limb sliding below with one futile, grasping reach.

Then it was gone.

We stood on a small patch of slightly higher ground covered in wiry sedge, chests heaving, clothes plastered to skin. The water around us rippled in protest, then stilled. The air smelled sharper, as if whatever long-held breath the swamp had been holding there had finally been released.

For a few heartbeats, no one spoke.

Then the surface of the new-formed hollow broke.

Elisah clawed her way out like something the swamp had tried and failed to keep. She came up coughing, gasping, eyes wild, coated head to toe in thick black muck. Her hair was a single dripping rope. One dagger was gone; the other she still gripped in a death-clutch, its blade pitch-dark with the elemental's residue.

She got her elbows over the edge. The mud tried to drag her back. She hissed through her teeth, kicked, gained another inch.

I was already moving. Jaime was faster. She hit the bank on her knees, reached down, and caught Elisah under the arms. I got her wrists. Together we hauled her up, out, free. The swamp clung, then let go with a loud, obscene slurp.

Elisah sprawled on the sedge, coughing up water so foul I had to force my own throat not to join her. She rolled onto her side and spat black. Her shoulders shook. For a moment I thought she was sobbing. Then I saw her face. She was laughing, a thin, cracked sound that might as well have been crying.

"Lost... the knife," she got out between coughs.

"Of course that's your first concern," Jaime said hoarsely. She brushed mud from Elisah's face with her thumbs, making no real difference. Her hands shook.

"That was good steel," Elisah croaked. "You going to replace it?"

Jaime choked on something that might have been a laugh. Or a sob. "We'll steal you a better one when we get out of this gods-forsaken hole."

"Promises, promises," Elisah muttered, and closed her eyes.

Rygial sank down on a protruding root with the gracelessness of a man whose strings had been cut. His shoulders slumped. For a long moment he only breathed. Then he reached up and slid the cracked brass ring off his thumb. It came away in three pieces that clattered softly onto the root beside him.

"That," he said faintly, "was thoroughly stupid."

"It worked," I said.

He glanced at me sidelong. "Those are the worst kinds of stupid."

The tremor in my legs settled slowly. My ribs hurt when I drew breath. Elisah's coughing eased to small, occasional spasms. Jaime knelt beside her, eyes flicking up every few seconds to scan the trees and water, as if expecting the elemental to reform and come for us.

It wouldn't. Bog elementals do not hold grudges. They only remember weight.

Others do.

The sense of being watched returned as soon as the last of the elemental's mass disappeared into the water. Sharper now. Focused. As if something had taken note of the disturbance. Of us.

Of the fact that we had survived.

"We need to move," I said.

"We just did," Elisah mumbled into the sedge.

"Move more," I said. "Farther."

Jaime looked at Rygial. "You up to it?"

The dwarf grimaced, but he pushed himself back to his feet. His knees trembled. "If I fall over, leave me leaning against something picturesque."

"Elric's right," he added, more serious. "That wasn't just mud and old bones we kicked. That was history. This place will notice. Things that like the quiet will be restless."

Things like drakes. Things like whatever lay bound to that black stone.

WE WENT ON. SLOWER now. More drained. Every step felt heavier after the elemental—like the swamp had grown more interested in holding us down.

The terrain changed again as we crossed an invisible line. The trees thinned to gaunt, skeletal trunks with sparse, colorless leaves. The moss that hung from them was gray rather than green, swaying in strings like cobwebs. The ground beneath the water turned from brown to a sickly, sulfur-stained yellow.

The smell intensified. Not just rot now, but egg-stink and metal tang. It coated the back of the throat. Made your eyes water. Every breath tasted like the air over a blacksmith's quench barrel gone rancid.

"Drake," I said quietly. There was no need to. The sign was everywhere.

Claw marks along the trunks where thick bark had been scraped away like skin. Deep furrows in the mud where a heavy body had dragged itself ashore. Scattered bones half-submerged in the shallows—deer, boar, something bigger with a horned skull. All gnawed. All cracked open as if something had sucked the marrow.

Rygial stopped once, hand on a tree that bore three parallel gouges as long as my arm. He touched the edges of the marks, then sniffed his fingers.

"Recent?" Jaime asked.

"Days," Rygial said. "Maybe less."

I crouched by a broad, flat print in the mud, filled with murky water. The outline was clear even through the distortion—a three-toed forepaw, nails like knives. I laid my hand in it. My fingers did not reach the edges.

"Bigger than the mother," I said.

"Older," Rygial murmured. "Smarter."

Elisah wrung some of the muck from her hair. It came away in thick ropes. "Wonderful. Anything else? Wings? Spellcasting? A fondness for conversation?"

"All of the above is traditional," Rygial said.

She made a rude sign at the swamp.

Jaime gathered us with a glance. "We're close. Elric, senses. Rygial, that anchor—how strong?"

The dwarf closed his eyes again, hand hovering in the air like a man feeling for heat. His fingers trembled. "Like standing over a well," he said finally. "Deep. Straight down. The pull's just ahead."

I extended my ears, listening for something beneath the steady hiss of insects and the faint drip-plink of water. The swamp held its breath. No birds. No frogs. Even the little scavenger things that had been bold around the elemental's remains were absent here.

I inhaled. Under the omnipresent reek of rot and sulfur, there was another scent. Old stone. Cold iron. And something sharp and acrid that made my gums itch.

"We're walking into its throat," I said.

"Yes," Jaime replied. "We are."

She said it the way you might say we're going into town. That was her gift. She could take terror and wrap it in plain words until you almost believed it was manageable.

We moved slower. Each step placed. Each ripple watched until it faded. The world narrowed to a cone of attention ahead of us, the rest of the swamp blurring into formless threat.

AFTER A WHILE, THE trees fell away completely. The swamp opened into a basin.

We stopped at its lip.

Below us lay a wide, dark pool ringed by broken stone and the warped stumps of dead trees. The water was almost still, a black glass broken only by the occasional puff of gas that rose from its depths and popped at the surface, releasing small vomits of yellowish steam. The edges of the pool were lined with a crust of sulfur and mineral deposits that glowed faintly sick in the dim light.

A few bleached bones lay scattered near the shore. Not many. Drakes are tidy eaters.

The air over the pool shimmered with a heat that did not match the chill of the swamp behind us. It tasted like metal filings on the tongue. Every instinct I had screamed at me to lower my head, flatten my ears, and slink backward into the trees.

"That's it," Rygial said unnecessarily. His voice had gone very quiet. "The lair."

We had found a vantage point on a small rise of stone and root that overlooked the pool from the north. It offered some cover—a curtain of hanging moss, a few leaning trunks. From there we could see most of the basin. Nothing moved.

"Do you see it?" Elisah asked. Her voice did not reach above a whisper, as if anything louder might break whatever thin safety silence offered.

"No," I said. My eyes traced the shoreline, the collapsed stones that might once have been part of a structure older than the swamp, the few patches of muck solid enough to bear weight. Nothing. No massive shape. No coiled body. No wings folded along a ridge of spine.

"Under," Rygial said. He gestured weakly at the pool. "Beneath."

Jaime's knuckles were white on the handle of her sword. "Could it have left?"

"No." Rygial swallowed. "The anchor's here. It's... fused. This place is its heart."

A thin breeze stirred the surface. It did not make enough of a ripple to account for the faint, constant movement I thought I saw—a subtle, almost imagined motion pulsing from the pool's center outward. As if something large, slow, and sleeping breathed below.

My tail lashed once behind me. I forced it still. The fur along my spine would not lie flat.

"Plan," Jaime said. It was not a question. It was an order to herself as much as to us. "We need a plan."

Elisah leaned against a trunk, arms folded, every line of her body tight. "Do we? I thought we were just going to stroll down there and ask it nicely to die."

"We have to get it out of the water," I said. "On land, where it's heavier and slower. Or at least less able to vanish."

Jaime nodded, eyes still on the pool. "Lure it. Hurt it enough that it wants us dead more than it wants to wait."

"That stone," Rygial said. "It's tied to more than its body. You break that, you don't just kill meat. You cut a line. Whatever is on the other end won't like that."

Jaime's jaw set. "We came here to cut it."

I looked at her. At all of us. Four exiles on a damp rise of mud and dead wood, staring down into the throat of something that had outlived empires. My side ached. My legs felt like hollow reeds. Rygial's hands were still shaking from the elemental. Elisah had dark circles under her eyes, and her lips were tinged slightly gray from cold and swallowed swamp.

Armies turned away from drake lairs like this. Whole companies of knights refused contracts when the pay did not match the risk. And here we were, with a half-bag of arrows, a couple of swords, some knives, and a lantern.

If this sounds foolish to you now, you are right. It was. We knew it then, too. Knowing changes less than you might hope.

"We could leave," Elisah said into the quiet. Her tone was flat, not teasing. This was the first time she had voiced it plain. "We go back. We tell them there's more than a drake here. They can send priests and battlemages and men with more steel than sense. We don't have to be the ones."

No one answered for a long moment. The pool breathed. A bubble of gas rose, swelled, burst. The faint, rotten egg smell washed over us again.

Jaime did not look at her when she spoke. "You saw the stone, Elisah. What it did to the mother. What it was doing to the nest. You think waiting makes that better?"

"We're not heroes," she said.

"Heroes are just people who ran out of ways to say no," Rygial murmured. "And kept moving."

She shot him a look. "You would know."

He shrugged, beard shifting. "I'm still here. That makes me more stubborn than wise."

I watched the pool. My claws flexed against the damp ground. "If we go back without trying, we go back with this thing still feeding. Still bound. It keeps hunting. The next team in might not make it this far. Or they might bring something that tears more holes in the world than the drake ever could."

Elisah's mouth twisted. "You're all terrible at making arguments for survival."

"You can stay here," Jaime said softly. "You three. I can go down there alone. Maybe I won't make it. But at least I'll—"

"Don't," I cut in. "Don't you dare."

She looked at me then. Really looked. There was a sort of bleak calm in her eyes I did not like at all. The kind of calm that comes when someone has accepted themselves as the thing to be spent.

"Jaime," I said. "If you run down there by yourself, I'm going to have to risk my life dragging your stupid half-elf corpse back up. Spare me the extra work. We go together or we don't go at all."

Her mouth twitched, just enough to break the mask. "Bossy."

"Annoying," Elisah added. "Reckless. Smells like wet cat."

"Ungrateful," I said.

Rygial snorted softly. The tension around us shifted, just a fraction. Enough to let breath move again.

"All right," Jaime said. "Together, then." She drew a long breath and let it out slow. "We hit it from range first. Arrows for the eyes, if we can. Elric, anything soft you can smell, you call it. Rygial—any more tricks?"

The dwarf flexed his fingers. The tremor had not gone away. "Small ones. I can slow a limb if it comes for one of you. Once or twice. No more stunts like the elemental. That was... expensive."

"Noted," Jaime said. "Elisah. You stay in the shadows. If we can get on its back, its neck, you get there. Look for that stone. Any sign of it fused to scale or bone."

"If it eats one of you, I'm cutting my way inside after it," she said.

Jaime blinked. "That's not—"

"I am not being paid enough to walk away from whatever is on the other side of that rock," she continued. "If it's riding in the drake, I want eyes on it. Even if they're from inside its gullet."

"That is the most Elisah thing you've ever said," I muttered.

"Flattered."

Jaime checked her bowstring, then adjusted the strap on her shield. The motions were precise. Ritual. The last small things a soldier can control when stepping into something that will not be controlled.

"Rygial," she said quietly. "If this... if we don't..."

The dwarf held up a hand. "I am too old to listen to death speeches from children. Save your breath for screaming."

Jaime shut her mouth. Nodded once.

We pulled our gear into place. Quivers checked. Knife hilts adjusted for an easier draw. Blades ready. The lantern was unhooked from Jaime's belt and passed to me.

"You see better than we do in this gloom," she said. "Call where you need it."

I cradled the lantern in one hand, its weight small and absurd in the face of what waited below. The flame inside was steady, a bright little stub of stubbornness.

For a moment, on that rise above the lair, all the words and bravado fell away. The swamp receded. There was only the four of us, standing close enough that our shoulders brushed.

I remember the feel of that. The warmth of them at my sides, the smell of metal and oil and swamp clinging to them. The quiet humming tension in Jaime's muscles. Elisah's faint, restless shifting as she rolled her soles on the damp earth, ready to spring. Rygial's low, irregular breathing, like an old clock with a crack in its casing.

We were tired. Hungry. Frightened in ways we did not know how to name yet. But the line had been crossed some time ago. There was only forward.

"Lantern light and long knives," Elisah said suddenly.

I glanced at her. "What?"

"Street blessing," she said. "From the Warrens. Lantern light to see the trouble coming. Long knives to meet it halfway."

Jaime's mouth quirked. "I'll take that."

Rygial closed his eyes briefly. "Time be kind," he whispered.

WE STARTED DOWN.

The slope to the pool's edge was treacherous—slick stone veined with mineral crust, patches of mud that looked solid until you stepped and your foot sank to the ankle.

We moved slow. Every small sound we made felt amplified. Pebbles skittering. Fabric whispering. The faint clack of an arrowhead brushing its neighbor in a quiver.

Halfway down, the sense of being watched sharpened. Not the vague, creeping awareness of earlier. This was a weight. Directional. It pressed from below. From under the water.

I stopped. The others halted in a stuttering echo.

"Elric?" Jaime murmured.

"It knows," I said. My voice sounded thin. "It's awake."

"How—" Elisah began.

The surface broke.

There is no delicate way to describe it. The pool did not ripple. It did not gently part. It exploded.

Black water and viscous mud rocketed upward, flung aside as something vast surged from the depths. The shockwave hit us like a wall, soaking us, driving the breath from our lungs. The sulfur stench tripled, burning the inside of my nose.

For a heartbeat all I could see was spray and darkness. Then the bulk of it rose clear.

The drake was bigger than a bison by three and a half again. It's face easily twice times my height alone, its jaws when opened were like a cave mouth I could easily walk into. Its body was a long, sinuous mass of muscle and scale the color of wet coal streaked with veins of sickly green. Its forelimbs were thick and gnarled, ending in talons that could gouge stone. The hindquarters tapered into a powerful tail that churned the water behind it into a whirlpool.

Its wings were half-unfurled, membrane torn in places, the ragged edges dripping. Rot clung to it in patches where the swamp had tried to claim even this apex thing—fungal growths, pale and glistening, nested between plates of armor. The horns curving back from its skull were not smooth like the mother's had been; they were ridged, etched with old, crude carvings that made my eyes ache.

Its head swung toward us.

The eyes were a molten gold shining like twin firelight in the mist. Eyes that spoke only death, no pupils or slits in that molten light. Yet we could all tell it was entirely focused on us.

On the lantern in my hand. On the three other small shapes at my back.

Recognition.

Not of us as individuals—we were too small to merit that. Recognition of pattern. Tools. Light. Blades. The sort of creatures that came with ropes and hooks and spells. The kind that set anchors of black stone in lairs and whispered to things beyond.

It opened its mouth. The jaws yawned wider than a man was tall. Teeth like scimitars. The slow, glowing simmer of some inner fire deep in the throat, banked but present. A sound rolled out of it—not a roar, not yet, but a deep, grinding exhale that rattled my bones.

We had thought, in some stubborn, human part of ourselves, that we were the ones coming to strike from shadow. That if we moved carefully enough, reasoned bravely enough, we could meet the danger on some kind of chosen ground.

Standing there, water dripping from my fur, sulphur burning my eyes, the lantern's small flame shivering in my hand, I understood.

This was no ambush.

We were the ones who had been drawn in. Tracked. Measured. Allowed to cross lines and wake elementals and feel proud of surviving. Led, step by step, to the one place in all the swamp where its strength was absolute.

The drake that hunts the hunted looked up at us on the slope, its gaze slow and sure and old. Its lips peeled back from its teeth in something that was not a smile and not not a smile.

It knew we were coming. It had been waiting.

# Chapter 17

## THE DRAKE'S BREATH

THE DRAKE CAME UP like the swamp itself was vomiting.

Water and muck fountained around it. The air turned hot and sharp, like iron left in coals. I tasted old scales and stone and something bitter, like the inside of a coin.

"Spread!" Jaime's voice cracked the moment. "Off the line—move!"

I moved before I thought. Down-slope, to the right, boots sliding. Elisah's shoulder brushed mine, a quick flash of warmth and bone under wet leathers. Rygial's breath wheezed somewhere behind.

Maximus' sword bounced against my back, heavy and wrong there. The leather harness bit into my shoulder. I'd taken the blade because leaving it behind had felt worse. I had not yet found a way to make it mine.

The drake's head cleared the surface. Black-green scales ridged with dull bronze. Eyes like molten gold sunk deep, lidless, too calm. Each blink slow. Measuring.

The rest of its body followed. It did not leap. It rose. Like it had all the time in the world.

The slope shuddered under my feet. Mud oozed. Water sheeted off the thing in ropes, each splash a slap of stinking heat. Its neck alone was longer than a wagon. The body behind, bulk and muscle and old scar lines, just kept coming.

That was the first moment I understood the size. Not by what I saw. By what I felt. The way the earth complained.

"Jaime," I said, and didn't know what I meant to ask.

"I see it." Her sword came free with a wet metallic whisper. Her shield followed, leather and iron scraping. "Front arc's death. Stay flanks, use the roots. Elric—eyes for us. Call everything. Elisah, you're with him."

Her tone left no room to argue. It never did, not when steel was bare.

The drake's chest broke the surface. The black stone was there, embedded just below the throat. Fist-sized, slick, wrong. Wet mud ran over it and then away, around it, without touching.

It pulsed once.

A sound followed. Not a beat. A tone. Low, sick. Like a bell rung underwater.

The hair on my arms prickled. My cat-ears flattened on my skull before I knew I'd moved them. My tail lashed once against the back of my legs.

"Rygial," Jaime said. "Can you slow it?"

The dwarf stood a little up-slope, staff dug into muck for balance. The brass disk of his timepiece hung open from a chain at his belt, already ticking too fast.

"A moment here and there." His voice sounded like dry paper. "No more."

"That's enough. Keep its head off us."

The drake moved.

It did not roar. Not yet. It breathed.

Hot air rolled up the slope. Not fire. Not quite. Damp heat, like steam let loose from a cracked pipe. It smelled of sulfur and rot and old blood. My eyes watered. My lungs rebelled.

"Incoming," I coughed. "Jaime—"

The breath hit us. The wet heat slapped my chest and face. It clung. My tunic stuck to my skin as if oiled. My throat closed for a heartbeat. I dragged air through my teeth like breathing mud.

Jaime's silhouette blurred in the haze. "Stay low!" she shouted. "Stay out of the plume! Shield high!"

She sank into a fighter's crouch, her shield tilted to shunt the worst of the steam aside. The swamp-light flashed along her sword's edge in quick, hard beats as she tested distance.

The ground under me shivered. The drake was moving faster now.

Claws tore into stone. The sound was like someone sharpening knives on bone. Bits of shale jumped and pinged. My ears twitched toward each one. Useless, panicked reflex.

"Elric." Elisah's voice to my left, tight, close. "Where's it starting?"

I forced my eyes to stay open, to see through the shimmering heat. The drake shifted, weight settling. It coiled, muscles bunched under slick scales. The eyes tracked Jaime. Then slid. Past her. Up.

On us.

"Left foreclaw," I said. "Step coming. Wide sweep."

"Elric says left!" Jaime bellowed. "Off that side, now!"

I threw myself to the right. Mud gave way. My knee banged stone. Wet moss smeared my palm. Maximus' sword hilt slammed between my shoulders and drove the air from my lungs.

The claw came down where we'd been.

Stone split. A spray of black water and shattered rock rained where our bodies had been heartbeats before. The air boomed with the impact. My teeth clicked together hard. My ears rang.

"Now, Rygial!" Jaime snapped.

Rygial grunted. He lifted his staff and the timepiece together, the little brass guts spinning so fast they blurred. He muttered something in his own tongue. The air around us thickened for an instant, like walking into a hot bath.

The drake's massive leg jerked. Its motion stuttered, as if someone had stolen a frame from the world. The water hanging off its scales froze for half a heartbeat as glittering beads.

Jaime used that stolen breath. Of course she did.

She drove downhill at the inside of the stalled limb.

Her boots hit a jut of rock, then another. Her shield rode high to guard her head; her sword flashed low. A clean arc, no wasted motion. She slid under the drake's chest and cut for the join in the scales where its arm met the softer skin of the belly.

Sparks jumped.

Not from steel on stone. From steel on scale.

Her blade bit. Not deep. Maybe a finger's width. Maybe less. Dark blood welled, thick and slow, like tar in winter.

Time snapped back.

The drake's head snapped toward her. Completely. Too fast for something that large. Water flew from its horns in long, shining threads.

"Elisah, now!" Jaime barked, not taking her eyes off the limb she'd marked.

Elisah was already moving. A smear of shadow along the slope. She sprang from a root to a rock to the slick ridge of the drake's forearm, daggers reversed in her hands. Her boots barely made a sound.

"Joint behind the tricep," I shouted, the word coming out before I'd chosen it. "Narrow scale, two handspans above Jaime's cut!"

She adjusted mid-leap. Her knives flashed down, angling for that thinner line of armor.

One blade slid between overlapping scales. The other glanced off. She twisted her wrist hard, tearing at whatever she'd found inside.

The drake's whole shoulder shuddered.

It didn't scream. Not yet. It hissed, long and low, steam running between its teeth. No wild rage. An annoyed kettle. It understood pain. It did not fear it.

Its tail lashed in irritation. Water fanned out, drumming the bank.

"Jaime, out!" I shouted. "It's—"

The tail was already coming.

I did not see it at first. I felt the air move behind me. Pressure, a push, wrong angle. I turned and the world thinned down to a line.

"Tail low!" I screamed. "Ground-hugging! Jaime, duck! Elisah, off!"

Jaime dropped flat, shield angled over her head. No thought. Just obedience to a voice she'd trained into us.

Elisah threw herself backward, letting go of her buried knife. She pushed off the drake's foreleg, body folding tight as she fell.

The tail blurred past, a dark streak at knee-height. It hit a boulder the size of a cart and didn't slow. The boulder exploded into shale and dust. Bits of it whistled past. One shard scored my cheek. Hot blood. Cold air.

Elisah had been moving with me. But slower. She had taken a different angle.

The very tip of the tail caught her hip.

She spun. Once. Twice. Her body skidded on mud, hit a root, flipped. She vanished behind an outcrop, a rag doll, wet leaves marking the path she tore through.

"Elisah!" My throat cracked on the name.

"Alive later," Jaime spat, crawling out from under the drake's shadow, shield first. "Alive later or never. Eyes, Elric!"

I swallowed her words and forced my gaze back to the monster.

The drake rebalanced. The wound at its armpit oozed syrupy blood. Elisah's dagger still jutted from the upper joint, its hilt quivering. The limb moved a fraction stiffer.

Rygial staggered closer, staff planted, his shoulders heaving. Thin lines of blood ran from one nostril, bright against his beard.

"Rygial," Jaime called. "Give me his eye. Just a blink."

He lifted his timepiece, fingers shaking. The ticking inside swelled to a frantic clatter.

"Too—too deep in its own time," he rasped. "I can't—"

The drake's head blurred.

One second it was above Jaime. The next, its snout slammed into the spot where Rygial stood.

Or had stood.

He was two steps to the side now. Bent double. A globe of warped air clung to his shoulders, bending the light. His beard streamed backward in a wind only he felt, each hair stretched thin.

The drake's snout crashed into the ground. Mud and rock blew outward. The impact blew Rygial off his feet anyway. He went rolling, limbs loose, staff tumbling from his hand.

The sound of his body hitting stone was heavier than it should have been.

My stomach twisted. I scrambled higher on the slope, boots slipping, tail lashing for balance I did not quite have.

"Jaime," I said, barely more than breath. "He's down."

"I see him." Her voice stayed flat. Command held. "Keep it talking to us."

The drake exhaled again. This breath came with sound. A low rumble that buzzed in my bones and made my teeth ache. Not quite a growl. A question.

Its eyes tracked between us. Counting. It knew how many we were.

Truth that came later: some part of me knew even then that it had wanted Rygial drained. Had wanted him to spend his age-bent magic on the bog-thing and the stones. To come here empty. It had wanted us tired. It had waited.

In the moment, all I knew was that each breath of that hot, chemical wind was cutting us down.

"Elric," Jaime said. "Its left side is stronger. Favors that foreleg."

"Scar tissue on that shoulder," I said, squinting through the steam. Old pale claw-marks ridged the muscle there, scales grown back wrong. "Old wound, bad set. Right side's slower on the push."

"Good. We go right, then. We stay right." She flicked swamp water and blood from her sword, brought her shield up. "On my mark, we split. I draw its face. You and Elisah cut low. We tear that leg out."

"Elisah's—"

"Alive later," she snapped again, but softer. "I need your mouth now, kit. Not your feelings."

I shut my mouth. Breathed. Tasted. Sulfur, blood, algae, Rygial's sweat-sour, the iron tang from my own cheek. Beneath that, a dry heat that hadn't yet reached skin.

The drake shifted its weight to the right, testing the leg Jaime had nicked. The motion sent a shudder up the slope. I watched how the muscles pulled along its ribs. Saw the hitch when it put too much down on that side.

"We can make it misstep," I said. "Rock seam three paces in front of that bad shoulder. Smooth. Slick. If it lunges, you can bait it over."

"Good," she said. "There's my clever boy."

Warmth at the words, even then. Maximus had called me that once. The memory sat heavy under the sword across my shoulders.

"Rygial!" she called. "Can you give us one more slow?"

Silence.

Then a groan. Wet, ragged. "Enough...for half a heartbeat."

"That's all I need." She set her stance, sword low, point toward the drake's chest, shield angled. "Elric, when I move, you shout. Loud as you can. Its eyes, its claws, any twitch. Don't try to be brave. Try to be right."

The drake's gaze settled on her. It lowered its head. Mouth opening. I saw black flesh, ropes of saliva that fizzed where they dripped into the water at its feet. Steam rose from each drop.

"Now," Jaime whispered.

She ran.

Down the slope, straight at the drake's face.

It watched her come.

The world narrowed. Her boots hit stone and mud in a pattern my body already knew by heart. Left, right, leap, suck of swamp, grit of shale. My ears tracked the scrape of each of the drake's claws as it anchored itself or shifted weight.

"Head dipping," I shouted. "Jaw opening wider—breath coming."

The air thickened. The inside of my nose burned.

"Jaime!" I yelled. "Out of the center! Left plume!"

She veered right without looking, shield between her and the drake. The breath washed past where she'd been. A white-hot sheet of damp air roared up the slope. My exposed skin prickled. The smell of burned moss hit me like a slap.

Where the breath touched stone, it hissed. Dark slime bubbled and ran. Not flame. Something worse. A heat that sank in and stayed.

Jaime kept running. She slid in under the edge of that white haze, shield covering her face.

The drake reared slightly, bringing its right foreclaw up to swat her.

"Lift on right claw!" I yelled. "Telegraphing big! Wide arc!"

"Rygial!" Jaime roared. "Now!"

The world shuddered.

Everything got heavy. Sound stretched. I watched drops of swamp water hang in the air. The claw came down through syrup.

Rygial knelt where he'd fallen, one hand buried in the mud, the other clenched around the timepiece. His lips moved, blood running freely from his nose now, leaking from one ear.

Jaime ducked inside the slowed claw. Her blade drove into the softer skin at the base of the drake's toe, where the scale thinned to a thick, pebbled hide.

The tip sank in. A handspan. Two.

The drake screamed.

The sound was what silence makes when it breaks. A ripping. A tearing. My vision jumped with it. The slope under us cracked. Somewhere far off, birds exploded out of the trees in a panicked cloud.

Jaime's sword lodged. The drake jerked its leg. The movement shook her like a dog worrying a bone. Her hand tore free from the hilt before her arm could snap.

She flew. Up and out. Caught a jut of rock with her shield first. The impact boomed. Wood splintered. Iron rim bent. She slid down the rock in a smear of wet.

"Elric—now!" she coughed, voice shredded, shield hanging from one mangled strap.

I was already moving.

Down the far right side of the slope, keeping to the thicker roots. Mud squelched around my boots. Maximus' sword hammered between my shoulders with each stride, throwing my balance. My knives were in my hands without me remembering the draw.

The drake's leg was half-lifted, wounded claw tucked in. Blood dripped in thick ropes, each strand steaming. It turned its head to track Jaime, attention still on the larger threat.

Its bad shoulder rolled forward. Closer to that slick rock seam.

"Another step," I whispered.

Behind me, Elisah hissed like a kicked cat. "You suicidal little offspring. You couldn't wait five breaths?"

Her voice was thin, pain-clamped. I risked a glance. She was ghosting between shadows, her left side held stiff. One hand pressed against her ribs, dark wetness seeping between her fingers. Her other hand gripped a single dagger.

"You alive?" I said.

"Debatable. I'll answer after this isn't trying to eat us."

She slipped in alongside me, somehow making her limp look like part of her stealth.

"Elric," she said. "I see a gap behind that bad leg. If we can get under it, I can open the tendon."

"You can barely breathe," I said.

"I don't need breath to cut."

The drake tried to pull its wounded claw higher. Its weight shifted further forward onto the bad shoulder. The scaled skin around that joint bunched, then slid.

It stepped.

Its foot came down on the slick rock.

Its foreleg shot out faster than it meant. The weight came behind it a heartbeat late. The huge beast stumbled, chest lurching low.

"Now!" I shouted. "It's dropping! Right ankle!"

Elisah moved.

She became a smear of dark cloth and pale hands, sliding under the low-swinging bulk. Her knife flashed once, twice, at the back of the drake's ankle, where scaled armor gave way to gristled tendon.

The blade bit. I saw it go in and come out red-black.

The drake bucked.

It should not have been able to move like that with one foreleg wounded and the other slipping. But it did. Muscle surged all along its body, a wave of flesh. Its chest slammed back up, lifting a torrent of water with it.

Elisah vanished in the splash.

The tail came a half-breath later. A convulsion that ran from the base of the spine to the tip. It cracked through the air, seeking balance, striking anything it could to find a brace.

The bank right of me exploded.

Mud, rock, and a curtain of water slammed into me. The world went end over end. Maximus' sword twisted on its straps and tore at my shoulder. One of my knives ripped out of my hand. My other shoulder struck something hard. White flared behind my eyes.

I hit the ground on my side. The harness buckles bit. One snapped. The sword slid sideways, its weight suddenly crooked, half-hanging from its scabbard across my ribs.

I clutched at it on instinct. My fingers closed around slick leather. The hilt jabbed my shoulder.

Then I was on my back. Water over my face, filling my nose, my mouth. My lungs convulsed. I rolled, gagging, coughed swamp back up.

Sound came back next. A roar of displaced water. The grating screech of stone on scale. Rygial's raw scream. Jaime's hoarse cursing.

I forced myself to my knees.

The drake heaved itself further out of the pool, trying to escape the unstable bank. Its wounded foreleg dragged, the joint not quite right. Elisah's cut had done something.

Elisah herself lay half-submerged against a broken root. Her head rested at a wrong angle, eyes squeezed shut. One of her legs jutted out straight, the other bent under her. Her chest moved in short, sharp jerks.

On the air I caught the sweet-sour edge of punctured lung.

"Kit!" she rasped as I scrambled toward her. "Don't you—look at me—"

Her eyes flicked past me, wide.

I dropped flat without thinking.

The drake's tail slashed where my neck had been. It tore a furrow in the mud that filled instantly with dark water. Pebbles pinged off my back. Maximus' sword dug into my spine and shoved the breath from me again.

"Up-slope!" Jaime shouted. "Get clear, Elric! Elisah, can you move?"

"What do you think?" Elisah spat, then screamed through her teeth as she tried to roll. The sound cut off on a wet cough.

Rygial staggered into view on the left. His robes were split and soaked, beard plastered to his chest with blood and swamp. His right arm hung useless. With his left hand he clutched his timepiece, the small brass thing open, its guts spinning too fast. His staff dragged from a thong at his wrist, carving grooves in the mud.

"Enough," he croaked. "Enough of this beast."

He raised the timepiece toward the drake and spoke words that weren't any tongue I knew. The air around his hand twisted. Light bent wrong. The world seemed to trip.

The drake slowed. Just a fraction. Steam curled more lazily from its nostrils. Droplets hung longer in the air before falling. The tremor of its rage came to us a hair late.

Jaime used it. Again.

She'd found one of Dratmar's cheap swamp-steel spares where it had fallen in the muck, battered and nicked. Her own sword still protruded from the drake's toe joint like a silver splinter. Her shield dangled broken at her side by one strap; she ripped it free and let it fall.

She ran for its exposed throat.

"Jaime, the stone!" I shouted. "It's guarding the stone!"

The anchor-slick rock in its chest throbbed faintly, in time now with the strange heaviness in my limbs. The drake's forelimbs crossed instinctively to shield it, even as its maw swung toward her, even as its leg bled and its wrist tendons screamed.

"I can't crack that," she called back. "I can make it hurt."

She dove under the lowered jaw. The drake tried to close its mouth on her too late. Rygial's magic stole the moment it needed.

She came up under its chin and drove the second sword up.

The blade met armour first, then something softer. It slid in, grinding. Not clean. The hilt hammered into her palms. She screamed with the effort.

Dark ichor fountained. It smelled like old coins scraped on flint. Drops hit her arms and hissed. Her skin blistered in angry red arcs.

The drake howled.

The sound knocked me flat again. My ears rang like struck bells. Blood trickled warm at their edges. The trees around the lair shook. Leaves tore free and spun.

The stutter in time collapsed. Rygial sagged to his knees, the timepiece falling from his fingers. It hit the mud with a flat, final smack. His staff slid down the slope and lodged against a rock.

The drake thrashed. Its head whipped side to side, trying to dislodge the sword lodged in its palate. Jaime clung to the hilt as long as she could. But flesh won over steel. The motion ripped the sword free from her hands.

She tumbled away, rolled through mud, came up on one knee. Empty again.

The drake slammed its head into the stone ridge at the far side of the pool. Once. Twice. Each impact cracked rock, shook the slope. Shards rained into the water. The sword in its mouth snapped near the hilt. The broken length clanged off stone and vanished into the darkness of the pool.

The wound in its mouth spat blood with every roar. It shook its head more slowly now. Its breath whistled high through the new gap, a broken kettle shriek.

Its eyes found Rygial.

The old dwarf was on all fours, trying to push himself upright. His left arm trembled. The veins in his forehead stood out like cords. He panted, each breath a saw blade. New white threads streaked his beard that hadn't been there in Lantern Light.

The drake understood. It had learned the rhythm of his interference. It knew the frail one was the source.

It lunged.

I had never seen something that big move that fast when it chose not to be slowed. The distance between them disappeared in a rush of wet scales and hot air.

"Rygial!" I heard my own voice break.

He looked up.

The drake's jaws opened on him, red and black and lined with teeth like broken sickles.

Jaime hit it from the side.

She'd found a rock, nothing more. Fist-sized, jagged on one end. She threw herself at the drake's face and slammed that rock into the softer skin at the corner of its eye with a snarl that was almost a sob.

The drake flinched.

Its head jerked. Its teeth closed shut a handspan left of where Rygial had been. Mud and water and a scattering of broken stone vanished between them. The shockwave of that bite slapped my chest.

Rygial threw himself sideways, more a fall than a leap. The swing of the drake's muzzle caught his hip. Bone cracked like snapping twigs. He screamed once, high and thin.

He landed half in the pool. The water around his lower body changed color slowly, dark threads spreading.

"Move!" Jaime yelled at him, as if yelling could force his limbs to listen. "Get away from the edge!"

He did not move.

The drake blinked the pain from its eye. Its growl rolled up from deep places. This one carried words I could not understand. Old, slow syllables. A question. A promise.

Its pupils narrowed. It took in Jaime, panting and empty-handed. Elisah, broken on the roots. Rygial, bleeding into its water. Me, crouched and shaking, one knife left, Maximus' sword still half-slipped on its harness across my back like a weight I had no use for.

Insight that came after: it saw the shape of what we were. Not individuals. A pattern it had known before. Youth and age. Edge and shadow. Voice and thread of time. It understood more than we did.

In the moment, all I knew was that its gaze lingered on me longer than the others. Its nostrils flared.

"Jaime," I whispered. "It smells us."

"It smelled us the whole way," she said. Her breath came rough. She bent, fingers closing around the strap of my sword harness. With one savage tug she yanked Maximus' blade back into its sheath, re-seating it so it lay solid against my spine instead of half-falling. "Stay behind me."

She stepped in front of me without waiting to see if I obeyed. Her shoulders were shaking with effort. The swamp-steam had reddened the skin at her neck. Her leathers were torn, one pauldron twisted useless. Her shield was gone. Her sword was gone. She picked up another broken shard of stone instead.

The drake's chest heaved. Its breathing had gone ragged. Each exhale rattled in its chest. The wound in its claw bled steadily. The mangled tendons at its ankle made its steps uneven. Blood dripped from its mouth, mixing with slime.

It was hurt. Not enough.

It lunged for Jaime.

There was no time to shout. No time to warn. It came with the last reserves of its strength, all of its hate focused through teeth and mass and speed.

Jaime did the only thing she could.

She went forward.

Her charge was short, three stumbling steps. She ducked under the first crashing sweep of its muzzle and slammed her shoulder into the softer flesh under its jaw. With her other hand she drove the jagged stone into the pulsing vein there.

The force of their collision picked her off her feet. For a moment, she and the drake hung there together. Then its sheer momentum drove her backward, up the slope, ploughing furrows in the mud with her heels.

The stone sank in. Not deep enough. Never deep enough. Blood sprayed, hot and thick, washing her face. It burned wherever it touched.

The drake reared, jaws wide to pull free. Jaime lost her grip. Her hand slipped on her own blood.

Its head came down. Hard.

The top of its skull smashed into her chest.

I heard the armor give. A wet metallic crunch. The sound of a shield bent wrong in a forge.

Jaime flew.

She spun through the air, arms loose. Landed on her back against a half-submerged boulder. The impact cracked the stone. Her body bent around it and then slid down, limp.

Everything in me went quiet.

Not just sound. Thought.

The swamp-light dimmed at the edges. The air thickened until it was like drinking earth when I tried to breathe.

"Jaime," I said. Or thought I did. My mouth moved with no sound.

She did not move.

Her head lolled to one side. Mud slicked her curls to her face. Blood ran from the corner of her mouth in a neat line, as if someone had drawn it there with a careful brush.

The drake settled its forelimbs back into the water. It swayed. It was hurt. But it still stood. And the only one still upright before it was me.

I knew, in a clean, flat way, that we were all about to die.

Something broke.

IT WAS SMALL. NOT a sound I heard with ears. More like the feeling when you finally give in to a long-held shiver. Muscles unclenched I had not known were locked.

The world sharpened.

Not brighter. Not slower. Just...clean. Lines came into focus. The edges of each scale, the way mist curled at the drake's nostrils, the trembling of each leaf around the lair as its mass shifted the air.

Noise peeled apart. I could hear Rygial's ragged gasps as separate from the bubbling of his blood into water. I could count the rhythm of Elisah's broken breaths. I could hear every drip of the drake's blood hitting the pool—each one a different pitch depending on distance and temperature.

My heartbeat vanished. Or maybe it just stopped mattering.

I did not feel brave. Or powerful. I felt hollow. Like something had reached inside and pulled me out and left a shape behind to move.

My right hand found my last knife. I do not remember seeing it. One moment it was empty. The next the hilt pressed into my palm, familiarity settling like a weight.

The straps across my chest creaked as I straightened. Maximus' sword shifted on my back, suddenly light. Not absent. Not forgotten. A silent length of metal at my spine.

The drake's head dipped. Its gaze slid past me, toward where Jaime lay broken.

No.

The thought wasn't a word. It was a line. A cut in the world between what had been and what would not be allowed.

My body was already moving.

I remember that from outside, more than from within. Looking back, it feels like watching someone else put on my bones.

One step down-slope. Two. The mud that had tried to swallow my boots all night now gave way easily beneath me, as if it moved out of my path instead of resisting it. I slid along a line I hadn't known was there until my body found it.

My tail streamed behind me, perfect counterbalance. My ears tracked every tiny scrape of scale on stone.

The drake's head began to turn toward me.

Its eyes—those molten cores—narrowed. Recognition sparked there. A faint widening of the inner lid. Its nostrils flared, tasting something on the air it had waited for.

Bones in my hands ached. The small ones, at the base of each finger, twisted under the skin. My nails bit deeper into my palms, points sharper than they had been a breath before. The joints in my feet burned, the tendons along my calves pulling tight like bowstrings.

I took the last step without feeling the ground.

Its claw swept across, an absent-minded swat that should have cut me in half at the waist.

I saw the path of it the way you see a moth's flight in firelight—imperfect, but clear enough. I dropped my hips. My spine bent in a curve that did not belong to someone who had felt his back seize ten minutes before.

The claw passed over me. Close enough that one chipped talon grazed a line along my scalp, clipping hair and skin. Warmth ran down into one eye.

I came up inside its guard.

Everything huge about it—the bulk, the heat, the noise—fell away when I was that close. All I saw was the join between two scales on its chest. The tiny raised edge where a scar had pulled wrong. The faint purple discoloration where the flesh had not healed fully from some old battle.

My knife angled for that seam.

The blade slid in.

Flesh closed around my hand with a rubbery, sucking resistance. The smell of its blood hit me a heartbeat later. Hot iron. Cold stone. Something like the first air after lightning.

The drake bellowed. The sound went through me instead of around. My eardrums should have burst. They didn't. The noise became a shape behind my eyes for an instant and then was gone.

Its foreleg came up to crush me.

I let go of the knife.

The hilt vanished inside its chest, swallowed by muscle. My fingers slipped out slick with its blood. And then I wasn't there.

One step to the side. Not a thought. A correction. The world folded around the space where my body had been and bent to make room for the claw. It came down into mud and rock, smashing my previous self to pulp in some other line of moments that never quite happened.

My toes dug into the slope. Claws. That's what they were, then. Not full, not true, but more than nails. The mud parted around them instead of slipping.

The drake reared back, confused. It could feel the wound but not the weapon. Its heart pounded around that foreign shard. I could see it beating under the scales in a faint shiver.

Heat burned along my forearms. The fine, colorless hairs there stood on end, then thickened, darkened a shade. Not fur. Not yet. Just a hint of what my blood remembered.

The drake's tail lashed in a tight arc, a close-range snap meant for gnats like me.

I did not plan. My body folded and rose in the same breath. The tail passed under my boots by the width of a finger. For an instant I rode its slipstream, the pressure of air giving me lift. Then I came down on the back of its bad foreleg, just above Elisah's cut.

Bone moved under my feet. A living lever.

"Hamstring," something in me noted. Not in words. In direction.

I dropped low. My left hand braced on rough scale, my right tearing across the back of the joint. I felt my nails bite through the softest part of a tendon, that rope of gristle Elisah had already marked.

My fingers came away wet. The drake's leg buckled.

It tried to brace with its other forelimb. The one Jaime had carved. It found no purchase on the slick bank. Claws raked mud, gouged deep. The whole front of its body pitched forward.

I rode the fall.

Its shoulder hit rock. The jolt shuddered up through my knees, but the world stayed clean. My spine twisted. I vaulted along the ridge of its ribs, each plate a stepping-stone.

The drake brought its head around in a snap, teeth bared, eyes white-ringed for the first time. It guessed where I would be.

It was wrong.

My body went sideways, not back. A slip toward its flank that made no sense to the patterns it knew. Its jaws closed on empty air, water, and a sheet of stone. Sparks screamed where teeth met shale.

I slid down the curve of its side, fingers and toes gripping at the tiny imperfections between scales. The membranes at the join of its forelimb and chest stretched as it strained.

A seam. Always a seam.

My right hand speared up. Nails—no, claws—punched through the thin, pale line where the limb's underside met the softer belly. Flesh gave. Heat closed over my wrist.

I ripped.

Something inside parted with a wet, stringy pop. The limb spasmed. The drake's whole front sagged another handspan.

I dropped away before it could roll.

Mud accepted me like a friend. I slid, shoulders brushing roots, Maximus' sword a long, balanced weight down my spine. I had forgotten it was there, and yet my body moved in ways that never let it catch.

The drake tried to rise.

It pushed with its hind limbs, powerful muscles bunching under slick hide. For a heartbeat, it managed it, chest heaving clear of the water, one foreleg crooked, the other half-useless. Its tail whipped for balance, gouging fresh furrows into the bank.

I was already heading for those back legs.

I DO NOT REMEMBER deciding to hamstring it. I remember seeing the line of its spine and knowing what needed to break.

It turned as I ran. Or tried to. Its hindquarters churned, water exploding outward. The swamp became a storm around its body. To anyone watching from the shore, I must have been a dark blur darting along the edge of the spray.

To me, each drop fell alone.

The first hind leg came down, claws digging for rock. I slid in under the curve of its thigh, my shoulder brushing rough hide. Muscle vibrated above me with the strain of holding its impossible weight.

I drove both hands at the back of its knee.

My fingers sank into soaked hide. Not deep enough. My nails lengthened another fraction, tips tingling like they'd been thrust into snow. They caught the tendon instead of sliding off.

I hooked and tore sideways.

The leg jerked. The drake's body lurched. Water and mud crashed over my back as it fought for balance.

It tried to stomp with the other hind limb. The motion was pure instinct—crush whatever was biting.

By the time its foot came down, I was already past it. My world had narrowed to angles. Vectors. Where it was, where weight would go next.

The second tendon lay where it must. I slid in on one knee, pivoted, and cut. Nails across rope. Another wet snap.

The drake screamed again.

The sound went higher this time. A note of surprise. The back half of its body folded. Its haunches dropped into the pool with a force that sent a wall of swamp up and out. The bank where Rygial lay vanished under water for a moment. Elisah disappeared, then bobbed back, coughing pink froth.

I felt none of that touch me. It broke around some narrow space I occupied, refusing to smear the edges of what I saw.

I scrambled up the slope of its collapsed flank. My palms slid; my nails dug tiny purchase points. My toes found the ridges between ribs like I'd climbed this same creature a hundred times in dreams.

It rolled, trying to crush me against the bank.

I let go.

For a breath there was nothing under me. Just hot air, the stink of its breath, the silver glimmer of water. Then my hands caught the torn edge of its forelimb wound, the one Jaime had started. My claws sank into meat and scale, anchoring me as the world pitched.

Its jaw snapped shut inches from my feet. Teeth clanged on stone. Fragments of shattered shale spun away.

I hung there, swinging under its throat.

Its neck muscles bunched, cords thick as ship-ropes. Veins throbbed under tarnished scales. The black stone in its chest glowed, pulse matched to the strain of its heart.

I climbed.

Each movement was small. Elbow bend. Shoulder twist. Nails in, pull, toes braced, shift. I moved like something that had always been meant to clamber over a dragon's underside, not a half-breed boy who'd never owned a pair of proper boots.

The drake tried to scrape me off against the broken ridge. It drove its chest into rock, water and mud and stone exploding outward.

I flattened, pressing my body into the shallow groove between two scale plates. Rock grated furrows into my back. Maximus' sword rang in its sheath against stone, a low, angry note.

Steel. My steel. Not yet.

The impact forced air from my lungs. In the thin space that left, something else slipped in. Cold and vast, like air from high above tree-line. Thin. Hard.

A pressure coiled in my spine. My tail went rigid, every vertebra a bead of fire.

Up. The word was not in any tongue I knew. It was deeper than that. A pulling.

I obeyed.

My head broke past the line of its lower jaw. I was suddenly looking down at the swamp from just under its chin. Jaime's crumpled shape was a dark smear against the rock. Rygial's robes floated around him like dead weeds. Elisah clung to a root with white knuckles, her face grey.

The drake dragged in a breath to roar again.

My right hand shot up. Fingers spread.

For a moment my nails lengthened I could see it. Two heartbeats. Three. They sharpened to hooked points, black at the tips, the beds beneath them bloodless. Lines of pain lanced from knuckle to elbow as the bones adjusted to bear the strain.

I drove that hand into the soft, paler skin between its jawbones.

My claws punched through flesh and sinew. Heat swallowed my forearm.

I felt the shape of everything inside that throat. Cartilage rings. Pulsing veins. A slick, muscular tube for breath and a thicker one for swallowing. My fingers found the space between them.

I clenched and raked down.

The drake's roar came out a choking gurgle. Blood and air and slime exploded out between its teeth. Its head jerked, a convulsion that would have flung me free if my other hand hadn't found another purchase point on the ridge of its breastbone.

I hung there, arm buried up to the elbow in its neck, the beat of its pulse hammering against my skin.

The stone in its chest flared.

CHEST PLATES CRACKED OPEN.

I would like to say I did that. That the force of my hand, the angle of my claws, tore it apart. It wasn't me.

The black stone in its breast—what we would later call the anchor—pulsed in a way that wasn't rhythm. It convulsed. The plates of bone and scale around it shuddered as if something inside had swollen too big for the cage.

With a sound like green wood splitting, one of the main chest plates fractured along an old fault line. Jaime's first cut, shallow as it had been, gave it direction. The crack raced out from that nick in a jagged web.

The plate above the stone tilted. A wedge of raw, wet organ showed between.

Black veins laced outward from the anchor. Each pulse sent a sick greenish-black light along them, a glow that was wrong in the swamp's brown murk. It wasn't bright. It didn't have to be. It made every living color around it look sallow.

My arm slid free of the drake's neck as it thrashed. I dropped half a man's height, then caught myself on the broken edge of the plate. My feet swung over empty air above the churned pool.

The stone beat.

Not like a heart. Like a bell struck too slow.

Threads of that wrong light reached for my hand. They brushed my skin. Frost and fever both. My nails smoked where they touched.

I should have let go. Fallen. Run.

I reached in.

My hand went through torn cartilage, past a slipping rib. Flesh tried to close on my forearm, to push me back out. I forced my way deeper.

The stone wasn't smooth. It was all facets and corners under the slime, like a cluster of crystal someone had dipped in tar. It hummed against my palm.

Around it, the drake's real heart labored. I felt it slam against the back of my hand, huge and terrified and bound.

Something else moved in the stone.

For a heartbeat I saw another place overlaid on the swamp. Black stone. Red sky. A vast shape coiled around a mountain. Not this drake. Something older, the outline too immense to understand. A voice like molten metal poured slow spoke a word I did not know but understood entirely.

*Warrior.*

My vision doubled. My bones shook.

The thing behind the stone reached along the black veins, testing the hollow inside me. Curious. Cold. Waiting.

The pressure in my spine flared. Heat flooded my arm. My claws locked around one jag of the anchor.

I drove them in.

Cracks spiderwebbed through the stone from that point. They glowed brighter than the veins. The drake convulsed. Every muscle in its body fired at once. The pool exploded outward, bank and roots and rock all lifting in one ragged breath.

Behind the stone, something screamed.

It didn't have a throat. It screamed through the anchor. Through the black threads. Through my arm.

The sound was not sound. It was absence. It hollowed me out in a way the earlier break had only started. My eyes rolled. My teeth clamped together so hard I felt one chip.

I squeezed.

The stone shattered.

Not clean. It crumbled under my hand like burnt bone. Fragments tore through the surrounding flesh, black shards ripping red tunnels. The greenish light flared once—sick noon—and then went out.

The drake's entire body seized. Its limbs locked. Its tail went rigid, whipping water into a straight line that slapped the far bank and shattered saplings.

Then it fell.

The mass of it crashed back into the pool and onto the broken bank with a weight that shook the lair to its roots. The ground bucked under my feet. The rock Jaime had hit earlier split along a fresh vein. Mud geysered.

My claws tore free of ruined bone and muscle. I was flung sideways, into the shallows. My shoulder hit a root. My skull bounced off stone. For a breath, the world went white.

When it came back, it was loud.

DEATH RATTLES ARE NOT a single breath. Not for creatures that big.

The drake's lungs shuddered and shuddered again, each attempt to draw air meeting nothing that would carry it. Blood poured from its neck wound, its mangled chest, the broken gap in its palate. The water around it went from murky to near-black.

Something beyond the drake screamed as the anchor broke.

I felt it more than heard it. A withdrawing. A thousand tiny hooks pulling free all at once from the world's underside. The cold that had filled my hollow surged for one last, greedy try at taking more.

Then it, too, was gone.

What remained was only a swamp creature dying. Its eyes filmed. The molten gold clouded, fading toward the dull amber of old sap. Its limbs twitched. Its tail thumped an irregular beat, each strike weaker than the last.

My body remembered gravity.

The clarity shattered like river ice under a boot. Noise flooded in raw and too bright. My heart slammed into my ribs. Pain arrived from everywhere at once—shoulder, scalp, knees, lungs, nails torn down to quick in places where the stone had fought back.

I tried to push myself up and almost blacked out from the way my wounded arm screamed. My claws—such as they had been—were receding already, nails softening back toward human.

Mud sucked at my palms. My tail lay heavy in the water behind me, no longer a perfect line of balance, just an extra limb that ached from root to tip.

"Jaime," I croaked.

Silence.

No. Not silence. Bubbles. Small, thin ones. They rose from between her lips where she lay half-slumped in the shallows against the cracked boulder.

I crawled.

Each movement hurt. Maximus' sword dragged against my spine now, impossibly heavy again. It had twisted further when I was flung; the strap cut across my ribs. I clawed at the harness buckle with one hand until it came free, let the scabbarded blade slide down into the mud beside me.

It hit with a wet thud and lay there, hilt just above water, as if Maximus himself had set it down carefully.

I reached Jaime.

Her eyes were closed. Her chest armor was caved in along one side, leather and steel both bent wrong. Purple bruise-spread already discolored the skin at her throat. Blood painted a fine line from one nostril to her upper lip. Her curls were plastered to her face with mud and drake-blood.

"Jaime." My voice was smaller than the insects starting to buzz back over the water. "Jaime, please."

My hand hovered over her ribs, afraid to touch. Afraid I'd feel nothing move.

Her chest hitched.

Tiny. Shallow. But it moved.

A strangled sound ripped out of me. Not quite laughter. Not quite sob. My vision blurred.

Behind me, the drake's last breath rattled out. A long, wet exhale. Its massive head slumped sideways, jaw hanging open. Steam no longer rose from its nostrils. The swamp water lapped at its teeth as if nothing special had happened here at all.

"Elric."

The voice came from my left. Raspy. Wet.

Elisah.

She lay still against her root-ledge. The wrong-bent leg had not moved. Her face was white beneath the mud, lips tinged blue. Every breath she took sounded like it had to find its way past broken glass.

Her eyes were open. Wide.

They were not on the drake.

They were on me.

Rygial dragged himself half out of the pool on the other side. His right leg trailed behind him, limp. His hip jutted at an angle that made my stomach roil. His beard hung in clotted ropes. Deep furrows lined his face that had not been there that morning.

He caught his staff with his good hand and used it to lever himself upright onto his knees. The timepiece lay cracked open in the mud a few paces away, its innards still spinning in tiny, useless circles.

He looked at the drake once.

Then at me.

He had the same expression Elisah did. Wariness. And something colder than that.

I followed their gaze down.

My right hand was still half-curled. Blood—drake and mine—slicked it to the wrist. Under the red, my nails remained longer than they should have. Not the full hooked daggers I'd felt a moment before. But not the blunt, chewed edges I knew.

Thin, almost invisible fissures had opened along the backs of my knuckles, as if the bones beneath had tried to stretch and hadn't quite finished. A tremor ran through my fingers.

Behind my breastbone, the hollow yawned wider. The thing that had brushed it stirred again. Less curious now. More intent.

I closed my fist.

"Elric," Rygial said again. He tasted my name like it was a new word. "What did you do?"

"I don't—" My voice broke. I looked back at Jaime. At the shallow rise and fall of her chest. At the way her fingers still curled as if around a sword hilt that wasn't there.

Whatever answer I might have given died behind my teeth.

Above us, the swamp canopy swayed. A breeze moved through it that did not belong there. Thin, cold, high. It slipped between the wet heat and the rot and stroked the inside of my lungs.

Sky. The breath of heights I had never seen.

I smelled it clean, then. Beneath drake blood and mud and fear.

The Dragon Above. Or its echo. Or something older that did not care what name we gave it.

I felt it consider me.

The drake's molten eyes were dull now, but in death they still seemed aimed in my direction. The memory of that earlier recognition sat hot on my skin.

*Warrior.*

No one spoke the word. Not then. But it hung there. In Rygial's stare. In Elisah's ragged breath. In the way my own heart hammered, trying to beat out of a chest that no longer felt entirely mine.

Maximus' sword lay between me and the dead drake. The swamp lapped at its tip, trying to take it. I reached out with shaking fingers and dragged it back toward me until the hilt touched my knee. Slowly I hefted the blade, feeling something new with it, I quickly returned it to the sheathe on my back.

I sat there instead, mud cold under my legs, Jaime's breaths counting out the seconds we still had in this world, the drake's corpse cooling by inches, and the hollow in my chest no longer empty.

We were alive.

Later I would learn the old words. The dragon's dream. The warrior's stillness. The price stamped into the bones of those who woke to it.

In that moment, all I knew was that nothing in the swamp was looking at me the same way anymore.

Not my friends.

Not the dead thing at my feet.

Not whatever watched from above.

# Chapter 18

## WHAT THE SWAMP KEPT

WE DID NOT SPEAK at first.

The only sound was the swamp reclaiming the hollow the drake had called a lair. Water dripped from the ragged hole in the cavern roof. Each drop landed in some unseen pool with a soft, relentless ticking. Mud sighed and bubbled under the corpse. Insects resumed their work in cautious threads, a high, thin whine at the edge of hearing. The smell shifted as the drake's blood cooled. The sharp, metallic heat of it dulled into something heavier. Sick-sweet, almost floral. That was new to me. I knew the smell of deer blood, of boar, of men. Drake blood sat somewhere between pitch and overripe fruit.

My hands would not stop shaking.

The drake lay on its side in the mud, three of its limbs twisted at wrong angles. Its wings folded under its own weight. The hide that had looked like stone in motion now showed the weak seams where we had found purchase: white gouges where Elisah's blades had slipped beneath scale, the dark, caved-in patch where Jaime's blade had found the softer bone of its breastbone, the wide, obscene crater in its chest where the anchor stone had been.

Steam rose from that ruin in slow, curious curls. The meat there still glowed faintly, as if some ember remained beneath it. The air around that hole felt warmer than the rest of the lair. It smelled acrid, like wet ash and burnt bone.

My claws were buried to the knuckles in the flesh just below that cavity. I had not let go when it fell. The jaws had missed my head by less than a handspan in its death lunge. Chipped fangs now sat buried deep in the mud to my right. One of them brushed my ankle as I shifted, like a dead thing making a last attempt.

"Kit." Rygial's voice sounded wrong. Too thin, too far away. "Answer when I speak to you, lad."

It took me a moment to understand that he meant me. My ears were still ringing from the drake's last scream, the world moving a half-second out of step. His voice floated over the clatter of cooling scales and settling dust, thin and far away, before it finally snapped into place as my name.

"I hear you," I said. My tongue felt thick. The air grated on my throat. When I tried to pull my hands free, the flesh clung. My claws did not want to leave their new burrow. The tendons in my forearms twitched in a way that did not feel entirely like mine.

"Good," he said. A scraping sound answered him, metal on stone. Then a sharp grunt that ended in a hiss. "Stay alive until I reach you. I am too old to be explaining your death to anyone."

I forced my fingers to uncurl. The drake's meat gave way with a soft, sucking sound. When my claws came free, they left four clean channels through muscle and shattered bone. The sight of those grooves unnerved me more than the corpse itself. I knew how deep the breastbone lay there. I knew how hard it had been when we first engaged.

My hands shook harder.

Mud had plastered itself up my legs to mid-thigh, warm with the drake's leaking heat. My shirt hung in ribbons from where its talons had brushed me and failed to find purchase. There was blood on my chest and arms and face. Some of it was mine. Most of it was not. I could not tell by smell anymore. My nostrils burned from the copper and the strange, resinous sweetness of the drake.

To my left, Elisah lay half-submerged where the creature's tail had thrown her. Only her upper chest and head were above the thin scum of the surface water. Her hair, usually tied tight, floated around her like dark weed. Each breath she took pulled the murky water rhythmically against the leather of her jerkin. In, out. In, out. The sound had a faint burble to it.

Her right leg bent the wrong way just below the knee. Splintered bone pressed up against the inside of her trousers there, trying to find a way out. Her left side rose and fell too quickly, the movements shallow and sharp. Each inhalation caught on some unseen hook in her ribs and turned into a ragged cough before it could finish. Pink foam clung to the corner of her mouth, bright against the swamp grime on her skin.

On the other side of the corpse, Jaime knelt with both hands pressed hard against her own ribs. She had dragged herself clear of the worst of the mud. A broad smear marked where she had done it, her knees and hands leaving parallel furrows until she found a hummocked patch of half-dry ground. She sat there now, back hunched, face gray beneath the olive of her skin, lips pressed thin.

A bruise already spread beneath the hem of her tunic, dark and blotched. Swamp-murk colored most of it, but the edges showed the deep wine-purple that comes only from blood pooling where it should not. Her breathing came slower than Elisah's but no easier. Each breath pushed her hand outward a hair, then pulled it back as if it weighed a stone.

"Do not take deep ones," Rygial said to her, voice closer now. "Short. Shallow. Curse under your breath if you must. Not out loud. It wastes air."

"You are—" She broke off with a dry, humorless chuckle that turned into a groan. "—a tyrant."

"True," he said. "Which is why you still draw breath to complain."

He limped into my field of view then. His beard dragged in the mud, tangling in broken reeds and clotted blood. It had never been clean, but it had always been cared for. The braids now hung half-loosened, charms of bone and brass smeared dark. The left side of his body favored the right by more than his usual old wound. His hip was wrong. I knew it by the careful way his foot searched for ground before taking weight, the brief closing of his eyes with each step, the way sweat had soaked his collar and the edges of his hair despite the cavern's chill.

"Keep still, boy," he said as he reached me. His fingers brushed my jaw, turned my face left, then right. His thumb pressed my lower eyelid down. His breath smelled of bile and iron. "Pupils even. You are lucky. Or stubborn. Difficult to distinguish at your age."

"I feel strange," I said. It was not the right word, but it was the closest I could find in that moment.

"Yes," he said. "We will argue about why later. Bleeding?"

I shook my head. My ears rang. My heart had not yet slowed. It beat against my ribs in a hard, double rhythm, faster than it should have but steady. Reliable. For now.

"Then you will live," he said. "Jaime needs me more. So does our little eel there. See if you can reach her without falling on your face."

He left me with that and limped away, his boot making sucking sounds in the mud. I let my breath out slowly. My arms shook as I pulled my knees under me. My first attempt to stand failed. My legs carried me up halfway before something inside my thighs cramped hard. I went back down beside the drake's cooling flank with a soft grunt.

The second time, I went slower. The mud tried to keep me. It felt deeper than before, like some subtle shift in weight in the lair had called it down. My toes scraped bone beneath the surface, rounded and slick. I pushed past the quiet panic that rose with that. I kept my eyes on Elisah and Jaime and let the rest of the cavern blur.

The air changed as I moved away from the chest wound. The heat of it fell behind me. A damp chill took its place, rising from the low pools and the shallow channels between heaps of bones. The smell of long rot grew stronger. Old marrow. Rust. Leather left too long in water.

By the time I staggered to the hummock where Elisah lay, my legs shook with exhaustion. Not weakness, not yet, but the deep warning tremor that says the body has spent more than it should.

"El," I said. My voice sounded rough to my own ears. "You with me?"

Her eyes opened. For a moment they did not know me. I watched the focus return, like something swimming up from depth.

"Unfortunately," she said. The single word scraped. The corner of her mouth twitched up a fraction. "You look like shit, kitten."

"Feeling generous, are we," I said.

Her gaze flicked down to her own leg, to the angle of it. She did not look long. Her jaw clenched. Her eyelids fluttered once.

"That bad?" she asked.

"Rygial says you will live," I said. "Which means he plans to bully you for at least another twenty years. The world is not so lucky as to be rid of you yet."

I bent and slid my hands under her shoulders, careful not to press on her ribs. The mud sucked at her as I lifted. She was lighter than I expected. Or I was stronger than I should have been. My arms did not agree on that. They shook hard enough that my teeth clicked together when I straightened.

Her breath caught when her chest shifted. A wet sound came from deep in her lung, a crackle and a pop like sap in a fire.

"Easy," I said. "Short breaths."

"Do not...tell me...how to breathe," she managed, then hissed between her teeth as her broken leg bumped the hummock's edge.

I carried her the three paces to slightly higher ground, where the water only lapped and did not pool. My boots found purchase there on hard-packed silt and embedded bone. Rygial knelt by Jaime on the same rise, his back to us.

He glanced over his shoulder as I set Elisah down. His eyes had the bright, sharp look of a man forcing his mind to outrun his body.

"Good," he said. "Set her there. Prop her half-upright. If she drowns in her own blood after all this, I will be cross."

He handed me his travel cloak without looking. The wool was wet near the hem but dry higher up. I wadded it and slid it under Elisah's shoulders, lifting her until she lay on a slight incline. When her head tipped back, her breathing eased by a hair, the rattle less violent.

Rygial's hands hovered over Jaime's ribs without touching. His fingers traced shapes in the air, following lines of injury that only he could see. Close up, I saw how badly she shook. It was not the fine tremor of cold. It was the deeper shudder that comes when the body has taken more pain than it can safely store and has nowhere else to put it.

"How many?" he asked her.

She blinked. "How many what?"

"Ribs. Broken. You count them as well as I. How many?"

"Two for certain," she said. "Maybe three. Left side. One of them...grinds."

"Do you feel sharp points when you breathe in?" he asked. "Like a knife moving in time with the air?"

"Yes."

"Then your lung is pierced," he said. His tone did not change. "We fix that first. Relax."

"Easier said—"

"Lass," he said. There was iron in the word. "Do you trust me?"

She swallowed. "Yes."

"Then breathe as I tell you and do not fight me. In. Out. Again. Good. Keep that rhythm. Do not falter unless I say."

He shifted, braced his right hand above her sternum, fingers spread. His left hand hovered over her side. The crooked finger of it trembled slightly.

"Kit," he said. "Hold her shoulders. Gently, but firm. You as well, girl. On her hips. Do not let her arch."

Elisah made a noise halfway between a laugh and a groan. "You are...giving orders to the dying, old stone?"

"Not dying," he said. "Not while I am here."

I moved behind Jaime's head. I slid my hands under her shoulders, thumbs along her collarbones, fingers curled around the muscles that lay just inside her shoulder blades. Her hair stuck to my wrists, damp with sweat.

"Ready," she whispered. Her gaze flicked up to meet mine. Her pupils were wide. There were tiny red bursts in the whites of her eyes from blood vessels gone under too much strain. "Do it."

Rygial closed his eyes.

For a moment, nothing changed. The swamp ticked and dripped. Elisah's breath wheezed. The faint heat from the drake's corpse breathed across my neck.

Then the air shifted.

I felt it first as pressure, like being under a shallow wave just before it breaks. The hairs along my forearms rose. Inside my sinuses a peculiar ache bloomed, the way it does when the weather turns on a high mountain. Rygial's beard stirred in a breeze that did not touch my skin.

The light in the cavern took on a peculiar cast. It did not grow brighter. If anything, it dimmed. But the edges of things sharpened. Water droplets stole color from the torchlight as they fell. Shadows thickened under bones and under Rygial's brow. Time did not slow or quicken in any way I could name, but it felt as if the world had inhaled and held that breath.

Rygial began to speak.

The words were not in any tongue I had heard from him before. They were harsh and soft at once, full of consonants that grated like stone on stone and vowels that slid like oil. His voice stayed low, but each syllable seemed to land somewhere just behind my ears. The cadence of it did not match the breathing rhythm he had set for Jaime. It matched something deeper. Heartbeats. The slow drip of water. The nearly inaudible, constant settling of the swamp's bones.

Under my hands, Jaime trembled. Not from fear. This tremor ran through the muscle in a fine shudder that matched the unseen rhythm Rygial wove.

Her bruise changed.

At first I thought it was only my eyes adjusting to the strange light. But no. The deep purple at its center lightened toward red. The edges, which had been only faint green and yellow, darkened, then began to fade. Like watching a flower wilt and then bud in reverse, except it all happened just beneath the skin.

Jaime hissed through her teeth. Her right hand clawed at the mud. "Ribs," she gasped. "They...move."

"Do not fight it," Rygial said. His voice did not break the chant. The words rode over and under it somehow. "Let them find their way back. You glued them wrong when you fell. I am just encouraging them toward the proper angle."

Something clicked under my fingers. A thin, precise sound, like a knuckle popping but deeper. Then another. I felt bone scrape bone, a grinding slide, then a sudden smoothness. Jaime cried out once, sharp, then bit it off so hard I saw the muscles in her jaw bulge.

Her breathing stuttered. Then it deepened by a fraction. The wet rattle at the bottom of it diminished. Not gone. But less like drowning. More like air forcing a passage where there had been none.

Elisah cursed under her breath. I did not look at her. All my attention sat on the shifting structures under Jaime's skin and on Rygial's face.

Lines deepened around his mouth as I watched. The small creases at the corners of his eyes, usually hidden under bristled brows, etched themselves deeper as if something were carving them with a knife from inside. His beard, always more gray than black, sprouted a new streak of pure white that began at his left temple and ran down through the hair above his ear in a single clean line.

Sweat beaded on his forehead and then did not fall. It hung there, quivering, as if the air around his skin were too thick to let it drop. When it finally did, it fell faster than it should have, striking Jaime's tunic with a tiny sound out of proportion to its size.

Jaime's bruise had gone from purple to a blotch of angry crimson now, then to a mottled yellow edged with green. Finally it settled into the sickly greenish-brown of someone two weeks past an injury. The swelling around it went down as I watched. The skin loosened from its taut drum-stretch to something closer to normal.

Her breathing steadied.

Rygial let his hands fall. The strange pressure in the air released all at once, like a held breath finally allowed to escape. The sound of dripping water rushed back in.

He sagged sideways. I moved without thinking. With one hand still on Jaime's shoulder, I shot the other out and caught him under the arm before he hit the mud. He weighed more than he looked. Like a stone wrapped in leather and old cloth.

"Gently," he muttered. "I am fragile."

"You are lying," I said.

"Yes," he said. He panted a little. "Help me to the other one before you let me die. Her lung will not patch itself."

We did it again with Elisah.

Her leg came first. Rygial cursed under his breath when he saw the angle of the bone. "You never do anything by half," he said to her.

"Would be...boring," she whispered. Her lips had gone pale. "If I die, you are...not allowed...to sell my knives."

"I will not sell them," he said. "I will bury them with you so some vulture does not cut itself on your poor edge maintenance."

He did not touch the broken shin at first. He set his hands above and below it without contact, then began the chant again. The air thickened. That same wrongness of light and sound folded around us.

This time the sensations were stronger. I felt itching deep in the bones of my own forearms as if some part of me answered the call against my will. The hair on the back of my neck stood. My tail lashed once, involuntary.

Under Elisah's skin, the protruding angle of bone slid. There was a grinding noise, like rocks in a streambed forced against each other by a sudden swell of current. Her fingers dug into my sleeve until her nails pierced the fabric.

"Breathe," I said. "In and out."

"I will...stab you," she rasped.

"You can try when we are done."

The bulge of the bone smoothed. The wrong angle straightened by degrees. The skin over it bruised dark, then lightened, then blossomed into the same strange fast-forward of colors, aging the injury in moments instead of weeks.

Elisah's breaths came in quick, high gulps now. Each exhale rattled. Rygial's chant shifted. The rhythm changed. It slowed. The hair on my arms settled by a hair.

"Lung now," he murmured.

He pressed his left hand very lightly against her side, just below the armpit. His right hovered above. His eyes were shut so tightly that wrinkles fanned from the corners like cracks in dry mud.

I felt it before she did. A faint bubbling under my palm where it lay across her upper chest. Then a sudden, peculiar sucking sensation as if the flesh beneath my hand had opened to pull at the air. Her next breath came easier. The rattle lessened. She coughed once, hard, and a clot of dark blood and swamp water shot from her mouth, spattering the mud.

She stared at it, chest heaving, then managed to laugh weakly.

"Disgusting," she said.

"Lovely," Rygial corrected. "Proof I am still worth what you pay me."

"We do not...pay you," she whispered.

"Yes," he said. "You owe me."

The white in his beard spread as I watched. It crept along one of the existing gray streaks like frost along a windowpane, whitening hair that had been only salt-and-pepper moments before. The skin at his throat sagged a fraction more. His hands shook as he let them drop.

"That is enough," he said when I opened my mouth. "I am not healing myself. One of you must carry me if something else tries to eat us."

"No more?" Jaime asked, voice still hoarse. "Rygial, your hip—"

"Is mine to live with," he said. His tone cut off further questions. "I know its tricks. I will not bargain with my own time for mere comfort. Help me sit before I fall."

It took both Jaime and me to ease him down into a more stable position on the hummock, his back against a ridge of stone half-buried under the mud. When he was settled, he leaned his head back and closed his eyes. His chest rose and fell in slow, deliberate breaths.

The whole process had taken perhaps an hour. Perhaps less. The swamp light had not changed enough to mark time clearly. The torches guttered lower, their fat nearly gone, but that could have been from the damp alone.

Jaime pressed a hand cautiously against her ribs. She winced, then frowned, as if surprised the pain did not blossom into its former intensity.

"Hurts," she said. "But not like before."

"Good," Rygial said without opening his eyes. "You will remember to be modest next time you fling yourself at something with that many teeth."

Elisah flexed her foot. Her brow furrowed.

"My toes tingle," she said.

"They would," Rygial said. "You forgot how to use them for a moment."

She touched her side, prodded gently, then stopped when her breath caught.

"Still broken?" I asked.

"Not broken," she said slowly. "Sore. Like I took a club. No knife in there anymore."

"Then my work here is done," Rygial said. His head lolled a little to the side. His eyelids fluttered. "Wake me when you find something worth my last years."

We let him rest.

The swamp pressed close around the respite his magic had bought. The drip from the ceiling kept time, indifferent. Somewhere beyond the ring of half-submerged bones, something large moved in the water. It did not come closer. The echo of the drake's death still hung in whatever passed for memory in this place.

My own body hummed. The bruises I knew I had taken in the fight—on my shoulders where the tail had clipped me, along my ribs where a claw had skidded—throbbed with a hot, pulsing ache. I rolled my shoulder and felt something in there tick, a small realignment. The itch of healing crawled under my skin, deep and insistent. Rygial had splashed a little of his working over me and Jaime when it spilled into the air. He had not aimed it at us. It had found us anyway.

"You two can stand?" I asked.

Jaime pushed herself upright. Her hand left her side. She grimaced, but no longer moved like a cracked piece of pottery afraid of shattering with each step.

"I can move," she said. "Not fast. Not gracefully. But I will not slow us by much."

Elisah planted both palms beside her hips and levered herself up onto her elbows. Her face tightened as her mended leg took a little weight, but she did not swear aloud. That alone told me how much it hurt.

"If a frog breathes on this bone, I will scream," she said. "But I can stand. I think. With help. You will not get a somersault from me today."

"Tragedy," I said.

Jaime's gaze went to the drake's corpse. Her jaw worked once.

"We need supplies," she said after a moment. Her voice had that flat, practical edge it took on after a shock. "And anything of value this thing has pulled down here. Then we get out before whatever else lives in this swamp realizes there is a vacancy at the top."

"Elric," Elisah said. "You do not look like you should be lifting anything heavier than Rygial's bad mood."

My legs still felt hollow. My hands had stopped shaking, but there was a lingering tremor in them if I held them away from my body.

"I can manage," I said. "I am less broken than either of you."

"Debatable," she said under her breath, but did not argue further.

We started with the obvious.

The drake's hoard, such as it was, scattered in an uneven halo around its body. It did not glimmer as the stories said dragons' hoards did. There were no mountains of coin, no cascades of jewels. Just the detritus of years. Half-sunk chests, their wood warped and split. Leather sacks rotted through. Stray pieces of metal armor, some still wrapped around bones, some bent and twisted like cooked reeds. Bits of harness and tack. Broken blades. A dozen shoes with no mates.

We picked through it with hands and the tips of our weapons. The mud clung to everything, thick as congealed blood. Each step sent slow ripples through the shallow pools, disturbing slicks of fat and oil that floated there. The bones moved underfoot, clicking softly. Some were old enough to crumble when we touched them. Others were disturbingly fresh.

Flies had already found the new rents in the drake's hide. They landed in black smudges, their buzz a low, hungry drone. The smell of its opened chest deepened into something almost unbearable. There was meat in there enough to feed a village for weeks, but I knew better than to think it safe. The anchor stone had sat there. Its influence would not vanish as quickly as its physical shell.

"Here," Elisah said from near one of the half-submerged chests. I looked up.

She had moved with her usual quiet despite the limp. She stood with one foot braced on a stone, the other kept gingerly straight. The chest at her feet had split along one seam, its contents spilling into the water: rotted cloth, greened copper buckles, a dark stain that might once have been velvet.

Among the soggy mess lay a sword.

At first I took it for any other piece of long steel ruined by the swamp. Then the light caught the blade and slid along it without the dull interruption of rust. A thin line of silvered sheen ran the length of its edge, clean and bright despite the muck that slimed its fuller.

The hilt was plain, no jewels. Wrapped in leather that had darkened but not rotted, it bore the mark of wear in the places fingers would naturally rest. The crossguard was a simple bar of steel. At each end, a tiny engraving of a lion's head stared out, half-filled with mud.

"Elric," she said. "Come take a look. My leg will not appreciate me wrestling that thing one-handed."

I reached down and closed my fingers around the hilt.

It felt wrong in my hand at first. Not wrong in a cursed way, but wrong because it was too well-balanced, too ready. I had grown used to the small imperfections of my own cheaper blade—the slight bias to the left, the tiny shift of weight toward the tip. This sword had none of that. Its center of gravity sat exactly where it should. When I lifted it, the blade came out of the water with a sucking sound, shedding mud in thick sheets.

Under the slime, the steel shone. Not mirror-bright but with the low, even glow of good metal well tended. No chips marred its edge. A faint ripple in the surface spoke of pattern-welding, the marriage of different irons folded and refolded. Whoever had made it had done so with care and time. I could feel that craftsmanship thrumming up the hilt into my arm like a note held in the air.

"What do you think?" Elisah asked.

"I think someone loved this weapon," I said.

Jaime had picked her way over to us. She watched as I wiped the blade against a relatively clean patch of my tattered shirt.

"That is Lionel work," she said quietly. Her fingers brushed one of the lion heads on the crossguard. "High-forge. See the style of the engraving? They favor that elongated snout."

"You would know," Elisah said.

"It does not mean it came from the capital directly," Jaime replied. "Their steel travels. But whoever lost this...they were not poor."

"Not anymore," Elisah said.

I swung the sword lightly. It moved through the damp air with less resistance than I expected. I knew instantly however that this blade was not mine. I turned the blade in my hand and held the handle out to Jaime, who took it gently. With a quiet nod I pulled Maximus' blade out from it's scabbard and eyed it. It had a new sheen from the blood of the Drake which did not seem to go away. At that moment I decided the sword was truly mine.

"Drakeslayer." I said simply, giving it a name, now it was a legacy of both myself and Maximus. I could stop referring the old blade to it's former master. The metal seemed to sing with me at my claiming. A ritual in the blood of dragons that I had by some instinct invoked but for a long time would never truly understand.

Further among the junk, I found a shield half-buried under a collapsed heap of rusted mail. The boss glinted dimly under the grime. I heaved it free.

The leather straps on the back had gone stiff but not entirely rotten. The wood showed signs of swelling, but no soft spots. Someone had oiled it well before fate delivered it to the swamp.

On its face, beneath layers of mud and algae, a design showed. I wiped at it with the edge of my cloak until the lines emerged: a lion rampant, crowned, on a field divided by a diagonal stripe. The paint had faded but still clung. The lion's eyes had once been picked out in red. Now they stared blind.

"Lionel," Jaime said again. Her voice had gone quiet.

The crest was not only Lionel's lion. It bore a small addition in one corner: three vertical lines, like tally marks.

"That mark," Elisah said, peering over my shoulder. "Company insignia?"

"Regiment," Jaime murmured. Her eyes had gone far away. "Third Pike. That is their sign."

"Your father's regiment," Elisah said. It was not a question.

Jaime's jaw clenched. "One of them."

Silence settled for a moment. The drip of water filled it.

I hefted it on my arm and found it balanced quite well with Drakeslayer, they were of course both parts of a set made for Lionel soldiers, so that fit. The crest itself, the Lion's Claw that could so easily be mistaken for a Drake's claw to my new experience, felt right to me and I slung it over my back. "I think I'll use it. That way you can focus on offense."

We found coins too. Not many. The drake had cared nothing for shaped metal beyond what it could not spit out. They lay scattered through the muck, dulled and blackened. Some had fused together in clumps where time and moisture had welded them. We scraped them into a torn bit of cloth. Copper, mostly, with a handful of worn silver and two bright gold pieces that had somehow resisted tarnish.

Rygial roused when he heard the telltale clink.

"My second favorite sound," he murmured, eyes still half-closed.

"What is your first?" Elisah asked.

"Silence from the mouths of adolescents," he said. He cracked one eye at me. "Do not squander those on sweets, kit. We will need bribes more than sugar where we are going."

Near one collapsed leather satchel, I found a round object the size of my palm. At first I mistook it for a smooth stone. When I picked it up, gears rattled inside. Mud filled the hairline gap where two halves met.

"A trinket," I called to Rygial, tossing it lightly in my hand.

He opened his eyes fully then. For the first time since the fight, something like emotion beyond exhaustion crossed his face.

"Do not throw that," he snapped, sharper than he had spoken all day.

I froze. The object settled into my palm. I wiped it carefully on the inside of my shirt.

Under the mud, a clock face emerged. What glass it had once possessed had shattered or dissolved. The metal ring that had held it bore etchings worn nearly smooth by time. The hands inside had rusted, stopped at some meaningless arrangement. Their tips were delicate as insect legs.

Rygial reached for it with both hands. His fingers shook, but not from fatigue this time.

"I thought I had lost this craft for good," he murmured. He cradled the broken timepiece the way a man might cradle a small, wounded animal. "Look at you."

"What is it?" Jaime asked.

"A watch," he said. "From before. When we still thought we could measure the world properly." His thumb traced the cracked face. His expression went somewhere we could not follow. "She will not tick again. But perhaps I can coax one last secret from her bones."

He tucked it into the inner pocket of his coat with surprising care, patting it once as if to reassure it.

We found more bones as we moved outward from the drake's body. A child's skull, small and round, lodged in the fork of a root. A hand still wrapped in the remains of a leather glove, ring bones encircled with greened copper. A ribcage that had been partially crushed, its armor dented inward.

Most were old enough that they held no smell. A few still clung to tatters of flesh and cloth that oozed when we disturbed them.

And then there was the fresher one.

It lay half on a flat rock near the edge of the lair where the muddy ground gave way to a clearer pool. The upper body had escaped full submersion. The lower half had not. Water lapped gently at the waist, swaying a tangle of fabric and weed.

The smell found us before we saw him. A sweet, rotting scent that was not the drake. Human. The kind that coils at the back of the tongue and settles there, sour.

Jaime stopped dead. Her back went stiff. I followed her gaze.

The man might have been in his thirties once. It was hard to say. Death and the swamp had worked on him. The flesh of his face had sunk, skin tight against bone. His eyes were gone. The sockets gaped, half-filled with cloudy water. His lips had pulled back in a rictus that exposed teeth stained the color of tea.

He wore mail, or had once. The shirt had been of good make. The links that remained uncorroded showed fine craft. Rust ate most of it now. The leather straps that had held it together sagged.

Over the mail, or where it had lain, he still wore a tabard. The cloth had clung to his chest and stomach in dark, stiff folds. Mud and algae coated it, obscuring pattern. Jaime stepped closer. She knelt in the muck without seeming to feel it.

Her hands moved with a terrible delicacy as she peeled the fabric away from the dead man's chest. A faint gasp left her mouth.

Beneath the grime, faint but unmistakable, the Lion of Lionel roared. The diagonal stripe cut it. In one corner, the same triple-tally mark as on the shield.

Third Pike.

Jaime's fingers hovered over the symbol but did not touch it.

His hair, what remained, had been light. Hard to say if blond or gray. The swamp water leached color from everything. A close-cropped beard still clung in patches to his jaw and chin. His nose had been broken at least once in life. A thin white scar ran from his right temple into his hairline, puckering the skin.

I had never seen Jaime's father. I had only the rough sketches her mother had carried, drawn by some camp artist for coin. A man with a broad, laughing face, the lion crest clear on his chest, a casual hand on a spear. The likeness here had been eaten away by time and water. The lines were not the same. Or perhaps they were, under the ruin.

"His pack," Jaime said. Her voice was flat. "Help me turn him."

We did.

His body came up from the water with a sucking sound. Gas rose in small, iridescent bubbles from where his belly had bloated and then burst. The smell hit harder. I swallowed against the reflex to gag.

A leather pack, strapped across his back under the mail, came free with some effort. The straps had swollen and fused to the cloth in places. Jaime's knife made quick, precise work of them. She did not look at his face again.

The pack squelched when she set it on the rock. It had been oiled well before he died. Enough of that care remained that it had not simply dissolved. She slit it open along a seam.

Inside, things had not fared as badly. The outer layers of cloth and paper had rotted to mush. Beneath them, wrapped in oiled leather, a smaller bundle sat.

She opened that one more slowly.

I watched her hands, not her face. Her fingers did not shake. They moved with the same control I had seen when she drew a bow at full draw in a high wind.

Inside the second bundle lay a book.

Not a large one. The size to fit in a coat pocket or a saddlebag. Its cover bore the stains of oil and time but had held. The edges of the pages had darkened, but when she thumbed them, they parted cleanly.

She turned it so that any water might run off, then opened to the first page.

The ink had blurred in some places but remained legible. Small, tight, regular script. I did not recognize the hand. She scanned the first lines.

Her face did not change. That scared me more than any scream would have.

"What is it?" Elisah asked from behind us. Her voice came slower. She had taken her time crossing the treacherous ground on her mended leg.

"Journal," Jaime said. "Field notes. He was...this man was...recording something."

She flipped forward, pages whispering. Her eyes moved quickly. Now and then she paused, jaw tightening almost imperceptibly.

"Anything useful?" I asked.

"Mentions of...sites," she said slowly. "Strange stones in the swamp. Reports of men vanishing near them. Someone named Kerran giving orders to 'secure all anchor stones at any cost.'" She swallowed. "He wrote that phrase twice. Underlined it."

"Anchor stone," Elisah said softly. "Like the thing in that beast's chest."

Jaime's mouth pressed thin. She nodded once.

"He also mentions a tower," she went on. "To the northeast. A...monitoring post. He calls it that. Says, 'If the chain fails, the tower will be the first to know.'"

"The chain?" I asked. The words felt heavy in my mouth.

She scanned again. "He writes it several times. 'The chain must hold.' 'I fear the chain will snap.' Nothing more specific. As if he assumed he would remember the rest without writing it." Her lips twitched humorlessly. "Optimistic."

"Does he sign it?" Elisah asked. "Name anywhere?"

Jaime's thumb had reached the last few pages. The ink there had blurred more than the rest, as if water had seeped in at some point and then dried. She squinted, turning the book slightly toward the failing torchlight.

I saw her eyes catch on something. Her pupils tightened. The skin at the corners of her mouth trembled once, quickly.

She closed the book.

"Any name?" I asked softly.

She shook her head. "No. Either he did not sign or the ink is gone." Her voice stayed level. That more than anything else told me that she was lying.

"Jaime," I said. "The crest. The regiment. Your mother said—"

"It is not him," she said. The words came too quickly. Flat as falling stones. "He is too young. My father would be older. And his hair was darker. The nose is wrong. Anyone can wear a tabard."

"El—" Elisah began.

"It is not him," Jaime repeated. She slipped the journal inside her coat, tucking it into an inner pocket near her heart. Her fingers pressed it there once, briefly. "We do not know. We cannot know. So it is not him. End of discussion."

Silence spread in the space after that declaration. The swamp's persistent sounds seemed louder for it. A frog croaked once, then fell quiet again.

"As you say," I said. I did not believe her. I do not know if she believed herself.

Later, much later, when I had read that journal myself by firelight, when I knew the shape of the hand that had written it, I would trace the loops of the letters and hear her voice when she said those words, and I would understand a little better the cruelty of hope. But in that lair, with the smell of the drake and the dead man in our noses, I only knew that pressing her then would break something that could not easily be mended.

"We should burn him," Elisah said quietly.

"In a swamp?" Rygial's voice drifted over, dry again. He had pulled himself closer on his backside while we worked, using his good leg and arms. "With what fuel? Your hair?"

"We cannot leave him like this," she said.

"Jaime?" I asked.

Her gaze had gone distant, fixed somewhere beyond the cavern roof. "The swamp will take him," she said. "It has had him for a long time already. It will not help him now to char his bones. We remember. That is enough."

She stood abruptly, almost too quickly for someone who had taken a broken rib inside her chest an hour before. She swayed. I stepped forward, but she steadied herself with a hand on the rock.

"We have what we came for," she said. "More, now. The sword. The shield. The notes." She touched the journal under her coat briefly. "We know there is a tower. We know someone is playing with anchor stones like children with knives. We cannot fix the drake, or him, or my mother. We can go to the tower."

"Now?" Elisah asked. "After a nap, perhaps? A small sleep? I promise not to snore."

"Soon," Jaime said. "As soon as we are out of this hole and on firmer ground. Every moment we linger here is one more for some other thing to smell the blood and come."

Her logic was sound. I did not want to stay in that lair a breath longer than needed. The air felt fouler by the minute, thick with the exhalations of too much death.

We gathered what we could carry.

The new sword went to Jaime as she had lost hers somewhere in the chaos. At my insistence so did the shield, she needed the protection more than I seemed to. The bundle of coins we split roughly, not by exact count but by weight. Elisah tucked hers into hidden pouches. Rygial, once hauled to his feet with much muttered commentary, took none for himself, only patted the pocket where the broken watch lay.

"Time is payment enough," he said. "And I have spent too much of mine today."

We left the drake where it lay.

Its body slumped a little more as we passed, the ruined chest caving in under its own weight. Steam no longer rose from the wound. The flies were bolder now. They blackened the edges of the ragged hole, their bodies a dark, shifting collar.

We did not look back at the dead man on the rock.

The tunnel out of the lair seemed narrower than when we had come in. The wet stone pressed close, sweating. Roots dangled from the ceiling, dripping cold water down the backs of our necks. The torchlight wavered, its oil almost gone. Shadows flocked at the edge of it, waiting.

Rygial leaned heavily on me with each step, his weight a constant, grinding pull on my tired muscles. My legs burned. My breath came faster than I wanted. Each inhale brought the heavy, green scent of the swamp, layered over with the fading metallic tang of dragon blood.

Jaime went ahead, one hand on the tunnel wall, the other near the hilt of the knife at her belt. Her shoulders were tight. The set of her neck told me her mind was not in that tunnel, not entirely. It was already miles to the northeast, climbing some unseen tower.

Elisah limped behind us, using her daggers as makeshift crutches when the ground grew treacherous. She still found breath for a muttered complaint now and then, more for the rhythm of it than the content.

We emerged into the open swamp.

Dusk had thickened while we were below. The sky showed through the broken canopy as a smear of bruised purple fading toward black. The air felt cooler here, though it was still heavy with moisture. The drone of insects rose higher, a constant, dizzying hum.

Mist coiled low over the water, hiding roots and unseen holes. The trees crouched close, their trunks swollen and gnarled, draped in curtains of hanging moss that stirred in some faint breeze we could not feel.

Behind us, the hole that led down into the drake's lair gaped black among the twisted roots. No smoke rose from it. No light. If not for the faint urn of churned mud around its lip and the drag marks of our boots, it might have been any other dark in the swamp.

"Tower to the northeast," Jaime said. She did not raise her voice. She did not need to. We all watched her now. "We follow the firmer ground where we can. Avoid open water, but do not get lost in the thickets. Rygial, can you still tell north?"

"If the sun has not changed its mind in the last hour, yes," he said. He lifted his head, squinting up through the shredded canopy. "There. That faint brightness. The day dying that way. North is left of that. Good enough for a march in a swamp with no paths."

"Then northeast is there," she said, pointing.

The direction she chose led along a low ridge of hummocked earth where roots tangled thick. It would be slower going than along the open channels, but safer.

"No mourning," Elisah said softly as we started moving. "No cairn. No words."

"We do not have stones enough here for cairns," Jaime replied. "And words..." She trailed off. "The tower first. Then we will see what words there are to speak."

The hollow in my chest, the one the anchor stone's destruction had carved, throbbed in time with my heartbeat as we walked. My limbs felt both heavy and light, as if some part of my weight had been left behind in that lair and something else had taken its place, unbalanced, not yet settled.

My hands ached. The skin across my knuckles felt tight, stretched over something unfamiliar. When I flexed my fingers, the tendons stood out sharper than before, like cords under taut cloth. The backs of my hands itched furiously.

I scratched absently as we went, expecting bug bites. My claws rasped against something not like skin.

When I looked down, I saw them.

Small scales. Flat and red, not the deep stone-red of the drake but brighter, fresher. They clustered in irregular patches across the backs of my hands, each the size of a fingernail at most. They overlapped faintly in places, catching what little light filtered through the mist. At the edges, where scale met skin, the flesh looked raw, irritated, as if the new growth had forced its way through from underneath.

I touched one with the tip of a claw. It felt hard. Warmer than the surrounding skin. It did not move.

"Elric?" Jaime's voice came from ahead. "You are lagging."

"I am coming," I said. My voice shook. I did not think anyone else heard it over the insects.

Under my shirt, along my ribs, a similar itch crawled. I did not lift the cloth to check. Not yet. Each step scraped fabric against whatever lay there. The sensation was not pain. Not precisely. More like the awareness of teeth settling into new sockets.

A strand of hair fell into my eyes. I pushed it back. My fingers paused.

One lock, near my temple, shone not black-brown like the rest but silver. Not the dull silver of age, but a sharp, clean stripe like moonlight on metal. It did not lie flat. It curled slightly away from the others, as if it had its own ideas about gravity.

My eyes caught my reflection for an instant in a slick of still water at the edge of the path. The surface shivered as a tiny insect broke it, distorting the image. For a moment

I saw my own face as if through fog: the familiar angles, the wide-set cat's eyes, the dark pupils.

The gold at their edges was new.

It ringed the brown in a thin, luminous band, faint as yet, but there. Caught the last of the day's light and held it a second too long.

"Elric," Rygial said quietly at my side. "Later, you and I will speak."

"About?" I asked, though I knew.

"About what you did," he said. "About what you are doing now still. Scales do not lie."

"You saw?" I asked.

"I am not blind," he said. "And I am not entirely senile. That thing in the cavern. When you broke the stone." He hesitated, choosing his words with unusual care. "You did not move like a boy then. Nor like any beast I have hunted."

From ahead, Jaime spoke without turning. "We saw it too," she said. "The way you...lit. You were...glowing. Not like fire around you. From inside. Like your bones were coals."

Elisah snorted softly. "You ran up that beast's chest like there was no gravity," she said. "And your claws—" She stopped. "It was not normal. Effective, yes. But not normal."

I remembered moments. Flashes. The feel of muscle and scale under my hands, yielding where they should not. The way the world had narrowed to the stone in the drake's chest, everything else a blur around it. The absence of fear. Not courage. That would have required the presence of fear to overcome. This had been...nothing.

"I do not remember all of it," I said. That was true. More precisely, I remembered with a clarity that did not line up with how my body told me time had passed.

"Convenient," Elisah muttered.

"Not for me," I said. I kept my gaze on the path. The new weight of scales on my hands made the hilt of the new sword feel different where it rested against my palm. Less slippage. More surety.

"What do you feel now?" Rygial asked.

I searched for words.

"Different," I said finally. "Like...when you have worn a pair of boots for so long your feet forget they are there, and then you take them off and the ground feels wrong."

"Do you feel powerful?" he asked.

I considered that. The honest answer was complicated.

"I feel tired," I said. "And hollow. And like if I call on whatever that was again without knowing what it is, it will be less a tool and more a...fall. Like stepping off a cliff and trusting that something will build itself under my feet before I hit the bottom."

"Do not step, then," he said. His voice had no softness, but it did have care. "Not until we understand the ground beneath you. Fire that does not burn you still burns those around you if you wave it without thought."

"I will try," I said.

The hollow in my chest pulsed. It did not feel like absence so much as like a space held for something that had not yet arrived. As if my body expected a weight that was no longer there and had not received the message.

The swamp thickened around us as night fell. The insects' song shifted, lower. Frogs took up a call-and-response between pools. Things moved in the dark beyond the limited reach of our one remaining torch, now held aloft by Elisah despite her complaints. Eyes glinted now and then, too high or too low or too many to be comforting.

Jaime walked ahead, straight-backed, every line of her body angled toward a point none of us could see. The journal lay against her ribs, each step pressing it into her. I imagined the words inside: chain, tower, anchor. Her father's name, whether written or not, stamped between them.

"We go to the tower," she had said. No mourning. No discussion.

So we went.

We left a dead drake cooling in its own blood. We left a man who might have been her father to sink slowly back into the mud that had half-claimed him already. We carried a better sword, a shield with a lion crest, a handful of coins, a broken watch, and a book full of warnings we did not yet understand.

The relief of having survived sat in me like a stone I could not quite swallow. Over it, a new dread layered itself, fine as mist, insidious. Something had changed in the world in that lair. In me. In Jaime. In all of us.

We walked northeast into the dark, into the damp, toward a tower I had never seen but would come to know too well, our boots sucking at each step, our breaths loud in our own ears. The swamp watched us go and kept its secrets a little longer.

# Chapter 19

## A Hand Behind the Monsters

WE FOUND THE ROCK by accident.

The swamp thinned as we pushed northeast, sodden peat giving way to a smear of firmer ground that only mostly tried to eat our boots. Fog dragged itself along the reeds. The sun was just a dull smear behind cloud and smoke, the memory of daylight rather than the thing itself.

Jaime was the one who saw the stone. "There."

At first it was only another hump in the dark. Then the mist shifted, and the shape came clear: a low, moss-slicked outcrop like the hunched back of some buried giant. Bracken clung to its flanks, the top was bare, slick in places with old lichen and bird droppings.

"High ground," Elisah said, voice rough with fatigue. "Such as it is."

Rygial squinted up at it. The new lines on his face were cruel in the dying light. "Back to the rock. Only two approaches. I've slept worse."

We all had. No one argued.

Climbing it was an awkward scramble more than anything. My fingers, raw from the drake's scales and stone, slipped once on the wet surface, and something in my chest gave a small, hollow protest that I pretended not to hear. We hauled packs up by straps, pushed each other when legs trembled. By the time we were all on top, my breath sat hot and thin in my throat and my hands shook with more than cold.

The outcrop's crown made a rough crescent with the middle scooped lower. If you crouched, the rock would hide most of your body from the swamp. Trees ghosted around us, black trunks lost in fog below the waist. Somewhere, water grumbled to itself.

"We can't risk much fire," Jaime said. Her voice was hoarse but level. "Smoke will sit in this muck and glow like a beacon."

"Just enough to keep our fingers," Elisah answered. "Kit'll start purring if he gets too cold."

"I don't..." I began.

Rygial cut in. "Jaime's right. Small as you can manage, girl. No green wood. We burn the dry we carried or not at all."

Jaime already had her hands on the bundle of twigs and kindling she'd insisted we stuff into one of the packs. Her movements were clipped, almost too efficient. She arranged the little pyramid with care that bordered on reverence. When she sparked the tinder, she held her breath as if the flame might take offense and flee.

It caught. A little lick of orange, barely a fist high, breathing slow and quiet. Hardly any smoke. It threw out a mean, clean heat that did little more than announce how cold the rest of the night was going to be.

We huddled around it like beggars.

Cold rations again. There was dried meat, tougher than my boots, and biscuit dense enough to hammer nails. I tore strips of both with my teeth and chewed past the ache in my jaw. My fingers ached worse, though not entirely from the climb.

In the skittering firelight, my hands did not look like hands.

I saw them when I raised the meat to my mouth. The scales along the back of my fingers had deepened from a raw, inflamed red to something darker, wine-dark at the edges, catching light along each small, ridged plate. In the wavering orange, they gleamed faintly, as if they owned their own coal-dull glow independent of the fire, banking embers under skin.

The sight made the hollow behind my sternum clench. It felt as if someone had reached inside my chest and scooped out a piece that should never have been touched. A shape of absence, more definite than anything solid.

I curled my fingers into my palms. Claws. Nails, I told myself, just nails. Digging into callused flesh. My sleeves were already as far down as they'd go, but I tucked my hands into my armpits, hunching in as if against a deeper cold.

No one was speaking. The only sound was the small, decorous crackle of the fire and the distant murmur of swamp water. Each of us stared at either the flames or the dark beyond them. The air between us was thick with the things we weren't saying: the smell of the lair still in our nostrils, the memory of hot scales, the flash of teeth.

Maximus's eyes as he disappeared under that wing. The villagers' faces as the drake dragged them away. The anchor stone breaking under my hands, not like rock but like something bone-deep and wrong giving way.

Jaime sat across from me, the journal resting in her lap like something fragile and heavy both. It was still bound shut with its strap, she hadn't opened it since we pulled it from the dead man's chest days ago. The Third Pike shield lay beside her, propped so the regiment insignia watched us like a single painted eye.

Her gaze wasn't on either. She stared past the fire, jaw tight, lips pressed so thin they had almost no color. The only log softer than her eyes was the one feeding our flame.

Elisah stretched out one leg with great care, rubbing at her mended thigh. The soreness there was written plainly in the little purse of her mouth. She did not complain, she never did. Every so often her dark eyes flicked to me, then away, like a cat tracking something out of the corner of her vision. Her hair still smelled faintly of the marsh, of mildew and smoke.

Rygial sat with his back literally to the rock, as if ceding the job of guard to something bigger. His hands were steepled under his beard, fingers worrying at one another in a restless, involuntary pattern. His gaze kept returning to me as well, but unlike Elisah's quick checks, this was a long, slow watchfulness, uncharacteristically quiet. The lines bracketing his mouth were deeper than they had been a week ago. The white in his beard had spread like frost.

For a dwarf who had spent two centuries and more bending time to his will, he suddenly looked hunted by it.

I pretended not to notice. It's a skill teenagers have, it keeps us alive longer than it should.

Silence stretched. The swamp breathed around us. It would have been easy to let exhaustion drag us down there and then, to postpone choices until morning. We had survived the lair. That felt like more than we had any right to claim.

Instead, Jaime raised her head.

"I'm going to see," she said.

No one needed to ask what.

She ran her thumb along the edge of the journal, then unbuckled the strap with a soft leather whisper. For a moment she only held it open in both hands, staring at the first page. Whatever she saw there was hidden from me in the flicker.

Her fingers trembled once. Not much. Enough.

The little fire sent shadows stuttering over her face as she began to read.

"'Third Pike, Fort Kelran, day...'" She squinted, brought the page closer to the fire. "'Day 6 of first watch. Orders received from Centurion Kerran. Anchor stones to be set at marked coordinates by any means necessary. Priority: absolute.'"

The word lodged in the air like a stone dropped into shallow water. Anchor.

My chest seemed to echo around it.

She turned a page. The leather creaked in the stillness. "He writes like an officer," she muttered, mostly to herself. "Short. All facts. No..." Her mouth compressed, and she forced it back to neutral. "'Squad morale holding. Locals resent requisitions. Kerran insists time is critical. Stones must be placed before first thaw.'"

Rygial's head dipped, the motion small but sharp.

Elisah's lips curved without humor. "Always time for the locals to resent having their lives torn up," she said. "Nice to know some things don't rot with the monsters."

Jaime ignored the comment, eyes scanning line after line. "Here. 'Anchor stones react strongly near old growth and deep water. They hum when brought close together. Kerran says that means they're linking as intended.'"

I could hear the hum again. The way the stone in the lair had sung at the back of my teeth before I shattered it. It had been more feeling than sound, a pressure like a finger in the center of my bones.

"Anchor stones," I said, before I could stop myself. My voice sounded raw.

Jaime's eyes flicked up, met mine, then returned to the page. She read on.

"'Reports from tower: increased predator activity in sector three. Kerran pleased. Says it confirms amplification function. Notes from quartermaster: requisition more chains, more manacles. Creatures getting harder to control.'"

"Elaborate hunting," Elisah said softly. "They were...making them worse. On purpose."

Jaime's hands clenched around the journal. Her knuckles stood out white. "He keeps using the same phrases," she said, forcing detachment into her tone like stuffing into a wound. "'Amplifying natural aggression.' 'Drawing corruption out where we can see it.' 'Monitoring post will log responses and relay data to the fort.'"

"The tower," Rygial murmured. "We knew it was watching something. Not what."

More pages turned. The journal was not thick, but somehow it seemed to go on longer than it had any right to, words collapsing into one another. Jaime's voice stayed even, only the faint tremor at the edge of certain sentences betrayed her.

"'Encountered resistance from village near site three. Locals claim stones are attracting "evil." Priest tried to smash one with holy symbol. Minor injuries to sergeant before containment. Kerran's orders: secure stone at any cost. If locals persist, relocate them.'"

Relocate. I thought of the empty houses, doors hanging open like broken mouths.

"Elric," Jaime said without looking at me. "The village. The drake. It wasn't just...chance."

"I know," I said. I had felt it, without words, when my hands closed on the anchor stone below the monster and the wrongness had leapt for me like a live thing. "Keep reading."

She swallowed. The fire popped, spitting a small spray of sparks that died halfway to Elisah's boots.

"'Progress report to fort: five stones placed along projected perimeter, two more en route. Monitoring post at old tower fully staffed. Kerran satisfied but pushes for increased tempo. Says: "Chain must be complete before the thaw. We can't afford another lapse."'"

"Chain," Rygial repeated softly. "A linked array. Of course."

Jaime's eyes moved faster now, scanning for particular words. Her hand found the Third Pike shield beside her and rested on it as if unconsciously seeking something solid.

"'Day 19. Unusual readings from stone near swamp basin. Corruption levels higher than expected.'" She licked her lips. "'Creatures responding beyond projected parameters, even docile species showing increased aggression. Monitoring post recommends temporary cessation of anchor activation. Kerran denies request. Quote: "We only see what they're truly capable of when limits are broken."'"

Elisah's mouth twisted. "Of course he did."

My stomach clenched around the hard biscuit. Outside the tiny circle of our fire, the dark seemed to listen.

Jaime's next breath shook. She flattened the journal page under her fingers. "The name's everywhere," she said, lower. "Kerran. Giving orders. Countersigning reports. It's all 'as per Kerran.' 'On Kerran's authority.'"

She flipped ahead, a corner of the page tore under the suddenness of her hand. Her jaw tightened further.

Rygial watched her with a look I had never seen on him before. Not pity. He didn't do pity. Something like regret, or apology, or simply the weary recognition of one more young life colliding with a truth it had never asked for.

"Here," Jaime said at last. Her voice lost some of its steadiness. "'Day 27. Anchor at swamp basin overperforming.'" A humorless sound escaped her throat at the choice of word. "'Monitoring post reports subject, classified "swamp drake" by naturalists, is no longer following bait protocols. It has begun slaughtering indiscriminately, including chains, handlers. Stones continue to hum. Request to deactivate stones goes unanswered.'"

The little fire hissed as a drop of something, swamp moisture or a tear from someone's face, fell into it.

She read on, faster now, each sentence another blow. "'Day 29. The chain is breaking. Stones no longer responsive to our runes. Corruption factor exceeded all estimates. Creatures turning on each other, on us. Kerran missing, presumed in tower or at fort. No orders received.'"

Her fingers grew white on the leather again.

"'Day 30. We've lost control. They're turning on us. Those still sound want to flee, but where can we go? The stones are singing all the time now. Can't sleep. Feels like they're...'" She faltered, mouthing the next word before forcing it out. "'...calling.'"

Silence again, thick and close. The swamp made small, wet noises in the dark.

I tasted stone dust at the back of my tongue.

"There's no signature," Jaime said, after a moment. Her throat worked. "No 'yours faithfully.' No name. Just, military shorthand. Coordinates. Supply lists. Casualties." Her thumb brushed one list of names, lingering for a heartbeat on one entry. "They were all Third Pike. Same as the dead man in the mud. Same as this shield."

"And the sword," Elisah added. The new blade lay across her knees, scabbard still smeared with swamp filth. She had cleaned the edge, though. Of course she had. "Lionel's work, stamped with Third Pike. All of a piece."

Jaime shut the journal with more care than she had shown any living thing in days. The strap slid back into place with a soft, final sound.

"So the drake," she said. The contained fury in her voice gave each word edges. "It wasn't just some rogue beast. It was...pulled. Twisted. Driven mad."

"The stone did that," I said. "The one under its nest. It felt like..." I groped for words and came up hollow. "Like it was drinking everything dark in the swamp and pouring it into the nearest thing with teeth."

Rygial nodded once. "Anchor stones," he said. "Set "at any cost." Drawing corruption. Amplifying aggression. A chain stretched from tower to fort and gods know where else. Someone was feeding the worst in the world and then acting surprised when it bit back."

"Not surprised," Elisah said. "Unprepared."

Jaime's hand remained on the shield. Her knuckles had a fine tremor now, the after-shocks of too long holding steady. "Kerran," she said. "Whoever he is...was. This traces back to him."

Her eyes met mine across the little flame. There was grief there, yes, but it was cooling into something harder.

"They turned the monsters into weapons," she said. "They lost control. And we're up to our necks in what's left."

The silence that followed wasn't empty. It was full of the realisation settling into place, the drake had not been an isolated horror. It had been a symptom, one swollen node in a sickness reaching far beyond one swamp.

And beneath all of that, under my ribs, the hollow woke and turned.

The fire shifted. A tongue of flame licked higher, then dropped, throwing a brighter flash across all our faces before slinking down again. In that instant, there was nowhere for my hands to hide.

Elisah's eyes went to them first. She froze.

"Kit," she said. Her voice dropped, losing its usual lazy drawl. "Your hands."

Too slow, I tried to tuck them under my arms again. Her gaze pinned them in place.

"They're glowing," she said.

It was not a figure of speech. In the low light, the scales along my fingers and the backs of my hands gave off a faint, banked luminance of their own, not as bright as the fire but distinct from it. The red had deepened to a burnished, metallic hue, darker at the edges and picked out with tiny filigrees of gold around each plate, like veins of ore in rock. When I flexed my fingers, the movement caught the light with an odd, inner sheen, each scale reflecting something that did not quite match the fire's flicker.

I could feel them, too, more acutely than my own skin. Every ridge and seam, the way they lay atop tendon and bone like small shields.

Rygial's breath left him in a slow, deliberate exhale.

"Show me," he said. His voice had none of its usual dry amusement. It was stripped down, all old stone and deep water. "All of it."

I wanted to refuse. To tell him there was nothing to see. To insist that the light was a trick of the fire and our tired eyes. But his gaze on me was very steady, very tired, and very certain.

I had very little left in me for lying.

Silently, I unhooked my fingers from my armpits and held my hands out, palms up, then turned them. The inside surfaces were still mostly skin, though the color had shifted slightly, a faint gold along the veins as if someone had dusted them with metal. The backs and fingers were another matter entirely, scales layered where there had been fur and freckles, spreading now in a pattern that was horribly coherent. They left just enough bare skin for movement, each little plate overlapping the next in a way that would deflect a blade.

Jaime's breath caught. She did not look away.

"The ribs too," Elisah said quietly, as if prompting me before Rygial could.

My throat tightened. I hesitated.

"Elric," the dwarf said. "You won't thank yourself later if we guess in the dark. Up with the shirt."

It was not like modesty, not really. These were people who had seen me half-naked in river and rain, bleeding and bruised. It was the feeling that whatever lay under my shirt was no longer something I recognized as mine.

Still, I hooked my fingers into the hem and pulled it up.

The night air on my torso raised all the normal gooseflesh. Under the right side of my ribcage, just below the heart line, was something that had never existed before, a plate of red-gold scales sweeping in an arc from my sternum back toward my spine. They were larger than those on my hands, each about the width of my smallest finger, set in overlapping rows like a dragon's chest in a storybook engraving. The skin between them was flushed, as if freshly healed.

In the center of that arc, just slightly left of where my breastbone ended, there was a depression no deeper than the breadth of my thumb. An absence, not a wound, the skin there was whole, but when I touched it, the wrongness made my stomach lurch. It felt hollow, as if someone had scooped out a piece of the bone beneath and left only a smooth shell. Cold radiated from it in a shape, round and clear and too precise.

"That's where it was," I said, fingers hovering over the place. "The stone. When I...broke it. It felt like it went through my hands and into me." The memory shuddered through me, half pain, half some raw, blinding clarity. "Like it tried to...root. And something else pushed back."

Rygial's eyes tracked every word, every twitch of my fingers. "And this?" he asked quietly, reaching up without touching my hair. "The streak."

I had forgotten about that. Jaime hadn't. "It started when we were still at the lair," she said. "When his hands changed. It's been...getting brighter?"

Elisah snorted, though there was no heat in it. "He's fashionable now. Silver at the temples. All the old matrons in Tarris would swoon."

I pulled a lock of hair down where I could see it. She was right. What had begun as a few odd pale hairs had become a definite stripe, a streak of bright, clean silver running from the crown down through my dark mane over the left temple, stark even in the muddy light. It caught the fire like polished wire.

"And your eyes," Rygial said. He took a steadying breath before leaning forward. "Look at me, boy."

I met his gaze. He didn't flinch, to his credit. He did, however, exhale slowly, as if confirming a fear.

"Gold in the irises," he murmured. "Rings around the pupils, like molten coin settling. Early, but there."

"Is he dying?" Jaime asked. The words were almost level, but under them I heard something else, a thread of panic twined around old hurt. She clutched the journal to her again, the leather creaking under her grip.

Elisah's eyes swept my bare torso, the scales, the hollow, then flicked back up to my face. For once there was no joke ready on her tongue. "Is he going to explode?" she asked, more seriously than I had ever heard her. "Or sprout wings? Because I have logistics questions either way."

Rygial sat back. In the small, wobbly firelight, with his age written so starkly on his face, he looked like carved stone that someone had forgotten in a forgotten temple. His gaze never left me.

"No," he said. He did not say it quickly. He tasted the word, weighed it. "He is not dying. He is...becoming."

The way he said it made the word sit differently in my bones.

"Becoming what?" Jaime demanded.

Elisah's hand found the hilt of the Lionel sword where it lay. She did not draw it, but she did not let go either.

Rygial laced his fingers together slowly, the knuckles swollen with sudden age. He looked very tired. Very old. Very inevitable.

"There are things," he said, "we prefer not to name. Not because they are taboo in the priestly sense, but because names are doors, and some doors are best left closed until you have no choice."

He glanced at me. For once, whatever masking layers he usually wore were stripped. What was left was a kind of quiet sorrow and hard resolve.

"You, Elric," he said, "are opening one of those doors whether we like it or not."

Jaime's jaw clenched. "Plain words, Rygial. Please."

He nodded, accepting the rebuke. When he spoke again, his voice carried a weight I had heard only once before, when he had explained to me beside that village fire why my father would never come home.

"Warrior," he said.

The word itself was nothing special. Common, even. We used it in tavern boasts and children's games, in stories about kings' champions and mercenaries who survived three campaigns. I had used it about Maximus more than once, tossing it around with the careless admiration of youth.

On Rygial's tongue, it became something else.

"Not in the way you think of it," he went on, before any of us could jump in. "Not merely a fighter, or a soldier with more scars than sense. I mean it as my people meant it when the world was younger, and the sky had not yet forgotten how to burn."

He looked up, out into the dark swamp where unseen things skittered. When he spoke again, it was almost like reciting from a text memorized long ago, though no book lay open in front of him.

"Once," he said, "the world was simple. That's a lie, of course, but we tell it that way because our minds like clean lines. There was the Dragon Above, in the high purity of the sky and stars, all idea and will and the cold, bright clarity of law. There was the Dragon Below, in the deep places, mud, root, the wild heat of making and unmaking, hunger and growth and the blind surge of life. And there was the Dragon Here, in the middle, the breath between them, the balance that turned chaos into forests and oceans instead of just teeth."

"Elric, stop clenching," Elisah murmured. "You'll leave claw marks." I realized my hands had curled into fists again and made myself flex my fingers. The scales rasped faintly against one another.

Rygial continued as if we had all the time in the world.

"In those tales," he said, "these are not three separate beings, not really. They're faces of one thing we can't look at directly without going mad. But stories give them names, because that's what we do. We say the Dragon Above is what pulls us toward order, oaths, cities, the lines of a sword forged true. We say the Dragon Below is what pulls us toward breaking, storms, rot, the urge to rend and gorge. And the Dragon Here, the one we walk on and breathe in, tries to hold the rope between them so the world doesn't tear itself apart."

He turned his hands palm up, as if weighing invisible scales. "Most of the time, it works. Life muddles along. Wolves eat deer, rivers flood and recede, people are cruel and kind in equal, ordinary ways. But sometimes, the balance slips. The Below swells, war on a scale that drinks nations, plagues that don't end, someone clever and arrogant enough to build chains of anchor stones to drag corruption out of its secret holes and feed it. Or the Above pushes too hard, empires that grind everything under their "order," magic that tries to flatten the wild into neat geometries. When that imbalance grows too sharp, the Dragon Here, call it the world or fate or whatever story you like, does something...drastic."

He looked at me again. This time there was something almost like reverence in his gaze, though it sat bitter in the corners.

"It makes an immune response," he said softly. "A counterweight. It takes someone who shouldn't be able to stand in that storm and makes them into something that can. Not through birthright or training alone, but by...touching them. Burning them. Marking them."

Jaime's eyes went from my hands to my ribs, then back to Rygial. "You're saying the world is...doing this to him?"

"Yes and no," he said. He winced slightly, caught himself. "I'm saying there is a pattern older than any of our little nations. When the Below's influence swells too great, when monsters that even the oldest bestiaries don't name begin to crawl up out of stories and into fields, individuals appear who can stand against them. Not just well-trained soldiers with good steel. Warriors."

The way he said it made gooseflesh rise along my arms despite the cold.

"How often?" Elisah asked, ever practical. "Because I've known a lot of braggarts with shiny armor, and none of them glowed."

Rygial huffed something that might have been a laugh if there had been more warmth left in him. "Not often," he said. "The last clear, agreed-upon instance was during the Riven War, five generations ago. Before that, the songs reach further back than my mother's grandmother could swear to."

He gestured vaguely eastward, toward lands I had only read about.

"In those days, the Dragon Below rose through the cracks of the world quite literally," he said. "Rifts in the earth that bled things out, horrors that made your swamp drake look like a fat housecat. Cities ate themselves from within. Armies broke not from losses in battle but from the whispers in their dreams. And in the middle of that, people started changing."

"Just...randomly?" Jaime asked.

"Not randomly. Never randomly," Rygial said. "Always at a pivot point. In the heart of a burning city. On a battlefield where something that was not mere steel and spear was walking. At the foot of a tower built wrong. People with no bloodline claims, no special rank. Farmers. Blacksmiths. A laundress, if the songs are to be believed. They faced something they had no right to survive. And in that moment, something in them...answered."

His gaze went to my scaled hands again.

"They hardened," he said. "They took on aspects of what they had to fight. Scales, sometimes. Eyes that could see the Below's corruption when others saw only a man, a deer, a river. Strength beyond what flesh allows. Resistance to venom and shadow. Some breathed fire. Some simply refused to die when they should have. The details differ. The pattern does not."

Warriors, then. Not as a tavern compliment, but as a category.

"The bards made them bigger," he added, almost grudgingly. "Gave them names with too many consonants and love affairs with queens. But under the embroidery, the truth holds, the world made...specialists. Monsters that could kill monsters."

He looked at my chest, at the place where the anchor stone's absence had eaten a hollow.

"And every account," he said, "agrees on one thing, it begins with a touch. With standing too close to something you were never meant to stand near."

"The anchor stone," I said.

He inclined his head. "Anchor stones are not natural. They're chunks of Below-leaning resonance dragged up and shaped by Above-leaning intent, then hammered into the flesh of the world by mortals who do not understand the scale they're playing with. They draw out what's already rotten, yes, but in doing so they make a fulcrum. A point where the imbalance is sharpest." He tilted his hand, miming a scale tipping. "When you put your hands on that stone, when you forced your will against its, you stood at that fulcrum. You let the Below's corruption try to root in you."

"It tried," I said quietly. The memory made my bones ache. "It felt like it was...pouring in. Like cold mud in my veins. It wanted me to...turn. To tear." My fingers spasmed, the scales whispered against each other. "Something else burned it."

Rygial's nod was almost satisfied, though there was no joy in it. "The Above," he said. "Or the Here, pulling on the Above, names are messy. Call it the world's need for a counterweight. Your nature, your choices, drew that in. It hurt the stone, broke it. It hurt you. But where it might have killed another, it instead rewrote you so you could bear it."

He spread his hands. "You had...room. More give than most."

Jaime frowned. "Because he's..."

"Half one thing, half another," Rygial finished for her. "People of mixed blood, catfolk, human, elf, dwarf, whatever, sometimes take change better. Your body is already a compromise. It knows how to hold two truths at once. That may be why you didn't simply burn out, Elric. Why instead the power that should have corrupted you is now...settling in. Finding channels. Growing scales and silver."

The thought that my heritage, which had mostly given me the joy of never fitting entirely anywhere, was now...helping...sat strangely in my chest.

"The hollow?" I asked, touching the depression again. The wrongness thrummed under my fingers, humming in time with a heartbeat that did not feel entirely mine.

"That," Rygial said, "is where the stone's pattern tried to seat itself. Think of it like this, the anchor was a knot tied in the swamp. You pulled the knot through yourself and then cut it. The rope is gone. The shape of the hole remains. A potential." He met my eyes. "The world abhors a vacuum. Power, of any sort, loves a path carved for it. You're feeling that emptiness because both Above and Below can find it easily now."

"Comforting," Elisah muttered.

Jaime's brows drew together. "So the scales, the eyes, this is just...what happens when that power settles?"

"Not 'just,'" Rygial said. "But yes. Your mortal frame is adjusting. Thickening where it needs to bear strain. Changing pigment to handle...heat. Your senses will sharpen where corruption brushes them. You may feel...hungers." His mouth twisted slightly. "For meat, certainly, but also for...confrontation. For the clarity that comes when you're close to something that needs killing."

The thought made something uneasy wake at the back of my throat. I remembered the moment, in the lair, when the drake's gaze met mine and the world had narrowed to a point, just teeth and scales and the need to end it.

"Warriors," he said again, carefully, "are not common heroes. They are...doses of poison the world makes to cure a worse poison. They arise only in times of great need, when ordinary means have failed. They are specifically...blessed is the word the priests used, though it sits sour on my tongue, touched, then, to fight monsters never meant to be set against mortals."

He looked at Jaime. "The kind of creatures your Kerran thought he could chain and measure."

Jaime's fingers tightened again around the journal. "You keep saying 'Warrior' like it's a title," she said. "Why does no one speak of them that way anymore? Why did my father..." She bit that last word off before it could fully escape, but it hung between us anyway. "Why has no one told stories like this in the open?"

"They have," Rygial said. "Just not honestly." He sighed, the sound like old leather creaking. "After the Riven War, when the last of those touched ones died or disappeared into whatever dark or bright places claim such souls, the powers that remained agreed on something for once. They did not like being reminded how close they had come to losing everything. They did not like that salvation had come not from their bannered armies and wise councils, but from...accidents. From farmboys and laundresses and bastards who broke all the pretty hierarchies. So they took the stories and they...filed the names off."

He counted on his fingers. "In some lands, Warriors became saints, holy figures whose deeds were miracles, not the consequence of the world itself fighting back. In others, they became demons, excuses for new witch-hunts. In most, the word itself fell out of use in that meaning. People still had soldiers, fighters, heroes. But Warrior, with a capital W? That was a reminder that civilization had failed. That it had needed something wild and uncontrollable to bail it out."

Elisah snorted softly. "And no lord wants to look his people in the eye and say, 'If you see one of these walking around, it means we have well and truly made a mess of things.'"

"Precisely," Rygial said. "So the bards turned them into half-myths, and grandmothers told their names as bedtime tales stripped of blood. And anyone who kept older, truer knowledge...kept it quiet. Because if you stand up in a marketplace and shout 'Warrior' when some poor boy's hands start to glow, the consequences are unpredictable."

His gaze slid to my ribs again. "Fear. Worship. Both are...dangerous."

Jaime's eyes were bright now, anger and something like grief behind them. "So when you say Elric is becoming a Warrior," she said carefully, "you mean...he's going to keep changing until he's one of these things in your old stories. And that means...what? For him. For us."

Rygial rubbed his thumb along the edge of his beard, buying himself a moment. When he answered, he did not soften the words.

"It means this is not the end of his changes," he said. "It's the beginning. The more he confronts corruption like what you saw in that lair, the more he breaks anchor stones, fights creatures twisted beyond their natural bent, the more the...pattern in his chest will fill. Each clash will give that hole shape. The scales will spread. His senses will sharpen. He will get stronger. Harder to kill. He will begin to...sense...when something in the world is wrong. Not in the moral sense," he added dryly, perhaps sensing Jaime's flinch, "but in the structural one. He'll feel tugs, like...an itch under the skin, when corruption pools."

"That sounds...useful," Elisah said slowly. "Given where we're going."

"It is," Rygial said. "Immensely. That's the point. Warriors are very, very good at killing the things that crawl out when anchor stones hum and forts meddle with what they don't understand. The world did not make you this way to have you sit in a village and cobble shoes, Elric."

There was a bitter comfort in that. Maximus would have laughed, I thought, and said of course the universe couldn't let me simply fix boots.

"But," Rygial went on, and the word hung heavier than the ones before, "useful is not the same as kind. This," he gestured at my hands, my chest, my eyes, "comes with cost. Multiple, in fact."

He started counting again, not for his benefit but ours.

"First: your body. You will hurt, boy. Things that are not supposed to move will move. You will wake with bones aching as if you've outgrown them overnight, and sometimes you will have. Your ribs, your spine, your teeth. You will get hungry in ways you don't have words for yet."

"Hungrier than now?" I tried to make it a joke, but it came out thin.

"Yes," he said simply. "And not just for food. For...the feeling you had when you stood in front of that drake and knew, absolutely, what needed to be done. Warriors talk, in the few honest accounts, about...itching...when they go too long without facing something that triggers their pattern. It can make ordinary life...unbearable."

He held up another finger. "Second: your mind. You will start to feel corruption as...a pressure. You will walk into a town and just know that something under the well is wrong, or that the nice old woman at the bakery has a shadow that doesn't quite match. If you let that run your life, it will drag you into every dark corner until you forget why you cared about light in the first place."

Jaime looked ill. "Compulsion," she said quietly. "Obsession."

"Call it what you like," Rygial replied. "Imagine a splinter you can't reach, magnified to the size of a city. Warriors are...driven. The world doesn't make them to be comfortable. It makes them because something needs doing."

He ticked a third finger. "Third: other people. Once word spreads, and it will if you keep glowing like that, folk will...react. Some will venerate you. Build shrines. Ask you to bless their children, their pigs, their turnip harvest. They will forget you are a person and treat you like a...useful storm. Others will fear you. They'll remember half-told stories about demons in human skin, about men whose eyes turned gold and then their village burned. They will call you cursed. Some will try to use you. Others will try to...remove...the perceived threat."

I swallowed. My throat felt dry as the biscuit.

"Can he control it?" Jaime asked. Her voice, when it came, was steady. "Any of it. Or does he just...ride along while the world rewrites him?"

Rygial's gaze softened, if only a fraction. "To a degree," he said. "You cannot choose whether you are touched. That is already done. But you can choose how you walk with it. The early stages," he nodded at my hands, "are...malleable. If you recognize the impulses when they rise, if you learn where they come from, you can decide when to lean into them and when to resist."

"And if he doesn't?" Elisah asked.

"Then he becomes what the world made him to be, without remainder," Rygial said quietly. "A tool. A very sharp one. The stories about Warriors who lost themselves talk of them as little better than the monsters they fought, only better aimed. They won their fights. They also burned out. Fast."

My heart had been beating faster as he spoke, a hollow drum echoing in the space behind my sternum. Each time he named some cost, some consequence, something in that emptiness thrummed in agreement, as if ticking boxes on a list.

"So what you're saying," I managed, forcing my voice to stay even, "is that I'm now a monster-slayer made by the world because someone else fed monsters too well." My scaled hands clenched and unclenched in my lap. "And if I'm not careful, I'll end up as much a threat as the things I'm supposed to kill."

"In the bleakest terms, yes," Rygial said. He did not look away. "You asked for none of this. But it has found you anyway."

The unfairness of it surged up in me so sharp it almost had teeth. I had not gone into that lair to become anything. I had gone because Maximus had pushed me out of the way and died, because villagers had screamed as they were dragged into the dark, because I had thought, in all my adolescent arrogance, that I could at least swing a sword in the right direction.

Now the world itself had apparently taken that swing as consent.

At the same time, beneath anger, beneath fear, there was another feeling. A sense of...alignment. Of being slotted into a groove I had not known existed. The moment my hands had closed on the anchor stone, I had felt something sharp and clear burning through me. For an instant, I had known, with a certainty that had nothing to do with thought, exactly what needed doing and exactly what I was capable of. It had been terrifying. It had also felt more right than anything I had ever done.

I looked down at my hands, at the way the firelight picked out each scale. They still looked like they belonged on someone else. But they were mine.

"We can help him," Jaime said suddenly.

All eyes went to her.

She held the journal tight against her ribs, as if it were armor. "You said he can learn," she continued, glaring at Rygial as if daring him to contradict her. "That he can choose. That with training, with...self-awareness," she made the words sound like curses, "he doesn't have to just...slide into being a legend and nothing else."

"Legends are only stories told about people once they're gone," Elisah said quietly. "I'm not interested in that version of you, kitten. I want the miserable, snoring, too-tall boy who complains about swamp water and burns the porridge."

"I don't burn the..." I began.

"You do," she said. "And I would very much like you to keep being that person, scales or no. So. Control. What does that look like, old man?"

Rygial's mouth twitched, surprised into the ghost of a smile.

"It looks," he said slowly, "like time. Which we have little of. It looks like teaching him to tell the difference between urge and need. Between the world tugging on that hollow and his own choices. It looks like not feeding the change more than necessary when we don't have to, and accepting that sometimes we will have to if we want to live."

"Practical terms," Jaime said. "He shouldn't go looking for anchor stones to break for fun."

"No," Rygial agreed. "Terrible recreational activity. But when we find them, and we will if that journal is any indication, he may be the only one among us who can destroy them without...abruptly ceasing to exist."

Elisah's brows rose. "That's one way to say 'explode.'"

"Is that...true?" I asked.

He nodded once. "Anchor stones are dangerous to touch even for trained mages. They imprint. They...seduce. You have already had one try to claim that hollow and fail. That makes you...resistant." His eyes met mine. "But every time you do it, the pattern deepens. It will make you stronger. It will also carve away other paths you might have walked."

"Meaning?" Jaime asked.

"Meaning that "normal life" grows further," he said. "Warriors do not retire to farms easily. They find it...intolerable to sit by a hearth when they can feel something wrong howling beyond the hills. Many try. Most do not succeed."

Silence again, but a different kind now. Less stunned, more...considering.

Jaime's eyes were on the fire, but I could tell she wasn't seeing it. "So we're walking toward something that made these anchor stones," she said. "And you're telling me the world just turned my best friend into the only kind of person built to tear them up."

"I'm not sure about "best,"" I muttered, because seventeen-year-old me could not let that pass without deflecting. "You still owe me for that card game in Tarris."

She shot me a look that was half glare, half something softer. "You beat me by cheating," she said. "And you're an idiot. But you're my idiot. So yes. Best." The word came out rough.

Elisah cleared her throat. "Sentiment aside, we have...data." She tapped the journal. "Anchor stones, set in a chain from tower to fort. Kerran making decisions he had no business making. Stones amplifying whatever nastiness sits under the skin of the world until it breaks its leash. Monsters not...innately malevolent being whipped into froth."

"And somewhere," I added, "villagers taken. Men dead in swamps. A tower that still hums if that drake was being pushed recently." The thought of that place, squat against the horizon, made the hollow in my chest throb.

Rygial nodded. "The monitoring post mentioned in the journal, the tower you two discovered first, it was part of the system. If the drake was still under influence, some of the chain remains active. Perhaps damaged, but not broken. The fort...the larger installation the journal references...that will be the hub. Where the anchor array was conceived, if not where the idea started."

"Kerran," Jaime said again, like a curse. She looked down at the journal in her hands. "His name's all over this. If he isn't dead, he's at that fort. Or went back there before everything fell apart."

"And if he is dead," Elisah said, "then someone else is using his work. Or trying to fix it. Or make it worse. None of those options thrill me."

"We go to the tower first," Jaime said. There was no quaver now. Decision had given her footing. "It's closer. It told the fort what was happening. Maybe it still has...records. Wards. Something." Her fingers brushed the broken dwarf's watch at her belt, then the journal. "We see what they did, how far it went. We find out if Kerran's still...pulling strings. Then we go to the fort."

Elisah made a face. "I was hoping you'd say 'we go to the fort.'"

Elisah made a face. "I was hoping you'd say 'we go literally anywhere else,'" she said. "But no. Sense. Always with the sense."

"It's not just sense," Jaime said. "It's answers."

The unsaid word father lay under that. None of us touched it.

Rygial inclined his head. "The tower will also give us a chance to test our...theory," he said. He nodded at my chest. "If there are still active segments of the anchor array there, Elric will feel them." His eyes went distant a moment, old memories chasing. "When I was a boy," he said, "one of my great-aunt's stories mentioned a Warrior who walked into a ruined temple and vomited blood before he crossed the threshold. There was a stone under the altar. He dug it out with his bare hands and crushed it, and when he was done he couldn't stop laughing or crying for an hour. Said it felt like being...scratched in a place he didn't know itched."

"That's...vivid," Elisah said.

"He might not vomit," Rygial added, almost hastily, as if realizing that he might be making the prospect less appealing.

"Thank you," I said dryly. "That reassures me greatly."

"The point," he said, "is that you will have...a sense. Learn to listen to it, and you will find stones. Learn to...argue with it, and you will remain yourself."

"Or he'll burn himself out," Elisah said, no malice in it, just fact. "Trying to scratch every itch."

"Yes," Rygial said. "That too."

Jaime's hand rested on the journal again, fingers splayed. She looked from me to the dwarf to the dark around us.

"We don't have the luxury of pretending we didn't hear any of this," she said. "There are people still alive under whatever mess this fort made. Creatures twisted that weren't meant to be. Elric...is what he is now. That's not going to...un-happen because we wish it." She took a breath, letting it out slowly. "We go to the tower. We find out what they did. We stop it. As much as we can."

Her eyes met mine. Under the determination there was fear, and under that, a fierce protectiveness that startled me.

"If that means he has to break more stones and grow more scales," she said, "then we make sure he doesn't do it alone."

Elisah bumped my shoulder lightly with the back of her hand. "And we reserve the right to smack him," she added, "if he starts snarling at villagers or talking like a ballad."

"I do not snarl," I protested.

"You do now," she said, eyes flicking to my teeth. "A little."

Rygial pushed himself to his feet with a grunt that sounded older than it should have. He moved stiffly, the magic he had burned in the lair to keep me alive had taken more from him than he wanted to show.

"Decision made, then," he said. "Tower at first light, fort after. Unless the tower kills us, in which case I expect appropriate bitter 'I told you so's on the way down."

"No martyrdom speeches," Elisah said. "I have a quota."

He gave her a look that might have been fond if the creases around his eyes hadn't been so deep. Then he turned back to me.

"You," he said, pointing a knotted finger. "Sleep. That stone may have failed to plant itself, but your body has had...a day. Your heart needs to remember its old beat before it gets too used to the new one."

"I can take first watch," I started. Habit. Guilt. The urge to do something, anything, to make up for all the ways the world had just changed without my consent.

"No," he said, sharper than I had heard him in days. "If something comes sniffing, I'd rather have you fresh than half-dead on your feet. Elisah can watch first, she's already halfway in the shadows anyway. Jaime second. I'll take third if the old ticker agrees." He glanced down at his chest with a wry grimace. "Elric, you take the last. Dawn. When your...new bits will have had a few hours to settle."

Jaime opened her mouth to argue on my behalf, then seemed to think better of it. "You heard him," she said instead, firm. "Lie down before I knock you out and call it an accident."

I snorted, but the thought of stretching out on stone and moss and not moving for a while made my bones sigh with anticipation. Exhaustion didn't so much settle in as reveal that it had been there all along, waiting.

We shuffled into arrangements that had already become familiar, each of us claiming a sliver of the rock. Elisah took the side facing the widest stretch of swamp, eyes already scanning the dark as she settled with her back to a convenient protrusion. Jaime positioned herself near the shield and the journal, as if she could protect them or they could protect her. Rygial leaned back against the outcrop's highest point, head tipping back, eyes closed but not quite relaxed.

I lay down with my back to the stone, knees drawn up slightly to make my too-long limbs fit. The rock was cold and unyielding under my scaled ribs, but whether because of them or sheer fatigue, it wasn't as uncomfortable as it should have been.

The fire had burned down to coals. Their light was softer now, a low, pulsing glow that echoed a different thrum inside me. I lifted my hands, turning them slowly in the dim red.

The scales caught the dying light like small embers, each one edged with a faint glint that didn't seem entirely borrowed. When I flexed my fingers, they rasped together so quietly I could almost convince myself I was imagining it.

Under my sternum, the hollow pulsed. Not a sound, but a sensation, a faint, echoing throb that answered my heartbeat half a beat off, as if some other heart were trying to learn the rhythm.

I hadn't asked for any of this. That unfairness sat heavy, a stone of my own lodged in my gut. But lying there, feeling the too-cold night seep into my skin and the slow, inevitable warmth growing under it, I knew something with the same clarity I had felt in the lair.

Pretending it wasn't happening would not save anyone. Not the villagers. Not Maximus's memory. Not Jaime, clutching her dead man's words to her chest. Not the swamp slowly curdling around chains it had never consented to bear.

If I was becoming something that could stand in front of things like that drake, that could put hands on anchor stones and break them, I could either run from it and let someone else, or no one at all, take that place. Or I could lean into it and learn where the edge was before it cut my friends.

The world had reached into me without asking. I could resent that. I did. But I could also reach back.

I curled my fingers. Scales whispered like tiny coals being stoked.

Somewhere in the murk, a night bird called, thin and desolate. Elisah shifted, nearly silent. Jaime's breathing evened out by degrees. Rygial snored once, softly, then swallowed it down.

I lay awake longer than I wanted to, watching the faint red shimmer along my hands, feeling the hollow in my chest beat time to a rhythm that was mine and not mine.

I did not know then that choosing to become something is easier than choosing to remain yourself once the change begins. I would learn that lesson in the days ahead, written in fire and stone and the screams of things that should never have existed.

# Chapter 20

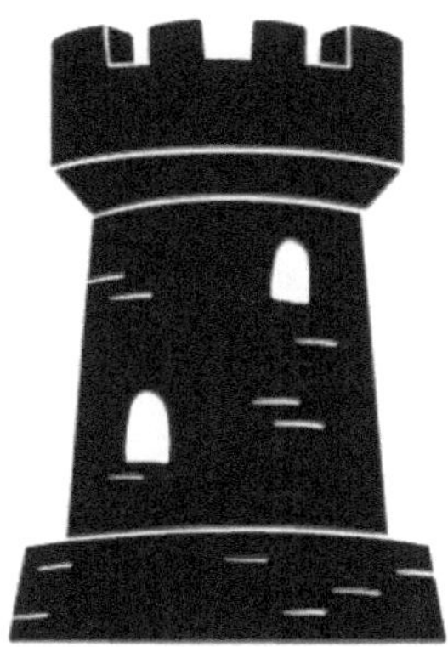

## THE FORT ON THE BLACK RISE

THE SWAMP THINNED AROUND us, one slow step at a time. Water gave way to mud. Mud gave way to black, packed soil that sucked at my boots and held on. The air changed first. The rot-smell from the marsh faded under something heavier. Metallic. Like wet iron left too long in the sun.

The sky still held the last color of afternoon behind us. Ahead, over the rise, it dimmed faster than it should have. The line of trees there looked closer than they were. The angles were wrong.

The hum in my bones woke as soon as the ground firmed. At first I thought it was the memory of the swamp stone. Old pain. Leftover echo. It started as a faint vibration under my ribs. It crawled along the scales on my hands, along the thin line of them that wrapped under my shirt. The hollow where the first stone had burned out felt colder than the rest of me.

I shifted Drakeslayer on my shoulder. The leather strap dug into my collarbone. Every step jarred a small ache in my chest.

"Shorter strides," Elisah said softly. "You're stamping."

I looked down. My boots had left a torn line in the black soil. I forced my feet to roll instead of slam. The ache did not ease.

"Sorry," I said.

She glanced back. What little light we had turned her eyes into two flat pieces of night.

"Don't be sorry. Just quieter." Her knives were already out. She had them held flat along her forearms, points back. Casual. Like another person might carry loose rope.

Jaime walked a few paces off to my right. She had the shield slung on her arm, edge down, Third Pike sigil facing her leg. The journal was strapped at her side. Her hand kept drifting toward its spine as if to check it was still there.

Rygial had taken the uphill side. The dwarf moved slower than any of us, but his feet found the driest patches without looking. He had his staff in his left hand. His right kept brushing the stone beads on the thong at his belt. The lines in his face had deepened in the weeks since Maximus died, but the aging from the swamp spell sat on him worst of all. His beard had gone more grey than brown. His back had a new bend.

"How far?" Jaime asked. She kept her voice low.

Rygial squinted ahead. "Half a mile to the base of the Rise," he said. "From there, another half up." His eyes shifted to me. "Unless our young Warrior has a more precise measure."

I did not. What I had was pain.

The hum in my bones gathered weight as we walked. It pulled in one direction. Forward and a little east. Another pressure grew lower and left, out toward the marsh. A third pulsed like a slow heartbeat somewhere deep under the earth. The different pulls braided into a constant ache. Sweat prickled along my spine.

"More than one," I said. "Three I can feel. Maybe more. The closer we get, the more... crowded it is." I rolled my shoulders. It did nothing. "Hard to separate them."

"Network spoke and hub," Rygial murmured. "Kerran did not do his work by halves."

Jaime's jaw tightened. "Third Pike was guarding this place," she said. "We were the ones on the ground while he was building his network. While the generals signed the orders." Her hand tightened on the shield strap. Her knuckles went white. "My father marched past these stones and never knew."

"Nobody knew," Elisah said. "Or nobody who cared." She tipped her chin at me. "Head clear enough to do what we came for?"

I wanted to say yes. The word stuck behind my teeth. The itch under my skin distracted me more with each breath. It felt like something pressing from inside and outside at the same time. A pressure front rolling through my bones.

"I can walk," I said. "I can fight." I flexed my fingers. The scales along my knuckles caught the dim light, dull silver. "Just noisy in here." I tapped my chest.

Elisah gave a brief nod. "Then we keep it simple," she said. "Get in. Find the hub stone. Break it. Get out. We do not tangle with anything we do not have to."

"Assuming the stone is not buried under a few tons of masonry," Rygial said.

Jaime looked toward the dark trees. "If this place is really the center, there will be records," she said. "Orders. Names. Kerran. My father. Others. We cannot just leave that behind."

"We take what we can carry without dying for it," Elisah said. "Dead, you get no answers."

"We will do both," Rygial said. His voice stayed level, but the skin around his eyes had gone tight. "If the hub stone is what I think, removing it may change the behavior of everything else here. Including whatever is guarding this fort."

The word "whatever" sat in my ears longer than it should have.

We climbed. The ground angled upward in a long, slow swell. The swamp behind us spread out into a dark, flat sheet. Ahead, the Black Rise earned its name.

The trees that covered the slope had needles and cones like any fir, but the color was off. The needles were almost black, but when I looked straight at them I saw a greasy green sheen. They seemed to drink the light instead of reflecting it. The trunks leaned together in strange patterns, not quite straight. Branches knotted around each other in ways that made my eyes ache if I followed them too long.

Birds should have been singing. Something should have been moving in the undergrowth. Instead there was a stillness that wrapped around us. Even our breathing sounded too loud.

The hum in my bones grew teeth. It scraped along the inside of my ribs. My heart found a rhythm that did not match my steps. It matched the deep, slow throb under the hill.

"Smell that?" Elisah whispered.

I lifted my head. Beneath the metal tang in the air, something else rode the wind. Old smoke. Oiled leather. Latrine pits. Cooking fat gone rancid. It was a fort-smell, one I had lived in for years, but it had turned sour.

"Garrison," I said.

"Or what is left of one," Rygial said.

We pushed through the last line of twisted firs. The ground leveled. The trees thinned.

The fort sat on the crest of the Rise like an old scar. Low stone walls encircled a flattened crown. The walls were not tall like city ramparts. They came up to three times my height at most. They had simple battlements, straight and practical. The stone was pale grey under a wash of grime and lichen. The corners still held their angles. This had been built by engineers who knew their work.

Third Pike banners clung to the outer wall. The fabric that had once been deep green had gone almost black with age and weather. The sigil was still visible where the cloth had not rotted through. A pike in three segments, head and butt crossing in the center. They hung limp in the still air.

Jaime stopped when she saw them. Her breath left her in a soft sound. Not a word. More like something caught. She reached out, then caught herself and dropped her hand before she touched the nearest post.

"I trained under those banners," I said. The image of the fort yard back home rose up sharp and unwelcome. A different wall, smaller. Banners fresher. Maximus laughing after a drill, sweat running down his neck. His hand on my shoulder, heavy and real.

Jaime swallowed. "My father marched under them," she said. "He wrote about a fort on a rise. The journal said it controlled river traffic. If this is the same place..."

Her voice thinned out. She cut it off.

"Later," Elisah said. It was not unkind. It was clipped. She nodded to the slope before the walls. "We make it to those stones alive and we can argue over their history all night. Rygial. Light."

He cupped his hand. A small, soft globe of yellow came to life in his palm. It lit no more than a few paces ahead. He closed his fingers around it until only a leak of glow edged between them.

"Dusk is closing," he said. "Best if it finishes before we reach the main gate. Sentries see worse in the shift from light to dark."

I felt them before I saw them. The hum in my bones sharpened as we walked toward the outer wall. One tug pointed straight ahead now. The ache behind my sternum deepened. It felt like fingers pressing from inside, searching for a way out.

We kept low and moved along a shallow wash cut into the slope. Elisah led. Jaime followed, shield close to her side, body turned so the emblem did not catch any stray gleam. I went next, with Rygial at my heel. Our boots sank into old ruts left by cart wheels. Rocks shifted under each step, but no bird rose, no frog croaked.

"This was busy once," I said under my breath.

"Yes," Rygial said. "Places remember their uses."

"Quiet," Elisah hissed.

We reached a point where the wash angled up toward the outer wall. Elisah flattened against the bank and lifted her head just enough to peer over the lip. I watched the line of her shoulders. They did not tense. That was its own sort of warning.

She dropped back down. "Two sentries on the north wall," she murmured. "One over the main gate. One walking the east run. You were right, Rygial. Sloppy patterns. Long gaps in cover. They are not watching their blind sides."

"Can you tell what they are?" I asked.

"Used to be soldiers," she said. "Now..." She searched for a word and did not find one. "You will see."

We waited while she counted patrol beats under her breath. The sky darkened in layers. The last band of red on the horizon faded to a bruise-colored strip. The wrongness of the light sharpened as we lost the sun. Shadows under the firs grew opaque. The only sounds were the faint chink of armor from the walls and the slow rasp of my own breath.

"On my mark," Elisah said. "We move when the east runner passes the tower cut. Hug the shadow of the ditch. No talking. No stumbling."

My legs coiled. The hum in my ribs climbed to a whine.

"Now," she breathed.

We went up the bank and out into the open ground.

The outer approach to the fort was bare by design. No trees. No large rocks for cover. In full daylight we would have been seen at once. In the failing half-light and with Elisah's timing, we were just four dark shapes crossing darker ground.

The nearest sentry stood at the north corner of the wall. I saw him clearly when we came close enough. He wore Third Pike mail, patched at the elbows with scavenged plates. His tabard hung stiff and cracked around the hips. The pike in his hand was held too close to the center, badly balanced. His shoulders were square, his head up. It almost looked right.

Then he moved.

The turn of his head came in one clean, jerky click, as if he had no motion between still and turned. His eyes swept across the slope. They passed over us. There was nothing in them. No focus. No flicker of interest. They were pale and flat, swallowed by dilated pupils. His jaw hung just open, teeth set, lips drawn back a little too far.

His fingers twitched on the pike shaft. Once, twice. Little spasms that did not match the rest of his posture.

He looked past us, then turned back in the same stiff segment. He did not shift his weight. He did not stamp his feet against the cold. He did not yawn or mutter. He might have been a doll hammered into armor.

My skin crawled. The scales on my hands prickled like they were held near heat, though the air had cooled with the evening. The hum in my bones rasped across itself. I could taste metal at the back of my tongue.

We slid into the shadow of the outer ditch, a shallow trench along the base of the wall. The stone blocks above loomed over us. The Third Pike banner nearest my head flapped once in a wind I could not feel.

Jaime's shoulders brushed mine. Her breath came quicker than before. She stared up at the sentry. Her jaw worked like she was grinding her teeth, though no sound came.

"That is not Third Pike drill," she whispered, so low I barely heard her. "We did not stand like that."

Rygial's reply was a breath against my ear. "Their wills are ridden. That makes them brittle. And dangerous."

"More brittle than a drake?" I asked.

"The drake had a mind of its own," he said. "These have only what is pushed into them."

A soft creak carried down from the gatehouse. Elisah shot us a hard look and started along the ditch toward the main gate. We followed.

The big iron-bound doors were closed, but a postern cut into them stood ajar by a handspan. Someone had wedged a stone at its base. The gap leaked a sliver of dim light.

Elisah placed one hand on the wood. She waited, listening. Her eyes went distant in the way they did when she paid attention to small noises. Faint movement sounded from within. A boot. A drag of something across stone. Farther away, not right behind the door.

She nodded once. "Inside," she breathed.

One by one, we slid through the gap. I turned my shoulders sideways to make it. Drakeslayer scraped the jamb. The sound flashed up my nerves like a spark, but no shout followed. No alarm.

The air inside the wall hit like a wall of scent. Sweat. Latrine. Horses. The endless tang of steel and oil. Under it all lay the same wrongness in the air that I had first felt on the Rise. It settled on my tongue like soot.

We stood in the shadow of the back of the gatehouse. Torches flickered in iron brackets along the inner wall. The flames burned with a faint green underlight. Smoke curled in slow, lazy spirals instead of rising fast. The courtyard on the other side stretched out in a wide, hard-packed oval.

It should have been alive with sound. Boots on stone. Shouted orders. Clatter as weapons were cleaned. The ring of practice from the yard. Instead, the quiet yawned around us.

There were people.

Near the far wall, a line of wooden cages had been built against the stone. Six in a row. Rough lumber. Iron bands from broken barrels reforged into hinges and locks. Shapes huddled inside. Blankets wrapped around shoulders. Bare feet tucked up under bodies for warmth. Faces lifted toward the gate when the torchlight shifted. Eyes watched through the bars. They had thought they heard something. The hope in those movements cut more than any shout.

Jaime gasped. She almost stepped out from behind the gatehouse instinctively. Elisah caught her arm and hauled her back.

"Locals," Elisah said. "Farmers. Fisherfolk. See the hands? Soft. No callus for weapon grips."

"Why cage them?" Jaime's voice had a ragged edge.

Rygial's face had gone very still. "Anchor stones change faster and feed better on fear," he said, so quiet the words were more formed air than sound.

My chest tightened. The hollow where the destroyed stone had been felt as if someone had pressed a thumb into it. The ache that had been general before now pulled hard toward the far side of the fort, past the cages, toward the central cluster of buildings. A second pull, sharper and closer, came from somewhere under our feet.

"They know we are here," I whispered.

"Do they?" Elisah asked. Her eyes scanned the wall walks. Two sentries. One over the gate. One near the far corner. Both had the same stiff posture as the man outside. Their heads ticked back and forth in that same unnatural rhythm. None of them looked inward toward the yard. They watched the fields beyond, but without real focus.

"They are not reacting," Elisah said. "Whatever is running this does not prioritize the inner yard. Strange."

Rygial's gaze had gone distant again. His fingers tapped along his staff in a counting pattern, as if he were measuring something none of us could see.

"There is a focus," he said. "A central constraint. It keeps them on pattern. It does not waste effort until a threshold is crossed."

"In common," Elisah said, "we are safe until we are not." She turned to us. "Outer wall is done. We are inside the first ring. Next, barracks and stores. Inner wall before the tower. Keep your eyes on the ground and on the corners. Ignore the cages for now. We cannot crack them open without raising the whole place."

Jaime's hand tightened on her shield strap again. I could see the cords in her forearm. She nodded once, short and sharp.

My own instincts were not as clear. Every part of me wanted to go to the cages. To cut them open. To put something between those people and the anchor hum that had started to vibrate in the stones around us. Another part of me, deeper and less familiar, screamed wordless warning.

That new part did not care about cages or banners or Third Pike history. It cared about angles and shadows. About open gates. About the fact that nothing had truly challenged our entry yet.

I shifted my weight. The feeling of wrongness pressed at the base of my skull. I forced it down. We had a plan. Get in. Break the hub. Come back for whoever we could.

"Move," Elisah said.

We slid along the back of the gatehouse and into the deeper shadow of a storage shed. The courtyard spread out. Barracks lined the left side, two long stone buildings with narrow windows cut high up. Stables sat to the right, doors half-open. I could smell old hay and animal musk, sharp and sour.

Beyond the barracks, an inner wall cut across the width of the fort, rising a little higher than the outer wall. A wide gate stood open in its center. Behind that, half-obscured, a squat central tower reached up two more stories. It was not grand. Just thicker walls, fewer windows, more stone.

The hum in my bones pulled straight toward that tower. The ache behind my ribs took on a pulse that did not match my heartbeat. It felt like someone else's heart beating against my sternum from the outside.

As we crept along the base of the barracks, Elisah's eyes never stopped moving. She pointed once at a guard tower at the far corner. "No one up there," she murmured. "They have abandoned high view. Short sight."

Rygial frowned. "A fort commander who puts no one on the high posts is either dead or replaced."

"Or very sure his enemies will not come that way," Elisah said.

Jaime's gaze snagged on the barracks doors as we passed. One hung half open. Inside, I saw rows of bunks, blankets still on them. A helmet lay in the doorway, half-crushed as if someone had stepped on it on the way out and never picked it up.

"Discipline's gone," she muttered. "Pike captains would have had our skin for leaving gear like that."

"Third Pike captains are not here," Rygial said.

We crossed an open space between the barracks and a row of low sheds. My skin crawled as I stepped into the center of the yard. There was nothing there. No mark on the ground. No stain. No trap that I could see. The feeling came from inside, not outside.

The hum under the earth scraped louder. It rose from a vibration to something like sound. My ears did not hear it. The bones in my face did. The back of my teeth ached. The silver streak in my hair felt like a cold thread laid along my scalp.

I paused without meaning to. My boot hung half an inch above the hard dirt.

"Elric," Elisah hissed.

"Something's wrong," I whispered.

"Everything is wrong," she said. "Pick one wrong to follow and we will never move."

She was right. That was what I told myself. I put my foot down and kept going.

We reached the base of the inner wall. There were no sentries here. No one in the shadows of the gate arch. Torches burned along the inner face of the wall, their light greenish again, their smoke slow and thick. The gate itself gaped empty.

My chest hurt. Not the steady ache from the anchor pull, but a sharp knot low and center, like the start of a stitch after a hard run. My breath shortened by a fraction. The scales on my hands itched.

"Open gate," Elisah said softly. "No one posted. No crossbeam ready to drop. Thoughts?"

"It could be a confidence," Rygial said. "They assume their outer layer holds."

"Their outer layer did not even notice us," Elisah said. "Nothing about this place counts as confidence."

"Maybe the sentries are inside," Jaime said. Her gaze had gone hard. She kept looking at the stonework, searching for familiar cuts, old marks. "Third Pike always doubled guards on inner access. This would have been the choke. That is what the manual said."

"Then where are they?" I asked.

No one answered.

The feeling of wrongness hit a new peak as we approached the arch. Not one gradual climb now, but a sudden coarse buzz, as if I had pressed my tongue to a piece of metal thrumming with power. The hollow in my chest throbbed, answering the unseen stone under the fort. Pressure built behind my breastbone until each breath felt too shallow.

My feet wanted to stop. My legs kept moving. I told myself this was just nerves. Just anchor proximity. The deeper pull under the tower had shifted, too. It felt closer now, though the tower still sat ahead past the inner yard. The network tugged at me from multiple angles at once, a headache in the shape of stone.

We reached the threshold of the inner gate. The arch overhead was simple. No carvings. Just stone blocks and a wooden beam that had once held a heavy iron portcullis. The rails where the gate would have dropped were empty. There were no chains, no winch.

"Why is it unguarded?" Jaime whispered.

"The commanders are gone," Rygial said. "Or something else has made them... extraneous."

"It is an invitation," Elisah said. Her lip curled a little around the word. "I do not like invitations."

The feeling at the base of my skull sharpened. It crawled down my spine in tiny, insistent claws. Every instinct that had woken in me since the drake and the swamp stone screamed that something waited beyond that arch.

I looked at the open space under the stone. It was just a gap. Dark. Torches beyond. No movement. No sound but the soft crackle of the wrong-colored fire. I had walked through hundreds of gates like this in my life.

"We do not have time to circle," I said. "We cannot climb the inner wall without rope. The longer we stand here, the more likely someone actually sees us."

That was true. Reason said move. There were no clear signs of a trap. Just a feeling. A new, unreliable feeling dragging at the back of my mind and the meat of my bones.

"Warrior instincts are not adornments," Rygial said quietly. His eyes were on me. "If something in you claws at the air, listen."

I thought of the drake's lair. Of the way my body had moved before my mind formed the plan. Of the instant when Drakeslayer had found the gap in scale that I had not seen until the sword was already moving. That same deep part of me shouted now. Not a clear word. Just raw, bright warning.

We stood there one heartbeat too long.

"I am listening," I said. "It feels bad. It also feels like the stones. We knew that would hurt. That is what we came to break."

Elisah's eyes tightened. She looked like she wanted to argue. The need to move overrode it.

"Then we go," she said. "Fast. In and to the left. Do not stand framed in the opening like targets." She glanced once at the empty gate top. "And pray there are not archers with a better schedule than the rest of this place."

She slid through the arch, low and sideways, hugging the left-hand wall. Jaime went next, shield raised. I followed close, Drakeslayer in my hand now, not over my shoulder. Rygial came just behind, his staff held like a quarter pike.

Crossing that threshold felt like passing through a thin film of cold water. The air on the other side tasted different. Denser. The hum in my bones flared, then dipped, like stepping into then out of a minor wave.

We were three steps into the inner courtyard when the trap sprang.

Something huge unfolded from the darkness along the right side of the gate. It had crouched there, pressed tight against the stone, so still and close in color that I had taken it for part of the wall. When it moved, the stone seemed to come to life.

Its shape filled my vision. It rose and uncurled in segments. Grey skin like old rock stretched over knotted muscle. Its arms were too long in proportion to its torso. They ended in wide, blunt hands with fingers like broken branches. Each digit carried a nail like a chipped piece of slate. Its shoulders hunched, almost touching the underside of the battlements.

Its head was squat, jaw-heavy, with small round ears pressed close to the skull. A wide, flat nose sat over a mouth full of thick, yellow teeth. Its eyes were pits. Not empty. Not glowing. Just deep and lifeless, like stones polished by a river and then set into a skull.

In the center of its barrel chest, half-sunk into grey flesh, a hunk of carved stone glowed a sick, pulsating green. It was the size of both my fists. Veins of darker color webbed out from it under the skin, like roots, running along ribs and shoulders and down into arms. With each slow flash of light, those veins brightened, then dimmed.

The hum in my bones leaped from ache to agony. The hollow behind my sternum clenched as if an invisible hook had sunk into it and yanked toward that embedded stone. The rest of the anchor pulls dropped away. There was only this one. It filled everyone I could feel inside myself.

"Elric," Rygial breathed, somewhere behind me. His voice sounded far.

The troll took one heavy step forward. The ground shuddered under my boots. Dust sifted down from the arch above us. Its gaze swept over us. Not curious. Not hateful. Just turning, the way a tower might slowly find the wind.

Its movements did not match the jerky puppet-stiffness of the corrupted soldiers. There was weight and slow calculation in the way its shoulders rolled. Because it did not have to look like a man, the wrongness in its motion lay deeper. It moved like something that had grown for one purpose and had been given another.

Behind us, with a grinding crash of stone and iron, the gate we had just passed through slammed shut. The postern we had slipped in through thudded at the same time. Something heavy slid into place above. The muffled clank of a bar dropping.

Jaime spun, shield up. The wooden gate loomed behind us, closed and implacable. We were in the archway's throat. Inner yard ahead. Outer yard behind. Nowhere clear to run.

The cold film feeling at the threshold had been the line. Once we were across, the fort had closed its jaw.

I felt it hit me then. The knowledge sank into my gut with a weight that outmatched the ankle-deep dread I had been stepping through all evening.

I knew. I felt it. And I walked us in anyway.

The troll's embedded anchor stone pulsed. The light that bled out of it washed across the courtyard in a sick tide. The air itself seemed to warp for an instant. The stone under my boots vibrated, matched by the vibration inside my chest. My hollow seized and answered with its own dull flash of pressure. Pain stabbed through my ribs and up into my throat.

My knees wanted to buckle. I locked them.

The troll opened its mouth. The sound that came out was not like the drake's scream. It was not like any animal roar I had heard. It was low, layered. A grinding bellow of rock shearing against rock. The broken echo of voices trapped in a cavern. It shook dust from the inner wall. It set the torches flaring green-white for a heartbeat.

The villagers in the cages cried out. A thin, ragged chorus. The corrupted sentries on the walls twitched, then stilled back to their patterns. The troll did not glance at them. Its whole attention rested on the four of us in the arch.

Elisah shifted into a fighter's crouch, knives up. Jaime raised the Third Pike shield. The old sigil faced the new monster. Her jaw clenched so hard I heard her teeth grind. Rygial brought his staff up across his body and muttered something under his breath that tasted like copper and dust in the air.

The hum in my bones drowned everything. Drakeslayer's grip felt hot in my hand. The blade seemed to drag toward the troll's chest, hungry for the glowing stone there. Or maybe that pull came from me.

The troll took another step. Its shadow swelled. Its hand lifted, fingers splaying, nails scraping deep scratches into the stone as it brushed the wall.

The air between us thickened. I could feel the exact moment when talk and plans and doubts fell away, leaving only the tight, pure thread of what would happen next.

We were trapped in the fort's throat. The anchor stone in the troll's chest beat in time with the pain in my own hollow. The green light swelled.

It lunged.

# Chapter 21

## THE TROLL AT THE GATE

THE TROLL MOVED BEFORE I finished my step. Stone cracked out from the wall. Dust burst. Its arm came first, thick as a tree, gray skin stretched over stone plates. Its claws scraped the floor and threw sparks. The wall around it broke like rotten teeth.

Jaime swore and shoved me aside. Her Third Pike shield came up. The troll's hand hit it with a flat smack that shook the air. Jaime's boots slid. Her heels carved two white lines in the grit.

The inner gate slammed behind us. Iron rang on stone. The sound bounced around the chamber and did not fade. Rygial flinched. His staff tipped. The amber crystal at its top knocked against the wall and chimed once.

Elisah vanished from my left side. One heartbeat she stood there. The next she was already moving for the shadow under the arch.

The troll dragged its torso free of the wall. Mortar dust spilled off its shoulders in slow curtains as its head tore from the stone with a crunch. Its face looked half carved and half grown. One eye was a dull yellow pebble. The other was a deep green glass that shone from within. It did not blink. It turned toward the sound of Jaime's shield.

In the center of its chest, something glowed. Sick green light pushed under cracked stone skin. The anchor stone sat there, the size of my fist, its surface smooth and wet. The air tasted wrong. My tongue felt coated in old coins. The light from the stone made Jaime's armor look pale and dead.

It pulsed once.

The troll roared. Its breath hit like a furnace in winter. It smelled like old graves and wet earth. Its voice was too deep. The floor shook with it.

It swung for Jaime again, the arm low and fast. I moved without thought. My shoulder hit her side and we went down on the stone. The blow passed over our backs and scraped the wall. Chips of rock rained on us. One cut my cheek. The sting brought my mind into clear lines as I pushed myself up, my palms slipping in dust.

The troll planted its feet. Its toes dug into the floor and cracked the stone. It pulled on the rest of its body. Fractures spread in the wall where its hips still stuck. One more wrench and it stood free, taller than the gate by a head, its arms hanging to its knees.

Its skin had the same dull gray as the fort walls. Plates of natural armor ran down its spine and shoulders, like stacked shields sunk inside it.

The anchor stone pulsed again. The pulse pushed at my chest. It pushed at the hollow place where my own stone had once rested. The scar there felt raw again. I put my hand over it. My fingers met only cloth and bone and the hard edges of scale around the hollow. I still felt the echo. I could almost feel the missing weight.

The troll took one step toward us. Its foot crushed a fallen chunk of masonry to powder. The green light from its chest painted the dust. "Move," Jaime said. Her breath came fast. Her eyes did not leave the troll. Her shield came up again. Her sword lined beside it.

Rygial was behind us by then. He limped to our right, along the wall. His beard had dust in it. His face looked thinner than it had that morning. His hand around the staff shook.

"We cannot stay in the center," he said. His voice came low and flat. "Off the line. Now." The troll's head turned a fraction at the sound. The green glass eye slid across us. It did not seem to hurry. It opened its mouth. Its tongue looked like a strip of dead leather. It stepped again.

Jaime did not give ground this time. She planted her feet, shield edge to stone, and braced. "Elric. Left flank. Make it look at you."

My claws flexed inside my gloves as I moved. I broke right, then cut hard to the left. My pupils narrowed against the green glare, heartbeat loud in my ears like boots on hollow boards. My throat felt dry. My mouth tasted of iron. The air thickened near the troll, a cloying grave smell that coated my tongue.

"Now," Jaime shouted.

Sound tore up out of me. It started low in my chest and scraped through my teeth, something between a hiss and a roar. My throat burned.

The troll's head snapped toward me. The green glass eye fixed on my face while the yellow pebble eye rolled outward. It swung for me this time.

The arm blurred through the air. I felt the wind of it on my fur as I jumped back. Stone claws tore long grooves in the floor where I had stood. Shards of stone shot up into my shins and pain lanced up my legs.

Jaime crashed into its side as the swing finished. Her shield slammed into the troll's knee. The crack of something hard on harder snapped through her arm. I saw her shoulder dip, but the troll staggered. Its weight shifted and its other foot slid half a span. Its torso tilted. The arm that had swept for me skidded along the ground and scraped sparks.

Jaime stepped in and used the moment. Her sword flashed and cut across the back of the troll's ankle, just above the thickest part.

The blade bit. Pale stone flesh split open. Gray-green ichor spurted and hissed when it hit the floor. The smell of it was worse than its breath. It smelled like deep pits and rotted vines.

The troll roared, this time with pain in it. It pulled its foot back and its knee buckled. Its great bulk dipped, just a fraction.

A flick of motion came from its shadow. Elisah appeared there. She did not look up. Her eyes stayed on the joints. Her cloak clung close around her. A knife glinted in each hand as she went in low. Her shoulder brushed the troll's heel. Her right blade plunged into the gap Jaime had cut while her left slid into the back of the other knee. She twisted both and pulled.

Ichor sprayed. It painted her forearms. It beaded on her dark sleeves and rolled off as the troll screamed. Its leg dropped. The knee gave. Its upper body lurched toward the wall.

"Back," Elisah said. Her voice came tight as she dropped and rolled toward the arch. The troll flailed. Claws tore at the air where she had been and its fingers gouged a chunk from the stone pillar. Rock split and crashed down in slabs. Dust splashed over Elisah as she slid behind the fallen stone.

Rygial raised his staff. His arms shook as he lifted it. The amber at its tip flared bright, then dimmed, then flared again like a faltering candle. "Hold it," he said. His jaw clenched. "Jaime. Elric. Hold it where it is."

Jaime grunted. She jammed her shield edge up into the troll's hip as it sagged. Her boots slid again. Her jaw muscles stood out like ropes.

I darted to the other side and leaped, catching a broken stone block with my claws. I hauled myself up and sprang for the troll's reaching arm. Its skin looked like plates fused together, but there were seams. Thin lines. Places where it had grown around old stone.

I landed on its forearm. Its hide felt grainy and oddly warm. The muscles under it bunched and rolled like cables. My claws dug for purchase and scraped over something that rang faintly. I slashed at the eyes. I did not think. My body knew that target. The troll snapped its head aside faster than I expected. My strike glanced off the ridge of its cheek. Sparks flew where claw met stone. The force jarred my shoulder. The green eye fixed on me from too close. Cold pulled at my gut. The hollow in my chest throbbed sharp and deep, in time with the anchor stone's beat.

"Now," Rygial whispered, and the air thickened. The green light from the troll's chest flared and pushed at the inside of my skull. It tried to draw my gaze. It tasted like old dreams and fresh blood. Sound went thin. The weight of the world pressed close. The troll's head turned at half speed. Its drool hung in the air. Sparks from my missed blow drifted like lazy fireflies. My own body still moved at normal pace. My heart hammered in my throat.

Rygial groaned from somewhere on the ground. "Short span," he rasped. His voice sounded strained, as if pulled thin. "Make it count." Jaime moved. She drove her sword into the back of the troll's other knee. The blade sank to the hilt. She tore it sideways with both hands.

Stone cracked. Ichor poured in a slow curtain. Elisah flowed from behind her cover like water. She climbed the ruined leg in three quick steps. Her boots found every jut. Her knives flashed. She opened lines along the back of each joint she could reach. Ankles. Knees. The tendon-like cords behind what passed for its heel.

I pulled myself along the troll's arm toward the shoulder. My claws dragged through slowed dust. The texture felt like thick air. The troll tried to pull its arm back, but it moved as if through honey. Rygial's spell pinned its mass in the moment. The idea of the troll lagged behind reality. His magic bit into the thread of its time. My muscles burned. I gritted my teeth and climbed higher, hand over hand.

The anchor stone glowed below me through the cracks in its chest. The green light pushed harder at my mind. It pressed behind my eyes. It tried to hook my thoughts and turn them inward. My stomach turned. The hollow in my chest throbbed sharp and deep with each pulse. The rhythm beat in my bones and claws. The world around that glow felt thin and pale.

The amber at the tip of Rygial's staff flickered. The thick air shuddered. The slow droplets and drifting sparks quivered. For a breath I felt caught between heartbeats, between one step and the next on the troll's arm. Then the weight of time broke loose. The world snapped back.

Sound slammed back in. The troll's roar finished. The air hit like a shove, its arm jerked, and I lost my hold as I whipped sideways.

I tumbled, claws scraping. Gray skin tore under me. Three long gouges opened along the arm, bleeding ichor that hissed on my scales. Not enough to matter. I hit the floor on my side, breath gone in a rush, pain lighting my ribs. The scales there took some of it, but not all.

The troll crashed to one knee. Its bulk still dragged forward, but its arms caught the stone. Claws dug furrows as it stopped its fall.

Jaime panted, sword arm hanging heavy, blood darkening the padding at her torn shoulder.

Elisah slid off its back and landed light, rolled, and came up near me, chest heaving, hair plastered with sweat and troll ichor, knives dripping. Rygial leaned against the wall, staff braced, legs shaking, veins standing at his thin-skinned temples.

For a moment we only breathed and listened to the troll struggle.

Its wounds oozed. Cracks in its knees and ankles showed darker stone within. Rents along its arms leaked. The anchor stone pulsed again. The green light brightened until it hurt to look, filling the chamber with a sick glow. My shadow stretched long and thin away from it, and every broken stone shard around us shone from one face.

The light felt like cold hands in my chest. It pressed into the hollow place and searched for something that was not there. The scar tissue burned. The scales there prickled as if they grew new edges. The pulse from the anchor stone slowed, then steadied. The light did not dim. It now matched the beat in my chest. That new beat did not belong to my heart.

The troll's breath hissed from too many directions. Its wounds bubbled. The ichor from its knees flowed backward. Droplets broke from the puddles and slid up into the cuts. Splinters of stone along its ankles drew toward the joints and knitted. The cracks closed like mouths.

Jaime watched with her jaw a little open, her sword tip lowering.

Elisah spat on the floor. The spit hit one of the green-lit puddles and burned away in a hiss of steam. "Of course," she said, voice hoarse. "Of course it does that."

I watched my own claw marks along its arm. The three deep gouges drew together. Stone fibers crept across the gaps and pulled the edges tight. Within three heartbeats only faint lines remained. The light from the stone beat in my chest. Each pulse felt sharper.

Rygial straightened with effort. He swallowed, his throat working dry. "It anchors more than the mind," he said. "It holds matter to a pattern. It rejects injury. It pulls the body back to the shape it remembers."

The troll rose. Both knees worked again. It pushed off its hands and stood tall as before. Dust cascaded from its shoulders as the last of the green-lit ichor vanished into sealed stone.

Its eyes found Rygial. It smiled. Stone lips peeled back along carved lines as Rygial lifted his staff again. The grin looked wrong on its heavy face. It showed no teeth. It did not need them. His breath whistled. Sweat rolled from his brow and dripped from the end of his beard.

"No more of that," the troll said. Its voice did not fit its throat. The words came through stone and into the walls. Each syllable vibrated in the rock around us. The green glass eye flared with the sound.

Elisah tensed. Her shoulders drew in. Her fingers shifted on her knives. "Jaime," she said. "You hear that." "I hear it," she said. Her voice had gone low. Her shield came up again, back in place without thought.

"Elric." Her eyes were on me.

"Here," I said. My tail lay flat along the floor. I only noticed when my spine ached. I forced it to rise behind me. My legs wanted to step backward.

The troll lifted its foot and stepped over the deep furrow it had scratched in the floor. The stone shook. The iron gate behind it rattled in its frame.

The sound of its weight landing rang through my feet. The gate behind us rattled in its frame.

"You carry the same mark," it said, its glass eye narrowing as it looked at my chest. Heat flared in the hollow there. My hand went to it before I could stop myself. The skin burned under my touch. I felt each scale edge as if it were newly grown. The green light set faint shadows in every groove. "You are empty. They took it from you. They broke the chain. That is not allowed."

"I do not take orders from those below," Rygial said. His voice shook, but not from fear. He planted the butt of his staff hard into the floor. The sound cut against the troll's low rumble. "This is not your realm. You break the balance. The Warrior stands before you." Jaime flinched at the word. Her eyes slid to me for a breath.

Elisah's jaw flexed.

The troll laughed. Stones grinding under a glacier. Bits of mortar tumbled from the walls.

"He is not yet anything," it said. "He is a cracked vessel. I will fill him again."

The anchor stone flared. Its pulse slammed into my chest and my vision tunneled to the green. The rest of the room sank to ash and shadow. Under the grave-scent came old blood, copper and dry. Inside the stone something beat. A heart, slow and huge.

My knees wanted to fold. My fingers hooked into claws to stop the shaking. Breath rasped loud in my ears, too fast, too thin. Heat climbed my spine, from the small of my back into the base of my skull. Scales along that path prickled, then shoved against my skin. It stretched around them, a clean bright pain that wanted more.

A weight settled over me. Ancient. Vast. It rode the heat in my spine and the itch of new scales. It watched from deep below or far above. It looked through the hollow in my chest toward the stone in the troll's. Want and hunger pressed at me, not mine and almost mine.

"Elric." Jaime's voice cut in, ragged and far away. "Stay with me."

I dragged air into my lungs. I forced it slow. In. Out. In. Out. My heart still pounded like it meant to tear free, but I held the rhythm and I held myself while that other thing pulled.

The troll lunged.

It crossed the space between us in one huge step, arm rising, shadow falling over Rygial. Jaime shouted and surged forward, shield coming up, but she was too far.

The arm aimed for the dwarf.

I did not think. My legs drove. My claws found every crack as I moved. The world sharpened. Each grain of dust hung clear in the air. Each scrape of claw on stone became a distinct note.

Heat flared up my spine. My muscles felt full, cords pulled tight and ready to snap. The hollow in my chest did not feel empty now. It burned. My pupils narrowed to slits. The green light from the stone turned from sick to sharp. I saw the layered growth around it. I saw the hairline gaps where it met the troll's own bone.

I reached Rygial as the troll's hand came down. I hit him in the side with my shoulder and wrapped one arm around his waist. We spun as the claws crashed into the floor where he had stood. Splinters of stone blasted out and scored across my back. I felt them slice through cloth and into scale. Fresh heat bloomed along each track.

We hit the floor and slid. Rygial grunted. The impact knocked something from his belt. A small glass vial rolled away across the stone.

The troll's arm rose for another blow. Jaime slammed into its side, shield cracking against the ribs under its arm. The metal rang. The shock jolted her, but the troll barely shifted.

Its arm lost its full arc and bought a breath.

Elisah darted in under that sagging arm. Her knife flashed for the gap at the armpit. The troll twisted. Stone plates slid. Her blade skidded off a ridge and cut only a shallow line.

The troll's other hand came down toward her. She dropped to her knees as claws smashed into the floor on either side and pinned her cloak. The force shoved her sideways. Her knife spun from her grip and vanished into the dim.

The troll flexed its fingers. Black threads of its cloak stretched and snapped. Stone claws carved trenches in the rock, closer to her ribs each time. Elisah dragged herself backward, hauling torn cloth with her. Her chest heaved. Her eyes flicked to where the knife had gone, then up to the troll's face.

It turned its head and looked down at her. The green glass eye brightened. There was intent in it. Hunger, not for flesh. For something more solid than that. The anchor stone pulsed again. The beat inside it rolled into my own. The two tried to match.

I knew then, in a clean way, that we could not kill it with cuts and bashes. It would stand back up each time. We would grow slower. Rygial would grow weaker. Jaime's shoulder would fail. Elisah's knives would dull or her luck would fail. The troll would not tire. The stone would keep it at the pattern it loved.

I pushed myself up. My ribs ached where I had hit the ground. The scales there had taken most of it, but the bone had felt the rest. Rygial lay on his back. His chest rose and fell in short, shallow pulls. He held the staff across his body with both hands. His fingers looked white where they gripped it. He met my eyes.

"You feel it," he whispered. His lips barely moved. "You know where to strike."

I swallowed. The inside of my mouth felt dry as chalk. The heat up my spine pulsed with the anchor stone's beat. It matched it now. My scales hummed, if such a thing was possible. The hollow in me felt cold.

I did feel it. Not just see. Not just guess. The stone in the troll's chest pulled at something that had once been in me. That something had roots still, even if the stone itself was gone. The roots vibrated like a tuning string. I could feel where to put the blow.

Fear pressed low and heavy into my gut. It did not come as a sharp spike. It came as weight. It felt like Lightning Day, like standing under a sky that had picked me out and was taking its time. I saw the ash and the crater where my anchor stone had been torn from me. I smelled burned flesh. I heard my own screaming again, from a distance. I remembered the numbness that came after, the hollow where the stone had been. I remembered the golden eyes that burned that numbness away.

My hands shook. My fingers wanted to curl in, to claw at the scar. I forced them flat. The heat rose higher. It reached the base of my skull and spread through the back of my head. My teeth ached. The tips of my claws tingled. I could let that heat burst. I knew what that felt like. It felt like claws growing longer and thicker until they could carve stone. It felt like my mouth filling with fire. It felt like my bones ready to bend into something that could leap great heights. The last time that happened, I had lost the world. I had burned through it without sight. When I came back, all I saw were bodies and ash and the hole in my chest. If I lost control here, I would burn Jaime. I would tear Rygial. I would cut

Elisah first because she stood closest. The troll would outlast my frenzy. It had a stone. I did not. I saw all that. I knew it. I felt my hands shake again.

"Elric." Jaime's voice came from my left. It sounded strained and sharp. Her sword clanged off stone as the troll backhanded her shield. The blow threw her into the wall. Her head hit the rock. Blood splattered there. She slid down the stones and hit the floor with her teeth clenched so hard I heard them grind. Her shield arm hung at a wrong angle.

"Elric," she said again. Her eyes found mine.

They were clear, full of the same fear I felt. "We need you."

Elisah rolled clear of the troll's pinning hand. The claws snapped together behind her heel. The sound rang like a trap closing. She came up on one knee. She had only one knife left. Her other hand pressed to her side where a piece of stone had cut. Her fingers came away red.

She looked at me over her shoulder. Her lips were drawn tight. She did not say anything. I did not see blame yet. I saw a question.

Rygial forced himself to sit up. His breath whistled louder. He propped his back against the wall. The amber of his staff glowed dim, only a faint spark now.

"The stone ties it," he said. Each word came with effort. "If you break the tie. The body will fall. The Dragon Below will lose that hold, here. That is your work, Warrior."

The last word trembled. He put weight on it. He sent it into me like the old man had thrown the first training sword at me back in the yard.

*Warrior.*

The heat in my spine steadied. It stopped rising. It coiled instead, waiting to uncoil outward.

I looked at the troll. It moved toward Jaime. Its arms swung slow and confident now. It knew we could hurt it, but not enough. It did not hurry. It wanted us afraid.

The anchor stone in its chest shone like a rotten sun. It called to the empty place inside me. It promised to fill it again. It promised a full pattern, no hollow, no ache.

I felt my lips pull back from my teeth. The sound that came up from my chest tasted of iron and old smoke.

I let the change come. I did not let it rush over everything. The first wave wanted to cover me head to toe. My muscles wanted to twist and lengthen. My jaw wanted to unhinge. My hands wanted to become full claws, not half measures. I gave it my hands first.

The bones in my fingers stretched. Tendons popped with sharp relief. The claws lengthened, darkened, curved. The tips grew dull in color, but I knew they had grown sharp as glass. My palms thickened. Scales shifted there from soft lines into armor plates. My forearms followed. Bones hardened. Muscles knotted. The skin over them tightened and opened to let more scales push through. They wrapped my arms from wrist to elbow in neat rows. Each scale edge caught the green light and flashed it. Pain rode with the change. It felt like my flesh was clay someone kneaded into a new shape. It hurt, but there was rhythm to it. It did not feel like destruction. It felt like a forge. My chest burned. My heart hammered against bone. The hollow in the center filled with heat, not stone. The scarred edges there crawled as if they wanted to grow inward, to close. I held them where they were. I kept that place open. It would stay a hollow. Not all voids were meant to be filled.

I drew breath. It came in long and deep, all the way down. My lungs seemed bigger. The air tasted of grave and ichor and something else. Under it, I smelled the Dragon Below, but also the ancient breath of the one above that had marked me. My pupils narrowed further. The world lost its soft edges. The stone pits in the walls showed every grain. Cracks in the floor looked like maps. The troll's form came into perfect focus. The anchor stone shone the brightest of all. The heat coiled there, in the hollow, wanted out. Behind my teeth, a taste of lightning gathered. My throat felt tight, but not from fear now. From pressure. I clenched my jaw. I did not open it. I did not let the fire come that way. The last time it had, I had burned past thought. I would not risk that.

I kept my feet mostly as they were. My legs tensed, but I did not let them lengthen. My spine's scales stood up sharper, but I did not give them more. I picked my parts. I chose what changed.

The troll turned its head toward me. It had started to lower a hand toward Jaime. It stopped now.

The glass green eye widened. The yellow stone eye rolled inward. The grin faded from its lips.

"I know you," it said. Its voice dropped lower. The walls thrummed. "You are the broken one. They tried to unmake you. They only made room."

The anchor stone surged with light. The beat inside it sped up. It tried to call to the heat in my chest. It tried to pull it. To twist it. To claim it.

The hollow in my chest ached. My bones there felt soft. I could imagine that stone sliding into place. I could imagine the rush of not feeling empty any more.

My claws flexed. The new length of them caught my own forearm. I felt the point press into my scales. They did not break it. Not yet.

Jaime pushed herself up to her knees against the wall. Her shield arm hung limp. Her other hand planted on the floor. She looked at me.

"Elric," she said softly. It was almost a plea.

Elisah wiped blood from her hand onto her torn cloak. She repositioned her single knife. She stepped to one side, automatically finding an angle that might distract the troll if I needed it.

Rygial watched with sunken eyes. He did not speak again. His breath came as a long gravelly sound.

I stepped forward.

The floor felt more certain under my feet. Every bit of stone grip met the pads of my toes better. The sensations came through clear and bright. My tail balanced my center without thought.

The troll planted itself. It saw something in me now that it had not seen before. Its weight settled into its hips. It squatted a little. It braced, just as Jaime had done earlier.

"I will pull you back," it said. "I will set the stone. You will thank me when the hollow stops hurting."

The green light swelled. The pressure against my chest grew. I felt my pulse trip over itself. My vision shimmered at the edges.

I let myself feel the pull. I let it wash across the hollow. It hurt. It called to the scar. It promised.

Then I remembered the crater and the smoke and the screaming. I remembered the way the stone in my chest had felt when it cracked. It had not hurt at first. It had felt like numbness. That numbness had spread. It had reached my fingers and my thoughts. For a moment, I had not known who I was. I had almost welcomed it.

I remembered the moment after that. The weight that had settled above me. The golden eyes that had opened. The voice that had not spoken in words but in light. It had burned the numbness away. It had left a hollow in me. It had left space for my own self.

I would not let that space be filled with the Below again.

I took another step. The world narrowed only to the path between me and the anchor stone. My shoulders rolled. My claws flexed.

"Elisah," I said. "Knees. Now."

She did not question. She moved. She sprinted, low and silent, for the back of the troll's left leg. Her feet barely sounded on the floor.

"Jaime," I said. "Right side. Distract the reach. You do not need your shield for that."

She gave a short, harsh laugh that broke on the first breath. She shoved herself upright with her working arm, then picked up her sword. She rolled her shoulder and winced, but she set her jaw.

"On your mark," she said.

The troll chuckled deep. Its claws opened and closed. Its head tilted.

"You plan," it said. "You think claws and tricks will break stone."

"No," I said. "I will."

I started forward. I did not sprint. The urge to leap high and slash and tear was strong. The heat in my chest pushed at my muscles to do it. I held it in. I set my pace.

The troll waited. Its patience tasted like rot.

"Now," I said.

Jaime yelled and charged, sword lifted high. She ran to the troll's right. Her boots thudded hard. Her voice echoed.

The troll turned its head. That was all. Its right arm came up slow, ready to bat her aside again.

Elisah dove at its left knee. Her knife flashed once and dug into a line she had cut before. She dragged the blade along it and opened it wider.

The troll's leg dipped. It did not fall. It snorted.

I ran straight in. The anchor stone swelled in my vision. The green light hurt my eyes. I did not look away. The pull on my chest became a claw in my ribs. You are mine, it said without words. You were always mine. The air thickened around me as I pushed through a swarm of unseen hands. Pressure built along my limbs and tried to slow me. It felt like the time-slow, but reversed. This magic tried to bind me. To drag me back into the same moment. My bones hummed. My scales sang in a thin sound I heard through my teeth. The hollow in my chest screamed.

I roared back. The sound tore free of my lungs. It shook dust from the ceiling. It hurt my own ears. It came out in two tones, one high and one deep. It carried heat on it. The air in front of me shimmered. The green pressure faltered. It had not expected its call to be met with that kind of answer.

I drove my feet hard. My steps came quicker. My claws bit deep into the stone. Chips broke under my weight. I launched myself the last distance.

The troll swung its arm across my path. Its forearm loomed. The stone plates there would break my spine if they hit full on.

Jaime threw herself into that arm. She did not try to block with the shield. She used her whole body like a battering ram. Her good shoulder slammed against the troll's wrist. The blow knocked her sideways. Her body spun. Her sword flew from her hand. She crashed hard and lay still, but she had done enough.

The arm swerved a fraction.

The arm swerved a fraction.

I twisted in the air. The claws on my right hand scraped the underside of the troll's forearm as it swept past. Stone shards flew. My momentum carried me through the space now open before its chest.

The anchor stone filled that space. It jutted from the heavy muscles. The skin around it had stretched thin to make room. It gleamed wetly, though no moisture sat on it. The green inside swirled.

The pull from it ripped at me. It tried to seize the hollow and tear it outward into the world.

I raised both hands.

King's Edge lesson. Always strike on the weak line. Do not slam broadside. Find the seam.

I saw the seam now. The tiny fault where the stone met the not-quite-living bone. It was a ring of hair-thin darkness.

I brought my claws down in a tight rake.

The impact felt like hitting a bell with my bare hand. Pain shot up my wrists into my elbows. Sparks flew, not of fire, but of that green light. It stung my eyes.

The surface of the anchor stone cracked.

A spiderweb line shot from the point of my blow across its face. The pull from it faltered for a breath. It came back stronger.

The troll screamed. Its voice dropped into a soundless range. My bones shook. My teeth rattled.

Its hands rose to tear me away. Its claws reached for my spine.

"Elric," Elisah shouted.

She drove her knife again into the back of its knee. This time she threw her whole weight into the cut. The joint gave. The leg buckled.

The troll dipped. Its hands swerved. The claws missed my spine by two finger widths. One hook raked my cloak and tore it from my shoulders. Fabric shredded and spun away.

I clung to the stone with both hands. My claws sank into the cracks I had made. They met a sick, smooth resistance, like sliding into packed mud that had bones in it.

The green light flashed. It tried to burn through my scales and into my blood. It wanted a path.

The heat in my chest jumped to meet it. It flowed down my arms. It filled my hands. It turned my claws from bone and horn into something more.

I smelled lightning again. The taste of it hit my tongue. A thin line of fire crawled from my chest along my shoulders and into my arms. It did not burst outward. It chased itself in a tight loop.

I roared again and squeezed.

The cracks in the stone widened. The ring of hair-thin darkness became a thicker band. The pattern inside the crystal fought back. I saw shapes like teeth and scales in the green. They shifted and struck at the inside of the stone. They left no marks.

The troll tried to stand. Its damaged knee wobbled. Its good leg pushed anyway. Its chest heaved toward me. Its own flesh pressed the stone against my hands.

Rygial's voice rose in a hoarse chant. I did not know the words. They came from his old language. They grated like gravel poured across slate.

Time shivered. Not as it had before. Not a slow. A hesitation. The troll's upward push faltered. The strain on my arms did not lessen, but it did not surge.

The heat in my chest boiled. I let it move further.

I opened my mouth. I did not breathe fire. I could have. I felt the flame at the back of my throat. Instead, I growled the sound the old man had taught me in the training hall when he wanted me to focus the power instead of release it.

Three short, harsh syllables that did not belong in any language. The noise pulled the heat down and out through my arms.

It hit the anchor stone.

There was no flash. No arc of flame. No burst of light. The change came inside the stone.

The green inside roiled. It twisted. The patterns broke. The sick light tangled with the brighter heat that came from my hollow. The two fought. They chewed at each other.

For a moment the stone swelled. Its surface bulged under my claws. Microfractures spidered through it.

Then it shattered.

The sound it made came in two parts. One my ears heard. It rang sharp and high like glass crushed under a hammer. The other sound happened in the hollows of bone and in the spaces between my thoughts. That one coughed out and left a silence behind it that hurt.

Fragments of the stone exploded outward. They hit my scales. They cut without cutting. Thin lines of rawness opened along my hands and arms where they passed. Each piece burned cold where it touched flesh.

The green light died.

It did not fade. It stopped. One moment the chamber lay in sick light. The next it lay in the dull gray of the fort again, with only the torches on the walls to give any glow.

The pull on my chest vanished. The hollow there flared with pain, then went blessedly numb.

The troll froze.

Its eyes went wide, uneven stones trying to understand. Its mouth hung open. A low breath rattled there, then stopped halfway.

Its legs gave out.

I leaped clear as the huge body tipped. It crashed sideways. The floor shook. Dust blew in a wave. Bits of broken anchor stone scattered across the stone and lay still, like small, dark-green teeth.

The troll's surface cracked. The lines started at the empty hole in its chest, where only torn flesh and broken bone now gaped. They spread along the ribs, across the shoulders, up the neck. The smell changed. The grave-scent thinned. It turned to simple dust and old stone. The troll's yellow stone eye rolled out of its socket. It hit the floor and broke into powder. Its body slumped further. The skin and internal stone did not hold together. They shed. Plates fell away. Chunks collapsed. Ichor dried where it lay and flaked. Within heartbeats, what had stood as a troll became a half-collapsed statue of rubble. Only the shape of the torso remained clear. The rest melted into a heap of stone and muck.

The green glass eye stayed intact for a moment on the ground. It stared up at the ceiling. Then a fine crack appeared in it. It shattered into sand. Silence filled the chamber. True silence, not the kind that held breath before a blow. Torch flames hissed along the walls. That was all.

My claws hit the floor to steady myself. My knees wanted to fold. The heat in my arms retreated, but not fully. My fingers throbbed in time with my heart.

The partial change did not vanish at once. The scales on my arms stayed thick. My claws stayed longer. My chest still burned.

I tried to roll my shoulders. Pain flared along my ribs. The wounds there spoke up now that the fight ended. I tasted blood in my mouth that was not troll's.

"Elric," Jaime said. Her voice shook. "You all right?"

She leaned half sitting, half slumped against the wall. Her face had gone pale under her olive skin. Blood ran from a cut at her temple. Her shield arm hung useless. Her other hand pressed against her ribs.

I swallowed. My throat felt sanded.

"I am standing," I said. My voice sounded lower than before. The word scraped.

I walked to her. My legs felt heavy. The hollow in my chest ached with each step, like a bruise struck over and over.

Elisah pushed herself up from where she had fallen when the troll's leg gave way. She limped slightly. Her side still bled, but less. She held the pressure with one hand. Her remaining knife was slick with ichor.

She looked at the rubble that had been the troll. Her eyes tracked the broken stone, seeking any twitch. Her nostrils flared once. She relaxed a fraction.

"Stay dead," she said under her breath.

Rygial still sat against the wall. His head had dropped forward onto his chest. His beard hid most of his mouth. His hands lay open at his sides. The staff propped between his shoulder and the stone, its amber dark.

"Rygial," I said.

He did not answer.

I stepped closer. My claws clicked softly on the floor. I crouched. My knees protested the bend.

I put two fingers against his neck, scales and all. For a moment I felt nothing. Panic rose cold in my throat. Then I felt a faint beat under his skin. It fluttered irregularly, but it went on.

He stirred. His eyelids moved. He took a slow breath.

"I am not done yet," he muttered. His tone carried irritation. That, more than anything, eased something in my gut.

He opened his eyes. They looked more sunken, but they were focused. They found my hands first, still half changed.

"You held it," he said quietly. Pride sat there, plain. His voice did not need to say the word itself. "You did not lose yourself."

He lifted one shaking hand and brushed the back of my claw with his fingers. His skin looked like parchment against the dark curve.

The contact woke a new ache. I looked down.

My hands had changed more than I thought. The claws were thicker than before. The scales ran further up, past my elbows. On the back of my hands, a new pattern had formed in faint gold lines, like fine cracks in old glass.

I turned one palm up. The skin there looked darker. The pads had grown thicker, more like armor than flesh.

My chest throbbed. I lifted my shirt.

The hollow in the center did not look the same.

It had grown deeper. The edges had sunk inward another finger width. The scar around it no longer looked like torn flesh. It looked like stone worn smooth inside. The scales encircling it had thickened and edged in faint gold.

I pressed my fingers to the hollow. The skin felt cool there, almost cold, while the scales around it burned warm. The contrast made my stomach flip.

"Elric," Jaime said softly. Her gaze had followed my hands to my chest.

"It took something out of you."

"I broke its stone," I said. Speaking the words steadied me.

Elisah stood a little apart. Her eyes flicked between my altered hands and the deepened hollow. She rolled her knife in her fingers, slow, thoughtful.

"That is twice," she said. Her tone stayed even. "Twice an anchor stone has left its mark on you."

Her words did not hold awe. They held caution.

Rygial let his hand drop back to his lap. His breath came shallow, but more steady now.

"The Warrior's work is never clean," he said. "Each design leaves countermarks. The Dragon Below does not let go easily. The one above does not mark without cost."

He closed his eyes again briefly. His lips moved as if whispering a name.

I lowered my shirt. The cloth brushed the hollow and made me shiver. It felt like brushing cold metal.

My arms still throbbed. I focused on my hands. I pictured them as they had been before. Shorter claws. Thinner scales.

The change did not reverse as easily as it had flowed out. The scales stayed. The claws shortened a bit, but not all the way. I felt bone shift, but the new shape did not fully retreat. Some part of it wanted to remain.

I met Rygial's gaze.

"This will not go back," I said.

"No," he said. "Nor should it. You stepped closer. That is how it works."

Jaime pushed herself to her feet with a groan. She sheathed her sword with her one good hand. The motion made lines of pain stand out along her neck.

She stepped to the rubble pile that had been the troll and prodded it with the tip of her boot.

Stone crumbled. No new green light rose from within. Only gray dust.

She looked at me over the stones. Her eyes were steady, but wary.

Not of the troll. Not now.

"What are you, Elric?" she asked. She tried to make it light. The strain in her voice made it fail.

I swallowed. My mouth tasted of metal and ash.

"I am still me," I said. The answer felt thin in the air. It did not change the way her shoulders stayed tight. It did not ease the way Elisah's knife stayed in her hand.

Rygial nodded once to himself.

"He is a Warrior," the dwarf said. "Whether he wants it or not. The world chose, as it always does when the Below overreaches."

Elisah let out a slow breath. She wiped her knife on a clean corner of her cloak, though it barely helped.

"Warrior or not," she said. "Next time one of those things shows itself, I vote we stay home."

The edges of Jaime's mouth twitched. The expression barely qualified as a smile, but it was there.

We still have to get out," she said. She looked back at the inner gate, still shut, iron bars thick and unmoving. "And this is only the inner fort."

She was right. The fight with the troll had taken up all of my sight.

Now the rest of the fort pressed in again. Stone walls. Sealed gates. The reek of old evil sunk into the mortar.

My arms ached. My chest burned. The hollow there felt deeper. My hands did not fit together as they had before. When I folded them, scales scraped against scale in new ways.

I looked at my claws. The gold lines across the backs of my hands caught the torchlight. They marked a path from my wrists toward the hollow.

I flexed my fingers. They felt stronger.

I lifted my gaze to the closed gate.

The troll at the gate lay in pieces behind us. The path ahead did not.

"We go forward," I said. My voice no longer shook. It sounded like stone scraped into a new groove.

Jaime nodded. Elisah's jaw set. Rygial drew one more breath and hefted his staff. His arms trembled, but he did not drop it.

We stood together in the ruined chamber, in the silence after the stone fell. The air still smelled of dust and grave. The torchlight made small pools on the walls.

My chest ached with emptiness and new weight at once. The anchor stone's echo lingered in my bones. The deeper hollow reminded me of what I had done, and what it had cost.

I placed my altered hand on the iron bar of the inner gate. The metal felt cool against my hot scales.

The Warrior in me stirred.

There would be more anchors ahead. More marks. More choices.

For now, we needed to open this gate.

# Chapter 22

## THE MAGE WHO WANTED REVENGE

WE CLIMBED. MY LEGS shook with each step, but I kept moving. The stair wound up along the inner wall of the fort. The stone felt smoother here. Less like the raw tunnels below. More like carved duty.

The air thinned as we rose. It carried less of the troll's rot and more of old oil and cold iron. My lungs pulled in the chill. The hollow in my chest ached with every breath.

Rygial walked just ahead of me. His shoulders hunched more than usual. His beard still clumped with troll dust. He held the staff in both hands. I watched his knuckles. They had gone a flat white.

Jaime moved in front of him. Her steps had a soldier's rhythm again. Heel, toe, heel, toe. Each step a choice. Her braid stuck to the bloody slash along her neck. She had not cleaned it. She did not seem to feel it.

Elisah kept to the shadows where the stair wall met the inner curve. Her cloak brushed the stone. Her breathing stayed light and careful. One hand hovered near her belt where fresh bandages bound her ribs tight. The dagger in her other hand flashed dull in the low light.

I took the rear. The familiar place. Tail low. Ears half back. Claws flexing in and out against the hilt of Drakeslayer. The sword's weight felt different now. More like it set the rhythm of my heart instead of the other way around.

The torches on the stair lit themselves as we went. First one ahead of Jaime. Then another. They woke to a faint blue spark that crawled along the wick. The flames burned steady and pale. No one touched them.

"Rygial," I said. My voice came out hoarse. "Is that you."

"No," he said. He did not look back. "This is bound into the stones. A standing instruction. Someone liked their order bright."

The stone walls changed as we climbed. At first they still showed the rough tool marks we had seen in the lower halls. Then the scars gave way to smoother planes. The mortar lines straightened. The air lost the stale cave smell and took on something sharper. Discipline.

I could feel it in my whiskers. In the way sound carried. There were no leaks. No places for whispers to drift off and die. Every step echoed with the same crisp ring. Every breath stayed in reach of every ear.

We passed narrow landings with iron doors. Each one bore the same sigil. Three spears crossed over a mountain. Third Pike. The steel fittings gleamed. Someone had kept them clean. Even now.

Jaime's hand brushed one door as she passed. Her fingers caught on a fresh scratch across the sigil. She looked down at the gouge. She did not stop walking.

"How many men did they keep here," Elisah asked. Her voice came soft, like she did not want the stone to know.

Rygial answered. "At full strength, a Third Pike fort holds one hundred and eighty. Plus staff. Plus attached arcanists in this case. Plus contractors." His mouth twisted at the last word.

"Plus trolls in the walls," I said.

He grunted. The sound wavered.

We climbed higher. My thighs burned. The scales along my forearms rasped against the leather of my bracers. The gold tinge caught the blue torchlight and turned it sickly. I kept waiting for my hands to shake. They did not. The claws stayed long and sure.

The stair opened without warning.

Jaime stepped through first. The others followed. I came last and felt my stomach drop for a moment.

We stood in a broad circular gallery. The whole level encircled the central shaft of the fort. Narrow windows cut into the outer wall like arrow slits. The light outside had dimmed to a sullen iron gray. Evening pushed against the glass panes that had been set into some of the slits.

A ring of doors faced inward toward the shaft. Each door stood open. The rooms behind them glowed with the low light of mage lamps. The scent of ink, old leather, and polished wood drifted out in dry waves.

Between the doors stood the soldiers, lining the inner curve of the gallery, two dozen of them, maybe more, Third Pike tabards over chain, spears grounded, shields hooked on arms, helms shadowing their eyes.

They did not move as I froze, my tail bushing without my consent, the fur along my spine rising, Jaime's sword coming up in the same instant, Elisah's dagger turning, Rygial's staff humming as he hissed a word in the old tongue.

No one attacked us.

The nearest soldier's head turned. The motion creaked. He's dead, I thought. Then I saw his chest. It rose. It fell. A slow, steady rhythm. Not sleep. Not rest. A held pose.

"Stand down," Jaime called. Her voice snapped. "By Third Pike code, identify." The soldier stared at her. His eyes were human. Brown. The whites looked dull. Like the inside of an old shell.

He said nothing.

"Elric," Elisah whispered as her eyes brightened with clarity. "Do you smell it?"

I sniffed and the smell of rot threaded through the man's exposed skin. I nodded. He did not blink.

"Anchored," Rygial murmured. He spoke as if to himself, but we all heard. "Held in place through the network. Their wills have been arrested. Their bodies are on standing orders."

"Who gave the orders," Jaime asked. Her knuckles had gone white on her sword hilt.

Rygial swallowed. "Whoever holds the hub."

One of the men near the windows twitched. His finger flexed along his spear. Not toward us. Some inner command. The movement stopped halfway.

"Can they hear us," I asked. "Are they awake in there."

Rygial's jaw worked. "Perhaps. Perhaps not. It depends how deep the binding goes. The stones can freeze a moment. Or a mind."

Jaime stepped up until she stood arm's length from the nearest soldier. Her eyes narrowed.

"Soldier," she said. "Unit and name."

No response. She leaned in, the muscle in her cheek ticking. "Blink if you hear me." Nothing.

Her sword dipped, her shoulders sagged for a breath, then she straightened, turned without a word, and strode toward the open door directly ahead.

We followed.

The room was large. Not grand, but precise. A command chamber. A long table filled its center. Maps covered it. Layers of vellum and waxed linen and pinned parchment. Thin iron rods held some sheets above others so that they could be lifted and laid aside.

The walls held shelves. Each shelf lined with neat rows of leather folders. Stacked ledgers. Neatly wrapped scrolls tied with twine. A large slate board took up most of the far wall. Colored chalk marks scored it with lines and numbers and lists.

An iron brazier sat cold in one corner. The air smelled of wax and old smoke and the faint bite of dried ink.

Jaime walked straight to the table. Her boots scuffed against scattered chalk dust. She reached for a map and stopped when her fingers began to shake. She drew in a breath. Then she pulled the top sheet aside.

Beneath it lay a map of the lowland villages. The swamps. The river. The trade roads. Someone had drawn circles around settlements in red. Arrows marked movements. Dates sat in small precise script beside each mark.

Rygial came to the other side of the table. He set his staff down with care. His eyes moved too fast, as if they tried to make up years of oversight.

Elisah stayed near the door. She turned her head to keep one eye on the corridor. Her other eye took in the shelves.

I moved along the table toward the head. The chair there still held the shape of the last man who had sat in it. A slight depression in the cushion. One arm more worn than the other.

A leather folder lay open beside the chair. It held a stack of thin sheets. Requisition forms. Third Pike letterheads at the top. Wax seals on the edges. I had seen such forms in smaller posts. This felt like their mother.

"Look," Rygial said. His finger tapped the map. "These are not random raids. These patterns show a testing sequence. They increased anchor-stone discharge along the front. Calculated intervals. Measured responses."

His voice had turned low and flat. Like shovels striking bone.

"Testing with people," Elisah said. She had moved to a shelf. She drew out a folder and opened it. Her eyes went hard. "Supply tallies. They logged how much grain burned. How many homes. How many days until folk rebuilt."

Jaime did not answer. She was not looking at the maps. She had found a metal file box set into the table. It had a lock. She held the lock in one hand. Her sword in the other.

"Elric," she said.

I stepped to her. She held the lock out. "Claws."

I slid Drakeslayer into the crook of my elbow and took the box. My talons had lengthened with my earlier change. They caught the light in a faint gold sheen. I set one claw in the keyhole. Metal scraped stone. The lock resisted for a breath, then gave with a dull crunch.

Jaime snatched the box back before the lid fully opened. Papers rustled. She flipped through them with quick harsh motions.

Third Pike rosters. Deployment charts. Casualty lists. Names in columns. Squads. Pikes. Rotations.

Her hand slowed. Her back stiffened. I watched the fine hairs along her neck rise.

She stopped on one sheet. Her thumb traced a line.

"Jaime," I asked.

Her jaw clenched. I saw muscle move. She swallowed hard, then spoke. "Second Squad, Third Pike. Lieutenant Andren Vell. Swamp patrol detail. Cleared for extended deployment."

Her voice had no tremor. Her hand shook as it gripped the paper. Just enough to make the sheet whisper.

"Your father," I said.

She nodded without looking at me.

Rygial left the map. He came around the table. His eyes moved over the roster. "The dates line up with the second wave of tests along the southern marsh. They deployed his squad as... variable presence."

He caught himself. His lips pressed tight.

"As what," Jaime asked. The question cut.

Rygial stared at the page. "The language is clinical. They wanted to test anchor-stone behavior with trained fighters present. To see how raids adapted to resistance. And how command would respond."

Jaime's breath left her in a sharp hiss. She flipped to the next sheet. The next.

Each rustle felt like a blade scraping bone.

"Where is his recall," she said. "Where is his return report."

She searched faster. Her bandaged shoulder bumped the table. She winced, but did not slow.

"Elisah," I said. "Look for any correspondence with the nobility. Or with command in the capital."

"Already on it," she answered. Her fingers ran along spines. She pulled out a ledger bound with green twine. Her lips moved as she scanned.

Rygial moved to the slate board. He read the chalk marks. He whispered to himself. Names. Numbers. Predictions. Some lines had been erased, then written over with bolder hands.

I stepped back from the table. My gaze caught the outer wall. A framed notice hung there. Typed words on stiff parchment. The royal seal at the top. The ink had not faded much. It spoke of duty. Sacrifice. The threat below. It called the fort a bulwark. It spoke of necessary secrecy.

The words felt like grit between my teeth.

Behind me, Jaime stopped turning pages.

The silence that followed felt thicker than stone.

She stared at one sheet. The skin across her cheekbones went tight. Color left her lips. Her chest rose in a shallow, uneven rhythm.

"Found it," she said. The sound came low. Rough. "Casualty report. Swamp engagement, southern marsh. Four dead. Two missing."

Her finger pressed to a line. The nail whitened.

"Lieutenant Andren Vell. Presumed dead in action. Swallowed by mire. Body unrecovered. Marked for honorary commendation in absentia."

Her mouth twisted around the words.

I stepped closer. "There is no detail."

"None," she said.

Rygial looked pained. "Often, in field reports, detail comes in the attached narrative. Or oral accounts."

"Which they did not bother to write here," Jaime said.

Her shoulder trembled. She set the papers down with care. Too much care. Like if she let them fall they would turn to ash.

"Elric," Elisah called. "You might want to see this."

I joined her at the shelves. She held a ledger open. The headings read: Authorizations. Co-signed. Countersigned.

The list of names crawled down the page. Nobles. Generals. Ministers. Each with a seal mark.

Beside them, in another column, someone had written neat little notes. Short codes. Rygial leaned over my shoulder. He squinted.

"These," he said, "are notations by the overseeing mage. He recorded when each patron requested escalation. Or deniability." His finger traced. His voice quivered. "Here. Marquis Erenthal. 'Requires plausible bandit origin.' And Duke Haval. 'Requests visible carnage for internal leverage.'"

His breath hitched. "They ordered shapes of slaughter as if ordering new boots."

Jaime had not moved. She stared at the casualty sheet. Her eyes did not blink. The muscle in her jaw worked. A fine sheen of sweat had gathered along her upper lip.

The door creaked, and we all turned as one to see Kerran standing in the doorway.

He might have once stood tall. His shoulders had the memory of that set. His uniform, if it could be called that now, carried a commander's cut. The Third Pike tabard hung from him in rags. The metal plates beneath it had been warped. Some bulged outward as if something beneath them had grown. Others had sunk.

His skin had gone pale as chalk in some places. In others it looked stretched thin over dark rock. Faint lines of light traced under it. As he shifted, those lines pulsed. They had the same sick blue as the torch flames.

His hair had been cropped in the Third Pike style. It now lay damp and lank against his forehead. His eyes did not hold to one color. They shifted. Brown to gray to a flat stone blue. As we watched, one iris changed faster than the other and then caught up.

He took one step into the room. His boot scraped the threshold. He winced as if the sound hurt.

"No further," Jaime said. Her sword came up between them. Her stance dropped into a guard I had seen her use with captains she hated. Respect held by duty alone.

He smiled. It did not reach his eyes. It pulled wrong at one corner of his mouth, as if one side of his face remembered how and the other did not.

"Lieutenant Vell's girl," he said. His voice rasped. It had gravel in it. "You have your father's posture."

Jaime went rigid. "Name and rank."

He placed his hand over the rag of his tabard. The motion shook. "Commander Kerran of Third Pike Fort on the Black Rise. Or what is left of both title and man."

Rygial sucked in a breath. His staff dipped. "Kerran. You were the one who requested my order's counsel. Years ago."

"You never came," Kerran said. He glanced at the dwarf. The veins beneath his skin flared. "You sent letters. Notes. Concerns. Very proper. No one came when the stones began to speak in ways we did not choose."

"We were blocked," Rygial said. His voice nearly broke. "You must know that. Our summons were intercepted by your superiors. We tried."

Kerran's laughter came short and sharp. It splintered on the air. "Yes. You tried with ink. They tried with chains. You see the difference now."

His gaze swung back to Jaime. It lingered on the papers near her hand. The casualty list. The requisitions.

"You found my work," he said. "Good. I wanted it found."

"Your work," I said. The words tasted bitter. "You mean this fort. These experiments. Those soldiers outside, frozen on their feet."

He looked at me, really looked. His eyes caught on my chest. On the hollow carved there. On the faint gold along my scales.

"Ah," he breathed. "The half-born. The one the Warrior has marked. I heard the stones murmuring about you."

"The stones do not speak," I said. My claws extended a fraction. "They gnaw."

He tilted his head. A faint scrape came from inside his neck, like grit moving against muscle. "You think so now. We all thought something at the start. Then we learned."

Jaime moved one step closer to him. Her blade kissed the air between them. "Why are your soldiers held in place. Why did they not attack us."

Kerran's lips quirked. "Because I did not ask them to. They stand guard as ordered. They will not resist you unless I tell the network to use them."

"The network," Rygial repeated. His brows had drawn down. "You control it."

Kerran shrugged. The gesture made his shoulder plates grind. "Control is a strong word. I direct. I advise. I suggest. The stones learn. They anticipate. It is a partnership of sorts."

"Partnership," Elisah said. She snorted softly. "If that is what the scars under your skin look like, I will pass."

Kerran's jaw clenched. The blue lines pulsed. For a heartbeat, deep under his skin, I saw something shift. Like pressure in a fault.

"These scars," he said, "are the ledger of our mistakes. All of ours. Nobles. Mages. Soldiers. Villagers. Everyone who looked away when coin came. When security came. When the Dragon Below gave us a taste of its power and promised more if we obeyed."

"You speak like a preacher," I said. "With blood on your hands."

He looked at me and smiled again. This time it held a trace of warmth. Twisted warmth. "Blood makes sermons clearer."

Jaime's hand trembled. She steadied it on the hilt. "The villages. The raids. The anchor stones in the fields. How much of that was you."

"All of it," he answered. He did not flinch. "By design. By necessity."

Rygial made a strangled sound. "You orchestrated massacres to test variables."

"To reveal crimes," Kerran shot back.

His voice rose. The soldiers in the hall did not move. The torches flickered.

"You think the nobles would listen to letters. To quiet warnings. To your order's gentle memos about possible corruption." He spat the word. A small spray of saliva caught the light. It glowed faintly blue as it fell. "They wanted results. Weapons. A way to crack the Dragon Below's hide without leaving the capital walls. They built this fort. They paid for the research. They demanded we use villagers as living charts."

His breath came harsh. He took another step inside. Jaime held her ground.

"I obeyed," he said. "At first. I told myself it was for the greater safety. That some must die so that more would live. Then I saw what they did with the reports. They used the fear to tighten their grip. To crush dissenters. They profited on our dead."

He spread his hands, the veins under his skin flaring as his fingers shook. "So I changed the plan."

Rygial stared. "By becoming worse."

"By turning their own weapon on them,"

" Kerran spat. "By correlating patterns. By ensuring that when I sent my final report, it would be so damning that no lord, no minister could wriggle free. The raids show exact lines between order and outcome. Signature and corpse. There will be witnesses. Survivors like you. Evidence like this room."

His gaze flicked around. The shelves. The maps. The ledger in Elisah's hand.

"They will try to burn it," he said. "That is why we must strike again. Bigger. Sharper. A blow they cannot dismiss as an error. That is justice."

"You call that justice," I said. My chest tightened. The hollow burned. I remembered the girl in the flooded village. Her hand reaching from the water. My own claws on her wrist.

He looked at me. His eyes had gone a cold, smooth gray. "You think destruction itself is the crime. I know better. The crime is who aims it, and why. The Dragon Below eats. That is its nature. These men in towers choose. That is theirs. I will drag their choices into the light, with stone and fire if I must."

"The stones do not stop with the guilty," I said. "They spread. They break whatever they touch. You think you can aim them, but look at you. Look at your men in the hall."

He flinched. His jaw worked. "This is the cost of using the only language they understand."

Jaime took another step. The point of her sword almost touched his chest. Her face had gone very calm. Too calm.

"You speak of cost," she said. "Then pay yours. Tell me what happened to Lieutenant Andren Vell."

Kerran's gaze fell to the paper on the table and he hesitated; for the first time since he appeared, I saw his composure slip—his shoulders sagged, the glow under his skin dimming. "You know what the report says," he answered.

"I know what the paper says," Jaime cut in, voice sharp. "I want the truth about my father."

" Jaime's voice sharpened. "I want what happened. In the swamp. In your words. Now."

The room felt smaller. The walls leaned. My ears flattened without my will.

Kerran closed his eyes. His lids fluttered. When he opened them, they had settled into a soft brown. Human. Tired.

"Your father challenged me," he said. "From the first briefing about the stones. He spoke in council. He spoke in the yard. He told the men that no duty asked them to guard murder."

Jaime's fingers dug into the hilt. Her knuckles creaked.

"He was right," Kerran said softly. "I did not want to hear it. I had orders. Funds. A clear command structure. I had the terror of the Dragon in my bones, same as any of us who had stood near a breach."

He took a slow breath. It shuddered. "Your father proposed we refuse. As a unit. That we hold the fort as a true bulwark. That we report the nobles and refuse to fire the stones into villages. He had others with him. Good men. Stupid men. Brave men."

He swallowed. The faint sound seemed loud.

"The nobles knew," Elisah said. Her voice floated from near the shelves. "There are notes here. About 'unreliable elements within command.' They did not trust you entirely, Kerran."

He smiled without humor. "Of course not. They watched everything. They sent inspectors. They sent... alternatives."

He looked back at Jaime.

"I saw the choice," he said. "If I openly refused, they would simply remove me. Put a more eager butcher in my place. The work would continue without my hand. Without my chance to redirect it. To record it. To... twist it."

"So you sacrificed them," Jaime said. The sentence landed like a stone.

He stared at her. No flicker. No denial.

"I scheduled a patrol," he said. "Deep into the southern marsh. Right along a line where we knew the Dragon's influence seeped. I made sure your father and the others who followed him led. I made sure the watchers in the capital saw that the troublesome voices marched into danger. Not against orders. Not in defiance. But in brave duty."

The torchlight seemed to dim around the edges. My claws bit into the leather of my hilt. I smelt blood. My own.

"You knew what would be there," Jaime said. Her lips barely moved.

"I suspected," he replied. "We had measured hungry currents in that mud. Echoes from the Below. Creatures that answered only to its rage. I thought..." He laughed once. A dead sound. "I thought if I placed the problem before the Dragon, the Dragon would solve it sharper than any court. Too quick for word to travel. Too heavy for cover to hold."

"Say it," Jaime whispered. Her voice had sunk into something low and dangerous. "Say what you did."

"I left them to die," he said.

The words hit like a hammer.

"I waited until the marsh sang with screams on the stones," he went on, his voice gone distant. "I felt every anchor go hot. I saw your father on the scrying table, up to his waist in black water, dragging a wounded man toward a bit of moss. He shouted orders."

"He looked straight into the projection," Kerran said. Moisture gathered at the corners of his eyes; it did not fall. "He could not see me. But he stared through the image as if he could. He shouted for extraction. For stone discharge against the beasts. For his commander."

"And you did not answer," Jaime whispered, her sword trembling.

" Jaime said.

Her sword had begun to tremble. Only slightly. The tip wobbled.

"I ordered the anchors dormant," Kerran said. "I told my operators to stand down. I locked the command. I framed it as a systems test. I said we needed to see how the Dragon's spawn behaved without stone interference."

He gave a bitter smile. "The nobles loved that part. The pure observation. They praised the data. They sent commendations. They wrote that I showed initiative."

He dragged a hand down his face. His fingers left faint glowing streaks in his skin for a heartbeat.

"I watched your father vanish beneath the mire," he said. "The water went still. The anchors cooled."

Silence pressed on us. Hard. My ears rang.

Jaime did not move, the muscles in her neck bunched like cord, her eyes gone bright—too bright. "You left him," she said, each word scraping. "You left them. Because they made you feel small in a room."

"Yes," Kerran said, his voice turned flat, bare, "because I told myself that with them gone, I could steer the project, record everything, build a case so heavy that when I finally turned it on the lords, it would crush them. I weighed his life against that and chose the weight."

He leaned forward a fraction, his gaze locking with hers. "I have smelled burning villages since," he said. "I have heard children choking in dust. I tell myself every one is another stone in the avalanche I will drop on their towers. I tell myself it must mean something. You want me to say it does not. You might be right. But I have nothing else left."

Jaime's chest heaved; her wounded shoulder pulled at the bandage as a slow red blossom spread through the linen, her free hand curling and uncurling at her side.

For a moment I thought she might collapse. She stepped instead.

Her sword drove forward. She did not scream. She did not speak. The blade punched into Kerran's side. The sound was blunt, like metal meeting dense wood.

He grunted as his body jerked, blue light flaring under his skin while the crackle of stressed stone filled the air.

He did not fall. Jaime yanked the sword back, a gray slurry clinging to the edge where blood should have been. Pebble dust spilled from the wound as the edges of the cut shimmered.

Kerran's hand shot out, catching the table to steady himself as his fingers dug into the wood and the grain splintered under his grip. "I deserved that," he said through clenched teeth. "Probably more." Jaime's shoulders shook. Her breath came fast and ragged; I watched her throat work as she swallowed bile. "I will give you more," she whispered.

" she whispered.

"Elric," Rygial said sharply. "The stones."

I felt it then. A low tremor under my feet. Like a mountain clearing its throat. The maps on the table rustled. The ink in the wells quivered.

Kerran lifted his head. His eyes had gone bright stone-blue now. Both of them. The veins under his skin shone hot.

"In truth," he said, "I wanted to tell you myself. I did not want you to find out from some dry line in a book. I do not ask for forgiveness. I know its shape too well to beg for a ghost."

His smile twisted.

"I do ask you not to get in my way."

"You think we will let you send another wave," I said. My claws dug deeper into Drakeslayer's grip.

He straightened. The wound in his side had already begun to close. Stone plates pushed up from beneath his skin. They ground against the metal of his armor. The sound made my teeth ache.

"The next strike will break the pattern wide open," he said. "A noble hunting party leaves tomorrow from the capital. Their route passes within reach of our far anchors. Lettered men. Ladies with soft hands. Advisors with too careful eyes. I have their path mapped. Their names listed. I will send the stones. Then I will send the records. Let them weep over their dead while the truth claws their throats."

Rygial's face had gone gray. "You will murder unarmed travelers to make a point."

"They are not unarmed," Kerran snapped. "They hold laws like blades. They wield coin like flame. They bring the Dragon closer with every sealed order. If they choke on a taste of its hunger, good."

"They will not be the only ones hit," Elisah said. Her voice had gone cold. She slapped a ledger onto the table. "Your own maps show the spread. Three villages near that route. Ten farms. Forest camps. They will burn all the same. You know that."

He grimaced. His jaw clenched so hard I thought his teeth might crack. "Collateral."

The word hung foul in the air.

Jaime took another step toward him. She raised her sword again. Her arms shook, but she held it.

"You do not get to use that word," she said. "Not after my father. Not after the marsh."

Kerran's eyes darkened. "Tell that to the men who taught it to me."

"I will," she said. "After you."

"Elric," Rygial said. His hand wrapped tight around his staff. The tattoos along his forearms flickered with faint time-light. "We cannot allow another discharge. The network already strains. One more push at that scale could crack everything. It could wake something in the Below that never sleeps again."

I felt the tremor stronger now. It crawled up my legs. Into my chest hollow. The anchor-stone threads in the walls began to glow faintly. Hairline veins of light. The soldiers outside remained still, but their armor clicked as if under a distant knock.

"Elric of no clan," Kerran said. He addressed me directly now. "You of all in this room know what waits under stone. You have felt its breath in your bones. You carry its knife in your ribs. You think destroying these anchors will silence it. You are wrong. It will only make us blind to it again. That blindness built this fort. Built me. Built this moment."

"I know what the stones do," I said. "I have seen villages sunk. I have felt the pull in my spine. You think you can hold the leash. You cannot."

"I have held it this long," he said.

His voice had begun to tremble slightly. The lines of light in his face twitched. Deep cracks formed at the edges of his jaw. Pebble dust filtered down.

Jaime lunged as Elisah moved in the same instant and Rygial shouted a word in the old tongue. The room exploded into motion. Jaime's sword carved a bright arc, aiming for Kerran's throat. He jerked back with inhuman speed as his chest split—stone plates fanning outward to catch the blade. The edge screeched along them. Sparks spat. One shard flew off and nicked Jaime's cheek, opening a thin red line as the smell of hot rock filled the air.

I sprang forward. Drakeslayer came up from low guard. The world narrowed to line and target. The sword bit into Kerran's other side, just above the hip. The impact shuddered up my arms, like striking a quarry wall. The blade sank deeper than Jaime's had. My claws gave it an edge beyond human strength, carving through stone-flesh in a spray of grinding dust. No blood.

Kerran roared, his voice rattling the shelves as the map pins jumped. His hand whipped out and caught the flat of my blade. His fingers had turned into sharp stone talons that dug into the metal as blue light surged along them. Pain shot through my hands. The scales along my forearms flared hot. Gold flickered at the edge of my vision.

"Back," Rygial shouted, and time warped. The air thickened. My swing slowed, then sped, then caught in a strange drag as Kerran's outline blurred. For a heartbeat, I saw him in three positions at once—one taking my strike, one reaching for Jaime, one turning toward Elisah. Rygial grunted, strain standing out in the cords of his neck as he thrust his staff forward. The time-split narrowed. Two of the Kerran-images snapped back into one. My blade connected again. Kerran's hand slipped. Drakeslayer tore free.

A crack opened along Kerran's torso as stone and flesh parted, blue light pouring from the gap like gas and spilling across the table. The maps smoked where it touched.

Then the wound began to close.

The stone under-skin flowed. Edges fused. The crackling of regeneration crawled through the air. It set my teeth on edge.

"His pattern is anchored," Rygial gasped. Sweat beaded on his brow. "The network patches him. We cannot cut him down faster than he will rise."

"Then break the pattern," Elisah shouted.

She darted to Kerran's blind side. Her steps were light and quick. She slid across the table, boots scattering papers. Her dagger flashed. She aimed for the glowing veins at his neck.

Kerran's arm shot up. It bent wrong at the elbow, as if extra hinges had formed under the skin. His hand snapped around her wrist. Stone fingers crushed flesh. Elisah's dagger clattered to the floor.

She hissed and drove her knee into his knee. The impact did not even stagger him. He swung her like a rag and hurled her across the room.

She hit the wall near the shelves. Wood cracked. Books tumbled. She slumped to the ground, breath driven out of her. Her bandaged ribs took the blow with a sick wet sound. She sucked in air in sharp, shallow pants.

"Elisah," I yelled, and she lifted a hand—two fingers up. Alive. Hurt.

Jaime screamed.

Her sword hammered against Kerran's chest again and again. Each blow chipped stone plates. Each chip regrew almost before it hit the floor. Her arms shook. Blood from her reopened shoulder cut a path down her arm and crossed her fingers. It slicked the hilt.

Kerran's face had begun to warp. The jaw stretched. Jagged teeth pushed through gum. One eye sank deep into a pit of stone. The other bulged, threaded with bright blue.

"You should not have come," he snarled. His voice had deepened. It carried stone-grind. "You should have stayed in your village and rebuilt your father from stories."

He grabbed Jaime's blade mid-swing. The metal groaned. His other hand shot forward and struck her chest. The sound was wet and dull. She flew backwards into the edge of the table. The wood cracked. She slid down, gasping.

I lunged at his back. Drakeslayer rose for a killing blow.

The network pulsed. Every anchor-stone thread in the walls brightened at once; the light stabbed from all sides, sank through my scales, and hit the carved hollow in my chest like a hammer.

My lungs clenched. My heart stuttered. The world flashed white and I stumbled. "Elric," Rygial shouted, his voice suddenly far away. "The hub. He is drawing through it."

Kerran turned toward the inner wall, toward a door at the far side of the command chamber that stood open upon a narrow stair leading further up, deeper into the heart.

He began to move.

"Stopped him," I tried to say. My tongue felt thick. My arms shook as if someone had poured molten lead into the bones.

The Warrior stirred, the presence in my chest uncoiling as heat flared up my spine, fingertips burning while the scales along my arms shone brighter, gold deepening toward molten.

The anchor-stones called to it, their pulse matching my racing heart as their light poured into the hollow; they wanted something from me—or wanted to give—and the Warrior pressed harder against my ribs.

Rygial thrust his staff into the floor and time energy spread in a wave that washed over Kerran; the commander staggered, his limbs slowing for a moment as his twisted face jerked in fits, one arm hanging half-extended while the other drew back, caught between movements.

Rygial roared from deep in his chest, veins in his forehead bulging, tattoos along his arms flaring bright white as the skin around them reddened. "I cannot hold him," he gasped. "He rides the same streams I touch. The anchor songs run through his bones."

Elisah pushed herself up along the wall, her face gone pale, breaths coming through clenched teeth as she limped toward Jaime.

Jaime tried to rise. Her arms betrayed her. She pushed once. Twice. The third time she got to one knee, sword point propped on the floor. "Kerran," she rasped. "You do not leave this room."

He turned his half-frozen head toward her. For a heartbeat, his human eye softened. The stone one glowed. "I left him," he said. "I do not get to choose my exits anymore."

He strained against Rygial's time-lock. Pebbles snapped free of his skin and fell. The air vibrated as he pushed, the sound reminding me of glaciers cracking in the north.

The hub pulse increased. The whole fort seemed to hum. Distantly, deeper below, I felt answers—stones in fields, in village wells, in swamp pools—picking up the song and sending it back, a net of bright pain, the Warrior driving against my ribs in time with it.

I clenched my jaw. "No."
"

My claws dug bloody furrows into my palms. The pain helped. It grounded me in my own body.

"Elric," Rygial shouted. His voice had thinned. "If he reaches the hub, he will send the discharge. I cannot cut him from the stream. Someone must break the stone itself."

"I will," I said, and if I broke the hub, the network would shatter, the stones in the villages would go dark, and Kerran's link would die with them, but the hub sat through that door, up that stair, and Kerran still dragged himself toward it, inch by inch, even under Rygial's slowing field.

I took a step, knees almost giving as the anchor-pulse hammered my chest, trying to pull me into a different rhythm, to make my heart beat with the Dragon's, and I forced another step.

"Elric," Elisah called, her voice shaking. "If you do anything stupid, make it be something that hurts him more than you." "I will try," I said, and it came out as a growl.

The Warrior laughed inside my bones. Not amused. Not cruel. Hungry.

I reached for it.

Fear flared in my gut. Not just of the change. Of what would stand in my place if I called it fully. Of what it might do to Jaime. To Rygial. To Elisah. I saw again that flooded village. My arm around a child's waist. My grip too hard. The water too strong. I smelled the mud in her lungs.

My claws flexed, the gold along them brightening as small sparks arced between scale and scale.

"Elric," Jaime rasped, and I looked back to where she knelt amid scattered papers, her braid coming loose, blood streaking her face, her eyes locked on mine with no plea in them, only a steady, terrible courage.

She nodded once, fingers tightening on her sword as she dragged herself up another inch. "End this," she said. "Whatever it takes."

Her words fell into the hollow in my chest. They hit something deep.

I turned back to Kerran.

He had broken one arm free of the time-drag, stone fingers clawing the air toward the door as his form bulked further, plates jutting from his shoulders and hips, legs lengthening, joints thickening until he looked less like a man and more like something sculpted halfway from a cliff.

The anchor-stone threads in the walls blazed as the Warrior pushed again.

This time I did not retreat. I opened.

Heat roared up my spine as my vision flared gold and the edges of the room darkened, all the light seeming to pour inward toward me while pain tore through my bones; every joint caught fire, each rib cracking, lengthening, fusing as the hollow in my chest widened, drinking the anchor-light and spitting it back in a deeper tone.

My fingers stretched as claws erupted, longer, curved like hooked blades, while scales rippled along my arms, over my shoulders, across my chest, catching the torchlight and turning it into a burning sheen.

My teeth ached, then sharpened as my jaw extended a fraction and the world filled with new scents—fear, ozone, the grit of moving stone, the rank tang of my own changing flesh.

My tail lashed as the muscles in my back thickened; armor straps strained until one snapped with a sharp pop and leather fell away, and I did not care.

Somewhere in front of me, Elisah cursed while Rygial shouted my name and Jaime's sword scraped the floor as she tried to rise again, but I could barely hear them over the Warrior's beat in my ears.

The anchor network screamed. It tried to claw into my change. To steer it. To pour its pattern into my bones. Images flashed behind my eyes. Villages burning. Tunnels flooded. A face of scales and hunger deep below, smiling upward.

Not yours, I thought, or thought I thought. My mind had begun to shred around the edges, but I grabbed that thought like a rope. I remembered my mother's hands—fur and callus—the way she had smoothed my ears after bad dreams. I remembered the first time I held a blade, the weight, the choice. I remembered Jaime laughing once by a campfire, before this fort, before the troll, the light in her eyes then. I remembered Rygial's fingers shaking when he showed us his first time-freeze. Elisah's dry voice telling me not to get sentimental as she stitched my side. I anchored myself to them.

Then I let the rest go.

The Warrior surged up. It filled me. Bones lengthened. Muscles tore and reknit. The world snapped into frightening clarity. Every breath of air around Kerran stood out. Every grit of dust under his heel. I heard the slow drag of Rygial's heart as time pulled at him. I heard the faint hitch in Jaime's lungs.

I raised Drakeslayer.

The sword felt small. Light. Like a knife.

My roar tore the room.

The last thing I saw before the change swallowed my human sight was Kerran's twisted face turning toward me. For the first time, fear flickered there. Not of death. Of recognition.

"The Warrior," he whispered.

The anchor-stones answered.

The network's pulse and mine collided. For a heartbeat, the whole fort shuddered in place like a beast startled from sleep. A crackly, grinding thunder rolled up from the depths. The hub stone ahead bloomed with raw light.

My skin split and remade itself in scales and fire.

The world narrowed to target and stone and blood yet to fall.

# Chapter 23

## WARRIOR, AT LAST

THE WORLD SETTLED INTO edges and heat.

Stone lines in the floor shone like buried fire. Every crack in the flagstones breathed dust. The air tasted of iron and old ash and the faint sour reek of the swamp, dragged in on boots and armor and Kerran's ruined lungs. My skin itched where fur gave way to scale. Each breath slid past new teeth that did not quite fit in my old mouth.

I stood taller than I had ever stood. My shoulders brushed the dangling chains. My shadow climbed the far wall like a stranger. Red and gold scales chased each other over my forearms and up my neck in layered chevrons. They caught the hub's glow and threw it back in little flares. The patterns followed the lines of muscle and bone as if they had waited there all my life and only now came forward.

The Drakeslayer sword lay easy in my hand. Almost light. Its weight fit my arm as if the two had grown together. The blade's etched runes steamed with faint golden mist. Every carved curve along the crossguard was as sharp as the first time I had seen it, but now I realized the steel had always been meant for this grip. For these claws.

My fingers flexed around the hilt. Talons of dull ivory tipped each scaled digit. They caught the glow and made little points of light. When I curled them, the leather of the grip whispered and protested, then yielded.

I could hear everything. Jaime's breaths, short and tight, to my left. Elisah shifting her weight behind me, distributing pain away from her wounded side. Rygial's knuckles brushing the haft of his spear, the slight wood fibers catching on his calluses. The deep, slow thrum of the hub stone in its iron cradle at the center of the fort. The hearts of the soldiers asleep in stasis in the rooms below.

And Kerran.

He stood across the chamber, in front of the raised platform and the hub. Or the thing that had his voice stood there. Flesh swelled over armor plates in knotted folds. Muscle had grown beyond sense, ballooned and torn and regrown. Splintered bone jutted and then sank back beneath skin that never decided if it was scar or stone. Anchor-stone veins glowed through his body in hard, cracked lines. They pulsed with the same rhythm as the hub. His eyes were pits full of crushed granite and fever.

He stank. Not of rot alone, though there was that, a sweet, cloying odor of meat that had died and then kept moving. Under it lay stone dust, sharp and glassy, and the metallic tang of old lightning. It burned the inside of my nose. The Warrior in my bones welcomed it as warning. The rest of me wanted to gag.

"You see now," Kerran said. His voice had two layers. One rode in his throat, wet and thick. The other came from deeper in his chest and the stones in the walls, doubled and hollow. "What it takes. What it costs. Power, boy."

His left arm ended in a mass of fused stone and tendon that had once been a gauntlet. Fingers like broken pillars clenched and unclenched. Shards scraped each other. White dust fell from the seams. His right arm looked almost normal from the shoulder to the elbow, then dissolved into tendrils of muscle and dark gristle that flexed and snapped around a chunk of anchor-stone the size of a child's head. It beat like a heart.

I stood. Feet planted. Tail, new and heavy, curved down and balanced me, the tip resting against the floor with the faintest scrape of scale on stone. My own heartbeat had slowed. The fear had cooled into something else. Not calm. Not quite. A line of intention that ran from my jaw through my spine to the point of the sword.

"Elric." Jaime's voice touched the back of my shoulder. Small. Hoarse. "You in there?"

I did not turn. The hub's glow painted Kerran's warped body in a halo of cold light. Stone veins crawled from the base of the hub into the floor and out under the walls. All the anchors of the network met there like roots. I could feel it now. Not just see. Threads of pressure in the ground. Sluggish, dangerous. Coiled toward the villages, the marsh, the old road.

"I am," I said. My own voice had deepened. The words came out with a faint rasp, as if the air had to slide around new shapes in my throat. I felt them in my chest as if another creature spoke with me. "Stay behind. All of you. Until you must not."

Jaime's hand left my shoulder. She cursed under her breath. The words shook. The sound steadied. "Get him," she said.

Elisah's reply was a quiet snort. "Try not to bring the ceiling down on our heads in the first minute." She shifted, then sucked a breath through her teeth, pain sharp and held. "Rygial. Pattern we discussed. Focus on his connection."

Rygial's answer was a murmur, more ritual than speech. "Anchor unmoored. Weight recalled. I hear you."

The hub thrummed. Kerran raised his head and inhaled. His nostrils flared. Flesh rose and fell along his back like waves on silt. New bone pushed at his shoulders, half-sprouted wings of jagged stone spines and tendons. They quivered, then settled. In his face, for a heartbeat, I saw the commander that had once walked the palisade of Third Pike. The man who had handed me a canteen the day my parents burned. His gaze tightened. The twisted meat at the corner of his mouth tried to fold into a smile.

"You accepted it," he said. "You chose it. Good. Good. Maybe you will understand. When the orders come, when the map lies in front of you. When you know that to save ten you must throw away one. Or many more than one."

"You murdered Jaime's father," I said. "That was not an order."

He flinched. The anchor-stone in his hand flashed, then dimmed. One of the veins along his neck swelled, then cracked. Dust bled from it. His jaw trembled.

"He chose to stand in the way," Kerran said. "Like bedrock. Like a wall. The tide cannot argue with walls. It crushes them. It must." His next words came faster, head jerking. "Your father. Her father. All the same. Always the fathers." A ragged chuckle echoed in his chest, more stone than flesh. "You think you are here to save daughters and sons. You are here to keep the line. The King's line. The old line. The rest is meat."

The Warrior in me wanted to move. The delay set its teeth on edge. Muscles twitched along my arms. Tail flexed. Claws dug into the cracks of the floor for purchase. I felt strength sitting in my limbs, a coiled readiness that made the world seem slow.

"Whatever they are," I said, "I am here to stop you."

His head tilted. The meat-wings shuddered. A piece of stone broke off his left forearm and clattered to the floor. He did not notice. His gaze sharpened and for a blink the fever cleared.

"Then come," Kerran said. "Warrior."

He moved first.

He did not charge. He lunged. The stone mass of his left arm slammed into the floor and ripped him forward in a low, dragging rush. Tendrils from his right arm whipped out, their wet lengths cracking the air. The stone-heart at their center pulsed bright white. The ground bucked under his weight. The hub sang in answer.

I stepped aside. The new tail shifted my balance without thought. The tendrils carved the air where I had stood. One brushed my chest and scraped scales with a sound like steel on glass. Pain flared, bright and clean. The Warrior in me narrowed on it and memorized the arc.

Drakeslayer met the stone-arm in a ringing clash. The impact drove me back a step. Flagstones cracked under my feet. My claws held. The blade bit into the fused stone and tendon and stuck. Energy from the hub poured through Kerran's limb and up into the steel. It sang, high and arching. The runes along the blade flared.

Heat exploded up my arm. For a heartbeat the old fear threatened to break through the clarity. The memory of past transformations. Of pain without aim. Of scales coming in ragged patches and bone trying to be two things at once.

I set my weight. Accepted the heat. It flowed along nerves that had learned to carry it. It did not unmake me now. It filled.

Kerran roared. The sound hammered the air. Fine dust fell from the ceiling in a soft, steady rain. His free tendrils swept around for my ribs.

"Down," I said.

Jaime dove. I heard her leather scrap and the hard exhale as she hit the floor. Rygial muttered quick, cracked syllables. A surge of cold wind knifed across the room and caught Kerran's right arm. The tendrils wavered, slower now, as if the air had thickened around them. Elisah's crossbow thrummed. The bolt cracked into the exposed anchor-stone. Steel rang on stone. A hairline fracture appeared and gleamed.

Kerran snarled. He jerked his arm away from me. The force tore Drakeslayer free. We both staggered, then reset. The edges of his mouth foamed.

"Vermin," he said. His gaze flickered past me, to where the others crouched by the wall. Muscles swelled along his back. "Always scurrying around the feet of giants."

"Look at me," I said. I stepped in, cutting his view off. Scale neck to cracked stone throat. "You wanted a Warrior."

I struck low, then high. The sword cut a deep line in the flesh of his chest, then slammed into one of the glowing veins. Stone shards fountained. Grey blood, thick and sandy, spattered my scales and hissed where it hit. It smelled of wet quarry rock and iron.

Kerran howled. His free arm swept down. I ducked under it. The air above my horns churned with heat and grit. I drove my shoulder into his ribs. It was like ramming a cliff. Pain shot up my frame, but the solidity felt right. Real. He staggered half a step. The hub glared. Its glow intensified. The veins across his body brightened and knitted, slower than before but still working.

"Elisah," Rygial called. "The feed. The hub is pushing everything to him."

"I see it," she said. Her voice had gone thin, but her words stayed steady. "The glyphs along the base. They cycle the flow. If we break the pattern it should choke him."

Kerran swung wildly, stone-arm smashing sideways. I brought Drakeslayer up. The impact numbed my hand to the shoulder. The blade held. Stone chipped.

"Do not touch my work," Kerran spat. Spittle and dust sprayed. One eye rolled, then fixed. "This fort is a dam. The flood is out there." He jerked his chin toward the invisible villages beyond the walls. "I hold it back. You want to tear it apart for peasants in mud. For children who will never matter."

"You are pointing it at them," I said. I slid around his arm, used his own momentum, and slashed across the anchor-veins on his flank. The line opened. Light bled out. The hub's glow stuttered. Stone within his flesh crumbled and shifted. He sagged on one side. "They are not your flood. They are who you drown."

His face twisted. The man I had known fought the stone around his skull. The muscles at the corners of his eyes worked as if to squeeze tears from rock.

"You think this is my choice?" he said, words breaking. "You think I wanted the stones? The network? They brought me reports from Old King's Walk. From the Hall. The

villages were numbers on a page. Units. Like barrels of grain. Like bolts of cloth."
His gaze snapped to mine. "You think they look at you and see a boy?"

His tendrils lashed at me while he spoke. His arm moved with the rhythm of a soldier trained to talk and kill in the same breath. I blocked and stepped and felt the strain in my legs as the Warrior's balance met the stone-fed strength. He was larger. He had more weight. He had the fort in his veins. I had my body and the sword and the three behind me.

"Rygial," Elisah hissed. "On my mark. Cut when I say."

"Ready," he said. His voice shook but the word stood.

Jaime moved along the wall like a shadow. Her knives gleamed in the hub's light. She used the wreckage of the command tables as cover, slipping from broken leg to splintered tabletop, eyes fixed on the glowing lines that fed the hub. Her jaw clenched so tightly that a muscle in her cheek jumped. Grief rode her shoulders, a weight that made her steps careful, not slow.

Kerran saw her. His head snapped toward her. The skin of his neck tore with the speed and healed a moment later with a hard crust of stone. The tendrils whipped that way.

I stepped into them. One wrapped my forearm. It burned like plunged iron. Stone grit embedded in its length scraped my scales and dug in between. Another whipped around my waist. It pulled. For a heartbeat my feet left the floor. The world tilted.

I snarled. The sound came from deep in my chest, older than words, and shook dust from the rafters. The tail that had seemed awkward a moment ago lashed out and struck the floor. The shock of it sent me back upright. My claws dug into the stone. I twisted my trapped arm and brought the sword down. The blade sheared through tendon and stone. The severed length of Kerran's arm flopped to the floor and writhed, then stiffened and cracked.

Grey blood sprayed my face. It stung my eyes. I blinked through grit and light.

Kerran screamed. His right side convulsed. The anchor-stone heart flared with a blinding rush of light and then flickered, confused. For an instant the veins along his body dimmed.

"Mark," Elisah said.

Rygial's chant peaked. Sound warped. The hub's hum shifted from a steady drone to a jagged, off-key grind. Air chilled, then compressed. A ripple moved through the carved glyphs around the base of the hub. Lines of glow broke and stuttered like a sentence forgotten mid-word.

Jaime slid in low at the hub's pedestal. Her knife drove between two cracked anchor veins that fed into the stone. She carved, hand sure, hatred a straight line in her arm. Stale heat blew across her face. Hair whipped back.

Kerran convulsed. The remaining tendrils on his right arm snapped and twisted like snakes thrown on a fire. The stone veins in his chest flared, then suddenly went dull. The flesh beneath them sagged. He dropped to one knee. The floor shook.

For a breath, the chamber quieted. The hub's light thinned. The fort felt lighter under my feet, as if it had exhaled. Far below us, through the stone, I heard faint voices stir. Soldiers waking from the cold hold of the anchor. Confusion, fear, the edge of anger.

Kerran hunched. The skin over his spine rose and fell in knots. He pushed his stone hand against the floor and forced himself upright again. His breath rattled. One eye had gone milky. The other burned.

"Clever," he panted. Blood and stone dust bubbled at his lips. "Choke the feed." He laughed, a broken sound that shook loose bits of stone from his shoulder. "You forgot something."

The hub's glow spiked.

The fractured glyphs along its base blazed back to life, too bright, too fast. Threads of light shot along the anchor veins that ran out under the walls. Not slow and steady now. Wild. Hurtling. Flares along a fuse.

A low boom rolled under our feet. Distant. Out toward the marsh.

Kerran's ruin of a face stretched into something like triumph and horror combined. His voice was both his and not as he spoke.

"I already lit it," he said. "While you played at severing roots. The order went through. The network is firing. Every anchor. Every stone. Every village marked." His gaze locked on mine. "This is what your Hall chose, boy. I am only the hand."

Jaime froze. Her knife stayed buried in the cracked conduit. Her shoulders rose. The word left her like a wound.

"No."

Another distant boom answered. The floor shook harder this time. Dust poured from a new crack in the ceiling, a thin dry waterfall. The hub sang high, keening. The air tasted of lightning and crushed rock.

The Warrior in me measured the power in the room. The draw and release through the veins. The timing of the pulses. I saw the path like lines of fire on the inside of my eyes. Out along the network to the anchors at the edge of the villages. The old stones standing in farmers' fields. The cairns built as landmarks. All bent into weapons.

To stop the wave I would have to break the basin that held it. The hub, root and heart. The stone that fed Kerran and took his instructions and passed them along. The anchor that had him the way it had the soldiers below, only deeper, crawling through his flesh.

"Can we cancel it?" Jaime shouted. Her voice had sharpened to a blade of its own. "Tell it not to fire?"

Elisah's hands hovered over the runes she had half-disrupted. Sparks bit her fingers. She flinched, then forced them back. Her face creased. "It is an order, not a question. The pattern is already running."

Rygial's chant faltered and stopped. His breath came ragged. "I can slow, not stop. The stones are listening to him, not to us."

All eyes turned to Kerran. He jerked, then straightened on ruined legs. The veins along his jaw blazed. The hub's light pulsed to his heartbeat. He was the fulcrum. The signal passed through him.

I knew then. There was one clear path. It ran through the hub and his body together. There was no line that cut one without breaking the other. The stone in him and the stone in the pedestal had grown too close. They shared a pulse.

The Warrior in me did not hesitate. It did not weigh lives in ledgers. It saw the joint. The break point.

The boy from Third Pike, who had once stood on a palisade and thought the commander kind for offering water, hesitated for him. For the man whose hand had rested on my shoulder and pointed out which fires in the valley meant danger. For the broken thing in front of me who had become what the Hall had asked, and more, and then too much.

Kerran saw that in my eyes. For a heartbeat, the madness receded. The stone around his mouth eased. There, beneath the horror, was a man who had been young once, and proud, and certain that if he held the line hard enough no one would starve.

"Do it," he said. The words scraped his throat raw. He forced them out like something he had carried too long. "Warrior. You wanted the truth. Here it is. Sometimes there is no other hand. No one above you to blame. You hold the sword. You choose where to cut."

Jaime stared at him as if he had struck her again. Her father's ghost moved between them, unseen but solid. The man in front of her had left that father to die in black water. Now he asked for his own death. For hers, by inaction, if I did not move.

Elisah swore, low and ugly. "Elric. The charge has not fully built. If you break it now, there is a chance the wave will collapse before it reaches the far anchors." Her voice cracked. "A chance. That is all."

Rygial's eyes glistened. He clutched his spear as if it were the only thing tethering him to the room. "If you miss," he whispered, "the discharge continues. And we lose you as well."

The Warrior did not care about me. It cared about the line. About what stood on one side and what on the other. It loosened my grip on fear. It made the muscles in my back coil and teeth bare.

I stepped toward the hub. Each footfall sent a dull shudder through the floor that answered the hub's song with my own presence. The sword in my hand thrummed. The runes drank the air. A faint gold light grew along the edge like dawn under a horizon.

Kerran laughed once. A short, broken sound. There was no triumph in it now. Only release.

"Make it mean something," he said. "Do not be like them. Counting barrels. Counting bodies. Call them by their names."

I thought of the villages we had passed. The woman with the crooked braid who had pressed a crust of bread into my hand. The boy in the flooded field who had waved at us with both arms. The old man mending a net on his stoop, humming to himself. I did not know all their names. I knew they had them. That was enough.

The hub sheeted light. Cracks ran spider-like across its surface as the charge built too fast. It hummed high enough that my new teeth ached. The glow painted Kerran's ruined body in stark relief. It turned the grey blood on my scales into coins of molten gold.

"I am sorry," I said. I did not know to whom.

Then I ran.

The tail that had felt foreign now drove each stride more sure. My feet found the cracks I had made earlier in the floor and pushed off them as if they had been placed for this. The air in the room thickened, solid under my hands. The Warrior in me burned white and clean. Every sense narrowed to the point of the sword and the heart of the stone.

Kerran tried to step in front of the hub. His stone leg buckled. He fell to one side. His arm, the one I had half severed, flared with last power and flung a fan of tendrils toward me.

I did not turn the blow aside. I drove through it. Flesh and stone whipped across my ribs. Something tore under my left arm, deep and hot. Pain roared. I let it be and came on.

Drakeslayer rose. The runes along the blade blazed. The air screamed past the edge. For an instant, the sword was not a sword. It was a line between one world and the next. Between a village here and cinders there. Between Kerran breathing and Kerran gone.

I brought it down.

Steel met stone. Not like earlier, when the blade had bitten and stuck and chipped. This time the hub was overloaded, strained past its own shape. Its inner lattice sang in terror. The sword cut through the outer shell as if through fired clay. The first third of the blade sank in, then the second. The runes drank the gathered power like water poured down a crack.

Light exploded. White, then gold, then an ugly, bruised violet. Sound vanished for a heartbeat. The world went empty. My body shook as power rushed up through my arms and spine, trying to use me as a path. The Warrior hurled it back out. Scales along my forearms flared and then darkened, some cracking under the strain. Horns rang in my skull.

Then the hub shattered.

Stone burst outward in a storm of shards. They whirled and hissed past like a thousand thrown knives. Scales on my chest and throat rang as they deflected a few. Others cut fur and skin where the scales had not yet come. Hot beads of blood dotted my arms. Slivers slammed into the walls, into the floor, into Kerran's body.

The hum cut off. For a breath there was only the hiss of falling debris. Then a deep, terrible groan rose from the bones of the fort.

Kerran screamed. Not as he had during the fight. Not in rage. This sound tore through the throat of what was left of the man and the stone together. The anchor veins that had lit his body flickered and went dark in patches. Where the light died, the stone flesh sloughed. It fell away in chunks, revealing raw meat that had never meant to be seen.

The anchoring lines that had run from the hub into his chest and spine tore loose. Each one pulled a length of calcified tissue with it. His back arched with the force. He clawed at the air with his stone hand, as if groping for the vanished pulse of the hub. Failing, that hand found me instead.

His fingers closed around my upper arm. They were not strong now. The pressure barely dented the scales. But the gesture held weight. He dragged himself up along that grip until his ruined face was level with mine. His breath stank of blood and dust and something that had no name.

"You hear it?" he rasped. "All that power. All that cost. Gone. No glory. No song. Just you and me in a room."

My hearing returned in a rush. Outside, distant, no more booms. No waves of pressure racing along the stone. The anchors still hummed, faintly, but the surge had collapsed back on itself when the hub broke. The line had snapped. The force had nowhere to go. It would bleed off in harmless cracks and failed sigils. Some stones would break. Some would sleep. The villages would stand.

"Yes," I said. The word felt heavy, like stone set into place.

Kerran's grip slackened. Stone along his fingers flaked away. Flesh beneath shriveled, the blood supply cut. His arm crumbled, starting at the shoulder. He watched it, eyes wide. Then he laughed softly, almost soundless.

"So simple," he whispered. "In the end. I held this for years. Do you know how many nights I stayed at this table, counting numbers on a page, telling myself the cost was worth it? All the speeches. All the Hall's fine words." His gaze found mine again. It cleared for one last heartbeat. "Do not let them say this was madness alone. Tell them what they did to me. To us. Make them say the words."

"I will," I said.

His lips twitched. "Liar," he said, but there was no bite in it. "They will never listen." His head sagged. Stone around his neck cracked. "Tell her I am sorry. Not for her father. That I would do again. For this."

His eyes slid toward Jaime. She stood a few paces away, knife still in her hand, face streaked with dust and tears she had not let fall. Their gazes met.

"Jaime," he said. Her name left his ruined mouth almost clean, shaped by the memory of a better tongue. "Your father asked me if it was worth it. I said yes. I see his face every time I closed my eyes. I still said yes." His voice shook. "That is what the stones do. They make you say yes. To anything."

She did not step closer. Her fingers clenched around the knife until the knuckles whitened. "You left him in the dark," she said. Her voice was flat. Thin. As if the weight inside had compressed it into a thread. "You walked away."

"Yes," he said again, almost inaudible. "I walked away from the swamp. I never left the fort."

The last of the anchor light in his veins guttered. Stone along his chest cracked into dry plates and slid free. Beneath it, his heart fluttered once, a small, frantic thing, then stilled. His body sagged. The grip on my arm fell away entirely. What remained of him crumpled, folding in on itself. Flesh cooled and dulled. The stone trying to grow through it lost its cohesion and sloughed into heaps of dead rock.

The smell of blood and dust thickened, then settled.

I stood there, sword in hand, breathing in harsh pulls that tasted of iron and grit. My chest ached where the tendrils had struck. My left side throbbed in time with my heartbeat. Hot liquid slid under my scales and fur. I could feel each injury with a clarity that kept them from becoming a blur. They were part of what I had bought for the lives outside.

Jaime knelt. Not by Kerran. By the fragment of the conduit she had cut from the hub. Her fingers touched the broken glyphs, the silent veins. Tears finally slipped free and traced clean lines through the dust on her cheeks.

"He chose it," she said. The words seemed to be for herself more than us. "All the way down. He chose it every time."

Elisah sank to sit against the wall, hand pressed to her side. Her shirt was soaked dark there. She looked at Kerran's remains, then at me. Her gaze took in the scales, the horns, the eyes that must be glowing faintly still. No fear there. Only assessment. Calculation. Then something like pity.

Rygial leaned on his spear. His shoulders shook. Sobs did not come. Only dry, rasping breaths. He stared at the shattered hub as if he could see the map of the network collapsing in his mind's eye. All that work. All those nights. All those justifications.

The fort groaned again. This time the sound traveled up through the walls and into the floor beneath us. Fissures raced across the ceiling. A slab of stone broke free and smashed into the far end of the command table, exploding it into splinters.

"We need to go," Elisah said. She pushed herself to her feet with a hiss. "Now."

I nodded. My body moved slower now that the immediate need had passed. The Warrior's fire banked. I could feel the drag of the injuries as if the air had thickened. My horns felt heavy. My limbs ached. The scales that had flared bright during the strike dulled to a more ordinary sheen. Behind my sternum, the power that had filled every breath settled deeper, like coals hidden under ash.

I turned from Kerran's corpse. From the shattered hub. From the cradle where the war the Hall had wanted had died stillborn.

"We take what we can," I said. "Proof. Names. His journals. Anything that ties this to Old King's Walk."

Rygial shook himself once, like a dog coming out of water. He crossed to the wreckage of the command desk and began to stuff loose papers into his satchel. Maps, orders, letters bearing the Hall's seal. His hands moved quickly, practiced. The tremor in them did not slow him.

Elisah limped to the side cabinets and kicked one open. Inside, rows of ledgers lined the shelves, some bound in leather, some in cheap board. She grabbed the most recent and shoved them into a bag, biting back a groan with each reach.

Jaime stayed where she was another heartbeat, fingers resting on the ruined stone. Then she forced herself up. Her face closed down. The grief retreated to sit coiled behind her eyes. She moved around Kerran's remains without touching them and joined Rygial in clearing the table. She found a small wooden box and opened it. Inside lay a cluster of sigil-stones, each marked with a different region of the marsh. She swept them into her pack.

The floor lurched. A crack shot across the chamber under Kerran's corpse. One of his stone-sheathed legs slid and fell away, breaking on the new-made fault.

"Elric." Elisah's voice cut through the rising noise. "Stairs will not hold long. Move."

I took one last look at Kerran. Not the whole of him, just his face. Or what was left of it. The features were barely human now. Yet the angle of his jaw, the line of his brow, still hinted at the commander who had walked the palisade. Stone had not erased him. It had grown through him.

It would be easy, later, to say the horror was all the stone. That the man was innocent beneath it. Or to say the stone was only a tool and all the blame lay with him. Both lies. He had chosen, and been shaped, and the two threads had twined until they could not be parted.

Smoke began to coil from a cracked brazier. Dry wind whistled through new gaps in the walls.

I turned away.

We ran.

The stairs from the command chamber shook under our feet. Fine grit had already turned them slick in places. Twice Jaime slipped. Each time I caught her with my good arm and steadied her without speech. Each time she nodded once and pushed on faster. The walls around the spiral stair quivered like the inside of a throat swallowing too large a bite. Stone dust hung in the air in a pale fog. It coated my tongue.

On the level below, the corridor that had held the anchor-bound soldiers seethed. The stasis had broken with the hub's collapse. Doors hung open. Men and women in Black Rise colors staggered into the hall, clutching at their heads, their chests, the walls. Their eyes were wide and unfocused. Some wept. Some cursed. Some laughed, high and wild.

One saw us. His face twisted. He snatched at his sword. His hand shook so hard he dropped it. The blade clanged off the stone and skittered in front of my feet.

"You," he said thickly. "You did this. The hum is gone. The weight is gone." His voice cracked. "What did you take?"

"Move," Elisah said. She had no patience left for their confusion. "The fort is coming down. Get out or die in here asking questions."

Some listened. The instinct to survive cut through the haze. They lurched toward the stairs. Others tried to gather their wits. One woman, younger than me, looked past us toward the stairs up.

"Commander Kerran," she said faintly. "We have to secure the hub. The procedure…" Her voice trailed off as she saw my face fully in the flickering light. Her words died. Fear, then something like awe, flared. "Warrior."

Not a question. A name learned in childhood stories, now finding something to cling to.

I met her eyes. They were bloodshot, rimmed with the red of broken vessels from the strain of release. She had not known where the anchors' power went. She had only known duty.

"Get your people out," I said. "No one else needs to die for this."

She swallowed. Nodded. "Yes." Her gaze flicked to my horns, my eyes, my scales. "What are you?"

"I am what happens when you ask too much," I said. It was all the explanation there was time for.

We pushed through the crowd. Hands brushed at us, some seeking help, some seeking to hold, to understand. Rygial murmured directions, guiding them toward side passages that led to outer courtyards instead of the central halls already cracking. Jaime's jaw was clenched so tightly that blood had beaded where she had bitten her lip. Elisah moved like a knife, sharp and direct, ignoring pleas and protests. Her own blood left a dark trail on the floor.

The corridor to the main gate had buckled. The floor there rose in a long swell, like a stone wave frozen mid-crest. We clambered over it, slipping on loose rubble. Above, gaps had opened in the vaulted ceiling. Through them, I could see thin slices of sky. Grey, low, heavy with impending rain. It smelled like relief. Like the world outside did not know the fort was dying.

An inner wall had already cracked through. We had to squeeze past, sideways, through a narrow gap where the stone had split and leaned together again. My scales scraped rock. The horns caught once and sent a spear of pain through my skull. I grunted and ducked lower.

At one turn, a half-collapsed arch blocked our path. A young soldier lay pinned under a fallen block, his leg crushed to pulp. He screamed when he saw us, an animal sound. His fingers clawed at the air.

"Please," he gasped. "Please. Do not leave me."

Rygial moved to him at once, dropping to one knee. He put his hands on the stone and strained. It barely shifted. The soldier sobbed.

"There is no time," Elisah snapped. Her voice shook. "We cannot move that rock. The whole arch is waiting to go. We die here if we try."

Rygial's jaw set. "I will not leave him."

"You will," I said. The words came out flat. In that moment I hated the sound of my own voice. Hated that it carried the certainty of the Warrior. "Rygial. Look."

I pointed with my chin to the crack running up the side of the arch. Dust trickled steadily from it. With every breath, it widened a hair. The block pinning the man was part of that weight. Moving it would unbalance the rest.

"If we pull it off," I said quietly, "the arch comes down. On him. On us. On anyone behind us."

Rygial's eyes shone. Anger flared there, real and sharp. "Then we cut it," he said. "We break it apart. We find another way. We…"

"There is no other way," I said. The words fell between us like another stone. "Not here. Not now."

The soldier's hand clawed at Rygial's sleeve. "Please."

Rygial bent his head. Lips moved. A prayer, short and rough. He put his hand on the man's forehead for a brief moment. A whisper of green light flared, easing something in the soldier's eyes. The pain eased, or the sense of it dulled. The sobs quieted.

"Forgive me," Rygial said.

We left him.

The Warrior in me accepted the choice as another line drawn. Another cut made where none felt right. The boy who had watched men die on the palisade had new images now to carry beside them. The sound of stone sliding into place behind us as the arch finally fell. The silence after.

At last, after too many turns and half-fallen corridors, the inner gate loomed. One leaf hung crooked, its hinges warped. The other had collapsed outward, leaving a ragged opening. Beyond it, the outer yard sprawled, strewn with debris. The outer wall of the fort had cracked but not yet failed.

We stumbled into the yard as another deep groan went through the structure. Behind us, the command tower listed. A plume of dust rose from its base as part of the lower level gave way.

"Keep moving," Elisah said. "The cliff path."

The path down from Black Rise had never seemed so narrow. It clung to the cliff face in a thin line of stone, the drop to the marsh yawning on one side. Rain began to fall as we stepped onto it, light at first. The stones slickened.

The fort shuddered behind us. A section of wall near the base tore free and plunged into the forest below, taking trees with it. The sound came late, a heavy crash filtered through distance and rain. Birds exploded from the canopy in a black flurry.

We made our way down with slow, careful steps. My new tail helped, counter-balancing where the drop tried to pull. The scales on my feet bit into the wet stone better than bare pads would have. Jaime clung to the inner wall, teeth bared in a grimace. Elisah leaned on Rygial when she had to have support, and cursed him when he offered more than that.

By the time we reached the base of the cliff, the rain had thickened into a steady curtain. It washed dust and blood from our faces, turned the ground to sucking mud. The forest at the base of Black Rise smelled sharp and clean after the stone stink above.

We stumbled away from the fall line of the fort, across the narrow clearing to where the trees thickened. Only then did we stop and turn.

Black Rise loomed above, dark against the grey sky. Cracks webbed its walls. The command tower leaned at an angle that made muscles in my back tense just to look at it. The hub chamber within was already a ruin. The rest of the fort followed, piece by piece, in slow, reluctant surrender.

One last, long groan rolled across the clearing. Then a deep section of the structure sagged inward. Stone toppled. Dust bloomed outward in a huge, slow wave, pale against the rain.

I felt something give inside myself with it. A tension I had not known I carried un-coiled, leaving emptiness behind. The Warrior's full form receded. Muscles shrank. The heaviness in my limbs lightened. My tail withdrew, curling up and in until it was gone, leaving a ghost of weight at my spine. Horns tingled, then steadied. My perspective sank back toward the height I had known before.

I blinked. The world changed scale. The trees grew taller again. The fort higher. My clothes hung looser where they had strained over the larger frame. The Drakeslayer sword weighed more in my hand. Not crushing, but definite now.

I swayed. Jaime's hand caught my elbow. Her fingers felt very small. Very warm.

"Elric?" she said.

I looked at her. At Rygial. At Elisah. Their faces had not changed, but the way I saw them had. No longer from high above, from that narrow line of focus. The edges softened. The smells of wet earth and rain and their sweat after battle came back into balance instead of spiking sharp.

I drew a slow breath. It hurt along my ribs, but in a familiar, human way.

"I am here," I said.

Jaime stared. Her gaze flicked to my eyes. I saw the moment she noticed. Her brows drew together.

"Your eyes," she said softly. "They are..." She searched for a word and failed. "Not brown."

"No," I said. The world around us reflected in them faintly now. I could see the gold in the corner of my vision if I shifted my focus. Like I watched myself from somewhere just to the side. "They will stay this way."

Rygial stepped closer, peering with a scholar's interest despite his exhaustion. "The horns too," he said. His hand started to reach up, then stopped, hanging awkwardly in the air. "And the scales. They did not fully recede."

I glanced down at my forearms. Fur still covered much of them, wet and clumped from the rain, but through it ran patterns of red-gold scale, denser along the outer edges, fading thinner toward the inner arm. They caught the grey light in small, stubborn sparks. I touched them with my opposite thumb. They felt cool and smooth now, not hot. Fused. Part of me.

"Yes," I said.

Elisah sank down on a fallen log, hand still clamped to her side. Blood had slowed, but her face was pale. She watched me with hooded eyes.

"Is this... permanent?" she asked. She did not frame it as hope or fear. Just a question that needed an answer.

"This is what I am now," I said. The words came easier now that I had used them, in some form, in the command corridor. "The full form. The height. The old voice. That comes when it is needed. Not always. But these." I tapped one horn, felt its solid curve, the slight ache at the root. "These stay."

Jaime's hand tightened briefly on my arm, then fell away. "Does it hurt?" she asked.

"Less than it did," I said. "More than it used to." I searched for the right way to put it. "The Warrior sits closer to the skin now. I do not have to reach as far for it. It does not have to push as hard to reach me."

Rygial nodded slowly. "That has a cost," he said quietly. "It always does. But the villages..." He looked toward the marsh, though we could not see beyond the trees. "They will not burn today."

"No," I said.

Silence settled for a few breaths. Only the patter of rain on leaves and the distant, intermittent crashes of the collapsing fort broke it.

Jaime's shoulders slumped. The knife she had carried since the command chamber slipped from her fingers and sank point-first into the mud. She stared at Black Rise as if trying to see Kerran fall inside it.

"He asked us to tell them," she said. "The Hall. About what they did to him. About what he did. About my father." Her jaw worked. "I do not know if I can say his name in the same breath as apology."

"You do not have to forgive him," I said. "That is not what he asked."

She gave a humorless little laugh. "You listened better than I did." She wiped her face with the back of her hand, smearing mud and tears. "We have his letters. His orders. The ledgers. The sigils." Her gaze cut to Rygial. "That is enough to make them listen."

Rygial let out a slow breath. "To make some of them listen," he said. "Others will call him a rogue commander who went too far. They will say the system worked, because we stopped him."

"And we will say," Elisah added, "that he worked exactly as they designed. That the stones and the orders and the maps led here. To that room." She nodded toward the fort. "To that choice."

I looked down at my hands. At the faint traces of grey dust still caught in the seams between scale and skin. I rubbed them together until the dust smeared away. It did not make my hands cleaner. Only less obvious.

"We have enough to show what they wanted," I said. "What they asked men like Kerran to do. What they did to people like Jaime's father when they stood in the way."

Jaime's eyes found mine. "People like yours," she added quietly.

I inclined my head. The memory of my parents' pyre flickered in the rain. The Hall had called that necessary too. Containment, they had said. To keep the sickness from spreading. Always the numbers. Always the ledgers.

"We go back to Old King's Walk," Elisah said. She shifted, winced, then forced herself to her feet again. "We put this in front of them. We speak where they cannot ignore us." She smiled, sharp and thin. "And then we see who survives the telling."

Rygial huffed a tired laugh. "You make it sound so simple."

"It will not be," I said. I looked at each of them. Jaime, standing with mud to her ankles, rain streaking her face, grief and resolve braided tight. Elisah, pale and hurt and still calculating, eyes already tracing the paths of names and evidence through the Hall. Rygial, shoulders bowed under guilt and purpose both, hands stained with ink and blood.

None of us were who we had been when we left Old King's Walk. None of us could go back to fitting into the spaces we had filled before.

"That is why we go together," I said.

Jaime bent, picked up her knife from the mud, wiped it once on her trouser leg, and slid it back into its sheath. "We owe them the truth," she said. "My father. Kerran. The villagers. The soldiers in that fort."

Rygial hefted his satchel. It sagged with the weight of papers, stones, and whatever else we had stolen from the dead. "We owe ourselves not to look away," he added.

Elisah took a shallow breath and held it as she adjusted the bandage at her side. Blood seeped through again, but less. She nodded once. "We should move before the rain turns the path back to the road into a river."

I glanced back at Black Rise one last time. The fort still stood in ragged silhouette against the sky, but every moment took more of it. A corner tower broke free as I watched and fell in slow ruin, swallowed by the trees.

In its stones lay what the Hall had tried to build. A machine to move death at a distance. To crush people into lines on a map. We had broken that machine. Another would be built if we did nothing more.

The Warrior coiled quiet in my chest, no longer pressing, no longer surging, but ready. It had taken a place in me that could not be given back. I felt its weight like a second heart.

I did not know yet if I would be better with it or worse. Only that I could not pretend to be less. The eyes I would walk with now were the eyes that had watched Kerran die and chosen the hub. The hands that would carry the Drakeslayer sword through the gates of Old King's Walk were the same that had left a soldier under stone because there had been no time.

"You are quiet," Jaime said beside me.

"I am thinking of home," I said. The word tasted different now. Not of safety. Of duty. Of a place that would not want to see itself, and of the three of us walking into it like a storm. "And of what waits there."

She followed my gaze to the distant line of the old road, half-lost in mist and rain. "Do you think they will listen?"

"No," I said. Then, after a beat, "Enough of them might."

She nodded. "Then let us go make their lives difficult."

We turned from the fort. From the broken stones and the ghosts that would cling to them. The rain washed its dust from our hair and clothes as we stepped into the trees. Each footfall pulled us farther from Black Rise and closer to Old King's Walk.

The road back would be longer than the map showed. There would be questions and accusations and walls of polished words. There would be those who saw my eyes and horns and scales and flinched. Those who whispered the word Warrior like praise. Those who spat it like a curse.

All of that lay ahead.

Behind us, another section of the fort collapsed with a distant, heavy sigh. The sound rolled through the forest, dulled by rain and leaves, then faded. No cheers followed. No song rose. Only the steady patter of water, the rustle of branches, the soft squelch of our boots in the wet earth.

We walked.

The Warrior sat in my bones. The boy walked on the road. Between them, I carried the sword and the names of the dead.

# Chapter 24

## HEROES COME HOME

WE LEFT BLACK RISE before the smoke finished thinning.

The fort still smoldered behind us when we crossed the outer ditch. Stones sweated heat under a gray sky. The air tasted of lime dust and burned pitch. Crows circled the broken tower in a slow, patient wheel. We did not speak much. There was nothing left to say about that place.

My arms ached under the weight of the pack. Straps caught on the edges of my new scales when I shifted it. The chevrons along my forearms had darkened overnight, red-gold against my skin, like embers laid in flesh. When I flexed my fingers, the scales pulled and settled with a faint rasp, like dry leather on stone. Jaime had wrapped bandage cloth around them for the march, to keep people from staring on the road. The cloth did not hide the horns that pushed through my hair, or the way my eyes caught the light.

The evidence rode in Rygial's pack. He guarded it with a care he did not grant his own sleep. Kerran's letters, the ledgers, the sigil-stones wired into their little brass frames. They had their own weight. I felt it in the way he walked.

Elsiah kept to the edges of the road, as if stone had less claim on her than shadow. Her cloak had been cleaned since the last fight, but faint stains still marked the hem and cuffs. Dry blood. Rust. Mud from the corridors where we had broken the anchor-lines. When the wind rose, the cloak smelled of oil and old smoke. The smell matched the fort behind us too well.

Jaime walked at my side. She carried the Pikes shield, dented and drity from the battle with the troll. She had polished it anyway. Sunlight gleamed off the rim. She did not strap it on her arm. She held it by the handle, letting it ride against her leg as we walked. When the shield's rim tapped her greave, it made a low, hollow sound. The rhythm of our steps.

The swamp lay two days to the south. We cut inland, but the air remembered. The ground turned softer under our boots. Flies thickened in the hollows. Water stood still between the reeds, dark and slick, showing pieces of sky. The smell shifted from burned stone to mud and rotting grass. Somewhere under those waters a man's bones lay wrapped in weeds.

Jaime did not look toward the south when the land dipped. Her jaw stayed tight. Once, when the road bent close to a broad span of standing water, she stopped. The others walked on a few paces before they noticed. She just stood there, staring at where the reeds bowed and rose in the faint wind.

I joined her. My boots sank a finger's width into the soft earth. A frog called from somewhere under the mat of floating leaves. It sounded like a hand tapping the underside of a kettle.

"He never liked still water," Jaime said. Her voice was flat. "Said it did not tell you where it meant to go. A river speaks its mind." She lifted her eyes from the water and resumed walking.

We did not hold a ceremony. That had happened long ago, in the moment he died, when none of us could name it. We had done what needed doing for him in another place. Kerran's blood had fed a different stretch of earth. It was enough.

Three days later we saw the city walls. The same city that had chained us. The same towers where we had sat in iron and waited for other people's decisions. They looked smaller in the pale afternoon light. A gull wheeled above the main gate and cried. We had come from the north road once, under escort. This time the guards at the gate saw four travelers and a heavy pack. Their spears leaned against the wall and their attention drifted between passersby and the dice cup on a barrel.

I had my hood up. It did not hide the horns. One guard squinted, then looked away. His eyelids twitched like a man who had almost seen something and decided not to. Jaime's badge from Black Rise—Kerran's seal, scorched, with the ink-threads inside dead and gray—sat in an outer pouch where a trained eye could find it. No one asked.

Inside the walls, the city smelled as it had before: tallow smoke, boiled barley, sour ale, chamber pots emptied too late. A wagon rolled past loaded with timber. The boards slapped and creaked. Horses snorted. Children ran behind, hands outstretched, hoping for scraps of bark to play with. A woman leaning from an upper window threw dishwater into the street. It splashed and ran toward the drain. Dirty foam lapped at my boots.

I remembered the walk from the prison house to the Hall of Correction, wrists chained, flanked by armed men. Maximus was with us then. He had joked about the guards' boots to keep Anya from crying. His voice had bounced off the stone and made the corridor feel less like a grave. We passed the corner where he had turned his head to wink at me. The stone looked the same. My chest tightened and eased with the next breath. We walked on.

No one stopped us this time. We did not seek the Hall. We needed only the road that led out the far gate. Rygial muttered under his breath when we crossed a plaza lined with engraved pillars. Time-sense work. A habit. His fingers moved through empty air as if tracing sigils. Elsiah watched everything and nothing, eyes never still. She flinched once at the sight of iron manacles hung as a warning over a side door. Then her expression went blank.

We took a room at an inn we had never seen before. Cheap. The straw smelled of mice and beer. The door had no lock. Jaime still wedged the shield against it that night. The boards creaked when someone walked in the corridor. Each time, my hand went to Drakeslayer's hilt where it leaned against the bed. Sleep came in fits. In one of them, I felt again the anchor-stone's hum under my feet, deep and wrong, and woke with my hand clenched on empty air. In the darkness, Rygial's snore started, then broke, then started again. Elsiah breathed without sound. Jaime murmured, voice thick with old dreams.

By morning, the city's noise pressed in. We left before the sun fully cleared the roofs. Out the south gate, the road unrolled between fields and hedgerows. The air changed again. It grew wider. Wind moved freely, with nothing to catch it but grass and the odd stand of trees. The smell turned to turned earth, sheep, smoke from scattered farmhouses, the faint sweetness of early blossoms. My shoulders dropped a fraction.

We walked.

Days blurred together, the way they do when there is nothing hunting from behind and no fixed fear ahead. Boots on packed dirt. The rut in the center of the road where wagon wheels had cut their mark. A crow on a fencepost, watching with one bright eye. The squeal of an iron gate on a pasture. The taste of hard cheese gone sour around the edges. Nights in roadside shelters or under hedges. Once in a hayloft, the sweet dust making me sneeze until I pulled my facewrap over my nose. Jaime laughed then, just once, quick and startled.

We did not speak much about Black Rise. We did speak of what came next. Not in grand plans, but in pieces.

"There will be questions," Rygial said one evening. We sat by a fire barely big enough to cook a thin stew. "About why I did not come to them sooner. About why I built what I built in the first place."

"You answer them," Jaime said. She stirred the pot. "You wrote the numbers that let them think villages were cattle. You can unscribe them."

Rygial did not argue. He held one of the sigil-stones up so the fire lit its dead veins. Once they had glowed. Now the crystal's surface was dull. He turned it between finger and thumb. "I can try."

Elsiah lay on her back, hands folded under her head, looking up where the stars were only a suggestion beyond the smoke. "They will not thank you," she said. "Not the men with titles. They will twist it. They are better with knives that look like words."

"That is why we carry both," I said. My hand rested near Drakeslayer's hilt. The leather of the grip had molded more to my palm since Black Rise. "Paper and steel."

Jaime nodded once. "We are not alone, either. The villages will listen. People know what almost happened to them, even if they do not yet know the names."

We had Kerran's letters. We had ledgers where men like him dropped their masks when they wrote to each other. We had names. We had ink. We had time, for the moment.

On the sixth day after leaving the city, the land began to look familiar. The line of the hills to the west took on shapes that lived in old memory. A notch there where Bobo had once sworn a giant had taken a bite. A crooked elm that leaned like an old man over the path. The air tasted drier. Dust rose with each bootfall. Somewhere ahead lay Old King's Walk, and the house that had been home.

THE FIRST SIGN OF the village was the smell of bread.

We came over a low rise and the wind shifted. Warm, yeasted air touched my nose, cut with wood smoke and the faint metal tang of the river. My stomach tightened. It had been months since I had smelled that oven. My feet slowed on their own.

A lane of flat stones led down between fields toward Old King's Walk. Rye stood knee-high on either side, green-gold, heads just starting to fatten. Grasshoppers clicked and sprang away from our boots. The sun sat halfway down the sky, light slanting, shadows long.

Old King's Walk had never been large. A double row of stone houses, their backs to the river, their fronts to the road. A smithy. A tanner's shed. The inn. The old cracked statue of some forgotten king at the village's center, his sword's tip broken off, his face worn smooth by lichen and too many winters. Smoke rose from chimneys in thin blue-gray threads. Chickens scratched in the dust. A dog barked once, then again.

We had left as fugitives and conscripts. We came back on our own feet.

A boy carrying a bundle of kindling saw us first. He was maybe ten, thin as a sapling. His eyes dragged over the four of us without catching, then returned. He slowed. His mouth opened a little.

"Ma!" he shouted, voice cracking. "Ma, they're back!"

His words rippled ahead of us like a stone tossed in a pond. Heads turned. A woman straightened from a washtub, water running from her forearms to the ground. An older man lifting a sack of grain paused with it on his shoulder. Someone at the inn's door shaded their eyes.

They saw the ears first, as they always did. My catfolk ears twitched under my hood at the rising buzz of voices. Then they saw the horns.

"Elric?" The woman by the washtub took a few hesitant steps forward. Her bare feet slapped the packed earth. Her face was sun-browned, fine lines at the corners of her eyes. I had once patched her roof. "Is that...?"

I pushed my hood back. The air felt cool against the base of my horns. They were not large yet, but they curled back through my hair in short, ridged arcs, black at the base shading to dark bronze at the tips. The woman's gaze fixed on them, then dropped to my eyes. The world shone in their reflection, small and clear. Golden, not brown. In the sunlight the color held threads like molten metal.

"Aye," I said. "It is me, Terla."

She made a sign with one hand without seeming to think about it. Old warding against strange things. Then she caught herself and let the hand fall. Her cheeks colored.

"Walk take me," she said, half whisper and half laugh. "They said you went to fight. They did not say…" Her eyes flicked over my arms. The bandages covered the scales, but edges of red-gold showed where the cloth had slipped. "Is it…does it hurt?"

"Sometimes," I said. "Less when I keep moving."

Jaime had stopped with me. Villagers' eyes turned to her next. Her hair was shorter than when she left, hacked off unevenly after a fire had singed it. Her armor bore new scars. The old defiance in her posture remained, but something had settled under it. Her gaze met each person's in turn. There was no apology in it. There was no need.

"That is Durandal's girl," someone muttered. "Jaime. Dratmar's blade daughter." A murmur of respect followed. Durandal's name still carried weight here. He had died making sure it would.

Elsiah and Rygial drew more curiosity than recognition. Elsiah kept her hood up and her head slightly bowed. Even so, her eyes moved under the shadow, taking everything in. The villagers read a dozen wrong things into the set of her shoulders and the slow pace of her step. Some backed a little away from the road, not quite meeting her gaze. They smelled the alleyways on her.

Rygial walked in plain view, his staff a simple length of smoothed oak, his beard trimmed shorter than most dwarves in these parts wore theirs. His clothes had more stitches than cloth. His boots were city-made. He might have been any traveling craftsman, but for the heavy pack and the sigil-stone lens hanging from his belt. A boy's eyes fixed on it as if it were a jewel.

"Is that a mage?" someone whispered. The word held more fear than wonder.

"Chronomancer," Rygial said mildly, without breaking stride. "Less fire. More numbers." His tone carried the dry humor of a man used to explaining his work to people who only half believed it. The villagers blinked, unsure if he was making a joke.

We reached the square around the old statue. The stone king looked down on us with his empty face. Children clustered near his base, staring. A little girl with her hair in two rough braids tugged at her brother's sleeve.

"His eyes," she said, not softly enough. "They're like the coins Pa keeps for sacred days." Her brother shushed her. He did not stop staring either.

I let Drakeslayer's tip rest on the packed earth. The sword's weight had become part of the way I stood. Villagers' gazes settled on it in turn. They remembered Maximus carrying it, the day we all left. A few faces tightened. A few set.

"Dratmar'll want to see you," the grain sack man said gruffly. He had lowered his load while we stood. Now he hitched it back up with a grunt. "He near wore a groove in the floor, waiting. Go on. The Hall can wait its answers. Old King's Walk sees its own first."

That suited us well enough.

I glanced at Elsiah and Rygial. "The inn has rooms," I said. "You can take quarters there until you decide what the future holds. It is not grand, but the roof keeps the rain out. Mostly."

Rygial gave a short nod. Lines of tension around his mouth eased a little at the word "roof." Elsiah's eyes flicked from the villagers to me.

"You sure?" she asked quietly. "They look at me like I stole their chickens."

"You stole worse," Jaime said, not unkindly. "They will get used to you. Or you will decide to go on. For now, eat a meal you do not cook for yourself. Sleep in a bed that is not a stolen pallet. That much you have earned."

Earned. She looked away for a second at that word. Then she shrugged, a quick, sharp movement.

"All right," she said. "I will try not to rob the place."

Jaime's mouth twitched. "Try very hard."

We crossed the square together. At the inn door, Rygial paused.

"You will come back here, after?" he asked. "When you have spoken to your family."

"Yes," I said. "We will need to plan with all of us. And I owe you a drink that is not watered beyond taste."

Rygial's smile was small, but it reached his eyes. "I will hold you to that." He and Elsiah stepped into the dim of the common room. Voices rose and faded behind them.

Jaime adjusted her grip on Maximus's shield, took a breath, and turned toward the lane that led to Dratmar's house. My heart had been marching forward for days. Now it stumbled. Then it found a new pace. We walked.

The Blackenstone house sat where it always had, halfway up the slope east of the village, its back wall cut into the hill. Stone, low and broad, with a slate roof patched in places with whatever Dratmar had on hand. An old yew tree leaned over the yard, dark needles stirring in the wind. The training posts stood where we had left them, scars from wooden blades and real ones not yet healed by time.

Someone had swept the front step recently. The dust lay in little ridges at the edges. The iron latch on the door had been polished until it shone. That meant Anya had been restless.

I stopped at the gate. The wood was rough under my palm. The yard smelled of damp earth, metal filings, and the faint sour-sweetness of cooling oil. Home. My throat tightened. My new scales prickled as if they, too, remembered.

Jaime did not stop. She pushed the gate open. Its hinges creaked the same old complaint. She walked up the path and set her hand on the door without knocking. Then, for just a moment, she rested her forehead against the wood. Her shoulders drew in, breath held.

Bootsteps sounded inside. Heavy, measured, with the familiar weight of a dwarf who had spent his life on solid ground.

The door jerked open.

Dratmar Blackenstone filled the doorway like a rooted stone. He had not grown smaller. He had grown more worn. His beard was more white than black now, the braids shorter where they had been singed months before. Lines dug deeper into his forehead and around his eyes. Those eyes were the same: clear gray, steady, missing little.

He took in Jaime first. The set of her mouth. The new scars. The older ones. The shield in her hand. He wrapped her in his arms before she could speak.

She went stiff for a heartbeat, then sagged against him, breath leaving in a long rush. Her face pressed into his shoulder. The shield bumped his knee.

"Da," she said, her voice breaking in the middle of the word.

He said nothing for several long breaths. His arms were thick as always, the strength in them undiminished. When he did speak, it was a rumble in his chest.

"You came back," he said. "Good. Good."

Over his shoulder, his eyes met mine.

"Elric," he said. His voice changed on my name. Something gentler threaded through the gravel.

I stepped forward. He let Jaime go with one arm and reached for me with the other. His hand closed around my forearm, just below the bandage line, before he saw what lay under the cloth. The edge of a scale scraped his palm. His eyes dropped.

"Hmm," he said. The sound was not surprise, not entirely. He loosened his grip by a fraction, careful, then tightened it in a measured squeeze. "You feel different."

"I am," I said. The words felt too small, but they were all I had.

He looked up at my face. His gaze did not flinch at the horns. It held, searching, at the eyes. Whatever he was looking for, he found.

"All right," he said. "You are here. That is the thing that matters first." He stepped back to let us in. "Come. Anya has been talking about nothing but your return since you left. She will wear out her wings if I do not give her something else to do with them."

We crossed the threshold. The house's cool air wrapped around us. It smelled of forge smoke, stew, leather, and the faint feather-dust Anya left wherever she perched. The main room lay as ever: hearth on one wall, long table in the center, weapon racks by the door. New nicks marked the rack where someone had been taking blades down and putting them back with less care than Dratmar liked. Bobo, then.

A clatter came from the side hall. Small feet thumped against stone.

"Elric! Jaime!" Anya's voice rose high and bright. She shot into the main room like an arrow loosed too early. Her wings—white, with gray tips from the ash she always forgot to shake out—beat the air hard enough to stir the banked fire. She crashed into me at chest height.

I caught her with both arms, grunting against her momentum. She wrapped her arms around my neck and her legs around my waist, wings flaring wide to balance. Feathers brushed my horns. She smelled like chalk, soap, and the outdoors.

"You took forever," she said into my shoulder. "You were supposed to be back when the winter ice broke. Then when the lambs came. Then when the swallows did. Bobo said you probably got eaten by a dragon. I said you would cut your way out and ride it home."

"Did you now," I said. My voice came out rougher than I liked. "I am sorry to prove Bobo wrong. I know it pains you."

She leaned back in my arms to look at my face. Her eyes, wide and silver-gray, traced the line of my horns and the color of my eyes. Her wings stilled.

"Oh," she breathed. "You look like a story."

"A scary story," another voice said from the corridor.

Bobo Arkenwright lounged there, a little more grown than the last time I saw him, though still shorter than Dratmar by a head. His beard was wispy yet, more a determined attempt than a true dwarf's growth. Soot smudged his nose and cheek. A leather apron hung crooked over his shirt, showing he had come from the workshop in a hurry. He had a hammer in one hand and a piece of chalk in the other. A half-finished rune, shaky but ambitious, marked the side of the chalk.

"He looks like the hero in the cheap broadsheets," Bobo went on, pushing off the wall. "The ones in bad woodcut. Horns and glowing eyes and a sword as long as the table. You need a cloak that goes whoosh when you turn." He mimed a swirl.

Jaime snorted. "He has enough dramatic accessories," she said. "He does not need cloth help."

Anya swatted at Bobo with one wing. "Do not tease. I like his eyes. They are like the sun on the river."

"Blinding?" Bobo said.

"Warm," Anya said firmly.

Ianteen Craigsil emerged more quietly, drying her hands on a rag. She had been at the forge too. Her dark hair was pulled back in a knot at the nape of her neck, a few strands escaping to curl around her pointed ears. Her skin had deepened in color from hours at the anvil and the kiln. Fine ash dusted her forearms. When she moved, I glimpsed the thin chain around her throat, her most prized work, links thinner than a grain of rice, each one hammered and shaped by hand.

She took us in with a craftsman's eye, noting detail. The new scars on Jaime's armor. The way Drakeslayer hung at my hip. The slight drag in my left step from a wound I had not bothered to mask. Her gaze softened.

"Welcome home," she said. Her voice had always been calm, the slow water to Bobo's quick sparks. "We kept your places at table. Anya would not let us move the chairs."

Anya tightened her grip. "Someone might sit in them," she said. "Then they would turn into you and that would be confusing."

"That is not how chairs work," Bobo said.

Anya sniffed. "Just because you do not know the old wing-magic does not mean it is not real."

Dratmar cleared his throat. The sound cut through the banter without harshness.

"Enough," he said. "Let them breathe. They have marched gods know how far. They need to sit on those chairs before they turn into anything. We have stew. It is not fancy, but it is hot."

Anya slid down from my arms at last, though she kept a hand hooked in my belt as if to make sure I did not vanish. Jaime set Maximus's shield carefully against the wall by the door, in the place where he had always put it when we came in from drills. The sight of it there, with no one else to claim it, turned the air in my chest thin.

Dratmar's eyes followed the motion. His jaw tightened once. Then he turned toward the table.

"Come," he said. "We will eat. Then you will tell us what needs to be told."

We sat. The benches creaked under familiar weight. The stew smelled of barley, onions, and cured pork. Anya heaped my bowl until it threatened to spill, then did the same for Jaime. Bobo tried to sneak a second ladle for himself and got his wrist smacked by Anya's wing.

"Guests first," she said. "Heroes second. Pests last."

"That is not a traditional order," Bobo muttered, but he waited.

We ate. At first the sounds were only spoons on wooden bowls, quiet breaths, the crackle of the fire. Food filled the hole battle always carved. Warmth spread from my stomach to my fingers. My scales tingled as the heat reached them.

Anya talked enough for all of us, as if to patch the silence with words. She told us about the winter storms, about how the river had frozen solid and Bobo had tried to skate on it in his forge boots and fallen three times. She told us about the new foal in Harim's stable, born with a white blaze like a crooked star. She told us about the owl that had nested in the yew and stared in at her window every night until she named it Inspector and saluted it.

Bobo broke in to correct details. Ianteen added small, precise notes—how the new ore from the north had different impurities, how Dratmar had shown her a way to temper blades that left a faint ripple along the edge like water.

Jaime listened, one hand around her bowl, the other resting on the table. Her shoulders loosened by degrees. The set of her mouth eased. Lines of tension around her eyes smoothed. For a little while, we let the talk be about things that did not bleed.

It did not last. It was not meant to.

Dratmar waited until the bowls were mostly empty and Anya's words had finally begun to run out. Then he set his spoon down, the wood tapping the bowl's rim. His eyes met mine, then Jaime's.

"All right," he said. "Now. Tell me how my son died is answered."

Anya's head came up. Her wings lifted slightly. Bobo's gaze dropped to his hands. Ianteen's jaw clenched.

They had been there. They had seen Maximus fall under the anchor's backlash, fire and stone tearing the ground open. They had seen his body burned where it lay to keep it from feeding the corruption that twisted the land. There was no new news to give on that wound. But there were edges to lay down. Names to place on causes.

Jaime's fingers tightened around her bowl. She set it aside carefully, as if it might break if she gripped it any harder. Her eyes found Dratmar's.

"Kerran did it," she said. The words came out low, but each one was clear. "Not by his own hand on that day, but by everything he set in motion. The network. The orders. The lies that sent us to that place."

Dratmar's mouth compressed. "I suspected," he said. "A man does not order a field test in a village without knowing what he is doing. But suspicion is not the same as hearing it from the mouths of those who stood there."

I set my hand on the table. The boards were smooth in the center from years of use, rougher at the edges where dishes had scarred them.

"We went to Black Rise," I said. "We broke his anchors. We killed him. We took what he thought would bury us and brought it back instead."

Jaime drew breath. The room's air felt thick. Even Anya stayed quiet, her eyes moving from face to face, as if piecing together a story she had not been trusted with yet.

"We followed the network," Jaime said. "Village to village. Anchor to anchor. Each one stronger than the last. Each one threaded into the land like a hook. They were not just...accidents. They were placed. They were meant to wake, together, when the Hall gave the word."

Bobo frowned. "Why?" he asked. "Why in the Walk would anyone build something like that? There is no sense in it. Villages feed the cities. They send coin and grain and men. Killing them is like...like breaking your own fingers so someone else cannot count with them."

"Numbers," Rygial had said by another fire. I heard his voice again as if he sat at the table with us. "To them, villages are numbers on a page."

I repeated the words.

"That is how they saw us," I said. "Villages as tallies. Each one a line in a ledger. They thought if they could wipe some away, they could move the others. Consolidate. Control who starves and who eats. Who freezes in the winter and who keeps warm. Then no lord or councilor would dare cross them. Because they could say, 'We remember what happened to Old King's Walk. To Craighold. To all the others. Do not make us choose again.'"

Dratmar's hands had curled into fists on the table. The thick veins on the backs of them stood out like cords.

"They played with lives like tokens," I went on. "Kerran oversaw the work. Rygial did the numbers. Others in the Hall signed the orders. We have their names. Their letters. They knew what they were building. They called it a safeguard. They wrote about acceptable losses."

Ianteen's lips thinned. Her fingers tightened around his rag until the cloth bunched hard. "Acceptable," she repeated softly, as if testing the feel of the word. "For whom."

"For men like them," Jaime said. Her eyes had gone distant, focused on more than the room. "Never for the ones under their boots."

Dratmar looked at us long. The fire popped. A curl of smoke drifted up the chimney's throat.

"You said you killed Kerran," he said. "Tell me that part. Not for the pleasure of it. For the fitting of the stone."

Jaime's jaw worked. She swallowed once, then began.

"We came to the swamp," she said. "You remember the orders he gave that day. How he told us to get you and the villagers clear. How he sent my father and his men down into the mire to 'stabilize' the anchor." Her voice twisted on the word, as if it hurt to shape it. "He told us the swamp had eaten them. That they fell. That the land took them."

Dratmar's eyes closed once, slowly. When they opened again, their gray had hardened.

"He lied," Jaime said. "There was no accident. No surprise. The anchor was still asleep. My father found the faults in the design. He saw what would happen if they lit them all. He told Kerran he would not go along. So Kerran made his own accident."

The room was very quiet. Even the crackle of the fire seemed to pause.

"He stunned him," Jaime went on. "With a sigil-bind. Took his men. Left my father in the water with his hands and feet bound. Then he told me we were too late to save him. He told me he had died in the work, like a good soldier." Her mouth pulled into a line that was not a smile. "He said he would make sure my service was noted. That my father would be proud of me. All the while, he knew my father was choking on mud a stone's throw away."

Anya's hand flew to her mouth. Her wings trembled. Bobo stared as if he could not quite hear.

"What did you do?" he whispered.

"In the swamp," Jaime said, "we found the place. Rygial's time senses showed us what happened. We saw it as if it were happening again. How Kerran stood on the bank and watched, just long enough to be sure the water would keep its secret. How he turned away. The anchorstones had sunk crooked. The mud clung to them like the land itself tried to spit them out. It did not matter. He pushed his will on them anyway. He chose to drown my father twice: once in the water, once in his report."

Her fingers dug into the table's edge until the wood creaked.

"I had always remembered his face like a picture," she said. "Standing there. Giving orders. I thought he had done his best. Failed, maybe, but tried. In the vision, I saw the truth. He did not flinch. He did not look back. He counted. He measured. He wrote my father off like spoiled grain."

Her eyes met Dratmar's. In them burned the banked coals of long-held fury.

"When we reached Black Rise," she said, "I put a blade through his throat."

The words hung in the air like a thrown knife.

Dratmar's exhale was slow. Not relief. Not approval. Something heavier.

"How?" he asked. "Not in the corridors, surely. He had loyal men."

"Kerran had wrapped himself in stone and commands," I said. "He thought the an-chors made him untouchable. He thought no one could reach him in his tower. We broke his network under his feet. Rygial unwove his threads. Elsiah slipped past her watchers. Jaime and I climbed the tower while his men tried to put out fires everywhere else."

The memory rose sharp. The stone stairs under my boots. The taste of dust and heated magic. The hum of the last active hub under my skin. Drakeslayer warm in my hand, its blade alive to the wrongness around us.

"He had tied himself to the last anchor," I said. "He thought it gave him more power. It did, for a time. It also bound him to it. When we struck the stone, it struck him. He staggered. His own magic turned wild. Jaime did not wait for his balance. She moved. She always was faster than me."

Jaime's mouth twitched, a humorless thing. "You cut the anchor," she said. "I cut him."

I remembered the feel of Kerran's presence in that tower. The weight of his gaze when he finally realized who stood before him. The flicker of recognition, then dismissal, when he saw my ears, my height.

"Halfbreed," he had said. "You meddle in work beyond your understanding."

I met his eyes on that tower. He saw himself in the reflection and flinched, just a little. That had satisfied a small cold place in me even as battle roared.

"He tried to call the other anchors, even then," I said aloud. "Tried to trigger what remained, to take something with him. Rygial blocked it. Jaime drove her sword through his throat. He died on his own stone floor, with his own work tearing itself apart around him."

Dratmar listened, unmoving. Then, slowly, he nodded once.

"Durandal would not have asked for that," he said. "But he would not have turned from it either. There are some men you do not let die in their beds."

Jaime's jaw trembled. She clenched it still.

"I thought it would feel like...more," she said quietly. "Satisfying. Clean. It did not. It felt like—like one stone set on another. Necessary for the wall. Heavy in the hand."

"Revenge is a sharp tool," Dratmar said. "Good for cutting, bad for building. You used it. Now you put it down."

"We did more than cut," I said. "We broke his network. We pulled the anchors out of the land or shattered them where they stood. We severed the lines that would have carried his will. The villages he would have burned still stand. The people he would have marked as 'acceptable loss' woke this morning and breathed. They do not know why. But they do."

Ianteen lifted her head. "And the men above him?" she asked. "The ones who signed the orders and stroked their beards while they weighed lives against coin. What of them?"

"We brought their words back," Jaime said. "We have Kerran's letters. We have ledgers with their names. We have proofs that what they call necessity was simply power dressed in numbers. We will put it before the councils. Before the masters. Before anyone who will listen. We will not let them bury it in some archive and pretend it was a miscalculation."

"And if they try?" Bobo asked. His eyes were bright. Anger suited him badly. It pulled his features into someone else's face for a second. "If they say, 'Thank you for your service,' and send you away while they burn the pages at night?"

"Then we tell others," I said. "Villages. Outposts. Garrison captains who still sleep at night. Priests who remember their vows. We make it so many people know that no one can cut all the tongues out at once. We carry copies like we carried the stones. Paper travels. Stories travel faster. We are not the only ones who will carry them."

Dratmar's gaze weighed me. There was something in it I had not seen before. A measuring that had nothing to do with how I held a blade.

"You speak like a man planning a campaign," he said. "Not just a fight. Where did you learn that?"

"At Black Rise," I said. "In the corridors. On the road. Watching how Kerran and his masters thought. If I know the shape of their knives, I can turn them."

Anya had been quiet too long. Now she burst.

"You mean to go back," she said. Her wings flared wide, feathers brushing Bobo and Ianteen. "Not to Black Rise, but to their halls. To the cities. You mean to stand in their chambers and tell them what they did wrong. They will not like that."

"No," I said. "They will not."

Her eyes filled, the tears standing without falling. "You just got here," she said. "You just walked through the door. You have not even seen what I taught Inspector to do."

"Anya," Dratmar said gently.

She shook her head, feathers shivering. "They will take you away again. They will lock you up. They will say you are lying. They will say you are dangerous." Her gaze flicked to my horns, then away, ashamed.

"They will say all those things," I said. "Some of them will even believe them. But I am a Warrior now." The word sat in my mouth with the weight of an oath. "My work is not just swinging a sword at whoever someone points out. It is choosing which fights matter. This one does. For you. For Bobo. For Ianteen. For every village that looks like ours and does not have someone to carry its name into those rooms."

Jaime's hand found mine under the table. Her fingers curled around my wrist, thumb resting over the ridge of a scale. Her grip was steady.

"We will go," she said. "Together. But not tonight. Not tomorrow. We just spent months cutting through stone and swamp and worse. We will take a breath. We will sharpen our blades. We will let Anya show us her owl salutes."

Anya sniffed. A smile cracked the edge of her fear. "He bows," she said. "If you do it first. It is very dignified."

"We will plan," I said. "Rygial will help us make copies of what we brought. Elsiah knows how shadows move in cities. We are not walking into this blind. We are not alone."

Ianteen exhaled slowly. "If you are to build something that lasts from this wreckage," she said, "you will need more than blades and papers. You will need symbols. Things people can point to and say, 'That is what stands against the dark.'" She glanced at Drakeslayer. "You have one already, whether you like it or not."

I looked at the sword. At my reflection in its faintly gleaming steel. Horns. Eyes like coin-gold, as Anya had said. A line of scales peeking from under the bandage at my wrist.

"I did not ask to be a symbol," I said.

"Real ones rarely do," Dratmar said. "They come from what you do when you are given no good choices. That is the burden."

Bobo leaned forward, elbows on the table.

"Tell us everything," he said. "Not just the strokes. The pieces. How did the anchors look when they broke? What did the magic feel like? How close were you standing when it all went sideways? Did you see time twist, like Rygial says it does, or is that just something he says to sound interesting?"

Despite the weight in the room, despite the ache in my chest, I found my mouth quirking.

"Eat your stew," I said. "Then I will tell you how it feels when the ground hums under your feet and you realize it is because someone has tied a piece of the world to their own heartbeat."

Anya's eyes grew huge. "Really?" she breathed.

"Really," I said. "Though you are not allowed to try it yourself."

She nodded solemnly, though I could see the wheels turning behind her eyes.

We talked then. For a long time. The story came in pieces, drawn out by questions, anchored by small details. How the swamp's stink clung to our clothes for days. How the sigil lines in the anchor room at Black Rise pulsed like veins under skin. How Elsiah had slipped through a barred window that no one else could have fit through and opened a door from the other side. How Rygial's hands shook when he first refused a direct order from a Hall superior, and how they steadied when he saw a village's anchor stone crumble harmlessly under his reworked spell.

We did not make ourselves grand in the telling. There was no need. The work we had done was ugly and necessary and hard. That was enough.

Dratmar listened more than he spoke. Sometimes he asked a sharp question that cut to the heart of a choice I had made. "Why there?" "Why that risk?" I answered as best I could. Sometimes he only grunted, a sound that carried pride and worry and something like sorrow.

When at last the fire burned low and Anya's head began to nod where she sat, wings drooping, Dratmar pushed his bench back.

"That is enough for tonight," he said. "We will have more nights. More questions. For now, you rest under my roof. If the world wants more of you, it can come knocking at my door and explain itself to me."

He stood. His chair scraped the stone. He put a hand on my shoulder, solid, warm. The weight of it steadied more than my muscles.

"You did what you had to do," he said. "You came back. You brought pieces of the truth in your packs instead of gold. I am proud of you."

The words hit harder than any blow. My throat closed. I managed a nod.

Jaime's eyes shone in the low light. Dratmar turned to her.

"You too," he said. "Your father would have wanted me to say it. So I do. You carried his name into the swamp and out again. You broke the man who drowned him. That is a thing."

She bowed her head. A tear slid down her cheek, cutting a clean line through the grime. She let it fall.

We rose from the table. Anya darted ahead to make sure our beds were "properly fluffed," as she said. Bobo offered to help with the packs and nearly toppled backwards under the weight of Rygial's, just to prove he could carry it. Ianteen lingered in the doorway, looking at Drakeslayer where it rested against the wall.

"You have work to do with that," she said quietly. "More than fighting. People will see it and think of Maximus. Then of you. It will carry both your ghosts."

"I know," I said.

She nodded once, then turned away to bank the fire for the night.

The house settled around us. Old beams creaked as the temperature fell. Somewhere above, the owl hooted once, as if marking the moment. The echoes of Black Rise followed me into sleep, but they shared space with the smell of stew and the feel of Anya's arms around my neck. The two lives met and did not break.

MORNING CAME SLOW AND soft, as it tends to in places that have survived.

Light seeped in through the small window in my room, pale and gray at first, then warming toward gold. The air had the chill of spring that had not yet given itself over to summer. I lay for a while listening: the distant rush of the river, the creak of wood as someone moved in the next room, the faint clink of metal from the forge where Dratmar liked to start the fire early.

My body expected danger in those sounds. It took a few breaths to let that go. There were no alarms. No anchor hum. No shouted orders. Only home.

I swung my feet to the floor. The stone was cool under my soles. When I stood, my reflection caught in the small polished plate of tin that Anya had insisted on hanging at the end of the bed so she could "practice expressions." My horns framed my ears now, the curve of them sharper than when I had left Black Rise. My eyes caught the thin morning light and returned it deeper. The scales at my forearms showed where the bandages had slipped in the night, red-gold glinting faintly.

I flexed my fingers. The skin tugged. It did not hurt. It would, when I gripped a sword for hours. I would learn that new line.

The house's main room was already warm from the hearth when I stepped into it. Jaime sat at the table with a mug of tea, her hair damp from a quick wash. Anya perched on the back of her chair, wings half-open for balance, chattering about something and making swooping gestures with one hand.

"...and then Inspector does this." She demonstrated a stiff, solemn incline of her head. "But only if you salute first. He will not waste his dignity."

Jaime tried to mirror the movement. It made her look like she was trying not to sneeze. Anya giggled, then clapped a hand over her mouth when Jaime raised an eyebrow.

"It is a work in progress," Anya said.

Dratmar stood by the hearth, stirring a pot of porridge with a spoon large enough to serve as a cudgel. Bobo fumbled with a small metal disk in his hands, lips moving as he muttered the lyrics of a rune he tried to recall. Every so often he glanced at the sigils etched into the iron and corrected a line.

Ianteen had a piece of chalk and the table's corner. She sketched a pattern there, a design for a hinge that could bear more weight without thickening. His fingers were sure, chalk leaving fine white lines on the dark wood.

"Morning," I said.

Anya's head whipped around. She nearly toppled off the chair back. Her wings flared, caught, steadied her.

"You slept," she said, as if this were surprising and praiseworthy. "Jaime was up before first light. She went to look at the training posts. She poked them like they had offended her."

"They had," Jaime said, not looking up from her mug. "They leaned."

Dratmar snorted. "You always say that when you have been away," he said. "As if the world cannot hold its own weight without you watching."

"Can it?" Jaime asked.

He shrugged. "So far. Sit. Eat. Today you do not lift more than a practice blade."

That turned into a small argument, familiar and easy. Jaime insisted she was fine. Dratmar pointed out that fine was not the same as ready. Bobo chimed in with an offer to spar "gently." Jaime threatened to tie his shoelaces together. Anya tried to referee and got distracted inventing a new rule.

We ate. The porridge was thick and plain, sweetened only by a drizzle of honey and a few dried berries Anya had hoarded. It tasted better than feast food in some keeps I had been in since. Warm. Uncomplicated. Mine.

After breakfast, the house fell into its old rhythms and some new ones. Dratmar and Ianteen went to the forge. The ring of hammer on metal soon drifted through the open window, regular and sure. Sparks flew when I went to the doorway and looked in. They smelled of hot iron and charcoal. Ianteen watched the color of the heated blade with a careful eye and said "Now" at just the right moment for Dratmar to quench it.

Jaime took me into the yard. The training posts stood in their usual row, scars on their surfaces catching the morning light. She handed me a wooden practice sword.

"Let us see what all that magic and stone has done to your stance," she said. "We will start slow. If Dratmar yells at us from the forge, we will pretend we cannot hear."

Anya insisted on watching. She perched on the fence with her knees drawn up, chin on them, wings folded behind. Bobo hovered nearby with a wax tablet, ready to note any "new moves" he could turn into something flashy.

We moved through the basic forms first. Step. Guard. Cut. Recover. My body remembered them, even before my mind did. The weight of the practice sword was wrong after Drakeslayer, but my muscles adjusted. The scales on my arms pulled in unfamiliar patterns when I twisted. I noticed every difference. Jaime did too.

"You shift more from your center now," she said, circling me. "Less from your shoulders. That is good. Less wasted motion. The scales will change how you take blows on your arms. We will work that next week. For today, get your feet under you."

We worked until sweat dampened my shirt and made the bandages itch. Jaime corrected my grip twice, swatted my calf once when my back heel rose too far, and said nothing else. That silence meant she approved more than any praise.

Anya clapped after each sequence as if she were watching a play. Bobo tried to mimic some of the moves with his hands while standing still, almost braining himself with his own gestures. We laughed. It felt strange and good in my chest.

By midday, Elsiah and Rygial appeared at the gate. They looked different already. An evening in a clean bed and a morning without fear had taken some of the gray from under their eyes.

Elsiah kept her posture loose, but her gaze darted, cataloging. She wore a plain shirt and trousers borrowed from Bobo, the cuffs a bit short. Her old cloak was gone, left folded in the inn room. Without it, she looked younger. More like the girl she might have been if someone had not taught her how to steal before they taught her to read.

Rygial carried his staff and his pack. The latter sat more comfortably on his shoulders now, as if he had decided he did not need to be ready to run every second. He had a small loaf of village bread under his arm and the faintest dusting of flour on his beard.

"Ha," Bobo said. "You lived. The inn did not swallow you. Did anyone coil you into some arcane debt?"

"Only for another night's coin," Rygial said dryly. "Your innkeeper drives a harder bargain than some Hall quartermasters."

Elsiah's eyes slid to the training posts. "You do this every morning?" he asked me. "Even when no one is trying to kill you?"

"Yes," I said.

He made a face. "You are all mad." He said it without heat.

"Stay long enough, we will make you mad too," Anya said. "Then you will be family."

His gaze shifted to her. For the first time since I had met him, he looked...unsteady. As if the ground under his feet was less certain than he liked.

"We brought these," Rygial said, lifting the loaf slightly. "As tribute. The inn had too much. We may have threatened them with unpaid songs if they did not share."

Dratmar emerged from the forge, wiping his hands on a rag. He eyed them both. The weight in his gaze had less suspicion now. More assessment.

"Come in, then," he said. "You fought beside my son and my blade daughter. You helped bring back what they carried. That earns you a seat and a bowl."

Elsiah's mouth twitched. "That easy?" she asked. "You do not ask where I came from. What I did before I met them."

Dratmar snorted. "If they trust you enough to bring you here, that is enough to start. If you had done something that needs answering for, it will follow you in its own time. Until then, eat my stew and stop fishing for exile."

Rygial's shoulders dropped a fraction. Elsiah's lips quirked into a small, genuine smile, quick as a flash of fish in a stream.

We crammed around the table again, more squeezed than before, elbows touching. Anya made room willingly, pressing herself against my side and tucking one wing close so it would not dip in the soup.

Conversation turned to smaller things. Rygial explained, at Anya's insistence, how time-sense felt from the inside. He spoke of tickle-threads at the edge of perception, of a pressure behind the eyes when a moment wanted to split in two. Bobo demanded to know if he could use time-sense to get more sleep in the mornings. Rygial told him no, unfortunately.

Elsiah watched and listened far more than she spoke. When she did speak, it was to comment on the best routes into the city markets, or how to spot a guard who had cheated at dice the night before. Her knowledge pared too clean for these walls, but it had its uses. Dratmar listened.

"Shadow work has its place," Dratmar said. "So long as you pick who you cast it on."

Elsiah's gaze met his. He nodded once. That was more trust than any formal pledge.

The day rolled on. Chores filled the gaps. Anya dragged me outside to see Inspector the owl, who did indeed bow, very slowly, when she saluted him. His round eyes tracked my horns with skeptical interest. I bowed back. He fluffed his feathers as if reluctantly impressed.

In the afternoon, I helped Ianteen haul a crate of ore from the river cart to the forge. The weight of it pulled my new scales tight. He noticed.

"How does it feel?" she asked without preamble. "The changes. I do not mean the eyes. I can see those. The inside."

"Like something finished growing without asking me," I said. "It fits. But I remember how it felt before."

She nodded. "When I burned my hands the first time at the forge, I thought I would never feel right holding a hammer again. The new skin was tight. It did not bend the same. I had to learn where it creased and where it did not. This is like that. Just...more."

"That is one way to put it," I said.

She smiled faintly. "If you want armor adjusted," she said, "or a new guard to protect the scales without pinching them, we can work on it. You should not have to choose between wearing your own skin and being cut to ribbons."

"I would like that," I said.

Evening came. The sky over Old King's Walk turned the color of cooled iron. The river caught the last light in broken ripples. I watched it from the doorway for a while, feeling the day's labor in my arms and legs. It felt good. Honest. No arcane hum under the ground. No sense of looming catastrophe. Just tiredness.

Inside, Anya fell asleep midsentence on the couch, a book about winged heroes slipping from her hands. Bobo covered her with a blanket, then sat at the table to scribble sigils in the wax of his tablet until his eyes crossed. Jaime leaned against the doorframe, looking out with me, her shoulder brushing mine.

"Feels wrong, being still," she said quietly. "After so long moving."

"We are not stones," I said. "We will move again."

"I know," she said. "That is the part that feels wrong."

We stood there until the first stars pricked the sky. Then Dratmar grunted from his chair.

"Enough brooding in doorways," he said. "Come sit. If you stand there any longer, you will wear a groove and Anya will complain about tripping over it."

We obeyed. We were home, for now. The world outside could wait at the gate.

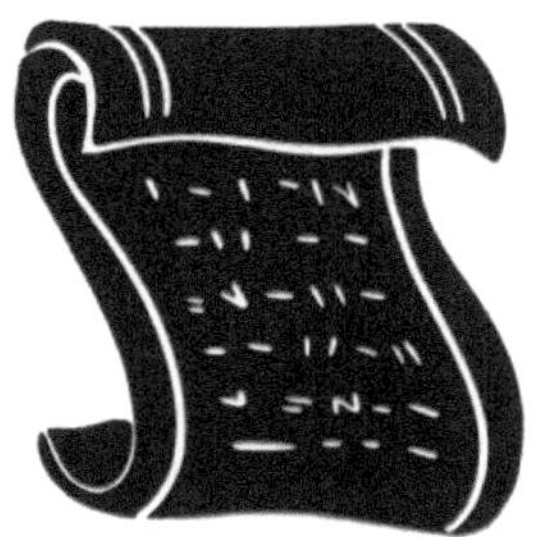

# THE PLACE WHERE IT ALL STARTED AGAIN

ON THE THIRD MORNING, before the sun rose fully, I walked down to the field beyond the last house.

Old King's Walk ended where the land sloped gently toward a shallow hollow. In spring, the hollow held standing water. In summer, it grew wildflowers and waist-high grass. The old path to the mill ran along its edge. I had stolen hours here as a child. Bobo and I had sparred with sticks until Dratmar shouted for us. Anya had tried to learn how to glide on low wind currents between the hummocks, tumbling more than flying. Maximus had shown me how to read tracks in the mud. Human. Wolf. Catfolk. Deer.

Now the dew clung to the grass, beading on each blade. It soaked my boots as I walked. The air held that clear, empty cold that comes just before the day warms. My breath made small clouds.

I stopped near a low rise where the ground was dry. From there, I could see the village's roofline, the faint curls of smoke from chimneys, the line of the river catching thin light. Behind me, the hills rose. Ahead, the sky opened.

I set Drakeslayer down on the grass beside me. It did not look like much, lying there. A long sword in a plain scabbard, its hilt wrapped in leather darkened by use. Only the faint pattern along the guard hinted at its making—the dragon-scale etching worked into the metal by a smith who knew old stories. Maximus had carried it first. Now it sat by my hand.

The scales on my forearms were cool in the morning air. They caught what little light there was and held it like banked coals. My horns felt heavier when I bowed my head. My eyes, if anyone had been there to see them, would have showed the field twice, once in flesh and once in memory.

Black Rise rose before me with my eyes open. The broken tower. The anchor chamber, empty now, its stones shattered. The humming web that had wrapped around the land and pulled at everything living within its reach. The way it had felt to stand at the center of it, to push my will against something larger than I had ever known and feel it give.

That moment had not been clean. It had been loud, and ugly, and full of fear. Rygial shouting numbers. Jaime swearing as she drove her blade through a plate-gap. Elsiah screaming in a way I had never heard from him before when a spell caught his arm and twisted the shadow there wrong. The anchor humming higher and higher, far past the point where anything should hold.

The choice had come not as a clear, shining line, but as a blur of half-realized options. Pull back and let the anchor complete its charge. Push forward and risk being burned from the inside out. There had been no guarantee either way. In that breath, all the drills Dratmar had given us, all the quiet talks by the forge, all the hours spent trying to understand who I was when no one else could name it—they all converged.

I had stepped forward.

The power had run through me, not around me. It had recognized something in my bones. The scales had flared, burning like metal fresh from the forge. My arms had felt both on fire and ice-cold. The horns had throbbed as if roots tunneled deeper into my skull. My eyes had filled with a light that was not the anchor's, but something I had always carried and never called by name.

I had survived. The anchor had not. Neither had Kerran's web.

In the quiet here, with only the wind and a few early birds for company, I could feel the echo of that moment as a low hum in my blood. Not constant. Not loud. Just...there. A new note in the song of my body.

Warrior. The word did not mean what it had when I first swung a wooden sword at a post and dreamed of glory. It did not mean what the broadsheets said it did, with horned figures on hilltops and banners snapping behind them. It meant choices that cut. It meant standing between people like Anya and people like Kerran, knowing you would be hit from both sides. It meant carrying the weight of proof in a pack and the weight of expectation in your own skin.

Dratmar had called me a Warrior by his fire when I came back bruised from my first real fight years ago. I had felt it like a reward then. A badge. Now it felt like a description. A simple statement of fact. I killed when I had to. I protected when I could. I carried truths no one else wanted to hold. That was the work.

I flexed my hands. The scales moved. They would never go away. Neither would the horns. Neither would the eyes. Children would point. Men in halls would mark me as other before I spoke. Some would fear. Some would try to use the fear. Some would try to use me.

I had a say in that, at least.

Behind me, in the village, Jaime was probably checking her gear, counting straps and buckles, turning Kerran's scorched badge in her fingers as she thought about what came next. Rygial would be at the table with his papers, drawing lines of ink between names, building a map of guilt as careful as any anchor web. Elsiah would be learning which doors in Old King's Walk stuck in the winter and which had loose hinges he could open without a sound, even though he had promised Anya not to steal anything unless it was "for the greater good." Bobo would be in the forge, trying to coax a spark into a spell. Ianteen would be sketching hinges and blades. Dratmar would sit in his chair for a moment longer than usual, eyes closed, listening to the house breathe.

We had work to do. The letters and ledgers we carried would have to be copied, safeguarded, sent in multiple directions so no one could snuff them out with a single hand. We would have to decide where to go first. To the nearest Hall? To a councilor who had once laughed at Durandal's jokes? To a captain who still remembered what it meant to swear an oath to people, not to ink?

There would be doors slammed in our faces. There would be threats. There might be prison cells again, or worse. Power does not like having its games exposed. Men who thought of villages as numbers would not stop because we asked.

I did not know, standing in that field, how each of those encounters would go. I did not know which names in Rygial's careful script would become our worst enemies and which would surprise us. I did not know which of us would live to see the network of anchors spoken of as a lesson in the Hall, or a rumor in village inns. I did not know that songs would be sung, badly, about the horned Warrior from Old King's Walk, or that half of them would get the details wrong.

I knew two things.

I would not walk alone. And I would not walk away.

The field was quiet. A lark rose suddenly from the grass at my feet, beating its wings hard as it climbed into the higher air. Its song spilled out as if it could not contain it, clear and fast and wild. I watched it until it vanished into the brightening sky.

I picked up Drakeslayer. The sword's weight settled into my hand. The leather of the grip felt familiar, molded to Maximus's fingers and now to mine. I drew it a handspan from the scabbard. The metal caught the sun as it broke the horizon, a line of light running along the blade's edge. For an instant, I saw my reflection there. Horns. Eyes. A line of scales. A mouth set in something like a promise.

I slid the sword back home.

Behind me, the village stirred. A dog barked. Someone called a greeting across a lane. The smell of bread reached me on the wind. Life, continuing.

I turned toward it.

There were stories to come. Battles and bargains and nights spent in places far from Old King's Walk. There were halls where we would stand before men in fine robes and make them listen, or at least make them afraid to pretend they had not heard. There were other kinds of anchors in the world, buried deep, holding worse things than stone, and we would find some of them in time.

That is talk for another time.

For now, I walked back toward the yew tree and the house that held my family. The sword rode at my hip. The sky arched wide over my horns. My steps pressed dew-dark footprints into the grass, a line leading from the past we had survived to the future we would make, one small choice at a time.

www.ingramcontent.com/pod-product-compliance
Lightning Source LLC
Chambersburg PA
CBHW050503110726
47899CB00005B/1312